The Angels of Resistance

LINDENHURST MEMORIAL LIBRARY
LINDENHURST, NEW YORK 11757

The Angels of Resistance

By David V. Mammina

A Dark Fantasy Novel

Published by David V. Mammina
Printed by Lulu Inc

The Angels of Resistance

By David V. Mammina

All rights reserved.
No part of this book can be used or reproduced in any form and by any means without written consent from David V. Mammina
Lindenhurst, New York

978-0-615-61880-7
Copyright © 2019
All rights reserved.
Printed in the United States of America
Cover art by David V. Mammina
Above illustration by Anne Clinton

Due to the dynamic nature of the internet, some of these websites may not still be active and others may have been established after the publication of this book and, therefore, are not listed.
www.Mamminabooks.com
www.lulu.com/mammina

Dedicated to my brother, for whom
I never had the honor to meet
in person.

Thank you, Joseph, and rest in peace.

PART I OF II
PROLOGUE
THE PRIMEVAL TRAGEDY

There was once a world, perhaps a thousand years ago, that was beautiful. An age of groundbreaking innovation, humanity was limited only by their imagination. Dreams were but a precursor to reality. Technological prowess illuminated the era and they performed wonders. These wonders came to define what it meant to be human in the modern world. But, ironically, all these things were never made to last.

No one can be sure as to how it all came to an end. There are theories. Some say that it was a super plague, fast-spreading and immune to all vaccines. Others believe that nuclear war enveloped the globe, explaining the various fallout bunkers scattered all about the earth and total destruction of all major cities. The third dares to blame the alleged apocalypse on an asteroid that unexpectedly changed course for earth. What is certain, however, is that their end was tragically inevitable.

The real tragedy was in the ignorance of how they lived. Despite the greatness of their civilization, they lacked a collective moral compass. That hubris was their undoing, for virtually nothing survived in their name. There were no real records of their triumphs or lessons learned in failures. The Primeval Tragedy serves as a cautionary tale for the arrogance of humanity.

A barbaric and feudal age, the new world suffered the consequences of the old. Ancient cities lay in ruins, consumed by nature or serving as the roaches' playgrounds.

Settled about bodies of water, survivors emerged from their bunkers and segregated in base cities. The new age, in consequence, had been forged by conflict. Chaos bled the new settlements apart, as human nature does not change. The need to survive in the dawning world cursed by their ancestors proved violent and without discipline.

Some believed that nuclear fogs from a thousand years ago altered some individuals with magnificent abilities to control the elements. To most of the world, those uncanny and mysterious attributes were regarded as a sorcery. Those granted with such abilities either blessed or cursed the lands with their powers, shaping the rising world. However, this magical phenomenon had faded away over the centuries, leaving only a few with the sorcery of times gone by. What remained after was an era of steel, feudal law and a drive for redemption.

In recent days, the sins of the old world had vanished, almost entirely forgotten and replaced by the recovering planet. Yet, there were some evils that remained dormant through the millennia, waiting for the perfect time to return. In the new world, stumbling forward in the hopes that humanity might yet flourish, a wicked force has risen again—a dark entity once buried at the fall of humanity so long ago.

PART I
CHAPTER I
THE ARRIVAL

Michael Miuriell, a man of great honor and power, was cursed with the memory of his people's slaughter. To evoke the living nightmare was for him to go mad, as no man could ever stay the same afterward. He was of the minority that survived the sudden onslaught from the Demon Plague, a demonic army as true to the definition of evil than any other. The famed man of peace, cast off in the middle of the ocean, was broken.

He couldn't remember how many days he had been stranded on the auxiliary boat in the open water. Famished, Michael peered far out across the ocean's horizon for a sign of hope. From his homeland, he was a hero—a beacon of wisdom in a perilous world. In the boat, however, Michael was but a man with a staff and a frayed cloak.

Wearily, he remained on his back and considered the blue, empty sky above. Accompanied by the tranquil rocking, Michael had pitied that he could not appreciate the peace. He had no fresh food or water. His mouth was as dry as ever, compelling him to choke and cough. But, in the fury of an instant, the calm water erupted like a volcano from the one side. Jolted into a sitting position, he slowly peeked over the side of his boat to face a vigorous dolphin with an awkward scar over its left eye.

"What do *you* want?" Michael uttered tiredly. "This boat is taken."

The dolphin seemed to smile and splash off. Michael watched it go, overshadowed by an enormous ship heading in his direction. He had to rub his eyes to make sure he wasn't hallucinating. It glided onward, coming into view as a sight of mercy. The ship's sails eased and began to luff, signaling that it would slow down enough to take a look at him. He waved for the vessel with his staff raised high in the air, expelling all of his energy to catch the vessel's attention.

Michael tightened his hold on the staff as he waved it, praying for deliverance. Given to him by his exceptional sage teacher, Urik, his unassuming staff contained remarkable power. Known as the Staff of Truth, by legend, it was a mystical article that helped him hone his special skills. Virtually indestructible, the artifact was told to have certain faculties that connected the user's mind to any event in time: past, present, and future. Michael had intended to master its techniques, something no one had ever been able to accomplish before him, including Urik. The staff was crafted intentionally to appear old and futile.

As fate would have it, the large vessel lowered a rescue boat right beside his own. Heaving himself into the fresh craft, the alert crew pulled him up portside with reeling machines. The flawless detail of the gorgeous auburn ship was stunning up close. Before he reached the crew on deck, a commanding voice ordered them to fetch dry clothes and ready a holding space for him in the cabin.

Their Christian dialect was familiar to him, for most of the West spoke the language for centuries. Men gathered to help him stand on his feeble feet. Others relieved him of his staff, but he didn't fear them stealing it. Even in his weak state, he had the article tethered to his mind. He only wanted to thank the strangers for saving him, but no words came out.

Michael was able to distinguish the captain from the rest of the men as he ambled forth. Many called him the "Sea-Sentinel," because of his great experience on the open water. He scrutinized Michael discriminately, "Do you speak the Christian dialect, son?"

"You from Ellium?" Michael answered with a question.

The captain rubbed his chin and insisted to his crew that he recognized him as a Pommelian from the West. Pommelians belonged to a bustling community well known by most travelers as a city that housed artifacts of the old world. A long series of questions were in order as to how and why he was stranded in the middle of the Great Pacifica without water or rations.

The captain beckoned his crew to tighten the sails and maintain course as Michael was escorted to a holding cabin. As for the ship, it would continue its route for the great kingdom of Tinaria, a sister kingdom of Ellium that dwelled across the sea. Michael leaned on the crew as they helped him walk to temporary salvation.

Michael was eating too well. Gorging his stomach with bread, fish, and water, he had no consideration for his company. Three guardsmen stood by the cabin door and nauseously watched him eat. Servants had just begun to offer him another piece of bread when the captain came through the door. After a briefing from the staff, Captain Marinaio approached him and began, "What is your name?"

"Michael," he replied in-between breaths. "Michael Miuriell of Pommel. I trust you've heard of me?"

"No, and you will address me as 'Sir Marinaio,'" the captain snipped in. "I am the commander of the Santa di Mare, the greatest ship in the world. If you were conceived just yesterday, you would have heard of it."

"Then you must be Tinarian," Michael countered when another man bearing a herald's mark on his breastplate came into the room and shut the door behind him. His aged face was cleanly shaven and his hair was like black straw.

"So, you *are* Pommelian," the man said while clasping his fingers at the waist, having overheard from outside.

"I am Michael—"

"You are speaking to Lancea Forra, the royal herald of Tinaria. We Tinarians have little patience for games, so do tell us the truth and nothing but. Our kingdom houses Antonis the Prophet, a man who could very easily see through your lies. Do you understand?"

"Yes," Michael replied, eyeing the second serving of bread, "but his powers are amateurish, at best, if you'll forgive me."

The Herald wasted no time in starting what seemed to be a firm interrogation, "Really? Okay, then, Pommelian. Let us see what sort of value you possess, besides a puffed-up arrogance for one stranded in an old dinghy."

"Indeed, sir," he said, shaking off the jaded spell. "It's been a while since I've spoken with anyone. In fact, I couldn't tell you how long I was stranded out there before your crew saved me."

Lancea quickly followed, "What were you doing alone in the sea? How did you become stranded like that?"

Such an innocent question awoke torment. His heart ached and his stomach turned just thinking about how he would even begin to explain it. A demonic force from the darkness stripped Michael's entire world from under him in a single night. Unable to convey it in words, his spirit broke down, compelling him to cry instead.

As a geyser needing to blow, Michael let loose and justifiably mourned for his family before them. Everyone inside the cabin awkwardly glanced at each other as he wept in his hands. Lancea was willing to wait just moments more. He was not known for his tolerance. The captain, conversely, had not seen a display of such sudden anguish in years. These were the sort of tears that told grim tales.

"What happened, man?" The captain asked mercifully.

In attempting to overcome his crying bout, Michael wiped his face with a tablecloth and started with breaks in his voice, "All of what I am about to tell you is true, so help me God. A demonic army of some kind enveloped Pommel and murdered everyone in it without warning—without meaning. I witnessed one of those things tear out my wife's beating heart and left her to die at its feet.

"When I could not save anyone else—when it appeared hopeless, I led others to escape along with my son. After that, I remember nothing. After we ran, I only remember blackness. I had dreamed that they killed everyone, including my son—my only child."

Following a dead silence, the captain uttered, "Demons, you say?"

"I thought they had killed me too, but I awoke in that boat." Michael held back persistent tears. "They plague my dreams! Those things were not of this earth. They were demons, whether you choose to believe me or not. I know what I saw. I know what killed my wife, my people—all those innocent—"

Dumbfounded by the stranger's impossible account, Lancea shook his head in a daze and said, "You expect us to believe that yarn?"

"Perhaps, seasickness?" Captain Marinaio immediately interjected. "I've seen this before in boys early in the service."

Hearing them, Michael could only laugh in disgust. Even he didn't believe his eyes back in Pommel. A sane person would be crazed to believe such a story, but there was no softening it. Michael had to convince them all, for the sake of all those who were butchered. He would make them all believe that truth was deadlier than fiction.

Lifting his head to meet the Tinarians' judging glares, Michael said gravely, "You had better take me seriously this day. Your kingdom may share the same fate because they will not stop at Pommel. They can do better than Pommel!"

"That's enough there!" The herald flicked his wrist and walked towards the door to leave the sordid scene. In his abhorrence for the stranger's outlandish responses to his questions, Lancea decided to return to his own cabin and let the captain deal with the insane Pommelian. Yet, when he was prepared to leave, his coin purse tore from his belt and jetted towards the center of the room.

As everyone in the cabin gawked at the breathtaking spectacle, a servant's helping dish was next to float up into the air. Stunned by the impractical display, they all witnessed Lancea's purse gently lay upon the floating dish as if a ghost had taken over. But Michael Miuriell was no ghost. Rather, he was telekinetic.

"I insist that you stay and listen to the rest," Michael said calmly from his seat. "If your money is that important to you that you must attach it to your hip, perhaps you should heed my warnings with an open mind? It could be your head served on a silver platter instead."

At last, they realized who they had taken aboard their ship. Michael's abilities were known far and wide by many. His training under Urik of Oron had given him a sense of control over this great power. If left unchecked, he was at risk of causing catastrophic harm. Even he could not say how he attained his unexplainable talent.

Gaining their attention, Michael proceeded, "If seeing is believing, then this performance should be easy for you to take in. Witnessing a demon slaughter your family and friends may be a bit more than one can chew. I think it's time that you come to terms with what I am trying to tell you."

After an immediate change of opinion, Lancea led the captain out of the cabin and pushed him back into the corridor's wall, hissing nervously, "What in the hell are we going to do? Do you know who that is? Do you know what this means?"

"Why would he lie?" The captain retorted with anxiety. "Unless you plan on making him angrier, we may have to accept his account of what happened!"

"And then what?" Lancea countered. "The king requests news of a trade deal, not him! He will never allow me to sail across the sea again if we entertain him with stories of demons!"

The captain peeked back into the cabin briefly before whispering, "That is the real Michael Miuriell in there. Surely, the king knows of his reputation. He would be more likely to hear his warnings directly."

"You don't have to face the king!" Lancea shouted. "Antonis would have foreseen this! Any prophet would have known that 'demons' were going to invade the earth! How ridiculous would you like me to look before him, Milo?"

Captain Marinaio moved in close enough so that their noses were practically touching and said, "That is not my concern. You are the Herald and that is your burden. Think about how ridiculous you'll look if Miuriell's story comes true for Tinaria and you did nothing to warn them!"

At last, Lancea was convinced. Sighing with a prolonged stare into the cabin, the Herald made his way back in and decided to hear the famous peacemaker of the West. His purse floated back towards him as he returned to the supernatural display, catching it in his right hand. Watching Michael guide the serving plate before himself without moving a muscle, Lancea clasped the purse to his belt and said, "Nice trick."

Michael chewed into another piece of bread before saying with a full mouth, "You must understand. They don't intend on stopping. This Demon Plague will destroy your kingdom as it did mine if your king does nothing. Accept my agonizing tale as an olive branch. I'm willing to help stop them if I can."

When the captain joined everyone else inside, Lancea cleared his throat and swallowed his pride, saying with a heavy heart, "We Tinarians have heard of you, Miuriell, but our kingdom is already in great turmoil. Before we departed for the West, our queen suspiciously became ill. There is no doubt now that she had come down with a sickness no physician could identify.

"Because our king is in despair, and we don't know if she's recovered since, he will not accept your story 'with an open mind,' as you say. The best you can do is present your message. From there, you are on your own. Since you have proven to us that you are the real Miuriell, we shall tread softly. We are not doing this for your sake, mind you."

"No, I am doing this for yours," Michael said, having filled his stomach. "I don't wish to see more people die."

Lancea Forra groaned before hastily storming out of the cabin, "May God be with us all."

Captain Marinaio ordered everyone but the guards to leave them. Michael remained in his seat and quietly reflected on his present state of circumstances. He shouldered a sacred responsibility to protect as many people as he could, having already sacrificed everything but his life thus far. He could hardly function as himself without his loving wife—and without his only son.

When the last man had shut the door behind him, the captain placed his hands behind his back and came in closer. He studied Michael's eyes for the truth one more time before saying steadily, "I don't like your story, gruesome and sorrowful as it lies, but I believe it. On the same token, there is one other thing you should consider. You never confirmed how you ended up in that boat. I don't accept your 'blackout' account of it."

Michael closed his eyes tightly in a last attempt to remember for himself. It tore at his heart, for none of it made sense to him either. He was always a lucid man—one who was not easily fooled. The sudden implosion of his world shook his understanding of all things. For the life of him, there was no reasoning for how he ended up alone in the water.

"Try to remember that you will be presenting your story to our king," the captain proceeded. "Our very lives may depend on how you convince the court. I have seen things on the water that I cannot explain to anyone still to this day. I've kept it all to myself. People will think us crazy until they see it for themselves. It's in our nature."

Nodding in accord of the captain's support, he returned quietly, "One of our greatest weaknesses."

After a tolerant pause, the captain signaled to his guards stationed around the room and said, "My crew shall escort you to your quarters for the remainder of the voyage home. I know that, if you wanted, you could turn this whole ship into shards of wood in just a few minutes. Please don't do that."

Taken aback by the captain's strange candor, he simply said, "Okay."

Michael massaged his tired eyes while his host described the many rules and procedures. His worried mind drifted off to the new mission. If Tinaria was as militarily superior as he remembered, then fending off demons was, in the least, worth trying. He prayed for his allies in the West, fearing that they were already suffering the brutality of the Demon Plague. There was no telling how much time had passed since his home was razed.

PART I
CHAPTER II
THE WORD

He walked through the misty forest, alone and confused. The sound of dead leaves crunching under his feet echoed with every next step. In the murky distance, he saw a figure of his wife, Opal, awaiting his return.

She sang a beautiful song from warmer times—the one she serenaded to their young son, Seth, when he was a baby. Michael's beaming soul chased away the fog of the woodland once they met. She seemed to hover above the ground in slow motion, riding the mist, until the loving embrace. Again, Michael was happy.

"Opal, I'm not living without you!" Michael cried into her breast, holding her tightly to prove she was real. "If this is the only place we can be together, I'd rather never wake up." He knew what came next, but he held her tightly still until the moment she suddenly faded away. Opal sobbed and vanished into the mist of the forest, as Michael remained there, heartbroken and begging for her loving embrace with outstretched arms. His hands just brushed through the mist.

Michael awoke from his recurring dream with a sweltering heat on his dampened skin, holding his racing heart. The folded cloth on his bed stand proved useful for wiping the sweat from his face. But when he was done, the cloth was crimson red, illuminated by the creeping moonlight of the cabin's porthole. Michael had bled from his nose at the dream's end. It was the first time he bled after a dream.

Finding it a battle to catch his breath amid the stale air of the cabin, Michael sought fresh air from the deck outside. A clear view of the universe up in the night sky would help clear his head. Escorted under guard, like the other nights, Michael emerged onto the main deck. He leaned over the starboard side to watch the tranquil crashing of the ocean far below him. The majesty of the stars coupled with the sounds of the rolling waves below offered a serene distraction.

"I'm so sorry." Michael tearfully imagined that his wife and child could hear him from the heavens. "I couldn't save you. God, help me, I couldn't save you from it."

Hanging his head, Michael gnashed his teeth over the deaths of his loved ones. It had been routine for the Tinarian guardsmen to escort him to the deck only to see him cry and groan miserably. He leaned on his spear tiredly until the moment Michael had mourned enough for another night.

The guard finally broke the uneasiness from behind him, saying, "We're not far from home, now. Word is that we could make berth sometime tomorrow. That seagull just a stone's throw away suggests that we're that close."

Michael turned to his left to acknowledge the gull not more than a meter away cautiously ambling closer, balanced on the gunwale. But, with closer inspection, he suddenly noticed its eerie defect. A scar over its left eye appeared strikingly similar to the one on the dolphin nights before. As he looked upon it more intently, the scarred gull squawked and flew away. *What were the odds*, he thought, *that two marine animals would bear the same mark?*

Taken aback by the oddity of it, Michael watched the seagull soar into the darkness and said, almost in a whisper, "You can escort me back. I am finished here."

It was not long before the morning cheers of joyous Tinarians reached the Santa di Mare. After the ship docked alongside the wharf, hundreds of citizens gathered around to see their heroes set foot on home soil again. The Santa di

Mare was ready to sleep once more as queen over the waters of the eastern realm.

"Do you hear them, Michael?" Marinaio exclaimed. "Is this how your people welcomed you home?"

"No longer, captain," he somberly replied, compelling Marinaio to rub his eyes in embarrassment.

"Forgive me." The captain decided to say no more than that, unwilling to risk any further awkwardness.

With the Santa di Mare docked, Captain Marinaio eventually emerged with his officers to formally meet the journalists waiting for his official report on the mission. Lancea ambled through the enthusiastic crowds with Michael close behind and under heavy guard. Many of the Tinarian people were garbed in wealthy attire, idolizing much of its sister kingdom across the sea in the West. The Tinarian flag of silver and gold was flown proudly for the sailors' glorious return.

Architectural marvels appeared to envelop the massive port city, rivaling even the most illustrious seaports back home. Towers that he had seen from the ship were even more awesome from inside the kingdom. Manors of all sizes stretched across the city borders as far as the naked eye could see and beautiful fountains highlighted the entryway into Tinaria's market square. Beyond the walls, he could see King's Tower in the center of the city where the royals lived.

Knights in intimidating, yet enchanting armor guarded the busy streets and many gateways to various sectors and districts. In heading towards the heart of the kingdom from inside a chariot pulled by a team of horses, Michael gawked at the Cathedral of Alchemiei. It was a gorgeous house of worship, serving as one of the world's largest cathedrals, second only to Remnants of Christ Cathedral in Ellium.

Lancea broke his trance, "We should be inside the Royal Crux in a few minutes. In all your travels, you never thought to visit Tinaria? Surely all of the stories you've heard from across the sea do her no justice when seeing everything from the inside."

Fixing his attention north, Michael laid eyes upon the famed Royal Crux, the beating heart of Tinaria. The colossal gates opened slowly and their chariot pulled in. Soldiers patrolling the crux donned splendid armor, which set them apart from their Ellium counterparts across the sea. A leather strap intersected the plated chest that centered their kingdom's symbol: two shields—the gold overlapping the silver.

Tinaria was originally founded over three hundred years ago, built over the foundations of the old world. As fate would have it, the old derelict fort served as a gold reserve. The new kingdom immediately flourished in the East as a crown jewel. It had become the only eastern port that Ellium and other major kingdoms would patronize. Rich in resources, Tinaria had also made its share of enemies in its thirst for power and global relevance.

"This is what you asked for, Miuriell. Prepare yourself," Lancea said, sitting across from him in the coach. Michael had reason to be nervous, for he had never officially met the royal family. While a famous figure in the West, he could not count on his accolades in Tinaria. His name would not be enough to sway the kingdom to prepare for a supernatural invasion.

The Tinarian guards greeted the Herald and then his entourage in tow. In entering the King's Tower, he became overwhelmed. Having been alone in a lowly boat for days without human interaction had shocked his system. An influx of wealthy citizens went about their way within the palace atrium, discussing politics and business. There were people of various cultures and races, some from across the sea, but most bred from within the vast kingdom itself.

Following the frescos and stained-glass windows, Michael proceeded up to the grand hall where an indoor creek flowed into the trickling falls. Statues of historical heroes and ancestors of Tinarian bloodline were scattered about the place like an art exhibit. He eventually scaled red carpet steps into another gallery almost as elaborate as the one before. While they ascended, a high-ranking official approached them, saying anxiously, "You must wait, ambassador. His Majesty debates over the Madam's curious illness."

"What do you mean?" Lancea asked, abruptly troubled.

"There is word that the queen has been poisoned. Her illness gets only worse by the day," the man whispered.

Lancea gasped, "My God. But, poison? How could anyone be so certain?"

"We think the Ziamons are behind it. Several spies had been captured within our very city in the past two weeks alone. Something is brewing," the officer said.

"Why her, then? Why the queen?" One of Lancea's consultants interjected. "The Ziamons wouldn't risk starting up the war again by poisoning Her Majesty."

Getting the signal from further upstairs, the official replied, "Indeed. I will show you to His Majesty. I hope you brought some good news."

Most of the king's court congested the grand throne room, standing in their respective places. There was a stench of fear in the air. When Michael and his Tinarian escorts came through the chamber doors, a daunting silence came over them. All heads turned as Lancea entered with his associates. The king breathed a sigh of relief, intrigued to see if Lancea had brought something positive to the court.

Approaching the king's throne while passing through his subjects and superiors in their segregated spaces, Lancea kneeled and presented the signed documentation of a mission well done.

He began, "Your Majesty, Manna Excallum of Falcus and Emperor Ellis of Ellium both signed the accord. Tinaria will, at last, have an embassy in the holy city. We may begin its construction immediately, as the lot belongs to us. All of the details are ready for you to read, sire."

"Finally, Tinaria joins hands with Falcus. At least there is some good to this day," the king said jadedly. "Rise on your feet. We can talk on this later. I'm too tired."

Lancea rose from his knee and said, "I can't understand it, sire. How is the queen?"

"She is brave," King Orgento returned, "but I've never seen her this diminished. She's—fading."

The princess had then suddenly burst through the side chamber doors, followed by her frantic handmaidens, "They're just watching her die!"

"What are you doing here, girl?" The king groaned, lowering his head, vexed.

She had silky red hair and striking hazel eyes, as even in her dismay Michael had to admire her beauty. Not out of her teen years, her skin was supple and white. Princess Shina, against the rule of the court, barged into the closed session and beseeched the chief physician, "Instead of sulking in board meetings, you should find a cure for her in a lab! Isn't that what you do?"

"Shina, girl, hold on!" Lord Drake Vitan seized her from behind and directed her out of the court.

"Drake, let me go!" she cried and began to thrash at him. "That's my mother who's dying up there! That's the queen you all swore an oath to protect!"

"That's why we're all here, princess. We're trying to figure out how to save her," the lord whispered into her ear.

"We will save her, princess," the chief physician called out to her as she broke from Drake's arms.

One of the king's advisors spoke out, "The Kajhic Ruins are a last resort we may just have enough time for. They have healing spells, even more powerful than Her Majesty's."

"Never," Drake said with disgust. "We will not mingle with those savage occultists! Out of the question!"

The king wiped the sweat from his brow and said from his seat, "So you see what has happened in your absence, Lancea? Right now, the Ziamons are probably laughing at our misery. They broke the armistice. They will pay, as God as my witness."

A consultant of the king declared, "That is if they are truly the ones responsible for this crime."

"Of course, they are, you ingrate! Are you sick?" Drake scolded him. "This could be war—that long bloody war all over again!"

Lord Drake Vitan was the most admired lord in Tinaria, governing most of the port districts. In his younger years, he led large armies against the Ziamons in the Ethereal Wars. Drake was a tall man with a slight shade of white in his pointed beard. The slight wrinkles around the corners of his eyes told a tale of how long he had been serving as Tinaria's esteemed lord.

"What about the Triad?" Lord Angola introduced the idea. "Those dirt dog wizards may have cast a spell on her. Poisons aren't the Ziamons' only weapon of choice."

Drake clapped, mocking his fellow royal, "Well done, Tyron. The Triad did it? From where—from Ziamon? Wow!"

"Enough!" the king roared. "Drake, you're making my daughter seem right about this whole thing! What are we all doing here, coming up with theories that lead us nowhere?"

"Your Majesty," he humbly kneeled. "It's just—we've been banging our heads—"

King Orgento explained, "If we panic in here, how long before the people panic out there? I don't want them thinking their queen is dying, do you all understand?"

In the midst of chaos, Michael mustered the capacity to speak over the crowd, "Your Majesty, if she *was* poisoned, as some of you say, then I can cure her."

Lancea glared at him, heated by Michael's foolish nerve. Everyone else turned to focus on the stranger who dared to speak out. As they all studied him, the king irately barked, "Who is that raggedy man?"

Humiliated by Michael's boldness, Lancea stepped forward and hesitantly proclaimed, "Forgive Michael Miuriell of Pommel, Your Majesty. He was in distress, alone at sea when we found him. He represents the western realms and brings with him some dire news, I'm afraid."

"Dire news, Lancea?" the king said, leaning in to take a better look at him. "I've heard of you, Miuriell of Pommel. *We* have heard some fantastic things, but toxicology was not one of them."

"No, but I can retrace the moment of Her Majesty's alleged poisoning and possibly uncover the components. That would be critical information for concocting the queen's antidote," he said. "But I will need my staff to help focus my skills."

"And where is this staff?" Drake cut in, curious to expose the foreigner's intentions—and powers.

Before one of Lancea's associates could confirm the staff's whereabouts, Michael interjected, "In the herald's royal carriage in the rear chest."

Lancea turned to look him in the eye, astounded by his omniscience. The party nearly gasped aloud after hearing his prophetic knowledge. The Staff of Truth, still tethered to his mind like a string, was safe and in waiting of its true master. Amid the hushing silence of the court, King Orgento gestured for his guards to bring Michael closer, saying, "I have read about Urik and the other sages like him. Are your powers as real as they all say?"

To answer the Tinarian king best, Michael closed his eyes and opened his arms to the side in deep concentration. In but seconds, Lancea's entourage of eight men began to gently float into the air. Their legs dangled and shook wildly as they hovered, weightless under Michael's control. The entire court reacted to the shocking spectacle. Princess Shina grasped Drake's arm tightly in disbelief as even he winced back, utterly astonished.

Opening his eyes to witness the king's wonder, he said, "They are pretty real, Your Highness."

Sitting back into his throne, King Orgento thought aloud, "So it is true. By God, man, let them down."

Michael obliged and carefully returned the men to their feet, overhearing another lord utter, "What sorcery—?"

"Not sorcery, sir," Michael replied. "I was born with these gifts and I use them only for the good of mankind."

Though many sorcerers of the new world had faded out, their very own queen was quite the prodigy. Her powers were wondrous, yet it barely showed. Males who possessed great magic in their core naturally grew white hair on their heads. It was a telltale sign of their capabilities. The same natural rule was not so for women. The queen's auburn shade offered no clues to her magical prowess. It was considered a miracle that she had such gifts, compelling her subjects to believe that old sorcery still existed elsewhere.

After Drake exchanged glances with the king, he asked, "And what is your price, Miuriell? You're evidently here for something."

Michael took a heavy breath before saying what he had come to say, "I am here to deliver a warning from across the sea. A great and terrible force has awakened on this earth. I know this because it routed Pommel in one night. It's possible that they're wreaking ungodly havoc as we speak here. If we don't stop them, they'll surely come here too."

From silence to alarm, the king's hall erupted into an awful state of fear. Whether they believed him or not, the message brought further unrest into the castle. Guards prevented anyone from leaving the hall, for the king forbid any panic to sweep into the streets. They desperately worked to keep order until Antonis had finally arrived.

From the side chamber door, a tall dark-skinned man ambled forth. His cloak was a pearly white that nearly swept the floor as he walked. His hair in long braids, the prophet pulled back his hood and joined the assembly.

The king stood out of his chair and said to him, "We have been awaiting your return for some time, Antonis. What visions do you have? What did you see?"

Antonis declared in a somber tone, bowing before the king, "This kingdom is in peril."

"No shit," Drake scoffed. "I supposed we're all prophets then."

"Quiet!" the king implored. "My wife—the Ziamons are responsible, aren't they?"

"Not in the manner you suspect," Antonis answered, prompting the assembly to prattle on behind him. "I saw a very different truth. It is more complicated."

The royal mob had been struck with another blow. After Michael's terrifying news of evil invaders in the West, Tinaria appeared to have their own dreadful problems. The plot regrettably thickened. Antonis the Prophet continued brazenly, "My latest visions cannot wait. We must speak in private."

Michael could only assume that the alleged prophet had seen the Demon Plague in his visions. Antonis, a mystic immigrant from the neighboring Tofauti Confederation, would have sensed a rift in the welfare of the world. If he refuted Michael's story, then there was no chance in convincing Tinaria of the threat. The Tofauti people were as far from the Demon Plague's clutches as any other eastern nation.

Antonis continued in his thick accent, "There has been an evil done to our queen from inside this kingdom. She was poisoned by someone of Tinarian blood."

The crowd blew up in a panic yet again, as anyone among them could have been the traitor. Drake's eyes widened in his outrage, impulsively sweeping out possible suspects with daggers in his eyes. Michael sunk his head. Tinaria dealt with its own demons. How would they ever believe his story now?

"Well, this heinous traitor was able to get close to the queen! He will die a traitor's death!" the king shouted in tears, faced with the truth that one of his own betrayed them.

"I cannot say here. There are more urgent matters to discuss," Antonis said as he folded his hands in front of him.

King Orgento turned to Michael, trying to compose himself, "Miuriell, they will fetch your staff! As vulnerable as we may seem to you, I will see you dead if you betray my trust!"

King Orgento silenced the mob with his towering arms and delivered his last order before departing with the prophet, "No one leaves this city until the traitor is revealed!"

The king had spoken. Michael had to fulfill his missions one at a time. A small throng of officers hastily led him outside to retrieve his staff. He was determined to find the origin of the poison before her condition proved fatal. Earning the king's trust was the main hurdle to being believed. For the memory of his loved ones and the people still threatened by the demonic army, Michael swore to find a way to end it. Somehow, he had to stop the Demon Plague.

The king and his prophet had their own work to do. They sat and spoke together in a secured chamber. A servant offered them red wine and opened the shades, welcoming the bright sun. The king was visibly pale with his grayish, white beard almost drooping lazily from his tired face.

At last, Antonis offered his first premonition to the king, saying carefully, "Your exiled son will return to Tinaria tomorrow."

"What? On top of all these things, you saw that?" the king shouted with trepidation in his voice. He could never forget the tragic fall from grace of his only true heir a decade ago. As king, he ordered Eric's banishment from Tinaria due to a sexual escapade with a spy. A dark-skinned beauty from the Waasi Tribe, a rebel tribe disaffiliated from the Tofauti Confederation, swindled Prince Eric of his lineage ring. Tinarian royalty passed the ring throughout generations as a sign of loyalty to the crown and honor to their ancestors.

The spy had stolen it during a night of drunken fornication. She slipped out in the dead of night like a ghost, never seen again. Her motivations for stealing the ring were never determined. For that public humiliation and dishonor to the royal family, the king exiled his only son and relieved him of his inheritance. Queen Orgento was distraught, but she, too, upheld the integrity of the code. Eric, the exiled prince of Tinaria, would be sure to seek his ill-timed revenge on the king. But the many scandals that shook the kingdom were trivial in comparison to what conceivably ravaged the lands of the eastern realms.

PART I
CHAPTER III
THE CALLING

Lord Drake Vitan slowly approached the door to the queen's quarters where she laid in her bed, tired and weak. Upon entering her chambers, it became clear to him that the rumors were true. Michael sat in a comfortable oak chair beside the queen with King Orgento, Princess Shina, the physician and the handmaidens looking upon her in bed.

Michael then stood to the far side so that the physician could examine the effects of the antidote. He surmised that she had been poisoned with a complex toxin designed to weaken her gradually until she died. He also claimed to know where the poison had come. Because the antidote seemed to have almost an immediate impact, the king was open to trusting the famous outsider that much more.

Shina held her mother's hand tightly with great trepidation, fearing Michael and the terrifying message he carried with him. She prayed to God that he could save her mother, but after that, wanted her father to send him away.

"How is she?" Drake feverishly uttered.

The physician tried to respond, but was cut off by Shina's haste, "We think the antidote is working."

"She is still very weak, my lord," the physician started. "The medicine will take the night to become truly effective. The poison may not be out of her system entirely for another two weeks."

Shina jumped in, "I will look over her, father. I know that you have many things to attend to."

King Orgento moved a red wisp of hair away from Shina's face, "You have been such a wonderful daughter, Shina. Your mother will need you."

Interrupting the warm moment, Drake cleared his throat and said, "If the king permits, I would like to begin with my investigation into Miuriell's presence here and the awful tale he claims to be true."

Eager to fulfill his mission, Michael bowed towards the king and princess before handing himself to Drake's authority. As Michael began to leave with the lord's thanes, the king said to him, "Miuriell, if you've saved my wife, you've saved this kingdom and I will hear what you have to say."

Michael lowered his head in reverence and then left the chambers. Drake shut the door behind them and remained to ask the king, "Your Majesty, if there is anything I need to know, please tell me now."

With everyone else wondering about his intentions, the king answered wearily, "You can check on your queen's health after your duties are completed, Drake. Find out what Miuriell has to offer, but don't harm him. He is like the Jesus Christ to the West. We do not need that sort of infamy."

Not satisfied with the king's answer, he insisted further, "Who has done this?"

The king offered only a stern look and Drake nodded before leaving, realizing that he had suddenly been demoted to a "need-to-know" status. Shina looked to her father as if to ask the same question, but his eyes repelled her curiosity. The queen, under a deep sleep, would have favored Drake's company, for they were close. Aside from the chivalric code, he held a passionate love for her. He hid such treasonous feelings from the king and the rest of his court. If uncovered, it meant his execution.

In the afternoon, Antonis the Prophet decided to meditate in his quiet house just outside of the Royal Crux. Children would often try to sneak a gander at his curious ruminations through his windows. It was no mistake that Tinaria had the upper hand over any other kingdom in the East, because of his gifts. As long as Antonis served the Orgentos, Tinaria was nearly invincible. His six-month retreat into the Kajhic Ruins in the Far East was his key to foresight, as it recharged his prophetic power. In Tofauti, he was regarded as a treasure responsible for promoting the lasting peace between the two kingdoms.

Michael, in contrast, possessed the Staff of Truth. While his experience with the staff was limited, he defied the odds many times with it in his hands. At last, he was awarded the privilege of visiting Drake's manor by the docks. The enormous estate had a beautiful pasture and delightful fruit trees lined the perimeter. His wife came out in dashing attire to greet her royal guests.

Lord Kal Era and Tyron Angola were already in the manor eating and chattering with their thanes in the Vitan dining hall. Drake kissed his spouse and squeezed her buttocks as he sat down in his place at the table. She smiled and smacked him on the arm while all of their guests laughed. Michael, in the meantime, received less than charitable looks. It was a wonder to him how so little was known about his good works in the West.

Tyron was the first to speak up, saying, "I thought we all agreed on a night meeting, Drake."

Then Lord Castor said after sipping his wine, "The king asked him to do this, Tyron, so drink some wine."

Lancea arrived just in time before the conference started. Drake asked everyone to sit about the dining table so the informal meeting could start. Michael sat beside Kal and one of his men when Drake began, "This morning, Michael

Miuriell here on my left, may have saved our queen. This is why we're choosing to hear out his warning for our realm."

Amongst the applause of the stranger's benevolent deed, Tyron asked boldly, "Did you uncover the traitor?"

Drake replied as the clapping died, "The queen is recovering, but the king requested that we finish this conference. This investigation was designed to uncover the truth behind Miuriell's story. Because of his loyalty to our queen, we must allow him to speak freely about his message from the West. Is that clear?"

The assembly agreed, so Drake looked to Michael to begin his account. He stood up, glanced over at all of the assembly members at the table, and put the base of his staff to the floor, saying, "Pommel was a formidable country, and yet, we were annihilated in one night. When I returned home from Oron, a horrific force swooped down upon us. I have no proof of this, but one only needs to visit my homeland to witness the devastation for themselves.

"There were so many. These unholy things were sudden and vicious, like from your nightmares. They could tear off your limbs as you would tear the wings off a fly. They fed upon us like we were fodder. After losing my wife and my son to them, I found myself unconscious in a puny boat drifting for nowhere. That is where your ambassador found me. He can attest to that."

"I can attest only to his abandonment in the boat, not the demons he speaks of," Lancea interjected.

"Demons? I don't understand." Kal altered his position in the chair, taken aback by Michael's account.

"Call them what you will," Michael replied. "They were creatures not of this earth."

Kal then asked with gravity in his voice, "If what you say is true, then what will it take to kill one of these things?"

"You believe his story?" Tyron exclaimed. "You must be mad!"

Michael was quick to answer, "They were very strong. Not all of them were alike. Some of them flew, while others moved through the shadows."

As the assembly initiated a strange debate, Kal said sensibly, "How do we know that these demons even exist? You could be lying. I have never heard of any creatures like the ones you describe."

"Of course not! It's all preposterous!" Tyron bickered.

"Do not make the mistake of disbelieving my story." Michael shushed the arguing throng with his words. "I know how crazy this sounds, but it is better to be prepared than to fall as Pommel did—by surprise and in disbelief."

When the proceeding squabbles seemed to carry on with Drake fighting to restore order, a thane frivolously proposed, "Only Maxim Cavallo would stand a chance against them if they came to Tinaria."

After the hall plunged into silence, Drake reprimanded him, "Do not talk nonsense! In fact, don't ever intercede in a lord's conference a second time."

Cavallo's reputation was known all over the new world for his unmatched skills as a total warrior. Trained by a sage as Michael was, his name was synonymous with greatness. He was a legend in Tinaria, a brilliant soldier. Michael watched skilled warriors fall quickly during the raid of Pommel. Tinaria would need many Cavallos to match the Demon Plague's malevolent might.

"He was a great warrior, but he has been dead for at least fifteen years," Drake rejoined. "Maxim was the greatest fighter in all the land—all the new world. He was my childhood friend, but he was the heart of Tinaria."

Drake shut his eyes and sighed, visibly affected by the reminiscing. His bond with Maxim was profound. They both wielded a deadly sword, but Maxim's skills were far surpassed that of anyone he knew. No one truly knew Maxim's lineage story, except that his ancestors included a famed true paladin from Ellium over four hundred years ago.

Kal revisited the past as he spoke, "Maxim Cavallo was the greatest swordsman I had ever seen. He was braver, stronger, and more cunning than any one of us. He could kill his opponents with but one movement of his sword. Maxim was a warrior even as a child at six, for Malcusin of Oron had chosen him to be his pupil. The poor boy was twenty-five when he finished his training and thirty when he died. It was tragic."

"There is no use in speaking of him now. He was killed by the Ziamons in a cowardly raid in the night," Tyron said. "We're getting off track."

"I have regretted not being able to save him, but that was war then. Those were the Ethereal Wars." Drake raised his goblet, compelling everyone else to follow in Maxim Cavallo's name.

In their talks of better times, Michael's warnings had become diluted. He could have proved his legitimacy as he did when on the Santa di Mare by moving things with his mind, but a vision came to him. By way of the Staff of Truth, he saw havoc at the docks and felt the pain of hundreds.

"The docks!" Michael gasped in awe. "Something is about to happen at the docks!"

Before they could challenge his puzzling prediction, the alarm bell started to ring at the wharf. There were screams and cries heard from outside the Vitan estate. Progressively, more people started to shout and run for cover. Everyone at the table broke from their reminiscing and stared outside, watching a mob run about in a panic.

The party rushed out of the manor and meshed with the crowds running like headless chickens. In the distance, beyond the docks, there was a vast miasma moving towards them with tremendous speed. The skies above the sea were dark and eerie. Whatever advanced towards the shore was not an ordinary storm. It was something alive.

Isolated squalls sent angry waves crashing onto the waterfront. As the miasma rapidly soared closer to the shore, mobs of worried spectators ultimately realized that the ghostly fog was not slowing down. Captain Marinaio, stepping out of a dockside pub with young women at his sides, could not believe what he saw. He shouted into the crowds, "Everyone, clear out! Get away from the docks!"

Most of them listened to his warning, but others watched hypnotically as the sinister fog raced towards them. As it neared closer, Captain Marinaio's fears were realized. Hidden deep within the deadly miasma was a grand Tinarian trade ship coming in at full speed. Before there was any time to focus in on it, the monstrous vessel smashed through the harbor and turned the pier into splinter pellets.

With a deafening blast, the ship carrying guns and explosives bought from Ellium obliterated anyone in range. The ship instantly crushed them all, causing devastating explosions. The bow of the ship blasted into pieces as the vessel persisted to hammer through the quayside. The ghastly miasma continued to pursue the destructive ship as it destroyed everything in its wake.

When the ship finally settled into the waterfront, the towns erupted into chaos. As the smoke lingered about, people's cries filled the air. Final shards of wood came falling down over the kingdom, rousing everyone into a panic. Unable to stop the ship in its tear, Michael reclaimed his staff and looked around at the devastation. Moans and cries of shock claimed the dockside. He limped about the disaster site, aiding survivors and lifting away heavy debris with his telekinetic powers.

Hundreds came from the smog to aid their injured compatriots. Michael discovered the captain's corpse amongst others. A projectile from the killer ship jutted out from his face. Michael tried to help as many injured people as he could, placing himself closer to the devastated ship when he noticed something familiar within ground zero.

A loose dog with a scar over its eye had made itself known to him before running off into the mad crowd. He watched it go, dazed by the horrific omen. It was clear to him that the dog was another sign that something was watching. The dolphin, the seagull and finally the dog—there was a dark force at work and it may have followed him all the way to Tinaria.

There was simply no more time for debate. As he prepared to help more of the wounded, Drake came up from behind him and seized his arm, screaming, "You have led the demons right to us! It was you all the while—a sorcerer from hell!"

"What are you doing?" Michael shouted in return when a mass swarm of frightened Tinarians shoved them both out of each other's reach. Within the hazy smoke still swirling, the incensed lord unsheathed his blade and broke a path through the crowd to look for his suspected sorcerer. Yet, as he searched the town for him, Drake felt the butt of a staff buckle his knees.

When the lord turned around with blade in hand, Michael propelled him backward with telekinetic force. Watching him fall into the frantic mob, Michael raced towards King's Tower to warn of the impending doom. He couldn't trust in Drake any further, even while the lord finally believed that an evil hand was at work. He mistakenly pegged Michael as the demon himself.

But as Michael went on helping the lot around him, a sinister laugh conquered his mind. The raspy snickering compelled him to bend over and cover his ears in desperation, for it was the loudest laugh he ever heard. He wasn't surprised that the city couldn't hear the bloodcurdling cackle. It came from within his mind. Something sinister had possession over him.

After falling to his knees, the baleful laughter silenced and there was nothing, not even a natural sound as if he became deaf. It was then that the vile voice spoke to him, saying menacingly, "**Master, is this the next place? Yes, it is ripe for the taking! So sweet! So sweet a prize!**"

In fighting the evil voices within, Michael reached for his fallen staff and willed that his mind push out the dark forces. Focusing with his instrument in hand, he opened his eyes and was able to hear again. In shaking off the scary spell, he turned to the open sea and used all of his power to see into the future. He felt the energy flow from the staff, into his arm and then into his entire body. With great worry, he saw what was coming. From the darkness of the sea, Michael saw the Demon Plague rushing forth in hunger.

Drake had then come up from behind him and took the opportunity to knock him in the back of the head with the pommel of his sword. Michael's trance was over, as he fell to the ground unconscious. Drake then called for soldiers to help him carry Michael away, saying, "Not today, you son of a bitch!"

The cause of the ship's tragic crash was terrible as it was unexplained. When the Tinarian guards scouted the vessel for survivors, none were found alive. Everyone on the ship was dead. It was a bloodbath. The gruesome discovery left so many questions as to what happened and how so many could have died, leaving the ship to tear for Tinaria. Nothing was pillaged, but the sailors were butchered—some beyond recognition. And then, the cursed fog dissipated.

PART I
CHAPTER IV
THE REVIVAL

The king watched the sunset over the eastern horizon from a large open window in King's Tower. With his trembling hands folded behind him and his back hunched over, he emitted a sigh of grief. The cries of his people reached the crisis room high above, even with the bickering court behind him.

"This was an attack! Our kingdom is under attack!" Tyron cried. "The Ziamons wish to reopen the wounds—"

"The Ziamons can't be the excuse for everything, for God's sake, Tyron!" Kal shouted back, flustered.

Lancea pushed himself from the wall and retorted, "For once, I agree with Lord Angola. Can it be coincidence that all this turmoil can happen so sudden and so soon?"

"Exactly my point," Tyron said. "It could be a sign of things to come. Mind what Antonis warned us about."

"He did not warn us about a ship slamming into our ports!" Kal fired back. "He failed to mention that!"

"That's because Antonis failed us," the king said from the window, obliging everyone to stop in their tracks. It was a fact he had to set on the table. Their secret weapon, a seer, could not predict the catastrophe at the wharves. Tinaria was in a vulnerable position and Antonis was nowhere to be had.

"These circumstances have compelled me to think," the king proceeded. "My wife is healing well and the physicians say she will most definitely survive. Antonis did not foresee that, either. He didn't foresee this disastrous affair at the wharves, nor did he foresee Michael Miuriell's arrival. Wherever he is, I want him before me, right now."

"And what of Miuriell?" Kal asked, confirming his duties with a bow. "He was trained by Master Urik of Oron, much like Cavallo under Malcusin. It is to our benefit that the hero of the West is here when we may have the most use for him."

Taking his seat at the head of the meeting table, the king replied, "Yes, bring him, too. Seek out Drake and ask him for Miuriell. He saved my queen. Let us see what other things he can do."

After the final decree was given, the king asked that he be alone. His subjects agreed and went out to perform their roles. When it was only the guards outside his door, King Orgento looked out of the large windowpane once more, wondering where Drake was amidst all of the terrible confusion. When he just closed his eyes to pray, a familiar voice emanated from the darkest corner of the room. It jolted him, for there was no one left in his company a moment before.

"It is dangerous for a king like yourself to be left alone without—supervision," the voice said scornfully.

The king jerked about-face as his heart skipped a beat. From the shadows came a figure shrouded loosely in a black cloak. The shady intruder held up his advance and stood motionless with his arms crossed.

"Who dares?" the king growled his words.

"You've forgotten the only son you ever had?" the man said before removing his dark hood, revealing his long white hair. The king acknowledged his face instantly and backed himself against the window, utterly shocked to see his exiled son return so soon.

His whitened hair served as a sign that his former heir mastered the arts of sorcery. Like his father, King Orgento was certain that Eric did not inherit his mother's talents. Turning bug-eyed, he realized that there could be only one reason for his son's homecoming. Antonis was right. Eric was prepared to carry out his vengeance.

"Eric?" King Orgento murmured. "Your hair."

"Please, father. You knew I would come back. That pet you call a prophet must have told you," Eric hissed.

The king rubbed his eyes frantically, "What, in God's name, is happening? It's the end of all things."

"Always so dramatic," Eric continued as he neared closer to his father. "I'm gone for almost a decade and look what happens. Damnation."

"I suppose you've come to cut my throat?" the king said heatedly.

Eric sat in his father's chair, "Well, it had crossed my mind, yes, but in the end, I decided that it was too quick for the likes of you. In fact, I don't even know why I cared to see you again."

"How did you slither your way into my kingdom? My knights know to arrest you on sight!" the king said from across the room.

"Well, they can't take what they can't see." Eric took a date from the table and ate it, looking directly into the king's unsettling eyes. "So, do be merciful, father. Don't exile them."

"And your hair! White as a sorcerer's!" he cried out in a rage. "You always wanted your mother's powers, but to go to these pathetic lengths? I suppose you've gone mad out in the badlands!"

Before he could conjure up any convincing reaction to the king's nervous outburst, the guards knocked on the doors and asked if he was alone. Eric spun his head towards the banging and then back to his father, spitting out the pit, "In due time."

The abrupt sound of the chamber door bursting open startled the king once more if he was not startled enough already. In came the guards with Princess Shina behind them. The knights rushed in and paced about the conference room for themselves. There was only the king. Eric had vanished.

"What is going on in here?" Shina said fretfully. "We heard you screaming!"

The king, too stunned to respond, simply stared into the shadows. Worried about the king's unnatural manner, a guard investigated the darkest parts of the chamber only to find nothing. The other one approached the princess, "The king seemed spooked. There's no one here, Your Majesty."

The king thought of revealing the newest trouble to his daughter, but shook his head in dismay and waved off his guards. He remembered how much he once loved his son, but as he grew older, their bond had been torn asunder. Years ago, Eric became increasingly jealous of his mother's magical abilities. He wanted to wield the same power as she did. Eric loved her, but his radical views on politics and foreign affairs changed their relationship. His growing lust for all sorts of power plagued his mind forever since.

As King Orgento stood there, accompanied by his knights and daughter, he knew that his son would return. Believing that Tinaria was at risk of falling to pieces, the king proclaimed with a renewed composure, "I need to speak with the queen. She needs to know."

Shina peered into her father's eyes and held his face, whispering so his guards would not hear, "Father, what are you talking about? What's happening?"

"There's no time to explain." He took the princess by the wrist and led his puzzled guards out the door.

Shina said in worry as they walked down the hall, "We have time. We're walking through this damn giant hall! As king, can't you just—"

Riled by his overwhelming encounter just a moment ago, he took Shina to the side and fretfully whispered into her ear, "Shina, Antonis told me that your mother put the poison in her own tonic. No one poisoned her directly."

Shaken by her father's outlandish claim, she snapped, "She tried to kill herself? I don't care what that fortuneteller told you! Mother did not poison herself! He said it before. A traitor is responsible!"

"Well, he *was* right about something!" the king shouted, his voice echoing throughout the hall, "Just before, in the room—"

Shina tore away from her father's grasp before the king could tell her about Eric's return. She cried, "Antonis is gone! No one can find him! Let's go to your queen, as you said, so you can see for yourself that you've been betrayed!"

"Her depression is not new. She has not been herself for years!" The king followed his princess down the hallway and cried out. "We are desperate, girl!"

"The queen has asked to awaken, Maxim Cavallo!" Shina had to say it, leading her father out of the grand hall. "She wanted to awaken him before she—if she—"

"That's insane!" he rebuked her. "She will do no such thing! It'll kill her!"

"Then tell her yourself!" she said, scaling the stairs with the king in tow.

Maxim Cavallo, the symbol of Tinaria, was not wholly dead. Kept preserved by clandestine magic only the queen could provide, he rested in an extravagant tomb for fifteen years. His body was in a comatose state, yet ageless. It was the queen's most prevailing spell: Capsuli Scorpus, the Encapsulated Scorpion. Placing a fallen subject under such an enchantment required practically all of the sorcerer's magic. The awakening spell was even riskier than that.

Tyron's knights had searched the city for Drake and Michael, last in the lord's custody. Even in Drake's estates, his own family put their last sighting of him at the catastrophe by the docks. The waning moon struggled to break through the mysterious haze that seemed to settle about the kingdom. Tyron's knights gradually returned to him in groups.

The drained lord looked up at the night sky and sighed, "Where the hell are you, Drake, you fool?"

When he dispatched his last round of scouts, Tyron thought to look in one place himself. Drake, in secret, called upon some of the harlots in the southern alleys. He didn't expect to see him there, but it was worth a shot from an old friend who knew his faults. His hunch was not bearing fruit. Not even the prostitutes were in the alleyways that night.

With every next turn, he felt a lingering sensation grow stronger as if someone was watching him. Beyond the stalls of the marketplace, a dark shadow arose from the ground, portraying an old crippled hag limping into a thin alley. The shadow's movements, however, did not emulate that of a woman. It moved like a phantom, fading into the night. Tyron backed off against the wall and covered his mouth with his gauntlet, aghast with what he thought he saw.

"Come out, there!" His voice crackled as he hollered down the dark alleyway. The voices of the Tinarian populace leaving the marketplace provided small comfort when there was no answer. Sweating now, he decided to escape his sudden shame of fear and return to his men. He drew his sword and slowly crept down the dark corridor.

At the alley's end, he saw another terrible vision. The silhouette of a hairless head peeked out from the side of the market walls, scrawny and abnormally shaped. Tyron grabbed the handle of a closed shop in dismay, rallying the nerve to call out, "You'll be punished for your games! It is Lord Angola of the Northland you toy with now!"

The head remained where it was, except this time, two withered hands grappled onto the alley wall like a ghost.

Petrified, he then watched as two green glowing eyes opened to glare at him. He gasped like a girl and ran until he tripped over a lump in the blackened street. There, on the ground, lay the corpse of one of his men with his throat eaten out. The soldier's face was frozen in great horror with his eyes wide open and his mouth pried ajar.

Tyron had no energy to cry for help—just a gasp and that was all. He stepped away from the mangled corpse and panted like a dehydrated cow. Among his pants and racing heartbeat were the sounds of scurrying footsteps behind him. He heard the rasping breath of the creature and felt its warmth touch the back of his neck. Staring blankly into the dark, Tyron turned around slowly.

In an instant, his severed throat poured out his blood all about the street. He was barely still alive when the creature began to eat him. As if to mock his death, the moon broke free from the haze and shined over his mutilated body. The terrifying predator scampered off and hid amongst the shadows again, awaiting the arrival of its next royal meal.

The dungeon held hundreds of prisoners in its complex infrastructure. Deep below King's Tower, the dungeon's layout made it improbable to escape with one's life. Michael was imprisoned within a sector apart from the nucleus of the prison's virtual maze. The narrow corridor he saw outside his barbaric cage was one of many hallways that united to form a labyrinth.

Michael had effortlessly acquired an awareness of his surroundings in studying every aspect of the area with his mind. If he had his staff with him, Michael would have been able to determine his possible escape, but Drake seized it. Still, bars of any dungeon could hardly hold him for long.

"What are you thinking?" Michael asked bluntly from behind the bars of his cell. "Why tear me away from that scene? I could have helped them."

Drake replied, surrounded by his men, "You may have fooled the others, but you shall not fool me. I know who you are, Miuriell. Your name may ring 'hero' in the West, but this is the East! Your little song and dance will not work here."

"Have you gone absolutely crazy?" he said, appalled by what the lord was implying.

"Crazy?" Drake countered. "The king will hear of this betrayal, as Antonis predicted. Hundreds have died by way of your evil ship trick and I'll be damned if I let another die by the likes of you!"

"This is madness! The Demon Plague will slaughter all of you in the dead of night! I swear, they're coming here! I saw them before you knocked me out and dragged me down here, you idiot!" Michael exclaimed.

"You are the only plague I see here. This is where you belong." Drake signaled for his men to watch the cell as he proceeded to leave the dismal dungeon.

"You know these bars can't hold me!" Michael shouted for his back. "I could implode this entire dungeon without a drop of sweat!"

"Then, do it!" Drake said as he left. "Prove me right."

Michael let the crazed lord leave him behind bars. He didn't wish to harm anyone, but remaining underground while the Demon Plague festered above preyed on his mind. With a throng of guards watching his every action, Michael shook his head and sat in the center of the cage, incensed. He knew that the only way out was by force.

Michael's worry was short-lived, however, for a strong sensation tugged on his psyche from a different location. It came upon him suddenly, forcing him to open his eyes and look about the dungeon tunnels for a glimpse of the person.

The power was young and prodigious, belonging to that of a woman. To see how near this mysterious woman was to him, he placed his head against the cold bars.

"Away from the bars!" The guard struck the cell bars with his mace.

Feeling her aura draw closer, Michael said, "You're in danger. You need to leave."

When the guard instinctively turned his head, a fatal arrow pierced through his neck and killed him. The others immediately readied their crossbows, baffled as to how the assassin made it into the dungeon. At once, the prisoners started acting up in an outcry, screaming and banging their bars.

With every swing and jab from the guards' swords, the hooded assassin evaded and countered with grace. One knight gave another thrust of his sword, but the archer swiftly seized the blade and put it to his back. He let out a broken cry before she snapped his neck and dropped him limp to the floor. Drake's guards fired their crossbows and then ran the other way, seeing that their shots missed.

Only a few remained to challenge the mysterious warrior who had finally reached Michael's cell. With all of the killings had by the archer, Michael did not feel threatened. It was a rescue mission, albeit a bloody one. In the midst of all the screaming and cheering from the imprisoned, Michael probed the assassin's identity.

She removed her dilapidated cloak and revealed her beautiful dark skin. Her eyes were green, her nose was sharp, and her hair was long. She wore brown leather topped with traces of old copper, leaving plenty of bare skin open for nimble movement.

"I am Predella, but formal introductions can wait," she said hurriedly.

Astonished to see her again, Michael gasped, "Predella? You were but a child when I last saw you! My God, I forgot how long you've lived out here."

Firing another arrow down the corridor, she cried, "We have to leave, Michael! What can you do?"

"A lot." Michael gestured for her to leave him as he blew the cell door off its hinges. The bars clanged onto the ground. His captors looked on in awe as he stepped out of his cell, exerting only a fraction of his telekinetic force. The prisoners were shouting like rabid animals. While sprinting down the passageway, two alarmed soldiers turned the corner from the right tunnel and charged them down with blades.

Michael smashed them against the wall with his telepathic might and continued to run, seeking any possible escape route. Having already traced a way out in his mind, a slew of soldiers seemingly trapped them in a narrow hall from both ends. Using the only arrow left in her possession, Predella quickly fired an accurate shot into an oncoming knight's pelvis. The unlucky guard yelped as he tumbled in pain. The other knights refused to cower to her.

"There is no sense in killing these men," Michael said, urging her to stop in the center of the passageway. He shut his eyes and held on to her arm as if to keep her safe. An unusual array of psychic control engulfed the hall and put a fantastic strain on the soldiers' minds, compelling them all to stumble to the ground in pain. Predella looked on in wonder as Michael discharged supernatural energy complex enough to leave her unharmed.

Upon opening his eyes, Michael found his chosen soldier. He raised him by the neck and put him against the wall, saying, "You look like a good escort."

...

The Red Mausoleum was impressive. Built with reddened stone, the one-hundred-foot sepulcher housed the insentient body of Maxim Cavallo. A replica of his fire-sword, for which he nicknamed 'Mad Phoenix,' crowned the dome of the building. The real blade had the capability to summon the power of fire, pending on its master's wrath. Maxim was the only man alive who was chosen to wield the sword, perhaps by the sword itself. Any other who dared to hold the legendary weapon endured some of the ugliest burns known to man, if not melting their hand to a hot, bloody pulp.

Maxim's Mad Phoenix rested before his marble casket, sheathed into the fine white limestone. His armor and other articles were on display, locked in glass cases around the temple like in a museum. As weak as she was, the queen understood her duties to the realm, not only as ruler but as a rare sorceress. She was determined to awaken Maxim again, as she felt that all the signs pointed to it.

Preserved by her magic fifteen years ago, Maxim was deemed too great to lose forever. In defiance of the king's wishes, Madam Orgento stood on her feet and walked. All who saw her donned in royal garb, descending the stairs without assistance, admired her strength. She wasn't nearly through with her sickness, but she made a convincing case to the king and his court.

As the royal guard escorted them to the Red Mausoleum, cheering crowds flanked them. Seeing their queen walk with just the lightest limp was all the faith they needed to believe that the kingdom would prevail. She knew that Tinaria was in turmoil. What she didn't know was that her husband suspected her of suicide. As Shina alleged, the queen could never have poisoned herself. Regrettably, Antonis the Prophet was not present to defend his foresight and she did not give the king the chance to argue.

Drake had suddenly joined them in the temple with Michael's Staff of Truth in hand, nearly out of breath. Hearing of the plot to resurrect Maxim, the lord tracked the royal court into the Red Mausoleum. He was determined to persuade them that awakening the fallen hero was unnecessary, for the sorcerer responsible for all of Tinaria's calamities was uncovered.

"Where has that man been?" the queen questioned Kal, directly beside her.

"Drake is finally here. You can ask him yourself, Your Majesty," Kal replied, considering Michael's staff in Drake's possession. "Or, if you'll permit me, Your Highness."

"Leave him," Madam Orgento said boldly. "If this evil that Miuriell speaks of intends on killing us, we will need Maxim. Announce my starting. Lord Vitan will have to wait until I am finished. There can be no interruptions."

Before announcing it, he turned to her again and said, "Your Highness, are you sure about this? Are you sure your body can take it? Please, you don't have to do—"

"Look around you, Lord Era," she returned. "This is the time. What this country needs is a resurrection of faith. The king had forbidden it all those years before, but he wouldn't dare forbid me tonight. Now, announce it or leave."

After Lord Era regretfully announced the beginning of the spell, the many spectators moved away. When everyone was a safe distance away, the king came forth and kissed her on the forehead. As they embraced, she gently touched his face and said, "Luther, go with the others. When I am done, both Maxim and I will greet you there."

She summoned her powers once she felt her full power charge completely. As she raised her arms, the temple's interior began to change dramatically. A steady burst of energy emitted from her body and surged throughout the place, illuminating everything. They all tried to cover their heads as the supernatural upsurge flashed and crackled like thunder. Her subjects had forgotten the power of their queen, even in sickness.

Madam Orgento commanded the blinding light to compact itself into a tiny orb that hovered above her open palm. The orb, no bigger than an egg, spun rapidly before her. Chanting the Lights of Life mantra, the orb blasted away from her hand and entered Maxim Cavallo's resting place. Then, like a tremendous ray from the sun, a marvelous cylinder of the same great light exploded from the tomb and discharged a deafening blast.

"This will kill her! God save us!" Drake shouted amongst the spell's incredible display.

After the magical cylinder vanished, her duty to the spell had finished. The queen fell on her back in exhaustion. Kal, Drake and other nobles ran to carry her weakened body over to her physicians and maidens. Having completed the difficult spell, it was a miracle to all who witnessed it. She had not attempted it since she was a young woman in Ellium. Michael's opening for the right antidote served as the key to her rebounding strength.

After a skeptical silence, a bright yellow ray quickly rose from the tomb and reached the ceiling above. Following another shocking blast, rays shot out from the casket and lit the mausoleum a second time. The cry of a warrior filled the temple and confirmed the spell's success. Maxim lifted the heavy cap and sat up. The yellow light thickened even more until it finally revealed the legendary Maxim Cavallo rise to his knee. He crawled and then fell out of the raised casket, hitting the ground on his side.

The beams of light disappeared, leaving Maxim feeble, but very much alive. With the temple stricken with wonder and awe, Maxim attempted to stand. One thane grabbed Maxim's arms and another supplied a warm cloth to cover him. The fire-sword remained asleep within the stone just to his side, thirsting eagerly for its master's attention.

"Maxim, can you hear me?" Kal held his face, amazed.

He slowly opened his eyes and lifted his head to address his old friend, "Kal? Where are we? What's—"

"Welcome back, old friend," he whispered into his ear, thanking God in the process. The queen was frail, but she had survived the taxing spell. Hope was forming, as the king, himself, witnessed.

"Am I dead? Did I die?" Maxim asked his comrade, unable to take in the rush of life that surged through him.

"You are reborn. There is much to tell, but we must clean you up first. I can't believe it worked." Kal helped him by his shoulder and summoned the help of others. To his surprise, King Orgento had been the first to offer hands of support. He took the place of another and helped carry the awakened hero from the other arm

Light of Life, even earlier in the peak of the Sorceric Age, was hardly regarded as a trustworthy casting. Often times, the spell gave rise to not a person, but an undead creature. Other times, it reanimated the body but left the host dead. This spell was never guaranteed to work—not even by the most eligible magician. For the queen, she put more than her magic into him. She emptied her heart and all the faith in the world that he might live again.

Drake stepped back and remained hidden amid the blissful crowd, much too frightened to acknowledge what had just taken place. He never would have supported the decision to risk the queen's life. Surrounded by his enthusiasts, Maxim had reacquired his armor piece by piece. All he cared about was reuniting with the Mad Phoenix.

Unexpectedly, the colossal doors of the temple opened up and Michael Miuriell walked through with Predella at his side. The small army outside was no match for them. Drake tightened his grip on Michael's Staff of Truth from within the crowd.

"I'll take that staff," Michael said boldly before them.

Drake quieted the temple, exclaiming, "Miuriell, what have you done?"

Michael cried in return, "You threw me in a dungeon without cause!"

"Do you see it?" Drake addressed the hall. "He's working with Predella! He has come to bring this kingdom down with that terrorist!"

Michael beseeched the mass assembly, "I have come in peace and I will leave in peace, but not before I've achieved my purpose here! It's no coincidence that this woman and I are here at the same time—and now Maxim! All three of us were pupils once to the sages of Oron! The three of us have never stood together against a common foe before this night! Believe me when I say it, you'll need all of us if Tinaria wants to see daylight."

"Do not trust him, sire," Drake beseeched the king from the crowd. "Predella has terrorized our kingdom for years. Even the Tofauti cast her out! You didn't see what—"

"Quiet!" the king cried, leaving Maxim to lean on Kal. "You have no idea what's going on! You disappeared! We all feared you were dead, but here you are now! Did you know what your queen just did? Do you see Maxim here, alive? All that I see is Miuriell's staff in your hands as you cower among my subjects!"

"But, Your Highness, I implore you—" Drake couldn't find favor with the king as he staggered forth.

"I heard accounts of Michael's service at the docks and then you're assault on him from behind!" King Orgento went on. "We are all making sacrifices, Lord Vitan! Michael has done more for your kingdom than I can say for you!"

Amid the dramatics, Predella admired Maxim in his vulnerable condition. As a child, she was in love with the tales of Maxim's courageous battles against the pirates of Miguel Bay. Though some Tofauti denounced him as a war criminal, Predella saw him as a reflection of herself. She loved even the idea of him.

Maxim could hardly understand what Michael was saying, due to his delusional state. King Orgento, on the other hand, believed in Michael and chose to accept his warning. He stepped forward and proclaimed, "I have the word of Michael Miuriell and that is enough! He has proved himself to me. Maxim has returned to us! Together, we will face any evil, any doom that threatens Tinaria this night and any night thereafter!"

He then turned to Drake and said, "What comes for us, we will be ready for them. Return Miuriell's staff, at once."

Drake countered heatedly, "He is not what he seems, I swear on the—"

Before the lord could even finish, Michael utilized his telekinetic attributes and pulled the staff out of his hand. The staff drifted smoothly into the air and passed a number of people before pressing gently into Michael's hand. Leaving everyone in absolute awe, Michael said, "Your queen put her beliefs to the test tonight. I think we owe Her Majesty a return for her investment."

PART I
CHAPTER V
THE BLOODSTORM

Many Tinarians had already heard rumors of the impending doom and booked voyages for Ellium or Falcus across the ocean. It was clear that King Orgento had been losing more control over his realm as the night dragged on, despite the uplifting news that Maxim had returned. Some believed that if the crown had to resurrect him, then certainly something terrible was on its way. Similar to the fog that ushered in the death ship earlier, a sinister cloud had blotted out the moon.

The candles and lanterns illuminating the king's quarters were burning feverishly. Gusts of wind brought the feeling of malevolence in the cold darkness, flapping the Tinarian flags wildly. From his chamber window, the king helplessly watched three full ships disembark for the West. Not allowing the people to flee would have brought disaster in the streets. They knew that something was coming. King Orgento felt his kingdom slowly bend into the wicked night.

Just moments later, his guards at the door announced that Maxim Cavallo had come calling. Jerking from the window, he swiftly agreed to it. When the door swung open, Maxim stepped in. He was handsome with short untidy hair and a strong jaw. Donning his black chest plate with the Tinarian seal on his pauldrons, Maxim saluted the royal family with a fist to his heart. A small gold cape cascaded down his back, partly concealing the scabbard holding his fire-sword.

The blade was virtually indestructible and blush colored, waiting to erupt into flames on command. The ergonomic hilt made it easy to wield and the round translucent pommel, seemingly encasing the symbol of the Phoenix, caused for a perfectly balanced weapon. It was a timeless artifact, shrouded in mystery.

"Come closer, my son." The king opened his arms.

Both of them in tears, they embraced tightly. Maxim assured the king as they finished, "Worry not, sire. Whatever threatens Tinaria tonight will be sorry they tried."

Patting his face, King Orgento said, "You've managed to uplift my spirits, boy. You look like the man I knew, like a living, breathing memory right before my eyes. There were times, hard times when your queen begged me to let her bring you back, but I couldn't. I was too scared for her life. Now I see how wrong I was for not believing. Are you well? What does it feel like?"

"I feel like I've slept for the better half of my life. Seeing everyone so different from what I remember, it's so strange," he said, "I'm so grateful to Her Majesty. I know that whatever I do can never repay—"

"Just be the man worthy of her magic," the king replied with hope in his voice. "Just be the man you are—the beating heart of Tinaria."

"Kal sent me to escort you down to the war room," he said. "They're all waiting for us there."

Composing himself, the king looked to the royal guards standing at the ready and declared, "Good. Then let's get on with it."

With Maxim at his side, the king ambled down the hall and into the war room. It sobered him to see Tinaria's greatest standing around the conference table, waiting to discuss the plan ahead. There was still that grave feeling that Eric hid somewhere, waiting for the perfect time to strike. It was there that he surprised him last.

After bowing to their king, Kal presented Michael and Predella under armed guard. Drake eyed them carefully from across the way. While they permitted Michael to keep his staff, the royal guard confiscated Predella's illustrious bow. The king acknowledged the presence of his daughter when he began, "Let us waste no more time."

The royal guard closed the door and shut them in before the king permitted the assembly to sit. Just as he sat, King Orgento honed in on Predella and asked boldly, "I see the infamous Predella has joined us this evening. Aside from Michael's word that we can trust you, I'd like to hear it from the horse's mouth. Why are you here?"

Unafraid, Predella answered, "What is happening is bigger than our past, Your Grace. I came to trade supplies for a river tribe in want just twenty miles into the Ghost Forest. When the accident at the docks happened, I got a glimpse of Michael Miuriell doing what he does best. That's when I saw this man arrest him without any reason."

"There was plenty of reason, woman," Drake countered heatedly. "You have no voice or power here at this table. If you care to accuse me—"

The king interceded, "On the contrary, *I* gave her a voice at this table. She has skills this kingdom needs. We've employed her services before. I trust she'd be willing to lend her services for free."

"That is your trouble, Your Majesty, if I may be bold," Drake said. "She's a mercenary—a hired bow. Her allegiance is to no one but herself. She has no loyalty to any nation. In her breakout from the dungeons, she killed three men. These were good, loyal soldiers who pledged their lives to you, Your Highness. In our most desperate time, keeping her close is a dangerous proposition."

"Your impulsivity is dangerous," Michael cut in. "You made this city ever more vulnerable in arresting me. Those men died because you put them in a hopeless situation."

"Shut up!" Drake cried out, pointing at him from across the table. "You're an interloper, a wolf in sheep's clothing!"

"Drake. Breathe," Maxim finally interjected. "I've been gone for a long time, but I still know you better than anyone in this room. You're passionate, like me, but this isn't the man I remember. Look around you. Michael was right. The three of us, together, can't be chance alone. You need to listen."

"Maxim, you've been gone for too long and God knows I've missed you every day," Drake said in return, "but if you want to talk of coincidences and fate, then take a *second* look around. Predella is a spy—a dog of war. She's a killer."

"So am I," Maxim answered. "So are we."

Kal shook his head and raised his finger, trying to have a say in the debate when Drake retorted, "But we fight on the same side, Maxim. We fight for honor. We took an oath."

Michael then said, "The circle only has one side. At any moment, this kingdom you love, this kingdom you took an oath for, will need all of us to work together. When we survive the night, then you can put us on trial if you want. If that helps move this forward, then for the love of God, so be it! But we're running out of time! I've seen too much suffering. I've lost too much already! So, if you don't mind, can we talk about saving lives?"

At once, the room was quiet. Drake, nearly standing out of his seat, looked about the table and then sat. Michael's words had a sobering impact on them all. Even he sighed and leaned back into his chair, propping his staff against the bookshelf just to the side. When everyone reflected on the troubles at hand, Kal broke the silence, "Tyron's thanes said he disappeared. Search parties found nothing. Antonis likely fled, perhaps to Tofauti."

"What of my mother?" Shina quickly rose from her seat, refusing to stay quiet. "Doesn't anyone care about her?"

"Your Highness, the queen risked her life to awaken me, so I am indebted to her until I die—again," Maxim vowed, offering a consoling smile. "I went to visit her. She'll recover. She's strong, like you, princess."

Shina was told heroic stories of him, one of them being the famed rescue mission that he took on himself. A spy posing as a servant for years had participated in a plot to steal her as an infant and hand her off to waiting Ziamons. Before talk of war or even negotiations for her release could begin, Maxim singlehandedly infiltrated the Ziamon bulwark and broke her out. It was the most brilliant and daring act he had ever done, turning him into a living legend.

"The spies we captured gave us nothing," Drake said. "I saw their eyes. Tortured and deprived of provisions, they had nothing—just prowlers."

"Leave it." The king raised his hand tiredly. "We'll see to that once we've learned from Miuriell. It's time we heard him—without doubt, with an open mind."

Though Michael had finally the chance to warn them of the impending doom in detail, a chill ran up his spine. Impulsively, he grabbed his Staff of Truth and sensed the disturbance. From outside, in the hall, a supernatural force had come. The table looked on him with worry when he said, "Outside, something is here."

Almost immediately, a guard rapped on the door, shouting, "Sire, someone has broken through our preliminary defenses! He's coming this way—a sorcerer!"

The guardsmen readied their blades and blocked the chamber door. The table leaped from their seats and took positions within the war room. The king held Shina in his arms and the guards stood before them, ready to give their all in case the intruder reached that far.

"Stay here." Maxim unsheathed the Mad Phoenix and ran into the grand hall. Drake and Kal were right behind them. He stared down the mysterious foe as he casually ambled towards them. There were only two guards left to face the enigmatic foe. All the others were unconscious. Maxim stepped in front of the knights and prepared for battle. Michael and Predella came out to join them.

"I'll give you one chance to stop in your tracks now! After that, you'll just be a corpse!" Maxim cried, pointing at the hooded intruder with his searing blade.

When the hooded man halted, Michael said softly into the air, "This man is something more. He shares blood with the king."

Hearing Michael's whisper from far up the hall, Prince Eric removed his hood. The exiled prince had come to confront everyone this time. The party was stunned to see him return to Tinaria, defying King Orgento's judgment. Eric knew that he instigated his own execution by coming back, but the call for retribution was too great.

Maxim had not seen Eric since his death and the prince was but a boy then. Eric said proudly, "I see all of you have come to witness it. This is what I wanted."

Drake screamed in shock, "Traitor! I'll kill you for this!"

From inside his chambers, the king called out, "I'm coming out to confront him! I am what he came for!"

Losing his patience, Drake warned the guards beside him, "If the king comes out of that room, it'll be your heads!"

"His hair is white. Eric is a sorcerer? That can't be him," Kal said, shaken. "It can't be you!"

"I just want to talk to him," Eric said coolly while opening his arms to the side. "I want you all to hear what I have to say to him. Then, you'll understand."

Drake gestured to the floor with his sword, "Like you talked to those men?"

"They are only sleeping, Drake, you lout. You've aged badly," Eric riposted.

When Drake was sure to run up and cut Eric into pieces, Shina tried to force herself out through the door. The guards were ready to sneak her and the king out through the secret passageway. Eric dropped his smirk then, asking loud enough for the king to hear, "Does she know?"

Drake warned him, "You have to the count of three to kneel where you stand! This is one!"

Just then, Eric recognized her. Standing amongst the others, he sharpened his gaze on Predella. Gnashing his teeth, he cried out almost in a wine, "Is that her? Is that you? How are you even standing there? He took *you* in?"

"Two!" Drake cried out, prompting Maxim's fire-sword to start up in flames. Everyone near him moved away.

She knew Eric would want to murder her, given their history. Her dubious, intimate night with the prince was part of her plot to steal his lineage ring. The clandestine task fell to her, though she regretted it every day since. In many ways, she didn't have a choice. Her theft of the ring was not for greed or sinister intent against Tinaria.

"Since when did you allow this scum from the clans to stand among you?" Eric roared as he sauntered towards them. "She stands by your side, like an ally? Have you any idea who that woman is? Do you have any idea what she did to me?"

"Give me the word and he dies!" Maxim cried, gaining the attention of the king inside.

Shina then shouted in return, "No, don't kill him!"

Eric stopped again, eying Maxim's fire-sword rise in flames, and rejoined, "Your new black friend here stole my lineage ring. This whore is the reason you banished me in the first place!"

As they impulsively looked her over, the king didn't hesitate to answer from behind the door, "I could believe you, but there would be no profit. Von Vanna trained her and she has pledged her loyalty to me, as did Michael Miuriell!"

Eric countered with great anger, "You fool! Are you blind? Are you dumb?"

Drake persisted brazenly, "Then there is no one who can be trusted!"

"Father!" Eric cried, still seeking the king. "No king would ever send their only son into exile for that purpose alone! I was the only heir you ever had!"

When the tension was too high to bear for anyone, Michael felt the sensation of concentrated evil growing inside him. His staff rumbled an alarming energy up into his heart. Like on the Santa di Mare, a small stream of blood slowly crept from his nostril. Michael felt the blood as he worryingly touched it with his fingers. The stalemate in the grand hall stopped to witness the bad omen. With it came an uneasy feeling that everyone felt.

On cue, Lancea Forra came rushing into the great hall with a dozen wounded knights behind him. One of the soldiers had claw marks on the side of his face and another had a bloodied bandage covering his eye. Eric turned about and dropped his guard, for the men were in no position to arrest him.

"Your Highness!" The royal herald passed the exiled prince as if he was nothing and knelt frantically. "Almost every ship has sailed, full of people escaping the curse on Tinaria! There are creatures, sire! Creatures are—"

One of the knights cried out, "The fog is falling heavier upon us! We're being hunted in it!"

The king then emerged from the war room, seized by their accounts of the terror just outside. Michael made a fist, squeezing his blood out of anger. He knew that it was too late.

"Tyron is dead and I swear it, sire!" Lancea went on, sweating profusely. "Look at these men! They can tell you what nearly killed them! Look out at the night sky shrouded in the fog! It is turning red!"

The terrified silence was daunting. Tinaria had never faced an enemy they couldn't see or understand. Drake suddenly moved in to run Eric through with his blade, growling, "And you're another one of Miuriell's emissaries, bringing your minions here to wipe us out?"

"I cannot take credit for this one," Eric proclaimed, bemused like the rest.

In the sudden turn of events, the king was ready to break a blood vessel. He ordered his guards to detain his son, but the order was muffled by Shina's screaming. Maxim dashed for the war room with everyone else following closely behind, leaving Eric to face Drake in the grand hall. When the party entered the chambers, they saw Shina in sheer terror amongst her knights, unable to turn away from the window.

The sky was red and a hard rain poured down over the city. The screams of horrified Tinarians outside confirmed the grisly truth that the rainstorm was red as blood. Kal extended his arm out of the window and let the droplets run over his hand. Jaws dropped at the sight. The rain crashed onto his open hand and pooled into a red puddle.

"Blood! God save us, it's raining blood!" he uttered chillingly as he pulled in his bloody hand.

A relentless rain of blood painted the city of Tinaria a sinister crimson. Those in the streets were soaked with the heavy blood from the reddened sky. As Shina cried at the disturbing calamity, King Orgento laid his back to the wall and surrendered into madness.

"Drake, take the king!" Maxim shouted desperately as he dashed out of the room in a flash.

"No, Maxim!" the king called for him, but to no avail. He was out to save his people. Accepting that Maxim was gone, he grabbed Kal's arm and said in distress. "Protect your queen! Go now!"

Kal ran off to safeguard Madam Orgento in her chambers. In his hurried run, Drake followed, leaving Prince Eric there. Lancea looked to the lords for help as they raced by, but they couldn't stop for him. Eric glared down on the petrified ambassador and groaned, "Useless."

Shina eventually sat back down at the conference table and hypnotically glared out at the supernatural nightmare. Predella closed her eyes and sighed, then turned to Michael, "I need my bow."

In disgust, Michael extended his arm out of the window and let the blood pour over his hand. Feeling the evil run through him, he took in his bloody fist and answered, "Your Majesty, I never thought the Demon Plague would come here so soon. It followed me somehow. I'm sorry."

The king said nothing. He only looked on blindly, as if in shock. Shina, too, was overwhelmed by it all. Michael and Predella shared a look of accordance, coming to terms with the circumstances, and left together. Leaving through the hall, they passed Lancea and the wounded soldiers. Michael helped the ambassador to his feet and said, "Your king and princess need you right now. Please take care of them."

When they left, Predella looked back and realized that Eric was gone. She knew that he would return again to settle scores with his newfound powers. However, there was time for that later. Michael used his gifts to find her elemental bow as they prepared to meet the others under the rain of blood.

Michael had the belief that those who doubted him would swallow their pride and follow his counsel. They would have to if they wanted to survive what came for them. Surrounded by dozens of others as he watched the blood pour from the atrium of King's Tower, a small child ran into his side. Michael broke from his trance to acknowledge him.

It was difficult to make out the child's face. The boy was covered in blood, having just escaped the rain. Using the inside of his cloak to wipe some of the blood from the child's face, Michael took in the boy's brown eyes, button nose, and round face. Seeing these features reminded Michael of his lost son, Seth.

They looked so alike that it nearly brought tears to his eyes. He smiled like a father, almost determining to hug the small boy. He said something in a petrified state with his eyes looking up as a puppy, but Michael could not hear a thing on account of the havoc around him. The clicks and clanks of the knights' armor and the stampedes of helpless Tinarians racing to find sanctuary from the bloodstorm muffled his hearing of the boy's utterances. People slipped on the blood that dripped off their bodies as they ran into the atrium for shelter.

From his left, a young woman approached the boy and asked, "Where is the rest of your family, young one?"

Pointing out towards the bloodstorm, the child started to cry. She frowned before taking his hand, "Come, I will take you to the medical ward where it is dry and safe. Then, we'll find your parents. How's that sound?"

Michael admired her compassion through all the mess, while he could hardly feel anything other than the evil of what lurked in the rain. The most eloquent kingdom on that side of the world was painted red. Birds fell to the blood-soaked ground and small alleyways were flooded. The realm was helpless against the storm.

However, as fast as the blood came, it died, leaving hell in its wake. Along with the cries of powerless Tinarians in the late of night, Michael tightened his hold on the Staff of Truth and focused on the task at hand. He knew that the end of the storm was but a precursor to the invasion. When Predella had come up beside him, armed with her elemental bow, they bravely went out into the night together.

PART I
CHAPTER VI
THE STAND

The aftermath of the bloodstorm revealed more devastating results than any war fought in Tinaria's history. The air smelled rank of blood. Because the torches were smothered by the storm, Tinaria was at its darkest. Maxim had just made it out of the tower when he saw his beloved kingdom in a ravaged state. He fell onto his knees, overcome with grief, and glared over the Tinarian flag stifled by red mud. He unearthed the thrashed symbol and pressed it hard onto his breast, letting his Mad Phoenix plunge into the bloody ground.

Soldiers assured the people that it was safe to come out into the open night again. Commotion and cries developed as the people emerged to discover the extent of the damage. They were all too shaken to comprehend how something so inexplicable could have ever happened. Panic had won the night.

Despite the queen's frailty after Maxim's awakening, she was able to dwell about her concerns. Because Madam Orgento was in need of rest, her maidens helped her slip into her nightgown. Drake entered unannounced before she could fully strip down.

"Drake! For God's sake, can't you knock?" she scolded.

"My apologies, Your Highness." He softly shut the door behind him. One of her three maidens laid the nightgown on the divan, while the others prepared the queen's clothing for the next morning. Drake nervously cleared his throat and said. "The king wishes to know that you are safe. As do I."

"Did he also wish for you to barge into my room like a bandit?" she said, juddered by the night's incredible trials.

"Forgive me, Your Highness," he panted and shook his head. "The kingdom is in ruin and I have my theories as to—"

"Then bring your theories to the king," she interceded. "I am heavily guarded by competent soldiers. Tell him that I do not require one of his babysitters."

Taken aback by the queen's rebuke, Drake hesitantly bowed his head and left. Once the door shut behind him, she held her heart and peered out her window yet again. One of her ladies encouraged that she continue to undress. She did so, still incensed that her husband didn't reveal the traitor that poisoned her evening tonic so many nights ago. *Why did he keep it a secret?* she thought.

As Drake passed the guards and into the war room again, soaking up looks of surprise from those sitting at the table. Lancea and the king had suspended their conversation while Princess Shina propped up her head in waiting of Drake's report.

The king was busy hearing further accounts from his herald when he turned to his lord, asking him, "What are you doing here?"

Shutting the door, Drake leaned into the conference table and said dejectedly, "The queen does not wish to see me. She called me a babysitter, in fact."

"That woman!" The king smacked the table.

Shina griped at her father almost instantly, "That woman brought Maxim back to life!"

Before the king could have at her, Drake grabbed one of the chairs and sat, starting cautiously, "Perhaps now is the time to inform her about the prince?"

"Is it? *Now* is the time?" the king groaned, pointing at him. "Stand up."

Guards in the room were heavily armed and numbered with General Grasso on his way up. Upon entering the meeting, Drake ordered some of the men to step outside and help guard the grand hall.

Picking at the banquet of food before him, the king said, "We must put our trust in Miuriell from this moment on. We act fast before this plague hits us with phase two."

"Municipal Hall seems to be the best place to congregate and discuss our plans for defense," Drake said. "I can intercept the general and lead him to gather the others."

The king thought on it before saying, "Find Miuriell and have him join you. Find out all you can about what's coming."

"Yes, Your Highness." Drake saluted before heading out.

King Orgento, as the lord was leaving, called him back and continued brashly, "And if I hear that you've done something to sabotage him in any way, you will be punished."

Drake bowed and left, incensed with that last part.

From inside Municipal Hall, right in the center of the Royal Crux, Drake and Kal observed the greatest officers come in for their orders. Under heavy guard, Predella and Michael followed Maxim in. As the night went on, Tinaria's finest discussed how they would defend the kingdom from the most terrifying evil ever to threaten their world. Tinaria was finally willing to make a stand.

The dimly lit hall crowded brave warriors into one place. The first order of business was to uncover the whereabouts of the initial attack. General Grasso, heavy and sporting a thick beard, asked Michael from across the table, "What kind of incursion are we likely to expect from these things?"

Kal furthered Grasso's inquiry, "Where did they come from when your land was attacked, Miuriell?"

Michael looked down at the large print of the Royal Crux and replied, "They will come from everywhere. We will need to station fighters all around the kingdom, even unassuming places where there are some traces of light. Some creatures can emerge from the shadows."

"This is insane!" Grasso threw up his arms. "How can we possibly prepare for things like that?"

"We will need crossbowmen at the parapets and gunmen at the turrets all over the city," Maxim said, leaning over the table to inspect the prints of the kingdom. "The local militia can guard all of the places Michael was talking about. They can guard their towns."

Grasso pointed to stations on the prints, "Then I want a man behind every arrow loop that can be had. If they will invade us from the west, then we will station half of our catapults and cannons towards the Great Pacifica. We will blast them out of the sky and into the water."

Drake added, "Be careful. The Santa di Mare will be in harm's way with your strategy."

Amid the dwindling numbers and festering trepidation within the hall, fierce bickering transpired. The infighting resounded throughout and hindered any chances of developing a sound defensive plan. Michael knew that they would never fend off the Demon Plague like that. There was no time. Hence, he proceeded to pound his staff into the floor until the madness died down.

When the hall was silent, Michael said, "We can fight together or die divided."

Agreeing with him, Maxim asked, "Do these things have any weakness?"

As the hall awaited anything that could give them courage, Michael remembered the worst night of his life and said, "It's possible that they can't stand the sunlight. If they could, the Demon Plague would have come earlier. Other than that, I don't know. I can tell you that they strike fast and hard from the air and the darkness."

The hall was never so quiet. If they could resist until sunrise, then there was a chance. Tinaria had to last until the sun rose again. While Michael struggled to think of anything else, he felt an overwhelming presence. People began to look upon him with apprehension, for some had already witnessed the omen hours ago. Again, a thick stream of blood slid down from Michael's nostril and ran over his lips. He sopped up the blood and shook his head. His body had given him signs.

Maxim knew what it meant. He backed away from the table and called out, "Time's up!"

He unsheathed the fire-sword and headed for the door. There was no time for special tactics. The meeting was adjourned. Drake followed his ally and mobilized his knights. Michael came to terms with what he was going to experience a second time. Believing that he led the demons across the sea to their new directive, he pounded the table with his fist in guilt. A deep crater in the table shook those near him.

The warriors roared like savages, holding their weapons high in the air as they charged into the dark city that became Tinaria's battleground. The militia lit torches all about the nation. The word spread to the entire kingdom that the oncoming assault was nigh. Every brave soul gathered their armaments, kissed their loved ones, and ran out into the night, prepared for combat.

Michael caught one of the priests standing outside of the Cathedral of Alchemiei and interrupted one of his blessings, saying, "Father, you must allow as many as you can to hold up here. For those who can't fight, they need to hide."

The cleric responded after he finished a knight's blessing, "The cathedral is already filling up with people. We are in God's hands now."

As the king and his daughter awaited any word from his officers about the night's defenses, Madam Orgento and her exiled son walked down the hall and accompanied them under the guard of twenty men. The sight was almost too absurd for the king to bear. They stood together in stunned silence, surrounded by armed guards.

"You must be joking," the king finally griped through his teeth, unwilling to let Eric enter.

With her arms outstretched, the queen answered, "Invite us inside so that we may be a family—at the end."

"Mother? Is that—" Shina covered her mouth in shock of seeing her brother again.

"He came to me when I could not sleep," the queen replied. "Please, Luther. He has given up his misguided campaigns out of hate. What is happening out there changes everything."

The king regretfully permitted his soldiers to let them enter, "You don't know him anymore, woman. I can't stress that enough! As king, I forbid it!"

"Do you even know *me* anymore?" she shouted, stampeding over his proud rant. "As queen, I brought Maxim Cavallo back into our world! As queen, I delivered you a daughter and a son! On this night, we are not going to be separated by our past! I forbid *that*! We must remain as a family, at the very least, tonight!"

Stupefied by his wife's unexpected reproach, the king brought his finger up to her face and fired back, "Do not dare challenge me on my—"

"On your what, Your Majesty?" she interjected. "They are my children, too! Will you prevent their reunion even after all this? You are not that man. You are a better man than that."

Almost on impulse, Shina moved into Eric's welcoming arms, despite their father's disapproval. The king felt betrayed by his family and guardsmen for allowing the gathering to take place at all. Even now, he believed that his son plotted something sinister, playing his own mother like a pawn. As the queen stood her ground, King Orgento scowled at the reunion. Eric hugged his loving sister genuinely and watched his father with a baleful stare all the while.

While the city scurried to prepare for the incoming attack, Predella equipped a bushel of arrows in her quiver at the crowded armory. She knew that her fate was sealed even if she singlehandedly saved Tinaria from the impending assault. She killed dungeon guards in her attempt to free Michael from his imprisonment. For now, however, she put her mind to task.

Predella placed her slender boot on the edge of the square's courtyard fountain and tightened her laces. While doing this, she watched Maxim come to join her. Fully armed to take on the Demon Plague himself, the swordsman splashed water onto his hands just across the way of the fountain's falling water tainted with blood.

"So, the infamous Waasi huntress is ready to defend a bunch of Tinarians?" Maxim started. "Surely, you have better things to do than risk your life in hell."

"Of course, I do," Predella replied playfully.

Maxim smirked and said, "Then you're as crazy as they all say. I guess that's good. We can use some crazy people."

Adjusting her leather attire, she indulged him, "When I was a child in the West, the elders would pass on the stories they heard from traveling tradespeople. People said you were a half-demon. Some even said that you were a demigod. I knew that Malcusin had trained you as Von

Vanna trained me. I wanted to meet you in Ellium, but I was just a kid."

"So that's why you came here then?" He moved in closer to her position. "You wanted my autograph?"

Brushing off his sly words, she said, "You were dead."

"I was." Maxim came in close and looked deeper into her striking eyes, saying. "When I was alive, I heard stories of *you*. As a young girl, you mastered the art of that special bow. It fires arrows of fire and ice at will like the bow was enchanted. I've never seen that for myself."

Smiling into his brown eyes, she said keenly, "There's a certain magic here in the arrow rest. When the arrow rubs against it, the bow recognizes the fire or the ice that I want in the grip and I just let it fly. It's that simple."

Captivated, Maxim took one of her hands in his and answered, "And it only recognizes one of these hands?"

Predella pulled her hand back and started to walk away, ending her flirt session, "The bow gets jealous."

Maxim watched the provocative archer saunter off into the city, instantly enamored. As she walked on, Predella eventually turned back to look at him again, then shaking her head when she had her answer. Maxim dipped his head into the fountain, tainted with blood, and then instantly regretted it. He frantically shook off the foul water right after.

PART I
Chapter VII
THE INCURSION

In the square, not far from the fountain, Michael and Kal met up with torches in hand and looked down upon a mutilated corpse. The body lay disturbingly twisted on the blood-soiled ground. His throat gouged out and one of his arms ripped off, the poor man died in fear and agony.

"What in God's name?" Kal covered his mouth by way of his wrist in disgust.

Michael peered around the grotesque scene in search of further clues. Scar marks on the body revealed the telltale signs of a shadow demon's work. They were stealthy creatures that set the stage for full-scale assaults, causing confusion and panic. Scrawny claw mark imprints littered the bloody mess.

Michael looked at the lantern's eerie light as it enabled a shadow to develop beside the corpse. Horrid flashbacks raided his mind about Pommel's last stand with them. Kal, in spite of his own fright, reached over and grabbed Michael's shoulder in order to awaken him from the trance.

A loud, thunderous crackle preceded the sounds of demonic sneering. Civilians ran for cover, holding their heads in an attempt to block out the nefarious noise. The sneering turned to uncontrollable laughter of different reverberations, causing animals to shriek in terror. Some horses escaped from their stables to seek refuge from the horror. The kingdom, within a matter of minutes, lost its mind.

Responding to the horrid sounds, hundreds of people ran to find refuge somewhere—anywhere. Those with hearts of valor remained steady during the distressing mob's chaotic retreat, becoming anxious, nonetheless. Women and their children favored the Cathedral of Alchemiei for their sanctuary. However, many other churches and chapels were filling quickly.

"This is like nothing I have ever—" Kal gasped, meeting Maxim by the bloody fountain.

"Watch it!" Maxim cut him off, just scarcely dodging a shadow demon's lunging attack from behind. The hideous creature regained its balance and stood on its hind legs.

Maxim could not believe what he was seeing. Kal minded the shadows on the gate's wall, determining the origin of the demon's assault. Knights nearby unsheathed their blades but hesitated. Michael followed the screeching cries near the main gate and found the irrefutable proof that the Demon Plague had come. He raced towards the foul monster in a fitting rage, wanting to crush it into a bloody pulp.

"Is that your demon?" Predella said in disbelief as she chased Michael to the scene.

Evading annihilation, the demon sunk back into the shadows of the ground. One of the knights exclaimed, "It's happening! Brace yourselves!"

And then, from the shadow belonging to one of them, the demon returned. It swiped its razor claws for the knight before one of his compatriots pulled him to safety.

Finally revealing itself for all to see, the scrawny creature of black scaling skin glared at its prey with green eyes blazing in the night. Its fangs dripped with saliva, having waited long enough to feed. Before it could pounce on anyone, Predella fired an accurate arrow of fire into its gaunt torso. Once it fell to the ground, wounded, Maxim split the demon's skull in two. He looked upon the slain thing with revulsion, now that he was close enough to study it.

"They're real!" A knight proclaimed from the alarmed crowd. While mobs of people scurried away from the disturbing scene, their sights were directed immediately upwards and out towards the docks. Dense gleams of green illuminated the night sky from the west like the clouds of a storm. Michael watched the familiar spectacle and held his staff tightly, knowing that the invasion was on.

Predella acknowledged his reaction to the green lights and loaded another arrow. Maxim watched the oncoming army of flyer demons advance in the black distance. Michael perceived the townspeople scurry in slow motion, like in his dreams of Pommel. He prayed that the outcome of the looming battle would be different.

In time, the prevailing sounds came from the moans of bows that stretched forcefully with arrows in place. Archers and crossbowmen watched the green spectacle advance closer to their positions on the Royal Crux's crenellations. With their soaring speed, the green lights began to spread apart from each other. Suddenly, the manifestation appeared to form figures, seeming more like reptilic bats with green eyes. Men-at-arms soon lost men to fear.

One archer mumbled, "Holy hell, what are they?"

"Fire now!" The captain pounded his fist on the stone crenel. In a sudden flash, a winged horror plowed through a bowman, instantly killing him. The flying demon continued to glide into the kingdom, allowing the butchered archer to fall a hundred feet into the petrified mob below.

The crossbowmen fired their bolts upon the charging monsters before them. Some of the creatures fell and slammed into the lower walls of the ramparts, crushing into the stone like missiles. Flyer demons continued their assault and swept over the men-at-arms like a never-ending squall.

Many quit loading their arrows and ducked for cover behind the crenellations. By the dozen, exposed archers were pounded from the turrets and fell to their death, the captain included. Startled bowmen hacked at the demons above with their short swords, staying down to avoid the concentrated rush of flyers.

Catapults loaded with heavy stone, burning wood, and other crude missiles were aimed for the invading demons of the sky. When the colonel gave the word, the catapults sent a virtual wall of missiles into the night. The fiery projectiles were never fiercer and never more beautiful as they soared like meteors towards the deadly swarm.

Droves of demons were instantly caught in the counterattack, some clipped by the missiles and then falling into the city. Many, however, evaded the projectiles and swooped down to cause havoc on the people below. As the flying beasts lashed out at their prey, knights quickly discovered that a sword would not be enough. The demons countered the warrior's attacks with powerful slashes and blows lethal enough to pierce armor. The war raged on, for the demonic assault came from the sky and shadows all at once.

"Too many!" Maxim panted, intensely focused on the blazing missiles blending into the flying mass of demons above.

"Look at that. My God, just look at it all," Eric uttered in awe, peering out of the windowpane to take in the mayhem. Madam Orgento insisted that he step away from the window and pray with his sister, but he refused to budge. Therefore, Shina moved in to speak with him in private. In her angst, the princess did not know where to start.

Flustered by the awkward silence, Eric started, "There is nothing to say, Shina. I don't expect you to remember me fondly."

"Come, brother," she replied while staring out at the hellish spectacle from the same windowpane. "Let's try to believe that we can be siblings that love each other."

"An optimist." Shaking his head, Eric sighed, "You were innocent in all of this. I loved you, as a brother should, regardless of what he may have told you."

Offering a crooked smile, Shina replied tenderly, "I believe you, brother."

"I still love you." Eric wrapped his arm around his sister, reminiscing the better times when they were younger. "Sometimes, you were all I thought about. You'll be queen in time, now that I'm out of the way."

She then pulled away just enough to look into his eyes, asking in a whisper, "Where did you go when father made you leave?"

Dreading the question, he closed his eyes and said, "It's better you don't know."

"But all those years." She prodded further. "You must have stayed somewhere special to become a sorcerer."

"Not now, Shina," Eric cut her off, holding her ringed hand. "This ring was more important to him than his only son. There was nowhere a man could go to replace the feeling a rejected son has for his father that won't love him."

Thinking over all that he must have experienced in the badlands, Shina asked even quieter this time, "Will you try to kill our father? Tell me you won't do something like that."

Eric could only smile, conflicted, "If I really was going to do that, you'd be queen already."

Finding opportunity in their dialogue, King Orgento sat beside his queen in a comfortable chair and offered her a glass of wine. She nodded and received it, observing her children rekindle their long-lost relationship. They sat in silence, amongst the company of the armed guards, for several moments before the king mustered the will to settle an insufferable controversy.

"I need to ask you something." Upon attaining the queen's attention, he began, "Antonis predicted that Eric would return. Of that he was right."

Puzzled by her husband's intentions, she said, "Go on."

"Now that he has fled, as cowards do, I shall just come out and say it." He put down his wine and held her hand, saying, "His second prediction was that I would uncover the one responsible for placing the poison in your tonic. He said that you poisoned yourself."

Appalled, she pulled her hand back, "What sort of insolence—"

"I want only the truth, my queen." The king took her hand again with his eyes glazed over in heartache. "I'll believe all that you say, for you are the woman God had chosen to sit at my side, still after all these years. You, alone, made me a better king and a better man. Tonight, over all nights, let us keep no more secrets."

Entranced by his heartfelt words, she touched his face and said in return, "Then you already know the answer, my love. How could I do something so weak, when I have lived so strong by your side?"

Taken by both love and fury, the king realized that Antonis was wrong. He believed his queen's words and cursed his prophet's lying heart. When he tried to understand why the Tofauti seer would misguide him on such a matter, the chamber door flung open without warning. A throng of soldiers barged through with one kneeling to report, "Your Majesties, we have word that the demons are advancing into the Royal Crux! Lord Vitan has ordered that we evacuate you straight away!"

"Already? My God." The queen rose dolefully. "Then this *is* the end!"

"Tell Drake that I refuse to flee," King Orgento retorted defiantly. "That repulsive army of fairy tale creatures has a leader and it shall find Tinaria's king standing his ground."

"Then he stands his ground with the queen, as well," she quickly rejoined, taking in the king's alarming stare.

"But Your Majesties—" One of the knights exclaimed.

"Take my children and lead them away from here!" Madam Orgento commanded him.

The king cried as he seized her in his arms, "You are leaving with them!"

"I am by your side still after all these years," the queen said, gesturing that the prince and princess be escorted out immediately.

"Wait! No, we can't separate!" Shina ran to her parents and received a kiss from them both before the guards took her away. While Eric could have vanished as he had done before, he chose to remain with his sister. He took a final glance at the king and queen before leaving the war room. There, the two rulers of Tinaria stood as one, guarded by brave knights that dared not let an evil soul enter.

The human barricade blocking the gates to the Royal Crux tightened and cried rhythmic chants, inspiring everyone to give it their all if only to save their country. The Demon Plague pushed through the outer defenses and tore their way nearer to the center of the kingdom. Shadow demons emerged from nearly every shadow, causing strife within the army's defensive strongholds.

As the demonic forces pushed in closer, a flyer demon dropped from the sky and landed just feet away from Kal Era. The monster was unlike the scrawny shadow demons, for its body was strapping and portrayed that of a flying lizard. But, like the shadow demon, its green eyes shined brightly.

The demon unhurriedly rose tall, towering over every man. Its tail also had reptilian characteristics, highlighting small, yet serrated spikes all the way to the tip. The wings on its back resembled that of a hairless bat.

Kal tightened the grip around his sword and pulled himself away from Maxim's sturdy grip. Michael worked tirelessly to warn Tinaria of what was coming. Now that it had come, he made it his duty to destroy them all, in honor of Pommel. As a gesture of faith to rejuvenate the masses, Michael would exploit his full power upon the Demon Plague, starting with this demon.

Without moving from his spot, he called upon his telekinetic powers and crushed the demon's black heart with little effort. To the laymen, it looked like it suffered from a heart attack. As the demon fell lifeless to the ground, Michael anxiously tightened the grip on his staff and exerted all of his power towards the sky, grounding every flyer in his sight.

PART I
Chapter VIII
The Fight for Tinaria

Michael pulled hundreds of flyer demons out of the sky, slamming them back to earth. In scores, they came crashing down. Some had died instantaneously, while others were critically injured. Easy picking for brave soldiers, the surviving terrors struggled to lash out at their human attackers. Though still horrified, rushing warriors found some courage in slaying the beasts up close. Even while injured, the beasts lunged at the men.

The key, as the leaders of the battlefield proclaimed, was to prevent the demons from forcing everyone into a death trap. The army fought to push the demons away from the Royal Crux and back into the carnage of the towns. Because Michael had temporarily cleared the skies, archers and crossbowmen above the city rained their arrows and bolts down upon the demons below.

Formidable gunmen in the towns blasted their demonic adversaries with powerful makeshift shotguns. The combat within the townships was ghastly, for alleys filled with the gory carcasses of man and demon alike. Unbeknownst to the military, militia there began using unorthodox methods of keeping their enemies out of pathways, igniting fires and laying explosive traps. The strategy backfired. Searing demons spread the flames to all areas where they stalked, engulfing parts of towns with wild blazes.

Maxim cried frantically as he hacked three flyer demons dead with his flaming sword, "Fires are building up in the east! If the demons don't squeeze us in here, the fires will!"

"I'm on my last two arrows!" Predella cried over the sounds of war within the Royal Crux. "I've got to scavenge for more! Don't die while I'm gone!"

Michael raced towards the Cathedral of Alchemiei with hopes of defending the innocent from any evil that tried to break through. Predella salvaged some arrows from dead archers as she started to follow him there. She quickly glanced back to find Maxim in the square, almost consumed by the hordes of demons that tried him. His fiery blade twirled and sliced about like a phoenix in the violent night.

As they ran, a crying soldier fell from the sky and would have fallen before Michael's feet if not for his lifesaving powers easing the fall. He quickly leaned his head up to find more flyer demons littering the sky as before. Predella leaped over flattened carcasses in her pursuit of arrows. The winged demons dropped multitudes of Tinarians from above, having already left scattered pieces of body parts all about the ground in response to Michael's similar tactic on them earlier.

When Michael saw a small girl drop from a flyer's claws, he caught her ten feet from the ground by way of his telekinetic gifts and set her safely into his arms, still running for the holy site. Predella fired off a shot, targeting an incoming flyer demon. Utilizing the enchanting force of her bow, the soaring arrow lit up into ice and froze the creature into a statue. Like hail, the demon broke up into pieces on impact.

Seeing that Predella was nearby, he offered the girl to her and stopped in the street with the cathedral in view. He then focused his power to catch all other victims falling from the demons' cruel maneuver. He shouted for them to head for the cathedral for refuge. Predella used the last of her arrows to cover the people who ran for the holy place as Michael took on the demons that soared above.

Amid the utter confusion in battling the demonic army, Grasso's generals withdrew from their posts and took shelter under Lord Tyron Angola's manor. One general declared, "Be swift, Grasso! Our men are giving their lives out there!"

"Yes, I know!" Grasso began as he waved his arms around with frustration. "These things catch on fire fast. Luring them into the town fires is just kindling! We must execute a final solution."

"What final solution?" The only injured general spoke up, his arm bandaged over claw marks.

"We must position ourselves on a five-pointed star around the Royal Crux and begin pushing the monsters back into the towns where we can entrap them." Grasso used the bloodied map of the city center as an aid.

"The towns have suffered enough! These things use the shadows! The others fly! The militia is giving their lives as we stand here scheming! Now we're going to feed them more demons? To hell with that, Grasso!" One of them stormed off and headed for the door.

Grasso hung his head in frustration when the chamber door erupted into splinters, walloping the despondent officer to the ground. The explosion cut up the general's face and gouged an eye. After the unexpected blast, they all peered through the smashed doorway, seeing nothing but smoke. It hovered throughout the corridor like there was a fire inside.

Suddenly, the grayish smoke quickly rushed into the chamber and twirled about like a whirlwind. Understanding that the formation was anything but natural, the fallen general scurried away from it like a crab. The smoke finally began to form into something with a life of its own. When the dark haze finished its fusion, a gray phantom stood before them, wearing a gray toned cloak that seemed more like an ancient rag.

The hood hid only more smoke within its empty space, conveying a precarious eeriness. Finally, it solidified and formed a gray skull with fangs and glowing red eye sockets. The arms under the cloak conformed just the same and exposed the phantom's skeletal claws that enclosed into fists, emitting crackling clatters. From its tattered sleeve, a crude scythe formed, fitting slickly into its right hand. The emphasized blade of the scythe reflected the candles' flames amid the generals' petrified stares.

With a long, deep tone, the demon snarled, "**Death.**"

Once it uttered the word, the generals knew they were doomed. The demon plunged the scythe into the fallen general's chest. He couldn't elude the blow, spewing blood from his mouth as he exhaled his last. The other generals ran towards the escape door behind them, leading them to an auxiliary ladder up into the lord's courtyard. The only officer too wounded to run stayed behind to give the others time. He gazed at the demon and unsheathed his rapier.

The phantom patiently pulled the bloody scythe out from its first victim's chest and veered its skull to the wounded general, pinpointing its next target. Emitting a hellish growl, the phantom demon came in closer. Knowing that his comrades had started up the ladder, he stood up straight like a nobleman and steadied his sword vertically parallel to his face.

"Long live Tinaria," the general said gallantly.

He shut his eyes as the scythe came across his face like a sudden surge of wind. His sword came apart from the center and clanged to the floor. The upper half of his face did the same, leaving only the bottom of his jaw. The general's carcass thudded to the ground and covered another section of the ground with blood. After admiring its work, the demon broke down into hovering gray smoke as before and pursued the other generals seeking refuge.

...

Maxim joined the heaviest resistance at the Royal Crux's main gate. There he witnessed the last remaining barricade preventing the many demons from raiding the heart of Tinaria by ground. Maxim sprinted in the direction of the main gate of the crux where his allies had been giving their very lives to protect the kingdom's nucleus.

His comrades' cries pierced his heart and the sounds of war shook his nerves. His Mad Phoenix accumulated heat as his anger raged on. Blood from perished knights and demons spattered around his body as he went. When the first demon tried him, it suffered a swift death by the sword.

The fighting intensified as he joined his brothers at the gate, combating hordes of monsters even his darkest imagination couldn't conceive. Once he arrived with rage in his heart and hand, the defending masses had a burst of confidence. They fought as one in a gory mess, screaming and cursing. Both sides slipped on the pooling blood under their feet, still fighting to overcome each other.

From behind them, numerous shadow demons emerged from the shadows of flickering lights and flanked the barricade. The well-timed maneuver was devastating, for it trapped the blockade in a cordon of hell. Suddenly, it turned into a battle of survival. Maxim, despite the demoralizing scheme, raised the fire-sword and roused his fellow Tinarians to fight on.

Maxim cut and slashed his way through the demonic flank, trying to scorch a path out of the trap. With his blade blazing, he torched the blackened horrors and pushed through, suffering from bites and slashes in the process. He led the way as a throng of warriors managed to tear themselves loose from the demonic obstacle at the gates. From there, the shadow demons breached the barricade and hopes of holding the Demon Plague there were lost. Instead,

Maxim surged through the lines and witnessed the next great hold fall under siege. They were overrun.

Finding no cause for staying there, Maxim fought through the shadow demons to lead his compatriots deeper into the crux. Leaving the barricade to the demons, Maxim raced towards the holy fortress. He hacked at demons nearby as he pushed onward. When a flyer demon swooped in to kill the highest threat with the fiery blade, Maxim swiped his sword overhead and sliced the demon's abdomen open, forcing its intestines to break loose and spill out. It collapsed onto the ground and cried out in anguish. Maxim resumed his run while lopping off the demon's head, finishing it off.

He continued to thrash his way through the demonic army. His stamina began to wane as they slashed, gnawed, and hammered at him without mercy. Mad Phoenix expelled answering flames as he fought back his enemies. Though he fought well and dodged most of the attacks against him, a shadow demon changed Maxim's luck with a stealthy blow to his side. Along with other demons that hungered for him, it tore his chest armor to futility with one swift strike. The demon's claw gashed the inner right side of his torso, leaving four incisions over his ribcage.

The pain was great, as he could feel every open lesion. He knew that if he stopped, the demons would finish what they started. Losing his endurance, Maxim screamed a warrior's cry, using all his will to sustain his charge. Leaving sizzling pulps of devils behind him, he stormed toward the masses of demons before the gates of the cathedral. Refusing to slow down, Maxim slammed through the hordes and then through the gates themselves.

Like a missile, he induced a devastating explosion as hot as his fury. After seeing Predella looking back at him, both baffled and content to find him safe, he let down his guard. His sword cooled off, leaving a blue trace of lingering heat about the blush blade. Safely behind the frontlines of the cathedral's defenses, he stumbled into a mob of soldiers who carried him over to a medical division.

A flyer demon came in for an attack on an injured knight, but Predella saw it. Her arrow hit the incoming beast directly into its chest, immediately freezing its entire body and forcing it to fall short and shatter into cold pieces all over the ground. Other knights scattered around Maxim to guard him against any further danger. He was the best they had.

"Cover him and head for the line!" the colonel disbanded from the party and headed for Michael, who carefully considered the demonic horde suffocating the cathedral walls. He closed in on him, but Michael did not respond.

"Miuriell!" he panted shakily, watching the hundreds of demons crawl like insects all over the cathedral's outer walls.

"They are waiting for the word," Michael said.

"What word? From who? From what?" the colonel retorted, functioning only by adrenaline.

Michael tightened his fist and looked into the colonel's eyes, saying grimly, "They are waiting for one of the generals to arrive. That is when they will enter the cathedral and slaughter everyone inside. When their general arrives, that's checkmate."

"How do we stop them?" the colonel shrieked.

Predella approached the colonel and forced him to step back. Watching the demons above her very closely as she placed her hand onto Michael's shoulder, she said, "You mentioned they don't like sunlight?"

Michael turned to her, "We need to survive the night. Stay with the line. I have to do this."

"Do *what?* Where are you going?" she probed hastily.

Michael walked away from her and headed for the guarded gates to the cathedral grounds. The knights were heavily armed with spears and stalwart shields. Not only would they need to withstand the demons' relentless attacks on them, but also save hundreds of innocent Tinarians from the cruelest of fates. Michael would never allow another massacre. In order to save the kingdom, he would need to pretend to be a Tinarian commander.

Predella, in the meantime, went to survey Maxim's condition for herself. It was a miracle that he survived the bloodbath at the barricade at all. A team of knights detected her rapid approach and intended to prevent her from any sort of contact with Maxim, not privy to their connection. Maxim erratically rose to his knee, tolerating the medic finish his work, when he saw her.

She inspected Maxim's wounds on his side, saying, "Your wounds are bad."

"More survivors are coming in. Thank God." Maxim inspected the consequences of bravery over his torso and arms. "I'm one of them."

A knight vigilantly raced over to their position and said, "Maxim, sir, you saved the lot of us by leading the way, sir! We're in your debt, sir!"

"Debt don't mean shit, you know that," Maxim growled as a medic began to treat his wounds. "Just do what you can to keep those things away from this church until I get going again."

The knight responded, "Sir, strict orders are for you to stay out of the combat zone until you've recovered!"

"That's what I said, isn't it?" Coughing, Maxim lowered his head and said, "No one can survive out there. Nobody."

Blood from his arm trickled down to the handle, reminding him of the trauma he had just endured. Flyer demons still conquered the skies as the shadow demons imperiled the streets. Maxim knew that more people were going to die. It was clear to him that, despite his injuries, his sword needed to burst into flames again soon.

"Quickly, indoors, sir!" the knight beseeched.

"No," Maxim boldly snapped, caught in a trance as he looked upon the carnage outside the gates. "No lights. Keep the shadows down. They'll overrun this place."

"Maxim, don't pretend you can go on like this." Predella could predict his future on the battlefield. He barely survived the fray earlier.

"The queen did not bring me back to bitch about my scrapes! I'm here to fight until the end!" Maxim cried out, riling his spirit for the next contest. Predella admired the fire in his eyes, though it hurt her to think that the man she idolized when young was about to throw himself to the demons again. As a warrior, she would have done the same for her people. Still, she knew the battlefield. Another skirmish and he was dead.

Michael approached the line of knights stationed at the cathedral's main gate. The demons were pushing the battlements back into the center of the kingdom, killing off hundreds in the progression. Though there were multitudes of demons within the Royal Crux, the bulk of the demonic army continued to devastate the towns and villages. It was an extermination.

"Turn down the lights inside the cathedral! Tell them inside, fast! We can survive the night if the cathedral is protected!" Michael hollered from behind the lines.

Hearing this, the colonel replied, "We won't survive the hour at this rate!"

"Just go!" Michael pushed his way up to the front of the line and held his staff securely. Once at the gates, he looked over the masses of demons that overran the crux. Enraged by the carnage, Michael stepped out into the intense battle and took immediate control. Grabbing a dozen of the creatures with his telekinetic might, he smashed them all into one another, killing them instantly. When a flyer came in to take another life beside him, Michael seized it from the sky and propelled it into a horde of shadow demons nearby.

Demons dangerously close to him suffered the batting of the staff, for Michael trounced anything evil in his direct path. As if he manipulated gravity itself, he stretched out his open hand, tore all of the flyers in his sight from the sky, and panned them straight into the ground. He then used select demons as missiles and sent them hurling into their kin, tearing limbs and snapping spines.

In moments, Michael killed masses of demons around the gates. Shadow demons that dared to emerge from the shadows within the cathedral's walls felt the wrath of his telekinesis. The Tinarian guards met those he could not find. His great surge of anger freed many knights from the burdening front line, for his great power was unsurpassed. The soldiers formed a cordon around the cathedral, preventing demons from entering or leaving the gates.

Hundreds of demons, both flyers and shadows, swarmed the outer walls of the cathedral in waiting for their generals' directives. Strangely, all the demons situated there constrained their aggression and merely clung steadily upon the cathedral walls, overshadowing its structural beauty with repugnance. They looked on but didn't budge.

Hordes of demons retreated from the gates and reformed around the cathedral, amassing their strength for another rush soon. Michael glanced over his right shoulder and considered the injured soldiers receiving treatment within the line. Most of them were not going to survive their wounds. He prayed for them, as Maxim and Predella came to help him.

"That was the most amazing thing I ever saw!" Maxim cried, referring to his incredible assault on the demon horde.

Michael answered with a new course of action, saying, "We'll need to kill the generals before they order the attack of the cathedral."

"Generals?" Predella said. "The demons have generals? What are they waiting for?"

"Where are they is the better question?" Maxim brashly interceded.

Michael searched the skies as he spoke, "They can be anywhere. But I know that they're waiting patiently for the perfect time to commence their assault. They want us all in one fell swoop."

"And when is that gonna happen?" Maxim asked.

"A good question to ask them." Michael locked his eyes towards the peak of the cathedral. Atop the high spire, an evil figure crouched over the kingdom and considered the conquest from on high. It was a slender demon with a vast wingspan. He watched the silhouette of the mysterious fiend against the moon, holding its firm position before it retracted its bat-like wings and moved out of view. Everyone around Michael could only wonder what he saw. He ignored his violent surroundings and walked towards the enormous chamber doors, still glaring into the sky in hypnotic fashion.

"Michael!" Predella ran to him and stopped his rhythmic march to the front doors. "What was it? What's going on?"

Michael faced her, "Speak of the devil and she appears. One of the generals is on the cathedral's roof right now. She's the one to order the attack!"

"She?" Predella became profoundly confused. "Are you sure?"

"It's a she-demon," Michael answered. "Whatever she is waiting for, we had better keep her distracted!"

"Distracted? I'll *kill* the bitch," Maxim boldly claimed as he unsheathed his fire-sword.

"Don't underestimate her," Michael stressed. "Consider her a demon with superior capabilities. I saw what she could do back in Pommel."

Predella gasped as she looked up at the roof a second time, "Every one of them has superior capabilities!"

The three heroes converged with the hopes of planning the perfect counterattack upon the Demon Plague. Michael returned to his divisions and strengthened their resolve around the cathedral's walls. Maxim volunteered to hunt down the demonic general on the rooftops. Predella insisted that she join his mission to ensure the she-demon's defeat. Michael remained with the throngs of fighters who trusted in his leadership. He had to keep the hordes away.

"Thank you for looking after me. You are most kind," the child uttered as one of the nurses washed his dirty face.

"My lord, 'You are most kind'?" the woman repeated, taken aback by the boy's eloquence. "What a little professor you are! How did you learn how to speak like that?"

"It's so bloody out there—so much violence," the boy replied. "It's very clean and safe in here."

"We cannot have you out there now, can we? It's just not safe out there." The nurse put her damp rag back into the basin and checked the child's neck for filthiness. "It's so safe in here. This is a place for lost children. When children get separated from their families, as you did, they wind up here and so—"

"That lady was so nice to take me here," he said, just staring at her. "So safe."

Suddenly, she sensed something off in the child. A dark sensation ran up her spine. She thought to call for help, if just for the company with him, when the boy said sinisterly, "I've got to do something about that."

She backed away from him, realizing that he wasn't what he seemed. He sat awkwardly in his little wooden seat and glared mischievously right back at her. His eyes widened like a mad joker as he slowly expanded a grotesque smirk that painfully stretched from ear to ear. A dribble of bloody saliva skulked from the corner of his despicable grin and his neck muscles swelled up under heavy strain.

She covered her mouth in disgust and let out a whimper. The boy said in a dark, sinister utterance, not of himself, "**Afraid of a mere child?**"

She screeched helplessly in watching the boy's skin melt from his bones and give way to a dissimilar form. A demon fully materialized from the child host and stood tall, tearing what little flesh of the child was left. Gaunt with an auburn hide and bright, dynamic yellow eyes, the creature stretched and let out a raspy yawn. His teeth glistened like a snake before the attack.

When she ran to escape, the demon snagged her by the back of the head and smashed her face into the wall. Blood splattered from her skull, putting an end to her crying. He allowed her lifeless body to fall to the ground, spilling more blood onto the floor, and then studied his blood-soaked claw. The creature licked each appendage as he ambled out of the room and into the medic ward. Everyone fled the hallway and scurried down the staircase in a panic, trampling over each other. The small number remaining was hardly a challenge for him.

The demonic general gently closed the door behind him, never taking his yellow eyes off his competitors, and said, "**Splendid.**"

"We must not allow it to pass!" One of the guards declared as he unsheathed his sword, "Go alert the captain!"

"**I have a schedule to keep and I won't be late. Come closer and kneel, please, and I'll kill you. It'll be quick. My time is valuable,**" the demon said while he cracked the knuckles in his claw.

One daring warrior charged the demon from the side and swung his sword, lashing for the monster's head for a quick kill. The general anticipated the attacker's plan from afar and briskly caught the knight's wrist that bore his sword. Without any delay, he viciously snapped the warrior's wrist, compelling the sword to drop, and flung him into a desk nearby. He neatly salvaged the knight's blade and plunged it into the owner's neck, finishing the job.

Another attacker, much larger than the rest, came from behind him, wielding a crudely fashioned mace. The general rapidly spun around and clouted the weapon from the hefty assailant's hands. Not giving the warrior a chance to think, the demon punched his fist through his skull, instantly finishing another opponent. He allowed the corpse to collapse to the ground as he proceeded towards the staircase leading to the tower's atrium two floors below.

"**You clearly have no concept of time,**" he said. "**I'll make a deal with you monkeys. Step out of the way and I won't return here and disembowel all of the ill patients you have stored in here like rotting meat.**"

The demonic general had four more impediments before him. They banned together as they warily watched the blood of their comrades drip effortlessly off the demon's claw. The shield-bearing warrior volunteered to challenge him first, though the demonic general barely devised a combat stance.

"**I'll even throw in the little lost children,**" he snickered, advancing for them.

He caught the knight's most recent thrust of the sword by the blade, but the warrior pulled back his strike and cut through the demon's claw. The demonic general flinched as he studied the clean gash in his palm. Angered by the knight's successful assault, the demon closed his claw and snarled, **"You pretentious fool."**

"If you want to take this tower, you will have to kill us first," one of the knights pronounced with faith.

"I know that! Don't any of you monkeys listen?" the general raised his arm and extended forth his open claw.

From his palm came a small sphere of light, almost blinding to the eye. With a sudden flash, a bolt of lightning struck two of the knights, hurling them far beyond their other ally. One of them luckily absorbed the concentration of the shock with his shield, rendering it useless.

As if bored, the demonic general sighed frustratingly and spit on the ground. The injured knight used his sword as leverage to raise himself off the floor and made his way towards the stairway with intentions of blocking the demon's path out. Though he could hardly stand on his feet, the fearless knight removed his charred helmet.

Seeing how the man was not afraid, the demon frowned and suspended his advance, saying, **"You are a unique pest. Though I should shatter your bones, I feel obliged to leave with you my name. Remember Valkris. I'll be coming back soon to murder all these people, as promised, and I'd like you to scream my name."**

Valkris offered a vile smirk, revealing his sharp piranha-like incisors, and proceeded down the staircase. There, the last warrior looked over the narrow corridor and wept for his fallen comrades. Blood tinged the wall and ceiling, but bathed the floor, causing the passageway to smell like a catacomb. Patients that witnessed the horrific event moaned and cried out, traumatized. The knight then understood that his new directive was to avenge his friends and stop Valkris before he made it to his next destination.

With Valkris breaching the King's Tower, hosts of demons infiltrated the citadel from every vulnerable opening. Like termites invading an ant colony, shadow and flyers broke through. The king's decision to take refuge in the war room had become a mistake. As news of the breach spread, elite knights ran into the grand hall to warn the king that they had to evacuate. The room's escape shaft was made ready and the king and queen regretfully fled. They never left the tower during any war in Tinaria's history.

However, down in the trophy room, six knights escorted Princess Shina and her exiled brother to the eastern evacuation tunnel. The grandest place to admire the many treasures collected by Tinaria over the decades was built with a tunnel to carry in large pieces, doubling as an escape to the eastern forest. There had been no sign of demons down there, as opposed to the rest of the tower crawling with them.

Running by the many priceless statues and rare artifacts as if they were passing debris, the fleeing royals made it to the exit doors. Once making it there, the leading knight slammed his fist onto the steel in anger, discovering that it was locked. The large padlock seemed to taunt them while sealing their doom.

"What's wrong?" Eric cried. "Open it! Unlock it! Let's get going!"

"We don't have the key!" he replied, nearly crying.

"Then who does?" Shina screamed, looking back in fear of demons tracking them.

One knight frantically peered about the vast room of relics and said, wiping sweat from his brow, "There has to be some weapon in this place that can break through it!"

"The attendant must have run," another said. "I'll look if they left the keys behind! Stay here!"

"Hurry!" Shina exclaimed, feeling that she would not make it out in time.

He raced back from whence they came, bypassing the exquisite spoils and enchanted objects, to rummage through the attendant's key box just outside the room. The knight tried breaking the box open when he heard a jingling coming from behind. As he quickly turned around, he watched a young woman limp towards him with the heavy keyring in her hand.

She was strikingly beautiful. Her flowing blonde hair cascaded down the sides of her gorgeous face as she lifted her head up to look at him. Limping on her right leg and holding her lower back, the woman wore a frayed robe that covered only her upper body, leaving her naked legs exposed. The knight impulsively admired them, as they were firm without flaw like a goddess.

"Girl, what happened?" the knight said. "Where were you hiding with those keys?"

"I was raped." The girl shocked him with her admission as she continued to approach. She lost her footing and leaned herself against the wall, dropping the keys to the floor. He ran over to her before taking the keys, embracing her by her underarms.

"Up you go." The knight marveled at her stunning visage, close enough to notice her neon blue eyes.

"Bless you, sir. I am simply ravenous, is all." She smiled.

"Hungry?" The armed guard fell into an erotic trance.

"Yes. You can help me," she replied seductively, gently pulling his face closer to kiss him passionately. When she had him, her blue eyes turned a crimson red. Her fingernails turned into claws. Without hesitation, the girl stabbed her razor-sharp fangs into the knight's vulnerable neck and violently sucked his blood.

His ecstasy suddenly turned to horror as he felt her incisors drain him. The knight's blood discharged into her mouth and down her throat. Some of it dripped from the corner of her mouth and down her neck. Despite his strength, she held him down as an apex predator. As he faded away, her climax was at hand. She sucked him harder, more fiercely than before, until she vigorously pulled away, crying with ecstasy.

Throwing the lifeless corpse to the ground, she ripped off her filthy robe and brushed her blonde hair back with her gory hands, completely fulfilled. She arose from the floor, surprisingly clean with little or no traces of blood, naked and satisfied. Out of breath, she licked her fingers like a feline. Just then, Valkris descended the steps and glared into her red eyes, saying, "**Always prioritizing your meals, Kaila.**"

"**I am still *so* hungry!**" Kaila replied with a juvenile grin. "**Let me have dessert inside!**"

"**No, that's where the princess is. You can have what's left when I'm done.**" Valkris slowly put out his open claw. "**Where is it?**"

Laughing giddily, she slanted her head, "**I hid it in the treasure room.**"

"**In that decadent warehouse?**" Valkris, sensing the rod somewhere in the room, beckoned it to return to his claw. "**It possesses the basis of my magic. Treat it with more respect.**"

Valkris retrieved his golden rod as it floated out from the room and into his possession. The Seltek, as he called it, was a gold shaft about four feet in length, hosting a myriad of eyes that blinked and frantically gazed around at everything. The head of the rod bore a demon skull that hid another eye within its orifice, opening during powerful magical incantations. It was a disturbing instrument of malevolent sorcery.

The rod's magic circulated throughout Valkris's entire body. A gold helmet materialized upon his head and trinkets materialized about his wrists and ankles. A magician's cloak swathed his body down to the shins, concluding his ornate attire. He muttered with a malicious smile, "**Much better.**"

"**Now let me feast upon—**" Kaila's lips were suddenly shut but Valkris' magic.

"**Droves of humans are hoarded in their holy place—a false bulwark,**" he hissed. Kaila rolled her eyes and headed for the stoned staircase until Valkris spoke up again, "**There'll be plenty to drink there. Be patient. We'll be out in a moment.**"

"**I need to find some clothes first. That robe irritated me,**" Kaila said as she took to the stairs, still nude from head-to-toe.

When Valkris entered the trophy room, the party across the way jolted back like squirrels. Shina screamed and hid behind her brother's care. Eric, however, was faceless—completely stunned with terror. It became evident as to why the knight had never returned with the keys. Valkris walked onward and revealed the keys to the escape tunnel in his open claw, then melting them down into orange molten metal that oozed through his fingers.

"Oh shit!" A knight unsheathed his blade in a panic. "What the hell is that?"

"That's a new one!" another knight yelped. "We must defend the princess with our lives!"

Valkris gradually sauntered down the hall with his Seltek in claw, "**I need only the princess. Hand her over to me and I'll leave you to play in your little toy room. You have my word.**"

"We can't face the demon like this. Eric, aren't you a sorcerer or something?" one of the knights asked hastily.

Eric rebuked him, "I don't have—"

"**Prince Eric cannot use his powers in my company,**" Valkris interceded haughtily, already halfway down the hall. "**He shouldn't even be here, isn't that right?**"

"Why does it want me? It's looking at me!" Shina hid behind her subjects.

"**My patience is fading.**" Valkris stopped about twenty feet away from them and charged his magic rod. While the eyes were always awake on the Seltek's shaft, the lone eye within the skull's mouth opened, ready to perform another malicious enchantment. When the knights gathered and put up their defenses, a faint sound of running footsteps echoed throughout the room.

The knights saw a lone warrior, battered and beaten, quietly rushing up behind Valkris with his sword in both hands. The wicked general studied his victim's faces and realized the attack from behind. Scattered eyes from all over the Seltek promptly located the assailant. The brave hero had not forgotten his fallen comrades, nor did he forget the vindictiveness of Valkris's vile nature. The wounded warrior enhanced his charge to ensure that he would be able to strike the demon from behind before he turned around.

But, as he was wounded, his steps were too heavy and his charge—too weak. Valkris caught the sword and stopped the hero's attack. The stunned knight quickly tilted and leaned the blade in all directions to try and push it through the demon's grasp, but it was to no avail.

"Now is our chance! Let's move! Go!" one knight took Shina by the arm and pulled her towards the sides of the trophy room behind the columns and large displays. Two others ran beside the prince and followed quietly. The valiant warrior's struggle with the demonic general was a remarkable sacrifice.

Valkris, learning that the princess tried to run, shouted madly, "**No! You will not escape me!**"

He refused to meddle with the warrior any further and charged the magical force within him. Before the hero could realize what was happening, the demonic general discharged his magical energy. The powerful force sent his attacker flying backward for several feet before slamming into a display of ancient Ellium armor.

Outraged with their surprising progress towards the door, Valkris raised his Seltek and aimed the open eye at his fleeing prey. Out from the rod came a powerful red beam intended to kill the princess's guards, but it was off target and left a considerable crater in one of the pillars. Debris hurled into the air, breaking showcase glass in the area.

Again, he followed their running tempo and blasted another beam towards them. The second beam obliterated marble statues from the old world, raining down its debris over the princess. Another and another, Valkris fired the destructive red beam towards them and every shot was unsuccessful. With every soldier taking Tofauti shields from their stands for cover as they went, Valkris watched them run out of the trophy room and out of his grasp.

"**Sloppy,**" Valkris uttered, aghast. "**Curse their luck.**"

"You should have killed me, Valkris." The wounded hero coughed with a big smile.

"**Yes, undoubtedly.**" Valkris vaporized him with just a burst from his Seltek, finding a small measure of solace.

Then, tilting his head to the side and taking a deep breath, he charged a great magical spell and detonated all his power into the trophy room, razing everything inside. The explosion rattled parts of the tower like an earthquake. Parts of the ceiling came down and massive treasures crashed through the floor to the level below. Finally, Valkris charged his scepter for the large exit door padlocked shut and let out a destructive beam that blasted the steel into metal shards.

PART I
CHAPTER IX
THE UNHOLY BATTLEFIELD

Drake assumed command of the eastern walls when General Grasso never returned. The east end's ramparts lied on the edge of a steep slope, leading directly into the Barrier Forest. Armies of the undead climbed the precipitous hill to try what the Ziamons wouldn't dare. A seemingly endless horde, the living corpses marched for the eastern front. Archers and artillerymen under Drake's command fired relentlessly on the reanimated army. Gunners rained canister and shrapnel shots down on them from cannons. The ghouls, nonetheless, scaled the knoll from the forest, relentless.

Drake ordered soldiers to gather more ammunition for the desperate defense, as nothing appeared to stop the ceaseless horde. Upon giving his directives, he saw General Grasso scurrying away from the castle walls and charging down the hill in a frantic hurry. He lost his pace and rolled down the knoll until his cries were heard no longer. Drake watched, dumbfounded, as knights from his division ran into the darkness of the zombie-infested forest to find him.

It soon became obvious as to why Grasso had run crying into the woods. One of the demonic generals drifted over the ground like a ghost. The reaper of smoke had yet to slay all of Tinaria's major generals by way of its scythe. It's preternatural blade still thirsted for blood and Grasso was the last kill. The demon would never let him escape.

Knights raided the phantom from behind, but they only hacked through the smoke. Their blades simply swept right through the demonic general's murky cloak and their guns fired through a sinister haze. After frustrating attempts to damage the demon, the soldiers progressively stopped their futile strikes and helplessly stood there. The reaper proceeded down the slope and into the forest, still clear on its objective.

Grasso continued to roll down the hill until he crashed his side into one of the trees deep within the forests. Though the trunk stopped his hazardous plummet, he was practically defenseless. His persistent hunter felt his fear. His heartbeat echoed throughout its skull. Undead invaders knew better than to feast on him, for Grasso was Scythian's kill. However, Grasso was not alone any longer. Another demonic general pinned him to the ground.

"**Is this one yours, Scythian?**" Tenebrion pressed his foot deeper into Grasso's back, making him scream for mercy. "**This is my territory and no soul can pass. So, this one is mine.**"

Scythian looked over Tenebrion, the most ghastly of the five generals. Thanks to Scythian's glowing eyes illuminating from its menacing skull, Grasso peered over his shoulder and gawked at the necromancer's gruesome form. The beast's eyes were of a cat's that shined in the darkness and his head resembled that of a vampire bat. Long, hairy ears sprung from his head and black hair covered his hide.

A solid black breathing mask covered his mouth. Old, tattered armor loosely fit his formless body. Tenebrion's claws were of a reptile and his feet portrayed that of a crow.

He coiled his whip called Malevolence around Grasso's neck and said, "**Understand, Scythian? Mine.**"

Yet, without wasting any more time, Scythian raised its bloodcurdling scythe and plunged the blade into Grasso's neck, separating his head from the shoulders. Tenebrion's whip fell limp to the grass as he watched Grasso's head roll down the slope, further into the forest. He merely looked up into Scythian's cold skull with malice. Scythian retracted its scythe and moved in closer to Tenebrion's ugly presence to declare chillingly, "**Mine.**"

Maxim grabbed Predella's arm before they snuck into the cathedral, saying, "Here's the plan. We split up. I'll scale the walls up to the veranda. You check inside and make your way to the roof."

"The walls are infested with demons! And what about your wounds?" Predella said in distress.

"Take the staircase to your right once you enter. From there on you'll know how to reach the top. Be careful." Maxim embraced her wrist, as he would have done with any brother-in-arms, and left. Predella then fretfully watched as Maxim began his climb up the buttress greave by the porch entrance.

The flyer demons didn't see him during his quiet ascension as he climbed the gutter system. Scaling the pipe was no easy task. His wounds stung with each push. Making a sound would have meant his doom. As he used to do when he was a boy, Maxim focused on his climb and never looked down. It was not long before flyers caught his scent, then spotting him halfway up the pipe. Like predators stalking their prey, the creatures closed in on him.

Noticing them advance towards him, Maxim stopped and slowly raised his hand behind his back to grasp the handle of his sword. Seeing them encircle him, ready to strike, he whispered to himself, "Of course, this was a bad idea. You knew this was a bad idea and you did it anyway."

Before the violence ensued, Michael lifted him off the pipe and brought him down to ground level with his gifts. As he floated Maxim down, he exerted a force field around him to prevent the flyers from picking him off. Maxim looked on him as he floated down, never hovering in thin air before. Once he touched the ground, he sighed, "Thanks for caring."

"What the hell were you doing?" Michael asked. "You know I can lift you up there, right?"

Maxim rubbed his neck and replied with everyone at attention, "Then let's do that."

Predella rapped on the porch door and waited until she saw a priest appear behind the peep window. The frightened man looked her over and then quarreled with others around him, debating whether they should open the door for the dark-skinned woman. After a brief dispute, one of the priests slowly opened it a trace and said, "What do you want?"

Predella began, bemused, "What do I want? Are you in denial of what's happening out here?"

"We have no more room, woman. I'm sorry," he said.

Unwilling to muster what little charisma she had left to burn, Predella kicked the door open and pushed the clerics out of the way. Once safe inside, she slammed the door shut with the nock of her bow and said to the crowd, "Now that we solved that problem, I need to know how to get to the roof, fast!"

One of the clerics stammered anxiously, "Please, the stairs to my left will lead you up to the upper levels of the cathedral and a small door will—"

She bolted passed the masses who watched her every move. They came to realize quickly that she had not come in for refuge but to protect them. Many knew Predella by her infamous reputation, though never seeing her in person. She had taken covert mission contracts from Tinaria and Tofauti, but served the Waasi Tribes throughout the land for free. Her family had fled the Tofauti kingdom many years back when they didn't agree with the modernization of the nation. They believed it was an abuse of their ancient culture, forming the Waasi Tribes thereafter. Predella sympathized with them. Though she was a hired bow, she had a conscience.

Michael lifted Maxim up with his powerful gifts and then sent him soaring towards the cathedral's veranda. As he rocketed forth, Maxim sliced his way through vicious flyer demons trying to tear him from the sky. He slashed three as he went, leaving them falling for the ground like fireballs. Once he made it to the terrace, he flung himself over the top rail and rolled safely onto the balcony.

The masses below clapped and applauded the success of the supernatural maneuver. Once Maxim was safe, Michael tended to the city's battlefield again. While Maxim expected the many flyer demons to meet him on the long balcony for another bout, they became spooked and withdrew from the terrace. Maxim remained there, confused and uncertain. Just then, a woman's sinister voice emanated from behind him, **"How delightful—a plaything to quell my boredom."**

Maxim quickly spun around to see the she-demon standing haughtily in the middle of the veranda. Her skin was like a snake. From head to toe, dark green scales swathed her entire body. Her short black hair ran down the sides of her face and a pair of radiant purple eyes stared on intently. Razor sharp teeth and claws gave the she-demon a baleful appearance.

Wyvern wings extended from her back and a devilish tail from her rear. The she-demon's attire was scarce, if not for the silver chest plate to conceal her breasts and a plated sarong to screen her other seemingly feminine attributes. Wielding long dual swords, resting in crisscrossing sheaths on her back, the demonic general reached back and grabbed the handles.

The inner parts of the blades were black with tiny gold inscriptions, while the outer parts were purely gold, virtually indestructible like Maxim's Mad Phoenix. The hilts were black and the pommels were short golden daggers. Startled by her appearance, Maxim asked, "What the hell are you?"

"**Sattka,**" she said, slowly walking towards him. "**You made quite an entrance. I assume you're a special one?**"

"Are you the one charged with ordering the strike on this cathedral?" Maxim asked, steadying his sword before him. "Just want to be sure."

Sattka laughed through her teeth, "**It is not my place to initiate the final attack on this ground. Only the father of us can do that. He shall commence the strike shortly. Don't worry about that.**"

"It'll be dawn soon, you know. Is your dad taking his sweet time, or what?" Maxim hid behind a scornful smile.

"**You know, that pretty little sword will look wonderful with the rest in my collection,**" Sattka held up her approach and unsheathed her dual swords out to her sides. "**Shall we play?**"

Predella located the west quarter of the secondary level that led to the balcony, transparent with windows. Through light colors of the windowpanes, she saw the silhouette of her ally clang blades with the she-demon. An accurate arrow could have eliminated the threat at once. She hid within the darkness of the corner and aimed her arrow through the glass, following the demonic general's every move. Breathing heavily, Predella held the arrow still on the bowstring and waited for a clear shot.

Suddenly, something dashed by and slapped Predella's elemental bow from her steady hands. The arrow flung somewhere in the room as her bow slid away. Shaken by the strike, she ran from her spot and hid behind an old pew. Her bow lying in the middle of the floor, abandoned, Predella then watched the passionate duel through the rose windows.

Whatever deflected her aimed shot had tremendous stealth and speed, leaving her with a single arrow in her quiver. Spare furniture and old furnishings cluttered the area. When Predella quickly ran through the obstacle course for her bow, her stealthy attacker landed a hard kick into her belly. The forceful strike sent her into a set of empty chairs, knocking them all over.

As she eyed her deserted bow, a gorgeous blonde-haired woman ambled into the breaking moonlight. Kaila had found a silk black gown, fit for a princess, which hugged her magnificent figure. Her eyes were crimson red, glowing in the darkness, Kaila had already fed enough to fast for a week. She taunted, "**Creeping about, are we?**"

Predella refused to give the demon satisfaction of a reply. She merely raised herself off the ground, cluttered with glass and miscellaneous articles. She rested her back on the wall, holding her aching stomach. Despite her pain, Predella returned the vampire's sadistic stare.

"**Still standing? You're tough. It is too bad, you know,**" Kaila said, leisurely moving in closer. "**I have fed quite well so far, but I would love to drink some of you. Your blood smells luscious. Then again, I could indulge myself just for tonight, but I'll scream if I lose my flat stomach.**"

"A vampire?" Predella startlingly uttered. "It just gets better as the night goes on."

"**It won't hurt as much as you think. Actually, it's a gratifying experience.**" Kaila neared dangerously close to Predella's face as if to kiss her lips. "**Like having sex, you will never want me to stop. Well, until you begin to die, of course.**"

Predella gazed at Kaila's gory incisors and riposted candidly, "I'm not your type."

Before Kaila could bite into her neck, Predella thrust her last arrow into Kaila's stomach. The vampire cried out in agony and pulled away from her, attempting to extract the arrow. Immediately after, Predella gathered enough momentum to kick Kaila across the face, driving her back into the darkness. She heard the sounds of the demon tear the arrow out from her flesh, as well as her screams of anguish that followed.

Wasting no time, Predella quickly retrieved her bow and stood in the faint light of the room, out of arrows. From the darkness came the awry arrow, saturated with Kaila's blood. She tossed it to the floor between Predella's open legs. Her crimson eyes illuminated in the blackness even stronger than before.

"**You will pay for that, cow,**" Kaila sneered.

A daunting silence followed. When Predella lost sight of the vampire's red glowing eyes, she speedily reclaimed her bow and dove behind a dusty dresser. Because her eyes were futile in the darkness of the room, Predella focused on her other senses. Nocturnal, Kaila could see in the dark with ease, preparing for the pounce nimbly atop a breakfront only a jump away. She could taste Predella's blood discharge into her mouth and feel it warmly ease down her throat.

The subtle sound of stressed wood reached Predella's ear, compelling her to be cautious of the vampire's attack. Kaila sprung upon her, but Predella jolted out of the way. Faster than anything she had ever seen before, she found Kaila suddenly overpowering her to the ground. Her razor-sharp nails failed to reach passed Predella's outstretched bow. Kaila snapped and nipped at her, but she pushed the demon away from her neck.

When she found the opening, Predella jabbed the grip of the bow into Kaila's face until the vampire temporarily lost her bearings. She then thrust her feet into Kaila's wounded belly and tossed her into a cracked standing mirror.

Kaila smashed into it but instinctively rolled over onto her feet like a cat. She hissed and lunged for her again, slashing Predella at her thigh and chest. When the huntress backed away, feeling the sting of her raw lesions, Kaila rushed in again and kicked her into a pew. As she thumped into it, the bench tipped and knocked over the others like domino pieces. Part of Predella's top tore open, nearly leaving her chest exposed, as she tried shaking off the wallop.

"**I've suddenly lost my appetite.**" Kaila gathered the pieces of broken glass from the mirror.

His injuries still giving him grief, Maxim pressed on and denied every strike from Sattka's blades. She failed even to draw blood from her opponent, only aggravating the raw wounds on his side. But, Maxim, too, had failed to execute a critical strike on the demonic general. With every opening she had presented, she immediately parried and countered.

Maxim had her scrolling backward, but a shrewd deflection turned the tables again and he nearly lost his balance, allowing Sattka the chance for a decent strike to the gut. Maxim swatted her gold blade down towards the floor with the palm of his hand. The point plummeted into the ground, throwing Sattka into disarray. He came around to cut off her head, but she quickly recovered the blade in her other hand and repelled the strike. Sattka then shoved him away with her blades and regained some breathing room.

Roused, she said, "**You can't be human!**"

"So, what's *your* excuse?" Maxim replied as he tried catching his breath.

Sattka growled in frustration and charged him down. As they clasped blades, she kneed him in the stomach and, in clamping her blades, tugged the sword out of Maxim's hands.

The fire-sword fell to her feet, rendering him unarmed. Permitting no mercy, she kicked him in the chest and sent him pounding into one of the veranda's posts just feet away.

He let out a grunt of air, feeling the debilitating pain in his back and side. Maxim's tender wounds bled through the bandages. There, Sattka stood only ten steps away from her adversary, who was in a world of pain, unarmed, and hesitant to move. She bent down and seized the fire-sword by the blade, sheathing one of her own in a scabbard on her back.

"**Beautiful sword. Let's trade.**" Sattka fired her gold sword at Maxim's head, leaning on the post. Not a moment too soon, he flung himself to the side, just avoiding a deadly shave. The sword lodged into the wood, devastating its stability. Splinters and shards jetted out, showering Maxim's body. He looked up cautiously to find the golden and black hilt of the blade wobble.

"**You're a very difficult bug to squash!**" Sattka tightened her fists and ground her teeth, suffering from impatience. "**How fitting that you should die by your own sword!**"

She flicked the fire-sword up above her, waiting for the grip to fall into her open hand. Maxim watched her foolish move closely. The demon couldn't know that if any other being handled his sword by the grip, they would pay for it with a scolding palm. He ogled his sword twirl in midair, eager to drop in her hand.

Maxim's best friend was his sword and he would never allow it to be wielded by another in vain. He reached over his left shoulder and, in pain, extracted the demon's sword from the post, weakening its stability even more. With every breath of air left in his lungs, Maxim leaped from the floor and dashed to strike down his enemy while he had the chance.

Finally, the sword landed into Sattka's hand, obliging the handle to scorch her palm, razing her scaly green skin. She had no choice but to drop it and quickly tend to her hand. Her palm was awfully charred and she squeezed her wrist, screaming in disbelief. While the sword fell towards the ground, Maxim pressed on and cast Sattka's blade into her chest, propelling her a distance away from his fallen sword.

Refusing to slow down, Maxim scooped up his Mad Phoenix by the grip and proceeded to finish off Sattka with one fatal blow to the head. She realized that Maxim was going to finish her, so Sattka desperately unsheathed the sword from her back and pulled out the other from her chest, forming a transverse cross that, as planned, blocked Maxim's strike. She employed the maneuver skillfully, stopping the fire-sword in its tracks, but Sattka had not yet experienced the true power of the blade and she could never have predicted the enchantment to follow.

Maxim's sword was denied the kill, but it was not going to be denied the telling blow. His blade pressed hard onto Sattka's crossed swords, feasting power off of each other's might. Maxim's rage began to grow as a great current of flames erupted from the Mad Phoenix and consumed Sattka's body from her head down to her waist. She jumped away, screaming and squealing in anguish. The flames fed on her scaly skin and traveled down to her feet, overtaking her whole body.

Sattka shrieked as she twisted and jerked, gradually moving closer to the windowpanes in a loud demonic cry. When she faced him, though she couldn't see him over the sweltering flames, Maxim fought through the soreness and executed a leaping kick into her torso. She crashed back into the second floor rose windows, still enveloped in flames and screaming.

Maxim walked away from the shattered window, exhausted and shaken by the confrontation. His wounds needed fresh bandaging, but he was certain that the demonic general would never have the chance to see the war's end. As he limped over to the railing, a foreboding chill ran up his spine, convincing him to inspect Sattka's charred carcass to make sure it was really over.

As he carefully walked over to the gaping windows, a great smash emitted from only feet away. Quickly turning to see what came out from the shattered window, Maxim witnessed a scarred and beaten Predella slam into the weakened post. Her faint cry was nearly the final wind knocked from her lungs. Claw and teeth marks overran most of her body and some glass from the window drove into her skin. The fated post, weak as it was, started to break and she slowly followed the debris descending the walls of the cathedral. Maxim's heart dropped.

He ran after his ally, hoping to catch her before she fell over the edge of the veranda. Finally, the entire railing came apart. Predella's balance was off and she fell. Knowing that he would never reach her while running, Maxim dropped and slid on his thigh just in time to catch her hand as she tumbled off the edge. She dangled from Maxim's grip, saved just in time. He wedged his other arm behind the broken stump of the wooden post to stop him from falling along with her. He cried painfully, "Hold on! Keep a steady grip!"

The huntress foolishly looked down and watched the gruesome war below. Predella thanked his fast thinking as she dangled there. He mustered what strength he had left and lifted her up over the edge and onto his bruised chest. For a small instant in a very dangerous time, Maxim and Predella shared the eternal now. The hellish war slowed down and quieted. The feeling they had felt in that brief instant was intoxicating, as it came by surprise.

Maxim looked into her eyes and froze, blurting in an anxious trance, "Are your hands still jealous?"

Staring back into his eyes, she uttered in return, "So damn stubborn."

"Are you alright?" Maxim proclaimed from his back, considering her awful abrasions.

"No better than you," she replied, rolling off him and then helping him up.

However, Kaila adored killing the peace. They heard sounds of crackling glass and looked over to the destroyed windowpanes, discovering the vampire pick up Predella's bow from the glass-besieged floor. She held the weapon haughtily and said maliciously, "**Don't you two know when to be dead?**"

"What the hell are you?" Maxim gasped, leaning on his Mad Phoenix.

"**What the hell am I?**" Kaila responded, trying to hold back her laughter. "**Oh, you are *so* adorable!**"

Before Kaila could slaughter them with one strike, she smelled a strong, familiar scent. She gazed around frantically, desperately sniffing to trace the aroma. It was not long before the mysterious scent discovered her first. Michael shouted from inside the second level, just under the broken glass, "Demon!"

Kaila turned around, shocked to meet him. Seeing Michael stand in her presence had her weak in the knees. He put out his left hand and emitted a telekinetic blow that launched Kaila off the terrace like a cannon. She fell, screaming, into the hell of war below she helped create.

The bow, once in Kaila's possession, remained frozen in the air by his will. Michael guided it into his open hand and gave his telekinetic skills a well-deserved rest. Predella breathed a sigh of relief, knowing that his coming was not part of the plan. She looked at him with a new kind of faith and smiled.

"I believe this is yours," he said, handing her the weapon. She received her bow and then patted him on the shoulder. Maxim exhaled, as the three warriors converged once again. "That wasn't a girl you'd take home to mother."

"No," Michael put the base of his staff to the ground, "but you stopped the other one from ordering the strike. You saved a lot of people."

"I don't know about that," Maxim retorted, holding his side. "It hinted to something totally different—something about her father."

Before Maxim could explain what he meant, a precarious rumbling shook the shattered glass on the floor. To their amazement and despair, Sattka stepped onto the veranda from the gaping windowpane. Fierce gusts of a strong air encircled her as she came forth. There were no blazing flames eating her corpse. Shockingly, there was no harm to her at all. Her scales regained color and appeared as new. In searing hot armor, Sattka stared them down with haunting eyes of purple.

"**Miuriell!**" she shrieked wrathfully. "**Curse your spineless indolence!**"

None of them could fathom what they were seeing. Sattka had the ability to regenerate her body rapidly. Her hair grew back in a moment's time. Maxim was baffled. It was far from over. While Predella and Maxim appeared beaten and bloodied, their clothes torn up, seeing Sattka in perfect form was a demoralizing sight.

"I killed her!" Maxim cried, crouched in pain.

"She can regenerate," Michael said in dismay.

Predella, looking to Michael, heard what the demon had said and warned, "She called you by name!"

"If I cannot have this place, then let my minions take the rest!" Sattka howled with great rage, letting out an earsplitting cry. The howl was long and with great reach, summoning every demon.

She had bled all of her magic into her demonic army, doubling their power. The sounds of war changed into horrifying cries for mercy. Retreat was the only option. The east quadrant of the kingdom was Tinaria's last chance for survival if they could evade the undead coming from the darkness of the forest. With the dawn approaching, the kingdom was already in the hands of evil.

Michael peered over the side of the veranda in horror. Again, the bloodbath commenced. The inevitable conquest of the Demon Plague reopened the mending wounds in his heart. As he watched the flyers gather forces in the sky and plow through human opposition, Michael fell into a surrendering trance.

"Damn you!" Michael sobbed in a broken breath.

Sattka stood proud, admiring the work of her minions, though disappointed that the cathedral remained untaken. She heard Michael's pathetic utterance and said, **"Pardon me? I was not paying attention. Did you mumble something, Miuriell?"**

Sattka sighed indolently and moved in their direction. Maxim and Predella were burning with anger and sorrow, too dazed to move. They warned Michael that she was coming, but he mindlessly observed the chaos below, pressing his staff harder into the floor.

"I should have known that you were following me," Michael said inertly as Sattka neared closer to him. "I don't know what you are or where you came from, but there is nothing you can say that can justify this!"

Sattka crept over his left shoulder and whispered softly, **"Why didn't you order the strike on the cathedral?**

It is a holy place for these rats. You led us all this way only to grow weak?"

"Shut up!" He blasted her with his telekinetic powers.

Sattka endured the attack and advanced again, **"You don't admire your work? It is a true honor to find our father, even as diminished as you are."**

"I am not linked with your evil!" Michael cried and held the Staff of Truth before him, ready to crush her.

"You know the truth! You know the prophecies!" Sattka tried to rejuvenate his memory.

"I will tear out your deceptive tongue!" Michael blasted her again, sending her into the wall this time. Sattka was beginning to lose patience when she caught a scent. It came from the base of the cathedral, and for whomever it belonged, fright was evident. Her malicious smirk tore into him and before Michael could realize what had changed her, she put out her wings and said eagerly, **"There you are!"**

She ran over to the edge of the terrace and jumped off, catching the air in her wings. She glided about to locate the origin of the scent and when she found it, Sattka rejoiced with a squeal. The demonic general swooped down to claim her prize.

"Where did she go?" Maxim pressed, feeling faint in response to the slaughter of his people.

Michael did not respond, for he tried to understand what Sattka hankered after. His answer came to him quickly as Maxim cried out straight away from the ground, "Shina! She found the princess!"

"What?" Michael spun around to acknowledge Maxim's cry from the edge.

"She'll tear her to pieces!" he exclaimed, helpless from his place on the veranda.

The only way he could save the fleeing princess in time was to jump. Staring down over the edge of the terrace,

Michael affirmed, "I'm taking her away from all this. There is no other way."

"We'll find you!" Maxim shouted. "Get her out of here!"

Eliminating all doubt, Michael dove off the edge, plunging into the gruesome hostilities below. Predella tiredly leaned against the wall aside the shattered rose window and thought aloud, "Why does it want the princess? Why her?"

Maxim turned to her, suppressing tears, and said, "I don't know. I don't know what we're fighting against, but you heard what she called him. She called him 'father.'"

PART I
CHAPTER X
THE DEFIANT

Gliding above the hell of war, Sattka descended in an attempt to snatch Shina from the air. As a team, the prince and princess ran towards the eastern walls with a cordon of knights to protect them. The valiant soldiers promised them safe passage into the Barrier Forest if they could make it out of the city. Their escape seemed hopeless, surrounded by demons of shadow and the air.

As Michael dropped into the battleground of the cathedral yard, a blast of his power crashed into the ground, driving both demon and man away like sand in a desert storm. The telekinetic force lightened his fall. Michael immediately pinpointed Princess Shina's location, along with her brother and a throng of steadfast knights.

They ran towards the eastern outlet of the kingdom, gunning for the forest. Michael sprinted through the horrific arena, cuffing anyone and anything in his way with his staff and mystical mind. Just ahead, Sattka readied to swoop down for the strike. He watched her every move and pledged to slay her before she could complete her mission.

Flyer demons cleared the sky for their general and she came in swift and free. A knight caught a glimpse of Sattka's incoming approach and warned the others to safeguard the princess. They all raised their shields over her and prepared for the impact. As the knights braced themselves, Michael hammered through a wall of shadow demons and locked on to Sattka's fatal advance. With a tremendous burst of his power, he vigorously extended his open palm to the air and released an incredible force that pummeled Sattka to the side. Like a bullet, she smashed through the walls of King's Tower, beaten and covered in rubble.

"Miuriell!" Shina saw pieces of him between the spaces the knights provided.

"Don't stop running! Go!" Michael shouted, eventually catching up with them. More than ever before, hordes of demons attacked the squadron. A moving storm of steel smashed through the demonic barricade, some knights not making it out.

Closer to the eastern gates, they all desperately ran. Michael couldn't be stopped, as he overran the escaping party and opened up a wider path for the soldiers behind him to follow. Not letting up, the small cordon of knights reached the east gate and persisted with Michael as their gallant tank.

The flyers became restless and dove into the army of warriors from the air like dropping mortars. Shadow demons gathered into terrifying packs and collided into the cordon, trying to break the princess out. All efforts proved to be futile. Michael pressed on with stability, unwaveringly pounding through hosts of demons. Finally, the battered walls of the east sanctified them all as they made it out of the kingdom and headed for the forest.

However, Michael and the knights were not out yet. The unyielding masses of the undead clamored for them. He drove through the trees of the forest, bending them like asparagus. Though Shina had fallen down the slope, a pair of loyal knights scooped her up by her arms and carried on. The force of the undead was no match for Michael's strength of mind.

Tenebrion watched as the hollering squad of knights ran through masses of skeletons behind Michael's escort. The demonic general loosened his whip, but let it run limp on the ground, for Michael was already through the offensive line.

Tenebrion simply surveyed in dismay, understanding that he escaped with the princess and that not all of the Demon Plague's missions would be fulfilled.

The secret passageway down King's Tower and under the castle was five feet wide and six feet tall, providing the king and his queen enough space to escape the massacre above. The corridor led them spiraling down below the tower and under the ground where it then rose to the northeastern cemetery. Wielding torches, the elite guards trekked on until the corridor ended and a brief incline gave way to a doorway of stone.

"This is it, Your Majesty. We've reached the cemetery, but remain out of the light," a knight said as he and two others slid the door over enough to expose the mausoleum's interior.

He waved the rest of the group on as they guided the king and queen out. A narrow opening of the mausoleum's double doors permitted a vertical beam of light to peek in. The sounds of heroes fighting to their last breath filled their ear. Shrieks and angry growls from demons confirmed the ill-fated truth that the cemetery had become a battlefield.

Closing his eyes in honor his brothers-in-arms' brave stand, a knight said forlornly, "It's not safe to move you."

The queen planted her face into her hands and cried for her people. Her husband embraced her and shook his head in angst. When hope seemed distant, cries of valor blistered the night from the south. An enormous cavalry rushed the field, equipped with single-handed weapons and pistols. Dirtied with blood and filth, the cavaliers roared savagely through the cemetery in a last-ditch effort to clear the field.

From the thin space between the mock mausoleum doors, the knight witnessed fierce red beams wreak havoc on the battlefield. Emerging from the graveyard's main gate,

Valkris challenged the Tinarian's fighting force among his demonic horde. Then, something made him turn around to look towards the mausoleum. A wicked smirk infected his face, lazily holding the Seltek at his side. Though he knew Shina was out of his grasp, there was still some opportunity to eliminate the kingdom's foundations for its future. Passing the necropolis conflict, Valkris headed straight for the royals' hiding place and scoffed, "**I smell her blood.**"

He handed the golden rod over to a minion and stabbed his jagged fingers into the crease of the stone entrance to the mausoleum, strenuously opening the double doors with fervor. A knight immediately before him quickly winced back and drew his sword. The others shielded the king and queen, stricken with fright.

Immediately, the knights' weapons melted to a sweltering heap. They quickly released their blades and moved away from the sizzling red liquid. Valkris then moved in and blew them all into the wall with a tremendous gust of wind from his magical arsenal. A throng of demons stormed the mausoleum and finished them off, with one of the minions returning Valkris's Seltek.

"**This is as far as you go.**" Valkris extended the nefarious rod forward and fired a blast from the eye, hitting King Orgento in his heart and sending him back into the wall. The queen screamed in grief and ran over to tend to him.

"Luther! God, no! I beg of you!" she sobbed, holding his heavy head in her arms.

"My love—" the king uttered warily, fading fast.

"Monster!" she cried at the demon as her mouth caught tears running down her face.

The king was dead. Madam Orgento could only kiss her husband's hand in remorse, kneeling alone in a place of death. Valkris approached casually with his familiar sneer and stepped over the massacred bodies of the knights scattered about. He proclaimed down at her, "**Do not grieve, for he will be reunited with his hopeless people.**"

Hearing the wretched voice of the king's murderer, she regained her strength and wiped the tears from her face. She courageously arose and peered right into the demonic general's vile yellow eyes, surrounded by his demons. Even as Valkris towered over her, she refused to back down.

"Reunite me, you heartless creature," she said boldly.

Studying the queen's bearings, Valkris thought about it and then said, "**You possess magic, but you're weak. You have drained so much of it from your core, there's hardly anything left. Until I find the princess, you'll have to stay alive. You may yet serve us—as bait. Therefore, your request is denied.**"

The evil commander then simply turned away from her and ambled back into the fray. Madam Orgento remained there, staggered, as she watched him leave. It was a sentence worse than death. There would have been no effort in taking her life, but Valkris was not about the kill. He thrived on torment. His demons shut her back in the dark mausoleum with her slain subjects and dead husband.

The fighting went on, but Tinaria never surrendered. As fate would have it, the most beautiful and treasured light appeared like a lost hero returning to his children. With hell invading Tinaria, the wonderful glow upon the horizon slowly rose above the trees. Slight rays of light began to cover parts of the kingdom. The light colored the towns beginning from the east and gradually draped the west. A natural occurrence, often taken for granted, became profoundly cherished.

The demons tried desperately to stay in the comfort of the darkness, but there was hardly escape from the conquering sun. Like the prey they had hunted, the Demon

Plague winced from the daylight, which swathed the city like lava from an erupting volcano. Demons abandoned their murderous duties and struggled to keep away from the advancing light, causing them all to pile into dark alleys. Survivors found it easier to strike the demons down, while others simply ran the other way.

Before the sun's rays had completely engulfed the kingdom, Valkris stared indignantly at the unfinished conquest. His minions in the cemetery shrieked from the blistering heat that consumed them, crying from the razing of their grotesque hides. If there was any shade, the ravenous vermin leaped into its sanctuary. Valkris's own skin slowly started to burn, but he refused to gasp. He positioned the Seltek vertically before him and snarled.

A red beam of light launched into the sky and proliferated like a ripple in a lake. The red magic encased the Demon Plague in its entirety. Valkris then pulled the magical wave back into the Seltek's evil eye, instantly transporting every one of his minions. When the magic diminished into the initial red beam, the Demon Plague was gone. Valkris, himself, was the last to retreat.

The morning had come and the Demon Plague vanished, leaving Tinaria a city of ruin. The kingdom was gorged with bodies, both human and demonic. Before the night had fallen, Tinaria was the most dazzling kingdom in the Eastern Hemisphere. Memories of its majesty echoed in the hearts of all her survivors. They held weapons in their hands that, for some reason, failed to come loose from their grip. Those who had the willpower to walk strolled aimlessly throughout the devastation of the battle's aftermath. They had fought the entire night.

Daylight had revealed the extent of damage done to the city. Much of the eastern towns had burned down, ravaged by uncontrollable fires. The harbor was a bloody, broken mess of sunken ships and floating bodies. Corpses littered the streets of red, discharging the foulest of smells. Walking about the city brought great sorrow for the survivors who emerged from the cathedral. Demon carcasses had not vanished with Valkris, leaving their hides to rot in the sun. Tinaria was in ruins.

The queen, discovered lying on her husband's chest in the mausoleum, organized an emergency gathering of her court in Municipal Hall. Her most trusted officials sat around a large table, surrounded by high-ranking soldiers who survived the night. Like the congregation itself, the queen's intentions were strong-hearted and of great weight. The fate of Tinaria hung in the balance as they decided how to move forward together.

As they sat, too tired and broken to discuss defense for the next possible wave of attacks, Maxim and Predella came through the main doors. The queen was the first to rise and hug him there in the middle of the hall, overwhelmed by emotion. She cried tears of grief and hope on his shoulder, embracing him tightly. After they exchanged grateful words, the queen looked to Predella and nodded honorably. The huntress humbly returned the gesture.

"Shall we get down to it, Your Highness? There is much we have to discuss and with very little time." Drake called the gathering into action from his seat.

Maxim joined his allies at the table, his eyes bloodshot and face covered with filth. Predella sat beside him, her body riddled with cuts and bruises. At a closer look, everyone had the same afflictions. Their blood drained from their faces, it was evident that no one had slept since the horror just hours ago. Aside from the cries and moans from outside, the hall was eerily silent. The party was shattered physically and in spirit.

"Maxim, the princess was evacuated into the Barrier Forest," Drake started. "I can't begin to describe the danger she is in right now. Miuriell attracted these things—that army from hell—to our doorstep. His intentions may have been noble—"

Lancea cut him off, saying jadedly, "We're all in danger. There's no safe place for anyone—anywhere. If that army of death comes again tonight, we're finished. They'll finish the job and exterminate us for good."

"It's not guaranteed that the evacuation to Ellium and Falcus was even successful," the admiral added sullenly. "We all saw the ship smash into our harbor. Those things could have—"

"Please, admiral, don't," Queen Orgento interjected, her hand raised in protest. "No more of that. We don't have the time or the energy to revisit all those things right now. I want to hear countermeasures."

She almost broke down in front of them all, overcome by the tragic turn of events. While her subjects offered her consolation, she had to laugh looking at Predella sit across from her at the table. The queen said to her, sincerely, "And after everything, you're still here? Why?"

They all turned to Predella after the queen's remarks, putting the spotlight on her again. She lowered her head in humility and took her time, holding back tears of her own, "I know what it's like to lose everything—to lose everyone. How could I live with myself if I just turn away? This is where I have to be."

Moved by her answer, citing the mass destruction of her people years ago, the queen said, "We are grateful."

"And how much will this cost?" Drake derided.

Maxim pounded the table and glared him down with his reddened eyes, angered by his disparaging behavior. The queen, then, lowered her head and sighed. Drake defended his condemnation of her, yelling out, "What? We can't trust her, especially when we're most vulnerable! The prince singled her out as the one who stole his lineage ring! That's her reputation at stake here!"

"She nearly died for us—for our kingdom." Maxim took to her defense. "Predella is like me, a warrior of the sages. From the moment I returned, I've only heard disdain from you. All you do is bark fear and doom."

"I'm Tinaria's guard dog!" Drake countered angrily. "I barked for years without you to keep this kingdom safe! How long can we keep our borders safe without—"

"There *are* no borders anymore!" he shouted, quieting all who thought it smart to chime in next. "Tinaria has fallen! Look around you, Drake! We are in ruins! What the hell are you trying to save exactly? A kingdom? A city? All we are, all that Tinaria has ever been, is a people! We all bled for that idea! We watched our brothers die for that idea!

"You think I was fighting for our borders last night? A dream that was Tinaria lies at our feet! This is what we're fighting for now! Goddammit, nothing else matters except each other! Those people out there, screaming and crying, are counting on us to come up with something! In the end, chivalry matters. When we walk outside those doors, they're going to want something from us. They need to know that we're still a country—that we're still a family. It'll take years to recover from this, but, until then, it's us."

The hall was quiet then, reflecting on Maxim's passionate plea. While he missed years of Tinarian triumph and heartbreak in his absence, Maxim remembered his home as it was before the Ethereal Wars. He missed Eric's exile into the badlands and the uneasy armistice with the Ziamons. His fire had never quenched, even in his sleep. That undying loyalty brought deeper meaning to his rousing words.

"As queen, I shall not have my king's life count for nothing." Madam Orgento broke the uneasy silence. "When one of those monsters killed my husband and so many others, it made it very clear that Shina was more than a mission objective. It wanted my daughter—and then said that I would be bait. If Shina was with me then, I can't even imagine it."

Drake, beguiled by Maxim's stirring words, answered his queen, saying, "When I was defending the eastern walls from the army of the undead, I saw them. Miuriell ran in front and Shina and the prince were behind them, shielded by the knights and whoever else. I swear, my knees nearly buckled at the sight. Demons dove in to smash the princess loose and the shadow ones materialized from every dark place but to no avail. Miuriell crushed through everything in his path.

"Eventually, as they dashed downhill, it may have been the smoke from the cannons and the town fires in my eyes, but I watched—all of us watched Miuriell bend the trees so they could rush into the forest unhindered. He bent gravity at will like it was his to control. Not one of those things even touched his cloak. He saved the princess from certain death, of that I know. And still, as I sit here, I can't believe that she's in safe hands. After all these years, living on guard and digging out Ziamon spies from our ranks, my intuition has sharpened. As a blade on whetstone, I can cut through every deception.

"If Miuriell means to protect her, he can't possibly keep her safe with those demons following him wherever he goes. You all want me to have faith in him, but you know, as well as I, that the army from hell followed him to our shore. He may not have intended it, but they came here and now my home reeks of death and sulfur. How can I, or anyone, trust him?"

Lancea nodded and answered him, "I didn't believe him until he employed that power you spoke of. Hearing you tell your account of their escape, I remembered what he told me about Pommel. Miuriell couldn't save it and that was his home. Tinaria has fallen, but it can be rebuilt. The princess will rule as queen, because of him. We are not all dead."

"And suppose we bring her back home tonight?" Drake countered. "How can we be sure that they won't invade again and finish us off? The sun chased them away. It won't stay up there forever."

Predella said, "The generals. Michael said that if we can kill the generals, we can weaken the Demon Plague."

"Demon Plague?" Drake uttered. "Is that what we're calling them?"

"It defines our enemy," Predella replied. "They spread like a plague and plagues can be stopped."

"The generals can talk. They're more intelligent than the minions they control," Maxim added. "They know how to speak Christian and who knows how many other languages. I almost killed one of them. Predella had it out with another."

"Maybe they can be reasoned with," Lancea said. "They, perhaps, will leave us be if we give them what they want. We can make a bargain, so to speak."

"They want my daughter." The queen admonished him. "Do you still want to bargain?"

He sunk his head and sighed. Grief-stricken citizens started to angrily bang on the doors, fighting with the guards to appeal for help. They all heard the noise as if it was a jolt back to reality. The princess was a target for an unknown reason and the Demon Plague allegedly followed Michael to Tinaria. Whether she was safer in his hands or in a greater danger remained to be seen. It was a trap either way.

As knights from inside dealt with the pounding of the doors, Queen Orgento began, "Well, time is running out. We need to find Shina and the rest before nightfall. Maxim, take Predella and track them down. Once you do, you'll have to make a judgment call. I don't feel comfortable bringing her back here, and yet, all I want is to hold her in my arms and kiss her face. Predella, you know how to get to Tofauti the fastest, yes?"

"I *am* Tofauti, Your Highness," she answered. "I can lead the way if that's what you want of me."

"Maxim will decide that. I give authority to him," the queen said. "Don't let Eric intimidate you. He's not in control. Shina will listen to you."

Drake then spoke up, "Should I go along with them?"

"No, I need you here, Lord Vitan," she said. "The city is in turbulent times and I can't do this without your leadership. Do you understand?"

Nodding hesitantly, Drake looked to Maxim and then back to his queen, "Then perhaps you should give Maxim the Tinaris Seal. Shina will not be able to say no to that—like he is your ambassador. He'll represent us all."

In agreement, the queen turned to Lancea and said, "See to it."

The beating of the doors subsided, but the people were growing restless without seeing their leaders. She looked to Maxim, saying, "This isn't the first time you've set out to find your princess."

"Hopefully it goes a bit smoother than last time," he said, referring to his solo rescue mission in Ziamon. "We'll go and prepare for the journey, if it pleases you, Your Majesty."

"You and Predella should get some rest first. You both haven't slept, or eaten, for heaven's sake," she answered.

Shaking his head, Maxim retorted, "But, I must insist, Your Highness, if we don't start out now, there's no telling—"

"I will not have my daughter's rescuers half awake and hungry while her life hangs in the balance!" she snapped back. "You'll get rest and eat! That's a command, boy!"

Maxim then lowered his head and understood. They all understood. There was no place for reckless heroics anymore. When the hall finally realized their duties in Tinaria's lowest, they went for the main doors. As the guards opened the way, instead of angry cries and lamenting, the gathering crowds were singing. Despite their right to mourn, the Tinarian populace sang the national anthem.

Overwhelmed by the brave show of unity, the royal court stood together and watched them sing. The queen shed tears before them, unable to contain her emotion. Maxim, too, felt to cry as they sang the song of his home. Drake began to join them, followed by Lancea and then the others. With one voice, over a hundred strong took a stance against their enemies and breathed new life into Tinaria.

PART I
CHAPTER XI
THE SMOKING EMBERS

Michael's cloak, ravaged by war, hung jadedly from his shoulders, as he led the party deeper into the forest. Though the march was arduous, there was peace in the silence of nature. The faint sounds of busy creatures surrounded them as they walked. Having walked miles already, Princess Shina sighed jadedly, "We need to stop. My feet are hurting."

When soldiers came to her aid, the exiled prince turned to Michael and asked, "Where are we even going?"

Anticipating the sullen reaction from his party, Michael leaned on his staff and said, "I suppose this is far enough."

"Back home, then?" a soldier said hopefully.

"Not when your home is in ruin and marked for death," Michael returned. "We should camp here tonight. Rain will be on its way soon enough."

"*We* are marked for death," Eric chided. "You are not from these parts. This is the Barrier Forest—the only thing that separates us from Ziamon. If we're not careful, their rangers will encircle us and you'll come to realize what kind of savages they really are."

"What of your truce?" Michael replied among the rising arguments from the group.

"That means nothing," he countered. "Ziamon would do anything to get their grubby hands on the heir to the Tinarian throne!"

Leading by faith alone, Michael struggled to convince his party that they were not yet safe. He picked up a colorful leaf from the ground and said, "This leaf is beautiful. However, it is a fallen leaf. It has fallen from the tree's branches and is now condemned to live on the ground until nature consumes it, just like the princess. I don't know why they want her, but they seem to think I have a part in all this."

Eric moved in close to Michael's face and said sternly, "If something happens to her, I will not be forgiving. How do you intend on protecting my sister?"

"By keeping her close," Michael answered as he turned around and continued ahead. "Your pretentious mouth will be what gets us killed if those Ziamon rangers find us."

Eric watched in a trance as Michael passed him and sauntered further into the forest. Princess Shina, however, found a small measure of trust in the Pommelian and chose to follow him. He healed her mother and helped in their escape. Whatever her connection with the demons, she believed that she had more of a chance with Michael than the remainder of the Tinarian guard.

Therefore, they continued their walk through the Barrier Forest. After voyaging further eastward, a small creek rode alongside them. Castillo's Creek flowed peacefully towards the Ziamon territory, serving as a natural travel guide. Prince Eric and some soldiers scooped fresh water into their cupped hands and drank. In time, their hunger called.

One soldier spotted a deer and urged that they kill it for sustenance. Michael handed his staff over to a nearby soldier and carefully drew nearer. The party could not predict what he planned to do without any weaponry. He walked over and knelt before it. He reached out and gently placed both hands on its head. Within a matter of seconds, the peaceful animal insensibly collapsed to the ground without struggle or fear.

The party was astounded. Their mouths hung open in wonder. A low tear fell from the corner of Shina's eye and trickled down her cheek. A soldier asked in a whisper, "How?"

"Ready a fire," Michael said, leaving the deer to rest in peace where they lied. "I'll start foraging to make a shelter. It'll rain as we're sleeping."

A pair of soldiers stayed behind to guard the prince and princess, which left the other eleven to scurry for nature's provisions. They rationed the venison, huddled around the fire, as Michael created a large tent away from the creek by way of his powerful mind. Heavy branches, sticks, twine, and thick brush came together like magic in the air at Michael's will.

A small pack of wolves drank from the creek just down the way, making the group nervous. Michael promised that the wild dogs would not harm them as long as they stayed by the fire. Though some of the dogs looked over, curious, they kept to the creek and left the party alone.

As they sat about the growing fire, watching dusk creep upon them, a rustling sounded from the obscurity of the forest came upon them. Sounding like footsteps, the group readied their weapons and peered into the dark void beyond the light of the fire. They had already learned to fear the night. A respite out in the open hours of the coming darkness meant total vulnerability.

Visible to the light of the fire, two figures came into view, walking side by side. Predella carried a large shoulder bag as Maxim followed in behind with two. The greatest warriors of the East had found Shina's caravan at last. The princess ran up to her champion and jumped on him, clasping her arms around his neck. Michael shook his head in relief as he watched Predella smile at him from the distance. Eric, however, was sure to glare upon her. He did not easily forget the lasting effects of her deception. His soul still boiled for revenge, still, after all the hell they experienced the night before.

Michael made his way over and hugged her tightly. She embraced him just the same and stroked the side of his face when they split apart, thankful to see him alive. Prince Eric glowered into her eyes. She gave it right back. While the overcast sky seemed ominous to some of them, Michael knew that its clouds contained water and not blood.

Later, the party built a larger fire to sit around and ate the rations that Maxim and Predella provided. The soldiers conversed with each other, sharing their experiences of survival the night before. Tinaria's destruction had settled into their hearts. Some were fathers and others had sweethearts that sailed across the sea. While the prattling ensued, Michael sat beside a young, anxious soldier whose eyes frenetically scanned the darkness of the forest for any demons that might jump out.

"They're not here," he told him, empathetically. "I was as scared as you. Don't feel bad."

"How—I mean, how do you know for sure?" the soldier asked him.

Having overheard them from just feet away, Predella cut in, "Because he can feel them—and he doesn't have a nosebleed."

Michael turned to her and offered a crooked smile, "I see you've been watching me."

Others started to pay attention to their conversation as Maxim scooched closer to ask Michael, "Is it true what they say about that staff—that its owner can tell the future?"

Attaining the attention of the group, Michael admired the staff and said, "The Staff of Truth helps focus the power already within me. Urik taught me how to wield it, being its original owner. When he found me as a child in Pommel, he told my father that the staff led him to find me—that it chose me to be its master."

Princess Shina became aware of the relationship between the peculiar writing on Michael's staff and the similar inscriptions on Predella's bow. She remembered the same sort on Maxim's blade, realizing that there was a powerful connection between the three. She wrapped her arms around her chilly legs and asked, "What do those inscriptions mean on your weapons?"

Michael surveyed his staff and ran his thumb down the engraved inscriptions, saying, "Not even Urik could tell me."

Predella followed with an intuitive grin, "Von Vanna said that the writing was from the old world—some ancient dialect."

"Ellium has books from the old world and none match the runes on our weapons," Michael said. "It's beyond the old world."

"They'll *be* no world left if that army returns from wherever it came," another soldier said. "Ellium, Tinaria—all of it won't matter a damn."

As cynical as he came off, the party could only nod their weary heads in agreement. Shina hoped to steer the conversation away from the talk of demons. Michael thought aloud, "When I was alone on that boat, left to drift out to nowhere, I imagined what the Demon Plague had done to the neighboring realms. Never did I predict them coming to your kingdom so soon."

"So, they followed you," Eric said. "You brought them to our shores."

Michael could feel the eyes of judgment fixed upon him when Predella came to his defense, "They can't be following him alone. The west must be suffering as we are. They have to be fighting them even now as we sit here."

Thinking of his loved ones and all the innocent people who potentially endured the Demon Plague's wrath, Michael uttered, "It's possible."

"Well, they're not here, now," Shina said if only to give herself courage. "They didn't follow Michael in the forest."

A soldier replied, having thought of his family, "With all due respect, Your Highness, that doesn't mean Tinaria is safe. They could be fighting wave two right now, God forbid it."

"We barely survived the first," another said. "They will never—"

Michael cut in before he sparked a greater panic, "They aren't there, either."

Bemused, Maxim asked, "So where did they all go? You know as well as I that they weren't the type to give up on—"

He was able to catch himself, before mentioning the princess directly. She lowered her head as Eric asked, "Well, what about, Tinaria? Did they live? Are my parents alive?"

Maxim, after hearing the exiled prince's request, took out the Tinaris Seal from his pocket and presented it to the party, "The king and queen chose me to represent them here. The queen, herself, begged that I make the choice."

"Choice?" Eric repeated while the rest of the party sighed in relief, hearing that Tinaria yet lived. "What choice?"

Michael looked at Maxim intently from across the fire, knowing all too well that the king was dead. He knew the toll. He wouldn't dare speak of it, however, seeing Maxim return his gaze. He differed to his authority, as any mentioning of the titanic losses would have only set off a grief-stricken uproar. Maxim answered the prince, "The crown fears that if we return home, the demons will be waiting for her there. She planned for us to split up—some of us returning home and the rest escorting the princess to Tofauti."

"Tofauti?" Eric cried back.

Maxim continued, "Predella would lead Michael, the princess, and myself there in as little time as possible while the rest of you gentlemen returned home as witnesses."

"But I don't want to go there!" Shina protested. "My place is in Tinaria."

"You may regret that, Your Majesty," Maxim replied. "It isn't for the faint of heart."

Predella said, "And they will be sniffing around for you there, Your Highness. It's best that we're on the move. I vow to take you to Tofauti as fast as I can."

"I will be the judge of that," Shina retorted angrily, irate that her parents would send her away.

Maxim showed the seal to her again before returning it to his pocket, "Not this time, princess. In the morning, *I* will be the judge of that."

As Shina sulked in her spot by the fire, Eric griped, "That is debatable."

"No, it isn't," Maxim riposted, glaring him down. "You are an exiled prince. Your words do not carry any weight in this company."

"And yet, you sit beside that Tofauti rebel?" Eric chided. "You'd trust her to take you there? They'd jail her and curse the rest of you for bringing her to their doors!"

"Haven't you had enough?" Predella countered, refusing to keep her peace any longer.

Prince Eric fired back, rising onto his feet in an explosive rage, "No, I will *never* have enough until you feel the same pain I endured for too many years! Because of your whorish trickery, my own father sent me into exile! I was doomed to wander the decrepit lands of the east! If you only could experience the Kajhic Ruins for yourself. Maybe then you—"

Predella sprung from her spot and turned the tables with a rage of her own, crying, "Do you truly believe I have not endured hardship? Were your loved ones annihilated in a day? Did you have to witness the devastation of an entire people and then pick up the pieces after? I know what it is to belong to no country! I know what it feels like to call no place home!"

"Ridiculous!" Eric instantly retorted. "Your savage clan was destined for failure and dissolution when you seceded from Tofauti! Why blame anyone else? Why blame fireballs from the sky?"

Even one of the soldiers had to intercede, saying, "What is wrong with you, man?"

Predella shouted back, "The Waasi were exterminated! They were targeted by a sorcerer, probably one like you!"

"There *are* no sorcerers that can do that anymore, woman! You're a delusional liar!" Eric waved her off.

Predella was ready to react when Michael asked her in a calm voice out of tone with their fueled argument, "How did this happen to your people? I caught wind of it in Pommel—some kind of—"

"Attack spell," Predella said over him. "I saw it. I was there when—when it happened."

"Pardon me for saying, but how would you still be alive if you were there when it happened?" A soldier asked her.

Sitting back down, as if in a trance, she stared into the lively fire and remembered out loud, "We were in the grass, miles away from Waasi, on the Shahidi Knoll. We were making love on the grass and, as I laid there, I saw the clouds darken and thunder. A storm of fire swirled in place. Then, from the flames, a dragon—"

"Give me a break!" Eric cut into her story, grumbling, "You expect us to believe that story? A dragon emerged from the clouds and vomited all over—"

"Don't you dare make a mockery of it!" she countered, infuriated and shaken by his hateful derision. "I can't believe you'd have the audacity to laugh at me as you suddenly appear in Tinaria, unwelcomed by your own people, while the army of the undead arise! Care to explain *that*, sorcerer?"

Silence conquered the party again with only the sound of the campfire's crackling having its business known. Eric and Predella maintained their fuming stares. Eric remained standing, unable to answer her claim against him. He looked down for his sister, but she stared deeper into the fire with hurt in her heart. Feeling defeated, the exiled prince, laughed at the insinuation, "You're trying to say *I* brought this calamity upon us?"

From her seated place, Predella said, "Tofauti built a memorial in the crater that once was the Waasi Tribe and, in the same decree, offered amnesty to all the dissenters. When we arrive there, I and all of us will be welcomed. I cannot say the same for you."

His hate quickly turned to remorse when he realized that he was alone yet again. The party was not in his support. Hoarse, he asked her, "Why did you do this to me? What was it that brought you to ruin my life? How did you even do it?"

Finally, Predella lifted her head and answered him, "All these years, you've probably cursed my name, but I was just an instrument in the machine that took you down. It was part of someone else's plan and they knew I could get the job done on the inside."

"Whose plan?" Even Maxim had to ask.

Predella shook her head, saying, "It was a long time ago. My contact was a Tinarian emissary. He had money and connections. He placed me where I needed to be and told me that all was fair as long as I relieved you of your lineage ring. My job was done after that. My contract was finished."

A soldier then said cautiously, "Tell me you didn't take part in the poisoning of our queen."

"I would never do that," she snapped back.

"Speaking for most of us here who took the pledge and recited the oath before Her Majesty, I had to ask," he defended his implication.

Michael, then, upheld her character, "She shared some very private matters to us in detail. I can tell you, she didn't do it."

"I'm more concerned about the inside job," Maxim said, steering the conversation back. "Someone wanted to set him up. Who would benefit the most from his exile?"

Eric added, "Or how did they know my father would go so far as to exile me? It was a death sentence—the badlands. The Ziamons were watching me, wondering if it was really the prince or just some wandering doppelganger. I could have surrendered to their custody. I could have given them everything for some comfort. In my anger, I very well could have betrayed the kingdom that betrayed me."

Maxim said, "And did you?"

"Don't insult me," Eric scoffed. "You're a fossil. If there's anyone who shouldn't participate in Tinaris Seal business, it's you—a man out of time. You're just learning all the fun you missed while you were sleeping."

"While I was dead, theoretically," Maxim corrected.

Eric sneered back, "Oh, do forgive me, champion. Don't let my semantics offend you. While you were dead asleep, I was crawling in the hot barren lands of the old world."

"Into the Kajhic Ruins, right," Maxim mocked. "And that is where you dyed your hair white as a master sorcerer from the good old days or did those Kajhic mages actually make you into something? It wouldn't be the first time those radical occultists birthed something wicked into the world."

With the party's undivided attention, Eric capitulated for the first time. Everyone leaned in and quieted their minds to hear everything. While gazing into the dancing flames, Eric cautiously began, "After I wandered the arid wastelands of the Kajhic Badlands, I lost consciousness. Kajhic women took me in and cleansed me of the desert filth, nursing me back to health. They knew who I was, somehow.

"The chieftain sensed a suppressed magic within me and vowed to uncover my true potential, for a price, of course. I agreed. For years, they trained me to root the powers from within my core. They taught me how to tap into the elusive particles handed down by my mother, as I expected.

"In time, I was able to channel the elements and command them to perform the basics, but that was not enough for me. I wanted to become as powerful as my mother. I wanted to be better—stronger. My first great achievement was the Mimican Essent."

"The mimicry of another magician's spells," Michael declared. "I never thought that was a real thing."

"Anything can be a real thing if you believe it. With that spell, I copied any enchantment a sorcerer had cast and added it to my arsenal. But the spell was weak in that I could only keep the magic within me for a brief moment and my casting of the magic was merely half the potential of the magician's I stole it from. They urged me to learn other spells, but I had an agenda of my own.

"I continued to feed off the magical cores of the Kajhic sorcerers, enhancing my skill of the Mimican Essent. After rigorous years of refining my spell, I reached the apex and became a sorcerer. The Kajhic people began to fear my power and avoided the use of their magic around me." Eric raised his eerie eyes and addressed everyone around the fire, "You see, I have mastered the Mimican Essent to the level where no other could. Instead of waiting for a novice magician to cast a spell, I could peer into the core of their arsenal and literally copy every last enchantment they had."

"My God, what have you done?" a soldier said, visibly appalled by the prince's dark triumph.

"What have I done? I conquered the rules of sorcery! I could copy the spell exactly as is, rather than settle for the half-life. I was able to have full possession of magic for an extended period. That is what I have done!" Eric proclaimed brazenly.

"What happened to your magic last night?" Maxim retorted with heartrending passion, counting the lives that Eric could have saved.

He responded heatedly, "I don't have the same magic I once possessed! My core has withered since then. Those crafty occultists found a way to hide their cores from me. So, I lost it all."

"Bullshit. You have something. That's a fact," Maxim groaned, clenching his fist.

"Watch your tongue, 'hero.' You're just another fool that assumes he knows the workings of the world!" Prince Eric fired back. "I alone have seen the ruins of the badlands and left on my own accord."

"You were banished, boy—banished from Tinaria and banished from the occultists' sandcastles. Our people died last night. If you had the magic to save them, I want to know why you suppressed it. What was your agenda this time?" Maxim asked in a bold tone.

"I am done talking!" The exiled prince glared over his opponents with a low brow.

"You are not telling us something. Your story does not tally," Predella expressed her judgment fearlessly. "Those hermit magicians don't just let people walk away—"

"That's enough, I think," Michael ended the debate before tensions boiled over the pot. "I hope you got a lot out of your systems. I really do. We won't settle all this in one night."

Unsatisfied, Eric turned to him next, saying, "Well, what about you, savior? Any dirty laundry you'd like to air since it's evident you like playing the spectator?"

Shina was first to answer him, "Leave him be, brother. He saved us all. You saw his power—what he did to get us out of trouble."

"Well that's what has got me so curious, Shina," Eric returned. "He has unparalleled mystical powers and you don't want to know more?"

Before she could answer for him a second time, Michael raised his hand for silence and then set out to satisfy Eric's provoking question. He began, "Even in my youth, I knew that I was gifted with abilities. Through all my life, like waves of energy, it came to me. In dreams, in sorrow, throughout the happiest times, the power would encircle me like an aura—like a feeling I can't describe. And with all these powers, sharpened and centered through Urik's training, I couldn't see it happening—the Demon Plague.

"They invaded from within Pommel, not like here. It was as if they were already among us, waiting. I dreamt nothing that night—no warnings, no sensitivity to it. Just the screaming. My God, how they screamed. I'll spare you the details of what I—of how—well, you've all seen how they work. You see how they butcher everything. Couldn't save my family. Couldn't save my wife's family. God, help me, I couldn't save my son.

"Then, after many escaped, the rest was just a blur of flashing memories that don't make any sense. I awoke in a boat, where your people found me, and it was as if I slept my life away. You know, I thought I was floating in a casket—a coffin? Thought I was dead—that maybe it was fitting, and that everyone I loved would be somewhere so that I could reach out and hold them. I just wanted to hold them, and feel them in my care, and comfort them with words like, 'It's all going to be okay now. Nothing can hurt you anymore. I won't ever let anything do that.' And then I'd feel their breaths and feel their kisses and—"

Wiping tears away, Michael composed himself and had started again, "It's certainly over for them now, anyway. They all can rest in some sort of eternal peace. But my sins are too great, you see. I failed, with all my 'unparalleled mystical powers,' as you put it. I failed to protect them. Who knows how long I've been away? The West could be giving their very lives to save their children and their family and their soul mates and I'm not there. But, at least, I was here. Thank God."

Michael's sorrowful bluster struck a hard cord for the entire party, putting them into a sad stupor. He opened his broken heart and, in turn, revealed a grief that festered in all their hearts. Most felt that the only right thing to do was sit in silence, honoring their shared hurt. Suddenly, Eric, himself, sat down and internalized Michael's regret. In searching the faces around the fire, he came to understand that they all had scars. Scars were simple mementos that told their stories. Some scars were left unseen, however, deep within the soul.

A soldier was the first to break the gloomy silence, "If you're serious about the fate of the West, can't you use your staff to see? You can see the present anywhere, right?"

Breaking out of his spell, Michael said, "It doesn't really work that way, actually. To see the past, present, or future of anything, I need to be there in the place where it happened. And even then, it can only go so far until things get fuzzy."

"That's how you found the poison used on my mother's life," Shina said, enlightened. "You were there to see all the ingredients."

"I know how it was prepared," Michael replied, then turning to look at her, "and I know who prepared it."

The party leaned in, open to the scandalous news that Michael kept close to his chest. He could have shared it any time, but there never seemed to be an appropriate hour. More pressing matters were at hand. Shina asked him, almost too anxious to know the truth, "You know who did it? You saw?"

"I told you that Predella wasn't responsible, because I witnessed the assassin poison the tonic," he went on, holding his staff close. "Following the phantom of her past, the woman mixed the ingredients in the kitchen, as the crumpled letter in her dress instructed. After stirring the poison in the goblet, she handed the two cups to a servant who, in turn, delivered the evening tonics to the king's quarters on a serving dish."

"So, this mystery woman poisoned both goblets?" one of the soldiers gasped.

"No, just the one," Michael answered, struggling to replay the scene in his mind. "I can't remember whose goblet was poisoned, but the king was fast asleep so Her Majesty took the liberty of drinking both."

Maxim gnashed his teeth in ire, "So she just poisoned the one? How did the bitch know that she was targeting the right person? If the queen didn't drink both—"

"Then maybe the toxin was meant for the king instead," Predella construed.

Michael answered, "Or the agent didn't care. It's viable that she didn't care who drank it, so long as one of them did. I couldn't make out the fine intricacies of the goblets if they were labeled or something or other."

"Bastards!" A soldier reacted in a sudden burst of rage. "They got away with it, whoever they are!"

"The queen lived and she still lives," Michael replied. "Their mission was, in the end, a failure. I can be of service in tracking down these conspirators. If it serves the kingdom to bring them to justice, I'd do that."

"You could have told them," Eric murmured to himself.

Incensed by his brash demeanor after everything that had happened, Michael rebuked him, "I'm sorry, Your Grace, but when demons come to kill everyone, that sort of takes precedence, don't you think?"

Maxim interceded, saying, "What the exile means to say is we would be grateful to have your help. Tinaria would be in your debt."

"Tinaria is already in your debt," Shina added, looking to Maxim after.

"But there is something you need to understand," Michael said sternly. "The Demon Plague must be stopped at the source. Their war on us started in Pommel, so, on my life, it'll end in Pommel. That's priority over anything else. If I don't stop them, then nothing we do matters."

The party gazed about the fire to catch brief glimpses of each other's expressions. They all fought demons of their own, suffering through trials others could never know. And yet, Maxim said to him, "You won't fight them on your own, Michael. I will fight by your side. I'll go west with you."

"That goes for me, too," Predella followed.

Some of the soldiers and guards had already fallen asleep, just too exhausted to stay awake. The soldiers that were awake wouldn't dare say anything, for they were not prepared to join such a quest. They barely survived the first battle. Maxim and Predella were of a different breed. Michael, appreciative of their noble gestures, rose to his feet and said, "It's too early to make those plans now. Your home needs us. The enemy is here and so are we. For now, we should think about turning in. The rain is finally here."

As he said it, sporadic raindrops began to fall on them. They looked to the night sky, darkened by the clouds, and marveled at his clairvoyance. None could argue with his suggestion, either way, for they had not slept properly for well over days. Retiring in the sturdy shelters Michael created hours before, the soldiers settled in. Predella made a place for herself inside another one of his makeshift tents, robust as the next. Maxim, however, didn't trust the exiled prince in the company of the princess, let alone the rest of the party. With Michael looking on from a distance away, standing in the falling rain, Maxim tied up Eric's hands and then hitched the rope to a nearby tree. Eric just looked into Maxim's eyes, even smiling.

As Shina sat in the last tent, watching the scene play out from inside, Michael thought to use his staff and see what the future had in store for them. Leaping into the ambiguous future, he watched events transpire around him. The rain had continued to fall, ultimately quenching the campfire. He looked all around the site for even the slightest manifestation of demons. He went as far into the night as he could, just to be sure. But the future was never certain, containing several possible timelines.

Nothing seemed to alarm him until a member of the party caught his attention. In the dead of night, when his foresight started to blacken in ambiguity, Michael watched as Eric awakened and left the tent. Standing in the pouring rain, the exiled prince burned the rope from his wrists until they fell to his feet. The line, still tethered to the tree, fell limp. Free, Eric entered Shina's tent.

Michael pressed into the fragmented future as far as he could to see the rest, focusing only on that tent. Though everything else went black, he saw Eric stroke his sister's red hair and then kiss her gently on the cheek. And then, showing regret, the sorcerer crept out into the darkness. Having vanished from his sight, Michael tried to pursue him deeper into the forest. It was to no avail.

Snapping back from his oracular journey, Michael took care to outline any small details he may have missed in Eric's escape. When Maxim finished tightening the rope around the prince's wrists, he escorted him to the soldiers' tent where the tree offered the least slack. The exiled prince retired with the other men without a fuss. Yet, as he lay there, Eric leaned his head up to look at Michael in the rain. He felt his stare as if he knew that Michael was on to him.

Maxim, soon after, approached him and asked up close, "Michael, what is it? Come out of the rain."

With Eric's eyes on him the whole way, Michael replied, "I just wanted to make sure there weren't any surprises as we slept. I'm damn tired, but it wouldn't be good if I missed something."

"Let the night take care of itself," Maxim said, patting his shoulder as he headed back for his tent. "We have important business tomorrow morning. Get some sleep."

Michael just smiled and nodded. In his walk back to the shelter, Maxim stopped midway and turned back. Predella stepped out into the rain then, wondering what was going on. Michael met him halfway. Maxim, looking troubled, finally asked him, "Since we're alone out here. I wanted to put something behind us."

"Go ahead," he replied.

While Predella looked on in the distance, her dark skin glistening in the rain, Maxim said, "In Tinaria, when that she-demon came to speak to you, she called you 'father.' She said 'our father.' Why did she say that?"

Michael knew that Sattka's chilling words would come to haunt him among his allies. He didn't foresee Maxim's petition in his premonition, so it came as a surprise. Looking up at the rain as it fell on his face, Michael sighed and then answered him, "There's so much I don't know, Maxim. I know there's a lot I don't understand yet, but I can promise you this one thing. I am not part of their plan. I'm not one of them. She can call me whatever the hell she wants, but, in the end, they'll know me as their destroyer."

PART I
CHAPTER XII
THE RIVAL REVIVAL

Michael dreamt of Opal, standing in wait for him within the density of the mystical woods. He headed towards her, ready to embrace her again. There was never much time for them in his lucid dreams, for their touch ended the fantasy. Yet, while he moved towards his wife, he saw a small army of ragtag soldiers advance from behind her. They marched straight through her as if she was but an apparition.

"Michael! Wake up!" Predella awakened him from outside his tent. "We have a big problem."

Roused from his vision, Michael rubbed his eyes and groaned, "Of course we do."

In crawling out, he needed only to look up to observe a slew of Ziamon soldiers encircling the camp. Droves of them, armed with crossbows and blowguns, axes and rapiers, swords and halberds, had closed in on them before sunrise. Predella showed him the trouble, joining the others by the stifled campfire. Using his staff, Michael perused the size of the Ziamon taskforce. He counted seventy-six.

"Our problem," Predella revealed.

"Good morning, Mr. Miuriell. A bit late to our modest social gathering, you are," the haughty Argall Francisco said from behind the kneeling Tinarian knights, bound by their wrists. A rich Ziamon colonel, he sported a pencil mustache and long black ponytail. Colonel Francisco had led numerous raids against Tinaria and the Tofauti in his time.

"Predella, you look as beautiful as always!" Argall remarked in the Christian dialect. "Did I mention that?"

She responded, after enduring the squadron's pompous snickering, "Save your venom, snake."

Argall laughed exaggeratingly with his hands on his hips, "Of course, so much venom these days with the truce and all."

Maxim retorted, standing before the cowering princess, "We can reconsider that, if you want, Mustache."

"How I miss that nickname," he answered, surrounded by the full protection of his squadron. "You look like him, you sound like him, but you're not him. The Red Menace is dead."

"I was, once," Maxim countered, still holding the handle of his Mad Phoenix in the scabbard. "Come closer and get a better look."

"It's Cavallo's ghost! Don't go near it!" one Ziamon warrior cried out from the group.

"Shut up!" Argall shouted. "He's a double of some kind—an imposter. Believe me, I would have liked the real thing. I would have liked to gut him right in front of his timid little princess."

For fifteen years, the eastern realms believed Maxim was dead, killed in a night raid within Tinaria itself. There had been an absence of war since, compelling Ziamon to sign the armistice or face Tinaria and Tofauti's full strength. In the standstill, Captain Aramis spoke out from behind his colonel, "I say we kill anyway, just to be sure. We can't take the risk of bringing them back for the Trials."

"Quiet!" Argall screeched, pondering his options.

Michael then called out, "I may just be an outsider, but I must remind you of the armistice you signed. There isn't anything you'll accomplish by threatening us. We're not here to cause trouble."

Argall turned to him and smiled crossly, answering, "Ah, well you *are* an outsider, after all. And, Mr. Miuriell, you wouldn't know, as an outsider, that one of the stipulations to that truce was the death of the Red Menace—this murdering scamp. And since Tinaria has fallen to some terrific army, according to my scouts, there isn't much room left for negotiation. If this is the real Maxim Cavallo, as he seems to be, then the truce is void and all of you are fair game."

"That stipulation is a lie," Maxim returned. "No other kingdom would have signed that accord."

"But, evidently, a Tinarian would sign an amendment, at least, to that very end," Argall said proudly.

Taken aback by the charge, Maxim countered, "I don't know what you're trying to convince me of—that they set me up to die for you? The king would never—"

"You know, maybe you are the real Red Menace," Argall snootily interjected. "The real Cavallo was fierce on the field, but not very bright. This is becoming burdensome. Lay down your weapons and you will not die where you stand."

Michael stepped forward, "You may not have heard me. The armistice was clear, stipulations aside. Tinaria suffered an invasion from a terrible, evil force and it's not likely to stop there. Your kingdom could very well be next. Whatever scores you have to settle, it won't be settled here. Leave us be and we'll do you no harm."

"No harm?" Argall uttered. "You still seem to think you can call the shots here? Only I call the shots, Mr. Miuriell. For instance, if your armistice logic applies, then Predella, a thorn in Ziamon's side, can be executed right now without consequence. She's wanted 'dead or alive' by Ziamon and she calls no county home. So—"

Argall motioned for his marksman to fire a bolt straight for Predella's heart. As he pulled the trigger of the crossbow, the bolt sprung forth and soared for her. Michael redirected the bolt away from her body and guided it deep into the bark of a tree behind them. To be taken seriously, he then cast his staff far across the way and struck the marksman in his breastplate, knocking him hard into a throng of his allies. As the Ziamon squadron gasped at his power, Michael beckoned the Staff of Truth to return to his open palm.

"Do not test me," Michael said, clenching his teeth.

Stunned, Argall began to clap, convincing his squadron to follow. In seconds, the cordon of soldiers applauded the outsider's powers, confusing the party. Maxim looked back at Michael as if to validate the lunacy of their adversaries. Shina could take no more of it and tore away from Maxim's shield. Out in the open, she shouted, "That's enough!"

Slowly, the clapping died down, inducing Argall to retort, "Your Majesty, please, we are only marveling at your companion's tricks! The stories were not just tall tales! Are you in the mood to negotiate the terms of Predella and the Red Menace's release into our custody? For sure, that is the only way we will leave you alone, princess."

Pulling out the Tinaris Seal from his pocket and raising it for them all to see, Maxim shouted over the princess, "She will not be negotiating with you, today! By the authority of King Luther Orgento IV, I represent Tinaria! And, as Tinaria, I *won't* be negotiating with you filthy, feral, inbred asshats! If you so desire, your new friend, Mr. Miuriell, would be honored to crush you into a bloody paste with just a wink of his eye!"

Amid the squadron's uproar, Michael shook his head and said to him, "That isn't my way."

Maxim warned, standing before the princess again, "It may have to be."

"Inbred?" Argall yelled angrily, inciting his squadron to curse and call out threats. "Perhaps, we can fire a hail of bolts and arrows to kill the whole lot of you once and for all! Even Miuriell can't stop that!"

Michael answered for himself, "You'd be surprised."

Shina, again, tried to put out the fire, crying out, "We *are* traveling to Tofauti! They won't be pleased to hear that Ziamon delayed our trip with threats! Would you risk pulling Ziamon back into conflict? Tinaria may be diminished for now, but Tofauti will lend all they have at their disposal to wipe you from the face of this earth! And you know that!"

The soldiers, incapacitated on their knees, collectively kept their mouths shut as Argall walked by them deep in thought. He contemplated Shina's intimidation tactic, finding it credible enough to be the truth, though he smelled a bluff. Maxim, Predella, and Michael awaited the colonel's reply. Maxim was ready at a moment's notice to unsheathe his blade and bring the fire. Predella could have planted three arrows into three skulls before anyone had a chance to fire back.

Michael, however, watched Argall intently as he gaged his options. Shina knew enough to speak the language they understood. Finally, the colonel stopped and said, "You've certainly gained some wisdom since I last saw you."

"Last you saw me, I was an incarcerated child in your country," Shina fired back

"But now, you're a cat with claws. I like that," he said. "I think we can come to terms. In respect of our truce, while ill at ease, perhaps a deal can be made. Understand, this is the best I can do."

Maxim grunted, too tired to deal with the colonel's draining overconfidence, "You're as boring as I remember. Just get on with it!"

"Very well," he declared eloquently. "Ziamon is willing to grant you safe passage to Tofauti, if that *is* where you're actually going, on one key condition. Cavallo, seemingly back from the dead, must face the Trials for his crimes against Ziamon. Of course, your entire party will be present to watch the proceedings. Ziamon will treat you as our distinguished guests, in accordance with the armistice.

"If he survives our most challenging test, be it fair and balanced, then all of you will be free to go on to Tofauti. That is my word. But, if he dies, then Predella dies with him. Her sins against Ziamon are almost as equally heinous as the Red Menace. So, it's only fitting that her life be bound to his. Either way, the truce, as it was written, remains intact and the princess may leave Ziamon in peace with Mr. Miuriell and all her knights. What do you say to that?"

While the party thought on Argall's proposal, Predella spoke out, "You fired a bolt for my heart just minutes ago. How can we be sure that you'll—"

"We accept." Maxim, with scores of his own to settle, agreed to the colonel's challenge.

Even Michael had not expected Maxim's bold move. If Michael was not going to destroy them, then Maxim would be the one to do it in the pit. An arena in the center of the city, the Crater tested the fate of prisoners with trials of combat. Maxim was more than willing to compete against Ziamon's best, despite his injuries. He looked to Michael for insurance. If they violated the truce, if Argall went against his word, then Michael would make them pay. There was too much at stake to spend even one angst-ridden day in Ziamon.

Delighted, Argall proclaimed, "Then, we'll finally see the ageless Red Menace enter the Crater. I know you won't disappoint."

The colonel ordered that the knights be released from their bondage under guard. Argall then welcomed the party to join them in the march for Ziamon, even allowing them to keep their weapons so long that Michael was part of the equation. His power was greater than the sum of their parts. The Ziamons were careful not to anger him. Captain Aramis personally chained Maxim's wrists tightly.

As Michael walked up, Maxim hissed loud enough for Shina to hear, "If Eric is behind this, I'm going to kill him."

"He left the camp in the middle of the night," Michael said. "He vanished."

Shina felt as if she had to throw up, overwhelmed by each terrible circumstance. She never endured anything close to the trauma she experienced over the last few days. Holding the promise of home in her heart, Shina sought what little bravery she had stored away somewhere. Her mother's influence peeked through when she was pressed against the wall.

"When I woke up, I felt his absence," she said while the Ziamons started to escort them to the march.

"That's because nobody was complaining," Maxim said, following the squadron out of the camp.

In their walk, Captain Aramis came up from behind him and went to take his sword from the scabbard, "Don't mind if I relieve you of this sword, do you?"

It had been so long and Aramis was too young to know the way around the fire-sword. Maxim let him try it just as Argall had warned him to leave it. Too late, Aramis grabbed the sword by the handle and jerked away in searing agony. Holding his hand, scorched and blistered, the captain screamed frantically. Maxim just smiled, making sure to connect eyes with the colonel on his horse.

Argall then knew that there was no doubting it. Maxim was the real thing, back from the grave. It shook him to his core, even if it was a little exciting. There was a last-minute alteration to the triangular armistice, signed in secret just outside Ziamon in neutral ground. Only a handful was privy to the clandestine meeting. Argall was one of them. Seeing Maxim alive and practically torn from the past raised too many questions.

Predella, her wrists chained like his, joined Maxim in the line, asking, "I hope you know what you're doing."

Turning to her and then back front, Maxim answered, "So do I."

She gave him a look, gauging his level of insanity with just her facial expression. He knew Predella was not on board with his reckless plan, betting everything on his skills alone. Michael, however, walked up behind them with Shina by her side. Ziamon soldiers were quick to move out of his way as he came, fearing his supernatural powers. The princess made it her objective to stay near him, if only for that reason.

Shina looked back at the encampment they left behind, hoping to find some last remnant of her brother's puzzling whereabouts. The squadron marched back to Ziamon, just as apprehensive as the Tinarian soldiers, for some of the deadliest figures in the east were in their company. There, in the encampment, one soul in hiding watched them leave. From behind one of the tents, Eric removed his invisibility spell and whispered to himself, "What are you hopeless fools doing?"

Later in Tinaria, Madam Orgento presided over the services for the dead. She had a difficult time attending the ceremony from the time when her husband was laid in the catacombs. The queen was a strong woman and the entire kingdom was well aware of her potential to rule over the kingdom while Shina was gone. They cremated hundreds of their loved ones in the eastern towns alone.

Drake finally came and sat by her side, having inspected the quality of the water reservoir. Almost in a blank stare, he uttered dimly, "How long do you intend on punishing yourself, Your Highness? You need rest. For God's sake, we buried the king this morning."

Madam Orgento replied, "Where is your family, Drake?"

"On a ship to Ellium," he said, sighing.

"Oh, so they're safe? Thank the Maker. All of these people before us weep for their families. Some of them weep for courageous men and women who gave their lives two nights earlier. Some were killed in hiding, relying on hope to protect their families. As long as Tinaria weeps, we must weep also," she said, looking straight on. "They *are* Tinaria."

"I understand, Madam, forgive me, but if Tinaria is going to survive, we have jobs to do," Drake urged. "There is not much that we can do for them by weeping."

The queen turned to speak directly to his face, "Tinaria's destiny is in Maxim Cavallo's hands. My children may very well have met the demonic army again in the Barrier Forest. Once the princess is back in my arms, we'll play it your way. If you wish to make some headway before then, please Drake, do what you must."

Drake rubbed his tired eyes and capitulated, saying, "I am grateful that the demons didn't return in the night. Even in the darkest parts of my spirit, I was sure they'd be back to finish us off. It rained, instead, washing some blood away. I was never so joyful to see such a beautiful storm. Some of us just stood under it for minutes at a time, just letting the rain wash us clean. Now, whenever it rains water, I'll thank God it wasn't blood."

Moments later, an anxious man, filthy from head to toe, ran up and knelt before them. Drake waved the guards and commanded the exhausted Tinarian to proceed with his news. He exclaimed in-between breaths, "Your Majesty, my lord, we've unearthed Lord Era from under the rubble of the southwest quarter! Our lord is injured, but alive!"

"Where is he now?" Drake rose from his seat.

"The King's Tower Infirmary, my lord," he quickly responded from his knee.

The queen embraced his forearm tightly, "Go to him, Drake. Ask for me later. You know where I'll be."

"Yes, Madam." He bowed, taking his leave.

The queen simply nodded graciously and went back to the ceremonies, as if mesmerized. Drake nodded in return with a feeble smile and headed off. While making his way to the Royal Crux, he turned back to have another look at his queen. She stared over the burning corpses, witnessing the scores of citizens and soldiers in mourning. Her face locked in an expression of bereavement, the queen seemed more like a statue than a living, breathing monarch. Drake left her there, broken and still in shock of losing so much.

In the infirmary, Drake reached his wounded friend, lying in a used cot with a splint on his right arm. Kal Era was moaning from the pain pulsating from his broken bones. A slew of medics corralled him, trying to keep him steady while the surgeons and doctors inspected his substantial injuries. The ambient commotion was overwhelming, coming from every direction. Screams and cries enveloped the ward. The odor was gut-wrenching.

Dried blood riddled the lord's body, especially his face, where there seemed to be numerous cuts from demons' claws. He was breathing with pain, due to fractured ribs and a broken arm. The doctor coolly enlightened Drake on the lord's status. Hearing that he could survive in spite of his injuries, he nodded his head and thanked the doctor for his work. He then stood over his old friend and joked, "So, I heard you were there when the world broke."

"Drake," Kal began sluggishly, "I suppose I still have a purpose here. Is Tinaria—"

"Tinaria lives, old friend, just barely." Drake sat beside him as the doctors continued their work. "What do you need from me? Anything I can do?"

Kal stared into oblivion, saying lethargically, "Can you imagine what the world must have been like for the people living before the Primeval Tragedy? One thousand years later and we have still not been able to come close to their potential. I have always wanted to live in a lifetime of surgery without pain. I want to see machines fly men into the sunset. If we had their weapons, my God, we would have blown those demons back to hell! For heaven's sake, are we moving backward through time?"

Not expecting Kal's weary rant, Drake replied, "This world learned from our ancestors' fatal mistakes. They abused their creations. One day, we'll return to Ellium across the sea where they share your vision."

"We could really create a utopian kingdom. You heard the stories." Kal chuckled, but then groaned after aggravating his ribs. "Why were we born now? We were born in the wrong time. You know that, don't you, Drake?"

"We survived the demons, Kal. It's now critical that you rest." Drake rose from the bed and stood over him, preparing to leave. "Your purpose lies in the ruins of Tinaria."

Suddenly, Kal snatched Vitan's arm and cried in a withering, mad whisper, "The demons are hiding in the darkness of every corner, watching us and smiling. I know they're smiling, Drake!"

Startled by his old friend's feverish outburst, Drake cautiously guided Kal's arm back to the cot where it was stable. His grip was strong, despite his condition. Before Drake could even consider a reply to Kal's chilling warning, one medic came by with surgical tools. They were prepared to amputate Kal's arm before it became infected.

"Stay strong, friend. I will return before long," Drake said with anguish in his heart, ready to leave him.

While two of the surgeons provided the tourniquet, Kal addressed one of the doctors in a fatigued manner, "I presume you have a steady hand?"

"We will perform quick work of it, my lord," the doctor replied.

"But not painless work," Kal said in return, looking for his friend. "We don't have the benefits of our past—only the costs."

Ziamon, the easternmost realm, was more of a bulwark than a kingdom. The warring nation had the Broken Gate Mountains to their east, separating them from the badlands—a virtually unending desert world. Occultist wasteland dwellers inhabited the badlands for decades until freak sandstorms shattered their civilization. The Broken Gate spared Ziamon from the same fate.

With the density of the Barrier Forest blocking Tinarian aggression from the west and south and the Keota River separating them from the Tofauti Empire to the north, Ziamon was wholly protected by natural borders. Its founding fathers built the Ziamon bulwark around the Crater, an ancient basin that marked the impact of one of the meteorites that ravaged the old world. It served as the nation's training center and provisional water reservoir.

Generations later, the Crater became an arena, built to entertain the Ziamon populace as political and war prisoners battled it out. Rivaling the Colosseum of the Ancient Romans, the Crater once highlighted the execution of slaves as well. Tinarian and Tofauti prisoners alike were condemned to slavery. Until a decade ago, when the armistice was ratified by all three nations, Ziamon avoided an all-out war and freed their slaves. Yet, because the Waasi Tribe had seceded from Tofauti, they were excluded from the terms of the truce. The Waasi, in turn, became easy prey for slavers.

Predella fought against the Ziamons for the sake of her people as a hostile abolitionist, slaying slave hunters and freeing Waasi from bondage. Entering the slave nation in chains dishonored her. Walking through the large clay arch meant that the party had crossed into Ziamon territory. The kingdom marveled at them from the sides as they marched on in captivity. Cheers and jeers greeted them for a mile before reaching Ziamon's main gates.

Walking into the bulwark city, Maxim looked up and connected eyes with Mistress Emmanuella Ayden, fifteen years older than he remembered her. The Supreme Ruler's only daughter, Emmanuella had the privilege of serving as his most trusted advisor. Her many brothers looked to her for their father's ear. As a lesbian, she would not provide the kingdom with children, so her position was promised for life.

She returned Maxim's gaze from the gable window, having flashbacks. When she was young, Emmanuella feared him more than any Tinarian. Maxim infiltrated her city when Shina was in confinement. Witnessing the path of bloody men, women, and children in his wake gave her nightmares for most of her life. Seeing him in chains compelled her to smile, knowing that the Crater waited to feast on his blood.

From his horse, Colonel Argall Francisco asked Michael, "How do you feel, now being a guest in Ziamon? I hope the death of your friends doesn't ruin your opinion of us."

"It's an impressive city," Michael replied boldly. "If you break your word, I'll raze it to the ground and make another crater."

Argall had to laugh, though sensing that Michael really wasn't joking. He saluted the mistress in glory, saying, "The ruler will have to make me brigadier for this. You'll like him, Mr. Miuriell. He, too, hates to see his people die."

PART I
CHAPTER XIII
THE TRIALS

Michael lost himself as he looked out from his special seat in the Crater, marveling at the aroused Ziamon audience cheer for the looming battle. On the sides of the actual crater, thousands of seats built into the earth leaned down over the open arena. The architecture was nothing short of ingenious, as it contained a retractable canopy, steps for every major aisle and megaphones for announcers to call the play-by-play over the noise of the mob.

The sandy circular arena covered a thousand feet in diameter, equipped with obstacles and structures to keep the battles interesting. Like a giant playpen, the Crater contained dips and mounds of sand in certain places and flat, smooth dirt in others. Doors and tunnels lined the perimeter of the arena, leading into larger chambers such as storage rooms, medical bays, armories and disposal ducts behind the scenes.

Supreme Ruler Dask Ayden sat comfortably in his chair over fifty feet about the showground, anticipating the epic trial about to commence. His Staff of Truth confiscated upon arrival, Michael sat beside Colonel Argall, just twenty feet from the supreme ruler. Ziamon guards placed him there at the colonel's request. As Michael unhappily settled in his seat, the colonel laughed, "Ah, so you *did* come! So very good of you to partake in our culture!"

"It's easy when you aren't given a choice," Michael said.

"Of course, it is," Argall replied. "You're welcome."

Looking down as the band played the entrance song, marking the beginning of the Trials, Michael noticed a small shrouded figure in the center of the arena. Without his staff, it was impossible for him to know who was under the sheet. Then again, it started to make sense as to why Argall asked for his company. He asked the colonel worriedly, "I assume you're going to tell me that one of my friends is under that canvas?"

"Well, you *are* a master of the obvious." Argall grinned. "I wanted you to be here for the unveiling. The Trials are just about to begin."

Only a few moments later, the Seven Justices emerged from the Channel of Legends, walking as a group into the arena. The applause was deafening. Equipped with unique armor and weapons, the Seven Justices were gladiators burdened with testing the innocence of those accused. Under the legitimacy of the Trials, the number of justices correlated with the crime. With all seven justices coming out to judge a single defendant meant that the Ziamon public expected to see a true villain to their nation.

Led by Justice Esker Vasquel, the seven justices encircled the sheeted person in the center dais. Barely out of his twenties, Esker was the most feared justice of them all. Two serrated swords rested in scabbards clinched onto each side of his waist. His hair was wild and jet-black, as he also sported stubble on his jaw to hide a scar from years past. Esker's most prevailing characteristic was his eyes. His left eye was brown, but the other was grey.

He walked calmly to the center of the arena and tightened the black gloves on his hands on his way. Women in the crowds tossed articles of clothing to express their true adoration for them all. They waved back, aware of the Trials' significance to the people. Much of the spectators already knew that Maxim Cavallo was in Ziamon hands, but they did not know who was under the sheet in the middle of the Crater. The arena took bets earlier for the person's identity.

"You know the Red Menace, thought dead for years, has been captured by Colonel Argall Francisco's task force! The rumors are true! He will finally face justice this day!" Mistress Emmanuella Ayden proclaimed through the large megaphones of her elevated balcony. "Brace yourselves for the relentless tyrant who cheated death! Once our greatest scourge who slaughtered hundreds of our people, I give you, the defendant, the Red Menace—Maxim Cavallo, himself!"

Never before had the arena been so exultant. The dusk was soon approaching as they brought out Maxim in heavy chains, surrounded by a small army of skilled soldiers. Even Dask Ayden jumped out of his seat to witness his nemesis enter the Trials. His daughter continued amid the acclaim of the crowd, "There walks Maxim Cavallo, the most ruthless of all enemies! We have confiscated his fire-sword—the sword spit out by the underworld because of its unspeakable evil, proves his identity!

"He will undergo the highest sentence ever to be administered in this arena! He must partake in vicious combat with the Seven Justices for seven minutes! The Seven Justices, in accordance with the statutes for the most heinous crimes, may wield any weapon of their choice, but the accused must do battle unarmed! He cannot wield or steal any weapon of any kind from any justice while the trial has commenced!"

As expected by the mistress, the crowd was restless, clamoring for Maxim to undergo his dreadful sentence. Several justices had taken it upon themselves to find an appropriate position among the obstacles of the arena. They liked the hunt, as did the masses. Attaining the mistress's approval from above, Esker moved over to remove the sheet concealing the bound defendant within.

"If he dies, then Predella shall share his sentence!" Emmanuelle shouted as Esker unveiled Predella's restrained form. Her hands chained behind her connecting to the shackles of her ankles induced Predella to lean forward.

Amongst the cheers, Michael looked on in utter shock. His eyes wide and his teeth clenched in anger, he gasped, "What kind of savagery—"

"We don't claim to be saints, Mr. Miuriell," Argall said, "but we are not merciful to our enemies. Besides, this night's trial alone will pay for the goodwill for hundreds of struggling families in Ziamon. It's all for a good cause."

Michael stared at him, incensed, as Emmanuella went on, "His death results in her throat being cut wide open before you all! If he is found not guilty, then she will have the opportunity to participate in her own trial in a later date! People of Ziamon, let your justices hear you!"

The crowd roared with anticipation as Maxim moved over to her, speechless. Horrified, Maxim knew that Predella's life was in his hands. He asked her, "What did they do to you?"

"Doesn't matter," Predella groaned through her teeth. "Just win. This is what you wanted."

While the cleaning crew rejuvenated the sand, Esker had unsheathed his blades and stared Maxim down. He wanted to be the first to kill him before the others had the chance. Maxim returned his hateful gaze, like two alpha wolves at each other's quarry. Enraged, he left Predella there and walked in closer to his rival, saying to her, "I'll make it up to you right now."

It was then that the flashbacks of his training with Malcusin rushed through Maxim's head like a drug. Visions of battling mercenaries blindfolded and unarmed reentered his mind. He remembered Malcusin's teachings. *"Leading the dance of combat will guide you to triumph and burden your adversaries with disbelief and distortion."*

Maxim remained in a state of meditation and recalled all of his training, including his purpose. Esker was the leader, so he was the first to confront the convict in the center of the arena. The other six justices scattered about the place, some behind obstacles. Esker stood before Maxim and instantly unsheathed his cruel blades. Scrutinizing, Esker clanged the two blades together and said in Christian, "Wake up sleepy head."

Maxim broke away from his meditation and peered back into the justice's irregular eyes. By then, he already mapped out his combat strategies. When the last Ziamon soldier unchained Maxim and ran off, Esker said brusquely, "My father so wished to kill you that he fought every battle in the hopes that you would be there to face him. He died looking for you. How fitting that I may kill you myself in honor of him."

Maxim replied, nonchalantly rubbing his freed wrists, "I will reunite you."

"And I will disembowel you," Esker retorted angrily.

"Well then, good luck with that," Maxim riposted.

"Save the luck for yourself," Esker raised one of his blades into the air to incite the crowd. The gong ringer held his instrument tightly in his hands and awaited the mistress's signal. With Esker directly before him, Maxim briskly examined his other adversaries. Naturally, Justice Fabian Marine and his Jalvolt, a long slender metal spear, stepped up onto one of the boxes on Maxim's far left.

The third justice was Addax, wielding a heavy poleax. He was a large, dark-skinned gladiator who armed his head with a large iron helmet. The fourth was Justice Corona, who wielded the reaper sticks. Her weapons were unorthodox, yet wildly renowned by all of Ziamon. They were two cylinders of sanded oak, both containing a hooked blade. She was the only woman on the league, though she was mistaken for a man on account of her muscular physique.

The fifth was Justice Reyes, who wielded a bow and ten arrows. He was a fan favorite for his cruel trick shots. The sixth was Justice Dampas, wielding two sickles. Regardless of his scrawny build, his savage ways of killing had forced some grown men to turn their eyes away.

Lastly, the seventh was Justice Attar. Born a Tofauti, he joined the Ziamon brotherhood when he was only thirteen. His supreme combat skills made his deadly machete seem impossible to avoid, for it also carried a lethal spike at the bottom of the hilt. As Justice Reyes hopped up on an obstacle to assure himself good firing accuracy, Maxim shut his eyes again and memorized their positions.

Finally, the mistress signaled the gong ringer to commence the trial. The scrawny man struck the gong with tremendous force. Immediately, Esker swung one of his blades for Maxim's gut, hoping to slay him in one blow. Maxim swatted the blade away with lightning speed and spun around the justice's body to chop the back of his neck with the side of his hand.

The counterattack numbed Esker's entire body as he fell onto his knees limp and then toppled over onto his chest, unconscious from the shocking blow. Then, Maxim opened his eyes and observed his first victim lying in the sand. To all the other justices, Maxim's blindingly fast maneuver was a warning. The crowd died down as soon as the best fighter hit the sand, out cold.

Reyes fired his first arrow for Maxim's head. He let it whiz past him, almost hitting Addax's charging foot. Taking advantage of Addax's size, Maxim grasped the poleax and slammed his elbow into the justice's gut. With the wind knocked out of his adversary, Maxim pulled the poleax to his side and kicked him into a nearby obstruction. The weapon came out from Addax's hand, but Maxim quickly discarded it. By trial law, he could not use any of their weapons.

Justice Marine had a clear shot at him but knew too well of the Tinarian's supernatural skills. Maxim awaited the casting of the Jalvolt, but the justice hopped off the box with the silver spear loosely in his hand. Just then, Justice Attar came from Maxim's right side to lop off his head. Maxim swiftly caught his wrist and punched him in the bare chest. Reyes fired another shot, forcing Maxim to dash aside, still grasping Justice Attar's armed wrist.

The justice punched him in the side of the face to free himself. When Maxim let go, Attar spun around to put a fast gash into his chest. Maxim hastily flipped backward and, when his hands reached the sand, kicked the machete out from the justice's grip. After Maxim returned to his feet, he kicked Justice Attar in the stomach, came around to lodge his elbow into his lower belly and rose up with a tremendous uppercut, knocking the justice out of the fight indefinitely.

When the machete fell to the ground, Maxim kicked it under a nearby obstruction. He hid beside the same obstacle for cover from Reyes's accurate arrows. Once kneeling beside a wooden box, Justice Marine sprinted towards him and aggressively plunged the Jalvolt for Maxim's lower stomach. Maxim caught the slick spear by its shaft with his two hands and forced himself onto his feet.

Already, Justice Reyes had loaded his third arrow and Justice Addax, pulling himself together, had recovered his poleax. Maxim had no time to dawdle. Marine was becoming impatient. He pulled his left hand away from the Jalvolt and reached for the crude dagger in his utility belt. The foolish move allowed Maxim to fully manipulate the spear away from him and produce a clean kick behind the justice's right knee. When he faltered, Maxim released the spear, came around for a fierce hack in Marine's lower belly, and then executed a rising kick that broke his jaw.

Justice Marine hit the sand hard, then holding his face in pain. Reyes fired another accurate shot, but Maxim heard it whistle through the air. He leaned back and allowed the arrow to sink into the wooden barricade behind him. After four misses, Reyes screamed with rage and threw his quiver with six arrows to his feet. Shaken by his incredible aggravation, the justice reached into the quiver to pull out three arrows and slipped them all between each of his fingers.

Before Maxim could respond to Reyes' desperate onslaught, Addax came up from his left side to challenge him again. The justice swung three times, failing with each strike. Addax's relentless offensive proved to be no match for Maxim's evasive maneuvers. Finally, he swung the poleax a fourth time, having spun about to muster all his might.

Prepared early for the attack, Maxim swiftly rolled under the swing and came up to the justice's side. When the poleax's blade clanged into a metal bar, Maxim assailed his opponent with a flurry of powerful blows. Overwhelmed, Addax fell onto his back and coughed blood.

Maxim swiftly turned to Reyes, the bowman troubling him since the beginning of the trial, and decided to silence him for good. As the justice fired three arrows for him, Maxim quickly advanced. He dodged the first arrow, which zipped by his head. He then dodged the next and subsequently allowed the third to continue its course, plummeting into the sand and almost hitting Addax through the helmet.

As the knight raced to pound the justice senseless, Justice Corona came out from one of the obstructions and thumped Maxim's shin with the back of one of the reaper sticks. While he abandoned his run and grunted in pain, the feisty justice emerged from behind the box and slammed Maxim's side with the back of the other reaper stick. His wounds spewed blood from the new bandaging, compelling Maxim to withdraw for the fight.

Justice Dampas ran up behind Maxim and planned to lodge his sickles vigorously into his back, taking advantage of his vulnerability. From a distance, Predella saw him coming and shouted for Maxim to be ready. Finally sensing the justice behind him, Maxim spun around and connected with a flying knee. He clobbered Dampas square in the chin. The impact was such that the justice stopped dead in his tracks, nearly knocked out on his feet. Maxim, enduring the smarting pain in his side, kicked him square in the throat. Dampas toppled limp onto the ground, suffocating from the fierce strike.

With the scrawny justice down, Maxim left him for later and focused on the woman. She adjusted her reaper sticks and awaited Maxim's first move. Reyes was loading his bow with another arrow, with only two remaining in the quiver. Maxim kicked both of the sticks out of her hands with stunning speed, using only his sweeping right leg. The two sticks jetted from her grip, leaving her baffled.

He jabbed her in the face, and then even harder with his elbow. Maxim finally swung around to launch a backhanded uppercut into her jaw, breaking her defenses altogether. When she was still strong enough to put up a counter-attack, Maxim evaded each strike, kneed her in the stomach, and then turned over a rising spinning kick straight in Corona's face. She twirled in the air before thudding into the sand. Unopposed, he hurled into the air and came down blasting his heel into Corona's forehead, rendering her unconscious. Once he rose onto his feet, Reyes released the fiercest arrow he had ever shot that day, screaming as he fired. It soared with intense speed for Maxim's back.

He attempted to evade the arrow, but it grazed through his right arm before stabbing into the ground. Blood spouted from his arm once but did not prove to be significant. He put pressure on the abrasion and growled, fed up with the annoying archer. Maxim turned and stared him down maliciously, charging the justice yet again.

Reyes threw his bow down and kicked his quiver off the obstruction. Glaring Maxim as he advanced closer, Reyes reached to his left arm and manipulated a secondhand weapon. A device vigorously latched onto the wrist provided a small lever, presenting a retractable double blade that extended far beyond the fist. It served its gruesome purpose well in close combat, providing lethal razor-sharp blades for offensive and defensive functions.

After pulling out the forearm blades, Justice Reyes hopped off the platform and charged down his oncoming foe. They both cried as the two adversaries charged each other, craving for conflict. The crowd cheered as they were already anticipating the brutal outcome of the collision with Predella seemingly in the center of it all. When they were dangerously close to one another, Reyes aimed his blades for Maxim's throat. Maxim slid on the sand, deflecting the blades, and swept his leg under the charging justice's feet.

Maxim grappled his rival's armed wrist and tossed him over his shoulder. The counterattack sent the justice flying to one of the boxes ahead. Maxim spit into the sand as he carefully watched the justice return to his feet, holding his back. He had three more justices to defeat. Maxim visualized them in the dirt.

Yet, as he glared at his enemy rising from the ground, Maxim tasted blood in his mouth. He then regurgitated a small dose that ran down his chin. Wiping the blood from his lips, he began to feel an ache in his lower back. Reaching, he felt the hilt of a small dagger. Maxim pulled out the knife and examined it, stained with his blood. He dropped it on the sand, feeling had by his underestimated foe, and inspected his minor wound.

"You should be more careful, Tinarian," Reyes taunted.

Maxim ground his bloody teeth. By the lightness in his head, the heaviness in his eyes, and stiffness in his muscles, he realized the knife had been poison-tipped. He regulated his breathing and channeled his energy to finish the job. Despite his blurred sight, Maxim was sharp enough to act upon Reyes's next attack. The Ziamon casually ambled up to his position with his arms extended out from his sides. The razor-sharp forearm blades lingered in the air, though tightly secured to his wrist. He smiled before driving the blades for Maxim's throat a second time.

Fearing Maxim was in a daze from the poison, Predella cried out, "Maxim! Watch it!"

However, by surprise, Maxim caught the justice's arm in action and manipulated his wrist, almost breaking the arm. Reyes shouted and aborted the strike. Because Maxim had him, he punched him in the torso and forcefully kicked the justice in the stomach. Maxim then released his arm and permitted Reyes to stumble on before collapsing to the ground.

Maxim then fell to his knee, dizzy and thirsty for water. The poison's effects were taking a toll. The audience started up in a thrilled frenzy, thinking that Maxim was, at last, out of gas. Predella shouted for him from the center of the arena, "Get up! Maxim, snap out of it!"

Her life was on the line and Michael knew it. He, too, started to sweat in his seat. Whispering for him to wake up and shake off the spell, Michael's pleas had seemingly made it into Maxim's spirit. Predella's cry, muffled by the booming ruckus of the masses, induced him into finding the strength to fight on. When he finally staggered onto his feet, Maxim made out the blurry figures of both Justice Marine and Addax carefully approaching him.

Dampas, too, had come limping from behind to try at him one more time. Maxim understood that he would need to hold nothing back if only to survive a while longer. As they came to finish him off, Maxim breathed in deep and found his discipline. Despite the cold shivers in his sweaty skin and the pain in his stomach, he obeyed Malcusin's rule of combat. He readied his stance as leader of the dance.

While the other members of the dance joined in, Maxim went to work. He sized up Dampas approaching from behind and dashed for him, grunting with each push of his legs in the burdensome sand. Catching the justice off-guard, he leaped and crushed a flying knee into his chest. Dampas propelled backward and crashed into the sand, knocked out. Marine and Reyes continued their charge for him, knowing that Maxim couldn't have had much left.

With Predella looking on, realizing that something was wrong with him, Maxim took on the two frantic justices. They battled it out before the audience, intent on ending the bout one way or another. Maxim parried what he could, but in his weak state, Marine and Reyes found brief openings to stab and cut him down.

Unwilling to surrender any more blood to the enemy, he punched Marine's knee in and swung his elbow up through his jaw. When Marine winced back, dazed and bleeding, Maxim rolled into the sand and kicked out Reyes's legs from under him. The justice, however, recovered fast and tackled Maxim to the ground. On top of him, Reyes hit him repeatedly with thundering punches to the face. Maxim's vision betrayed him, as each strike found its target. The crowds reveled in every second of it.

But when Reyes went to slam his forearm into Maxim's throat, ultimately delivering the finishing blow, the mob was denied. Maxim blocked that strike, prolonging his life, and then deterred the following strikes thereafter. Fueled by rage alone, he grappled Reyes's last punch and yanked him close enough to dislocate his elbow. Shouting in anguish, Reyes held his useless arm and cursed. Maxim took the fleeting opportunity and emptied his whole life into one unyielding punch for the justice's jaw. Screaming all the way, his blow dislocated Reyes's jaw next and sent him tipping over into the bloody sand.

The crowd cried out and jeered in disapproval, almost shaking the seats. Ayden looked over the state of all seven justices in the arena amid the booing of the audience. Turning to his far-right side, the ruler hastily asked the gong man, "How much time left?"

Showing the large bead counter, the gong man shouted over the crowd, "Two minutes, sire!"

Time was an estimated construct in the new world, relying on the sun, moon and the shadows. Ayden pounded the armrest in frustration, knowing how close Maxim neared to exoneration. But, in his apprehension, he saw one glimmer of hope. The masses erupted in exultation when Justice Esker began to awaken. He slowly rose from the sand, coming back into the fray. Looking around him, he shouted in a bitter rage upon seeing his fellow justices routed.

Drooling like a mad dog, Justice Marine lifted the silver spear above his shoulder and positioned himself just right. Maxim did not attempt to budge, too tired and beaten. With all of his hatred, the justice fired the Jalvolt precisely for Maxim's scarred chest. The magnificent weapon spiraled fast for its target. When the terrifying tip of the spear neared but five feet from his breast, Maxim hastily grappled it with his left hand as if catching a fly. As he forced the tip downward, the smooth shaft propelled upward into his other hand. In a second, Maxim had caught the speeding Jalvolt, claiming full ownership.

Justice Marine was utterly dumbfounded. His shot was perfect and Maxim could never have dodged it. His eye twitched as he observed Maxim holding the Jalvolt comfortably in his hands. The justice, hunched over with his arms hung to the side, had tried everything.

Esker came like a ravenous beast, swinging his blades angrily. However, Maxim was awaiting Esker's attack, unsurprised to see him back in the fight. When his blades reached his bare torso, Maxim positioned the Jalvolt vertically with a stone hold. Once he parried the serrated blades, he twirled the Jalvolt and, subsequently, loosened Esker's grip. He then pitched the silver spear far to his right and countered with a fierce punch to Esker's stomach.

While the justice hobbled backward and knelt to recover from the blow, Maxim fell to his knees again. Spitting up more blood, he resorted to deep rasping breaths to keep his focus. Esker, then, stabbed his blades angrily into the sand and challenged his foe, unarmed. The crowd, though, cried foul over Maxim's use of the Jalvolt. He broke the rules in wielding another justice's weapon during the Trials.

Michael was visibly shaking in anticipation, while the dictator of Ziamon slinked in his seat, humiliated. Argall then started to whisper, "Come on, damn you. Come on! Don't let him! Don't let him do it!"

When he found the opportune moment, Marine drove his small dagger for Maxim's stomach. Instinctively, Maxim seized the justice's armed wrist and pulled it down to his waist, forcing Marine to flip forward and come down on his back. The justice quickly rose onto his feet again, assuring Esker that he wasn't done yet. However, none of the pride in the world would be able to recover his dagger from Maxim's fast hands.

Maxim derisively lobbed the knife onto the ground by his side, glaring at his last foes. Refusing to surrender, the justice carefully stepped over to his adversary and timed a well-delivered punch for the face. Naturally, Maxim blocked the blow and delivered a counter punch of his own. The bemused justice stumbled backward before falling back into the sand. Before he could finish him off, Esker rushed forth.

With a flurry of strikes, Esker put his rival to the test. In his weary state, Maxim blocked and evaded what he could, but Esker held nothing back. The fight was intense as each Ziamon leaned off the edge of their seats in hopes that Esker could deal the telling blow before time ran out. Marine tried to rise to his feet, but couldn't. He simply collapsed in the sand and left Esker to try and kill the Tinarian.

Ayden turned again to the gong man, finding that only one bead remained before the trial ended. The ruler cried out to him desperately, "Don't you dare hit that gong! Do you hear me? Under no condition!"

Michael heard it from his spot not far from the Ziamon dictator. Argall was too enthralled in the fight to notice, but Michael did not intend to let the tyrant stretch his own rules only for Maxim die. Watching them battle it out right in front of Predella, fearing the worst, Michael knew he had to do something. Maxim was losing the fight, unable to keep the pace with his adversary. Finally, Esker slammed Maxim into the dais where Predella was bound. She cried out for him to fight on, but he had nothing left. As Esker knelt before him to end it, Predella could only hang her head and close her eyes.

But Michael knew that the trial had to have extended beyond eight minutes already. Assuming that the gong man would leave it alone, Michael blasted the gong himself with a supernatural force. It was the loudest the gong had ever rung out, jolting the masses into shocking disappointment. Ayden jerked to the side, ready to order the death of the gong man, only to see him standing there, bemused and emptyhanded.

Argall shouted with all the breath in his lungs, fighting over the jeering of the crowds, "Do it!"

Esker held his shaking fist out, ready to crush Maxim's skull in one bloody blow. Yet, his strike lingered in the air. He heard the gong ring louder than ever before, knowing the law of the Trials. He so wanted to violate the code, bringing his fist higher to deliver his fiercest blow, but, again, couldn't bring himself to do it. Against his anger and broken pride, the justice stayed his hand. Maxim jadedly raised his head to look Esker in the eyes, admiring his honor. Predella, too, warily saw the justice leave Maxim there, alive and acquitted of his crimes.

At last, the masses had expressed their final discontent. Screaming expletives and throwing things into the arena, the Crater blew up from the disillusionment of the glorified trial. The soldiers fought to cool the meltdown before it turned into a riot. Esker backed away from Maxim's thrashed body, propped up against Predella's dais. He couldn't believe it. In a daze, Esker went to help his comrades. Droves of guards and medics had then rushed in to tend to them all, as well as the defendants.

"Maxim!" Predella sobbed in disbelief. "Talk to me! Are you alright down there?"

Gradually sliding over to his side, he said, trailing off, "I told you I'd make it up to—"

He slid over into the sand, unconscious. A pair of medics had come to carry him out of the arena, bloodied, poisoned and catatonic. Michael rose up in his seat, fearing for Maxim's life. Predella worriedly cried out for him and Michael heard it from up in the seats. Argall, still disappointed from the thrilling upset of the trial, said to him, "Mr. Miuriell, do sit down. Your despicable friend isn't dead.

If he was, they would have called it and I would have joined my compatriots in a full night's reveling."

"Your Trials have really opened my eyes, colonel," he said, still standing. "Where is the princess? When can I see to it that both Predella and Maxim will survive the night?"

"Your princess is quite safe, indeed, in my temporary custody." Argall stood up to face Michael head on. "As for your friends, it's become a bit more complicated."

To pacify the angry masses of the Crater, Emmanuella called out from her gallery, "Ziamon, listen to the stipulations of the trial! It has not yet concluded! Do not fret! The Red Menace has yet to survive the night! If he dies from the wounds your loyal justices inflicted upon him, then his trial shall end in defeat! You must be patient with me!"

The guards unshackled Predella and carried her off just behind Maxim. She knew that if he died within the night, it was her neck. Still, his survival only meant that it was her turn to face the Trials and the Ziamons would want revenge. But Predella would rather have her day in the Crater than see Maxim dead. Emmanuella went on to appease the crowds as Michael confronted Argall again, "You won't let him survive the night, will you? You'll just let him fade away."

"If it's any consolation, the princess didn't see anything here today. One of my favorite courtesans is pampering her, much like what she'd expect as a royal in a time of peace," Argall said, ordering that Michael be taken away.

As the guards came to move him out, Michael answered back, "Remember, we were just passing through. It was you who brought this hell upon Ziamon."

"More threats, Mr. Miuriell, will not save your friends," Argall retorted.

Michael shook off the guard before replying in a grave tone, "We barely escaped Tinaria. What brought that place to its knees could easily come here and wipe Ziamon off the face of the earth. You better pray that when night falls, your city doesn't fall with it."

Meanwhile, in Tinaria, night had fallen and the kingdom warily awaited the Demon Plague's return. Under Drake alone, the harbor swelled with all the warriors Tinaria could provide. With only the crackling flames of the night torches, the entire city kept eerily quiet. Drake maintained his position, standing over his cannon and gunnery divisions. Queen Orgento sat on her horse beside him, refusing his request to take refuge.

"Your Majesty," Drake began awkwardly from his horse, looking straight out towards the darkness of the sea, "I am obligated to ask you again. Tinaria stands ready to escort you to refuge somewhere—anywhere."

The queen responded, "Oh God, give it up, Drake. Why does my place always have to be in a secluded shelter somewhere—anywhere? If they come again, no place is safe and you know that. I will not die in hiding."

Sighing, Drake reluctantly accepted her demand to remain on the line. Her presence induced the army to be ready to fight if only to defend their queen. However, there was no imminent sign of any attack. They looked up to the night sky, observing the moonshine. There were no signs of a bloodstorm and the scouts reported nothing suspicious. The gusts blew and lifted his cape now and again, offering the only excitement.

However, Drake had a familiar thought as he stared into the blackness of the open sea. His theory that Michael, absent from the city, was a deceiving warlock and the bringer of his demonic army, became a justifiable argument. He was willing to speak his mind concerning Michael's mysterious connection with the attack nights before, but for the queen's sake, he bit his tongue.

As the night dragged on, the crickets sang. The knocking of the feeble waves into the broken wharf echoed throughout the shore. By midnight, the queen broke away from the army and everyone lowered their guard. Drake permitted his men to retire for the night but decided to visit the east of the kingdom and scout the forest for himself. His division waited for him there and reported no activity. Instead, he peered out into the forest, dubious of Michael's real intentions.

PART I
CHAPTER XIV
THE SIEGE

Colonel Argall Francisco granted Michael permission to visit Maxim in the Pits of Pain, the medic chambers where gladiators and justices were kept until they recovered or died from their injuries. Escorted by Captain Aramis, Michael came upon the wing where Maxim laid thrashed. In and out of consciousness, his right arm hung from the side of the cot, sopping with his blood. His face was beaten red and his body was covered in lesions. Medics had patched him up with the least amount of care.

Shaking his head in disgust, Michael said, "You'll just let him die down here, as I expected."

"The staff reported that he was poisoned," Aramis said. "He has to survive the night in order to be absolved of his crimes against the citadel. He also violated the rules by using one of the justices' weapons in combat. The Red Menace—"

"I'm staying here to look over him and offer him the care he desperately needs," Michael cut in loudly enough for the medical staff and their guards to hear. "Did you apply the antidote for the poison in his system?"

"No. That's not our business." Aramis countered.

Michael moved by his friend's side and said, "Of course not. You specialize in poisons, not the antidotes, right?"

He demanded a bucket with clean water and a tray of fresh bandages and alcohol to tend to his friend for the night. Aramis allowed it, unwilling to anger him any further. The captain remembered his god-like powers from the Barrier Forest. Michael knew the whereabouts of the rest of the party, including Princess Shina, Predella and the soldiers in case he needed to break them loose. Spending the night in Ziamon was not part of his plan, but he would stay up for as long as he was able just to safeguard Maxim from his worst enemies.

    The citadel housed Ziamon's most esteemed officers and nobles. Colonel Argall Francisco, held in high regard by Ziamon, dwelled in a large apartment in the citadel's higher levels. After a delicious dinner in Argall's dining hall, Princess Shina spent the rest of the evening with Huruma, the colonel's favorite Waasi slave mistress. They eventually retired in Argall's guest quarters, at his request.

    Shina somehow dozed off, despite her draining anxiety, in her single bed with Huruma sleeping in the bed beside her. In the dead of the night, Argall had drunk himself into a bitter stupor and intruded on them as they slept. He watched the princess asleep. The glow from the moon illuminated the room considerably, as the candles on the bedside table flickered to death. Still fuming from the humiliation of Maxim's shocking victory in the Crater, Argall unsheathed his dagger and slowly slithered over to Shina's bed five feet away from Huruma's.

    Wanting vengeance in his drunken state, he began to consider the consequences of taking her in the night. He admired the tiny nightgown they gave her to wear. Her body fit snug and the gown ended high above her knees. Unable to wait any longer, he pulled off the thin sheet covering her body and dropped it at the foot of the bed. He marveled at her fine legs retracting from the lack of covering. He started from her calf and slid his hand up her leg until reaching her gown.

    Argall then slipped his sleazy hand up between her legs. Finally, Shina awakened to find her nightmare become real. She shrieked and fired profanities at his stoned face. She tried to tear his hand from between her legs, but he was too strong. Still, she fought harder, finding new ways to fend him off. She screamed uncontrollably and woke the colonel's dark-skinned mistress. Once Huruma was awake, she looked on in sorrow, but couldn't interfere. The princess had fought Argall enough for him to become incredibly frustrated.

He pulled his hand out from her gown, held her throat firmly with the same hand and waved the dagger over her face. Her cries stopped instantly as she fearfully studied the knife. When he had control of her, Argall moved his hand from her neck over to her mouth, silencing her. He said angrily, "I do not wish to kill you, princess, but I will if you compel me."

Paying attention to the colonel's glossy eyes, she saw no hope in fighting on. She loosened her muscles and laid motionless in the bed, giving herself completely to him in the hopes that he wouldn't kill her. He smiled sickly and stuck the dagger deep into the wooden desk beside Shina's head. The candle shook lazily.

In control, he turned her head towards the candle and dagger on the table to lick the side of her neck like a vermin. She cringed as he moved down to her chest, tightening her fists. He tore the gown straight through the middle and exposed her naked breasts, for which he toyed with next. While he spent his time on her, Shina felt feelings of shame.

Gradually, her muscles began to tense up again and her breathing escalated, suddenly replacing dishonor with hatred. Shina's adrenaline pulsed throughout her entire body when she fixed her eyes on the dagger lodged in the table only a foot away from her nose. She awakened something deep inside of her. A frightening and powerful presence that even Argall hadn't recognized swelled from within.

Bursting, Shina broke the dagger out from the wooden desk, sending small pieces of timber into the room. The colonel's pupils shrunk as he realized just what she had done. Before he could react, Shina angrily thrust the dagger firmly into the side of his throat. The knife sunk into his neck until the hilt couldn't go any further.

Argall's blood poured out from the wound, slid down the hilt of the dagger and then dropped onto her lower neck and chest. Before he died, Argall gargled something in shock of his fate and rolled his eyes back into his head. Within the moment, he faded away and fell heavily on top of her. Letting out a shrieking cry, Shina pushed him off the bed until his body fell sluggishly onto the floor. She still held the bloody dagger in her shaking hand, too afraid to let it go. The sopping blood slipped through her fingers and ran down her wrist and arm.

Huruma looked on from her bed in astonishment. She came out from under her sheets and wrapped them around her body as she stood off to the side. Shina finally let the dagger drop onto the bed. She then jumped off and pinched the front of her torn gown with her left hand. Realizing the murder she committed and the incredible strength it took to pull the dagger from the table, the princess was frantic.

The mistress slowly walked towards her and stopped when she saw Shina tensing up. Instead, Huruma said from a safe distance, "Many Waasi women will salute you."

Princess Shina looked back at the colonel's corpse on the floor, surrounded by his draining blood. She covered her mouth again and sobbed, smudging his blood on her chest with her fingers. She fell onto her knees and ultimately cried like a child, weeping into her bloody hands, "Oh God, what's happening!"

Huruma came and knelt before her, saying cautiously, "You freed me from his filthy hands. You have become a hero to the Waasi people this night."

Taken aback by the slave's words, Shina raised her head and whispered in fear of the guards hearing from outside, "What am I going to do? The Ziamons will kill me!"

The woman smiled and answered, "Predella is with us. She will save us all, if we are brave and save her first. Do you understand, girl?"

Shina, still shaking, asked, "What are you going to do? How do we set her free?"

Huruma frisked the colonel's body for keys and other articles, "I will free her. I can make it."

Shina was appalled, "No, they'll stop you! They know you are just a slave!"

She replied, "I am charged with keeping you company but keeping my eyes on you, as well. The colonel granted me more authority over his others. See, I will take his keys and tell them that he was too drunk. They saw his condition."

"They'll kill you!" Shina moaned.

"No," Huruma replied while embracing her. "The Spirit Mother granted you the power to pull that dagger from the table and strike him down. Now, She will grant me the power I will need to free us all."

In the highest levels of the citadel, Emmanuella was enjoying her feminine company inside her quarters. The magnificent corridor leading to her chambers, dimly lit with small torches, served as a runway for a chillingly beautiful caller. She walked, unopposed, down the corridor with a jet-black cloak and a hood hiding her face.

When she finally reached the chamber door, she knocked three times and awaited a reply. Within the instant, Emmanuella opened the door and examined the mysterious hooded figure before her. In response, Kaila removed her hood and allowed her stunning face to glow amongst the wall torches. She deviously smiled and said in Espanion, "**I am a gift from your repentant colonel. Won't you let me in?**"

Seeing her face alone triggered her inner desire. The mistress was taken by Kaila's beauty and could not respond. Kaila opened the inside of the cloak, still smiling seductively, and revealed her nude form, saying, "**I am sure to please you, mistress.**"

Emmanuella inspected her perfect figure in delight and bit her lip, finally allowing her in. When she shut and locked the door, the two soldiers who left their post broke out from their trance and looked at each other, dumbfounded.

Deep within the Crater, Michael and Maxim shared a rank clinic room, separated by a single row of strong metal bars cutting through the midpoint of the chamber. A lonely torch on the outside dungeon wall, emitting a small amount of light through the door's vent, broke the darkness of the room. Moans from other justices reverberated throughout the Pits of Pain, enduring the hardship inflicted by Maxim in the Trials.

Michael could not sleep, for he pondered the right time to exploit his powers. Maxim, however, hoped for a miracle recovery. Given no antidotes for the poison still in his system, he was sure that they lied about the midnight deadline. With Michael, still patting his friend's forehead with a damp rag, cleared his dry throat and asked, "I'm concerned about the rest of our party. These people like to stretch the truth."

Fighting to stay awake, Maxim said jadedly, "I doubt they're getting the five-star treatment if that's what you're asking."

Michael said with his head towards the ground, "I can almost feel them—the Demon Plague. We shouldn't be apart like this if they come. We're stronger together."

"Let them come," Maxim grunted. "Let the arena players up there have their turn with it."

Following a stint of silence, Michael said, "Whatever they gave you hasn't killed you yet."

Maxim eventually responded with uneasiness in his voice, "If I sleep, I'm not waking up."

"You're making me think that I should have crushed them all in the forest after all," Michael groaned.

"Forget it," Maxim uttered.

"No, I dragged you here, so I'll drag you out." Michael tightened his fists in frustration.

"I fear more for the princess—for Predella," Maxim said with all of his might.

At the moment Michael closed his eyes in thinking of them, a small stream of blood slowly crept from his nostril and ran down his face. The droplets fell onto Maxim's bare chest, one at a time. He stopped the nosebleed with his cloak and sighed in dismay, "Careful what you wish for."

Princess Shina tried to clean up the bloody mess after Huruma had fled. Before anyone could discover what she had done, Shina briskly pulled the sheets off the bed and sopped up the blood around the deceased colonel. A ferocious bolt of lightning frightened her during the toiling task, inducing her to scream.

She dragged him under the bed and hid the blood sopping sheets in the retracting closet in the far corner of the room. The place still looked like a horror scene, no matter what she tried to do. Finally collapsing and crying in her hands, the door blasted open without warning.

Two soldiers maintained a nervous pose at the door, hastily looking for the colonel. Before the head soldier could beseech Huruma for his whereabouts, he instantly noticed something wrong. Princess Shina knelt at the foot of the bed, covered in blood, feeling to crawl backward in trepidation. She covered her naked chest with her hands, tainted red.

The head soldier cautiously entered the room with his hand fretfully caressing the handle of the sword on his side. The other soldier remained at the door with a shocking glare. Looking over the bloodstained bed with a closed fist, he unsheathed his sword, pointing it directly towards her and spoke frantically, "Did one of them do this? Did it come in here?"

Shina was too terrified to speak. She couldn't comprehend who "they" were. All that she thought to do was nod her head, holding in her hysterics. The soldier cried recklessly, "Did they harm you? Where did those things go— *where* dammit?"

"It ran out of the door! We tried to save the colonel, but he was already dead!" Shina lied in their native language.

"The colonel? Where?" the soldier howled madly as he uncovered Argall's corpse beside the bed, covered in his own blood. He then proceeded to thrash the place in an unbridled rage, "What are those things?"

The soldier paused and placed his hand on the wall trying to catch his breath. After the uneasy hiatus, the sound of a club hammering through a watermelon echoed throughout the room. In chorus, Shina and the shaken soldier brought their attention to the doorway, where the soldier maintained his frightening posture.

"Leonis?" the soldier inside asked hesitantly.

In response, the soldier spit up a mouthful of blood and died. A black claw replaced his chest cavity, sodden with blood. The claw swiftly retracted back through his body and violently stabbed its sharp fingers through the back of his head and out from his eye sockets. The demon's thumb easily shot through the back of the man's neck and erected inside his open mouth. The shadow demon then maneuvered its prey by the skull and slammed his face into the floor.

Shina screamed and the soldier retreated beside her with his unsteady sword. Their bodies grew cold and numb as the hellish creature pulled out its claw from its victim's skull and fed on his cranium, chewing through the bone before tearing away at the brain. It was far too hungry to care about the two humans trapped inside.

The demon rose its dark head up to inspect its other victims as it finished chewing on the last portion of its meal. Its sharp incisors were drenched with wet chunks of flesh, justifying its hideous nature. The shadow demon scrolled the chambers with its beady green eyes, illuminating the nearby area. Emitting a detestable hissing, it then focused on them.

Catlike, the nefarious creature leaped onto the wall within the chambers and off again to pounce on the armed soldier. Shina scurried away and knelt beside the bed hosting the colonel's corpse. She watched in utter shock as the creature tore out the crying man's throat with its fangs. The mutilated soldier twitched as the shadow demon fed on him.

When it finished, the monster sniffed the rest of the soldier's body vigilantly and raised its head again to search for more game. Peeking out her quivering head, Shina prayed that the demon would leave satisfied. Her hopes dashed as it jerked its head up and glared in her direction, hissing. She hurriedly ducked below the bed and huddled next to the miniature cabinet alongside the mattress.

The bed shuddered. It was close enough for her to feel its detestably warm breath, stinking like death. Directly above them, it hissed threateningly with its prey's blood dripping along with saliva from the maw. Its green eyes gleamed upon her as she cried for her life.

The demon quietly growled to itself as it inspected her authenticity as Princess Shina Orgento of a fallen kingdom.

After recognizing her, the monster snarled and pulled Shina up by her red hair and delicate chin. With her torn gown open and her chest exposed, the demon extended its long, blood-soaked tongue in-between her naked breasts, licking up the colonel's blood. The test proved that she was unharmed and she wasn't covered in her own blood after all.

It then turned her face from side to side and painstakingly examined the shape of her skull. Once pleased with its finding, the demon placed her back onto the floor beside the bed and simply watched her. Shina soon came to realize that the nefarious beast did not intend to harm her in any way. The shadow demon easily sprung onto one of the bedposts and maintained its freakish posture. There was no chance of escape. The fiend smoothly waved its black tail through the air. It also admired the murdered man lying cold on the bed before it. Though tempted to desecrate the corpse further, it remained on the pinnacle of the bedpost.

Sounds of war outside found the inside of the chambers. Judging by her vile guest, supernatural forces were at work in the citadel. Then, suddenly, another guest came calling at the doorway. The demon reacted accordingly by dropping from the bedpost and vanishing into the shadows of the room. Within seconds, it was gone. The glow from its green eyes evaporated into the darkness. Now, only the advancing figure from the hallway was to fear.

Kaila said softly, "**You are not so easy to find, princess. What a feisty little thing you are.**"

Kneeling, Shina turned herself around to find a gorgeous woman standing under the doorframe. Her hips slanting lazily to one side, Kaila licked her lips and snickered. The faint light from outside the chambers revealed her blood sodden hands. The vampire general wore Emmanuella's nightgown as if tailored for her. Finally, she walked into the room and admired the bloodshed.

"**What lovely decoration. Did you take part in the decorating, too? It looks so.**" Kaila sat on the bed, looking over Argall's corpse. Her mannerisms were dominant and seductive, but Shina easily saw through her charms.

"Are you one of those—those things?" Shina nervously whispered.

"**Things?**" Kaila answered with a meager smile.

"You've come to finish me off, right? You're here to kill the future of Tinaria once and for all," Shina tensely replied, squatting before her.

"**Goodness, no!**" Kaila smiled as she hopped off the bed and knelt to face her. "**I've come to save you.**"

"Save me?" Shina said, trembling.

"**Of course! I am an angel—a killer angel. My name is Kaila and I have been sent to take you away from this wretched dustbowl of human filth.**" Kaila gently clasped Shina's trembling hands in compassion but forgot the condition of her own. The blood from her previous victims saturated Shina's soft hands. Pulling away, she looked upon her own hands, stained with blood.

Unable to convince the virgin princess, Kaila decided to exploit her hypnotic talents and seduce Shina into compliance. Kaila held Shina from behind her neck and passionately kissed her lips. Shina tried to break free from Kaila's kiss, but something prevented her from struggling. Within seconds, Shina was charmed.

When Kaila sucked Shina's bottom lip, she snickered and revealed to the princess her bright crimson eyes. The taste of blood was now in Shina's mouth. Kaila's fangs extended, though she fought desperately to retract them. She couldn't feast on her, for that was not her right. Her purpose was to deliver her to the Lord as quickly as possible. There was no time to waste.

"**Your true destiny waits.**" Kaila raised her from the floor and held her hand. Shina had no control over herself, even though she realized what was happening. Her heart begged her to escape, but her body urged her to follow. Kaila easily walked towards the door with Shina directly in tow, joined by the hand.

As their silhouettes started to pass the large center window, a wounded flyer demon violently smashed through and collided into its general. The arrow-stricken demon plowed Kaila into the wall supporting the guest room bed, which crumbled some and emitted debris. Amongst the terrifying scene, Shina swiftly broke away from Kaila's spell. She shook her head and regained control. Finding no other option, she dashed out the door.

Pinned on the bed, Kaila broke the routed demon's neck and, with profound power, kicked it right back out of the window from where it came. Shrieking in a rage, Kaila scurried off the mattress and obliterated the dresser cabinets under the shattered window with her bare hands.

Shina had never run so fast in all her life. The red-carpeted hallway was redder than it had ever been. Blood was everywhere and the scattered bodies of Ziamons cluttered her way. Nonetheless, Shina evaded the grotesque scenes and made it to the corner where a grand staircase led to the high atrium. She hurriedly turned the corner and spotted a throng of soldiers blocking the staircase.

She covered her chest with her hands and cried unto them in Espanion, "Please! Please help me!"

Startled by her frantic approach, the soldiers all recognized who she was, but the horrid night had already burned its mark on their minds. Not one of them was certain how to respond to the Tinarian princess. Shina cried again and looked behind her.

Two of the five soldiers begged her to stop, but she was too terrified to try that, for she knew that Kaila could not be far behind. Not knowing where she was running to, Shina burst through the soldiers who tried to detain her. One of them grabbed her gown and worsened its condition. Shina disregarded her appearance and tore herself away from his hold, racing down the open staircase. The left portion of her gown had been completely torn away, draping from the soldier's hand. She didn't know where she was running, but she knew better than to linger with the soldiers. They would not be able to protect her.

When she disappeared, Kaila whipped around the corner like a ravenous lioness. She tore through the hall on foot for a moment, but then leaped onto the bare ceiling and sustained her rush. Suspended from above, Kaila sadistically prepared herself to pounce. The soldiers were besieged by the demon's bloodcurdling advance from above. Her movements were too fast for them and not one soldier was primed for her strike.

Kaila trampled all five of the soldiers with her catastrophic ambush. Two of them died instantly while another fell victim to her bite. She tore out his throat and ferociously cast him down the full scale of the hallway until he smashed into the corner. The other from behind tried to attack her by way of his sword. Kaila evaded the attack with no trouble and then came from his side to swipe off his head with her single hand. The last remaining soldier twitched in incredible horror and dropped his blade. Kaila seized him by the neck and put his back against the wall, two feet above the floor.

"**I smell her! She's close! Which way?**" the vicious vampire snarled in Espanion.

He could not respond, his heart beating against his ribcage. Losing all patience, Kaila plunged her fangs into the side of his neck and butchered his artery. His blood splattered all over the wall and her face as she sucked him dead. She then forced her hand through his mouth, grabbed his spine and tore off his head with it. Immersed with the blood of her frail prey, Kaila resorted to her talented sense of smell. Sniffing, her senses led her down the staircase.

Running to wherever she could hide, Shina stumbled upon a sitting room leading to what seemed to be a dining hall. Shina refused to pass the chance. She came off the stairway and headed down the deserted vestibule. There were no blood or half-eaten corpses anywhere. A small stairway led to the open hall. As Shina scurried for sanctuary, she witnessed the governing reason for the awkward silence.

A dozen shadow demons inhabited the hall—some feasting on old meat on the table and others fighting over corpses. In unison, the demons raised their heads and observed the traumatized princess, half-naked and ready to faint. A demon squatting on top of the long dinner table finished chewing up a wad of meat and slowly inched its way to the edge of the table. Shina instantly darted for the slaves' entrance door to the left side. The demon hastily scurried off the table to seize her but fell in between two wooden chairs. The others hissed together in curiosity, providing her with horrid ambiance.

She blasted through the door as the majority of the demons came after her. With haste, Shina squeezed herself into one of the large serving carts and pulled close the side hatch. Only seconds later, the door blasted open again with the sounds of growling. She maintained her tight composure inside the cart. Though her breathing was heavy, she tried desperately not to make even the softest sound.

She heard their sinister presence as they sniffed the area. It was not long until the demons closed in on her hiding spot. As she began to pray to God in her head, Kaila had lifted the entire serving cart and dropped her to the floor. The demonic general then said with disdain, "**There's no hiding when you smell that delicious.**"

Considering Shina's torn gown, Kaila shook her head in disgust and ripped the dress off her body. Shina screamed. Hating to leave her that way, Kaila raised her to her feet, slipped spare tablecloth over her and tied it. Shina was too frightened to respond to Kaila's unpredictable actions.

"**There, you see?**" Kaila ran her fingernails through Shina's red hair. "**A true treasure shouldn't look like that. You're a princess, after all.**"

Kaila softly clamped Shina's chin with her fingers and passionately kissed her mouth. The princess fell unconscious and Kaila mounted her on her right shoulder, saying in her ancient demonic tongue, "**Let's leave Shit City, shall we?**"

When Michael was primed to break out from the Pits of Pain and encounter the demons for himself, something in the corner of his eye demanded his attention. He turned to the side of the room and saw a cat. The stray feline meowed loudly before scurrying off through the room's entranceway. Before it could make it out, Michael caught it with his telepathic gifts and brought it closer. As the confused cat floated in thin air, he looked for the scar over one if its eyes. In seeing it, he sighed miserably and let the animal run off.

Disturbed by the Demon Plague's ongoing torment, he turned to Maxim, still fighting for his life, and said, "I have to go and assemble our party. The Demon Plague is here."

Maxim coughed, "Go. Make sure the princess is safe."

PART I
CHAPTER XV
THE SECOND COMING

Predella had been stripped of her clothing and chained like Maxim before the Trials. In the bleak darkness of her dungeon cell, she meditated. The soldiers gawked at her from the sliding window of the door and made jokes. Yet, their jests were put aside when a woman's voice sounded from outside. She awakened from her meditation and listened carefully. It was the Waasi accent.

After a brief dispute, the soldiers opened the prison door and permitted Huruma to walk inside. Holding a torch, she looked her over and nodded, ordering them, "Free her."

"Don't reach too far, slave," one replied. "The colonel might have given you this moment with her, but you're not in the position of making demands for him."

Dangling Argall's keys for them all to see, she said, "But I'm his favorite. He trusted me to keep watch on the Tinarian princess and now he wants me to bring Predella up to his quarters—under your guarded escort."

Knowing that Colonel Argall was a scoundrel with his women, they reluctantly permitted the Waasi slave to free Predella as long as they chained her in transit. She agreed and went to unlock her from bondage. Predella knew she was one of Argall's slave women, but the look in her eyes was unmistakable. There was a plan afoot.

"What is this?" Predella asked in her Waasi dialect.

"Spare weapons are in the armory somewhere in the Crater," Huruma replied in her native tongue. "We'll go there next after we deal with these men. Just follow my lead."

In allowing Predella to put on her clothes, the soldiers came to chain her wrists. Connecting eyes with her rescuer, Predella permitted them to extend the chain up to a collar around her neck. Then, with just one soldier staying behind, the others corralled the Waasi women and headed for the colonel's quarters. As they went, one of them kept his spear at Predella's back. They hated when Argall sent his slave women on errands.

As they marched for the stairway, a Waasi ambush had caught the soldiers off-guard. In the desperate fight, the men and women, once slaves to the Ziamons, overpowered their oppressors and freed their best warrior. She had saved so many of their people and it gave them pride to return the favor. As the soldiers were subdued, Huruma freed Predella of her chains and hugged her.

In unison, they sang the Wimbo ya Huru, Waasi's hymn of liberty. Over thirteen freed Waasi surrounded Predella, just to touch and bless her. Tearing, she kissed them on the foreheads and embraced them. Others chained the soldiers together in the middle of the corridor and stole their spears and swords. Predella asked Huruma, "How did you do this?"

A Waasi male answered for her, "She freed us from our cells. No soldiers standing guard. Ziamon is at war."

Knowing what came for them, Predella clenched her fists and said, "We need to get to the armory now. I fear that something far worse than Ziamon has come to kill us all."

As Michael left the medical ward long before in search of the princess, Maxim heard Predella's voice. At first, he thought he was hallucinating, but then she appeared in the entranceway with a throng of her people swarming the ward. Maxim tried to stand on his feet, but his body would not allow it. Predella ran to Maxim's side and lifted his sweaty head. She held his face, beaten and cut, and gasped, "Don't take this the wrong way, but I thought you'd be dead."

"Predella? You look good," Maxim said, his head still swirling. "Am I—is this heaven?"

"No time to be stupid," she replied, receiving a cup of water to serve him. He gratefully swallowed it in small sips and then coughed some out to the side. She wiped his mouth with her hair and said, "The Demon Plague is here, just like Tinaria, but you're in no position to fight."

"That explains the lack of company," Maxim said, holding her hand in gratitude for her care.

"It explains *our* company, though," Huruma interjected.

Predella added, "She and the others broke me out. Most of the soldiers were called to fight. Now is our chance to get you somewhere safe."

Maxim fought to sit up, but fell back. The Waasi came in and helped him rise to a seated position, holding him there. He then, in-between breaths, said to her, "Michael went to find you and the princess."

"I know where the princess is. She was with me all day," Huruma exclaimed from his side. "But we have to be careful. The citadel is a dangerous place and I don't know how long she's—"

"You left her there?" Maxim coughed, hunched over in pain. "Dammit! She had better be there, kid. Michael ran off to find her."

A Waasi man interceded, pulling Predella by the arm, "We have to take this opportunity to escape! The desert dogs are distracted!"

Answering in their native dialect, she turned her head and scolded him, "We can't leave him here to die! He almost died so that I could live!"

Maxim then asked after drinking more water, "Where are the justices? Are they still lying around here?"

"Everyone was evacuated, but you, it seems," Predella said, fixing his moist hair. "They left you here to die with no one to guard you."

"Michael guarded me," Maxim said, trying to stand on his own. "Now you're here, but I sense not for long."

Huruma joined in, "What are we going to do, Predella?"

Lowering her head to think, she sighed and said, "Go on without me. Get out of here with as many of us as you can."

One of them insisted, "Not without you!"

"You need to go!" Predella fired back. "Find a way to get out of here before you all die as slaves! Get out now before it's too late for you!"

"We'll never make it without you!" another said.

After a distant explosion made the chambers tremble, Maxim touched her shoulder and said, "Leave me a sword. You get these people out. Free the Waasi and I'll take care of myself. Besides, there's nothing down here but me and the dark."

Astounded, Predella uttered in reply, "Maxim, I don't know what to say. What about Shina? What if—"

"What if you forsake your own people?" He cut her off, saying, "Michael won't let me down, and neither will you. Get the hell out of here."

Grateful, the Waasi began to rush out of the medic wing with Predella joining them. One man offered Maxim a sword he stole from the Crater armory and nodded his head in thanks. Predella rushed back and kissed Maxim on the lips, passionately taking his face in her hands. He received it and leaned in when she broke away from his mouth, then looking into her eyes. She then said, "I'll come back for you."

When she left, he watched her the whole way, leading her people out from the Pits of Pain and then probably out of the bulwark city. He had the despondent feeling that it was the last time he would ever see her. In the silence of the dark,

Maxim felt the vengeance of the poison and languidly fell off the edge of the bed. He hit the floor, spilling the pitcher of water, and slipped into oblivion.

Meanwhile, in Ayden Square, a legion of demons wreaked havoc upon Ziamon. Many shadow demons had already infiltrated the citadel. Their frightening attribute of shadow teleportation shocked and confused the Ziamons as they desperately tried to defend their ruler's keep. Swarms of demons besieged the city, assailing Ziamon's greatest with horrifying brutality.

Inside the citadel, Captain Aramis and Argall's task force dispatched to Mistress Emmanuella's quarters as reinforcements. Aramis and his men had already killed three shadow demons in the fortress, but there appeared to be almost no resistance in route to Emmanuella's chambers. She never left the double doors opened and unattended. With crossbows loaded, Aramis and his men infiltrated the mistress's vestibule.

With two men on each side of the door, one of them carefully opened the chamber door and swung it ajar. The scene was more gruesome than anyone ever could have imagined. One-by-one they all walked into the large room, gradually removing their helmets, and fell into desperation. In her bed, Emmanuella and her women lie mutilated. Blood was all over, nearly painting the entire bedroom alone.

Emmanuella and her women's intestines were pulled out through their vaginas and intertwined at the foot of the bed. As horrific as the scene was, it portrayed a map. The intestines were in the shape of a trail to a specific place. Bowels on the right were clumped together to form the Eastern Hemisphere, the innards on the left were formed into the Western Hemisphere and the pool of blood in-between signified the ocean of the Great Pacifica.

From inside one of the citadel's armories, Michael had blasted the steel doors violently from their hinges. Walking out with the Staff of Truth, back in his possession, Michael emerged from the smoke of debris with Maxim's fire-sword and Predella's elementary bow floating just behind him. He retrieved their legendary articles, but had no time to deliver them all to their proper owners. He needed to find Shina before the Demon Plague could.

Reunited with his mystical staff, Michael awakened its power to view the area around him. Demons had infested the citadel and the city streets, overwhelming the Ziamons in a way Tinaria had not even seen. They were unprepared for the invasion, as well as the horrifying armies of the wicked beyond. Panic and carnage had already brought Ziamon to their knees—and without a bloodstorm.

He raced to Argall's apartment complex in the higher floors of the citadel to meet up with the princess. Using his staff, Michael found the fastest route to her last location. Yet, even that path was beset with horrors. Fighting time, he ran through scenes of desperate, blood-spattering battles and terrified defenseless Ziamons, crying for help. He pressed by them all, using his powers to keep them at bay if necessary. Shadow demons seemed to glare at him as he rushed by, as if they remembered him.

Once he made it to Colonel Argall's corridor, Michael's heart dropped. The sight nearly brought him to his knees. In walking passed the slaughtered troops to the colonel's guest room, he felt weak, feeling to throw up. Putting his hand against the wall to keep him standing, Michael used his staff to see what had happened. He found the princess's room to be a horrific scene, but without her corpse inside. She had gone somewhere or was abducted by something.

Delving into the past, Michael saw the appalling event play out before his eyes. Shina ran with the vampire in hot pursuit down the corridor and through the soldiers, killed in brutal fashion. Deeply troubled, Michael followed them both in his premonition of the shocking incident. Chasing after the ghosts of the past, Michael ran through the cocktail lounge and then into the servants' passageway. Shadow demons had infected the place, inducing him to blast them away with great force.

If in a trance, he witnessed Kaila bewitch the princess into unconsciousness. The vampire then carried her towards the stairway up to the higher levels, encircled by a horde of scurrying shadow demons. Practically invincible, she trudged through every opposition with her wicked minions clearing a pathway of blood. Michael followed them out to the highest lanai where his worst fear had become realized.

From the night sky, lit only by the fiery hell of war, Sattka swooped in to meet them at the edge of the open porch. There, she received the sleeping princess and flew out into the night, disappearing from Michael's vision. Kaila, too, leapt over the lanai's edge and out of his sight. Distraught, he returned to the present, alone on the open lanai. Staggering over to the edge where the princess had been taken away, he finally looked over the despairing fight to save Ziamon.

In anguish, he fell onto his knees. The fire-sword and elementary bow fell behind him, clanging and thudding to the floor. On his palms, he punished himself for letting them take the princess. Brokenhearted, Michael retrieved his staff and headed to the edge of the lanai in tears. Over the carnage below, he tried to locate Shina with some last-ditch hope that she was still in the city somewhere.

Searching Ziamon all over by way of his staff, Michael finally broke down and cried. He surrendered his fruitless hunt and sat with his back against the lanai's edge, in shock of another demonic raid. Flashes of faces rushed before him as a growing list of victims. Along with his wife, son and so many others, Michael suffered the guilt of failing to protect the young Tinarian princess. What was the worse than the failure, however, was that the Demon Plague targeted Shina for capture and he didn't know why.

At the gates of the Crater, Predella held up her party of brethren. Crowds of fleeing Ziamon citizens had held up in the arena's vestibules and it became impossible for her to sneak out with a group of runaways. She pushed them back into the dark subterranean passage of the Crater. Pulling the metal door shut, she said to them, "It's a mad house out there. There's no way we're getting out any of the Crater's standard exits. Besides, the way it sounds outside, we won't make it."

"There's a trash tunnel that we used to deposit garbage and bodies and all that to the landfills," one of them replied. "We could escape that way."

Another added, "That's a long tunnel and those landfills are guarded—heavily guarded. We'll never get out that way. It's fenced off and slave hunters are as many as flies."

Another said, "The rest of us are in the slave yards in the back of the citadel, Predella. You said we were saving all of us! What about the rest of us!"

"It's either us or no one," Predella replied boldly. "If we spend one minute out there in that warzone, we're all going to die and you're going to have to square with that."

Breaking down, the same woman cried out in grief, "My husband is in that—"

"We all have lost more than husbands and wives!" she growled back. "I will return for them, but it's impossible to save us all tonight! Out there is hell. I thought we could make a sneak for it, but it isn't possible. It's as bad as Tinaria—and that was very, very bad."

As the group tried consoling the woman, Predella abruptly asked one of them, "Where is this garbage tunnel?"

"Bottom level, all the way down. I know how to get to it," Motambo said.

"Then we go now," Predella declared. "In no time, you can expect more Ziamons to cram themselves into this arena and then inside these passages and then we're trapped. Hand over the recurve bow and lead us to the garbage shafts. You all will stay behind me the entire way. How many arrows did we salvage?"

"Over a dozen, I think," Huruma said.

"Then follow me. No stragglers." Predella received the bow and started down with the man who claimed to know the way. "We're going to make it out of here. On my honor."

As quiet as they could as a group, the Waasi scampered deeper into the Crater's lower ground. Passing a number of chambers, cells and tunnels in what seemed like a maze, the group finally came upon the refuse tunnel. What few torches they had, the deserted tunnel looked like a shaft straight to the depths of hell. The stench overpowered their dread.

Covering his mouth and nose with his wrist, Motambo said, "This is it. This is the tunnel."

"Smells like it, indeed," Huruma groaned.

"Disgusting," he replied. "Welcome to the Bowels. Now you get a taste of my world."

"Everything bad has one name in this shitting place," a woman said. "The Trials. The Crater. The Bowels."

"The Demon Plague is worse," Predella retorted. "So, we have to move. All of us."

While they were ready to leave, Motambo outstretched his arms and said, "Hold on. There's a wagon train down there, if the Spirit Mother is merciful. That's what we take all the way down."

"A wagon train? Good," Predella uttered. "Let's—"

Just then, the most fearsome sound resounded from the blackness of the passageway. Predella cowered at the first sound of them rasping and growling—a horde of them on the way. Somehow, they found shadows large enough in the dark of the passages to teleport. Out of time, she rushed them into the tunnel, screaming, "Go! Get down there now! I'll be right behind you!"

Terrified of whatever Predella was afraid of, the group rushed down the tunnel with Motambo leading the way. As Huruma passed by her, she clenched her by the hand, "Keep feeding me arrows and we might live through this."

Just then, a pack of green eyes materialized from both sides of the passageway. Down the tunnel, Motambo had sat in the head car of the refuse wagon train and asked for help pushing it down the slight slope. While the women filed into the open metal drums on wheels, the men pulled the cars of the wagon down the subtle ramp. Predella rushed Huruma to leap into the last car and she followed, pulling an arrow with her balmy hands.

"We'll have to go a lot faster than this!" Predella cried from behind, loading her first arrow.

Motambo cried back, taking hold of the front car's steering mechanism, "Everyone get inside and stay in there! I've never done this drive without the ceiling lamps!"

As the shadow demons scrambled for them in the darkness of the tunnel's descent, Predella fired for the closest one. Judging only by the illumination of their green eyes, she struck one in the skull and grounded it. Pulling another arrow from Huruma as the wagon train started to pick up speed, Predella fired another accurate shot from the recurve bow as her brethren screamed in terror. They knew too well that Predella's skills and Motambo's steering were the only things keeping them from enduring a horrible death.

Again and again, she picked off a pursuing demon, each time finding them gaining ground on her. Shaking her head, Predella fired on a demon that had gotten that much closer. There were more demons than arrows and the wagon train was only starting to fly down the slope. She had to make her every shot count. Flickering shadows from their torches were an ominous reminder that no one was ever truly safe.

An ambitious shadow demon swiftly dashed through one, but only partly. As the shadow moved away, it cut the creature in half from the waist. It dropped on the group anyway, wreaking havoc on them as they cried terribly. Clawing and chomping for their flesh, the demon feverishly clamored. Predella heard the bloody chaos and proceeded to shoot down oncoming terrors. She couldn't abandon the rear. She could only hope that they were able to repel the demon.

Repel they did, but for a price. One of their brethren stabbed the beast and, in turn, fell out of the speeding wagon train. The demon fell with him and tumbled into the dark. Predella saw him screaming into blackness as the wagon fled down the tunnel, besieged by the chasing horde. Many began to eat him alive before his body even stopped rolling. They all cried out for their Waasi brother, having finally seen the evil creature Predella warned them about.

As the wagon furthered down the tunnel, Predella just kept her head straight and fired on them. Only a handful of arrows left, she received another from Huruma and uttered in a subdued panic, "Please, no. Please don't let it happen this way."

The Demon Plague had all but claimed Ziamon as theirs by the dead of night, massacring thousands in just a little over an hour. Unprepared and petrified by the unearthly invaders, it seemed that Ziamon would follow the likes of Pommel. From the barren lookouts just out of the forest, Valkris waited for Michael's emergence. With Sattka growing impatient, Valkris determined to flush him out.

"I feel him, but where is he?" Valkris uttered.

"Father says he will come to us—that he is confused as to who and what he is," Sattka hissed back. **"Perhaps it would be wise to pull out. We already have her."**

"I am not so convinced that the Lord even knows who he is. There are ways of testing his theory." Valkris extended his Seltek and fired the magical red beam across the realm and into the highest tower. Like sawing through a tree, he started from one side of the citadel and cut straight through to the other side. Hundreds marveled at the red beam of light gleaming in the darkness of the night.

It was not until the beam disappeared that the true nature of its emergence was revealed. The slim sever around the tallest spire set off an explosion that tipped the summit over. Debris came hurling towards the ground and the many people of Ziamon ran for their lives. Gradually, the sound of bending metal and crumbling rock harmonized with the song of war as the spire leaned for the square. Ayden stared upon the threatening scene in awe from his keep. He knew that his time had come. He held on to whatever was close by and prepared to plummet into the heart of his city.

The spire finally broke loose and the head, along with several other severed pieces, came hurtling towards the ground. Having just descended the citadel, Michael sensed Valkris's presence in the forest as well as his evil hand in the destruction of the spire. With furious anger, Michael ran out into the square and telekinetically shoved a significant mass of debris off its track for the square thirty-four feet away over a separator. The debris of rock and metal crashed deep into the Crater's arena, causing for a tremendous blast.

Those sheltered in the Crater's inner complex took refuge deeper within. Surprised to witness the stranger's bizarre powers, masses of warriors fled their battle stations and droves of demons pursued them. The rubble fell in larger bulks, becoming more difficult to hold in the air. His powers tested more than ever before, Michael formed a basin of telekinetic might and felt the street break beneath him. All gasped at his tremendous power to keep the heavy masses hovered in the air. His eyes teared from the pain. His arms grew weak.

Groaning from the intense pressure, some of the debris fell to his side and deflected off other pieces, launching them all about. His body shook while the ground around him blasted into fragments. Still, the head of the tower was yet to come with most of the ruling family hunkered inside. They screamed and shouted, holding on tightly to whatever had not broken apart. Some had already met their end in the violent fall.

Within seconds, the summit was close to slamming into the square. Michael knew that he wouldn't be able to save everyone, but he'd do all he could to save some. When the main wreckage was upon him, Michael braced himself and unleashed a fury of his powers to catch it. The spire began to slow, but when it came too close, Michael gave everything he had. With tremendous strain on his entire body, Michael caught it all in midair. The sheer size of the tower's head compared to Michael's stature was staggering.

Trying desperately to maintain control of the wreckage, Michael's exertion of his telekinetic power forced the ground under him to erupt and form a deep crater. Feeling his body begin to shut down, Michael moved the huge wreck behind him. He moved it off balance, losing control over it. Finally, he gradually placed it all down around him. The spire broke apart further into the square.

Before the smoke could fully clear from the air, Michael lost all consciousness and fell limp into the wreckage.

Insignificant debris continued to fall from above, but did not hinder the mass amounts of soldiers from running to the chaotic scene. Before long, a vast cordon of Ziamons enclosed in on him. Elite warriors made the way for their dictator to pass. They shoved everyone in their path until Ayden was able to clearly see through the rubble.

They searched inside for any survivors, but many had succumbed to the fall. Yet, in his fortified chambers, Supreme Ruler Ayden and others in his royal court had lived. The dictator murmured within the wreckage, "What happened?"

One officer said, "A man had some magical abilities. He caught the spire as it fell. I've never seen anything like it."

While Ziamon endured the astonishing occurrence, Valkris was pleased. Michael Miuriell was indeed the one prophesized by the Lord. He happily utilized his Seltek and vanished within the red beams. His minions throughout the realm evaporated with him and the war upon Ziamon had ended for the night. There was no reason to waste any more resources. Another civilization had collapsed and the Demon Plague had, at last, seized Princess Shina.

Among the initial shock of the many creatures' instant disappearance, the people of Ziamon gradually emerged from their sanctuaries and joined their kin in the ruins of the city. The smell of death littered the air, merging with sulfur and cinders of their fallen world. Many slipped in the streams blood as they tried to make it through the city. The Crater, renowned for hosting a theatre of death, had been gorged to the limit with corpses dropped there by spiteful flyers. Their entire world was razed to the ground, just as Michael had inadvertently promised upon entering the gates.

Ayden, suffering broken ribs, a fractured arm and cuts and bruises throughout, sat upright in the auxiliary palace hall deep within the citadel. Treated by a slew of medics, he listened to the current figures of Ziamon's losses. They were too large to count. Worse than everything else, he mourned his beloved daughter, Emmanuella, who had been slain in the most appalling fashion. His advisors tried, to no avail, to convince him of just how fragmented Ziamon had become. His face never budged. He offered no reaction to anything the consultants said. He froze in a state of shock, enduring pains of the body and heart.

It was not until someone mentioned that Michael had awakened that Ayden sort of snapped out of his faint trance. Almost in a gasp, he uttered, "Miuriell?"

"Yes, sire," the advisor answered cautiously. "We also found some of these articles down Califia Street, shrouded in a cloak."

One official emptied the cloak of its contents: The Staff of Truth, Mad Phoenix and Predella's elemental bow. Ayden looked over the legendary weapons and said jadedly, "These belong to Predella and the Red Menace. They are Miuriell's companions?"

"It would seem, sire," he replied. "We don't know the whereabouts of Predella, but so many are missing already. It would be impossible to find her body any time soon, unless she escaped. Maxim, however, we fear could be as good as dead. The poison—"

Grimacing from the agony of leaning forward to make his point very clear, Ayden groaned, "No, we must not make Miuriell angry. No, sir. We must cater to his needs—to his friends. Administer antidote to Cavallo immediately! Now! If he dies, you die!"

While the official scurried off with his subordinates to alert the surviving chemists, Esker reported for duty. Having suffered injuries in battle, he knelt and bowed his head with a groan. All of the other justices had died. He was the last.

PART I
CHAPTER XVI
THE AFTERMATH

The mood was grim in Supreme Ruler Ayden's conference chambers. The morning light revealed the total annihilation of Ziamon. Facing the open window to the city square over two hundred feet below, Ayden perseverated on his losses. His army routed, his daughter slain, his kingdom's infrastructure broken—he was a leader without a nation. A dark force from beyond his most sinister imagination swept in and took everything he ever loved in one night—even his pride.

He sat motionless at the head of the ten-foot-long oak table with Captain Aramis and Justice Esker on his right. To his left, empty chairs awaited his newest guests. Personal guards surrounded the conference table. Esker looked dourly at his folded hands clasped loosely on the table and brooded the loss of his six fellow justices.

"Esker," Ayden called him in an almost inaudible voice, "don't do anything rash, you hear, boy?"

"Yes, sire," he responded quietly.

"And you, captain?" Ayden turned to him next.

Aramis nodded loyally, still scarred from uncovering Mistress Emmanuella's mutilated body. Ayden simply shook his head and turned to the open window from his seat, fighting back tears as the smoke of the devastation below passed his view. His eyes, reddened from lack of sleep, hardly had any tears left. What destroyed Tinaria had finished his kingdom after, ending their feud and leaving it in cinders.

Suddenly, there was a strong knock on the chamber door and he snapped back into the present. Startled, Ayden bid they enter. Coming through the chamber door were five heavily armed escorts who guided Michael and the frail Maxim to their seats at the designated side of the table. Cleaned and their bellies full from breakfast, the two men sat down. Maxim sat with discomfort and apprehension. Their weapons and gear safely packed away in chests outside in the lobby, they looked over the three men in attendance and felt that they understood the purpose of the summit.

Staring at Maxim, nearly defeated in the Trials, Ayden spoke in Christian with a faint accent, "I have recently encountered an enemy worse than you, Maxim 'Red Menace' Cavallo. If not for this man here, you'd be dead. But this man, Michael Miuriell, proved himself last night. He saved my life and surely would have saved my daughter's life if he was able. Thank him."

Sluggish, Maxim turned to Michael, "Thank you."

Michael, instead, asked the dictator with concern, "Well I was hoping to ask you about a third ally. Predella never—"

"Funny you should bring her up," Ayden said, incensed. "Witnesses say that slaves broke her out of her cell so she could then help them escape, which they did. Heron, my head slave master, reported to me this morning that every last Waasi slave had broken out from the yards, as well. If this is true, then, it is the last offense that I can accept this day. She, the scoundrel that she is, took advantage of Ziamon in our most desperate time to free the rest of her people. Now, for certain, our regime will have zero chance for survival."

Maxim, right on cue, retorted, "If you built your entire survival on the backs of slaves, then don't you deserve it?"

"Bastard cur!" Esker practically jumped over the table in his wrath. "I should have followed through with you and buried my fist through your skull!"

"Careful, Cavallo!" Ayden shouted after. "I'm a broken man, and testing a broken man will end badly for you! You're only an ally to Miuriell. There is a distinct difference between allies and friends, so shut that mouth or we'll sew it shut!"

Raising his hand in the growing intensity of the talks, Michael said, "May I interject for a moment? These monsters have done nothing but kill and destroy everyone and everything they find in their path. We can easily kill each other if you want, but the Crater is satiated with corpses already so I think we should consider our real enemy here. For once, you both can agree that a greater evil has come calling on us, so we need to wake up and join hands in resistance.

"Pommel, my homeland, is gone, Tinaria was brought to its knees just a couple of nights ago and now your realm has suffered the same fate. For some reason I haven't figured out yet, they wanted Princess Orgento and, just last night, they succeeded. I couldn't stop them. Who they kill and who they want has pressed on my mind like a vise. I've lost my fair share of loved ones—my wife and son among them. We have all lost. Maybe, together, we can take some things back."

"You're proposing a truce," Captain Aramis rejoined. "I should inform you that we've already made a truce, one that may not apply anymore after this."

Michael replied, "Your truce, or armistice, or whatever it was, merely keeps you apart. Let's talk about a treaty that bands you together. The Demon Plague crushed Tinaria and Ziamon one at a time. We need to talk about a lasting truce that binds our forces as one."

"To do what—counterattack that army from hell?" The dictator almost laughed from the implication, if not for his fractured ribs. "We don't even know what they are. They appeared from nothing and then, when they were satisfied, vanished into nothing. How do you fight that? Some of those things were crawling out of shadows!"

Michael replied, "They have weaknesses. Sunlight has some effect on them."

"And fire cooks them pretty good. They're flammable," Maxim added.

Aramis countered, "Fire cooks me pretty good, too."

Maxim then asked, agitated, "Wait, look, Tinaria's princess has been taken and I can't face the queen without some hope that she can be saved. If Michael believes that we can get her back safely, then I'll make a truce right here and now. I'll sign it in blood if I have to—and it doesn't have to be mine."

Ayden laughed under his breath, "You are not a voice for your king. Ziamon can only make such alliances with ambassadors and noblemen. You are neither—just a ruthless, unfeeling—"

"The king is dead," Maxim asserted, taking a bold leap of faith in the company of his enemies. "I answer in the name of the queen, now without a princess or a prince to take the throne. Cousins and uncles in Ellium will no doubt find out about his death and come to claim the throne as theirs. This realm is going to get pretty complicated pretty soon."

Ayden retorted, "I can see right through your lies."

Michael declared, "He speaks the truth. The king died so Queen Orgento named him as her representative."

Esker looked to his dictator, who looked right back at him. Ayden then turned to Maxim and replied warily, "Orgento wasn't poisoned by anyone commissioned by me. Might I suggest you start looking within your own kingdom if you haven't already?"

"I didn't say he died by poison," Maxim said, glaring over his rivals' shaken expressions. "You just assumed that he did, because your agents worked with someone on the inside to assassinate him. What you wouldn't know is that my queen incidentally drank the poisoned tonic herself. She almost died, too, if not for Michael saving her life."

Bewildered, Ayden uttered after a queer pause, "What madness is—"

After revealing his knowledge of the failed attempt on the king's life, Maxim, suppressing his fury, asked further, "How did your scum manage to sneak poison into Tinaria? What traitor were you working with under their noses?"

Aramis, anticipating hostilities, interceded, "Maybe we should proceed with—"

"I'm surprised they pulled off the whole operation," Ayden admitted arrogantly. "I found it farfetched when I first heard it, but he insisted it was good for our realms."

"Who insisted?" Maxim protested.

"No point in keeping secrets anymore. Our nations are on the brink," Ayden began. "Perchance you were away this past couple of weeks? Lord Vitan's associates visited my associates in the Barrier Forest on multiple occasions to discuss a real truce—a finite treaty. On their last meet, they fashioned a shadow treaty. Only Vitan and a select few of his people knew about it. Would you like to hear the terms of this clandestine accord?"

Maxim could not bear to hear the sick truth. He just offered a blank stare. Ayden proceeded, "Your king hired Waasi mercenaries to wreak havoc upon us, secretly attempting to violate the armistice. Vitan caught wind of it and set a few wheels in motion to save our kingdoms from another war. His schemes were very cunning. All we had to do was develop a potent poison—one that dragged on like a bad illness. Evidently, the plan failed.

"Originally, the king, as you no doubt already know, was supposed to drink the tonic and ultimately die. With the prince in exile and you dead, things would eventually simmer down and the armistice would be salvaged. Of course, the queen and her teenage daughter would not have posed much of a threat. But, you're right about the Ellium factor. I wonder if Vitan had a contingency plan for that as well."

Though he was more or less finished, Ayden reveled in his enemy's suffering. He found immense fulfillment in watching Maxim agonize over the details. He never imagined that his own friend could have orchestrated such a vile conspiracy. His blood boiled just thinking about the ring of traitors in Tinaria, led by his childhood comrade. Maxim muttered in a broken whisper, "If you're lying—"

"I have been known to lie, but I give you my word on this day. Every word is true," Ayden stated brazenly. "I have nothing left to lose, Cavallo."

Covering his mouth and laying back into his seat, Maxim soaked in the sore reality. The pain inside was too grueling to bear. Michael, heartfelt for him, grabbed his wrist and squeezed tightly. After he soothed his burning heart, Maxim inquired further, "Where are the others—the soldiers that came with us?"

Ayden looked to the captain, who said, "I can't promise anything, but they should still be here in the citadel. Demons infested the place. Our colonel was found slain in his own quarters, so no one was safe."

Michael cut in, steering the gathering back onto the same road, "Pommel, my home, is where they're based now. I can try to avenge your daughter's death. I can try to get Shina back safely. I can try to end all this, but the reality is they have a vast army and the only way to stand a chance against them is if we make an army of our own."

The very idea of building an army combined with Tinarian and Ziamon forces seemed ludicrous at first, but they all began to think on it. Maxim, having debated Michael on that very topic already, swallowed his pride and said boldly, "Under the authority of the queen, I will agree to a truce. In light of the common enemy we share, an enemy that can destroy us better than we ever could ourselves, I'm willing to join forces."

Michael breathed a sigh of relief, "Our very existence falls on what we do here—right here, right now. I pledge to lead our united army into battle, if not for vengeance alone. I don't know where your nations will stand after all of this is over and, frankly, I can't care. What matters is that we win as a human race to get us to that point. What matters is if we want to die divided, or take our chances together for once."

Responsive to their appeals, Ayden sat stoically and shut his eyes, deep in thought. A lifelong end to the bitter bloodshed by both kingdoms was idealistic. Yet, desperate times opened his stone heart to the real possibility of a new age for the two kingdoms. Ayden opened his eyes and proclaimed, "I will agree to the truce on one condition."

"Name it," Maxim said.

"Aramis and Esker will lead Ziamon's elite warriors into battle and concede only to Miuriell. If Miuriell dies, their contribution to the quest across the sea is over," Ayden declared. "When *this* is over, I cannot promise Predella's life. She still must answer for her crimes against Ziamon. That is not negotiable—not even by you, Miuriell."

Maxim held his tongue, letting Michael answer to the tyrant's conditions. Had he answered himself, there would have been another breakdown in the truce. He wasn't sure how stable he was already, still numb from learning about the traitors within his kingdom. Still, he knew better than to lean on the word of Ziamons alone. Burying it all inside, sure to never let them see through him, Maxim remained quiet.

Michael addressed the preconditions with just a word, "Agreed."

Maxim kept composed, hearing them condemn Predella for death, and said nothing. Inside, a storm shocked him to his core. Michael seemingly sacrificed her life for the sake of the world without hesitation. The proceedings that followed left a sour taste in his mouth, but Maxim pressed on with the details. As Tinaria's ambassador, there was no greater duty to his people than to draft a worthy treaty that lasted the ages. All of it hinged on the Queen's seal of approval—and his willingness to trust that Michael knew what he was doing.

By dusk, plans were already in place for Ziamon's Kill Force in the war against the Demon Plague. To commemorate the milestone, Ayden organized a supper at dusk, inviting Michael, Maxim, and the Tinarian knights as honored guests. In the face of Ziamon's greatest despair, there was a display of unity that none had ever seen before.

Awarded their armor and weaponry as a token of goodwill, Michael and the Tinarians drank to peace and the pledge to join forces against their nefarious foe. After their toast to the treaty, Ayden summoned Michael to address the assemblage. They applauded him as he rose from his seat and surrendered the Staff of Truth into Maxim's hands.

From his place near the head of the table, Michael thanked the supreme ruler and said, "What invaded Ziamon last night—what invaded Tinaria nights before—is an army. Like any army, they have soldiers, specialists, a ranking order and a purpose. Their purpose, so far, has involved nothing short of killing everything, but, now, it's clear they're here for something. They withdrew with Princess Shina unharmed. I don't know what they want with her, but it proves that they have intelligence. They have a purpose we can't understand.

"The only way we're going to defeat them is to understand them. And the only way to do that is to take the fight to Pommel, my home, where they struck first. To learn our enemy's weaknesses, we have to challenge them head-on. Here's what we know. They only attack at nightfall. This means, they could attack again tonight, but it isn't certain. Tinaria was spared the second wave. There are signs to look for that—signal—"

In hearing the rainstorm materialize outside the fort, Michael suddenly feared the worst. They watched his face emulate dread, unbeknownst as to why. In receiving his staff from Maxim, he peered out under the falling rain. Though he expected another bloodstorm, the darkened skies released only water. His anxiety subsided when soldiers opened the shutters, revealing the natural rain.

"There was no call for rain," one of them said. "The skies were clear before we even shut the doors."

Colonel Aramis turned to Michael and asked him, "Is this one of those signs?"

Soldiers lining the walls prepared for another battle as Michael hung his head in relief, saying, "No, but stay on your guard. I'll let you know when you need to worry."

Later in the night, as it proceeded to rain, Michael shut the door to his night lodging provided by the state and cried. Unable to pinpoint from where his emotions had come rushing, he couldn't stop it. He knelt by the bed and sobbed into the mattress. For minutes, he sobbed uncontrollably on his knees. He thought he was alone when a voice emanated from the darkness.

"So, you *are* human, after all." Prince Eric emerged from the dark, disabling his invisibility spell.

Taken aback, Michael jerked up and bid his staff fly back into his hand. His eyes glossed over and his face reddened, Michael growled in disbelief, "Eric, dammit! Where the hell have you been? How long have you been here?"

Advancing for him, Eric replied, "Since the demons left last night."

"You really should keep away from Maxim. He's aching to cut your head off," Michael said. "And I'm starting to think he has a point."

Eric sighed, "It's not so easy to—"

"You certainly have a knack for hiding like a coward when you're needed the most," Michael rebuked. "Your sister wasn't as lucky!"

"I'm aware," he said, putting up his hands in defense of his inaction. "I had to make her think I was gone. It wasn't my intention on following you to Tofauti, but when the Ziamons took her—"

"Well, now she's in much more sinister company. You know what they're capable of, yes?" Michael found a chair to sit in despairingly. "You know the danger she's in. Damn you for sitting this war out. When are you thinking of being a part of the team, I wonder? Have you ever used your sorcery for something productive, other than sneaking out from dark corners?"

"Where do you think this rain came from?" Eric replied. "The sky?"

Bemused, he looked up at him and uttered, "This storm was you?"

"Yes, and there's no need to thank me," Eric said. "The Demon Plague, as you like to call them, won't be coming this night as a result."

Michael countered, "As a result of what, the rain?"

"Think about it. It rained that night when we were all sitting around the fire. Nothing came for us. Are you listening to me? They could have taken her in the night while we were all asleep, but they didn't—they couldn't." Eric peered out of the small rectangular window to the open square and said, "They're afraid of water."

Replaying Eric's words in his head, Michael muttered, "Afraid of water. How can they fear water?"

"Like salt to a slug is my guess," he said. "These monsters don't belong on this earth, so, consequently, some elements of our world may be toxic to them. It isn't so mindboggling, Miuriell."

Utilizing his staff to scout the city for demonic invaders, Michael only replied, "It's a theory."

"I'm glad you think so. Too bad you're the only one who can appreciate it," Eric retorted, staring out at the falling rain from the window.

"And to that point, why are you here talking to me, Eric?" Michael had to ask. "There must be some scheme you are working that somehow involves me."

"You flatter me," Eric said, "but I suppose I came for a bit of closure."

In showing his hand, an illustrious ring sparkled in the faint light of the dusk's rain shower. The memorable symbol of Tinarian lineage fit snugly around his ring finger, leaving the exiled prince to smirk behind it. Once Michael looked upon it, he deduced Eric's primary motivation for visiting Ziamon. He asked him in his dazed stare, "Is that what I think it is?"

"And only a handful of dirt dogs had to pay the price for it. Tonight, while he sleeps, the supreme ruler will pay the ultimate price and my vengeance will be fulfilled—well, perhaps partly. Predella must pay for her—"

Michael then rose from his chair and confronted him in the center of the room, "Under no circumstances are you to harm anyone in this place. Do you understand? The truce is too important. If you kill him now, it'll set off a chain reaction that will doom the progress we've made in the past day to unite the rival kingdoms. We're *this* close to sailing across the Great Pacifica to challenge the Demon Plague head on. Your sister's life hangs in the balance of that."

Eric smiled defiantly before saying in return, "Do you know why my parents named me 'Eric' and not 'Luther' like my father before me and his father and his ancestors trailing all the way back to the first Luther Orgento of Ellium? Because my mother is an Ellison, related to Eli Ellis I and his many descendants. There is more lineage in my mother's royal blood than in this stupid, trivial ring my father stuck on my finger. I was to be the first king from both families—Ellison and Orgento. This ring only proves that I was born into the Tinarian royal family.

"But to me, Miuriell, it signified that I was significant. It reminded me that I mattered. Now, feeling it on my finger, it just feels tight, like a knot cutting off my blood supply. There is no love or admiration in wearing it. Tonight, the deep stiff feeling in my bony finger reminds me that I was mistreated. When every last perpetrator has suffered at my hands, I will return to my father and make him swallow this ring whole."

After letting him finish his passionate rant, Michael said boldly, "Your father is dead."

Then, Eric fell into a petrified stupor. His eyes welled up with tears as he made a fist, snarling, "That pompous fool lied to me. *You* lied to me."

Just realizing his rash mistake, Michael sighed before saying, "Eric, he didn't want to stir Shina into a panic. I know it was wrong to do, but he did it for the right intentions."

Eric stumbled to the window and then anxiously paced about the room, still shaking his ringed fist. Before Michael could try to bring him at ease, the exiled prince blasted into a bright flash of magic and disappeared. Left in the dark of his borrowed apartment, Michael lowered his head and groaned, "Shit."

In the early morning, after an uneventful night, Michael joined Maxim in the square to observe the assemblage of the troops. Just by seeing Supreme Ruler Ayden make his way into the bloody parade, Michael knew that Eric had not done the evil deed. He disappeared from Ziamon and took his vengeance with him. Michael could not know where, but by the power of his staff, he knew the exiled prince was nowhere in the city.

Because Ziamon had barely evaded decimation, Ayden could only provide a fraction of his best soldiers. Two legions of two hundred warriors marched for the main entrance, many of them chosen based on their total losses of spouses and families. A caravan of forest coaches approached for the officers, including Justice Esker and Colonel Aramis, had prepared to launch for the day's journey to Tinaria. Michael and Maxim were set to travel in the rear car, also the smallest one in the caravan. The hundreds of soldiers, donned in their finest armor, trudged along the sides as the small unit of Tinarian knights was at the rear of the convoy.

The journey was to Tinaria's eastern walls, but Maxim promised the Ziamons passage across the Great Pacifica by way of the Santa di Mare. Not only was it the fastest and largest of their ships, but it was the only vessel that survived the invasion nights ago. Most of the Ziamons had never even set foot on a ship in their entire life.

In the conclusion to the rallying parade, Ziamons from all over the city sang the national anthem in unison. Maxim found it ironic as their carriage finally set off by way of the cattle driver. Snickering to himself, he said, "Tinaria sung the national anthem before we set out to find you."

Michael, in admiring their departure from the bulwark kingdom, sighed, "I suppose that would make sense."

Twirling the signed treaty in his hands, Maxim said, "No demons last night."

Michael had not told him about Eric's presence in Ziamon and wasn't planning on it anytime in the near future.

Instead, he tried the prince's theory about the rain, uttering, "Perhaps the storm had something to do with it."

Intrigued by his notion, Maxim replied, "You think the rainwater kept them at bay?"

"It's possible," Michael said. "We should consider it."

Maxim only nodded, scarcely taking his eyes off the precious document. He had regret over dooming Predella to fall as a bargaining chip for the truce. Michael saw the shame of it in his face when he asked, "You're still thinking about the Predella stipulation?"

Shaking his head, Maxim admitted with guilt, "Predella shouldn't have been a part of that treaty, you know that. We just betrayed our friend—the friend who fought alongside us when she didn't have to. We dragged her along to Ziamon—"

"Where she freed her people," Michael interjected.

"And paid the price," Maxim retorted. "No matter how she did it, we didn't have the right to play the part in sealing her fate. What will she say when she discovers we sold her out?"

"I suppose we'll just have to keep her away from them. We can discuss this in further detail when Predella arrives," Michael said, smiling as he gently held onto his staff.

"When she arrives?" Maxim riposted. "And how can you be so sure she *will* arrive?"

"Because this staff here takes out the guesswork," he said, then turning back to yell out for the cattle driver to stop for a brief respite. When he argued with him about pressing on, Michael warned him, "Either you stop this carriage, or I will. I'm not asking twice."

Capitulating, the driver held up the cattle, causing the carriages in front to start slowing down. As the car came to a full stop, Maxim asked him, "Just what the hell is going on?"

Opening the door, Michael replied, "I suppose this is far enough from the likes of Ziamon."

As Maxim followed him out into the forest, the knights assembled behind them. Ziamon soldiers began to cluster in fear that something was following them. Instead, Michael put his hand on Maxim's shoulder and said, "She's been trailing us since we left."

From behind the wood and brush, Predella emerged. In appearing tired and sullied, she stared back upon them. The caravan of Ziamons threw her off, leading the way to Tinaria. She had kept a cautious distance away until realizing the two nations made some sort of agreement. Her presumption was confirmed when Michael sent her elemental bow all the way to her position from its place in their carriage. She extended her arm and received it from thin air.

Michael, in taking no chances, called out to all Ziamons that were listening, "In case you're not abreast to the terms of the treaty, Predella is one of us! She is to be treated as such or you will answer to me! Any objections?"

With only silence, Michael grinned and gestured for her to come and join them in the carriage. Strapping the bow to her back, she jogged over and embraced them both. They gradually made their way back into the carriage and the trek to Tinaria resumed. The knights, having become closer than they ever imagined, followed the carriage of heroes with a greater determination.

PART I
Last Chapter
THE ASHES IN THE WIND

The night was not far behind as the caravan approached the eastern walls of Tinaria, nearly lumbering uphill. Dusk prepared to consume the realm when the knights raced up to the city and bore the good news that they had returned home with a proposal of peace with Ziamon. Scouts and criers proclaimed that a Ziamon caravan advanced for the eastern walls with Michael Miuriell in command. What remained of Tinaria's army gathered their might and sprawled the kingdom's walls.

As the last carriage neared closer to the front of the line, a soldier from Drake's unit spotted a figure standing in-between the two drivers. Maxim stood eagerly between them with his sword strapped around his back, hidden by a cape. Gallantly dressed, he appeared alive and well amid Ziamon company. When he saw this, the soldier raised his hand and cried, "It's Cavallo, alright! He's got Ziamon enforcements at his back!"

Stricken with disbelief, Drake jogged over and snagged the scope from his hand. Looking through it, he saw it for himself. Maxim waved meticulously and white flags began to rise out of every carriage thereafter. Drake gasped, "This is impossible."

Maxim hopped out of the carriage and waved from afar, trying to attract attention. Drake had suspicions that he and the princess discovered the shadow treaty with Ziamon. This troubled him to the point of paranoia. A soldier asked, receiving the scope, "What is it, sir?"

Regaining his focus, Drake answered him crossly, "Don't you see that? Ziamon is at our gates! Don't drop your guard for a moment!"

Drake retreated into the city walls and ordered his men to fire upon the carriages if they neared too close to their defenses. Maxim did not miss his old friend's dramatic exit from the defensive line. Immediately, Tinarian soldiers came running down to meet Maxim before the Ziamons could make for the walls. He welcomed them with warm embraces and asked them to escort his allies to Municipal Hall where they would receive dinner and service.

Maxim informed the Ziamons that they would need to set camp outside Tinaria's walls, being that the queen did not yet sign the treaty. The colonel nodded in acceptance of the terms. He wasn't going to allow the Tinarians to ambush his men within the city overnight. By morning, if all went to plan, they would all be boarding the Santa di Mare for the West.

When Maxim proceeded up the knoll with Michael and Predella at his sides, Colonel Aramis moved beside Esker and said in Espanion, "They're stretching the terms of the treaty with Predella in our midst. We should kill her when we're on the other side of the world."

As Esker ogled them walking up the hill, he received a crossbow from one of his men, saying, "Damn, it would be so easy right now. One good flurry of bolts."

"He's lucky," Aramis replied.

"No," Esker said before handing the crossbow back to his soldier, "he just knows he's got us by the balls away from Ziamon."

Throngs of Tinarians flocked to Michael and Predella in Municipal Hall, eager to hear what had happened during their journey. Instantly, food and drink were prepared and dished for the pair of them. Maxim, in contrast, was greeted with acclaim. Men, women and children alike came running up to him just to have a chance to touch him. Almost the entire kingdom cramped up the city walkways to catch a glimpse. The city assumed that their princess was safe, but some started to suspect something was amiss when she never appeared.

The city, still in smoking ruins, was a taste of heaven. Maxim felt blessed to be back at home where many had been working tirelessly to rebuild it. In reaching King's Tower, he found it almost impossible to climb the steps. Weakened by his trial in Ziamon, he needed help to make due. Holding the treaty rolled up in his hand, Maxim entered the throne room and knelt before the queen. Drake and Kal were at each side of her. She bid him welcome, but with hesitation in her voice.

When he didn't raise his head to meet her, she asked him, "Maxim, where is my daughter? You sent her to Tofauti as we discussed, I hope?"

As the entire room awaited the news, Queen Orgento's body began to shake in anticipation. She clasped her hands together firmly and uttered almost in a whisper, "My God, Maxim, will you raise your damn head and answer me!"

"The princess was taken," Maxim blurted out amongst the rising wave of shock and dismay of the court around him.

"Taken?" Kal intercepted. "Taken by whom?"

"Michael's Demon Plague?" Drake screamed out in a sudden rage, compelling others to cry out in horror.

Certain that the queen was going to fall to pieces, Maxim rose to his feet and vowed passionately, "We will bring her back safely! I promise you! Ziamon has fallen, worse than us. They have nothing left but vengeance. This treaty has the potential to merge our two kingdoms together to fight this plague across the world. Together, with Miuriell's help, we can annihilate them and bring her back."

"At what cost?" Drake retorted. "How do you plan—"

"At *any* cost!" Maxim yelled back, already furious with him. "With the cost of our lives, if necessary!"

Trying to hear him among the hysterics of the court, the queen eventually shouted for everyone to be silent. Her voice was booming, bringing everyone to an abrupt stillness. As they were hastily learning to obey her as they would their king, she caught her breath and said, "There is no saving your princess or ending the Demon Plague with fits of terror! Now, if you can't hold it together for her, how can I trust you'll be of any damn use to me? Get out if your blood runs cold! Leave Tinaria entirely! The only Tinarians I want in my presence are those who are ready to fight!"

As the hall cowered under the heat of her wrath, she turned to Maxim and commanded, "Not another word from you. Bring me Michael Miuriell, now."

Maxim nodded, but then raised his hand in a petition to speak up. She rolled her eyes in her panic and barked, "For God's sake, what?"

"Your Majesty, I must insist that we discuss some urgent matters before you meet with Miuriell. Please." Maxim tried desperately to suggest the substance of the matters with his eyes.

Feeling the weight of his request in her spirit, she locked eyes on him and proclaimed to the open court, "Leave us until I summon you again. That means you too, my lords."

As the assembly began to disperse, Drake walked by him and growled, "Whatever it is you have to say to her, you'll say it to me in the Baron Room. I'll be waiting."

Maxim then said back, "I'm counting on it."

A time later, Kal Era himself escorted Michael to speak with the queen in her private quarters. Maxim, however, burst the door of the Baron Room wide open, flustering Drake's officers inside. As promised, Maxim commanded that they leave immediately. In a scurry, the men raced out of the room and Maxim shut the door behind them. In response to Maxim's rising fury, Drake rose from his chair and groaned, "What the hell is this?"

"I was intending to ask you the same." Maxim moved in.

"Don't play with me, Maxim," Drake countered. "I want to know what happened—"

Maxim cut him off, "What has happened to my world when I trust a Ziamon's word over my own comrade's?"

"What are you talking about? How did you come to mingle with those dirt dogs?" Drake replied wearingly.

Maxim said, clenching his teeth, "They mentioned you by name."

"Why?" he asked, defensively.

"You tell me! I wish to hear it from you now!" he cried.

"You idiot!" Drake spat as he yelled. "You speak like the Ziamons are your new friends! What are the terms of this treaty? You probably let them spit on our seal!"

"You must know. The previous treaty left a lasting impression. Frankly, I'm shocked that the king avoided your treachery for that long! Our queen was not as fortunate," Maxim paced around, holding back from strangling him.

"You think you know everything. You know *nothing!*" Drake shouted back.

"I know enough!" he answered. "You betrayed us all when you shook hands with that tyrant! Your 'treaty' was hardly that! You practically threw Tinaria in fire—for what?"

"I wanted peace, Maxim! Our king never would have considered a truce between our two kingdoms and you damn well know that! I bought us lasting peace!" he rejoined.

"That wasn't your choice to make!" Maxim countered fervently. "Our prince—exiled, our king and queen—targets for assassination and your best friend, killed—for peace?

How many of our men served as your sacrificial lambs for your shadow treaty?"

Drake whispered pitilessly, "How many men have *you* killed, Maxim? Your hands are drenched with the blood of those barbarians you despise so much. I think I recall a rash choice *you* made in running off to Ziamon to start a war. You defied the king. You defied Tinaria, just like I did, to do what you thought was right. At least my arrangement brought some sort of peace, even if it was fake peace."

"'Fake peace.'" Forsaken with a mix of truths and hurt, Maxim replied, "I was young and bold, but I didn't bring back a fake princess."

"It's not fake to the thousands in Tinaria and the dirt dogs of Ziamon," Drake said in reply. "I would sacrifice you a hundred times over if it meant an end to total war between our kingdoms."

"You look me in the eye and tell me this?" Maxim gasped. "I and the rest of my people refuse to serve as a sacrifice for your peace! And how did that treaty of yours play out? Do you know how many spies were inside our city when the Demon Plague struck that night? Droves. Like flies over sugar."

"And yet you deliver them to the outer walls of this kingdom? How can you be so sure that they will resist attacking us in the dead of night?" Drake answered.

"With four hundred troops? You know they'd never stand a chance, Drake," Maxim said. "Don't insult me."

Drake then riposted in the heat of the argument, "They killed *you* off with less than that years back, as I remember!"

Maxim seized him by the collars and pulled him close, "You looked just as surprised as they did when Her Majesty brought me back."

Drake broke from his grasp and yelled, "This idiot!"

"I want names. You'll give us the names of all the little peons that did your bidding! All the traitors of Tinaria will be snuffed out, even if I have to scorch them down myself! God help me, I'll cut them in pieces. I'll burn the rats out of their nest, including you. Don't think I won't!" Maxim cried.

Drake wiped the sweat from his brow and exhaustedly replied, "I'd die for Tinaria, but you won't dare touch me."

"She almost died for *you*! You almost killed your queen!" Maxim instantly countered him. "She might kill you herself."

"And Tinaria falls with me," he said.

"Only your family will miss you," Maxim could not help but laugh, forsaken with woe and disgust. He rubbed the back of his neck and walked over to the open window. As the sun began to fall beyond the horizon, Maxim prayed that the demons would leave them alone. He just couldn't bear another confrontation.

Changing the direction of the conflict, Drake uttered to Maxim's back, "Of all the days you and the others were gone, Tinaria wasn't visited by one single demon."

After a short pause, Maxim took another deep breath and said, "They were after the princess."

"Because Miuriell is their leader," Drake said. "Inside, I know you believe it, too."

"Shut up, Drake. You think you know it all, don't you?" he rebuked.

"I'm the *only* one who knows it!" Drake shouted. "That warlock may not understand how, but he is connected to that army from hell. Miuriell *is* a demon!"

"Then he's a demon I trust to lead us to victory—to return Shina to us," Maxim replied. "We all have demons. If his ever threatens the princess, I'll kill him, too. I'm not just an idiot with a hot sword. There's a lot I've been thinking on and some things take precedence over the others."

"You will not be able to stop them, Maxim," Drake said, nearing closer. "Miuriell or not, they are far too strong and far too many. There is no chance of defeating them on their own ground. Just imagine the scale of their power. Send Miuriell off and let that be the end of it. He led them to us. He should face them alone."

"And the princess? Will she be another one of your sacrifices?" Maxim challenged him.

"If they took her, she's still alive." Drake sat in a chair aside the table and rubbed his straining eyes. "But God only knows what they're doing with her."

"And that's why I'm going with him," Maxim returned to the sunset by the open window and sighed. "I remember, long ago, our silly adventures as childhood friends. We imagined the most terrible foes. Outnumbered, we always survived victorious in our games. And then, there we were, fighting alongside each other against true villains.

"But now, times have changed us. We must protect what little we have left. Make no mistake, I believe these are our final days. We will leave for the West at first light, but, this time, you'll stay here and I will go to battle without you by my side."

When Maxim started to walk out of the Baron Room, Drake leaped out of his seat and stopped him in his tracks, "Wait a minute! You don't make demands of me! Your words are ash to the wind! Only the queen can judge me."

"And so, she did," Maxim said as he started to walk for the door again. When he left, Kal Era took his place with a throng of elite soldiers. In a panic, Drake challenged them to no avail. As the knights overtook him, he cried out, "You'll die in hell! Do you hear me? You'll die in hell!"

Maxim replied from the hallway, making a declaration, "Then it will be a death of my choosing—one with honor."

. . .

As the night finally arrived, the Ziamon divisions outside were staggered. Colonel Aramis remained awake under the shelter of the trees, fearing every snap of the branch and lift of the wind. From the eastern walls, sixty fully armed Tinarian knights marched down the hill, carrying extra provisions. Though the Ziamons easily noticed the gunmen positioned right outside the walls, they focused on the knights at hand.

Colonel Aramis stood up and met the knights a quarter way up the hill. It was then that the officer spoke, "Courtesy of the queen, receive these provisions for the night's rest. In the morning, we sail as one."

Aramis commanded men to come and disburse the gear to their soldiers accordingly. When the last blanket was taken, the knights turned back and returned for the safety behind their walls. Aramis told the serving officer, "Please give the queen our sentiments."

Even after the knights withdrew behind the wall, Aramis awaited the signal for the ambush on his soldiers. It would have been the killing joke. To his surprise, the enemy delivered gifts without the sword. For Queen Orgento, in contrast, the night was less peaceful. She could not sleep with so much troubling her mind. She turned and twisted in her bed, dressed only in her nightgown. Finding no possible way to fall asleep, she sat up on the side of her bed, slipped her feet into a pair of warm slippers and walked out of her chambers. She passed the grand hall and headed for the princess's quarters.

Soldiers on guard followed her from a distance. There was no one watching the main doors to Shina's quarters. The queen easily slipped through the large doors and bothered to close them as she was in. Into Shina's bedroom she crept, closing the door behind her. The guards waited outside.

Shina's bed was neatly made with her pretty pillows. Her dolls and stuffed animals remained where they were, though some of her things were cluttered tightly in her closets. The large window allowed the moon to shine in, dimly illuminating most of the room. She couldn't know that Kaila, the demonic vampire general, had rummaged through her closets for a robe the night of the invasion.

Madam Orgento immediately stepped over the gowns thrown all over the floor and sat on her daughter's bed, feeling the sheets with her hand and smelling the pillows. She smelled her daughter's hair on them. She then snatched the stuffed unicorn at the foot of the bed and embraced it tightly. It was not long before she broke down and cried, desperate for her daughter's safety. Until she held her in her arms again, Tinaria's queen would mourn her deeply.

In the dead of night, a sudden cloud materialized and emptied rain over the city. Michael, in the quarters provided for him, smiled at the sight. Tomorrow was the beginning of a haphazard journey into hell on earth and the Demon Plague would have reveled in the chance to wipe out their combined forces, as trifling as they seemed. Admiring the storm, he had to evoke Eric's name in gratitude.

The Demon Plague was finished with their merciless campaign in the East. They would only need to wait. Michael would tremble sometimes as he remembered the gruesome and unholy slaughter of Pommel. He mourned the loss of his beloved wife and all of his people for whom he could not save. His stomach tightened when he dreamt of whatever happened to his son.

But under the rain, a dark figure seemed to materialize. Floating in place, it stretched out its arms and moved the raindrops away from hitting its hide. When it opened its red eyes, glowing like the bright embers of a raging flame, there was no question that it was a demonic visitor. But how did it last in the rain? Michael began to question Eric's theory of the Demon Plague's vulnerability to water. Suddenly, the figure came into focus and looked more like a man. His baleful black armor looked as if it was fused to his skin. His long black hair flowing in the gales of the storm, the supernatural figure turned his attention to Michael's open window.

His crimson stare seemed to break deep into Michael's very soul. The dark warrior of boding evil pointed for him from Tinaria's diminished skyline. Then, his ominous voice entered his mind, saying, "**Unleash me.**"

Feeling it in his heart, Michael backed away from the window and held his chest. A stream of blood fell from his nose as he withdrew. And when the figure found him by way of his mind, he vanished to ash. Starting from one side of his body, he faded away with the gusts of Eric's storm. Michael jumped out of his sleep and tried desperately to catch his breath, still holding his heart. In feeling his face frantically, Michael felt the blood that had streamed down the side of his cheek while he slept.

His waking nightmare was just the start of it. Leaping out of bed, he rushed to the window to see if his vision was real. In distress, he peered out and saw only the rainstorm. In his confusion, he reached out for the staff to get into his open palm, but there was nothing. He felt that the Staff of Truth was there, but it refused to come. As he turned to find it, Michael, at last, met the source of all his dread.

Flashes of lightning exposed a little girl with sloppy, filthy hair covering most of her face. A malevolent force emanated from her little frame, as she slumped over in the corner with the Staff of Truth in her tiny hands. Again, he had used his power to pull it out from her grasp, but she was too strong. It hardly budged from her grip.

"What are you?" Michael gasped.

"**I am the one you fear,**" she answered in a deep, rasping voice, hinting a chilling whisper. "**This artifact alone stretches the fabric of reality. And even with its extraordinary dominion over time and space, you are yet blinded. Is it truly wasted on you?**"

There was no need for Michael to decipher the girl's answer or her counter question. He knew that she was nothing more than a marionette with the highest evil pulling the strings. He asked, "I see the puppet. Now, where is the puppeteer?"

She replied, "**My true form is inadequate when absent from my refuge. This earthly environment compels me to use such abject methods.**"

"Where are your other puppets?" Michael asked.

"**I no longer require their services here,**" the spirit answered ominously. "**For now.**"

"Then answer my first question." Michael came back without delay, "Why have *you* come?"

"**For confirmation.**" The girl let the staff float over to its rightful owner. "**Ignorant creatures, born for greatness, live a liar's life.**"

He received the staff, then scouting the city for any presence of demons. The girl snickered, "**You'll find nothing. I told you.**"

"Quiet!" Michael shouted, trying to find the origin of the girl, rewinding the time as he was sleeping.

"**The cause you fight for has no merit. Your true place is with me,**" the demon continued.

"Where the hell did you come from?" Michael retorted angrily, unable to revisit anything before he awoke from his nightmare.

"**All that you have done means little in comparison to what you were born to do,**" it said.

Snapping back to his current struggle, he couldn't comprehend what the demon had come to do. Though he could not bear to hear the truth, he asked it a dangerous question, shaking, "What am I supposed to do, then?"

"**Disappointing**," it riposted. "**I am surprised that you have not yet uncovered your true calling. You have mingled with your beloved humans for far too long.**"

"Answer my question!" he cried.

While Michael feared the demon's response, he needed to understand why so many had to die because of him. The little girl's hair moved away from her face, allowing her to look Michael straight in the eyes as it said, "**You are the leader of us all—our creator.**"

"No!" Michael ground his teeth, retorting madly with tears swelling. "You will not—"

"**It is natural human behavior to first deny your destiny, but it is inevitable. You have led us to the lands of the East. When you join us, all the world will cower before your might alone,**" it proclaimed, finding elation in exposing his identity.

"I'd kill myself first!" Michael screamed.

"**Your death would be regrettable and I would assume command, as I have taken the liberty as of late.**" The demon's dark words ate through Michael's heart.

Though dismayed, Michael learned a useful truth. If he was as powerful as the demon said, then there was a chance he could finish it. He determined to kill the powerful demon, believing it was the only way to stop the Demon Plague for good. As he thought, the demon spoke, "**Ah, I can hear your thoughts. You want to finish it now, here with me?**"

Without hesitation, Michael answered avidly, "If it's all the same to you."

"**And you think you can defeat me?**" it went on.

"You said it yourself," Michael said, clenching his fists, "if I am your creator, then I can be your destroyer!

"Then let's play." The girl extended her hand, emitting a small, but bright sphere that simply hovered above her delicate palm.

Emitting a high-pitched tone that forced Michael to hold his ears, it spun faster until it exploded. The bright flash blinded him. He felt as if his feet lifted off the ground and turned completely upside down. In time, he felt the raindrops falling heavily upon him. In opening his eyes, he found himself laying in a giant crater somewhere, his body felt feverish and his vision was blurred. He then recognized that he was out of the storm and in a quiet, desolate place.

Feeling the dry ground, barren and cold, Michael had suddenly realized that he had been teleported. Nauseous, he hunched over and fought the feeling to vomit. From his spot in the ground, he looked up and saw a large boulder with a plaque of some kind glistening faintly in the moonlight. Upon closer inspection, holding his stomach, Michael read it:

Here lies the former settlement
of the Waasi Nation,
destroyed by a scourge with no name,
cursed evermore as a people with no country.
May this hallowed ground serve as a memorial
to their struggle for freedom in kinship.

He then knew where the demon had dropped him. Looking about, Michael found the girl dancing in the distance of ground zero. Skipping on the site where so many Waasi had died unexpectedly, she giggled sinisterly. In seeing her do this, Michael retrieved his staff from the dirt and shouted out, "Is this supposed to be some sort of—"

"All the dead souls give me strength!" the demon returned, her hair enlivened and her small eyes turning a bright green.

"Well?" Michael cried out among the desolation.

The girl's eyes discharged beams of green energy for him. He focused all of his power, absorbing the rays before they burned through his body. The force of the surprising attack nearly toppled him over, making him dig his feet into the ground. Seeing that it could not break through Michael's telekinetic barrier, the demon ceased its first attack and tried a better one.

It extended its hand out and sent out erratic bolts of power for him. In response to the awesome force, Michael extended his left hand and easily repelled the power away, sending it into the air. As he did this, Michael started running diagonally towards his target. Now with both hands, the demon emitted a more lethal charge. Purple in hue, the currents were like lightning. They stopped him in his tracks.

Michael attempted to deflect the power with his palms, but the force was too great. The currents jolted him for a moment as they raided his force field, keeping him off balance. Quickly, the horrible energy was beginning to scold his skin. Michael felt that he couldn't hold the electric current for long. Yet, something began to burn inside.

The sudden clench of desperation and the resolute in his heart produced a rush of power that consumed him. The sensation was dark and stronger than himself. It built up around him, like a globe of power.

In an abrupt burst of might, Michael's eyes glowed bright red and the terrible currents against him broke away, dispersing into the night. The remarkable blast forced Michael to fall and the fierce demon to succumb to its little knee. Though the girl was mildly rattled by the counter blow, Michael scurried to his knees and then onto his unsteady legs in a hasty attempt to recover. The red glow within his eyes dissipated. The demon, still hiding inside the child, rose in astonishment, exclaiming, "**Yes, that's more like it!**"

Now, feverishly determined to kill the powerful demon, Michael began to advance forward. Thus, the demon decided to unleash a terrible spell. When Michael was but twenty feet away, the demon sprung its tremendous trap. The ground began to break like thawing ice and steaming hot magma loitered in the cracks. When the ground began to quake, the demon raised her hand into the air. Upon reaching the mark, a colossal detonation of searing magma discharged into the air like a volcano.

The molten rock raged into the sky, eviscerating the ground below. The demon submerged him in the devastating attack. Nothing could have survived the blast of that magnitude. He should have died instantly. Though the ferocity of the spell was extreme, Michael held on to his force field. The senses were strong with him and he was able to hold the concentrated heat of the magma away from his body, screaming all the way.

Under severe duress, Michael tried to hold off the searing hot lava from consuming him. His strength started to diminish and falter. The magma's intensity was just too great. But then, it happened again. The absolute power and rage that flowed through him moments before had returned, but greater. His eyes turned to a fiery crimson red, fiercer than even the demon he faced.

Michael's power tripled and handling the hellish bombardment became instinctive. Screaming with rage, Michael exploded his telekinetic force field and reduced the volcanic assault to nothing. He blasted everything away as if it evaporated to gaseous matter.

In that meantime, Michael's nefarious powers had steadily faded away and he was himself again, except for his eyes. His body, exhausted from exerting everything he had, nearly gave out. He collapsed to his side, fighting the urge to lose consciousness. When his eyes returned to his natural brown, the demon found the opportunity to try its last trick. The girl ran over to him as he tried to stand and said, "**You're the real Miuriell—the one we have been waiting for all this time. Let me show you.**"

Then, the little girl smiled and raised her arms high into the night, calling upon some power. In moments, it abandoned the girl and transformed into a woman—one Michael would know too well. As his wife, Opal, the Demon Lord laughed over him.

Crossed by the demon's devious ploy, Michael groaned in despair, "You sick—"

"Dead!" the demon cried in her voice. "Dead because of you! I loved you and you let me die!"

Falling to his knees in the enormous crater, Michael held his head and cried out in fury. As he fought his guilt, the demon vanished and reappeared directly behind him, defiling his wife's figure as its shell. A crushing slap and Michael careened into the hot dirt, lying there in ire. When the Demon Lord came to strike him again, testing his madness, Michael stood up and revealed his glowing red eyes.

"**Your natural eyes?**" It mocked in its real voice.

As the fighting resumed in the storm, Antonis the Prophet, accompanied by five Tofauti scouts, climbed up the Shahidi Knoll and discovered the supernatural mêlée. The scouts were in awe of what unraveled before them in the distance. Antonis had already seen the battle in his visions a day ago. He watched as the Demon Lord, disguised as Michael's wife, thrashed Michael about like a cat playing with her prey.

"**What an unnecessary defeat.**" the demon proclaimed. "**This battle doesn't need to continue. Join me and live out your true destiny! Isn't that what you want, to uncover your purpose?**"

Still scarred from the demon's powers, Michael answered passionately from the ground, "You will not turn me against my own!"

The demon, disgusted with his response, said, "**Your own? Your absurd perspective has become tiresome and flat. This world has seen the last of humankind. Good riddance! This world would benefit greatly without their malignant presence. They alone destroyed this world. Look at what they did to your planet. You're living in the remnants of their sins. How can you defend that species?**

"**The human race is a cancer. You can't deny it. So, Miuriell, for whom do you stand? We will reform your world. Your precious humans have already ravaged it. Where do you stand?**"

The Demon Lord made an imperative mistake in pressing Michael in such a way. In real agony on his back, he knew better than to believe the demon's talk of fate and destiny. He alone had the power to choose. He was not going to surrender to the Demon Plague and turn into the creature he saw in his vision. Thus, his eyes returned to normal.

"You are wrong, demon!" Michael fervently professed from the ground. "I *am* a human. Humanity led themselves to their doom, but they're actions don't speak for mine!"

"**Indeed.**" The demon then showed him flashes of evil, thousands of years of human hatred, murder, rape and war in just seconds. Overwhelmed by the rush of vile atrocities, he hunched over and vomited. It was too much wickedness for any person to bear witness. The revolting visions cursed his mind. Hence, the Demon Lord told him, "**All the sufferings of humanity, caused by humanity. If anything, we're here to end that vicious cycle of man. Would you like more?**"

"Yes," Michael gasped after spitting up again. "Show me the love of humanity. Surely there are thousands of years of all that, as well?"

After the Demon Lord heard this, it knew that Michael's determination was too strong to break. Extending Opal's hands to discharge its greatest power, it declared in a crazed fury, **"Then *die* like the human you are, hopeless!"**

From the distance, the scouts looked on, but Antonis could not stand by and watch anymore. He seized one of their horns and blew as hard as he could. Instantly, the Demon Lord pulled back and withdrew its final strike. It turned towards the slope far to the left of the rainy plains and acknowledged the one who bellowed the sound.

"An admirer! The prophet," the demon mockingly stated with malevolent glee. **"Let's give him one last act."**

Michael swiftly called upon his senses and smothered the sorcery in its open palm, refusing to let even a trace escape. While the demon fought to overpower him, its magic backfired. The Demon Lord fell to its knees and shouted in agony as the spell rattled its feeble frame. Michael labored off the ground as it was debilitated and decided to destroy the hellish monster at once.

With everything he had left, he grappled its head with his hands and said in-between breaths, "This is for my wife and son."

Separating his hands from its head, Michael exploited his power and tore Opal's skull to pieces. The demon's shell exploded into bloody plods and his wife's body fell limp to the ground, decapitated. A ghostly aura emerged from her corpse and dispelled into the atmosphere, fleeing the fight.

Michael finally collapsed in grief and blacked out. The Demon Lord's shell of Opal's body remained on the ground as the Tofauti scouts came to help him. Antonis followed closely behind, sighing shamefully as he went.

Within the political dungeon of King's Tower, Drake couldn't possibly sleep. His head swirled with theories as to how

Maxim finagled a treaty with the Ziamons. The most hated enemy of the bulwark kingdom procured a peace after there was no kingdom left. There were too many facets at work and only so much he could resolve from inside a cell, fallen from the queen's grace.

As he brooded over it all, an eerily familiar voice came from the coldness of the corridor, "How bizarre it must feel to finally see the cage from the inside. Are you a rueful rat?"

Drake sat up in his cot and gasped, "Who is that?"

The exiled prince then came into view just beyond the cell bars, his white hair falling down the sides of his face, and continued, "Or are you still just an old, treacherous weasel?"

"You!" Drake grumbled. "Of course, it's you. Fitting."

"Fitting? Maybe." Eric grabbed one of the bars with his ringed hand. "It's tighter than I remember."

Ogling the lineage ring, Drake snickered in disgust. Eric spoke before Drake could say anything snappy, "You know, I can smell your blood. A tinny, sweet smell, you're not that different from other men. But, if I hone in on your scent, there is something unique about it—something distinct. Everyone has a distinct smell when they're scared. This makes me wonder if your offspring smell just like their old man—just before they know they're going to die."

"You son of a bitch, coward!" Drake leaped out of the cot and approached the cell bars to confront the exiled prince face-to-face. "I swear, you won't ever lay even a finger on my children's head! I'd slit your throat first!"

Suddenly, Eric phased right through the metal bars and walked into Drake's cell, compelling the lord to wince back and fall on his back. The sorcerer's eyes illuminated a glowing white as he entered Drake's prison space, seeming more like a god than a magician. While the disgraced lord retreated into the corner, helpless against his powers, Eric snarled, "I came with the intention of forcing my father to swallow this futile little relic. Given that he is dead, you're the next best thing, I find. So, in light of your scheming affronts against me, you'll swallow this ring whole, or I sniff out your family and turn their blood to dirt."

"Go to hell!" Drake spat on him in what he reckoned was his last act of defiance.

Hence, Eric removed his ring and seized Drake by the throat. While the lord struggled, the prince lifted him off his dungeon cot as if he was made of paper and forced the ring down his throat. Drake gagged and coughed, writhing in pain suspended in air. When the ring was halfway down, Eric let him drop so that he could watch him choke on it. Drake held his throat, choking, on his knees. Eric stood over him and said, "Hell is relative, Vitan. I'll hunt down every last agent that worked for you in plotting my exile. All your slimy conspirators will die a traitor's death. But you—"

Eric needed only to prod Drake with his finger to turn him into stone. From his head down to his knees, Drake had frozen in his state of suffering. He became a kneeling marker for everyone to take notice. Prince Eric had his revenge. He finally said over his enshrined body, "You'll always be a part of Tinaria now."

Satisfied, Eric left the human gravestone in his cell and walked out through the metal bars as he did before. He turned his rain into a drizzle, still steady enough to deter the Demon Plague, and walked out into the night. Because his magical arsenal was nearly depleted, Eric decided to let the raindrops fall on his face and began to cry.

When he opened his eyes, there was a clearing blur revealing Antonis's face above him. Michael was covered in blankets and his outer clothes were removed, plopped on a chair beside the mattress. His aches and pains returned along with his consciousness. Antonis, the disgraced prophet, patted his wounds gently with a damp cloth from his seat beside him.

Finally, Michael's vision improved and he focused in on the prophet's face. His jet-black hair was in braids and his skin was clean. In a forlorn voice, he said, "Welcome back."

Taking his time to reflect upon what had happened, he answered with an exhausted whisper, "Where am I?"

Antonis answered, "You're in my homeland."

"Tofauti," Michael promptly sighed, feeling every ache in his body. "I guess I've taken the full tour of the East now."

"For beginners, maybe." Antonis offered a crooked grin before splashing his own face with water. "Word has gotten around about you—and the demons that came after you."

Michael looked him over closely from his bed. "Tofauti knows about the Demon Plague? You warned them?"

"Warning is what I do." He fretted, "The chief here trusts my council and I assured him that you aren't any threat to the Tofauti people. In Tinaria, they were the highest bidder, and I served them for well over a decade. My visions are never foolproof, but there's no better seer in the East. In that, I am very certain, Miuriell. But when those things came to—when I tried to—"

Michael rested his head back on the pillow and closed his eyes, knowing the pain of the unknown better than most. He endured the shock of three demonic invasions, all of them by surprise attacks from nothing and nowhere. He breathed in deeply before saying, "I feel my staff somewhere in this place, wherever I am. Can you bring it to me please?"

"Miuriell, were you listening to me?" Antonis moved to the corner of the garrison to take the Staff of Truth to its rightful owner, inspecting its unremarkable qualities. There was nothing exceptional about it. He brought it over to him and let it float into his possession. When Michael had it, he immediately realized where and when he was.

His barracks were in an outpost region just south of the Tofauti capital city. With the dawn only a few hours away, there was no presence of demonic forces. Five native warriors were fast asleep within the barracks with just one on night watch. While he assessed his surroundings, Antonis interjected from the side, "Using that artifact, were you able to prophesize the demons' coming—at any time? Did you?"

Michael used the staff to help him sit up on the edge of the bed, uttering, "No. No, I couldn't."

Nodding his head and rubbing his chin frantically, Antonis returned, "Well, I didn't see them—ever. I didn't see any of it. The fall of Tinaria, the fall of Ziamon, the king's—well, you know. No one foresaw the invasion, not even the master chieftain of the occult himself. The Kajhic seers feed off the dark magic of the old world in the badlands, where it still lingers in the atmosphere. I've learned to draw from its power as well.

"But in the prelude of war, I tried to see. I focused in on the dark energy festering in Tinaria and the dark energy fought back. Some sinister force countered mine and invaded my mind. It was something like a mystic poison, draining my abilities—draining my very soul. All that I could do was run from it. I ran to live. Back in Tofauti, I warned Chief Madax of what happened. Shortly after, fragments of insight returned to me, but—"

"You need to feed off more dark energy, is that it?" he said, stretching his back. "Well, Pommel's got the motherlode you're looking for if you're interested. The Demon Plague is as dark as they come. What you saw from the hill was the Demon Lord in one of its forms. Its power is unlimited, or so it seems. A united force is going to the West in the morning. I don't suppose the Tofauti chief would be willing—"

"Why do you think we're stationed in a lonely barrack out here on the edge of Tofauti?" Antonis said. "Madax does not trust you in his kingdom. The demons tend to follow you around, don't they?"

Nodding despondently, he said, "I believe they do."

"Well, that's why we're out here. The chief doesn't want you anywhere inside Tofauti," Antonis replied solemnly. "But if it's any consolation, I want in."

Taken aback by his request to embark on the most perilous quest in history, Michael could only mutter, "You want in? You, of all people, want to come?"

"I am entitled to some sense of redemption. And, also, some answers to questions," Antonis said, fidgeting with his hands. "The warriors out here with us have been assigned by the council to guard me if you permit me to come. They are prisoners, criminals with a rare opportunity. By defending me, seeing the mission out all the way to the West and back, then their honor as Tofauti warriors may be restored. If you permit them, they will begin their Honor Quest at first light."

"I see," Michael replied. "Tinarians, Ziamons and a crew of Tofauti felons—"

"Don't bother asking them anything. They're sworn to silence until their mission is fulfilled," Antonis said.

Michael smirked and replied, "You all may join us on one condition: get me back to Tinaria immediately. We make for our departure in the morning."

Stretching out his hand, Antonis exclaimed, "Then it is decided! Thank the Maker!"

While he seemed elated at the thought of rushing to the devil's den to find some sense of redemption, Antonis had never been more scared in all his life. Aside from having to face his Tinarian comrades after his craven escape during their time of need, he had never seen a demon in the flesh. It finally hit him after he embraced Michael's hand in accord.

Michael felt the distress in his grip, compelling him to say, "You understand that this can very well be a death sentence for yourself and those men sworn to protect you? You saw the Demon Lord in the plains. It is helplessly driven to destroy humanity. And as surreal as that sounds and as hard as it is to believe when they kill all of the people you love—you believe."

"Why you?" Antonis asked, blankly staring through him. "How do you plan on snuffing out that army?"

He replied in a troubled tone, "I had a vision of a man consumed by evil. I don't know how to explain it, but I felt his power when I fought the Demon Lord in that crater. I felt his power in myself.

"I don't understand," Antonis said in a daze.

"I am not very far ahead of you," he said, "but it felt like I was becoming one of them."

"He's inside you? That evil is in your blood?" Antonis covered his mouth in shock as he spoke. "Of course. That is why they follow you, isn't it? You are one of them!"

Shaking his head in trepidation, he finally had to admit, "I don't know. I don't know what I am."

Antonis seemingly gazed into his spirit, saying, "If we do not know ourselves, then we are pawns in someone else's game."

Michael stared right back, "The man who truly knows himself trusts no one else. Are you sure you want to come?"

"I'd rather challenge demons than wait to be picked off by them. Of course, I still want to come," Antonis said. "What purpose can I possibly serve here? Tofauti is the only nation that has it's shit together now. They don't need a seer to see that. You will need me. I promise."

"And what about these warriors?" Michael whispered. "Whatever you have seen in your visions in the seclusion of Tofauti, they're nothing compared to the real thing. The smell of demons stays with you long after you've survived them. A time in their company is beyond terrifying—beyond words.

Are you really willing to risk their lives for your conscience? Do you honestly want to put them through that?"

Antonis thought on it. He went to the table and brought Michael his clothes, saying gravely, "If we don't do something to fight those unholy things, then those things are going to come here and kill them anyway—along with their children, wives, and everything else. To prevent that, I am willing to bring them to the afflicted pit of hell itself."

Michael received his clothing and leaned in to whisper in return, "Then you'll get to see what that pit looks like from the inside."

A clasp of thunder convinced Predella that there was no saving her sleep. It seemed like her adrenaline had never shut off since the Battle of Tinaria. Rolling around in her bed for hours, she surrendered to warrior's restlessness and went over to the window to watch the rain. Below, in the crux's courtyard, she saw Maxim standing in the storm. Wearing only his slacks, he put his head up and shut his eyes, permitting the rain to wash over him.

To most people, he would have seemed like a lunatic. It was late, approaching dawn hours, and the morning swore to an intrepid exploit to the demon-infested western lands. Out in the rain was the last place any stable person would have planned to be, but Predella shared in his fighter spirit. Only, she didn't want Maxim to be alone, even if that's what he wanted. She went to meet him.

Maxim had been praying when he felt her presence. He turned around to see her standing in the storm, just watching him. Predella's hair had cascaded like waterfalls on the sides of her face and her drenched nightgown became fused to her body. Gazing upon him, enamored by his radical behavior, he called her name. Predella said nothing. She just stared at him.

Comforted by her resolve to join him in the rainstorm, Maxim fought through his tears to admit openly, "There was nowhere else I could go. This could be the last night I ever get the chance to be with her. I just wanted to feel her one last time before we leave for what could be forever. I just, I don't know how to explain it, but, it's so quiet out here and I can't let her be alone. So many died in her streets and there was no place where it looked like my home after. When I'm gone—when we leave, Tinaria will only be a distant dream. Maybe in the storm, I'll remember what it was like here."

She continued to stare at him under the shower, getting soaked to the skin and said nothing. He couldn't make out her face, but she couldn't take her eyes off of him. Feeling his ramblings were lost on her, for Predella had lost her people long before Tinaria had fallen. Dropping his head, he thought on her and then continued, "But, you know more about losing than I ever could. You lost them to something worse than any army or horde, man and demon alike. How can one woman have that kind of strength? How did you do it? Alone, without a home—without a nation, in a hostile world and yet you still stayed here to face the Demon Plague. You fought for Tinaria with a valiance I haven't seen anywhere else.

"Broken, in the Barrier Forest, I put you in danger by taking on the Ziamons in that bloody shithole. I never should have made that decision for you. And, yet, even during the carnage of another demonic raid, you still freed your people. You set them free in the deadliest of—in the middle of the most—"

Stumbling over his words under the cracks of thunder, Maxim took a breath and said to her, "I admire you for everything you are in this mad world that doesn't deserve you. I never took the chance to tell you that."

Unable to stand it any further, she moved over to him, took his face, and kissed him passionately on the lips. She squeezed herself into his naked chest and capitulated to his touch. Like the storm, they became one for that eternal now, crashing into each other and driving an electric charge into their hearts. From Predella's window, Eric looked down upon them as they kissed and held each other. He had snuck into her room just minutes before, debating on whether he should kill her for her role in his humiliating exile. In seeing them share something real in the darkest hours, Eric decided to go and leave her be. Even he knew the power of love in the face of wicked spells.

Michael learned from Urik when he was just a child that human beings possess the ability to save and protect all life on the earth. The true problem lied with their sins. There was an overlong struggle between good and evil where they, the only creatures on earth, had to choose. Of angels and demons, they chose every minute—every aspect of life included dire choices. It was not easy for humans to handle such power. Michael was beginning to understand how real the struggle between angel and demon could be for himself.

Predella watched on from the docks as Michael returned with Antonis the Prophet and six Tofauti warriors. The commotion was fierce, as many deemed the prophet a traitor. In Michael's company, others were fast to trust him. There was speculation as to where Michael had gone and how he returned so quickly from the Tofauti border.

She was about to venture into the West, where Von Vanna had raised and trained her when she was young. It was right to say that her past would be her connection to the future. Predella undoubtedly believed that her destiny would be settled at the end of the quest. Regardless of where he was or whom he brought with him to join the mission, she had to trust in Michael. Her life was in his hands.

The warriors proceeded to board the Santa di Mare when Michael had made it back, exhausted, and in Tofauti attire. Predella embraced him with relief, then backing up to look over his armor of yellow and blue. He told her that he would explain everything on the boat and that he was sorry. While some angry Tinarians came to threaten Antonis for his treasonous escape nights back, the throng of Tofauti guards surrounded him and extended their razor spears. Michael had to come and ease the tension before things got worse.

As he did this, Maxim had come with an entourage of elite knights. Soldiers proceeded to board the ship when he asked Michael irritably amid the standoff, "Where were you?"

With others coming to find out that same answer, he said, "I was taken in the night. Antonis and other Tofauti had found me after—when I—"

When it didn't feel right for Michael to tell him in front of the others, he said, "Maxim, I'm tired. It's better if I tell you about it after we're on the ship."

"No, you'll tell me now!" Maxim cried back, distraught about something. Breathing heavily and sweating, Michael realized that Maxim had been through something when he was away.

Seeing that Maxim would not budge, Michael confessed, "I met the Demon Lord—the leader of the others. It tried to get me to join the Demon Plague."

"And did you?" Maxim replied from a place of wariness.

Predella gasped, "Maxim! What are you doing?"

"What?" Michael uttered in shock. "How could you ask me that? You, after everything?"

Shaken by even his own charge against him, Maxim had to say it, "They follow you like you're their master or —"

"Maxim, not here," Michael pleaded with him. "We can talk about this, but not here in the open—"

"They call you their leader!" Maxim said, pointing at his face. "How long have you known?"

Predella stood between them, "Maxim, stop!"

"You said the rains would protect us!" Maxim shouted. "But my friend is dead in stone! In stone, on his knees!"

While they all listened to his manic cry, Kal Era caught up with them, understanding that he had already revealed the truth about Drake's fate. Using his staff, Michael saw the lord for himself, frozen in stone and on his knees, suffocating in the cell Maxim arranged. Before he could admit to seeing his old friend, Antonis interjected, "And you'll find a lineage ring inside his throat."

"Antonis! I don't know where you've been—" Kal tried to condemn his actions, but the prophet interposed again.

"My powers aren't what they were, but even the blind can see it," he exclaimed. "The exiled prince returned to take vengeance on the traitor. He made him swallow the ring just before casting that spell on him, sealing his doom for good."

"This, coming from a hack like you," Maxim said. "They told me about you and your riddles and vague, mystical crap. Now, all of a sudden, you're as direct as they come."

"Prince Eric was in your room, as well, woman." The prophet looked to Predella, disregarding the swordsman's claims.

"Like hell he was," she snapped back.

"He was, but you weren't there. You left, if I'm not too mistaken," Antonis declared, then turning to Michael. "I must say, you may be the only dark magic I'll need from now on. You are like a beacon of dark energy. I'm draining it from you, but it seems like it's an unending well. It's unlimited."

Michael replied in a growl, "You're really not helping my case right now."

"On the contrary, I'm liberating you from what this old relic thinks of you," Antonis proclaimed before them. "Curse any man who dares to call Michael Miuriell the leader of the Demon Plague. He is *our* leader and I'd follow him to hell. He is ready to snuff out every last trace of them and if anyone is going to slow him down, or have doubt in his convictions, then maybe that person shouldn't come along."

Amid the quarrel at the dock, surrounded by hundreds of looming spectators, Maxim neared closer to Michael and said to him, "You and I will finish this on the ship. We have a lot to discuss."

As he turned and proceeded to leave, Maxim turned to Predella and contritely said, "I'm sorry."

Two-thirds of the Ziamon army had ventured into the Santa di Mare when Esker stopped mid-bridge to watch the confrontation unfold. He never set foot in Tinaria before, let alone boarding one of their vessels. With the exception of Tofauti, the Ziamons controlled almost the entire realm before Emperor Ellis V launched the expedition. Named after the emperor's birth name, the new kingdom drove the Ziamons from the shore and pushed them deeper into the east. Esker knew his history well.

He never trusted a Tinarian—especially ones like Maxim Cavallo. Yet, nothing could prevent Esker from what he wanted dead. It could rain fire, but he would finish what he started. Maxim survived the Trials and he vowed to honor the system. To honor the Trials was an act of reverence to his country. Esker's entire voyage would sit on his ability to focus on his true mission. But, if in the heat of battle with man or demon, he didn't plan on saving Maxim if it ever came to that. He would much rather watch him and Predella die by demons than make another pledge to fight as one.

As for Michael, he prayed that Urik was in the Holy City of Falcus. Under Master Urik's guidance, Michael grew from a child to a man who knew his abilities. Harnessing his telekinetic powers, he uncovered the Staff of Truth under

Bard Lake amidst Ellium's secluded caverns. Upon returning from his quest to find it by feeling the article in his soul, Michael knew that Urik was right. He was destined to wield it. No other warrior could have had the power, the will and the good intentions for the staff. Urik vouched for him in Falcus, leading to Michael's entrance into the Kai League—a band of heroes that traveled the western realm in search of peace and justice among the kingdoms.

The queen looked on from the King's Tower pulpit as the spritsails and the fore topsails were already catching wind, blown by the winds of fate. When the crew towed in the anchor cables, the Santa di Mare was free. Michael stood upon the marine's walk at the bowsprit of the ship, letting the wind flow through his hair.

Upon glancing behind him, Michael caught the sight of an omen. Tormenting him long since his solitude on the small boat out in the Great Pacifica, he saw a deep scar over the left eye of one of the crewmembers. It nearly stopped his heart. Running over to her, he tugged the woman's arm and saw her face as she turned to him. Her eyes were blue in her surprise as she looked upon him. No scars at all. She couldn't have been older than twenty.

Realizing his mistake, he let her go and apologized. A graceful girl, she nodded her head and continued with her work. Michael watched as the girl went about her business. When he went to look at the Tinarian shore for the last time, the same girl called out to him. He turned to see her.

With the scar plainly reappearing over her eye, she said over the chatter of the deck, "**We're waiting for you.**"

He rushed over to her in a panic, but she had already turned to ash and blew away in the wind—gone.

The End of Part I

Poetic Intermission

Amidst the sea of courageous hope,
the wind did carry sail and rope.
As one, they embarked, friend and foe,
to challenge an evil born ages ago.

On the vessel was time for understanding—
to break the hate long withstanding.
Over the days, no land in sight,
but angst and fear wrenched in the night.

Miuriell mended wounds of the soul,
while suffering quiet himself took toll.
Crying out in the dark,
dreaming for wife, for son and the evil mark.

By flaming sword, the knight did make
a war with many with nation at stake.
Yet, in light of his newfound mission,
he heeded the call—making new admission.

The archer huntress and liberator of slave
took to the West for the world to save.
What evil conquest the Demon Plague sought,
a greater band of humanity fought.

Thus, berthed a new age army of recompense,
the only hope—the Angels of Resistance.

PART II OF II
PROLOGUE
AN EVIL BEGINNING

During the chaos of war, a thousand years ago, a remarkable evil had awakened in the West. A decade before the end, warlords bent on winning turned to darker and more desperate means for an edge. Secret underground facilities practiced dark magic and performed callous experiments with hopes of creating the first paranormal soldier. The endeavor was called "Project Gambit."

But when there was no real fruit to the experiments, a new idea won the day. It was an idea that scarred the world. A portal to the depths of a sinister realm opened successfully. Despite the backlash, a daring band of scientists uncovered the means to transport profound evil into the world in the hopes of tipping the scale.

By controlling the terrible portal, evil spirits entered the lab. With that incredible feat accomplished, the scientists were prepared to sell their findings. One man, the founder of Project Gambit, realized that his formulas could sustain physical avatars for the demonic spirits. After collaborators turned down his plan countless times, claiming that there wasn't enough time or money, he decided to make some drastic modifications.

Ingesting the imperfect formula, he gambled his life in hopes of becoming the first real prodigy. He was stronger and more powerful, but it came with a price of madness. He brutally murdered everyone who worked for Project Gambit and enslaved his associates, chaining them to his dreams. In command, he and his enslaved assistants finally perfected the portal, discovering the secret means of creating true demons, ready for the stage of war. However, he did not consider what he had truly done. The portal expelled such evil from the nether-dimension that it fed on everyone in the underground lab. The terrible malevolence of the portal killed everyone except for the one man able to withstand the force of the evil charge.

A small stream of blood ran down from one of his nostrils as the evil force within slowly overtook him. In the end, the experiment had failed and without anyone to follow through with the research, Project Gambit was no more. He abandoned the underground facility and permitted it to rot. When warlords searched out their contacts from Project Gambit, they found something worse instead.

His afflicted followers came to call him Abaddon, an angel of torment bent on bringing havoc to humanity. His horrible demonic power became stronger until he could no longer find the man inside the monster. He needed to hunger on suffering. Abaddon killed everything in his path, becoming unstoppable. Warlords fell under his might as he vowed to murder everyone who posed a challenge to his plans.

No army was strong enough to destroy him. When every warlord that had ties to Project Gambit was destroyed, he turned to anything in his path of devastation. He moved things with just his mind and seduced droves of people to perform his bidding. Abaddon fashioned supernatural weapons that only he could wield. He became a force driven to end all war by ending all humanity.

However, on one fateful day, Abaddon chose to wander the valleys and seas, gradually surrendering his path of destruction. No one was sure as to why he chose to stop, but even his indoctrinated apostles, the infamous Omega Cult, faded into ambiguity. His wicked reputation compelled warring nations to band together in the hopes of killing him once and for all. A joint strike obliterated Abaddon in the island of Oron and the Omega Cult died with him.

At last, the half-demon was gone and Project Gambit was lost to the ages. The hellish portal stayed buried under the secret facilities underground. The portal remained closed—its evil contained and subdued. It was only a time after that the apocalyptic asteroid bore down on the planet.

PART II
CHAPTER I
THE ARRIVAL

Days before seeing land on the horizon, a looming storm had pushed the Santa di Mare off course. When the storm had passed, Michael understood that the ship careened further south than even he expected. They were to moor at Falcus's harbor, but it was not to be. The masts were too badly damaged to correct course, resulting in a forced berth somewhere. Feeling it through his staff, Michael realized that Falcus would need to wait for them a bit longer. It would have to be a march north.

Amongst the applause of the crew, having endured a long voyage across the Great Pacifica, Predella came up from behind him and said, "It's been so long. I haven't seen the likes of this place since I was a youngling."

"Since Von Vanna and the Amazons," he replied, trying to keep his composure.

"Yes," she said. "Those times were testing and magical. I only seem to remember the magic. The East made the trials of my early life here seem like a good dream."

Michael lowered his head in worry, "You may not have that same feeling over the next days."

Colonel Aramis then reported to Michael from behind them and called, "It's as you said—off course. We'd like to disembark immediately before we cause the wrong attention out here."

"Granted, colonel. Go to it," Michael declared, scanning the land in his mind. "Predella, give Maxim the word. We're setting our feet on Western soil now. The noon sun beckons that we get started. Our situation has changed."

Michael turned to look at the beach one more time and thought about his chances. His small army of unique warriors would add great power to the Falcun military. As the ship began to unload its warriors onto the beach, Michael felt his powers grow. There was a greater force in the West—a dark energy, as Antonis described it. Something spread out over the realm and it came from Pommel, as he supposed.

Michael focused on Falcus, the holy city, and shut his eyes. His sight traveled across the valleys and plains, across two rivers, between the memorial ruins of the Primeval Tragedy, through the forest and finally into the vast lands of Falcus. He estimated it would take two full days, maybe three to march there on foot. Manna Excallum, his mentor second only to Urik, surely awaited him.

After surveying his four hundred Tinarians form on the shore, Maxim awakened Michael with a pat on the shoulder and said, "Are you ready, friend? We'll need you."

Nodding, Michael embraced his ally and said, "We will need each other, more than you know. Come."

The crew stayed on the ship to repair the vessel in time for the short journey to Falcus. The army couldn't linger about. It was lucky that the Demon Plague never harassed the ship in route for the West. Many called it a good sign, but Michael saw it in a different way. The Demon Lord wanted him to come.

Across an open land of crabgrass, Merchant Pass was a road that led straight to Pommel. The land was home to many merchants and traders who camped along the pass, selling all sorts of things. Pommel claimed the land as their own, as Merchant Pass was built by Pommelian brokers. As of late, the pass belonged to no one. Pommel was dead.

Garvin Kane, known infamously as "Slayer," rode his black steed for Pommel. Armored from head to toe, Kane's helmet was that of a goat's skull with long wavy horns and empty eye sockets from which he peered. A fearsome adversary, Kane lived as a cruel destroyer, once leading the Blackhearts gang. After the Kai League virtually destroyed his faction, Garvin Kane went into hiding. The world had not seen him for well over a year.

His reemergence was not by coincidence. Kane experienced reoccurring dreams that revealed him as a god in Pommel. He believed the dreams to be real omens of things to come. He was sure that his new beginning was but a few miles away, eerily connected to the new demonic kingdom in some way. But he wasn't alone.

Masses of people trekked towards Pommel in hypnotic determination. They walked, like the undead, for the city. It spooked him the closer he came to the place, galloping near some of them. The hordes of travelers hardly noticed him at all, even with his notorious armor. Kane left them alone, finding the mesmerized vagabonds to be no threat. Still, they spooked him, nonetheless.

The closer he came, the more they appeared like moths to the flame. Yet, it wasn't the mindless hordes that disturbed his stallion, inducing it to balk. Dark energy from Pommel had ultimately caused the horse to frighten. It wildly bucked until Kane could no longer stay saddled and fell off hard to the side. The spooked stallion then bolted, racing with all of his weaponry and supplies.

He gathered himself and groaned from behind his helmet, trying to catch his breath after the wind had been knocked out of him. Down the road, he saw Pommel under the darkened sky in the distance. The Shadowland was a demonic refuge in the midst of sunlight. Demons of the night could saunter under the sinister miasma, making Pommel their earthly home.

The crowded road had taken him to the Shadowland, at last, after trudging miles among the spellbound trekkers. In stepping into the darkened land, Kane felt the weight of its evil power in his stomach, breaking also his nerves. After seeing mounds of corpses left to rot, he knew he stepped into hell itself. It looked nothing like Pommel, except for the tower bastion of the city. Everything else was in ruins.

Word spread of a demonic army, slaughtering anyone who invaded their province. The Merrier legions of five thousand soldiers were massacred in a day after trying to avenge their neighboring Pommelians. Merrieu suffered a plague of some kind, affecting people with madness. Their attempt to defeat the demonic army ended in utter failure. Only two men escaped to report of the bloodbath in its entirety. Eventually, they, too, succumbed to the madness and went to Pommel on their own accord. It was anyone's guess as to what happened to them.

There were no merchants or traders anywhere near the city. Instead, endless corpses lined the road, stuck onto tall spikes. The sight was profane, even for him. Any force that flaunted the deaths of children was either mad or of pure evil. Walking the remainder of the trail was intolerable. However, he wanted his glory, as promised. Kane would do anything for that. Hence, he endured the awful scenery. The others walking on with him were unfazed by the grisly surroundings.

When it seemed that he had reached his final destination, a large gate remained open before him and hundreds of deceased soldiers laid all over the field. Merrier flags and banners were left forsaken all about. Still advancing towards the gate, Kane collected a sword and ax from fallen knights and headed for the undead guards at the main doors.

They had no faces under the hoods—only emptiness. Their hands were of bare bone, like the skeletons in the heaps scattered about the field. They silently escorted him towards the tower bastion at the end of the village. Like in his dreams, they courted him as a king. Garvin Kane was chosen, as he predicted.

Inside the demonic castle, the highest court chamber held the Demon Lord's newly acquired throne. Sattka sat to his left. Valkris, the leader of the Five Generals, sat to his right. A spared Pommelian wearing a flyer demon's bleached skull bowed to the Demon Lord in honor of his advancement. Then, like the mindless lot he traveled with, the conditioned soldier left the hall without saying a word.

The dark room was silent with only a few shadow demons lurking about. The Demon Lord, in his true form, basked in the baleful aura around him. Appearing as some sort of phantasm, the lord said, "**The sunlight general has come at last. It is good that you obey your dreams—the rein to your soul's desires.**"

"**Our sorcerer is hiding among us,**" Sattka sensed.

The Demon Lord said, "**That human will join us after Kane reveals himself to me.**"

Kane's heavy blade shook fretfully in his trembling hands. His gauntlets could not stay still, no matter how hard he tried. Speechless, he refused to walk any closer to them. Finding the turn of events interesting, the great demon shut the arduous doors behind the warrior, prompting him to gasp. In an uncontrollable sensation of fear, Kane lost his grip on the blades and lazily dropped them. He fell onto his knee, trying to grasp reality.

"**What good are these monkeys if they keep their annoying faculties?**" Valkris growled, summoning shadow demons to corral him. The demons eerily rose from the darkness, thirsting for Kane's blood. Two manifested from the floor, while another arose from Kane's own shadow behind him. Feeling it was a trap, he sprung up like a cornered rat.

Kane swiftly picked up his heavy broadsword and swung it for the shadow demon's head. The creature was quick and evaded his strike altogether. Countering the attack, it slashed his enforced armor and vigorously pounced on him. Kane launched the beast far behind him by way of his legs. The initial strike by the demon's claws left residual gash marks on his armor.

The next two shadow demons could not wait to tear him limb from limb. The beast to his left struck first with a fast leap onto his chest, like a feral cat. He embraced the blow and tried to pull it off, but its grip was vigorous. The other two were eager to join in. Kane was helpless to combat the three demons with all of his heavy armor wearing him down. Despite his mail's fortitude, one of the monsters was able to lodge its claws into his upper side. As a reflex, Kane shoved it off and cut its torso straight down the middle, causing it to shriek.

He evaded the nearest demon's bite and swung around to clout the creature with his blade. His swing was forceful enough to propel the creature into the air before crashing onto the floor, dead. Behind him, a shadow demon swiped his ankle and tripped him flat onto his back. When the demon thought it had him for sure, Kane instantly gathered his bearings and slammed the sword's pommel into its face. When it was stunned, he twirled the broadsword upside down and stabbed the creature into its scrawny jugular.

Kane regained his form, pulled the blade out and then offered it a final blow while on his right knee. The last demon slashed the left side of his skull helmet. In no time, he released all of his rage and charged the demon like a hellish beast himself. He collided with the scoundrel and viciously chopped it to mulch in a fiery fury. He cried ferociously as he mutilated his nefarious foe.

With his heavy, animalistic breaths, Kane was too primed for combat to fear anyone or anything any longer. He peered around the cursed room for any other challengers. With demon blood running down his helmet and gauntlets, Kane heard the awkward sound of laughter. As it was, the Demon Lord found it equitable to show himself to his new sunlight general, abandoning the phantom veil.

His entire body seemed mechanical. There was hardly any skin showing through at all. His black helmet concealed his cranium and the top of his head. For his face, a large visor filled in the helmet, leaving a sizable slit for his demonic, green glowing eyes to shine through. An eerie horn erected from the front of the helmet and two other ones, which seemed to be sharper and more rigid, sprawled out from the rear like acute rabbit ears. His body armor was crude and even more intimidating. Blades, spines, and spikes were scattered all over his mail.

The brawl compelled him to speak, "**Impressive. I would have expected no less from you.**"

Garvin Kane, exhausted and confounded, responded in deep, unsettling breaths, "What are you? Have I stepped into the gates of hell or what?"

"**You have done just that, General Kane. But it was your will alone that has brought you to this place. You know that your destiny lies here,**" the Demon Lord said in his sinister voice.

Sattka attacked his pride from her seat, "**Kneel before your master!**"

Kane quickly kneeled, muttering, "What the—"

The Demon Lord declared chillingly, "**We are the new inhabitants of this lowly planet. For a thousand of your years, we have longed for this time. Our age has come** and mankind must submit to their inescapable destruction, for it is the eve of their holocaust."

"Then why the dreams?" Kane said still on the ground, "Why me? I'm a human."

"**Until our father is unleashed, our powers are inadequate. As a result of this, your sword is what I desire. You will lead two thousand and thirteen human soldiers under the sun to serve as the conquest's daylight fighting force. Your obligations will begin at once,**" the Demon Lord pronounced.

"Where are these soldiers? They live here among you?" Kane retorted.

"**No human possesses the claim to exist amongst us unless I see it fit,**" the Demon Lord growled. "**They are all stationed beyond the forests of these lands. They wait unweariyingly for my instruction. More flock to our refuge every day, as you've already seen.**"

He then asked his new master, "Oh, I've seen. They look like fuckin' zombies. If I'm gonna lead those zealots, I'd like to know what the hell I'm leading them to do."

Valkris interjected sardonically, "**So many questions.**"

The Demon Lord answered, "**Your dreams were not a farce. You will become the most celebrated man on the face of the earth. And, as an indispensable gift for satisfying your dreams, Sattka, my daughter, shall grant you regeneration.**"

"Regeneration! I would be invincible?" Kane realized that he made the most important decision of his life by joining the ranks of the Demon Plague.

Sattka griped, "**No human deserves this.**"

Valkris scornfully sparked Sattka's attention, "**You defy your father.**"

Hearing this, Sattka was willing to tear off Valkris's head and throw it to a horde of shadow demons to pick at.

Her hate for him was uncanny. Because the Demon Lord instated him before his own daughter, Sattka was naturally defiant.

"This is for the conquest—nothing more," she snarled as she rose from her seat and ambled over to the kneeling Kane. When the Demon Lord permitted him to rise, he did and left his sword at his feet. Sattka neared closer to him and, candidly, scared him half to death. Seeing her up close and too personal resulted in the shrinking of his bold stature. She removed his helmet and vigorously kissed him on the mouth, inserting her long, vile tongue. Kane gagged.

When she finished with him, she pulled her lips away from his and started back for her seat. Kane, petrified from what had just happened, felt something change within him. It was a rush of power flowing through his veins. Even his heart beat differently. He was much stronger than before.

"I feel—new," Kane said, clenching his armed fists.

"Would you like to test your new skill?" the Demon Lord said.

Before Kane could predict it, a shadow demon dropped from the emptiness of the ceiling. Without his helmet to ward off the demon's deadly incisors, the creature chewed into his throat as he gurgled in terror and agony. In seconds, he fell to the ground and died. The Demon Lord shooed off the beast with his hand and it vanished into the shadows below. As Kane lay dead, his blood spewing, Valkris laughed.

However, within seconds, he opened his eyes and inhaled, like fish craving water to breath. He pushed himself off the blood-sodden floor and held his mutilated throat. Gasping in anguish, the wicked gashes instantly closed up and healed. His wound was gone without a scar to show for it. Blood remained on his chin, neck, and armor, but his fatal wound disappeared.

He stared at his blood all over the ground and swiftly picked up his blade, screaming vehemently, "What, in the fuck, happened to me?"

"**Welcome to your new life, general,**" the Demon Lord said.

Kane did not hold his wrath, yelling, "What was *that*?"

"**You are no longer an ordinary human being. You are one of us now. Yet, your new skill comes with a cost. Whenever you regenerate, you become ever more demonic. A small wound on your finger would suffice. Your regeneration will bring you closer to our kind. Abuse your powers and you will become one of us. It is the binding to our covenant,**" the Demon Lord declared from his seat.

Kane was speechless. He was aware that his destiny would lead him to great and supernatural powers, but he could not bear the demon within him for long. He vowed to conduct battle with caution. Kane felt as if he sold his soul.

"**You asked me a question,**" the lord said. "**You shall serve as our sunlight general, leading your minions to overrun Falcus. That is where Miuriell is headed. That is where you will focus your strength. You'll represent us until the sky is shrouded in blackness.**"

"And what then, after I'm of no use to you?" Kane said.

The Demon Lord leaned in to say, "**Even the best slug is just a slug—but the last slug is most precious.**"

PART II
CHAPTER II
THE MADNESS

Michael climbed to the top of the dune valley until the beach was behind him and the green, lush planes were as far as his naked eye could see. The comforting breeze rushed from behind him and lifted his cape. He welcomed the feeling. The landscape was breathtaking. Michael knew that they would need to venture northwest until they reached the course for Falcus.

Maxim awed at the splendor of the land, "I have not seen such beauty for a long time. I have almost forgotten."

Michael replied, "In the night, it may not be as beautiful as you remember."

As for Aramis, he saw beyond the beauty of the landscape and remembered why he was there. The Ziamon colonel believed that his journey could have easily been a death sentence among his rivals. Thus, he barked, "Are we going to stand and look at grass all day or are we going to start off?"

"To Falcus, then?" Antonis said.

"They are expecting us there. I can only imagine what horrors have happened here at sundown," Michael said as he looked to the northwest. With the ramblings of the Ziamons behind them, the starting army began their march. If they were going to be serious about ridding the world of the Demon Plague, the quest would need to set out immediately. Michael lifted his staff into the cool air. As everyone saw him do this, the word was past and it was time to begin their march for the Holy City of Falcus.

As one long horde over eight hundred strong, they trekked up the dunes and started down the plains in route for the first river that they had to cross. Tinarians marched on the right side and Ziamons on the left, separated in the center by fifteen feet so as not to instigate trouble. Michael, walking front and center, knew the land like the back of his hand. The Plan River, the thinnest in the Western Hemisphere, was the gateway to the middle country. The Rehab Brotherhood, a team of thieves and outcasts, ruled most of the waterway.

The band of warriors hiked for two hours before they saw an odd occurrence. Scattered about the plains, scores of wanderers paraded south. With blank stares and lethargic movement, the drifters seemed to acknowledge nothing. None carried supplies or food, just the clothes on their backs. Then, more came down the path. They all migrated for the south, unwaveringly. As they headed towards them, Predella asked, "What's happening? What are all these people doing?"

"It's eerie," Antonis said. "They're drawn to something. It's as if they lost their sense of will."

A few strewn migrants had headed for them, as if an army wasn't there blocking their path. Michael walked ahead of the others to get a closer look at them. Each that passed by, stared him down. He couldn't understand it, but they broke away just enough to look at him, bending their necks. Still, it didn't sway them from their unnerving migration.

Trying to wake one of them from their weird stupor, Esker broke from his line and nudged him from his absorbed spells. The man stopped and gradually turned to look upon his aggressor's face. Sluggishly, he analyzed Esker before scaling the ground for a weapon. In finding a rock, he quickly charged with it to break Esker's skull, screaming.

Before the man could even try to hurt the justice, one of Esker's soldiers came up to punch him in the face. The strike put him into the grass, knocking him out. Michael heard the commotion behind him as other entranced drifters passed him by, gawking. Another Ziamon cried out, "They're cattle!"

"Where are they going, Michael?" Maxim cried out, then shouting louder when he didn't respond, "Michael!"

He shook loose from the disturbing trance of mindless drifters and used his staff to track where they were all going. Traversing the landscape south, Michael finally saw what he already knew to be true. Droves of them helplessly walked all the way to Pommel, shrouded in the Demon Plague's sinister aura. Just seeing his home consumed by pure evil was enough to push Michael out from his revelation.

The evil feeling lingered in his heart, making him fall to his knee and groan in pain. Tinarians came to his aid when Antonis walked closer and said, "It's Pommel, isn't it? That's where they're all going. But why?"

"We need to move," Michael replied, disturbed. "We have to get to Falcus on time. They'll have answers we need."

After another hour of marching north, they reached a valley bearing a sign that read: *Plan River up ahead*. As they moved down the valley to meet another trail, they saw a caravan of travelers and a dozen hermits walking northwest, following the road to the Plan River.

"What is this?" Aramis blurted out as Michael gave the signal to slow down. "More crazies."

"An exodus," Michael said. "They're headed in the right direction this time—away from Pommel."

"We're going to meet them one way or another," Maxim declared.

As Michael mulled it over, one of the hermits saw him and his standing army. Without hesitation or doubt, the man cried out in jubilation, "Michael Miuriell! It is Michael Miuriell! He has returned!"

Others shouted in praise, "He's come to save us!"

If a posse of hermits could identify Michael in the distance, he was as renowned as he claimed. A small group of men came running up the hill for him and the caravan stopped in its tracks. As their families waited for their return, the men climbed the hill in honor of the powerful peacemaker. His army prepared to draw their weapons in any case. After seeing his legion of foreigners, the men knelt on the grass and thanked him for returning. One cried, "We thought you were dead! Have you come to rescue us from this evil?"

"Where are you coming from, my friend?" Michael asked, pressing him to stand.

He said, "We're from Merrieu, but most of us worked at Merchant Pass. The evil there is too great and it's consuming everything! Our crops have failed and our livestock has gone mad! Even people, our families, have gone mad. We had no choice but to leave and seek salvation elsewhere."

"Where are you all going?" Michael asked them.

Another answered in heavy, arrhythmic breaths, "As far away from Pommel and Merrieu as possible! We will go anywhere!"

"What happened to Merrieu?"

"The army was mashed to bits in one day! Thousands of warriors—dead!" the same man replied. "In retaliation for Pommel's destruction, the Merrier sent hundreds of their knights to avenge your people! In a day—gone! After that, people started to lose their minds, screaming and convulsing in the night. After a few days of it, they just started to leave. They just left for Pommel. More and more of us fell to the madness."

"God save us!" Maxim couldn't believe what he heard.

"The madness is spreading!" another man exclaimed. "Haven't you seen them all walking south, programmed? It's happening everywhere!"

"Have any of you seen these demons for yourselves?" Antonis asked.

"Never," he said. "They don't come out from under that dark swirling cloud over Pommel. Whatever they are, they stay in there, just collecting people."

Michael realized that the Demon Plague had already established a reputation. What was shocking to him, however, was that they didn't invade kingdoms nearby. Something else was happening. The Demon Plague remained idle as if waiting for something. A hermit then beseeched Michael, "Can we please come with you? We dread the night!"

Michael considered the situation, as well as the time of day. Looking behind him, he considered the Ziamon army and their reluctance for company. He then considered his own connection to the Demon Plague. Michael couldn't drag more innocent people into his midst.

A Ziamon officer exclaimed from behind, "Can we move along? The day is wasting!"

"Shut your mouth," Maxim snapped, inciting others to grumble in Espanion. Tinarian knights started up after.

Esker came up closer to him, "You'd be wise to keep to your own, Red Menace. You wouldn't want a bloody—"

"Don't even try it. Just leash your dogs," Maxim said.

As he tried listening to the refugees, Michael only had to raise his hand and the two warriors silenced their feud. It wouldn't be the first time, but he was never going to tolerate any bickering amongst his army. When Maxim and Esker had stopped without question, Michael continued, "You can come with us, but we can't claim responsibility for your caravan."

The men agreed and ran back to their convoy. They waited until Michael and his army passed by, then followed closely behind. Advancing to the Plan River, Maxim jogged to Michael's side and said, "Michael, we were not prepared to march to Falcus. Speaking for our whole force, we only have enough rations for tonight and maybe tomorrow. After that, each individual soldier will have to go without."

"I know," Michael answered. "There's a small village near the river. We'll see if they can contribute something for the remainder of our trip."

Maxim declared, "Fair enough. Nobody is complaining."

Michael replied, "I couldn't blame anyone, though. It is not an ideal thing to do—to trudge through open land with a Demon Plague waiting in the night. You know I'll have to go and rest in another place, apart from the army. I can't chance it. They follow me—watching me even now."

"Tell me more," Maxim sighed. "We'll get through it."

Various onlookers praised Michael and his army of diverse warriors. They marched towards the holy city and everyone knew why. The spectators bowed their heads, waved and cheered. Eventually, there were fewer drifters stricken with the madness. As a ripple effect, it became clear that the Demon Plague's influence had not reached this far. But, as the refugees suggested, the madness was spreading like an airborne virus.

The Plan River was a worthy sight after a long trek. A large number of displaced families from the south had settled by the river village of Shopville. Seeing that room there was scarce, Michael suggested that they, at least, cross the Plan's bridge and set camp on the north side. Tinarians and their Ziamon counterparts made fast work of it. Again, scores of desperate people had come nearer to see Michael's return.

To prevent the masses from coming too close to the encampment, he went out and met them by the village. They surrounded him from all sides, touching his flesh and armor. He eased their hearts and heard their stories as his army set camp. They all watched Michael from afar, taken aback by his redeeming influence. Because they believed in him, the many people sent cartloads of food and medical supplies that any could spare for his army. Michael, then, remained with them.

By the time the night finally arrived, everyone had food in their belly, including Antonis's Tofauti guardians. Ziamons took turns singing old national songs in unison. Michael had not allowed alcohol consumption until they reached Falcus. But he had abandoned the campsite before night fell, trying to keep his allies out of harm's way. If the Demon Plague did indeed try an assault, they wouldn't have anyone to kill but himself.

As he slept in the dead of night, Michael awoke and felt a tugging in his heart. In checking his nostrils for blood, he found nothing. Coming out of his tent with the Staff of Truth, Michael found Valkris standing over the quenched campfire, awaiting his presence. There were no demons about the camp and none a mile up the river. Having scooped up a clawful of embers, glowing faintly in the dark, Valkris said, **"I've always wondered how savvy all your monkeys would be without fire. Perhaps controlling this element was the catalyst that set them apart from the other animals? Perhaps without it, they'd all be less—human."**

Cautious and wrathful, Michael obliged the demon's invitation and stood before him, saying, "What do you want from me?"

Valkris turned his glowing yellow eyes for him and replied, **"I offer you one last chance in the promise that maybe not all your sycophants may suffer."**

Unsettled, Michael retorted, "What have you done with the princess? What do you want with her?"

"Because you have lost your way, we have grown impatient. Abandon this misguided campaign of yours. It will only lead to the deaths of those you love," Valkris declared, dropping the ash from his claw. **"Including your princess, if need be."**

Staring back into the demon's eyes, Michael said, "As I told your puppet master, I'll do no such thing."

Valkris frowned, riposting, "**Then you have forsaken your true self. Let this be a warning, Miuriell. The next time night falls, so shall everything fall with it.**"

When Valkris teleported back to Pommel via his Seltek, Michael looked over the quiet campsite and sighed in angst. He wasn't able to get anywhere on Princess Shina's condition or reason for her capture. There was no guarantee that he'd get the chance again.

In the new morning, bands of soldiers washed by the river and equipped themselves for another trek north. The second day's journey began as the army traveled into the forest, following the road for Falcus. Ghost Thruway was a wide enough road for multiple carriages to take through the woodland. The journey proved to be an easy one until they came upon Rambler's Haberdashery. The large trade hut was in ruins. Michael held up the march to let Maxim and Predella investigate.

As they both approached the devastated hut, things already did not seem to appear normal. Windows were smashed outward and the main door remained opened and thrashed. The left side of the hut's foundation was destroyed. They walked carefully toward the front door when a man rushed out, screaming incoherent ramblings, and attempted to fire a loaded firearm.

Before the frantic assailant could pull the trigger, Predella charged her bow and shot an arrow into the man's hand, forcing him to drop the shotgun and fall to the ground in pain. Maxim dashed for the wounded assailant and detained him, ordering others to come out and identify themselves. While the aggressor cried in agony and trepidation, six others came out from the hut with hands up.

"Try me and see what happens!" Maxim shouted.

One of the men answered hesitantly in Christian, "He thought you one of those—things! He tried protecting us!"

"Protect you from what?" Predella pressed, aiming her arrow for them.

The same man said, "From the dragon lady."

His wife said in desperation, "We all thought you were her servants! Please forgive him!"

Maxim looked to Predella and shared the same bewilderment. After five long minutes of interrogation, they reported their findings to Michael. The haberdashery was attacked by a woman who appeared innocent at first, but in the night, transformed into a demonic creature and lashed out. Demons then infiltrated the shop and tried to take her. When she fled, the demons disappeared.

"How can that be?" Antonis uttered. "How could those things travel anywhere without you, Michael?"

Thinking aloud, he said, "I have no idea. There must be something I'm missing—something about that woman."

Maxim reported, "They told us she was young, pale and had red hair. That sounds a lot like Shina."

"It does," Michael said. "What else?"

Predella gave Michael the man's gun he almost used against them. He held it in his hand and then said, "This is one of Ellium's shotguns. They never sell their firearms, as I'm sure you know. This could have put a hole clean through you both, back-to-back."

"Shina may have escaped," Antonis announced from his place behind them. "Yes, she escaped Pommel, somehow."

"How can you be sure?" Maxim gasped.

"I see her running—fleeing for her life." Antonis looked straight out for the woods, glaring beyond the forest. "God is she fast!"

Maxim proclaimed, "There's no way she'd escape from them, is there? I mean, we've seen what we're up against. We're saying Shina got away from them, alone?"

Predella added, "They said the girl ran into the forest."

Then, Colonel Aramis approached the group and said, "I think we should start moving."

Michael returned the rifle to Predella and said, "I think you're right. We need to move on. Keep your eyes peeled. We may be heading into some questionable territory."

Marching forth with Shina on his mind, Maxim joined Antonis and asked him, "Any other signs of the princess you'd care to share?"

"Not that I can see," the prophet returned, biting into a fruit. "Nothing comes to me."

Finding little sympathy in his answer, Maxim grabbed his wrist and said, "Maybe you should look a little harder."

The razor tip of a spear came just inches by Maxim's throat, compelling him to grasp the shaft of it in shock. One of the Tofauti guardians stood firm and ready to split open his neck. Antonis then said, "Next time you wish to threaten me, remember that."

"Hold here for a moment," Michael raised his staff and stopped at a fork in the road. The Ghost Thruway curved for the west, where it then ran eighteen miles out. A straight run up north through the Ghost Forest saved time and mileage but proved to be a treacherous hike. He asked the main officers to his army about which route they were willing to take. They mulled it over for a few minutes before they all agreed to take the risky shortcut by way of the forest trail.

The party walked into the woodlands where most would never venture. Michael urged that the trailing caravan take the thruway and not follow them no matter what. There were dangerous clans of thieves and killers in waiting.

The Amazon women who lived in and about the Ghost Forest established a truce with the ninja clans there. The specifics were not known, but the two forces had not fought in years of living together. Michael's relationship with the Amazon women was agreeable, as he was one of the only men they ever allowed within their province. Predella, as a youth, lived with the Amazons when Von Vanna returned to Oron for his residency. Each sage honored their commitment to remain on the island for four months out of the year while the others trained their pupils.

The Eastern warriors, trained to fight in forests, never preferred situations where they were vulnerable. As their march proceeded into the afternoon hours, the first appearance of Amazons surprised them. From the brush, a lone Amazon girl aimed her bow and cried out like a rebel. Two others shouted the same from parallel perches hidden amongst the trees.

"You've got to be kidding me," Aramis scoffed.

"This hide and seek shit is ill-timed," Maxim groaned. "I assume these are the Amazons you were talking about?"

"They are indeed," Michael raised his hand to halt the party's march, then addressing the Amazon scouts. "There's really no need for that sort of reception. You know you can't hide from me."

"It's protocol," the woman replied, clad in light armor. "We heard you were dead."

"Well, I'm not dead," Michael replied with hundreds of soldiers in tow, "but we could use your help to keep that up. Will Kyra Tal let us proceed?"

The same woman snickered before saying, "With all those men? Unlikely. You know that."

"There's worse things than men out here now if you haven't heard. I think, under the current circumstances, Tal will see me," Michael insisted.

Predella interceded, "We're just passing through."

Then, from the same brush, Kyra Tal, leader of the Amazons for decades, revealed herself. Maxim remembered the Amazons when he was younger. He never knew any of them personally, because Malcusin advised him, wisely, to maintain his distance. She would not recognize Maxim, but Predella, Kyra Tal could never forget.

"Predella? Can it really be you?" Kyra Tal proclaimed. "They told me it was you. I almost didn't believe it."

"You remember me, after all these years?" she replied blissfully. "I was so young then."

Kyra Tal came over and embraced her tightly, passing Michael in the process. The women had been tracking the army's movements since they entered the density of the Ghost Forest. Kyra kissed her on the forehead and said, "We knew you'd come back, whether by fate or something else."

"I'm afraid this is the something else," Predella said.

Kyra then turned to Michael, saying, "We thought you were dead."

"Many have died, Kyra," Michael said. "These brave warriors of the East have joined me on a quest to stop the Demon Plague. We must go on to Falcus."

"We owe you one—more than one." She looked over his army. "If you vouch for these foreigners, then they can stay for the night if need be. It'll be dark before you're out of our forest."

"The longer we wait, the stronger they become," Michael affirmed. "Even now, their influence spans beyond the Plan. Scores of cursed drifters trudge mindlessly for Pommel."

Antonis added, "They're recruiting cultists for sacrifices. It could be anything like that."

Kyra said, "The Demon Plague is a good name for it. We've been safe here for some time until a girl possessed by the dark spirits of Pommel came running into our province. I was going to ask you to take a look at her. We've had her locked up in a cell for two days and even that can barely hold the girl in the night."

"Did she give you a name?" Maxim felt his heart drop.

Kyra answered him, "Shina—called herself a princess from an eastern kingdom."

"Tinaria," Predella said in shock. "She is his princess."

"I must see her," Maxim uttered in a trance.

Antonis gasped, "She *did* escape. Extraordinary."

From behind Michael, Aramis had marched ahead of his men to say heatedly in Christian, "We are not setting camp here in this place—this vagina sanctuary!"

Before anyone could respond, Michael turned back and looked over his army. He was aware of their loyalty to him and the mission, as brutish and crude as they came. He replied, "We have no choice but to camp here tonight. Our situation has changed."

"Ugly man," Kyra started on the Ziamon colonel, "we're permitting you and your army of men into our ranks. This is a rare and profane act, but I am honoring you as guests. You are welcome to camp outside our dominion, if it makes you any more comfortable, as long as you don't mind contending with rogue ninja clans content on raiding your divisions in the night. There's a shortage of vaginas out there."

Predella had to smile after Kyra was finished. Aramis, after a gawky pause, reposted, "We concede only to Miuriell's leadership."

Finally, Michael announced, "Then I guess it's settled."

The party followed Kyra Tal and her Amazon scouts back to their base deeper within the forest where Shina was kept. As the afternoon dragged on, Michael felt the presence of dark forces waiting for him to reunite with the princess.

PART II
CHAPTER III
THE DRAGON LADY

The Demon Lord peered out from the large windowpane on the highest level of the castle's keep, broken open during the invasion weeks ago. His evil cursed the air he breathed and his eyesight was omnipresent. Releasing Shina back into the world had promising results, connecting her with Michael as new and improved royalty.

He sat into his throne and summoned Garvin Kane to the hall. He predicted the daylight sorcerer to arrive in minutes. While they waited for Kane to arrive, a blinding light appeared from the center of the room. The scrawny demons about the chambers scurried away, vanishing into the comfort of the shadows. Valkris found the abnormal light trying. Unlike his master, he did not know the light's origins. The Demon Lord accepted the impressive entrance of the sorcerer and welcomed the magician's superior strength. For a human, the enchantment was remarkable.

On cue, Prince Eric Orgento revealed himself from the comfort of the shadows. He hardly seemed any different from when he lived in the East. His hair was long and white and still sustained his easy scowl. His only difference was his grim attire, retrieved from the Kajhic Ruins before teleporting to the West. Coveted in a dark purple cape, his hood hung sluggishly from his back. He was equipped well with a taut mail that concealed his entire torso in black.

Valkris smirked, "**The brother. Are you sure you are ready to fight for the right side?**"

"Save your comments for someone who can stand your voice, demon. You killed my people," Eric rebuked heatedly.

Valkris retorted, "**You were supposed to keep her close for easy extraction. Instead, you made it very difficult. And for what? We came to take her anyway.**"

"Only to lose her again," Eric countered.

As Valkris laughed uncontrollably, hearing Eric's ignorant response, the Demon Lord felt obliged to speak, "**One must first be willing to lose the bait in order to snag the significant catch. We don't have an interest in her alone. The conquest requires them both.**"

Eric could not understand the Demon Lord's chilling intentions. Awarded superior sorcery overnight, his magic core burned for release. It hardly made him feel human. Like Kane, his dreams came in three consecutive nights. Eric saw himself feared and exalted as the most powerful sorcerer in the world.

He retained the one ability that no demon was conscious of: The Mimican Essent. The slick spell of mimicry was never in the demonic arsenal of magic tricks. Eric knew this, for he was determined to sustain the secret from his new lord. Sadly, it was the only spell that he ever learned himself. It was the only spell that he mastered on his own.

"Where is my sister?" Eric ground his teeth, beginning to feel overpowered by the malevolence in his company.

The Demon Lord replied, "**She has run into a forest of women where Miuriell has discovered her.**"

Smothering a sweltering rage, Eric snarled, "Well, last I recall, you promised she'd be here."

"**Your sister's powers are greater than you know,**" the Demon Lord rejoined. "**In the dead of night, her true powers emerge. The longer we leave her out in the water, the more her spirit festers. As a seed—**"

"But you promised she'd be *here*!" Eric cried out.

After his outburst, Tenebrion materialized out of balls of smoke and light, unfurling his whip, Malevolence. From behind Eric, Scythian came into form, bearing its scythe. In seeing he was not in a position to petition, Eric said listlessly, "What do you want of me?"

"**That's more like it,**" Valkris grinned.

Sattka then brought Kane into the throne room. The new sunlight general barked as he walked closer to Eric, "Who is this loss? This is your sorcerer?"

Immediately, Eric looked to the Demon Lord and said, "What is the meaning of this? Who is that dupe?"

The Demon Lord answered freely, "**He is Garvin Kane, our sunlight general. You will operate under his command.**"

Eric hissed while vigorously clenching his fists, "Funny, you said I'd never have to take orders from any man."

"But you will take orders from me," Kane said proudly before briefly kneeling to the Demon Lord.

"Which proves that you are not one?" Eric became flustered and looked through Kane's rough skin.

"That's right," Kane rebuked. "Unlike you, I've become immortal. Your magic tricks won't work on me."

"They'll work on everything and everyone," he quickly retorted. "Including fleas like you."

Kane cried, "Care to try me?"

"I don't do exhibitions," Eric snarled. "You'll see it when the time comes."

Impressed with Eric's restraint of his magical gifts, the Demon Lord said, "**Keep the fire blazing in your hearts. The conquest may require your services as early as tomorrow. If Miuriell defies us again—if they reach Falcus, you will assault the city.**"

Eric protested firmly, "You can expect him to defy you and I don't want her to be touched by your demons. I'll take her during the attack on Falcus! All this just to see what she'll become? Why risk her safety?"

Sattka countered, "**Your sweet little sister is not so sweet anymore.**"

"She's come to be quite enlightened out there on her own," the Demon Lord said. "**Understand, boy, Shina is more than just blood to you. When we're done, she shall reign over you. You remember that in our covenant?**"

Eric had felt defeated in some ways, but triumphant in others. He embraced the superiority of magic bestowed to him, living his dream. He followed Sattka to his quarters and left Garvin Kane there on the floor, watching him closely as he went. When the she-demon opened the door to his chambers, Eric stepped inside and succumbed to a vision.

Eric felt as if he was a member of the Waasi Tribe when the fire dragon unleashed its rage over the settlements. The firestorm was like the apocalypse, as he could feel the heat of the inferno on his face. He watched innocent people burn away to nothingness under the wrath of the fireball from the sky. In just moments, the Waasi fell victim to the mystical genocide. Eric then watched the aftermath from a sky view, spotting scorched bodies strewed all about the encampment.

Eric pulled away from the vision using his magical aptitudes. In that short time, he found himself in tears, sweating. His chambers reverted to its normal state as if nothing had ever happened. Holding the doorframe to his chambers in case he collapsed, he gasped, "What was that?"

The cause of the destruction of the Waasi Tribe was, as Predella claimed, a fireball from the heavens. Eric saw the awesome beast that dealt it as if he was there. Sattka said, "**I wouldn't worry, prince. The visions will subside soon. Flashbacks of your covenant with us will come and go, I'm afraid.**"

Eric asked in a poor whisper, holding his heart, "What are you talking about, demon?"

She continued, "**Reknit Drakkat: the casting of the Reaper Dragon. Only the most capable of sorcerers could summon such a lethal creature. Our covenant required a sacrifice and you provided a crater of lives. The greater the sacrifice—the greater the covenant.**"

Fashioning the most exaggerated smirk on her inhuman face, Sattka leaned in closer, saying into his ear, "**Remember that last dream, the one where you woke up with your newfound powers? I know you can remember at least that. Consider that a promise fulfilled.**"

When she pulled away and left him in the doorway to his quarters, Eric finally realized his crimes. There was no one alive who could have defended themselves against that spell—just as there was no one else alive who could have cast it. He thought it was all a dream, but the price for all his magic was heavy, drenched in blood. Weak in the knees, Eric lumbered into his room and shut the door. Aside from learning that he was a mass murderer, he found proof that Predella had been telling the truth about her people's destruction.

Night had fallen in the Ghost Forest. As the reluctant Ziamons set camp in the specified perimeter of the Amazon's province, Kyra Tal escorted Michael and Maxim up to the tree quarters to see Princess Shina. Predella and some of her old friends started a campfire while the crickets sang. The camp was extensive, hosting multiple complexes that rose into the trees and connected to each other with bridges and ropes.

Kyra, upon reaching the hard-wooden door of the fire-resistant prison house high above the camp, warned them about the girl's outbursts and superhuman strength during the night. Hesitantly, she opened the door. The two men walked in and saw a row of cells sprawling the tree prison. One of the cells, all the way in the back, seemed to alight by a torch on the wall. Kyra closed the door behind them and insisted that they follow closely behind.

Reaching the cell, a warm bed was set in the far corner, a seeing window in the back, and a mirror on the wall. Shina was squatting peacefully in the center of the cell with her back facing the bars. Her wrists were shackled to her ankles, connected by chains.

"Princess?" Maxim uttered hesitantly.

As Michael held tightly to one of the bars, she propped up swiftly, turned around and revealed her face bursting with relief. She was jovial to discover that her heroes had found her, regardless of all the hell she had endured.

"Maxim! Oh, God!" Shina crawled up to the cell bars and touched them on the face and hands to prove she wasn't dreaming. "You've all come! You came for me!"

Maxim said with emerging tears, "Of course, Shina."

"How are we feeling, princess?" Kyra Tal asked her.

She didn't answer, for her joy had overwhelmed her senses. But, with the night upon them, Michael needed to speak fast. He asked Kyra to open the cell so that they could enter. She agreed but warned them that if she transformed again, they would be left to die inside.

She opened the cell gate and they entered, embracing Shina compassionately. Her skin was sweltering. Losing her happiness in an instant, she said to them, "I can tell you things that will make you sick."

Taking a moment before he responded, Michael said in return, "Nothing will surprise me. I'm so sorry for not being able to protect you. I failed, but we're here now. You're safe with us."

Shina sat on the bed with Maxim pulling up right beside her, holding her hand, asking, "Shina, how did you escape?"

She answered him after swallowing her angst, "I met all of the demons who are in control of Pommel. They sacrifice a person every night and torture people. But they treated me like a queen. Demons delivered food to my door and vampire women bathed me. The Demon Lord spoke to me one night about my 'true' destiny with them."

"Destiny?" Maxim uttered in dismay. "What destiny could you possibly have with those monsters?"

Shina held her mouth in shock, "He told me that I was the key to their conquest. He said that I was one of them the moment I was born!"

"Lies!" Maxim interrupted her. "They're deceiving you. The queen had given birth to you and your father was by her side. I was there."

She instantly followed, "No! They said that—"

Michael urged her to continue, but she was shaking. He took her other hand, asking, "What, Shina? Go on."

She finished off in tears, "They said I was the beginning of the end even before my conception—that I was destined for Abaddon!"

"Abaddon?" Maxim gasped. "Who the hell is that?"

She could not talk anymore. The conquest of the Demon Plague had been set in motion years before any inclination of their potential coming. The demons were in Tinaria before Michael had even arrived. The news hit them all like a bombshell. Shina was a half-demon. The Demon Plague came to collect their child—their demon child. Michael recognized that her unusual powers were her demonic heart yearning to break free.

"That is how you escaped?" Michael said softly, taken by the news. "Your powers were underestimated by even them."

Shina said while sobbing, "Escaped? They let me go! It awakened something in me!"

Michael had enough. He seized Shina's gentle shoulders and told her that she would need to stay inside the cell to sleep there for one more night. For her safety and the safety of everyone else, she agreed. Maxim demanded that he stay the night with her, but Michael denied him. As they left the cell and offered their sweet departs, Shina asked Michael what he was planning to do. Michael just smiled at her and told her not to worry. Again, he stressed to her that none of the antecedents were her fault.

Leaving the tree complex, Maxim asked him, "What was that? What are you planning, Michael?"

"They released her. Why?" Before Kyra guided them out, he said unto them in private, "I'm leaving the camp tonight and will convene with you and the others at the other side of the Lai River."

"I know," he replied.

Then outside, he held Maxim's arm and warned, "There is a lot more going on here. They think I resemble something from long ago. They only invade the lands that I walk on when I walk on them. But that also means Shina is born from something beyond time, as well. The demons may follow her, too. Be on your guard, Maxim."

Before it was too late, Michael bid them farewell and hurried north through the forest. The revelations concerning Shina weighed on his mind, holding major repercussions for what he thought was true. If they awakened something deep inside her soul, then she was something like him—a prophecy.

As the party prepared to turn in, the night ambiance was of some little comfort. Predella remained with her friends from her younger days and Maxim saw to it that his Tinarian brothers were turning in safely. But Antonis was of the belief that something was wrong. At once, the crickets silenced and the Ghost Forest became true to its name.

PART II
CHAPTER IV
THE DARKNESS WITHIN

In the dead of night, many warriors went without their sleep in dread of what stalked them in the darkness of the trees. As Esker kept watch while his unit slept, Ziamons on guard alerted him to Antonis's appearance. All six Tofauti accompanied the prophet as he sought an audience with him. Esker came to meet them just outside the Amazon base and asked in Christian, "What do you want?"

Antonis replied, repulsed by the sensation that an army of evil creatures awaited them within the trees, "I've come to propose something, from one Easterner to another."

Uninterested, the justice said, "If you're scared to sleep among women, there isn't much I can do for you."

"Funny," the prophet proceeded. "Well, if you haven't noticed, we're being stalked—right now. In just a matter of time, whatever is out there will close in on us and we'll all be quite defenseless."

Esker just stared at him, waiting for the point, as he knew just as well that creatures rustled about. Antonis, then, cleared his throat and explained, "There is only one way to stop them from coming to kill all of us. You must kill Princess Shina. Now, I can help you do this."

Mystified by the prophet's cold scheme, Esker uttered, "What?"

"These demons follow Miuriell, of that we know, but with him gone, they will come after the princess. It isn't what any of us wants, but to save us—to save millions after—we may have no choice," he elucidated.

Nodding his head, Esker came in close, prompting the Tofauti to be on their guard, and whispered, "If that's what it takes, then grow a pair and do it yourself."

Michael's lonely walk through the Ghost Forest was a terrifying ordeal. It had become so dark that it was almost impossible to navigate through the trees and undergrowth. The moon barely illuminated the way. Kyra Tal warned him before he departed about the disparaging ninja clans. After years of exile in the grim forest, the assassins grew brazen enough to challenge even Michael.

He could feel the tension around him as he went, hearing unnerving sounds from every direction. The Lai River was close when he sensed an impending attack. In an instant, three poisoned darts had jetted for his back. Sensing the assault, Michael swiftly spun around and stopped the projectiles in their pursuit. With his powers, he crushed them in midair and let them fall like powder.

Another throng of darts came whizzing for his head from the left side. He easily waved them away without moving a muscle. Allowing one of the poison-tipped darts to float into a tiny sack in his cloak, Michael shouted out, "This isn't a good time!"

With their feet equipped with climbing spikes, the fast ninjas darted from limb to limb, scaling the trees for better angles to catch the night wanderer in their sights. Michael knew what they were conniving to do. Within the minute, the ninjas would unleash all of their furies on him. Michael ran in the direction of the Lai River, knowing that he was close.

A surprising onslaught of arrows, darts and throwing knives came dashing for him. Dodging and deflecting all of the projectiles, Michael ran faster, staying alert. The ninjas scurried amongst the forest, following his every move and gaining ground. When one of them leaped onto another branch, he caught himself as something came into his sight from the branch across the way. A flyer demon chewed out a warrior's throat and then brutally tossed the carcass below. When he was about to gag from disbelief, the demon raised its head, revealed its green glowing eyes and dashed up towards him. He had no defense. The creature flew to his position and tore him from the branch. He let out a last shriek.

As the other assassins chased after Michael, another ninja was taken out of the hunt. The next ninja, close to Michael's position, readied his knife until another flyer had seized him from above. One by one, the pursuing ninjas were picked off and killed. Michael was too busy evading their attacks to know that they, too, were being hunted.

Finally, Michael ran over a mine, which jetted into the air and exploded. He immediately shielded the blast, but the shockwave dazed him. While any ninja could have finished him off and looted his every pocket, they were suddenly too preoccupied to care. From the darkness, the shadow demons appeared and vanished with sinister efficiency. Their quiet stalking had transformed into cries of terror. From everywhere and nowhere, shadow and flyer demons slaughtered the ninjas, allowing none to escape.

As Michael lay defenseless in the soil, not one ninja could harm him. The demons would never allow it. They protected their leader at all costs. All of Michael's attackers were dead. Finding it strange that they would abandon their assault, he used the staff to scout out his surroundings. Demons littered the forest, having feasted on the deadliest warriors there. He hung his head in realization that they saved his life. In the night, he was practically invincible—the father of the Demon Plague.

The demons had come. In her cell, Shina fought the evil within. Her wicked half tried to break free again, but even stronger this time. The demonic spirit hungered for release. The two Amazon women alerted Kyra as she slept. She awoke with trepidations of a demonic raid. Ziamons were on guard, as well, but less keen on surveying the forest like their female counterparts. Deep in the forest, Amazon scouts were asleep high in the trees. The demons were scattered all about. They cordoned the entire camp, simply watching the humans sleep. Ziamons watched the forest in distress.

Nevertheless, in time, additional scouts began to report sightings of demons. Kyra and Esker decided to join forces and patrol the camp together, accompanied by equal numbers of their subordinates. Tinarian officers joined in. An uneasy feeling awakened Maxim. He could not fall back into his sleep, for his chest felt heavy.

"I see them creeping about!" Some cried out. "They're upon us! We're surrounded!"

Maxim stepped out from his tent and looked about the forest, meeting with Predella by the dying fire. He heard the rustling of trees all around him. She said, "They're here. This won't end well. My heart is pounding"

The demons were everywhere. Green eyes snaked in from every part of the border. Antonis said bleakly in Ziamon company, "We're too late."

"What are they waiting for?" Esker whispered.

"Don't egg them on." Antonis slowly made his way back into the Amazon complex.

A man's terrified scream resounded from somewhere outside the encampment. Maxim unsheathed his blade, "Stay together! Everyone funnel in the center!"

His words went unheeded, for another soldier's cry had echoed throughout the camp. Amazons readied their bows for anything that emerged from the darkness of the trees. As they waited, trembling in fear, a deafening cry reverberated from Shina's cell high up in the tree prison. Her shout, long and feral, turned demonic. Everyone who was awake tilted their heads up to see it for themselves. They found what they dreaded. The prison hut was covered in shadow demons, but even they scurried away when the roof burst outward.

Shina crawled out from the top like a panther. Her eyes were as black as a shark and red pulsing veins consumed her white skin. As she stood over them all, gnashing her teeth as a beast, Antonis yelled in desperation, "Kill it! Shoot her!"

"Antonis!" Maxim screamed from his spot. "Don't!"

Shina sprung from the tree complex and landed onto the lush ground below, making a deep impression in the dirt. Then, she ran north towards the Lai River with fast speed. The forest was dangerously dense and crawling with spying demons of all sorts.

Maxim bolted after her into the darkness of the forest. Predella cried for him, "Maxim! Maxim, no!"

He heard her voice trail off in the distance as he ran, holding his sheathed sword in his hand. Maxim was able to spot her tearing through the forest at a feverish pace. Her terrible speed had outmatched Maxim's as he desperately tried to keep up, calling for her. As he ran, he felt the stalking presence of demons everywhere. He even smelled them as he went. An exposed root from a nearby tree tripped him up and he fell to the ground. The fall hardly affected him as he immediately propelled himself onto his feet. Yet, Shina was gone. In that split second, he lost her.

Maxim soon learned the penalty for his falter. Shina had not escaped him after all. He heard a thumping of the trees above. Looking upwards, Shina had leaped from tree to branch to come down on him, kicking Maxim in the chest before touching the ground. He grunted as he flew back into another tree. The impact stunned him.

Shina's sinister power was uncanny. She moved like a demon and growled like a possessed animal. She stared him down with black lifeless eyes. Before he could call Shina's name again, she pounced for him a second time. He rolled to his left to evade the blinding attack. Her fist smashed into the tree and set a scar in the bark. Since Maxim was not far enough from her reach, Shina tried to hit him in the face. Again, he dodged the attack.

"Shina, dammit!" Maxim cried. "Wake up, kid! Snap out of it!"

She charged Maxim and let out a fury of strikes. He evaded all of them, but he was too frightened to counter. He could not strike his princess. Shina was in there somewhere. Maxim needed to reach her heart. The demons surveyed them from the darkness of the forest. Shina let loose a kick for the side of his face, but he caught her ankle, then letting it go to evade another critical strike. Maxim had eluded attacks that left scars and abrasions on trees. Talking was futile now.

Frustrated by his reflexes, Shina remained still, eerily motionless, with her head hung down. Maxim tried catching his breath, keeping his distance from her. Raising his hand up, he whispered, "It's okay. Everything's going to be okay. Just relax and—"

Suddenly, she rushed him with ferocious anger and slashed his chest. He couldn't evade fast enough, as she had taken him to the ground. She bit into his arm, inducing him to cry out, before preparing to gouge out his eyes. But as Shina went for the kill, something stopped her. Frozen in fear, she looked at her bloody hands and touched the four lesions on his chest. With him shaking, Shina then touched his bite mark and started to cry.

Letting out a howl, she leaped away from him and ran off for the Lai River, disappearing in the darkness. He managed to sit up and then stand on his feet, knowing she was gone for good. Yet, he was far from alone. Demons corralled him from everywhere, hiding amongst the darkness. He felt them come in close, planning their strike. Unsheathing his Mad Phoenix, Maxim anxiously checked all around him. He was out in the open and vulnerable. Then, the attack.

A shadow demon tried him from his back, but he came around to slash it through the torso. In flames, the creature writhed and thrashed. Another came from his other side and pounced on him, thirsting to tear off his sweaty flesh. He did all that he could to fight it off, sensing a horde coming for him next. Maxim stabbed it in the abdomen from his side and then slashed its throat with a fiery hack. With more closing in on him, he swiped and swung his blazing sword everywhere just to keep them at bay.

As he fought desperately, shouting out and swirling his blade into an inferno, the forest began to catch fire. In just moments, he stopped and caught his racing breath, standing amid the flames. Waiting for the next assault on him, Maxim held his blade as if it was fused to his palm. But then, an icy arrow quenched a part of the brush in flames. Then another one doused a blaze just feet away from him. Predella fired two more ice arrows to stifle the last fires, leaving Maxim alone in the dark again.

Seeing that Predella had come for him, Maxim fell to his knees. She rushed over and knelt before him, checking the fresh wounds, adding to the collection on his body. She said, "They're gone. They just left."

Holding her hand on his bleeding chest, Maxim said in-between breaths, "Because *she's* gone."

"But I'm here." She lifted up his chin to look him in the eyes. "It's you and me. Together, we'll fight on tomorrow. You hear what I'm saying?"

Maxim pulled her in and kissed her on the mouth. He was beginning to fall for her, particularly in times of hurt. In the struggle against the Demon Plague, they found comfort in each other's companionship. Their warrior spirits found a small sense of relief in their compatibility, even as different as they were in their backgrounds. They rose up as one and headed back for the encampment emptyhanded, but with their lives.

PART II
CHAPTER V
THE TRUTH

Michael had made it to the Lai River before dawn and, because he was so exhausted, collapsed under a simple makeshift shelter. Gradually, the morning woke him, as tired as he seemed. The Staff of Truth rested near, feeling it with his mind. But then, while lying on his back, he felt someone cuddled up warmly on his chest. Shocked, Michael looked down to see Princess Shina sleeping peacefully against him, her head of hair resting on him.

Shina nestled herself in Michael's care, wearing her dirty gown. She clung to him like a lover, somehow finding him in the dead of night. It was difficult to imagine that a demonic spirit lingered within her innocent frame.

As the morning came, the army of eight hundred strong, having survived the Demon Plague the night before, continued their trek through the forest. Predella led the way, after Kyra Tal supplied her with fresh Amazon arrows, and bid them all farewell—and good riddance. It was the closest the women tribe had ever come to dying in a night raid. Some Tinarian scouts found Michael sitting up beside the princess at the river, letting the army know that they were both safe and ready to move out, despite the danger just hours before.

Amazon trackers escorted the army across the river and then to the edge of the Ghost Forest, encountering ninja lookouts as they went. None posed any threat, for they knew the army survived the demonic encounter. Having suffered casualties, some discussed the supernatural threat with the Amazons to learn more about the creatures.

With Shina a part of the group this time, scared and guilty of the unholy scourge within, they walked in unison and with a steady pace. Low on rations, their steps were swift as they hurriedly made it to the edge of the forest in the hopes of reaching the holy city's district before noon. Hiking out of the forest terrain had burned much of their energy, forcing them to take a respite out in the plains.

Finally, with the density of the forest behind them, Michael elected to take the trail northwest in order to connect with the road again. The army ventured forth, most having eaten the last of their rations for the journey. When they met the main road to Falcus yet again, bystanders came to watch Michael and his army march by. Spectators reveled in the awesome sight of the brave warriors from the East, but conversely feeling the gravity of their arrival. Maxim and Predella were only stories until the crowds found them in the march for Falcus.

The dungeon in Pommel was a rotting ground for those awaiting gruesome death. They were all deemed sacrifices for the conquest, required to suffer. Moans and cries filled the chambers, as well as the dreadful stink of human wastes and decay. The light was minimal, as only a few torches were placed about. The undead stalked the shadows and rusty cages of the unspeakable keep.

Amongst the putrid souls of the dungeon was a young boy, innocent as any. He was no more than twelve years old, but there was no way to tell in such a place. Everyone was as thin as twigs, if not as fragile. The young boy, however, was fed more than the others and treated better. There was a dark and devious purpose for him.

From the far-left corner of the chambers, a door at the head of the stairs opened and footsteps resounded off the walls, giving angst to the prisoners. With the little light the torches provided, the boy wearily observed Kaila kneel before the bars of his cage and watch him, gleefully. She ogled him with a pleasant smile as if she admired a pet swallow. She made playful sounds with her lips and grazed the bars with her fingers.

The vampire said with a sad smile, "**None of this was your fault. You didn't ask to be born.**"

As Kaila tormented the boy, who cringed into the far corner of his cage, Tenebrion sauntered up behind her. Kaila could feel his presence and she stopped her playful torture, waiting for the necromancer beast to say something. The boy cowered, even more, when he saw the creature come nearer. He feared him the most.

Tenebrion said while standing over her, "**Kaila, find something to do. This is my ward, not a pet shop.**"

Kaila retorted crossly, "**But he wants company, see?**"

"**Go suck something,**" he hissed down Kaila's smooth neck. Hence, she took one last look at the child and smiled, showing him her fangs. As he winced back again, she stood up and discarded the general's derision. Detesting Tenebrion and his pestering, Kaila sashayed towards the exit.

When Kaila finally took to the stairs and shut the dungeon door behind her, Tenebrion hunched over the containment cage to have a better look at Michael Miuriell's son. He was malnourished but alive. Michael never knew what happened to his boy when Pommel fell. He feared Seth was dead. Despite lapses in his memory of that dreadful night, Michael never witnessed his son's murder. If he ever discovered his son's cruel imprisonment, having been alive this whole time, he would have unleashed his worst powers.

Tenebrion's evil was too much for any child to stomach. He said sinisterly, "**You're a survivor. Good. Soon, you will face your father once again. I may need to warn you. He will not be the father you remember.**"

Seth refused to respond, while reassured that he would somehow look upon him with his father's face at least one more time. It was the only hope he had left, knowing his mother was dead. But, Tenebrion was not finished. He continued, "**Do you even know who your father is?**"

He provided no response to the theoretical question. Believing that he would never react, the demon snootily said, "**You were never meant to be born. You're bait—nothing more. When you have served your purpose, you will be disposed of.**"

Tenebrion could not physically torment the boy, but there were other methods of torture beyond physical pain. Before leaving him be, the demonic general declared, "**If he doesn't come to accept his true purpose here with us, then he will come to save you. When he does, you will lose the father you once knew—one way or another.**"

As the abominable creature left him, Seth fell over onto his side and cried. He had the ritual timed. In but a few minutes, an undead agent would come and deliver cold meat and water. Like a dog, he would eat it. He never quite knew where the meat had come, but he intended to eat. At least, he found confirmation that his father was going to find him. If his faith was strong, he believed that his father would save his life.

The Holy City of Falcus—a utopian kingdom stretching from the eastern harbor to the western peaks, belonged to everyone and answered to no one. All cultures, religions, and races were welcome. Facilitated by a council of nine members representing the people within its walls, the holy city did not run on a traditional economy. Instead, the people lived on credits, a value system where currency was based on the good works and generosity of its citizens.

Manna Excallum lived in Falcus for all his life, renowned for being the most prevalent prophet of his time. He was the elite advisor to the Falcun League. Shadisha, a master tactician, followed Manna as second most popular diplomat in the league. Thomas Excallum, Ellium's ambassador and Manna's only son, served as an honored leader to the paladins. Deemed as the most powerful Christian legion in the world, his paladins armed themselves with maces and holy shields bearing the cross.

Lai Kai, aside from losing the sight in his left eye, was the respected commander of the ninja warriors, the most skilled fighters in the Kai League. Second only to Shadisha, Lai served as general to his ninja warriors and Thomas's paladins when the Kai League was in full force. Like her older brother, Lana Kai served as a member of the fighter league. Once belonging to the ninja clans in the Ghost Forest, Shioda Shokan converted to the Kai League through Lana, having fallen in love with her while in her custody as a prisoner. Shioda dedicated his masterful sword to Falcus years later, serving under his wife's command.

And so, after an arduous journey, Michael's army had finally congregated with an ecstatic force of twenty guards at the main gate to Falcus. The Easterners marveled at Falcus's massive defensive wall, larger than any they had ever seen. An enormous wall of bleached brick extending around the city took three decades to complete, proving that a noble kingdom was worth protecting. A modest moat-encircled most of the city and drawbridges remained open during the day. Invasions, however, were nothing but suicide missions.

Falcus was unlike any other kingdom in the new world, or the world before it. Everyone was accepted, as long as they did their part in the community. Maxim said with enthusiasm, "Tinarians are behind that wall."

"God willing," Michael replied.

A Tinarian officer reassured them from behind, "Well, I know my wife and child took a vessel for Falcus. They are there. I feel it."

Other Tinarian soldiers eagerly awaited the chance to reunite with friends and family. Others had loved ones who sailed for Ellium. Shina was jubilant. All of her torments were finally fading away. Falcus was going to be her ultimate refuge where she'd be cured of her dark spirit.

As they all headed for the holy city, warriors eyed Maxim and Predella among Michael's army, surprised to see them in the flesh. For many, they were but legends lost to the East. Stories of their enchanted weapons spread all about to every kingdom. Masses watched them all enter their city with great anticipation, led my Michael Miuriell himself. As a hero returning from a long, perilous journey, he was met with terrific exultation. Easterners had ultimately come to realize the true level of esteem they had for him.

Children of all races and cultures raced up to Michael as he led his party deeper into the city. They all were eager to hug him and cheer his renowned name. The streets were cluttered with a diverse populace. The architecture was as white as the clouds in some places and rose almost as high. Michael led his army for the Tinarian embassy, still under construction. The space there was adequate for both Tinarian and Ziamon soldiers, having to settle as one army. Michael's orders for their encampment in the embassy was direct—surrender your sordid past as two warring nations or sleep outside the holy city's watch.

Hundreds of Tinarians came running when they saw what only their faith had promised. Families ran for the Tinarian soldiers with elation and embraced Princess Shina, cheering her name. They kissed her gentle hands and touched her smooth skin. Among his people, Maxim kept Predella close. His enthusiasts had to greet her, as well, when they came to see him. The four hundred Ziamons envied their rivals' reunion among families.

By the dozens, the Falcuns made a path for Shioda Shokan, their warrior captain of the guard. He came with other elite ninja warriors by his side, all attired in Falcun body armor and regalia. Unlike his troops, Shioda did not own a full head mask. He wore only a face shroud from his nose to his neck, used only for combat missions. For the occasion, he revealed a welcoming smile from his handsome countenance.

Dressed in dark blue garb, tied and secured by a gold sash, Shioda kept his one katana latched to his back, like Maxim's fire-sword. Stopping in his tracks and folding his arms at the chest line, Shioda called for Michael. When Michael met the guard captain halfway into the Tinarian commune, they embraced fervently, overjoyed to see each other alive. Shioda said, "We've missed you, Michael. It is a miracle that you have made it this far."

"I've brought friends from the East," Michael replied.

"So, you have," Shioda said as he saw the Ziamon forces gather to his left, then saying. "We have mourned your people in Pommel. This is an unforgivable tragedy and I could never imagine the loss you must be feeling."

"It only makes this quest ever more necessary. The army brave enough to join me have lost equally as much. I swear they have come to fight with all of their hearts," Michael declared.

"I hope so, Michael," Shioda said despondently. "Manna Excallum is gone."

"Gone? What do you mean gone?" Michael gasped. "He is—dead?"

Finally, the moment Michael had waited so readily for had slipped away. As he fell into a deep sadness, Shioda held his arm and said, "But there is hope, yet. Urik has come to take his place. He is waiting for you and promised to explain everything that has happened since your disappearance."

"Yes. I would assume so," Michael sighed, overcome with emotion.

Shioda showed him to his escorts for Principal Palace, the capital building. Michael started off with the guard captain's warriors in route for the palace. When he eventually reached the steps, making it through the jubilant crowds, Shadisha greeted him at the top. Her jet-black hair was tied behind her head and suspended down her back. She kissed him on the cheeks and said devotedly, "Thank the heavens you're alive! I have endured sleepless nights thinking about your safety!"

Michael clasped one of her hands, replying, "A man could live a long time before finding a friend like you. I just heard about Manna."

"Two weeks now," she said in woe, then leading him into the palace. He knew his way around, but it had been a while. A pair of women dressed in traditional silk garments simultaneously opened the double doors to the prophet's quarters. There, behind Manna's desk, the sage propped up his old head and smiled. An aged man doubled that of Michael, Urik sported a thick beard and a balding head. In royal Falcun garb, he came around to meet Michael in the center of the large room.

"Michael, my boy, I never thought that I'd be so shocked to see someone while knowing he was coming!" Urik teased.

Michael embraced him, replying, "It's a comfort to see you Urik, though I wish under better circumstances."

"Indeed," the prophet answered. "This inescapable evil has taken us all by storm. Manna tried to delve into its stronghold in Pommel and paid the price with his life. The man suffered an aneurysm and died. I wasn't too keen on doing the same thing, seeing how they killed him that way, but I was able to find out a few things before he passed on. He told me what he saw, so now, I believe, I'll be telling you, won't I? And trust me, you'll need to sit down for this, son."

Together, they sat and the women closed the doors. Sitting by the opened windows, Urik poured some tea for the both of them, "I think this might still be warm if you'd like some."

Michael said restlessly, "I just want the truth, Urik. Just that. I came a long way."

"So that's a yes on the tea. Good," Urik started. "So, since we're reunited under these new world conditions. Who do you believe you are now, after all that's happened to you?"

Michael replied, reflecting on his teacher's bold question, "I once was a husband and a father—a man of faith. I dedicated my life to peace. But now, wherever I go, I bring the darkness. I bring death."

Urik said in return, "You are still the man you were. You will always be that man. No matter what, this unspeakable evil will never have the absolute power to make you something else. However, there is a significant difference between a man's identity and a man's purpose. What I tell you now is the truth and nothing more. It can't affect who you are or what your purpose is and has always been. Do you understand?"

Thinking hard on Urik's pledge, he nodded his head. The prophet took another sip of tea and said, "Your powers are unique and foreign to this world. In fact, no other force like yours exists on this earth. That truth has led me to the nature of your purpose. When I discovered you in Pommel, I never felt a greater force emanating from your being.

"I had no knowledge of those strange powers, but I trained you to focus and manipulate your telekinetic abilities through virtuous means. However, your powers were never meant to be virtuous, were they? Your unique powers have vile origins. You were born to annihilate. You were born to father the Demon Plague, as you've come to call it."

Michael couldn't find the energy to speak. Even the idea of using his telekinetic powers shook him. He held his head in shame as the prophet continued, "Hope is not lost, son. Because I found you and trained you, I may have saved us all. If anything, you changed your destiny. And as a new fate would have it, you grew up with the goodness of humanity in your heart."

Shocked beyond belief, Michael pleaded, "Why didn't you tell me? For all this time, you knew?"

"Of course not, you fool," Urik retorted. "I'm a seer. This plague, or whatever you want to call it, was planned from the beginning, concealed for hundreds of years. I couldn't see it."

"What beginning?" he frustratingly proclaimed.

"A thousand years ago, Michael!" Urik rooted deeper. "You've had the visions by now! You know what walked this earth. As fable tells it, his given name was Abaddon and he was the first—the bringer of this plague.

"From the Primeval Tragedy to today, the Demon Plague designed their incursion. All of your ancestors wrought segments of Abaddon, but you were the replica of their creator. You returned and so have they."

"But how?" Michael beseeched. "How did they succeed? They were never here! What let them in?"

Urik stared blankly into Michael's eyes for a brief moment before answering cautiously, "They are very strong. Whatever power they are, I couldn't say, but they're blinding my mystical contact with Pommel. I can't see inside their fortress, but *you* can. Something lies underneath that city, Michael. It may be the place to their origin."

"I don't know anything about that," Michael answered despondently. "But I *will* leave this place before sundown."

"I know, and you'll be taking the Tinarian princess with you." Urik finished his tea, declaring, "Shina is the product of something, but my visions to her past are too clouded. What is certain is that the Demon Plague's conquest had started long before any of us were born. As I told you, this invasion may have been plotted after Abaddon was killed around the Primeval Tragedy."

Michael massaged his face before saying, "The Demon Plague follows me, not Shina."

"No. The evil within her is growing stronger and faster. Soon, she will no longer be Shina. They awoke something deep within her," Urik said. "She'll be like you."

Michael countered, "Why her?"

"I'm not quite sure of that, either, but she can never be trusted—not until the Demon Plague is destroyed. Because you are their reincarnated leader, only you have the power to stop them," Urik insisted.

Michael evoked the monumental battle with the Demon Lord in the Waasi crater. His sinister powers were aching to emerge even then. He said to his teacher after fighting back tears of guilt, "If I destroy the Demon Lord, then I become Abaddon all the way, erasing what is left of Michael Miuriell. If I fail, the Demon Lord assumes command. We're ruined either way."

Urik peered into Michael's soul and felt around his dark spirit, then saying, "You can win. I see it in you. Everyone has a spark that lights a fire. That fire can light the world, or help burn it down. The thing that makes us humans distinctive is that we have that choice. Even you."

Michael nodded and rose up before his loyal mentor. There was truth in Urik's eyes and no one could challenge his wisdom. The sage clasped Michael's hands together and said to him almost in a whisper, "When you leave with the princess tonight, meditate on all that we have said. Find a way to sneak inside Pommel. They must have a weakness. They must have a birthplace, too. Everyone and everything has each one of those."

As Michael began to walk out of Excallum's quarters, bidding his farewell for the day, he stopped and asked one final question. He said, "On the way here, I encountered a strange—"

"Ah, yes. The madness," Urik said, looking out from his window. "It's spreading. Soon enough, it'll reach Falcus. That is why time matters. I can't see why they are drawn to that evil place, but I can't see any of it. Another riddle, Michael. You never liked riddles, eh?"

"I never liked the ones you invented, because yours had no definite answer to them. Not even you knew," he retorted.

Urik laughed, "So true, but I taught you something. Not every riddle has—"

"Not every riddle has one definite answer, but every definite answer has one close-minded person," Michael said. "I was just a boy then. Those riddles, I miss."

"Just the same, this one can be answered, too. There is more than one way to defeat the Demon Plague, son. We can do our part here, but, unfortunately, this is that one riddle you'll need to solve on your own. That doesn't mean you're *on* your own. Understand?" Urik said.

Michael accepted his friend's counsel and permitted the guards to open the doors for him. He walked out with the guards and headed down the wide corridor, in route for the steps out of Manna Excallum's district.

By sunset, Michael and Shina had expressed their gratitude to the Falcuns and bid their goodbyes. Antonis agreed with Shina's absence, believing Urik to be wise enough to see the threat. Shadisha watched Michael and Shina ride towards the high edge of the cliff due east where the repaired Santa di

Mare had finally come to berth earlier in the day. They rode gallantly away from the holy city alone and cursed. Shadisha wept for Michael as he rode off with only the princess to accompany him. She had loved him for years. Because he married Opal, Shadisha never pursued him.

The Ziamons were already settled in the Tinarian embassy. Their respect for the Falcuns would gleam after the night's end. Such hospitality was alien to them. The East offered no generosity. Their realm was forged in blood.

The Tinarians had felt similar repercussions. Their ship rested safely at the Falcun dock where it should have berthed in the first place. Maxim promised to provide them all with the news of Tinaria's survival and Princess Shina's sad curse. Everyone planned to gather to listen to their tales told by the brave knights who lived them.

Antonis sat among his Tofauti guardians as he listened to the soldiers' tales. He watched Maxim slip out from the courtyard gathering and knock on someone's door. Antonis looked on when Predella opened up the door to her chambers and welcomed him in. The prophet then realized that the relationship between the two warriors had become more serious than he expected.

PART II
CHAPTER VI
THE EVE OF WAR

Between the high cliffs and the forest's perimeter, a ninja clan was compelled to investigate the suspicious activity. They hid in trees and ditches as they scrutinized the sounds of toiled assembly. A ninja spotted the first ghastly mark of the clan's suspicions of an incursion.

Torch lights illuminated the forest sector and a tall, heavily armored warrior with a shimmering skull helmet supervised his dark troops prepare for an offensive. The warrior was equipped with a deadly sword and black and silver armor that vindicated his warring intentions. From the high cliffs, hundreds upon hundreds of the eerie warriors came climbing horde by horde, making their way deeper into the forest.

With them, lethal and devastating bombards and rocket launchers followed. Substantial function cannons and mobile rockets were next. They all gradually progressed northwest towards the open land leading to Falcus. No ninja stationed there had ever seen such ferocious warriors. Never before had they ever been deceived by another force developing under their noses. They were shocked as to how the formidable army could have been concealed all this time.

Michael meditated aside the high cliffs miles from Falcus. Shina slept peacefully in their large, insulated tent that Michael had erected. Shina never would have agreed to leave Falcus if it was not for Michael's companionship. She beheld an instinctive attraction to him. It was a sensation she could not explain. In essence, she felt at peace, without the feeling of vice. None of it ever came about until after Pommel.

While sleeping on her side, Michael squatted outside of the tent, overlooking the Great Pacifica from the edge of the high cliff. With eyes closed for an hour already, Michael desperately tried to see through Pommel's new malevolent fortress. He searched for a weakness and an explanation for Shina's curse. He envisioned the evil bastion of Pommel, but could not peer inside.

As he searched for a weakness, a grave feeling ran about his spine. A mysterious power routed his sight from elsewhere. Something inside clued him into a crucial inkling. The sensation was overwhelming, filling him with an array of dark energy.

Though he searched up and down the city, it seemed that it was not until he focused on Pommel's lower levels that his sight began to improve. The impression originated from the lowest level of Pommel. There was something underground that called to him. At once, thereafter, more of the bastion became clear.

Michael's eyes stretched farther—deeper. There was something underground Pommel that connected to him most intimately. While exploring the bastion during his concentrated meditation, Shina had awakened and it was the dark sensation that woke her. Shina moaned and held her heart with trepidation.

Out of fear, she painstakingly called for Michael to soothe her sting. Michael broke away from the meditation and shook off the spell that came with it. Considering her cries, he ran back into the tent and came to her aid.

"It burns!" she squealed with a rapid heart. "The burning is back! I can feel it trying to take over!"

"You can fight it! I'm here with you," Michael said, seizing her moist hand. "Just breathe and try to calm it."

Within minutes of rhythmic breathing, the burning lessened. Michael, again, had soothed her and held in the evil that desperately wanted to explode. Shina lowered her heart rate. In calming her, Michael was left to reflect upon the dire secrets that had risen. They both felt the connection—the attraction. Regardless of Shina's young age, lust had taken them by surprise. He saw so much in her that reminded him of Opal when she was younger. He fell into a trance, blanketing himself in her eyes.

She, too, beheld a strong passion for him. The connection was not by coincidence, but by design. Thus, a serious enigma took him. Why was Shina the key to the Demon Plague's conquest? He thought heavily upon the terms. He was their leader and she was the key. With this menacing puzzle turning in his head, the answer developed deep inside his heart. They were meant to be together.

It was the very reason Opal was targeted and Shina was never harmed. They were destined to wed as king and queen of the Demon Plague. Both possessing demonic influences, their offspring would emerge as a true prodigy, more powerful than all the rest. The perfect demon king, or queen, would be born to serve as Michael Miuriell's heir.

Discovering that purpose for Shina, he proceeded to stroke her hair and reveal to her the truth. The only way to prevent the evil bond between them was to remain abstinent. Shina was cringing and trembling with an extreme lust for him. As his want for her escalated, his new discovery had justified itself.

"Take me now, Michael! It's alright. I need you inside me!" Shina yearned with desire.

He held the side of her face with his hand and said earnestly, "It's what they want us to do! If we do this, we doom this world."

"Please, I cannot stand it!" She seized his shirt robustly.

Slowly and gently taking her hand, he responded with ease, "It's not you, princess. It's not us. Let it go. Let it go for good."

Battling moments after his counsel, Shina toppled the lustful urge. She opened her eyes and understood. Overwhelmed, she started to cry, "Oh, God, what's happening to me?"

Michael squeezed her securely, "You can suppress it."

"For how long?" she answered from his shoulder.

Without breeding, they could delay the demonic conquest. They had to resist each other's budding advances. Michael did not leave her spot until she fell back to sleep. Maintaining focus, he decided to suspend his meditations for the rest of the night, fearing that Shina's demons would emerge again.

During the lateness of the night, the Demon Plague's Mad Legion emerged from the Ghost Forest. As the morning was upon them, Kane and Prince Eric would lead the daylight army for Falcus. As much as Kane wanted the princess in his grasp, Eric would never allow him to lay a hand on her.

Something woke Michael at the same time, compelling him to revive his perilous meditations. Searching the bastion with his mind, holding on to the Staff of Truth tighter than ever, a malevolent dungeon appeared. Amongst the suffering, there was a small boy crying out for him. Astonishing him, he saw Seth shaking with fear and in anguish, craving for his father's rescue.

Seeing this, Michael opened his eyes, gorged with tears, and fell onto his back. In dismay, he plastered his hands over his face and cried like a child. Pounding with his fists into the ground, he mourned his son's tortuous keep. With hateful, vengeful strength, Michael vowed that he would save his suffering son from that hell. They didn't kill him. Rather, they kept him as bait, knowing he would find him somehow.

Inside the city, Shioda and Lana's exquisite abode had just livened up. Lana awoke from an uneventful sleep as she turned her position on the bed. The bedside table was in her way when she slipped out from under the covers and walked towards the mirror, taking the bright lantern with her. Looking at herself in the mirror, she analyzed her slender figure. Wearing only a bra and thong, it was still too difficult to tell that she was pregnant.

The stages were early yet, but it was verified. Lana rubbed her smooth belly, still as flat as yesterday. From behind Lana, Shioda had surprised her from behind, hugging her. She touched his hands as she stared at him in the mirror, smiling. Shioda said, "You are so beautiful. Now you shall bear our child. A man should not pray for anything greater."

She answered, "Our baby is blessed with you as the father."

Shioda turned her around and knelt before her. Holding her waist and pressing the side of his face upon her belly, he uttered sweetly, "I now love two people in this world. Whatever happens, Lana, stay out of harm's way. Protect the baby and do nothing else. I cannot allow anything to happen to you. Never. I would have to die first."

Instead of sleeping the night away, Antonis remained awake in his temporary domicile in the Tinarian embassy of Falcus. On the balcony, he waited for the sunrise, anxious for the battle that was sure to come. He felt it strongly. Just a few levels above, Esker had felt the same sensation. Something was coming. He was an artist of war. He could smell it in the air. War was upon them at sunrise.

PART II
CHAPTER VII
THE MAD LEGION

Among the cool breeze that ran into Falcus's famed walls, Michael and Shina had returned safely with news. As Shina had revisited the Tinarian sector of Falcus, receiving unremitting praise from her people, Michael reported straight to Excallum's quarters. The guards welcomed him back as they opened the large chamber doors.

The moment he stepped into the chambers, a gloomy sensation ran through his bones. It was sickly. He felt that something was not right with his great friend. As he would have expected, Master Lai and Shadisha came out from his private quarters and displayed faces of distress.

"What's wrong?" Michael asked worryingly.

Shadisha answered after she looked to Lai for approval, "He is ill. Last night, he developed a rigid sickness during his meditations."

Michael asked, stepping closer towards the double doors, "What kind of sickness?"

"He has a severe headache and suffers from fatigue," Lai explained further. "This is how Manna started to decline."

Shadisha urged him to enter, nonetheless. As he started to enter Urik's chambers, she asked of him, "Are you alright? How is the Tinarian princess?"

Before entering the room, Michael replied, "It's quite complicated."

Leaving an enigma with the two Falcuns, Michael entered Urik's room and guards closed the doors behind him. There he observed Urik neck deep under his white sheets. Physicians lingered over him and Lana Kai held his hand.

Like a flashback, Michael reminisced about his experience with the queen's health in Tinaria.

He prayed that his mentor was not losing an incurable battle. Holding his Staff of Truth tightly, Michael steadily approached the divan. The prophet insisted that he come closer—that his illness was not contagious. Thus, Michael knelt beside him and bowed his head in worry. He then briefly looked to the nearest physician, hoping that his dearest ally was not deathly ill.

"Why do you always do that?" the prophet asked him jokingly with a raspy assertion. "Asking doctors about me when I'm right here."

Michael retorted, "Don't make this about me. You're the one who chose to get sick."

Urik started lethargically, "I was meditating last night. I couldn't see inside the Pommelian citadel as I expected, but I found something underneath."

Laying his staff against the bedpost, Michael asked, "I felt it, too. What was it?"

"I felt a door of some sort—a portal. Did you see this?" Urik asked as he looked directly into Michael's eyes from his pillow.

Michael proclaimed, "I felt it, like you."

"It was then that I developed this strange illness. Something knew that I was snooping around," Urik declared seriously. "I should have followed my own advice and let you do all the work."

"I wish you would have," Michael said. "I discovered a lot more than just that. Shina was born to bear a child—mine. Being that she is a half-demon, and I—"

The prophet interjected with trepidation, "Then a pure demon is their insurance plan? What better way to secure the conquest than have a demonic ruler carry on the legacy?"

"That is why Opal was first targeted. Shina was to bear my child all along, which can only leave my son—" Michael's frightening deciphering led him to Seth. If Opal was not meant to be his wife, then Seth was his illegitimate son. His true child was predestined to fulfill the Demon Plague's conquest. His pain returned from last night's cruel discovery. He could not help but to break down and cry, mourning the present and future fate of his innocent boy.

"Your son, Michael." Urik feared the same. "Your son is alive in that hellish place?"

Crying and clasping his hands together, Michael wept, "My son! He's alive but in so much pain! I felt him crying for me! How could this ever happen to my son—my poor boy?"

As Michael cried by Urik's side, the prophet placed his hand over his friend's head and said, "Seth is your legitimate son, Michael. You were a father then and you are a father now. That was ordained by God, which supersedes all other plots and schemes."

"I must save him!" Michael vowed between tears. "All this time, he's been waiting for me to save him."

Urik answered, "Then you will, even if it is a trap."

Trying to recover from his lamentation, Michael said, "They are holding him as bait to get to me."

Urik avowed, coughing, "They want you to return to Pommel. They will try to turn you there as they did with the princess. If they turn you, Abaddon would be enough to finish their conquest within the month."

"How do I defeat them?" Michael wiped the final tears from his eyes. "It's impossible. If I die, they win. If I destroy them, I become Abaddon. I still can't see what you see."

Kai guards helped their prophet prop the pillow higher so that he could sit up into his bed. After this was done, he coughed, "Never forget what I told you. You are more powerful than you give yourself credit for."

As they spoke together, Urik's door had burst open and several ninja warriors entered and bowed. One of them spoke forth, "The foreign warriors from the East are suiting up for battle, sir."

Bewildered, Shadisha asked from the hall, "Why would they be doing that?"

The same ninja replied, "They say that war is coming."

Hearing this, the prophet shut his eyes and focused. It had taken all but ten seconds to fully witness, in his extrasensory mind, over two thousand warriors advance towards the city. In shock, Urik opened his weary eyes and realized that the Demon Plague had sent a human commander to lead an army to invade Falcus. He did not recognize the armor they wore, let alone from where the men had come.

Michael was convinced that the Demon Plague was intent on reacquiring Princess Shina. Grave preparations were in motion to take her to higher ground where she would be protected. Without wasting time they did not have, Shadisha arranged for Shina to be kept in one of the high towers of the city. Throngs of ninja warriors stampeded into the Tinarian sector to take the princess to safety. Protected by the Falcun League, no man would ever dare try to capture Shina and escape from Falcus alive.

"What is the meaning of this?" Maxim asked, alarmed by their rushed abduction of the princess.

Shioda, who supervised the operation, said, "Michael is sure that the army advancing for us wants to take your young princess for the Demon Plague."

"Army?" Maxim gasped.

Colonel Aramis came over clad in full armor and said, "Time to prepare for battle, Red Menace. Let's see how our soldiers do fighting warriors other than our own."

By this time, Kane's Mad Legion reached the towers surrounding the open land to Falcus. To avoid any alarming signals, Eric was sent to dispose of the ninjas that scouted there. He dismounted his horse and took several steps forward so that he could cast his magical incantation properly. After all, he was doing it for his sister. There could be no mistakes, or Shina could become hurt.

From a tower straight ahead, one of the two scouts perceived the army from his high outlook. Cursing the day, he saw Eric beginning his dark incantation from the eye of a retractable telescope. Shaken from what he saw, he quickly dropped the scope and alarmed his comrade beside him, "Ignite the rocket! Invaders are coming!"

Yet, before his comrade could light the firework to forewarn their home of the army's advent, Eric cast his teleportation spell and faded away into nothingness. Kane smiled and shook his head after the impressive maneuver. Instantly, Eric simply appeared from a gust of black smoke over the tower, landing before the rocket and between the two scouts.

Taking advantage of their astonishment, Eric punched the shrouded scout to his left and sent him over the edge. The next swiftly reached for his short sword, but Eric summoned another spell and snatched the man by the neck, freezing his entire body with frigid ice. Without a cry, the ninja scout lost consciousness, imprisoned in a glacial skin of ice.

Eric, feeling content with his cruel spells, ignited his right hand in flames and struck the scout in the chest, exploding his body into thousands of solid pieces of melting ice that glistened as it burst from the tower. He was preparing to teleport back to his horse when he heard a hissing coming from his feet. The irony of his sadistic nature clobbered his objective. The flames from his fist ejected hot embers that ignited the rocket below. Not reacting in time, the rocket blasted off and his simple mission failed. Kane cursed the sorcerer's incompetence.

Maxim, among others, saw the rocket blast in the distance. Just as he collaborated with the Ziamons over their gearing up for war, the sound reached the city. Watching the people of the city scatter, he looked back to his temporary abode in the Tinarian sector. His Mad Phoenix rested peacefully there for a good while. Today, he was sure that it would be put to use.

Shioda cried from his high pedestal in one of the squares, "Prepare for defensive actions!"

Shina was taken to the highest level of one of the towers in the city. Various warriors defended her from inside and outside of the room. Thousands of ninja warriors stationed themselves behind the front wall of Falcus, awaiting the Mad Legion. Maxim, Predella, and Tinarian knights willing to fight began marching for the front wall as well. The Ziamons were already prepared and thrilled that they could finally spill human blood in the West.

Michael stood outside Excallum's chambers and onto the illustrious balcony. He oversaw the great front wall to his lower right and the thousands of warriors that waited for the invading army. From the looks of things, Michael couldn't understand how the legion of just two thousand men could even hold a candle to the Falcun League and the added might of the Eastern fighters. It was clear that the Mad Legion was a distraction. Somehow, as Urik had predicted, they would attempt to recapture Shina. He just felt it.

With the Staff of Truth in his hands, Michael foresaw the Mad Legion for himself. In an utter shock, he envisioned Prince Eric co-leading the horde. He prayed that he was mistaken—that the man attired in black armor with long white hair was another man resembling the exiled prince.

Also, with Eric was Garvin Kane, fully armed with his horrid body armor fit for a warlord. It was obvious that he, too, had returned from exile to fight for the Demon Plague during the light of day. Michael feared for Eric's life, but then remembered the path he chose for himself. He chose his allies poorly. He betrayed them from the start.

Shadisha mounted a tall horse in the far rear of the Falcun League. Shioda, Lai, and Lana commanded their divisions, ready to slaughter the new enemy. Maxim assumed command of his Tinarian knights and the two Ziamon leaders deemed control over the four hundred soldiers. How the Mad Legion would even consider challenging Falcus seemed outrageous.

The ninja warriors manned the several machine guns all over the crenellations, making up the firepower defending the massive defensive walls ten feet thick. Rockets and cannons also participated in the defensive. Its firepower rested chiefly in the hands of the paladins. The large spear launchers were placed on the various battlements at every thirty feet along the wall's crenellations.

At last, the Mad Legion came to the Holy City of Falcus. The installed general, Kane, raised his fist and brought the vast company to a halt. Falcus was close enough for them all to see the prepared warriors manning the crenellations ahead. From his horse, Kane pointed to his right side and then tightened his armed fist. Accordingly, the five catapults had trolled alongside the warriors, built and manned by the spellbound masses afflicted with the madness.

Kane then did the same to his left side. Seconds later, six massive rocket launchers stationed themselves in a chaotic line, ready to blast the top battlements and crenellations. When the machines were in place, he turned to his aide, grumbling, "Sorcerer, I hope this time you will not fail me. All the Lord wants is the girl. That is all you need to do. Is this going to be a problem for you?"

Replying to the contemptuous remark, Eric guffawed under his breath, "I mean, I could blow that wall to rubble if you'd like. Wouldn't that be a better plan?"

"My legions are trusting in your swift acquiring of the princess! *That's* the plan!" Kane snapped. "Find your sister! Don't fall short!" Surveying the enormous city from afar, the exiled prince exclaimed, "Just keep it hot!"

Kane raised his open hand and then made a fist. The Mad Legion roared with readiness and unsheathed their various weapons of choice. All armored in black and silver plate mail, the warriors leveled their axes, steadied their swords, tightened their shields and raised their spears.

Two hundred cavalrymen remained with Kane out of harm's way as the foot soldiers prepared to storm the city's great walls. Even beyond the two thousand warriors were the three colossal bombards and the double cannons. The bombards could easily devastate the great wall with a continuous beating. The double cannons fired two cannonballs at once, bound by a steel chain.

The thunderous roar of the legion was tremendous for two thousand. In the distance, Shioda had made his way up to the crenellations and viewed them from on high. In bewilderment, he said to the nearest ninja warrior, "How can they even attempt this foolish attack? They will never reach within a thousand feet of our walls."

Regardless of how the odds calculated, Kane was more than willing to utilize his mammoth artilleries rather than his infantry. With the constant cries for war amongst his legion, Kane raised his right arm and pointed towards Falcus. Three catapults and four rapid-fire rocket launchers started for the kingdom's walls. Two of each remained behind for later usage. Along with the heavy artillery, the Mad Legion hastily advanced for the kingdom with their weapons raised and their souls aflame.

As the Mad Legion made their way to Falcus, Kane and his cavalry watched the beginning of the battle unfold. When all of the infantry had dispatched, he called upon one of the bombards and all twelve of the double cannons to move in. The tremendous wall crushers would pave the way for the legion to enter the city and fight the Falcun League by hand.

To all those who could see the army approach, the colossal artillery seemed to blossom worry. The mammoth machines were never seen before. Michael reasoned that it was the innovation of the Demon Plague. Their lord had many illustrious tools to play with, using his human cattle to build and fight for anything.

Shioda cried out from the crenellations, "Ready the guns! Place the rockets! They are advancing!"

The warriors cocked the machine guns and staffed the rockets. The cannons were already loaded behind the walls and were good for action. Coming closer to the city walls, the Mad Legion ran into the sand, rather than grassy soil. They thought nothing of it until it became difficult to run. Their boots sunk in the density of the sand and their legs buckled. Slowing down as they charged the walls, the Falcun artillery was ready to attack.

With the drawbridges up, the troops holding the large planks of wood on one side and a ladder on the other came running up first. Little did they know that these innovative tools were useless against Falcus's great white walls. The moat was tiny and insignificant compared to Merrieu and Ellium, but it was cleverly not the moat that provided the city with its chief defenses.

Wasting no more time, Shioda ordered the nearest paladins to wave the enormous red flags, signaling the cannons. Shadisha cried out and waved her same flag abruptly. Progressively, the paladins fired the first rounds from the cannons stationed within the walls. The cannon balls and cannister shots came soaring for the advancing legion, smashing through them with brutal accuracy. Instantly killing some and mortally wounding others, the cannon shots tore through the advancing foes as if they were standing still. The Falcuns quickly reloaded the cannons for another round.

Shioda called for the rockets. He shouted forcefully for the fierce firing from the crenellations as the distant men-at-arms attained the signal from both west and east of the long wall. Then, the awaited round of the dragon-headed rockets blasted into the perimeters of the oncoming legionnaires.

The explosive missiles erupted after hitting the ground and sent percussion and fire into the enemies' advance. Cries from the blast engulfed legionnaires into charred corpses and enflamed carcasses. Others were sent into the air to fall elsewhere. Yet, with the initial defensive from Falcus, the rocket launchers to the city's right had been stationed correspondingly, prepared to launch.

As the legionnaires neared closer and the defensive cannons fired upon them a second time, the adversary rockets opened up and revealed a five-gage launcher able to set off five rockets consecutively with each firing.

"Fire the rockets for those things!" Shioda cried.

An officer waved the flag for rockets and pointed another of the same hue for the awkward enemy rocket launchers. As the Falcuns loaded their next rockets, the enemy launchers released their wrath. One after the other, the four rocket machines consecutively fired off five at a time straight for the crenellations. The discharges were surprisingly precise and the enemy rockets demolished the crenellations to the west.

Amid the devastation, the Falcuns tried to retreat from the oncoming onslaught. Awful eruptions lit the sky as explosions caused by the incoming and the defensive rockets' collisions. A hefty ton of debris had come falling from both sides of the western wall, killing those directly below and everyone who could not escape the regulated offensive.

Maxim shouted from the reserve lines within the city, "Where the hell did they get those?"

"We're no good in here, Maxim!" Predella exclaimed as she oversaw the demolition.

"Guns, now!" Shioda raised his hand and the officer to his left raised the corresponding flag that set off an assault from above. The steel arrows cut deep into the legionnaires' charge. Undoubtedly, there was no chance for them to even consider breaking through.

From the far distance, Kane shook his head and growled, "What are those assholes waiting for? Fire the damn bombard! Break the goddamn wall!"

Eric smiled and prepared to teleport to the first high tower in search for his sister, "I always found fireworks to be so primitive."

Kane would have slammed his armed elbow into Eric's face if he had not vanished from the seat of his horse. Now, with Eric teleporting to one of the towers, the bombard was set and ready to launch the strike. The commanders of the double cannons raced the artillery closer with hopes of reaching the top crenellations from a low location. Even so, the catapults started to fire upon the city.

Lai Kai, in full black ninja regalia, met with Shioda upon the crenellations and assessed the impending doom. He said coolly, "Forget the soldiers! They are of no consequence! Those strange contraptions are preparing to fire!"

"I'm ahead of you, Lai!" Shioda had just previously called for the rockets to his left to fire for the double cannons and catapults. The machine guns immediately concentrated on the artillery machines currently advancing.

"Arrows!" Shadisha cried.

All at once, the Falcuns unleashed their blazing arrows for the advancing legionnaires below. As the arrows struck the soldiers down, the catapults were already enduring machine gun fire. Even so, the catapults were able to fire off their first round. Three searing boulders hurled for the city beyond the great wall.

As the boulders came close, Michael caught one of them with his strong telekinetic senses and smashed it into the other. As a result of the strenuous tactic, the two blazing projectiles fell short and crashed into the moat, shaking some sections of the wall. He caught the last remaining fireball and steadied it in midair. Immediately after the legionnaires dropped their jaws in wonder, Michael guided the blazing missile directly towards one of the catapults to the far left. As he steadied it eight feet above the sand, the legionnaires ran for their lives, retreating from the oncoming fireball soaring for them.

It finally crashed into one of the contraptions and blew it to pieces. The Falcun rockets then tactically fired upon the remaining two, finally destroying them as well. The Falcuns cheered as Michael proved his worth. However, nothing was more dreaded than the terrible bombard that was in range and ready to fire. Kane called upon the other two bombards to roll into the offensive and assist the assault. Consequently, the last four contraptions set off to partake in the bout. The pair of catapults and rocket launchers rolled faster passed the huge bombards.

The infantry had dwindled to a mere nine hundred men. Kane was desperate to unleash the true power of the demonic bombard. Falcun rockets were able to strike a rapid firing rocket launcher inside the gages and totally destroy it.

The city cheered the fleeting triumph but became real to the fact that there was much more to fear. Within seconds, the enormous contraption detonated a large steel ball for the holy city's great wall. It still had some scorching powder razing off of it as it hurled for the city.

As everyone on the crenellations looked on at the terrible ball of destruction that seemed to coast through the air, they started running for cover. Now with a large section of the crenellations vacant and bearing down for impact, Michael decided to change the tides. Sure that it would strike the wall directly, he summoned his great powers with intentions of stopping the bullet.

As it reamed closer, Michael sized up the projectile's force and stretched out his arms. When he had it figured, Michael desperately seized the metal ball. Groaning and pushing himself to the limit, the ball shook and wobbled as it came dreadfully close with the same voracity. He pushed himself further, trying with every inch of his might to stop it from advancing. The crenellations began to crumble about him and break up under his feet.

When everyone was sure that his valorous act would end in tragedy, Michael stunned all. Within a split second of the ball's impact, Michael's eyes turned crimson red and an abysmal blast emitted from his being. He cried with rage until the enormous ball of disaster suddenly stopped altogether. It abruptly stalled in midair. The shockwave sent many back, but the destructive bullet was dead in the sky.

Then, with Michael's evil power still great, he screamed and impelled the steel ball back, faster than it came. He guided the projectile with furious anger and cried out like a demon. Michael's eyes illuminated a brighter crimson, his powers instilling fear in any who witnessed his impractical strength.

Especially for the Mad Legion, their cause instantly dwindled. The legionnaires manning the bombard watched their bullet come back for them in shock. Most of them began to run away, but there was no time to get clear. The ball darted right back into the hot barrel from whence it came and erupted the entire contraption into wild fiery pieces, evoking terror in every dark soldier.

After the Falcuns watched the spectacle unfold, they all cheered and celebrated the destruction of the awful weapon. Kane winced back on his horse and screamed in horror, "How? What in hell?"

One of the cavalrymen said from behind his helmet, "The lord warned us of this. Miuriell is with them."

Michael's furious outburst had taken much out of him. He needed to catch his breath. Lai ran to him, followed by other Falcuns, and held him up from under his shoulders. It was then that they noticed Michael's eyes. They remained the crimson bright red. Instead of fading away like before, his eyes remained as they were—a sinister red.

"Michael, your eyes!" A ninja uttered.

Another unsheathed one of his katana blades and allowed Michael to see his own face through the reflection. Stunned beyond belief, he peered into the reflective steel with fearful repercussions, not fully understanding why the crimson hue refused to dissipate. Rather, it remained and replaced his light brown eyes with an evil color. Abaddon had broken through that far.

The fighting did not subside after the dazing counterattack. In minutes passing, Shioda summoned a joint rocket assault in front of the main drawbridge where the mad infantry ran amuck. The rockets simultaneously fired their round upon the same location. The legionnaires were overwhelmed with the massive destruction that overtook them like sitting ducks. They had expected the wall to have come crashing down, only to be stalled in the most terrible position on the field.

The drawbridge slammed onto the ground, providing the pathway for the Eastern cavalry to charge out and cut down any legionnaires they found. The major target was the artillery contraptions. Once they were all silenced, the battle would be over. Once the drawbridge was down, Maxim rode ahead of the cavalry and unsheathed his fire-sword, leading the reserves to finish off the artillery divisions.

Like the rush of an avalanche, the Tinarians blasted out of the gate and completely overwhelmed the last of the Mad Legion's infantry. Horses trudged over and into them with ease. In the dense smog of the rockets' aftermath, the legionnaires were helpless to the hackings and stabbings of the rushing Tinarian cavalry. Predella, replenished with an array of lethal arrows, had already shot two foes with a single arrow. Its great power zipped through one of their necks and then poked into the next one's eye socket. Her aim was demoralizing.

After the Tinarians had cut down every last legionnaire in their sights, Esker's cavalry reserve division rushed out of the gate and targeted various contraptions from afar. The two collective Eastern forces quickly learned to combine their strengths, picking off feeble infantrymen. The double cannons turned away from the walls of Falcus and sized up the given number of cavalrymen charging them. Predella fired off an enflamed arrow that filled a cannon and blasted the contraption to pieces. Other cavalrymen tossed spears into their enemies' formations.

Maxim allowed his men to finish off the remaining enemies from the cannon line as he led a separate charge for the catapults. The two bombards were approaching from the south and Maxim was aware that those forces had to be neutralized first. The Ziamon cavalry had already taken off for the bombards when Maxim had initially headed for the cannons. As he watched Esker lead his men towards the advancing machines, the Tinarian knight raised his sword and ran to intercept the catapult division. The legionnaires there unleashed a surprising storm of arrows that rained upon them as they advanced. As horsemen fell to the fatal rain, Maxim pressed on with Predella close by his side.

When they jointly intercepted the catapult division due southwest from the kingdom, the bowmen couldn't prevent the legionnaires' rout. Maxim deflected as many arrows that targeted him until he met with the archers and spearmen down below his horse. With the enraged fury of his Mad Phoenix, Maxim left a searing wasteland of scorched infantrymen in his path. Like the god of war, Maxim set free his wrath upon the enemy. In despair, Kane ordered that all of his cavalry ride off to protect the bombards from the Falcuns' reserves. The last bombards were necessary to complete the distraction.

While the Eastern warriors finished off the Mad Legion, Eric teleported from tower to tower and from keep to keep all in the hopes of finding his sister. For reasons he could not comprehend, he felt Shina's presence in the nearest spire. The eerie feeling saddened his soul, for he never wanted harm to come to her. Yet, that was why he insisted on taking her to the Demon Plague instead. He believed that she would be safer with the winning force. Eric resolved that Shina was better off as a demon queen than a dead princess.

Finding the window pane from outside the balcony, he called upon a lethal spell. An explosive discharge of energy burst the glass inside the tower and paved the way for Eric's entrance. As he hopped into the tower and onto a landing between steps, Eric was certain that his sister was close.

However, scattered ninja warriors, already primed for the ambush, surrounded him.

Without hesitation, Eric kneeled and called upon one of his most vicious ice spells. Within seconds, an awesome expulsion of frigid ice swallowed the entire edifice. The high chamber had become a rime dungeon with cold silence. His enemies were frozen dead and in the room across the way, enclosed in ice, he felt his sister's frightened presence.

Eric extended his right hand forward and blew through the heavy door consumed by ice, tearing it from its steel hinges. The deafening explosion slammed the door inside the next room and demolished the icy surroundings. Amongst the mumblings for which Eric could not understand, Shina's terrified whimper ringed in his ear. Protected by ninja warriors inside, Shina was sure to fear the insanity of the beast that would come all this way to recapture her.

Readying himself for the slaughter, Eric propelled a force field around the blown doorway that only he could penetrate. As the ninjas prepared for battle, he sauntered towards the cursed entry. Shina couldn't clearly see her brother's face but was sure that her enemy was twisted with dark magic. The ninjas demanded their adversary to reveal his name before they flogged him with their deadly weapons.

Eric clasped his hands together and cast a sneaky spell. In due time, the ninjas realized that their darts couldn't penetrate the magical barrier. Finally, their weapons became so hot that none of them could hold onto them. Their weapons melted into the ground and were diminished to heaps of magma.

As the ninjas stressed over their futile weaponry, Eric dashed through his force field and struck everyone at once from his hands. The bolts of energy shocked every last ninja to their death and Shina finally discovered her adversary's true identity. She tightly swathed her arms around herself and anxiously stepped farther away from him, mumbling in a confused fright.

"Brother?" she gasped. "It can't be you!"

Eric stepped closer with his arms open, "Sister! I've come to save you!"

"What are you? Stay away!" Shina stepped as far back as she could until she reached the dome-shaped wall, plastered with ancient art. Refusing to waste any more time, Eric peered into her eyes and griped, "I promise that you will understand when this is over."

However, Eric underestimated the stealth of his enemies. Three ninja warriors had made their way up the frozen staircase antechamber and uncovered the evil sorcerer's force field with the Tinarian princess in his hands. Together, they tossed three grenades up to the doorway, tapping against the wall. Unbeknownst to him, the three shells detonated and devastated the force field, emitting a shocking blast. Debris screamed into the room.

The sudden shock from the explosion and the effect of the debris took Eric to the ground. Shina, too, fell to the floor and cried out. Fearing the worst, the sorcerer raised his hand and released bright charges of magic in all directions, destroying anything in its path. Despite the traumatizing effect of the blasts, he used the same deadly spell to blow a hole into the ceiling. Subsequently, he cried in agony of small pieces of debris that had lodged into his right arm, making its way inside his armor.

With a section of the dome roof blasted through, outside Falcun forces took their attention to the high tower. Rubble had fallen to the ground and warned the city of the breach. The three ninjas still took cover from the possible energy bursts from the magician behind the smoke of the grenades' aftermath.

Eric knew that he needed to escape without exceptions. He summoned a spell that had given him a pair of magical wings that grew from his back. The wings sparkled with radiant energy, making him airborne. Eric took his sister from the floor and soared into the air, bleeding from the blast moments ago.

Once he left the dome roof of the tower, he flew through the skies of Falcus and headed due south. Eric swallowed his pain with intentions of escaping with Shina in his arms, alive, flying in-between structures and scorching bystanders with his dark magic. But once he reached the front crenellations of Falcus, Eric outstretched his right hand and discharged concentrated energy blasts for the crenellations. The sections of the high wall took the vehement strike of the electric clouting. The explosions sent Falcun warriors into the sky along with geysers of rubble. Michael and Lai were amongst the line of carnage.

The destructive blow from the evil sorcerer, soaring away from the city, could not penetrate Michael's powerful force field. While it protected Lai as well, the magical strike still obliterated the wall around them. With the rubble that fell in destructive heaps, they plummeted. The unaffected sections of the battlements fired for the sinister warlock in vengeance. The shots were accurate, but Eric was able to endure the harsh assault. One of them nicked his left wing, though it did not foil his flight.

Kane saw a flying entity in the sky from his lone horse and whisked out a telescope. Steadying the eye, he discovered Eric soaring towards him with the princess in his grasp. Relieved, he allowed Eric to fly for him and watched his cavalry gallop to aid the other legionnaires defend the bombards. Their mission was almost complete.

Maxim and Predella had raced like fierce lions on horseback. The Ziamon cavalry had cut down many foot soldiers, preventing them from firing any rounds from the bombards. But the legionnaire cavalry had employed a counterattack. Becoming much more difficult for the Ziamons to kill their enemies for good, Maxim vaulted from his horse and allowed it to run off in fright. Predella remained on her charger and fired devastating shots for grouped opponents, killing them with fire and ice.

Jolted off his horse by a legionnaire cavalryman, Esker quickly rolled onto his feet and unleashed hell, thrashing his opponents to bloody cadavers with his cruel blades. Blocking and parrying every attack, Maxim overwhelmed his victims with great force. His fire-sword thirsted for flesh and flesh it was given. Lopping off heads and slashing stomachs open, he defeated every warrior he faced.

While Predella picked off the opposition with the abundance of arrows she had left, the airborne sorcerer caught her eye. He flew with recklessness over her head and beyond the bombards towards the distant forest. She fired one last steady arrow into an adversary's unprotected neck before crying Maxim's name. Maxim, though mesmerized by the brutal combat, heard her calling. She pointed to the sky and pinpointed the magician taking the princess away.

Without delay, Maxim leaped onto a foe's back and then propelled himself into the air. While airborne for a moment, he grappled onto a passing enemy cavalryman. Grabbing onto his helmet, Maxim pulled himself onto the back of the horse and broke the legionnaire's neck from behind. He tossed the limp foe to the ground and took full command of the dark steed.

Maxim withdrew from the battle and dashed in the direction of the flying villain. Predella urged those remaining to do everything in their power to disable the bombards. She rode off after Maxim and prepared for a grueling chase.

With the two Eastern warriors gone, the other knights and soldiers battled the remnants of the Mad Legion. The very legionnaire that boldly struck Esker from his horse earlier had met him again, armed with a long-bladed spear. He charged the justice on his horse, keen on finishing the job. A Ziamon soldier threw an ax and struck the horse's side. The animal cried and collapsed to the ground, throwing the legionnaire to the sand. He quickly regained his composure and fixed his skull helmet. Esker allowed his rival to come forth unopposed by any other warrior. The Ziamons knew the code. When a challenge was met amongst the arena of war, no other fighter could intervene until the bout was finished.

The duel was underway. The warrior swung his spear rapidly around his body and attacked the justice with great fury. Deeply engulfed in the gratification of conflict, Esker matched the blows and deflected every last strike with his two serrated blades. As the fierce battle continued, he found a prolonged opening and stabbed his vindictive blade into the enemy's flesh, underneath the arm. Rattled from the pain, the legionnaire became prey.

Esker tore the blade out from his flesh and hacked the challenger's knee cap to bits before carving a mortal scar into his helmet and face. Futile, the enemy fell to the ground and could not thwart Esker from finishing him off with two fatal plummets from two cruel blades into the torso. With his rival mutilated, he ripped the blood-sodden swords from the corpse and reveled in the cheers of his fellow Ziamons.

When the Eastern warriors finished off the remainder of the Mad Legion, Falcus applauded their fighting spirits. Women and children came out from their shelters and applauded the victory, realizing that the threat was over. Only one legionnaire survived as a prisoner of war. Shioda was not going to allow the attack on Falcus to go unpunished. He needed to discover why and how they assaulted the holy city. They all wanted to know what the Demon Plague was planning next.

The great wall was vulnerable near the gate. The moat was red with the blood of the enemy and the fields were littered with bodies. Large debris from the terrible contraptions was laid to rest and thousands of shells littered the dry ground. The Eastern warriors headed back to the city to revel in the glory of their victory. From the battlefield, it was almost impossible to make out Falcus on account of the smoke lingering in the air.

Among the mounds of debris behind the wall, Falcuns helped their architect, Lai Kai, from the mess. He was hurt, but not gravely injured. He removed his mask and breathed the free air. However, the true scene was Michael Miuriell's rescue. Out from the same rubble heap, Michael recovered his staff, his eyes still illuminating a sinister crimson.

Most of Falcus found out that an evil sorcerer escaped with Princess Shina. What they did not know, but were soon to discover, was that Maxim and Predella were chasing after him with great haste. Predella cried to Maxim from behind as they rode staunchly in the sorcerer's direction, "He is landing just up ahead! He may be hurt!"

As they both rode on, Kane had already started his full retreat. With Shina in Eric's hands, his mission was accomplished and there was no reason to remain there any longer. Clearly, his army of over two thousand was annihilated. While he rode in the direction towards the Ghost Forest, Eric swooped down directly behind him and cried out with Shina just dangling now in his weak arms, "Kane, take her! I can't hold on any longer!"

Coming to a stark halt, Kane arrested his horse and looked behind him in case others were following. Eric landed before his wings vanished into oblivion. Handing his sister up over to him, he cringed from the severe agony he experienced from his critical wounds. Strapping the unconscious princess to his back with twine, Kane looked down onto his sorcerer from the saddle and said with disgust, "What happened to her?"

Eric responded while holding onto his injured right arm, "She fainted while I was airborne! Harm her in any way and I'll—"

"Why didn't you just teleport, idiot?" Kane shouted.

"I can't in this condition!" Eric cried back. "I can't chance what might happen to her if I do!"

"You're such a useless tool!" Kane rode off after hearing the oncoming sounds of horses galloping near. He hollered for his steed to push on to reach the cover of the forest. Eric, still agonizing over his wounds, chanted a spell that turned him into transparent matter. He was as good as invisible to the fast passing warriors who rushed by on their horses. He easily recognized Maxim and Predella on the steeds.

"Where did he go?" Maxim cried out as they rode.

"There!" Predella pointed onward at Kane riding far ahead of them. "That horseman has her!"

"Whoever he is, he's dead!" Maxim compelled the horse to dash faster.

They pursued Kane with great speed. Knowledgeable of his enemies' pursuance, he rushed for the Ghost Forest just ahead. They could easily see that Shina was tied unnervingly to his back and to the horse by a rope just under her breasts. She was still unconscious, making it easier for Kane to steal her away without a fuss.

"I have a shot!" Predella shouted while she charged an arrow on her bow.

"Wait!" Maxim countered from her right side. "We can't chance it! I'll take the princess from him. Then you take him down!"

A surprise for the two pursuers was waiting in a small bag tied to the lead horse's girth. Kane dug his hand into it and pulled out a grenade. From his jarring ride, Kane lit the explosive projectile with a spark and tossed it behind him.

Predella saw the shell hit the ground and bounce for them, so she used a charged arrow to seal it. The arrow struck the grounded grenade, overcoming it with ice. The frigidness of the enchanted arrowhead silenced the explosive from ever going off. Kane, bewildered by the silence, figured that it was a dud. He pulled two out this time and lit them both with the spark plate, ultimately tossing them behind him frantically.

Predella shot one of them with a flaming arrow as it still lingered in the air. It exploded and stunned them both for a brief moment. The second grenade, however, rolled onto the ground and exploded beside Maxim's horse before she could silence it with another ice arrow. The blast shook the land and Maxim steered his dashing horse as far from the detonation as possible.

She wanted to pierce a hole into his artillery sack but didn't want to risk it detonating all of the other grenades inside. Maxim, however, was coming up fast on Kane's left side. The general readied his ax, as his broadsword was too heavy to steady while on horseback. Maxim buckled down and fueled his focus, fearing that Shina was already dead.

Maxim hastily steered the steed closer and then hurriedly sliced the rope that fastened Shina to her abductor. Still tied to the horse, Shina's body became limp and her right arm was in his reach. However, Kane swiped the weighty battle ax with his right arm, attempting to hack off Maxim's reaching hand. Maxim pulled away and countered with his fire-sword, unable to shroud his enemy in a fire for the princess's sake. Thus, he fought with Kane as they raced on horseback.

Maxim swatted the ax with the pommel of his sword and then stuck the sharp end of the blush blade into a piece of Kane's armor. In his pauldron, Maxim tried to maneuver the evil warrior so that he could steal the ax. Kane recovered and jolted him away with it. He then took swipes for the hero's head, but Maxim lodged his sword into the ax's designs and hindered Kane's lethal swinging of the weapon.

Just as Maxim thought he could disarm him, he saw Kane's left and open hand reach for the broadsword on the right side of the horse. He looked into Kane's mad helmet and ogled his wide angry eyes peering through the faceplate. Maxim barely dodged the fierce horizontal strike by leaning back and allowing the broadsword to just skim over his chest, missing his flesh. After rushing by a rogue tree, Maxim's wrist slammed it and knocked the Mad Phoenix out of his hand.

The fire-sword danced in the air until Predella caught it by the hilt. However, she had forgotten the excruciating effects of the blade. Her hand instantly seared from the mysterious handle and she shouted, letting loose of it. It fell into her lap as she cautiously handled the sword by its blade. She growled from the agony, looking down at the scar on her palm.

In the meantime, Maxim unsheathed a small dagger from his ankle scabbard and sliced Kane's demolition sack open, letting the futile grenades to fall out and scatter all over the ground harmlessly. Kane, infuriated, went to stab the hero in the stomach, but Maxim swerved away so that he could evade the attack.

Away from Kane's devastating blades, Maxim cast the small dagger directly into the villain's armed left hand, forcing him to drop the broadsword to the ground. In great pain and shock, Kane vigorously pried the knife from his leather gauntlet and the top of his hand. Confounded, he couldn't believe how someone could be skilled enough to throw a knife with such accuracy and strength.

Maxim, content with the attack, met up with Predella again and she tossed him his sword by the hot blade. Kane continued to race into the Ghost Forest, throwing the bloodied knife away. His hand healed straight away, but it had grown small measures of demonic skin. He didn't have time to worry about it. Pushing for the east, Kane decided to lose his pursuer in Evertz Caverns—an underground mining network of caves.

The jarring ride jostled Shina around on the horse since she was partially untied from Kane's back. The rope around her waist and hind legs connected her to the horse's hide, but barely. Maxim and Predella persisted as they allowed him to drive his horse into the dense forestry. Dodging trees and branches, the chase became even more hazardous.

Kane swerved through any obstructions to throw off his chasers. Maxim hacked branches and vines to keep steady on his foe's trail. Predella's horse caught her leg on an exposed tree root, compelling it to tumble to the ground. She rolled onto the forest soil and fired an arrow for Kane's helmet, hoping that it would kill him. The arrow whizzed through the trees and pricked Kane's armament on his left appendage. Due to the awkward angle of the arrow and the level texture to Kane's armor, it deflected into the grass.

His ghastly armor gained a new scar, sparing his life. Her shot may have been successful if the palm of her hand had not blistered from the fire-sword's handle. She could have pierced the arrow through the armor, otherwise. With

Predella incapacitated, it was up to Maxim to reclaim Shina for the resistance and kill the abductor once and for all.

Through the trees, Kane found Evertz Cave and was sure to ride into it with blazing speed. The cave contained miners' contraptions and warrens, though illuminated with torches. The fueled lights alerted them to the miners at work somewhere in the caverns. It was as good as a maze for anyone who had never explored the network, but Maxim, nevertheless, followed his enemy into the labyrinth. Pursuing him with a fit of passionate anger, he was willing to sacrifice everyone inside the caves if only to safeguard the princess.

The cave was too narrow to ride up beside him. He would need to pull off a miraculous trick from behind. Mining stations scattered about forced them to leap over and skirt inside the tight spaces. Kane led him into a different tunnel where the floor rushed with streaming water from up ahead, leading out towards the sea.

There, the miners had set traps to arm the sea cave so that intruders couldn't come in from the water. Darts shot from the walls after Kane's steed triggered the traps. Maxim blocked all that he could with his blade before taking one in his arm. He groaned and pulled it out. It didn't seem to be poisoned. Even if it was, it couldn't stop him anyway. Kane then decided to manufacture his own trap. He raised his blade above him with both hands and let the cutting edge scrape the ceiling. Fragments of debris fell into Maxim's path.

Enraged, Maxim pushed his horse to dash faster. He was going to risk everything to get Shina back. He rushed through the falling rubble and tried to ride beside Kane. His sword erupted with angry flames. Kane was on to Maxim's strong advance. He swung his ax with his left hand to bash the horse's head in and, in turn, hinder Maxim's pursuance. Maxim blocked every strike with furious wrath.

His left shoulder crashed into a protruding stone from the tunnel, but he accepted the blow and continued to challenge Kane's attacks. Finally, Maxim unleashed a vicious vertical strike that lopped off Kane's armed left hand. The villain cried in agony as the ax fell through his horse's running legs. Maxim then swiped the last rope clean from Shina's waste with his searing blade. As Shina began to slip off, he reached over and seized her by the blouse. As he held onto her tightly, Maxim cut the escaping horse's hide with his enflamed sword. Overwhelmed by the strike, the horse cried and stumbled to the watery floor.

Kane roared as he tumbled along with his dying horse, mortally injured and without a hand. Thankfully, Maxim remained strong and sustained his grip on the princess. The horse fell, but Maxim swung Shina onto his lap, slowing down his steed in the process. His horse was exhausted and could not help but fall onto her knees. He fell off into the water with it, dunking the princess. She awoke thereafter, thrashing about in the sea cave.

Maxim came to her aid, hardly able to keep himself above the knee-deep water. He embraced and kissed her, thanking God in the process, "Princess, are you alright?"

"Maxim? What happened?" she cried out, feeling the smarting pains of the chase all over her body. "Where are we now? I'm hurt!"

"Where are you hurt, princess?" he asked, still trying to catch his breath.

"Everywhere!" Shina screamed passionately. "What did my brother do to me?"

"Your brother? Eric?" Maxim said, confused. He figured that she was delusional from the trauma she endured.

Kane tried to scurry away from the brutal scene, pulling Maxim away from the princess. He supported her against the wall of the sea cave and told her, "Stay here and rest. I'll be right back."

As she sat in the water, leaning against the cave, Maxim approached the dying horse and general with his fire-sword. First, he stabbed the horse through the head, putting it out of its misery and into flames. But then, the true kill was at hand. Watching his newest enemy roll onto his back, Maxim raised the blade into the air and angrily plunged the sword into Kane's heart, setting his body aflame.

Maxim pulled out the Mad Phoenix, quenched with blood, and tiredly returned to his princess, safely seated by his exhausted horse. Kane shouted from the searing heat that scorched his skin, cooking him inside his armor. After rolling around in the rushing water, hollering from his mortal wounds, the water extinguished the fire. Yet, Maxim didn't attempt to kill him again. Though he lived long enough to wash out the flames over his body, he was dead soon after.

Lying lifeless in the small stream, Kane was finished. Maxim breathed heavily as he cleaned his blush sword in the tiny stream. The blood rushed off the sizzling blade and flowed behind him. His stolen horse was eager to escape the hostilities. Fearing what could happen next, Maxim's borrowed horse galloped for an exit from the cave, leaping over Kane's cooked carcass. He didn't care. Maxim was only grateful that Shina was safe and out of the Demon Plague's grasp.

Maxim sheathed his fire-sword and lifted Shina in his arms, holding her like a bride. He walked by the carcasses and hoped that the cave ended somewhere by the shore. He needed to breathe fresh air.

From one footstep to the next, the knight did not know where he was going. With hope, he figured that he would just stumble upon the exit—if there was one. He eventually met up with the origin of the water current, leading him to the sea cave's entrance. Maxim seemed to be marooned at the Great Pacifica. He simply looked out of the sea cave and admired the horizon.

"Maxim?" Shina uttered, still suspended in his arms.

"Yes, princess?" Maxim replied, joining her in looking over the beautiful ocean.

She started to cry again, muttering, "I'm sorry. I'm so sorry for all this!"

Maxim shook his head and said to her, "Shina, you have nothing to apologize for. We're in this together—all the way to the end."

When he was certain that no one would be able to find them there, miners had come following them out. He turned around to confront the four of them, staring at him in shock. When there appeared to be a standoff, one of them said, "We thought we saw two horsemen ride into this cave. We saw what happened to the other one."

Maxim, unsure of how to respond, held Shina tightly in his arms and said nothing. The same man said further, "Are you from Ellium?"

Taking time to answer, he replied, "Tinarian."

Another wheezed, "Tinarian? What brings you all the way out here, aside from killing warlords?"

"The Demon Plague," Maxim said with exhaustion as he moved closer. "Falcus was attacked. That's where we came from. That's where we need to return."

Hearing the thundering sounds of war for themselves, the miners agreed to escort him and the foreign princess to the mine's exit. Helping Shina through the cave, they asked Maxim to remember them in case the Demon Plague reached Shopville, where the miners were based. He patched up his bleeding arm with some medical equipment provided for him. In their gratitude for the miners' aid, Maxim and Shina walked out into daylight.

Just yards away from the cave, they saw Predella and some Ellium knights conversing civilly. When she noticed her Tinarian allies emerge from Evertz Caverns, Predella urged the paladins to meet them. Shina knew who they were, as she met the legate on her trip to Ellium years back. She spotted him among the other paladins, armed in silver plate mail and illustrious visor helmets. Knights equipped with maces and longswords, each carrying stalwart white shields with the red crucifix in the middle, ushered their commander to meet the Tinarian princess halfway.

"Is that Princess Shina?" Thomas exclaimed. "My God, it's been years!"

"Legate, it's good to see you again. A pity that it must be under these circumstances," Shina said while she extended her soiled hand to greet him.

Wearing his gauntlet, the Falcun ambassador took her hand and was going to kiss it until he saw the filth of the cave all over her fair skin. Donned in royal armor with a purple and white cape, the blonde-haired, blue-eyed paladin gasped, "Heavens, princess, you've been through hell. We must get you cleaned up proper, at once."

"You have no idea," she said, retracting her hand in embarrassment. "This is Maxim Cavallo, Tinaria's champion."

"Cavallo? I thought you had died!" he uttered in shock. "I never imagined—"

"I've died many times, I wager, but I've got some things to finish before I commit to staying dead, I guess," he said, shaking the legate's hand.

Thomas replied, "We shall take you back to Falcus and clean you up. We missed the fight, it appears."

"The real fight may just be upon us," Predella declared.

The legate asked her, "Is Michael Miuriell with you?"

"Yes, he helped defend the city," she said.

"Then we have a chance," Thomas sighed. "Ellium is prepared to join the fight against the demons, so let's get to Falcus as fast as it is practical."

Together, as a single unit, the party traveled back to Falcus. Thomas got word that Manna Excallum, his father, had died a small time before. Returning to Falcus was surely a bittersweet occasion. He hadn't returned for his father's funeral service, for his duties to the realm were far too great. Instead, Manna telepathically connected with his son and granted him his final wishes just before he breathed his last. His message: *Stay in faith, for I will always be with you now.*

PART II
CHAPTER VIII
THE AFTERMATH

Falcuns had scurried to stash the Mad Legion's massive artillery to study how they were made and with what materials. As the Falcuns did this, Colonel Aramis sat on the edge of the moat and resignedly dipped his large broadsword into the water, tainted with blood. He dipped the heavy blade with a trying sigh, catching his breath from the previous battle. The moat appeared to be filled with blood more than water. Officers reported that only three soldiers had fallen to the legionnaires. It was a stirring victory.

Other Ziamons had come to wash the blood from their weapons and out of their hair. One of them spit a jostled tooth out into the moat water and patted another on the back, satisfied with the outcome of the battle. Tinarians did the same by the entrance, congregating by the fallen wall. They waited for Maxim's return, hoping that their princess was with him.

The rubble from the wall's destruction was not as bad as they thought. Many parts were easy to repair, but the gaping hole where Eric obliterated the crenellations during his escape proved to be much more taxing. Arduous labor awaited the populace in ridding the city of debris. Michael's valiant defense of the city spread to every corner of Falcus. His nefarious transformation, however, was kept quiet, so as not to alarm the people. He remained with Urik in the Principal's Palace, worried about his eyes.

After the battle was done, there was not one person who could describe the nature of their new enemies. The Mad Legion was never encountered before, but there was no explanation as to how they were able to assemble at the edge of the Ghost Forest with heavy artillery without being discovered by the rogue ninja clans. Michael recognized that the Demon Lord sent this human militia to distract the city as Eric recaptured Princess Shina—betraying the world in the process.

Bursting through Urik's double doors, Michael made his way to the prophet's bed. His crimson eyes gleamed with anger, reeling the Kai guards that tended to him. The prophet understood that the battle was over and Falcus was victorious. From his propped-up position, the prophet gazed into Michael's eyes and declared, "You exerted your powers."

"I had no choice," Michael said. "What's happening?"

"Abaddon is pushing through," Urik coughed before firmly grabbing Michael's shoulder. He said sincerely, "And have you changed? You are still Michael Miuriell. The color of your eyes can never change this. Your soul remains intact, especially with this old man. You may look a bit more like them, but you'll always be who you choose to be."

Moved by his mentor's genuine words, Michael nodded gratefully. He wished that he could have given him better news, but Shina was taken. The Mad Legion was decimated, but their mission was ultimately accomplished. He said with tension in his voice, "Shina was taken by a sorcerer."

Before Michael could use his powerful abilities to search for her, Urik gasped, "A sorcerer, you say? I assume your old friend from Tinaria has thrown his lot in with the Demon Plague?"

"The Demon Lord uses him to perform his dirty work in the daylight," Michael answered heatedly. "God knows how long he's been—"

"Whatever it was, that man is motivated by one thing. He's not an idiot. Find out what they've got on him and you can use it against him. Perhaps you can even turn him. But consider this. There are no sorcerers powerful enough to do what he did," Urik explained. "This magician's powers were granted to him."

"He had magical abilities back east," Michael said. "All that time, he was working for the Demon Plague. It's hard to believe."

"Both the warrior and the sorcerer were coaxed," Urik deciphered. "Yet, the sorcerer would have needed knowledge of the elements to wield the magic. He must have already learned some."

"Yes, but that's not my point," Michael said. "The only thing he cared about was his sister. He couldn't even imagine the idea of any demon touching her. For him to steal Shina from where she was safest and deliver her straight into their hands doesn't make sense."

"It certainly doesn't." Urik coughed again. "Like I said. Find out what they've got on him. It's not too late."

Michael nodded in gratitude and then asked him, "Is there anything I can do for you? What do you need?"

"These aids here have given me everything I need." The sage smiled. "What you can do for all of humanity is get back out there and learn what you can about our enemy."

Using his staff as leverage, Michael rose from his knee and left his teacher, saying, "Shioda took a prisoner today. I'll pick his brain, or what's left of it."

Urik called out to him just before he left the room. As Michael turned around, the sage said to him, "When your son looks upon you, he will see you as you are inside. He'll see you as we all do."

Shedding tears from his reddened eyes, Michael heard his teacher's words and internalized them as he went out.

Lana Kai had launched a search party to find Princess Shina and the two sage apprentices who went after her. They could not have known that Shina was asleep in a warm carriage alongside Thomas Excallum. Maxim and Predella walked alongside the car with paladins leading the way. The party approached a small ridge in the grass that led them to a higher level of the land. From there, Falcus was clearly visible. However, before they could advance up the slender slope, a frigid wind had come whooshing down upon them. The wind became colder and its ferocity had escalated to the level where everyone was forced to stop and cower to the ground.

As everyone cried for mercy in the bitter cold confusion, a sudden gust of winter had burst through, consuming them with freezing anguish. A soldier cried out amongst the squalls, "Where the—what's happening?"

"The sorcerer!" Predella shouted. "He's here!"

While the fierce blizzard winds had compelled the horses to flee the scene, a figure manifested atop the head of the slope. Long hair flowed violently from the rushing winds. It looked like a woman for a moment, but Predella was not fooled by the person's gestures. She tagged him as the same sorcerer that stole Shina from the Falcuns.

With a strong supernatural tone, the sorcerer cried out amongst the drafts of the flash blizzard, "Deliver the princess to me at once!"

"Go to hell, you son of a bitch!" Maxim hollered amid the storm.

The sorcerer raised his hand and the snowy winds stopped. Standing up in the snow, Maxim and Predella readied their weapons for another possible attack. As the party frigidly awaited the sorcerer's identity, the winds finally stopped and Eric revealed himself.

"Eric?" Maxim panted in bewilderment. "Is that you? It can't be you!"

Eric cried out again with more passion this time, "I will not ask again! Give Shina to me before I kill every last one of you mindless fools!"

Fearing the Demon Plague's power and dreading his soiled stature amongst his companions, Eric was, once again, an interloper. Seeing Predella jogged his memory of what he had done to the Waasi settlement. The more his conscience battered him, the greater his hatred for the world became.

Maxim riposted with hatred in his spirit, "You betrayed us! You killed Drake!"

"My cause is beyond Shina's or your understanding! Do as I ask or I will not spare a soul!" Eric erupted.

"Why?" Predella screamed. "How could you?"

"Him? *That* is the sorcerer?" Thomas emerged from his carriage, stepping into fresh snow.

"Stay inside, sir!" A crusader shouted.

Eric hissed, "You've wasted enough of my time!"

Before Predella could respond with an arrow to the skull, Shina followed Thomas out of the carriage, inducing Maxim to shout out, "Shina, stay inside the—"

Seeing his sister out in the open, Eric seized the chance and she simply disappeared into a flurry of magic. Maxim ran to protect her, but it was too late. He plowed through her ghostly self before the magic had dissipated completely. Eric teleported her elsewhere.

"Where is she?" Maxim cried belligerently.

"She is safe—safer than the rest of you," Eric said before teleporting himself, glaring into Predella's eyes as he vanished.

Confounded by abhorrence, Maxim screamed into the air. One of the paladin officers muttered, holding snow in his hand, "Not since centuries ago was there sorcery like this."

"Who, in God's name, was that?" another asked.

Predella responded frustratingly, "One who chooses demons over his own kind! He lied about his sorcery back in the East."

"He's nothing we thought he was!" Maxim continued his outburst, shouting, "He's a demon-lover!"

"It's treachery," Thomas said. "Why does he want your princess? What is she to him?"

"His sister," Predella replied.

"Holy hell," he gasped. "Are you sure that's really him?"

The Mad Legion's sacrifice had ultimately reared fruit. There was no one who could predict what the Demon Plague would do with her now. While they all conferred about what they would do when they returned to Falcus and how they would do it, Predella sensed a throng of steeds heading their way from over the slope. Maxim soon heard the horses and the broken calls of a hunting party.

Thomas scaled the slope himself and stabbed his rapier into the soil, relieved to finally reunite with his fellow Falcuns. Maxim and Predella joined the others atop the hill and watched Lana's party engage them with great enthusiasm. They were overjoyed to see that their legate had returned.

As the party converged with them, Maxim proclaimed angrily through his teeth, "I will not allow this day to be forgotten. Regardless of what the queen says, I promise that her son will meet the fiery edge of my sword."

Atop an ancient building marvel amid the ruins of the Primeval Tragedy memorial, Shina found herself nauseous and, on her knees, high above the world. The rusty roof of the old building seemed to break apart as she tried to stand up. Looking out over the remnants of a city from the old world, she covered her mouth in shock and went back to her knees. The wind howled up in the thin air, making her feel like it would blow her off the rickety structure. While the ancient skyscraper was not as unstable as she thought, it lived long past its due date to collapse. Many of the materials used for such edifices were synthetics made to withstand the years.

As part of the fenced-in memorial, dozens of stubborn city buildings from the old world lived on after death in a far-west sector of the realm. Many edifices had fallen over the years, causing giant clouds of perilous smoke to lift high and wide. People from all over the West had grown to see each building fall one at a time over the years. In time, there would be nothing left, as nature consumed the skeletons of the past.

Finally, the wounded sorcerer appeared before her on the roof, just hovering. Seeing her so scared and desperate pierced his heart, but he was certain that it was the only way to protect her. Eric said amidst the pain of his injuries, "These are the remnants of the old world. There are others far out west beyond the mountains, but few ever venture out there. This is a glimpse into our past—and our future."

Shina was unable to utter a word. She was stunned. He gently lowered himself onto the roof and walked towards her, then stopping when he saw her wince. From his place, Eric said, "I know this is not what you wanted of me. I know that you hold a precious innocence in your heart, but I'm the one who wants to save you. I can save you from all this."

When she just stood there, taken aback by everything, Eric outstretched his hand and said, "Take my hand, Shina."

She shook her head apprehensively, saying, "You are *not* my brother! I don't know who you are, but you are not my brother!"

"Sister, I have sacrificed more than you know! Some things that I've done—" He then yelled out of frustration, "You don't understand what I am trying to do! You're not safe! Only with the Demon Plague will you survive the day of reckoning. Your friends can't save you, let alone save their own hides!"

After grumbling from the throbbing pain, Eric inched closer to her and griped, "They told me about your true fate—your born purpose. You are to be their queen. Don't you see it, Shina? You'll then have the strength to watch over me, instead! We will be written in history as the humans who ruled the world!"

"What history? Demonic history?" Shina backed away from him. "Michael will not let you do this! He will stop this from happening!"

"No!" Eric cried, before grieving from his upset injuries. "There is no one who can protect you now! You must accept your fate or you will be prey to it!"

Hearing this talk come from her brother, she backed away further and started to cry, "Father was right about you! You are wicked!"

"Damn our father!" Eric cried vehemently. "Damn him! He's dead! A lucky break for the old coward! The rest of us will suffer far worse if we don't—"

Shina then continued to walk backward until she unknowingly headed for the edge. Watching her move too far back, he called for her, "Shina! Wait, Shina, be careful!"

"You are banished from God's eyes!" Shina cried just before heedlessly walking off the roof of the old building and falling into the pit of the city's graveyard.

In her fall, she screamed out hysterically, until Eric had materialized just beneath her. Joining in her fall, he held onto her and said something she couldn't hear amid the wind in her ears. The archaic buildings of an advanced civilization had seized her senses, erasing all her fear. The further Shina dropped, the more she marveled at the decaying wonders of the old world. As if in slow motion, she saw how nature had consumed them from the bottom, crawling up their bodies like a beautiful virus.

Eric teleported them both out of the sky just moments before they hit the ground. Instead, the remnants of his magical incantation showered over the vestiges of the world from long ago, conquered by flora and fauna. A pair of butterflies fluttered about, startled by the intrusion of magic.

Within the Falcun dungeon in the western prison, some officers started working over the only living captive from the battle an hour ago. The stripped legionnaire sat in a cold chair with his wrists bound behind him, seeming to stare right through them during the interrogation. One of them put a dagger on the table as if to frighten him. The threat had no real effect. The attack on Falcus was a suicide mission and he was prepared to die.

There was no use going any further on him until there was time. They waited until he became hungry, or thirsty for water or had to use the facilities to work on him for any information. He appeared languid, yet not scared. It was as if all human emotion had been removed from him. The Demon Plague programmed their warrior slaves well.

Finally, Michael asked to enter the interrogation room. With two officers already inside the cell, the guards allowed him in. His red eyes glowed amid the dimness of the room, making the officers yank their chairs to opposing sides. They had not seen his transformation before. Not many had.

But when he entered, the legionnaire propped up his head in sudden fear and straightened his posture. His eyes opening wide, the prisoner muttered, "Father."

"Don't call me that." Michael rebuked, standing over the others who looked on in surprise. "What is your name?"

"We have no name, father," he said, shivering from the anxiety just being in his presence.

Saying sternly, Michael pressed on, "I told you to stop calling me that!"

His chair ran backward and hit the wall, taking him three feet away from the table. The show of force had the prisoner shriek and comply straight away, "Yes! Forgive me! Forgive me for that! I'm sorry!"

"You will answer my questions truthfully and directly. Is that clear?" Michael said over him, realizing that the brute of the Mad Legion obeyed him absolutely.

As the prisoner nodded his head frantically, one of the officers said, "We've been trying to get him to say one word for over an hour! Just a word and he's yours?"

Disregarding their astonishment, Michael went on, "I want to know why you came here to wage war. Tell me now."

The prisoner said, "To send a message to the world that there is nowhere we cannot go—even in the daylight. I am your servant until my death, which I am—"

"Why do you serve them?" Michael asked.

"To serve the conquest. To spread dominion. They are within my head, within my spirit, and within my soul. I am a soldier of man, made in the image of Abaddon. You are our eternal savior! To death, I shall go, for the conquest. Do you wish me to die, my savior?" he said passionately, saliva running down his chin.

"My savior?" an officer uttered, looking to Michael for any clues for his insanity. After seeing the red of his eyes, he started to understand that Michael was more than a man. It was something evil.

"You will tell me why the Demon Plague wants the girl. What is the girl to them?" Michael said, his eyes glowing even more vibrant than before. "Why Shina?"

"Oh, she is your bride!" he said with an inflated grin. "Together, you shall birth a new breed of man! A new breed of humanity, thanks to you, savior! She is the Eve to your—"

"What are they doing with my son?" Michael hollered, making even the officers jump in their seats.

Baffled by his question, the prisoner only gasped, "I know no son, savior. Your bride has yet to have a son. But she will, by the—"

"Quiet." Michael stopped him from going any further. He just hung his head and tried to focus on the hard silence. It was evident that each person stricken with the madness knew only what was necessary as good slaves. The officers were sweating, feeling that something bigger than anything they thought they knew was happening right before their eyes. In the quiet, Michael turned to them both and sighed.

With his eyes shut, he said delicately, "I may appear different because I *am* different now. But, do not fear me. I'm the Michael Miuriell I will always be. Understand?"

As they agreed with shaking heads, he continued, "You may unshackle this man now."

The officers looked to each other with anxious stares before Michael insisted, "You'll have to trust me. He is under my power."

With others looking on from outside the cell, one of the officers came and released the prisoner. The man felt his sore wrists but remained in his chair. There was nothing he was going to do without Michael's command. Hence, he said to the prisoner, "Stand up and come to me."

When the prisoner did all that was demanded of him, Michael said directly into his eyes, pronouncing every word with care, "As father to the Demon Plague, I, Michael Miuriell, am bestowed with supreme authority over you. From this day forth, you are free. There is no more that you can do for the conquest. Any bonds left with them are hereby broken. Now, go out and tell others like you that they, too, are free. I have no more use for your services. You must tell them these words, 'Michael Miuriell releases you from the binds of conquest. You are now free.' Repeat that back to me."

And, with a sudden shift in his behavior, the man said, "Michael Miuriell releases you from the binds of conquest. You are now free."

Embracing him by the shoulder, Michael said, "Go on. Tell the others and find peace."

Michael signaled for the guards to open the door and let him leave without trouble. As directed, the guards opened up and escorted the man, wiped of demonic influence, out of the dungeon. No one asked him what he had done or why he had done it. They just watched as he took command of the prisoner, portraying the role of a master, and washed him of any connections to the Demon Plague.

Finally, one of the officers still inside the cell had the courage to ask him, "Miuriell, what did you do?"

He said before following the others out, "I just created a walking antidote for the madness, it would seem."

Deep inside Evertz Cavern, a lifeless warrior confirmed the signs of life. Kane should have been dead, but his terrible new gift beckoned him to live. His sweltering skin cooled to a gruesome end and his hand was separated by the wrist. There was nothing that Maxim could have done to prevent the Demon Lord's dark magic.

His opened left wrist began to bleed, tainting the cave's water current. From the aperture of the scorched wrist, tiny new bones protruded all the way through. Belligerently, the bones formed, not into a hand, but a claw. Idolizing that of a flyer demon's, the hand was absolutely demonic. It formed muscle and then skin. The completed appendage was hideous. With it came other ghastly attributes.

His scorched skin gradually healed at a dramatic rate, defying the laws of nature. From his fast reconstruction, a dark reddish hide swathed his entire body, forming demonic flesh. As the Demon Lord promised, his former being was replaced with a hellish substitute.

Finally, after the brunt of his demonic transformation was complete, his eyes opened wide with embellishment. The new eyes were serpent green. It was then that he realized the sheer agony of the transformation. Kane cried with his acquired beastly voice and pounded his doubly powerful fists into the watery ground of the cave.

Enraged with madness, the dehumanized warrior rose onto his knees and his roar reverberated throughout the mine. His teeth glistened with razor edges and his new left claw finished its reanimation. It was larger than his right hand, still concealed by his scorched gauntlet.

He felt the breach of his chest plate's battle scar with the demon claw. His memories returned to him as he remembered his ordeal with the Tinarian knight and the princess. Kane then stood onto his feet and considered his new form. He removed his helmet and looked upon his reddened face in the reflecting water. His sharp teeth and green eyes amid his red demonic skin startled him.

Spitting up settled blood from his stomach and throat, Kane clouted the cave's rock-solid wall with his demonic left fist. Growling monstrously, he unwaveringly headed for the cave's exit. He was going to return to Pommel as a warrior with substantial modifications. Vengeance was the first sin that teased his mind. Two miners who came to remove the body found a reanimated monster in its stead and ran the other way.

The glum party had returned with the two mystic warriors and Legate Thomas's paladins. Away for long enough and surviving the most nightmarish peril, Thomas tightly embraced Lana. He explained that he would describe Ellium's contribution to the resistance further over dinner. He was famished. The Falcun populace praised his return.

Yet, he became overwhelmed by the scene of damage at the wall. He marveled at the amount of scattered dead still in the stages of removal from the property. The smell of gunpowder and putrid death lingered. Masses of Falcuns worked to clean the rubble and assess the damage when Thomas's party finally arrived.

Gathering in one of the temples beside the Principal Palace, Michael left a conference with Shadisha to encounter the paladin legate. After agreeing to the conference dinner, Michael raced to the main square and tried to find Maxim and Predella, praying that Shina was with them. Ultimately finding them with Lana Kai, he discovered the ill-fated truth.

Predella's face presented sorrow for the lost princess and Maxim's guilt was evident. Lana nodded to Michael as he made his way through the dense crowd of Falcuns, displaying her discontent. Michael's crimson eyes were shocking to the two warriors, but it did not faze them as it could have. Their real shock lied with the princess, returned to Pommel by her own brother.

Maxim looked into Michael's eyes and considered the new, sinister aura. There were no conversations and no cringing. Instead of condemning Michael's scary appearance, Maxim finally seized his collar and sobbed, "What is going to happen to us, Michael? Are we going to stay human after all this is over?"

He expected Eric's treachery to be a result of Shina's certain capture. Michael caressed his head, still cold from Eric's spell. Allowing the wretched truth to sink in, Michael answered, "It wasn't your fault. I didn't see this betrayal."

Predella looked into Michael's eyes and said with fragments of fear, "Eric was too powerful."

"Sorcery gifted to him by the Demon Plague," Michael said. "The real question is why Eric thinks he's helping Shina and not destroying her. We're planning something big with Thomas in our company now. I'll expect to see you then."

He squeezed Maxim's arm with encouragement and insisted he get some rest until then. Michael was still bewildered by Eric's sudden deceit, but he was too overwhelmed with his own battles inside of himself to brood over it. In two hours, the gathering would finalize Ellium's participation in the fight against the Demon Plague and how they would assist in the operations to come. With Seth and Shina in the Demon Lord's grasp, evil yet had the upper hand.

Thomas had gone to pay his respects to his father, just buried a week earlier at the Pious Cemetery. His mausoleum was fresh and clean. He walked into the edifice and shut the door behind him—the last heir to the Excallum legacy.

The conference had initiated in the Metadome, a large dome structure strictly utilized by the Falcun League. The well-lit chambers were surrounded by clear glass windows and a white stone floor. The elongated table was waxed and polished to perfection as only the architects of Falcus conferred in such a place. Surrounded by Kai guards and elite paladin knights, the milestone conference, known by everyone inside the city as the Metadome Harvest, was underway.

Michael Miuriell and the ailing Urik sat at opposing ends of the table. Thomas, Shadisha, Shioda, and Aramis sat on the left side. Opposite them were Maxim, Esker, Predella, and Lai. At the ringing of the ceremonial bell, Lai called the Metadome Harvest into commencement. As dinner was served by the esteemed servers, Lai gently raised his hand and invited Michael to start.

From his seat, Michael said, "My good friends, all of us have lost together, but we have also triumphed where evil expected us to fail. I wish that I could convey to you my gratitude for combating this unwavering terror across the land. I know that you are apprehensive and suspicious of my role in this war. You see how my appearance has changed.

"My eyes are forever altered, but it changes nothing. My past is shrouded in evil, but it's that reason they fear me. They fear my power. They fear water and daylight. Five generals submit their dealings to an even more powerful Demon Lord. They can only follow my movements alone. Furthermore, I have—"

Colonel Aramis interrupted him, grunting, "We know this, Miuriell. How do we kill them? That's all that matters."

Maxim was quick to retort, "They stole the princess again—"

"Because of your traitorous prince," the colonel said.

"Enough, colonel," Michael admonished. "Let's stick to what comes next."

"I agree. The fact is that it's time to commence the rally assault on Pommel," Shioda interjected.

"Not so fast," Thomas said. "Ellium has a reservation about a full-scale assault as our first action. We don't know what we'd be charging into."

"He's right," Michael followed. "An assault on Pommel will only lead to disaster."

Shioda could not understand the downside to a combined offensive on the Demon Plague's bastion. He rubbed his face with bewilderment as he pondered Falcus's fighting force. A monumental attack from all of the Western realms would devastate any force, man or demon. That was what he believed.

Urik smiled empathetically and pronounced from the end of the table, "I can feel your frustration, Shioda. There is a difference between doing the right thing and doing things right. This threat is very real and we are still uncovering secrets that may reveal to us their weaknesses. We must engage these creatures cautiously, rather than ambushing them without scrutiny. Can Thomas inform the assembly of Ellium's response to our proposed alliance?"

Thomas nodded first and then began, "Yes. The emperor was reluctant at first, but he decided to reconsider—as long as we ambush Pommel with one great combined strike. The only stipulation is that we scout the bastion and provide detailed schematics to ensure victory. An attack like that, if unsuccessful, means that we lose everything in one fell swoop."

The predicament left a lasting impression on the assembly. Shioda shook his head in dismay, knowing that the Metadome Harvest would not commence as smoothly as he had hoped earlier. Lai looked about the table and focused on the troubled faces. Michael, more than anyone else, believed that the joint strike was reckless, for a simple error could jeopardize the lives of thousands.

Breaking the silence, Lai declared openly, "I am all for the combined assault on Pommel. A swift attack from every kingdom at once would only help our chances. Do we really want to shun the help from the emperor?"

Maxim, on the other hand, countered, saying, "They have the princess again. Eric can destroy us with his sorcery. The last thing I want to discover is the extent of the Demon Lord's powers firsthand. Perhaps they're waiting for us to attack them together. What better way to kill all of us off than gather every warrior and slaughter them at the front door?"

Urik instantly followed, "We must learn about our new enemy. Firstly, the Tinarian princess is of great value to them. Though, without Michael, their strength may not be complete. A weakness in Pommel is the only way to face the

Demon Plague. If we rush them at once, then we will fall as the Mad Legion fell this morning. Brutish violence is not the answer here."

Esker had a response for the prophet, "Then what do we do? Ziamon was massacred in one night. They'll find a weakness in our passive strategy if we fail to move quickly!"

Brimming with impatience, Aramis bluntly exclaimed, "My men can infiltrate that fortress and kill every one of those things. We Ziamons crave for retribution."

Maxim reposted angrily, "Then go have a party."

"Afraid to fight, Red Menace?" Aramis fired back.

"Wait a moment." Michael thought as he placed his fist over his mouth in wonderment. As the two rivals proceeded to argue each other, Lai ordered that they silence immediately. He easily could see that Michael was developing an idea. Once the enemies ceased their bickering, Michael was ready to deliver his design.

Snickering to himself, Michael had finally discovered the only practical means to rescuing the innocent victims of Pommel and destroying its evil hosts. With a nod of his head, Michael said, "I believe the colonel is on to something. An infiltration of Pommel's bastion would catch them off guard. We can free the innocent captors and assassinate the generals from inside. Quiet and quick."

Shioda had not laughed that hard in years. The thought of crawling into the demon-stricken fortress was nothing more than suicide. However, those who were gallant enough to consider the operation started to think.

Maxim asked Shioda and Lai, "How competent are your ninjas, anyway?"

Lai replied, "They're better than yours."

Before Shioda could question the mission, Maxim interjected nervously, "But the generals? Michael, you must be joking! Only we have seen them in battle. On their own turf, they'll be nearly invincible!"

"Invincible?" Shioda gasped. "Michael, what are we dealing with here?"

"No." Michael held his head and sighed from exasperation. "They can be beaten. Even they know this."

Predella held Maxim's shoulder and proclaimed unto the table, "So what do we do about that?"

The following moments led directly to the hope of bringing the fight to the demons. Urik asked Michael to reveal the known weaknesses and strengths of the Demon Plague. The promise made by the sage apprentice was encouraging. Michael vowed that his evening's meditation would enlighten him of the ultimate map to Pommel's bastion. He promised to find any promising loopholes.

As for the rest of the table, they agreed that the following day would be committed to preparation for a tactical strike inside of Pommel. Shioda and Lai were keen on arranging the ninja warriors for the missions. The paladins were only to be used for cover fire in the event that the escape was perilous. Only the stealthiest of warriors were applicable for the mission. The use of Tinarian knights was strongly denounced by the assembly.

The Ziamons, like the paladins, would provide cover fire. It was highly probable that Esker would partake in the operation. Aramis, as well, could never turn down the tempting work. Further arrangements for the silent and swift attack would unveil the next day, but only if Michael uncovered enough knowledge of the demonic stronghold. It was up to him to lead them into a sure path for victory. One mistake risked everything.

Before they retired, Urik coughed and addressed the table, "When I discovered Miuriell as an infant, I knew that there was something brewing within him—something not of this world. Do I take credit for raising him to be good? Yes. I definitely deserve that credit. But the Demon Plague doesn't see it that way. They know the Miuriell name and, from beyond the vale, they've been watching him. Michael was not just embellishing when he said that they fear him. They do. He has a connection with them. In a way, he *is* one of them. Michael is their leader, or they think he is. Either way, this man is the key to their downfall. We are all just playing along. We're playing our parts."

Nodding to his mentor in thanks, Michael admitted, "I recently discovered that my son is alive. He is alive and in the furnace room, suffering. He's been suffering this whole time."

The table was stunned to silence. Lai eventually said, "Michael, I'm at a loss for words."

"How did you find this out?" Maxim asked. "I mean, we talked about your ability to see things. How did you see your son in Pommel? How do you know it's really him?"

"I can see into Pommel clearer than anything I've ever seen in my life," Michael replied. "My vision has tripled, especially in Pommel. At the moment I touch my staff, I feel this rush of authority. When I stalked that place, my child had reached out for me. When I did, his face was as clear as all of yours before me now. It's him. Give me the night to peer into Pommel again. There is something there that I'm missing. If you can put your trust in me—"

"I'll trust you to hell and back, Michael," Predella said with resolve.

"That's the point, Predella," Michael said to her. "If we choose to do this, it's up to me to get us back safely. If there's a chance we can't, then I can't ask you all to come with me."

"No disrespect, my friend," Thomas countered, "but I'm afraid that isn't up to you. What we do from here, we do together."

"Agreed," Maxim added, raising his glass.

Others followed in the pledge to work as a unit, even the Ziamons who were not familiar with alliances. When there seemed to be a lot to discuss in the hopes of finding a way to defeat the Demon Plague, Urik felt faint. He had been out of his bed for too long. Putting down his glass, the sage said, "If you'll excuse me. This old man needs to lay down and continue to be futile for a while longer. Bless you all."

While some officials came to escort the ill sage back to Excallum's quarters for rest, Michael watched him go and hoped he would not follow Manna to the grave. He needed his teacher's guidance more than ever. In a way, he felt like his training had only just begun. Michael was a new person, one that he needed help understanding. There was a lot of pressure on him. If he failed, then the world was doomed. A man destined to either save or conquer the earth needed the support of an old man who loved him like a son.

While night fell, Predella stood upon the high crenellations of the great white wall of outer Falcus and watched Michael gallop off on his horse alone. As he rode away like before, she felt an utter sadness for him. He was forsaken with an evil spirit but blessed with a good soul. It was expected of him to leave their presence every night. The dust of the sand discharged from the horse's hooves and left a dissonant trail of the earth in the air. He was to sleep, once again, on his own in the chill of the night.

Maxim eventually met up with her and said from her side, "I noticed that someone treated your hand. I'm sorry."

"Remind me never to catch your sword," she jested.

Maxim replied, "I should have offered to help with those burns. It was my fault."

She smiled, looking him over, "You're a warrior, not a nurse."

"Nice one." He led her by the left hand and walked into the calm night of the holy city. Antonis spotted them walking together, closely tender as if they were in love. He was certain that their relationship was unhealthy for the quest.

Shina was adorned in a new dress fit for a demonic queen. The entire dress was a blood red from top to bottom. Her red hair was tied into a long ponytail that suspended down her half-naked back. Her Tinarian principles rambled through her mind as she stood before the Demon Lord yet again. This time, Valkris stood closely by her side, for it was his charge to watch over her. As Scythian looked on from his dark corner and Sattka admired her father's plans from her chair, the Demon Lord came down from his high seat.

The ruler was as dark as she remembered him. Chills ran up and down her spine. Her legs fell limp. When he looked over her provocative attire, he spoke, "**How do you feel?**"

Shina mustered enough courage to say, "Filthy."

"**Not bad,**" Valkris declared.

The Demon Lord neared closer to her and looked her over, saying from behind his dark helmet, "**For a girl so naïve, you've finally had a taste of the darkness hidden deep inside. A brief venture out into the world has made you something else—something less credulous. Nothing can stop it now. You've been awakened.**"

Besides her creeping fear, Shina fought the evil within. It demanded that she let it go free, but she had spent many long and terrible nights learning how to hinder its full manifestation. Sensing the struggle, the Demon Lord peered inside. She could feel his powerful eyes probing her psyche.

"**Fighting yourself? You were made to be so much more than just a meager little sack of meat and bone.**

You were predestined to father his child—born to rule over the new world," the Demon Lord declared.

Refusing to respond, she simply shut her eyes and tightened her muscles, battling her burning spirit. Valkris was beginning to feel Eric's presence drawing near. Thus, the demonic general telepathically reiterated his sensations to his leader. The Demon Lord had no doubt in his mind that Shina would turn within the night. Hence, he decided to send her to spend the night with the vast numbers of virgin girls that lay to waste, naked and cold in a dungeon keep. Their pure blood would spur her thirst to feast on the weak. They were all Shina's in one way or another.

Valkris nodded and gladly seized Shina by the arm and led her to her dungeon for the night. She could have screamed and tried to fight, but the shock of her capture remained in her still. The undead opened the double doors and permitted Eric to enter. His wounds treated, he came into the dark chamber and looked about. From her seat, Sattka sarcastically applauded him.

Eric said, disregarding her scorn, "My sister is safe?"

"**Tonight, she'll break. There will be nothing left of the old girl you once loved. The new woman shall be your queen,**" the Demon Lord said as he started back to his throne. The terrible creature stretched out his enormous wings in the meantime. Sattka searched Eric's obscure face for falsehoods. He could easily see that she peered into his soul. Her sick eyes unsettled him to no end.

When the Demon Lord returned to his throne, his daughter spoke up with indictments, "**How is it that only you survived? Where is the smutty pig for which my powers were wasted?**"

Trying desperately to prevent himself from falling into the dazed stupor that every human being received when they looked upon Sattka's evil countenance, Eric hesitantly answered, "He and all the others are dead."

The Demon Lord snickered from his spot and leaned in to counter, "**No. He will return in time to kneel before Miuriell when he arrives.**"

"Miuriell?" Eric said. "You have misplaced your savior with a cleric. I have endured Michael's discipline enough to tell you that he is not going to submit to you as I have."

The Demon Lord sat deeper into his throne, "**All sheep become dependent on their shepherds. They fill the need to follow something and, in turn, surrender their freedom for a feeling of belonging. They give up their natural instincts to be domesticated. And they trust all the way to the end. You, boy, have been a sheep all your life. You're not here for your sister to be safe. You are here to save yourself.**"

His pride swelling under the weight of his heart, Eric countered, "And Michael is the shepherd? Is that it?"

"**He is the shepherd,**" the Demon Lord leaned in to say, "**and the butcher.**"

Eric had ultimately come to understand that his place in the world was twisted. A traitor to his own people and lemming to the Demon Plague, all of his sorcery could not break him from the truth. Eric was owned by evil and there seemed to be no way to save himself, let alone the only person he ever loved. For him to live beyond the conquest, he would first have to kill the man and become the sheep.

For the night, Shina was forced to stay with the enslaved virgin girls inside the vast dungeon. Out of admiration, Valkris allowed her to remain clothed. The demon general shut the door and summoned a large spider, the size of a bull, to serve as a guard. The arachnid was Valkris's eyes to probe Shina's behavior for the entire night.

Seeing Shina again, the other girls rushed to the far corners of the dungeon. They shivered in her presence, knowing what she was behind all her pretty innocence. She was able to smell their fear. It aroused the beast within, though she still fought to bury it there. Shina believed them when they said there was no turning back. Yet, she was not hopeless. She had a morsel of faith that her allies would find a means to rescue her. In rescuing her, they could rescue the world and everyone in it.

PART II
CHAPTER IX
THE HARVEST

Peering over the high cliff of the land, Michael meditated and embraced the freshness of the atmosphere. The rumination had led him again inside the Pommelian bastion. He, reluctantly, looked upon his caged son a second time, mourning the poor boy's fate. As if he was there, Michael scoured Pommel's interior. His powers were only growing with each time he meditated on his home.

He witnessed torture chambers where prisoners suffered without mercy or hindrance. Blood-wringing skin slid off their backs after hours of vicious whippings. The undead pulled teeth and gouged eyes. Tenebrion's crew broke bones and extracted organs. For certain, it was hell on earth. The travesty had twisted Michael's mind, spoiling his concentration. He pulled away from his explored visions and gasped, feeling to regurgitate.

Suddenly, it seemed that his son was being well kept in comparison to the rest of Pommel's tenants. Finding the courage to continue, he immersed himself back into it. In visiting the women's keep, he came upon the large chamber door, where a grotesque spider stood guard. The spider was large, bulky and black with thick hair all about. Its eyes were many as to see everywhere.

Inside the dungeon was another ghastly sight. Naked women and girls were spread all around in iron chains. They all appeared either dazed or terrified. Phantom spirits danced about the room, especially in Shina's company. She was equally frightened. Though he was relieved to find her safe, Michael still mourned for those who would endure the gruesome murder as a sacrifice. While mapping out all of the Demon Plague's headquarters, Michael wondered why the virgin females were sacrificed at all. Why only one sacrifice per day?

The dungeon was dimly lit by ghostly light from the walls and candle stands. After discovering Seth and the princess's keepings, Michael attempted to test the extent of his abilities. He held the Staff of Truth closer and summoned enough dark energy to view the past day in Pommel. He wanted to know what the demons were up to during the day.

With his entire body shaking from the energy, a great evil swarmed and hissed about his spot. Sweat beads began to form and cascade down his head. Gradually, the powers greatened and Michael ventured through the past. Rewinding the day, as the holy city was under attack, there was a strange period in the Shadowland.

For some peculiar reason, Michael noticed that there was no sign of demons scurrying through the halls or stalking the courtyards. For a significant fraction of the day, the halls were silent, without activity. More importantly, the Demon Lord and his daughter were nowhere to be found. Michael searched the entire fortress but could not place them. For a moment, he realized that something was taking place during that two-hour span. It appeared that the evil forces of the Demon Plague slept.

Finally, Michael searched for the two demons in the place where he could not see before. Even Manna Excallum could not break through its dark secret. With his new and improved powers, he prepared to search again for that mysterious portal. He had come across the horrid sensation yet again as his visions neared closer to the haunted location. It was the enormous fireplace that rested unlit by fire for weeks. Something treacherous was behind there—hidden from even prophetic sight.

As his telepathic vision crept closer to the vast fireplace, a strange sensation mangled his senses. Though he tried, not even his greater powers could make it through the portal without harming his mind. He was compelled to pull away from it. Yet, the feeling grabbed his soul, tugging at him. Something terrible was beyond that fireplace. He had sat by that fireplace many times before and felt nothing.

With certainty, Michael believed that a mysterious portal dwelled behind that front of a hearth. Because Sattka and the Demon Lord were nowhere in his foresight, it was only logical that they were inside the secret portal for the sleeping period. Trying again, Michael considered the past and discovered that Sattka and several shadow demons seized one of the imprisoned girls and led her towards the unnerving place. The girl went willingly as if spellbound.

Michael knew that she was the sacrifice—but for what? What did they benefit from virgin blood? Upon opening his eyes, Michael suddenly realized that he had been floating high above the ground. Startled by his unsettling power, he cried out and fell. Just before hitting the dirt, he propelled his telekinetic forces and softened his landing. His heart raced as he settled himself on both his feet, shaken by the strange occurrence.

While holding his chest, he heard a sinister voice—one he remembered long before in Tinaria. It said, "**Unleash me! Revel in the torment of the unworthy. Unleash me now!**"

Peering around his lowly encampment by the sea, he found nothing. As he searched further out to sea for the origin of the voice, it spoke again, "**Blessed be the pure blood of virgin women. May their selfless sacrifice replenish the conquest!**"

"Not *my* conquest!" Michael cried back at the cryptic voice, then coming to realize where it originated. The voice was coming from inside. When the voice stopped, he hissed, "You're never getting out. You'll never take me. Never."

As the sun began to rise over the Great Pacifica, the second and final Metadome Harvest came into session. It was the most memorable conference ever held in the holy city. Michael sat at the head of the table as Lai came in with Pommel's interior diagrams. Despite Maxim's protest, Michael invited Antonis to join the conference. He needed his foresight, as Urik was too ill to attend. Maxim and Predella were at Michael's left while Thomas, Shioda and Shadisha sat at his right. Esker and Aramis shared the opposing head of the table across from Michael.

With the most influential figures of the new world assembling, the great plan was fashioned. The stratagems were swiftly revealed to the table as Michael laid out the entire setting in Pommel at an hour before noon. When brunch was served, Michael began from his seat, "My friends, I know our enemy's weakness. Our window of opportunity is not opened long, but it should leave us enough time to perform our mission."

"I have to hear this." Shioda leaned his chair in closer to the table.

"For two hours during the day, Pommel is asleep. Only a small number of men stricken with the madness guard certain dungeons and chambers. This is the perfect time for an organized invasion of the bastion to kill sleeping generals and rescue as many prisoners as possible," Michael explained.

"Prisoners?" Maxim uttered.

Reluctant to convey the violent and disturbing images that cursed his mind during his meditation, Michael directed his red eyes to the face of the table. Feeling that it was inevitable, he answered with woe, "Inside that unholy place, hundreds are tortured and killed in the most horrific manner. My son is among them. We can't leave them there."

Breaking the uneasy silence, Aramis barked, "How can we possibly pull off a mission like that? With respect to the suffering, it cannot be done!"

"Where are these prisoners you saw?" Lai asked from across the table.

"These two main holding cells." Michael referred to the plans on the table. "On the sixth level, the women, including younglings, are kept like animals. They are naked and chained to a cold, dank dungeon. Those virgin girls are kept for the purpose of some sort of sacrifice. It is because of this ritual that we are able to infiltrate the bastion."

Shadisha grieved almost instantly, "Your incursion is at the expense of a child's murder?"

"There's no other way, Shadisha. I checked. It's why we have to save as many as we can," Michael replied. "We also steal their sacrificial ammunition in the process. Princess Shina was among them."

"And the victims of torture?" Thomas prompted.

"It's bad. They're held up here in the furnace sector, below the main level. That's also where my son is caged. I lost my wife. I can't lose my son too," Michael said with grief.

Shadisha said, "I can't believe they had him this entire time—alive."

"For now," Michael said somberly. "Probably as bait."

They were stricken with disbelief, looking over the floor plans in worry. The terrible acts against humanity done by this unexplainable evil force were too much for them to tolerate. It was assumed that the Demon Plague took no prisoners. Apparently, their conquest craved for the torture of the helpless. Michael's account of what he saw staggered everyone at the table.

Perturbed, Shioda held his forehead and pronounced, "What kind of monsters are they?"

"The worst kind," Antonis retorted. "Killing even one of these demonic generals will be very costly."

Esker interjected without heed, "I watched as the best fighters in Ziamon fell to just one of those bastards. If we are able to catch them as they're sleeping, I'll saw their heads off. If they expect us coming, we should be prepared to lose many lives in a short amount of time."

Predella looked to Michael, bouncing off of Esker's warning, "So, is this a rescue mission or a seek and destroy?"

Aramis interjected, "I will lead only a kill squad."

Maxim turned his seat to face the Ziamon colonel and said, "You continue to remind us of what you will and will not do. I'd be amiss if I didn't warn you, it's frustrating."

"So sorry to hurt your feelings, Red Menace," Colonel Aramis countered.

"There are too many in misery. We have the chance to save them," Michael explicated further. "Doing this isn't just the right thing to do—it takes away their fuel for sacrifice and torture."

Antonis then said, "But they have flocks of hypnotized human sacrifices ambling for Pommel as we speak. We saw the caliber of these twisted people charge these walls in an act of suicide for the sake of distraction. What we save, they can readily replace."

"Perhaps I can remedy that," Michael said, folding his hands before his chin. "I may be able to control them—break them from their mind-control. When we come upon Pommel, there will be a dark cloud shrouding the realm. Under that place, the demons can roam freely without fear of daylight. In the time of inactivity, shortly after noon, members of the Mad Legion stand guard. I may be able to turn them."

"Turn them, as in, work on our side?" Thomas said.

"I believe I can," Michael answered.

The tension was thick in the harvest, built on belief and assumptions. While many trusted him with their lives, there was still a sense of uncertainty. The amount of planning needed for the mission proposed at the table was massive and without the promise that the Demon Plague would stay asleep during the stealthy incursion.

After the justice whispered to him in Espanion, Aramis echoed, "Our kill squad is designed to do as the name suggests. We will slay the generals, but take no part in the rescue mission. If we die, we die in battle."

"I see." Michael reacted perceptively, allowing the Ziamons' influence to sink in. He expected as much.

Maxim had to interject again, "I suppose we should all hope that your so-called 'kill squad' can kill the generals if they suddenly wake up from sleepy time."

"Miuriell points and we kill. That's the deal," Aramis retorted boldly.

"In two hours?" Maxim countered. "We're in a kingdom full of ninjas. They're a lot quieter than the horde of you."

Before the Ziamon colonel could rebut Maxim's challenge, Shioda interposed, "The Tinarian has a point. Will we have enough time to rescue all of these people? It doesn't seem possible."

Lai chose to address his comrade's contention. With the entire table turning his way, Lai said, "If we chase two rabbits, they'll both escape, won't they? Granted, we're not trapping bunnies, but dividing our forces is the only means to accomplishing our mission. Because the Ziamons are eager to fight, I believe that it would be only fitting to station them on the assassination front. Another team can save the women and another can rescue the other prisoners. Time is of the essence, so if we split up, we may be able to rush in like a storm in the night and make our exit."

"Trusting that Michael has faith in the strike," Shadisha added. "Urik trusts in him and I do, as well. If he believes that this is possible, then he should be the tactician."

Almost instantly, the Ziamons agreed to the terms. They were not a rescue party, but a wrecking crew. Their talents involved the shedding of blood and nothing more. With the first step taken, Maxim volunteered to save the females on the sixth level and annihilate anyone or anything that mired his mission. With him, Predella, Shioda, and several ninja warriors proclaimed their loyalty to the party. They were in it to the death. Michael approved the team.

For the tormented prisoners in the lower dungeons, Michael, Lai and a small army of elite ninjas would rescue them from their cruel lot. Michael assigned the colonel to lead a party of stealthy Ziamons to kill Valkris, the head general. Esker, then, preferred to kill Tenebrion with his number of men.

Michael was able to predict where these demonic generals were going to be, marking the schematics accordingly. There was no mistake in anyone's minds that this mission was a dire one. There would be no other operation of greater peril or importance. If they succeeded, they could possibly cripple the Demon Plague. In defeat, the hopes of resisting the demonic forces were all but lost.

He stationed Thomas and his paladin reinforcements outside the Shadowland to provide cover fire if a daring and deadly escape was unavoidable. Shadisha agreed to provide tactical carriages to transport the army to and from Pommel under the condition that the new base is situated in Merrieu. It sparked another debate.

"Merrieu is a shattered kingdom, full of people afflicted with the madness," Antonis interposed. "From what I've seen and heard, that place is cursed."

Lai then said, "But what better place to gather forces and coordinate our attack? It's the closest nation to Pommel and Michael can cure the madness."

"So he believes," Shioda interjected. "Forgive me, but I have no interest in succumbing to the madness myself. Michael, are you sure you can persuade those people to break free from their spell? I mean, is Merrieu even a nation anymore?"

Nodding first, finding resolve at the table, Michael said, "Shadisha is right. Merrieu will be our base of operations for a while until it's safe for us to return to Falcus. I have faith that there is more to my powers than just moving things. Yes, maybe I can control those afflicted. Yes, maybe we can take it to the evil forces that occupied my home. I believe that this one assault will weaken the Demon Plague enough for a final, massive attack. This one mission will set the stage for Ellium's advance from the south. When Falcus is ready and able, our combined army can crush the remainder of—"

"What about Eric?" Antonis interrupted Michael's plan, dropping in serious concern for the mission.

Everyone lowered their heads and sighed, coming to terms with Eric's indomitable powers. Michael's moving admission had to be cut short to handle the wild card of the enemy. Maxim, Predella, and Antonis, in particular, felt the sting of his betrayal the most. The full plan was in jeopardy. All that they discussed had to be rehashed.

"The sorcerer." Lai broke the sullen silence. "Michael, even if the entirety of the Demon Plague is asleep, that mage alone can wipe out our whole force."

Antonis furthered, "The joint attack which you spoke of would be useless, just the same. Our world hasn't seen that sort of magic for centuries. Something has to be done about that traitor."

"I wouldn't mind cutting him into a few pieces," Maxim growled, "if I can get close."

"We all have some score to settle with him," Predella said, "but only you, Michael, have any chance of defeating him."

Regretfully agreeing with her, Michael said, "Where Shina is, Eric is most likely to be."

"And that is where you will need to be, also," Antonis explained. "I am sorry, Michael, but we can't assume that she is any more human than the creatures we're up against."

"Of course, you'd say that," Maxim snapped. "All you've wanted to do is kill her since—"

"Since finding out she was a demon? Yes," Antonis had countered irately. "Everyone wants to destroy the Demon Plague, but very few are willing to make the hard sacrifices!"

"I'd give my life for this cause. *That's* sacrifice!" Maxim returned. "Killing others in fear is what tyrants do. It's what cowards with agendas do."

"I came all the way with you, humbling myself, to find redemption at the end of this hell!" Antonis cried. "To do that, I will do whatever is appropriate."

"Killing the princess is inappropriate," Maxim said.

Michael finally raised his hand to silence the debate. As everyone listened in to what he had to say, Michael declared, "I will find the princess and take her back. Eric will have to face me. He believes in some misguided, self-righteous plan to save his sister. He thinks that we've already lost—that the Demon Plague will make Shina a queen of the afterworld and me, the king. He has believed their lies. Truth—lies. Everything is gray until it finally happens. I swear on my life, I will never let what is wrong hide in what's right. We write our own prophesy and see it through to the end. If you're with me."

Following a silence at the table, Thomas said, "I'll send some scouts ahead to Merrieu so they can inform us of its conditions before we arrive. If it's not in our interest, we return to Falcus after our mission is complete. Fair enough?"

Nodding in agreement, Shioda said, "Fair enough."

Predella then said, "I am with you, Michael. All the way to the end—no matter what that end may be."

Smiling ingratitude for her unwavering loyalty, he said, "As my friend, I can tell you that, together, we can make the end what we want. Hope is a fire that can only be quenched by those who wield it. Keep the fire alive and, as one, we can light our enemies aflame. If I didn't believe it, I wouldn't be here to say it. After tonight, when we finally set out for Pommel, we become demon-slayers like the angels casting out evil. We'll let them know that humanity refused to kneel. When we set out tomorrow, we'll be angels of resistance."

The party, though anxious and afraid, let Michael's stirring words settle in their spirit. They began to eat their breakfast, rivals, and friends—souls from different paths. The goal was the same, even if their beliefs were not the same. A solid unit broke bread and came together, knowing that the next day was the start of something daring. They knew that, for some, it would be their last mission. Courage was always a choice—a decision to face the greatest fear, win or lose. It was a virtue where they all found some common ground.

After the Metadome Harvest had concluded and the group went their different ways, Thomas came up to Michael and shook his hand, saying, "The Angels of Resistance. Would you mind if I gave our army a name? I kind of liked it."

Embracing his arm in return, Michael said, "History will remember that name. They'll remember what it stood for, long after we're all gone. Thanks, Thomas—for everything."

Thomas replied, "When the smoke clears, I will still be standing as an Excallum, here on this earth, or beyond life in heaven. My duty is clear. I'll see you tomorrow, old friend."

Mastering the martial arts of the ancient ninja, Lai primed his spirit for combat in the open courtyard. He chose his most capable warriors to gather there, hearing of their bold roles in the mission. Shioda, on the other hand, could not possibly concentrate, for his wife, Lana, disturbed him with a frightening request.

While clothing himself in his renowned blue garb, only concealing his face under the bone of the nose, Lana entered his prominent dojo in a similar fashion. A red headband was wrapped snug through her loose hair and a darker-hued garb finished inches under her thighs. Witnessing his pregnant wife suit up for combat training, Shioda uneasily confronted her by the entrance.

"What are you doing, Lana?" Shioda grabbed her arms.

She responded passionately with her eyes looking up into his, "I'm preparing myself for the mission."

"No." He shook his head in fright. "This, I will not accept. You cannot partake in this mission. It is shrouded in danger."

Releasing herself from her husband's grip, Lana said, "I am a leading member of the Kai League, Shioda! You will not prevent me from serving! You don't even have that authority."

He cried, visibly shaken, "Free yourself from this dream! You are bearing our child!"

As two ninja warriors entered the dojo entrance, Shioda pulled her away from the public and scolded her in a persuasive whisper, "Listen to me. This mission will not be like the ones you fought in the league. You have never even seen these demons!"

Lana replied to his close-ended question defensively, "Neither have you! Don't patronize me, guard captain!"

"You are a mother now, Lana! We can't chance it," he countered.

Shioda would have said more, but his eyes welled up with tears. The thought of losing his wife and his first child stopped his heart. He loved nothing more. This mission was for her safety and the safety of all of his people in Falcus. In Shioda's solid view, it was not Lana's place to partake in the perilous assignment.

Like her husband, Lana was helplessly stubborn. She loved Shioda too much to see him leave for the deadliest mission of his life without her. Without question, Lana possessed uncanny might. Shioda, himself, knew that she was more than capable, but the risks were inescapable.

Lana seized his trembling hands and clasped them together under her chin, asking earnestly, "At least agree to my joining Thomas and the paladins on the outside lines. I will not remain in Falcus while the Kai League takes on its greatest challenge! I will be there personally."

Terrified of what could result from his decision, Shioda hesitantly answered while looking straight into the wall, "You must promise to remain there and without any exceptions will you leave that paladin line."

Lana simply tightened her clasp on him and nodded her head in compliance. It was her will to go. Shioda was forced into understanding this truth as he felt her head move up and down on his chest. There was no greater love than a love shared. It was his worst fear to lose what no-one else could ever provide.

A different bout developed in the Tinarian sector of Falcus. Inside Antonis's temporary abode, a Tofauti guard had spotted Maxim approaching the front door. He opened the door and stood there, drawing his spear as the Tinarian warrior advanced. Maxim, upon reaching the prophet's dwelling, breathed in deeply and said, "Go tell your Tofauti brother that he has a visitor. I promise to be civil."

Of course, Antonis expected him and signaled for the silent guard to allow him in. Maxim shut the door behind him, asking the prophet straight away, "What are you doing?"

Coming to meet him in the atrium, Antonis replied, "I'm preparing for the journey to Merrieu. How is it that I may be of help?"

Maxim responded, perturbed, "You're not serious."

"Oh, I'm quite serious," Antonis replied, walking back to his case of meditative supplies. "You'll need me at the ranks. Even Miuriell knows that."

"Does he know that you want to kill the princess?" he retorted.

"That again? My God, boy, I have to hand it to you. You just don't give up," Antonis said.

Maxim persisted, "Don't think I forgot. Whatever you're planning, the last place I'll allow you to be is anywhere near the princess."

"These are my guardians, not my assassins," he said. "I can see you're intimidated by them, but they cannot harm you unless you provoke them—or me."

"The Tofauti pledge of silence. I'm not an idiot and I rarely feel threatened by babysitters," Maxim replied. "You're here for redemption, which means that you are here for one main reason, right? You."

"Don't be a fool," Antonis retorted. "I will not die for the sake of debts! I'm here to set things right! I ran during the raid on Tinaria, you have me there. But then again, what good is vengeance in death? We're all fighting for something here. Everyone leaving for Pommel tomorrow has something to prove, even you and your Waasi girlfriend."

Taken off-guard by the prophet's venomous strike, he replied, "I would be very careful if I were you."

"Let's just throw it all on the table, shall we?" Antonis started. "You've become smitten by the Waasi huntress and it's not by accident. She is fantastically attractive, but as you may not know, Predella is even more cunning. She shrouds herself with tenets of honor and meekness amid her valiant aura, but there is a panther waiting to pounce. Predella does not care who is her prey—an unsuspecting, arrogant prince or a powerful champion out of time. Through and through, Predella is a mercenary and she fights for herself first."

Maxim neared closer to him with closed fists, making the Tofauti warriors begin to close in on him. When he saw them move in just a few steps, Maxim remained in place and said, "Whatever you're—"

"Oh, but I haven't started on you, yet." Antonis put up his finger and continued, "You're a brash, thick-headed blade with a nationalistic agenda that can't see past the point of your sword. You'll sleep with her as long as it benefits you because, in this new world, for which you've awakened, the one thing you long for more than anything is someone just like you.

"She was far too young for you when you were alive, but now she's a ripe, voluptuous fighter with the same spirit. She's also a woman who lost everything—her own people. Her whole family—gone. And you, you hardly know anything of your bloodline, let alone your own parents. All that you have is that fiery sword, which allegedly confirms your blood ties to a paladin and his descendants. Yet, no one can rightly tell you the truth, really because no one knows where you fit in. So, as you can see, you're both a perfect distraction for each other. And that is why you'll both die in Pommel."

Maxim endured the prophet's attack on his character, as well as Predella's, surprisingly well. Having been called brash had something to do with it. Thus, he assessed his odds in battling his way out of the atrium before saying, "I know that the only reason you allowed me in this little abode of yours was that you knew I wouldn't start a fight, particularly without my sword and a few Tofauti guards in the mix. I came unarmed because you'd be an idiot to sick your mute brethren on me. But, in reality, I've had enough time on the water to think about your motivations.

"You've picked us apart, and that's fine, but it isn't going to save your ass in the end. Your foresight is pretty useless around here, as I think we've established already back in Tinaria. We can't rely on you anymore. You're a hack, scurrying to any kingdom that will give you some sort of purpose. That's why *you're* here, isn't it? Stay back and leave the real fighting to those willing to bleed for something. And, if I find out you're scheming to murder the princess one more fucking time, I'll plow my way through these rent-a-guards and beat you into a bloody pulp. Now, *that's* something you don't need foresight to see coming."

Leaving the atrium with fire in his soul, Maxim looked over the two guards at the door and walked on. They stood firm as he left. Antonis, sighing through his nose, shook his head and went back to packing his things. In an ironic twist, he trusted Maxim more than any other warrior in the party, even Michael. Maxim could hardly hide his passionate stance on almost anything. He was an easy book to read, which also meant that his threats were real. The next time they met, he was sure to be ready. Antonis knew that Maxim would surely come armed to kill when Shina was dead.

As the sun began to fall, Michael rode out into the dark horizon once again. And again, Predella watched him gallop off alone from the high crenellations. If not for Michael's extra senses, the impending mission could never have been attempted, though some still wished just for that. Slowly, the sun faded and Predella's face was empty with the cool breeze of the darkness. Michael's withdrawing could not be heard or seen anymore. He was gone and the city was safe for another night.

For Michael, the mission meant everything. After losing everything once already, he had to be sure. Overseeing the dark water far below the cliffs, he meditated. Instead of inspecting Pommel further, Michael envisioned his past life there. He saw how beautiful Pommel was before the invasion. He could even smell the flowers. Seized by the powerful memories, he vowed to retake his homeland and plant new flowers himself.

It was an infamous night in Pommel. Shina could not prevent the evil inside from overtaking her body. In her new chamber, she waited in chains for Valkris to arrive and desecrate her soul. The chamber was elaborate and fit for such a queen, but Shina was not willing to surrender herself just yet. She fought the spirit within and desperately tried to resist it from taking her over.

Valkris drew closer to her as he sarcastically slammed the gruesome Seltek into the solid ground with each step. In full garb, Valkris opened the chamber door with his demonic sorcery and stepped through, allowing the door to shut behind him at his command. With horror in her moist eyes, Shina watched helplessly as the general sauntered nearer to the exaggerated throne for which she was shackled.

Valkris planted his hideous quarter staff directly before her. The many eerie and manic eyes of the staff all peered in her direction. They remembered her. She was the prize that eluded them during their previous encounter in Tinaria. Shina was conscious of Valkris's needed visit for the sake of vengeance.

"**At last, you are ready,**" Valkris hissed sardonically through his sharp incisors. "**When you turn, and you *will* turn, these shackles will keep you complacent. This time, you will lose that weak, feeble child. You will become a true queen. You see, little princess, this is your night.**"

Still oppressing the evil within her from bursting loose, Shina riposted heatedly, "You'll soon wish that you never played with me!"

Snickering, it was clear that he enjoyed the foreplay. Valkris lifted her delicate chin with the ghastly head of the Seltek and said, "**How dear! Your fear has lessened since the last time we met. I will shower my queen with the most elaborate gifts when your transformation is finished. In honoring you, I shall present throngs upon throngs of bludgeoned children at your feet. All in the sanctity of your name, I will murder them as a sacrifice. When you and Miuriell conceive, we will no longer require their sacrifices to the sacred portal. Miuriell will command his minions to rise—as it is foretold.**"

After Valkris laughed again, he proceeded to vanish into thin air. The sorcerer was much more powerful in his birthplace. Thus, Shina was left there in her glorious throne fit for a demon queen. She had no energy to cry, so she just sunk her head downward and allowed her red hair to veil her face. Though her sorrow was best dealt with by her lonesome, she felt a presence. She insisted that there was someone else in the chambers with her.

Her feelings were justifiable. From the wall beside the door, Eric materialized. Utilizing his concealment spells, Eric easily hid from his sister. Valkris, however, was aware of his company. Hesitant, Eric approached his sister's large throne, fashioned with demonic skulls, bones, and skin. Viewing her in such pain was agonizing for him. She was chained like a slave to her grotesque seat. Matching the high ceiling and the gorgeous sculptures about the room, Shina's aura leaked insidious greatness.

Shina, in knowing that her brother was watching her from only feet away, said feebly, "Are you surprised to see me like this? It was your doing that brought this burden upon me."

Unsure how to answer, Eric looked her over and replied gently, "I did not expect this. They told me that you would be handled as a queen."

Taking her time to answer his inexcusable plea, she said with her head still towards her lap, "There is your trouble. You trust demons."

Eric could not find the words to respond. He imagined that his sister would be acclaimed and exalted like the princess that she was. Instead, her true character that he cherished was useless to the Demon Plague. Her malevolent spirit was the true essence that the conquest required. He should have known that Shina was not going to rule as queen with her amiable soul. Eric felt duped.

Feeling to hold her, he moved in closer. Her head remained downward and he could not see through her falling hair. Thus, he extended his hand to touch her shoulder. It was Eric's fatal mistake. Shina suddenly lifted her head and screamed in a terrifying tone, "**Never touch me!**"

Her hair danced in the air and her eyes were black. Taken aback by his sister's sadistic outburst, Eric jerked away, his spine-tingling with dread. Shina's delicate wrists jolted up and slammed the chains so tightly that he thought she would either break her arms or break free. She wanted to obliterate the shackles of her bondage and kill her enemy, who she once believed was her brother.

"Shina, stop!" Eric cried, but her rage was too great. She would not stop. Her recent and sudden hatred of Eric fed her evil soul well. As supernatural veins crawled up her pale skin, Eric came to the realization that his sweet-hearted sister was that evil creature. He could not witness Shina suffer in that way.

Watching her lunge for him and fail, Eric understood that he destroyed the last person that loved him. The exiled prince stumbled out of the sophisticated throne room and closed his ears, trying to shut out his sister's cries. Her cries were not of the kind he remembered. They were not cries of sadness, but cries of hatred and raging pain. He blamed himself this time. There was no one left for him to rebuke.

PART II
CHAPTER X
THE MISSION

It was a four day and three-night journey. As one stable force, the Angels of Resistance trekked around the Ghost Forest and toured the famous trail between the cliff over the Great Pacifica and the forest to the right. Fleeing refugees passing by gathered in awe to watch the historic army march forth. With Michael Miuriell in front and Maxim and Predella to his sides, the skillful caravan met no odds. There was not a force foolish enough to meddle with them.

Every night, Michael galloped off to a distant location so as not to attract demons. In his absence, the army rested amid a large encampment with scattered campfires. Rogue ninjas observed them from the trees but dared not harass them. They recognized the members of the Kai League. Their patrolling of the bluff was no coincidence. In missing the Mad Legion's impressive stealth along the shoreline days ago, the rogue ninja clans were taking no more chances.

Outside of the Ghost Forest, the army mingled and had nightly discussions of history and philosophy. The Tinarians had no scuffles with their Ziamon counterparts but were in no hurry to intersperse as one. Yet, each soldier selected for the mission knew their duty. They were willing to die if only to lay a crippling blow to the Demon Plague. It was the one drive that banded them together. There was never a question of their charge.

When Michael met up with them on a hill overlooking Merchant Pass, Shioda peered through his telescope. With great terror, they all took turns looking over the Pommelian realm, shrouded by the daunting Shadowland. In the sky, the swirling miasma lit up with lightning and concentrated evil. Droves of the afflicted ambled for the wicked bastion like cattle scattered all about the field. To all those who stood before the horrific spectacle, a sudden dread struck them ever so sharply. It became real.

"Merrieu is just a day's trek southwest," Thomas said in shock of seeing it a second time as if he never laid eyes on the sight before. "We should keep moving."

Michael added just to his side, "It's exactly as I saw it in my visions. I can feel it trying to pull me in. Thomas is right."

Marching with greater tenacity, the army headed for the blighted kingdom of Merrieu. In their pressing march southwest, paladin scouts met them halfway by an abandoned checkpoint gate. They updated the army on Merrieu's daunting condition. While there were no threats or maladies, the government had all but collapsed. The king had killed himself in disgrace as many of his people succumbed to the madness. Most had already fled the cursed kingdom.

With the king's nephew and niece as the only surviving sovereigns of Merrieu left to the greet them, the Angels of Resistance entered the main gates and gathered about the barracks. Setting up camp inside the near-derelict state, Michael's army prepared for their final supper before the next day's fateful mission. From their encampment, they watched as masses of feeble souls came running to crowd around the members of the Kai League, mainly Michael. To lessen the pressure on his officers, he emerged from the barracks and came to meet them all himself.

Some ran in terror just at the sight of his eyes, but others saw through his frightful appearance. The faithful knew him as he was, coming to touch his cape and armor. His hair had grown longer and his stubble turned into a small beard. Multitudes came for what little blessings he could provide, not caring what he did for them so long as he was in their company. From in the crowd, he felt the many who were afflicted, suffering from disturbing visions and recurring nightmares. The symptoms were often the same for those who eventually left their life behind to walk mindlessly for Pommel.

Before the masses of the Merrier populace, Michael summoned the many who suffered from the creeping signs of the madness and cured them. As their theoretical leader, he told them to free themselves and obey the call to Pommel no longer. His sway over the demonic forces was a relief for the flocks who felt the itch disappear. It only took his words for them to find instant freedom.

"It worked. He did it," Lai said in wonderment from outside the barracks' rotunda. "He *can* do it."

Shioda followed, "He just spoke to them. That's all he had to do."

"Words have power, Shioda," Lai returned before going back to tend to his officers. "One who speaks from authority speaks the loudest with but a whisper."

Thomas and Lana had met with the young sovereigns of Merrieu, expressing their gratitude for their hospitality as well as asking what the Kai League could offer in return. The palace, having faced the death of their uncle king and the loss of various royals to the madness, was in turmoil. Within the month, Merrieu was sure to implode. Lana promised support.

In the meantime, Michael tore away from the masses and headed into the dungeons, working on a tip from one of the citizens. Convincing the guards to let him through, he had come to realize how many innocent people suffered at the hands of their own government. Stricken with the madness, droves of prisoners gorged the dungeon. Emaciated, they cried to escape, but not for freedom or sustenance. They all wanted the torment to stop. The drive to trudge for Pommel plagued their minds. The smell inside was rank.

Appalled by the incarceration of the many who couldn't help it, Michael caught their attention and started to cure the lot of them. Cell by cell, he went and commanded them to free themselves. Their manic cries began to fade from sorrow to salvation. As a group of guards came to witness the event for themselves, Michael told them, "You must let these people go. They will no longer serve the Demon Plague. In fact, they will cure each other and everyone else in this place."

The guard captain then said in awe, "Sir Miuriell, we have orders to not to release them under any circumstance."

"Did that circumstance include me?" Michael retorted angrily. "What about feeding them—keeping them from dying? No animal deserves this treatment."

The same guard dared to answer, "Sir, our resources are limited. There is hardly—"

"You can let them out or I will take this dungeon apart. Your sovereigns will answer to me if they disapprove." His red eyes grew vibrant in the darkness of the prison, forcing the guards to wince back. In self-reproach, Michael breathed in deeply and said, "Go fetch others to help me release these people. They won't cause any trouble. We have food to spare as a token of our gratitude for allowing us to stay here."

The Merrier guards did as he asked, opening the cells and funneling the enervated people to the medical sector for treatment. Michael cleansed all of Merrieu from the madness, finally making his way back up to the barracks. Meeting some of his allies there, he told Maxim and Shioda to expect him at the border of Pommel on Merchant Pass in the late morning. Seeming tired, he sat on a bench just outside of the rotunda. Some knights brought him water from the well.

Predella had come to meet them there, asking, "Are you feeling alright, Michael? You look sick."

Drinking some water, he said, "I've never been this close to Pommel since—it happened. In some ways, I feel as strong as ever. In other ways, I feel diseased. They know I'm near. Tomorrow will mean everything—our surprise assault. Before nightfall, before I leave this place, we'll discuss our final plans. I want this attack and rescue mission to be the beginning of their end."

While the sun began to set in the western mountains, Michael bid farewell, as he had done consecutively since his enlightenment in the hemisphere. With his provided horse, he rode off and blessed everyone with a good night's rest. As he went, his many allies cheered in favor. They knew that Michael departed for their sake. The next time they would see him would be at Merchant Pass for the quiet invasion.

When he was gone, the vast encampment settled in Merrieu's barracks. The Ziamons sang war folksongs to enrich their fighting spirits and the paladins prayed. Thomas's scouts rode off to alert Shadisha back in Falcus that the Angels of Resistance had made it to the kingdom safely and were ready to attack Pommel.

Maxim and Predella slept close. Tightly embracing their bodies, they stared into each other's eyes. They never needed to utter words to express their growing feelings for one another. Instead, they kissed passionately as their souls burned. Predella slid her fingers across Maxim's face and vowed to survive the deadly mission. Moving wisps of black hair away from her face, he vowed the same—both of them not uttering a single word.

Predella's palm, imprinted with the handle of Maxim's sword, was still raw. It was difficult for her to retract her bow, though she, like her counterpart, was trained to ignore the pain. He kissed her hand before moving again to her lips.

Shioda and Lana, in another room, held each other with a fierce love. The anticipation of what waited for them when the sun ascended from the east was harsh. Falcun warriors had never surrendered to any adversary since the founding of the city over seven hundred years ago. In love and in dread, the two fell asleep in their arms.

Antonis couldn't sleep. Something picked at his mind. He felt a thousand eyes on Merrieu, as if an entire army had been raring to strike. As a pair of Tofauti warriors departed with him, the prophet left his quarters and stood out in the barracks' yard. Under the moonlight, he felt it even stronger. Something was coming, but he couldn't identify what.

When the sun rose from the Great Pacifica, the Angels of Resistance had already assembled their forces. There, they met up with Michael on Merchant Pass. Much closer than ever before, the army had their first glimpse of the realm's horrific Shadowland. Like living a nightmare, soldiers came to look upon the land reeking of visible death. Spikes impaled hundreds of people, warriors, and children alike, along the perimeter of Pommel. Undead soldiers guarded the dark land as the Demon Plague began its session of sleep.

Most stunned to silence, the army stopped just yards away from Michael's position. The officers organized their troops along the border as planned the night earlier. Thomas and his paladins formed the defensive line with Lana Kai by his side. The paladin legion developed a strong barricade of armored knights and cannons to cover their allies' escape if things became messy.

Before joining his incursion team, Shioda met Lana at her post and kissed her. After their loving embrace, he put on his mask and said, "Remember what we discussed. You are not to leave this line under any condition. Is that clear?"

"Yes, dad," she replied, as he ran off to join the others.

At the front line, Maxim met Michael at his side and said, "You know, that tool of a prophet you dragged along has the whole base on guard, warning everyone about an imminent attack on Merrieu. Is there anything to that?"

"I've tried to throw off the Demon Plague by leaving a part of my psyche at each camp—some off the Falcun coast and others by the Ghost Forest," Michael replied stoically, looking on the realm of his homeland. "If he thinks there's an attack, then he did the right thing. We must be cautious, but our minds have to be on that bastion right now. Nothing can distract us. This one moment is too important."

Digesting Michael's words, he inhaled deeply before asking him, "Michael, tell me you'll save Shina."

Taking him by the shoulder, Michael said earnestly, "I grew up in that place. I found the love of my life there. My son was born in the clinic just three levels up there if you can see that far. Maxim, as far as I'm concerned, Shina is family. You're my brother. Predella, charged with saving my boy, is my sister. You've all come to join me on this wretched homecoming and none of you had to. I swear to you that I'll do every last thing to save that girl because we're all in this together."

Embracing him as a brother, Maxim said, "I will not let you down."

Maxim caught sight of Colonel Aramis in the distance, his torn cape blowing in the wind. The Ziamons knew where to find their assigned demonic generals. As long as they abided by Michael's directions dictated on two individual maps, they vowed victory. Their only concern was killing the demonic generals in the first place. The challenge was as real as it was dire.

When it appeared that the invasion was set, the Angels of Resistance streamed quietly passed Thomas's defensive line. Before them was the path to Pommel, guided by the border of the impaled. The bastion was not far and reaching the iron doors on the left side of the bulwark was critical.

One foot away from the shadow of the high twirling miasma above, Michael accepted the dark energy that flowed through him and moved onward.

One step into its cast and the undead could instantly move in for the kill. It was their land. Michael, entering first, commanded that Tenebrion's skeletal soldiers submit to his will. In but an instant, they moved to the sides and knelt. The intensity of his power was difficult to control, but, on the other hand, felt right. Centering himself by way of his staff, he turned to his divisions just beyond the Shadowland and let them know it was safe to follow.

With silence in mind, the teams advanced. On the far left, the first rescue team led by Shioda and Predella stepped forth. The ninja warriors amassed in total black concealment. It was necessary that they be able to hide amongst the shadows like the shadow demons themselves. Next, the second rescue team led by Maxim and Lai came forth. Maxim had been wearing a foreign mail unfamiliar to him by most regards. It was brushed with a dark red hue, providing optimal flexibility as it was primarily designed for heavily armed ninjas in open warfare. His fire-sword and scabbard were attached securely onto his back, allowing the hilt of the sword to protrude above his right shoulder.

Lai, as expected, was completely concealed by his ninja garb. Not one portion of his skin was visible, with the exception of his one working eye. Lai, above all others, was blessed and cursed with partial blindness. His heightened senses were a welcome tool for Maxim and his team of ninjas within the darkened halls.

The last pair of teams were all Ziamon. Esker and his dense number of men, equipped with blades and shields, knew that Tenebrion was a foe that none of them had encountered yet. However, the fact that the demonic general wielded a supernatural whip forced each of them to keep their shields out in front at all times. Aramis and his heavy broadsword were thrilled to face Valkris, the feared leader of the five generals. Vengeance was Ziamon's principal law in the theatre of war.

Michael, on his own, had stepped forth and tightened his grip on the Staff of Truth. As tempting as it was to investigate the mysterious fireplace in his visions, he needed to concentrate on Shina and the success of the mission. Hundreds of lives hung in the balance. The evil essence consumed his soul and offered him a strong aura of power. He felt stronger and faster. The more he lingered in the land, the greater the power that flowed through his veins, reaching into his glowing red eyes. Groaning from the surge of evil, he clenched his fist.

"Michael?" Maxim uttered. "You alright?"

"Better than alright. Let's go," Michael replied coolly, adjusting to the great enhancement in his abilities.

With no creatures to assail them, the Angels of Resistance cautiously followed behind Michael's lead. It was warrior instinct to unsheathe their weapons as they marched through the road leading to Pommel's walls. On each of their sides, brushing the road, the army of the undead remained reverent on their knees. For those warriors that had never seen such fetid evil, an even more egregious army likely awaited them inside.

As they finally reached the walls of the fortress, collected bones of the vanquished laid at their feet. They had no choice but to step on the remains. Corpses and skeletons were everywhere. When Michael uncovered the side entrance into the bulwark, covering his nose from the putrid stench of death, the task force split up and entered the fortress of hell together. Each and every warrior was aware of their targets and how to find them. At last, the incursion had begun.

"We have a limited amount of time. Get in and get out as fast as you can. Keep it concise and don't waver," Michael said unto the officers that were close enough to hear him. "I will be with you in spirit. Godspeed, my friends. This is it."

The bastion was gloomy and rank. Yet, it was clear that the ceremony had begun, for the entire citadel was silent and without action. For the moment, the Angels of Resistance could explore the corrupted fortress without quarrel. The different teams split up and dared to deal a telling blow to the Demon Plague.

Sattka had taken a young girl of her choosing and carried her through the fireplace. The ceremony was commencing. The first team to reach their designated target was Aramis and his party of twenty-five Ziamon soldiers. They silently crept through the hall, under the large staircase, and through the suspended drape of linked finger bones to reach the tall double doors leading to what should have been Valkris's private chambers.

The doors were swathed in blood. The bronze door grips were tainted by cursed claws. Already, the Ziamons could feel the evil air of whatever waited inside. Aramis wielded his heavy broadsword vigilantly and signaled for two of his men to open the doors. Six crossbowmen loaded their steel bolts for the incursion once the doors were pulled open. Amid the foul smell of rancid meat, the crossbowmen rushed into the chambers with weapons ready.

However, the room was still. They looked about the chambers carefully from corner to corner, but could not find the demonic general. Aramis passed through to survey the repugnant room for himself. He found nothing. The colonel stepped in further and signaled for his men to scout the entire area.

They dashed in and explored the terrible dungeon room. Bloody skulls and human bones portrayed all of Valkris's furniture. Every bone had a purpose in this mad scene. His throne was carefully constructed with a flyer demon's skull at the top and then human spines that crept down the exterior of the chair's backside. The vertebrae met the armrests of the seat fashioned out of arm bones.

Beside the in-ground pool of blood, a terrifying stand, molded out of human flesh and obscured with living eyes, housed the infamous Seltek. It hovered over its dais magically on its own. The room was dark and shards of flesh hung from the ceiling. It was difficult for Aramis's warriors to focus on their elusive target. Most of them believed that he was elsewhere and that their mission was over. But, when it seemed that Colonel Aramis was ready to leave the gross chamber, the double doors slammed behind them.

They quickly turned to find themselves locked inside the sinister compartment. As the warriors cried out in panic, Aramis smashed his hefty sword into one of the skeletal desks and shattered it. Screaming in Espanion, Aramis led by example, "Converge in the center!"

They quieted for a moment, but eerie noises spooked them to no end. Coming from behind and under them, the petrifying sounds irked Aramis's battle-hardened men. One warrior resorted to trying to barge the double doors open, but a shadow demon lifted him into the air by its claws. Upside down, the creature twisted the warrior's neck, killing him instantly. It dropped the lifeless soldier onto the ground and retracted back into the comfort of the dark.

The crossbowmen fired their bolts mercilessly as the others cried out in horror. The bolts tore through the suspended flesh and devastated old wooden planks above. Other than that, nothing dropped to the floor. With one man down, it was time to panic.

From the blood pool, Valkris slowly broke the surface. Drenched in gore, Valkris rose out from it, disturbed out of his slumber. The Ziamon team looked on in sheer terror. Aramis, himself, could not utter a sound, not even a pant. Behind them all, Valkris opened his glowing yellow eyes and stepped out of the blood pool, moving towards his prey.

Those close to the demon backed away from it, realizing that their sneak attack had failed. There would have to be a desperate fight. Tilting his head to the side, the demon hissed, "**You sneaky monkeys.**"

Colonel Aramis shouted out, "Kill it or die!"

Once Aramis raised his greatsword, Valkris had outstretched his right claw and produced a shockwave that blasted the squad back, sending them into every obstruction. Valkris then awoke the Seltek and bid the quarterstaff's eyes to move about sporadically. His regal attire formed about his body.

"**If you wanted to surprise me, you should have checked the blood pool,**" Valkris rasped. "**But, of course, I can understand. You're anxious.**"

Responding to the demon's provoking taunt, the colonel's soldiers gathered themselves from the floor and charged at him. Valkris had taken all of them on at once. The eyes of the Seltek kept a close watch on all of his human adversaries. In Pommel, Valkris was practically a god.

As he killed one man and struck another, the soldiers became more daring. They fought back with broken limbs and ravaged skin. Valkris had detached himself from an attacker and snapped his clawed fingers, causing the stumbling man to suddenly burst into flames. Though his sorcery wreaked havoc upon them, they still persisted. The Ziamons fought to the end. Within moments of the fight, Valkris summoned a poisonous tremor that jolted everyone back, poisoning them all simultaneously. Marked for death, their last act of defiance was the slaying of the demonic general in its own dwelling.

As the battle continued, Michael had finally reached Princess Shina's disturbing domain. The other teams still had not made it to their targets, though they were not intercepted by any foe. Michael cautiously snuck his head around the corner to find an enormous spider guarding the doors. Without permitting one more second to scratch away, Michael apprehended the arachnid with his telekinetic ability and swiftly crushed it. The guts leaked out of the forced orifices and all seven of its eyes burst like squeezed eggs. The spider squealed once before it was finished.

Valkris's watch through the arachnid's eyes quickly perished. Now, the demonic general was fully conscious of the surprise attack on Pommel. Feeling a sadistic rage pulse through him, Valkris tossed the prey presently in his claw into the pool of blood and cried maliciously. If Shina was taken, then the Demon Lord would surely destroy him for his futility. He now had no choice but to finish all of his enemies off in an instant to prevent Shina's escape.

In a fury, Valkris smashed his foes aside before conjuring up a devastating spell. Raising the Seltek, the orifice opened to expel a deafening noise that stunned the warriors in their tracks. From there, he blasted them all to their death by the red ray of his staff. He melted their armor and smoldered their bodies. The crimson rays tore through his opponents, finishing the conflict with little effort.

While Valkris's quarters were spoiled by the surprise assault, he retracted his Seltek and headed for the doors. Colonel Aramis ran out from the cover behind the bizarre throne and swung his huge sword to kill the demon once and for all. Valkris spun quickly to repel the attack, but he underestimated the Ziamon's strength. The Seltek was clouted from his claws. It was not until the quarterstaff knocked about the floor when the demonic general realized that the colonel had survived one of the Seltek's best incantations.

Shouting in intense pain and anger, the valiant warrior raised his tremendous sword and attempted to cut down the demon again, killing him this time. With all of his troops dead, destroying the monster was the only task left so that their deaths would not be in vain. Valkris, however, was too fast for the brave hero. He seized the sword's hilt and both of Aramis's shaken hands before punching his chest in with a sorcerer's might. The last man fell to the ground and coughed, realizing the severity of his injuries.

Now wielding the broadsword in his left claw, Valkris stepped onto the colonel's stomach and plunged the heavy blade into his heart. As Colonel Aramis took his last breath on the ground, defeated by an inhumane fiend, visions of his lover and children burned into his mind. Letting go, the great warrior, admired by all of his people, died. His own sword remained implanted into his chest.

Valkris wiped the saliva from his mouth before departing from the mad scene. Loyal Ziamons laid dead in his chamber, resulting in the first tragic defeat of the mission. The demon then hurried out to stop Michael from ruining him totally. Yet, as he went, he felt his power wane. Valkris ran back in to retrieve his Seltek. Michael was not above his sinister magic anymore.

Amid the deaths of the colonel and his team, Michael forced open the large doors to the gallery. Dozens of paintings and sculptures from the old world were strewn about, some torn to shreds and others matted with blood. Priceless artifacts, soiled by the bastion's new inhabitants, were smashed to bits. The gallery, once attracting hundreds of dignitaries and illustrious art enthusiasts from all over the realm, had become Shina's lair.

The vast hall was beaming with the flickering light of a hundred candles. They rode along a red rolling carpet, directing him to an empty throne. If there was an evil present, Shina was a part of it. Michael searched everywhere in the hall until he took the set of steps that led to the upper level of the derelict exhibit. With his staff, Michael saw her there, sleeping in a skimpy red dress. Before entering the hall, he took a deep breath and centered himself.

Lying on a bed fashioned from bone and flesh, she slept like an angel. She ruffled the red covers and twirled her young legs into the sheets. Michael could not believe the sight. Droves of servants knelt all around her, cloaked in red. They were more victims of the madness, trapped in a wicked cult none could have chosen themselves. Nearing closer to her, slipping past the cultists, Michael looked upon Shina.

The only explanation remaining for him was to endure the reality of Shina's turning. Her pale skin was aggrieved with pulsing veins that ran up her neck and into her jaw. As beautiful as she was, Michael knew that the old Shina, the true Shina, was probably gone. Before attempting to find out who he was about to awaken, Michael looked to free the entranced disciples from their bondage.

He said to them with a resounding voice, "All of you are free from this curse. Leave this place, at once and never come back."

After he said it, not one of them moved. He stood there, unable to comprehend how his words had no effect on them. As he looked on the hooded figures, Shina's voice emanated from behind, "**They are mine—not yours, my sweet.**"

He jerked back from the bed and placed his staff into both of his hands before him. Awake, Shina rearranged her figure on the bed and smiled lustfully. Her eyes were as black as oblivion. She licked her top lip and proceeded, "**Jealous?**"

She was Shina no more. Michael understood that there was no sense in negotiating. Feeling that time was bleeding away, he focused his strength and then discharged a surge of power around them. Every last one of her disciples flew back and slammed into all four walls, knocked unconscious. After all of them were neutralized, Michael looked at her and said, "You're coming with me, whether you want to or not."

"**I don't wish to fight, love,**" Shina said with a devil's intent as she rose onto her legs and put her hand on his chest. "**Stay here where you belong.**"

"I want to. It's everything else that doesn't belong here and that includes you, princess," Michael replied, seizing her hand and guiding her in the direction to leave.

"**Queen,**" she said, walking along with him. "**I'm your queen, even if you don't want me.**"

"I want Shina and you aren't her," Michael said, pushing her out towards the steps. "Maybe you'll feel better with the sun in your face."

"**Maybe you'll feel better inside me. Your first wife was a poor concubine. Only a single son and such a meek, sad little thing. Her womb was infertile, to say the least,**" she said, prancing ahead of him.

Her demonic intuition was a venomous bite. Stricken with sudden grief from her words, Michael stopped and put her up above the floor. Her feet dangled just a foot above the ground when he turned her around to look her in the lifeless eyes. It was far from the woman he knew, but Michael had to face the demon that possessed her body. She only smiled at him, saying, "**If your intent is to hurt me, then please don't make me beg for it. I'm up for everything.**"

With only his wrath to suppress his tears, he brought her closer and growled through his teeth, "You'll say any damn thing to bring out the darkness inside me, but it isn't going to work. I mourn the woman I love, but I will save her son, yet. I assure you. He is much stronger than you think. He survived this hellhole for this long. I'd call that astonishing."

"**And that was just half of what you *could* have. Our children will make him look like a sniveling pup,**" Shina declared.

Before Michael could defy her again, he sensed Valkris's advance. Michael envisioned the demonic general teleporting to their location in just seconds. To cover his escape, he smashed open a sector of the wall and then bashed the floor beneath them. He finally broke another gaping hole into the wall behind him and hauled the princess as he went. Pretending to fly, Shina spread out her arms and legs as Michael brought her along through the hole and out of the gallery.

Arriving seconds too late, Valkris materialized from the beam of his Seltek and realized Shina was gone. As his sorcery dissolved, Valkris wasted no time in sniffing about the scene. Not fooled by the cavities Michael made to throw him off, he followed Shina's scent and pursued them.

Meanwhile, on the sixth level, Maxim and Lai's team had reached the vast lobby leading to the holding cells. The stealthy team glided through the dark and remained close to perimeter walls. The lobby was a perfect octagon that merged with a straight running corridor to the north. Lai led the team down the hall as Maxim maintained his march at the master ninja's left side.

Following Michael's instructions exactly, Maxim looked for the only steel bolted door guarded by undead warriors. It was not a difficult task. Two hefty knights, breathing with dark magic, stood guard on each side of the chamber's entrance. Their skulls showed through their helmets. With red gleaming eyes, the two undead warriors sensed a human presence.

Lai signaled for six ninjas to ride the darkness and overwhelm the demons with arrows and knives. As ordered, they broke free from their positions and devastated the warriors, regardless of their robust shields. In seconds, the threat was eradicated. It was free for the rest of the team to follow through with their task.

Maxim and Lai led the ninjas out of the exit corridor and into the hall—a dead end. The only place left to go was the holding cell. From there, they would need to follow their trail of powder back out to the main vestibule of the fortress. Every warrior could feel the evil impression. It sent shivers up Maxim's neck. They knew they were in the belly of the beast.

From inside the holding chamber came the sounds of startled women. So as not to frighten the bemused females, Maxim entered first with his fire-sword sheathed behind his back. His features gave the scared captors some sign of respite. He walked into the large holding dungeon only to choke from the rank smell.

Nearly all of the virgin girls were naked or with only fragments of clothing. Most had lost almost all sanity. Walking through the wretched scene, Maxim acknowledged all of the women chained from their wrists and ankles to some section of the wall. Eight pillars in the middle of the dungeon hosted chain clamps as well. A strange smoke floated about the place like shifting mist. Among them and the imprisoned females, blue flames lit the chamber by a supernatural force. The entering party had never seen flames like that in their lifetime.

One of Lai's officers had followed Maxim in and called out, "If you are able to move, please try to stand now. If you can't stand, stay where you are. We're going to get you all out of here. If you can't walk, we'll carry you out. Please, as this is most important—please try to stay as quiet as you can. We don't have much time."

Lai stood by the opened door with his arms crossed, surveying the operation. Fortunately, most women had the will to flee on their feet. Some of the younger girls were too emaciated to walk out on their own. Trembling, one of them muttered to Maxim as he helped free another girl nearby, "They took my sister. They took her away."

Working to pry the shackles from her ankles with tools provided by the craftsmen of Falcus, Maxim said to her, "I am sorry for your sister, kid. Her memory will live on in you once we've got you out. That's all I can promise."

When he pried off the last shackle, Maxim removed his cape and wrapped it around the girl. He lifted her up in his arms and started to head out when a ninja met him in the center and offered to take her. He gently gave her up and offered a reassuring wink to calm her. As he stood there, taking in the traumatic scene in slow motion, all of the women were taken out. Lai shook him out of the spell, warning him that they had no time to think about it. They had to go.

Maxim gave the obscene dungeon one last glare before he followed the party out. The odd mist lingered above the cold floor, empty. Like a miniature twister, the mist began to take shape. It was not long after that Scythian had formed. The skeletal phantom emerged from the low miasma, shaping its skull. Its gray torn cloak floated sinisterly as its red eyes emerged from the sockets. Fully formed, Scythian unleashed its deadly scythe and followed the intruders not far ahead.

On route to his escape with Shina, Michael had come upon the infamous fireplace that burned in his visions. The Demon

Lord and his daughter were slaughtering a girl as he stood there, unable to tear himself away from it. His mind couldn't see beyond the trap door, even with the Staff of Truth. Having lost his focus for but a moment, Shina met her feet with the floor.

"**Finally, on my own feet again!**" Shina exclaimed.

Michael then turned to her and remembered what was happening. He felt Valkris advancing closer. Unable to locate the demon with his staff, Michael left the fireplace behind and said, "Come, girl. Let's leave this place."

"**Aren't you going to take a closer look at that door?**" Shina mocked, stretching her body like a feline. "**It's where it all started, you know. You—me—all of us. Don't you want to take just a little peek?**"

Unwilling to succumb to the temptations, Michael put her back into the air and moved on.

Below the fortress, the dungeon of torment awaited Shioda and Predella's team. The steep stairway down was impractical for pairs. Like a hunting colony of ants, they resorted to descending the steps in a straight line. It slowed them down significantly, but, when they reached the lower level, six undead guards met them there. Instinctively, Predella loaded two arrows and conjured up a fire. She struck two of them in the skulls, engulfing the others cluttered too close to the flames.

In a mad dash for the sake of time, Shioda ordered that his team dart into the dungeon and free any survivors inside. They quickly came to understand what Michael referred to when he described the level of suffering in the prisons. Aside from the rank smell of death and excrement, the sight of entrails and body parts littered about brought the many warriors to wretch. The degree of anguish so many had to endure broke every man's heart. If they had anything to say about it, Shioda's division swore that each and every survivor would never have to suffer such torment ever again.

Seth was asleep, knowing that the demonic generals slept as well. Predella searched for him among the others in cages. As the other ninjas poured into the dungeon, various undead minions began to impede the rescue mission. Ready for Tenebrion's skeletal soldiers, the warriors split up into strike and salvage teams. Shioda joined his strike force and cut down the first three animated corpses that entered the fray. The battle was on.

Amid the fight, Predella discovered Seth's cell. Before she could even attempt to break open the lock to the cage door, a ninja rushed by and picked it within an instant. Taking advantage to her comrade's skillful deed, Predella opened the door and pulled Seth out of the cell. The poor, thin boy made a fuss. He was too ill to know what was stealing him from his vile dwelling.

She hushed him down and caressed his weak face. Seth still continued to struggle, but she would never let him loose. After a short while, Predella soothed him enough for him to finally realize that she had come to save him. She took him from his deplorable cage and held him in her arms. The care of a woman reminded him of his mother's loving embrace.

Seth's feeble limbs hung down as she raced out of the dungeon with her quiver of arrows and legendary bow secured tightly on her back. She then joined others who had already made it back to the narrow stairway out with a weak captive. A small group of lockpicks opened the cages for each subsequent warrior to assess for themselves. Not every captive was salvageable.

Feeling as if he had sinned worse than the devil himself, Prince Eric visited the church to pray for forgiveness. Finally finding himself, he came to realize that his path of greed, murder, and hatred had come full circle. He lost the only person who loved him to the Demon Plague, abandoning his allies for a false and immoral sense of security. Notions of suicide crept in, for the visions of his crimes upon the Waasi never let up.

As Eric defied God in casting his lot with demons, he believed that forgiveness was most probably out of reach. The once arrogant sorcerer had, at last, seen himself as he truly was. The church was the only place left for him to find some sliver of salvation. It was the only holy place in Pommel left untouched by the Demon Plague. Like smoking a cigar, the Demon Lord wished to burn it out after Michael Miuriell took his rightful place in the conquest over mankind.

The initial noise that came with the Ziamons' rush passed the church had startled him. If the Eastern warriors were slithering around the Pommelian bastion, then Michael and the resistance were inside. He couldn't believe it. Eric marveled at Michael's strategic timing to invade Pommel during the demonic kipping hours. There was no doubt he had come to rescue Shina and his son.

The Ziamons proceeded up the corridor to find their target just up the way. Little did they know that the colonel and his warriors were slain. Eric exited the ancient church and watched Esker's division go towards Tenebrion's perch. There were easier ways to die.

Michael blasted out from Pommel's second story wall and dropped into the main field. With Shina floating closely behind against her will, he ran with great trial, trusting that he could cure the princess of her demons when out of the oppressive darkness of the Shadowland. While he neared closer to the Falcun lines, Michael could hear Thomas's paladins cheering. Michael had been running since evading Valkris at Shina's dormitory. He was exhausted and in need of respite. A dozen paladin knights came running into the Shadowland, coming to take Shina off his hands. They could not know that it was much more complicated than that.

"**Let me down! What are you doing? Why?**" she had screamed and squirmed just feet above the ground as he brought her closer to the edge of the Shadowland.

When he didn't answer, she cried out louder, "**Do you mean to kill me? I'll burn out there!**"

Michael ran, wheezing each breath, when the oncoming paladins shouted out for him, "Watch it! Behind you!"

A mad soldier came from his left and tackled Michael to the ground, tripping up his run. Shina, having willed the man to intercede, finally dropped to the ground and rolled until she made it to her feet again. When Michael recovered from his fall, he called out for the paladins to stop in their tracks. There was no telling what Shina was going to do.

"**Kill yourselves!**" she screeched, leading all of those stricken with the madness to turn the swords on themselves.

Each soldier, over fifty scattered about their position, began to kill themselves. Along with the reinforcements at the front lines, Michael looked on in horror as they all took their lives. He then turned to her and hollered, "Shina, stop!"

"**You think you're the only one who can control all these human sheep?**" she cried out to him, defiant.

Rising up from his knees, Michael exclaimed with tears falling, "Shina, I'm so sorry for putting you in this position! I tried to save you from this! God save us."

With just a flicker of his fist, Shina lost consciousness and fell over onto her side. He put her into a deep sleep and, just as soon, punished himself for not doing it sooner. Finally, the paladins rushed over to check on Michael's condition. A team of Tinarians scurried to check on Shina's. They put her on a stretcher and awaited Michael's instructions.

Michael called out to them, "Keep her in the sun, but cover her from direct sunlight! I don't know what it'll do to her in that state. She could burn."

A paladin then said to him, "Michael, we're sorry, but the Mad Legion came onto the field when you immobilized the undead warriors. They just waited in the Shadowland. I didn't think they'd do—what they did."

"Just make sure they keep her under a sheet, but in the sun. Do you understand?" Michael said as he started back for the bastion.

"Legate Excallum wishes to see you, Miuriell," another paladin said through his helmet. "What should we—"

"Tell him I'll be back with survivors! We'll be coming fast, God-willing," Michael replied while running back for the perils of the bastion.

Holding his staff in his right hand, Michael made it back to the same door from which he began the mission a time ago. Once he made it back into Pommel's citadel, a loud scream from Valkris's Seltek came to greet him. Just catching the devastating ray from nowhere with his telekinetic shield, Michael was cast into the wall. Display cases of priceless old-world artifacts crashed under his back. He lost his staff amid the impact. Michael had his quick reflexes to thank for saving his life. The beam would have easily killed him.

While he squirmed in the hazard of obliterated glass, Valkris calmly strolled up, holding the Seltek in his left claw. Michael tried to focus in on the great demon, though dust dispersed from the crash hindered his eyesight. Valkris revealed his right arm previously hidden behind his back to show Michael his lost article—the Staff of Truth.

As Michael came to his senses, cut and bruised, Valkris proclaimed, "**Looking for this? Who would have imagined that even with Abaddon's staff, you still wouldn't see the truth? It has only been a stick to the likes of you.**"

Finding his way to his feet, Michael asked, jaded, "What happened to them?"

"**Your pathetic troop of monkeys? They died miserably, of course. You see, no one ever thinks that when spying through the looking glass there is often something else spying back.**" Valkris tossed the staff aside like it was nothing more than a hollow twig. He aimed the Seltek for Michael's heart. The erratic eyes about the evil weapon focused on him and nothing else. Thus, Michael summoned his staff and commanded it to dash into his palm. Once it did, Valkris fired the red beam of devastation.

As quick as he was able, Michael nudged the Seltek's position in Valkris's claw just an inch to the side with his telekinetic ability. The ray just missed his chest and obliterated the wall behind Michael further. The protective shield that he sustained prevented the energy of the beam from affecting him.

Countering the demon's strike, Michael cast the Staff of Truth with as much strength as he could muster. The butt of the wooden shaft landed into Valkris's chest and compelled him to wince back. The blow disoriented the great demon and offered Michael some time to summon the staff, once again, to return to him. He then outstretched his hand and tried to crush Valkris to death.

Protected by a forcefield that already started to crack under Michael's fury, Valkris roared, "**How much longer do you think you'll hold out before you end up like Shina? It should be comforting to know that she has finally turned. Now, they're only waiting for you—but for me, I have grown impatient!**"

Valkris fired another powerful beam for him, compelling Michael to abandon his attack and defend himself. Staving off the wicked beam with his palm, Michael summoned all his strength and shouted, "So have I!"

Unleashing a concentrated force from his mind, Michael pulverized the source of the Seltek's magic. The skull at the head of the quarterstaff backfired, sending Valkris back. He lost grip of his Seltek shortly after Michael's unsuspecting counterstrike. It laid idle feet away from him. Michael took the fleeting opening in the battle and brought forth all his might. He leveled the vestibule's ceiling and let it come raining down to squash Valkris underneath.

Crushed by tons of rubble and wreckage, the demonic general had become buried by the second floor. Michael had no time to revel in his victory over the creature. Nor did he mourn for Aramis and his team. He couldn't lose his focus. Michael ran for the lower dungeons to help Predella and Shioda rescue the prisoners, along with his son.

It was not long before the Demon Lord realized that something was wrong. His omniscient sight, even from the enigmatic place underneath the bastion, saw that Michael had returned. Time was short. He would need to exert all of his power if he wanted to save his friends, flirting with Abaddon's hankering to consume his body and soul.

PART II
CHAPTER XI
THE RECKONING

Esker and his team climbed the levels of the bastion only to find an old abandoned astronomers observatory. The hall hosted a long empty table with dozens of empty seats. An elaborate chandelier hung high above the long rectangular table and lit the way for two swooping staircases that met at the top, providing two routes up to the doors leading to the observatory. The lab was eerily quiet, as Michael had said it would be. Somewhere, Tenebrion, the necromancing beast, was sleeping.

Because Pommel was essentially a living museum of the old world, the hall was kept in perfect order. The Ziamons gathered inside with their weapons drawn, waiting for a potential ambush from the cursed creature. Esker noticed fingerprints of human digits on the arms of chairs and on the astronomers' advanced tablets that hadn't worked since the Primeval Tragedy. Old documents and accomplishments in glass casings were set by each chair like a dinner table serving of archaic data.

A pair of warriors climbed the swooping staircase and approached a large inset wooden door, already partially opened, to the actual observatory. Esker gestured for them to open the door for others to rush in. Their target was most likely sleeping inside. He ordered more troops to ascend the staircase and assist in the intrusion. As the warriors scurried up the steps with their diverse weaponry unsheathed, the door exploded from the other side and shook the entire hall.

Men had fallen over the balcony's edge and others tumbled halfway down the stairway. Shards of wood from the old door encompassed the place as their target demon was up and ready to take them on. Beyond where Esker's imagination could carry him, nothing prepared him for his unbelievable first sight of Tenebrion.

The great demon gradually made his way through his entranceway and onto the balcony's landing. Unraveling the supernatural whip, Malevolence, from his reptilic claws, Tenebrion planted his left talon on a soldier's back and crushed him into the marble floor. The warrior cried once before losing air and his life. Looking over his invading challengers, the beast chucked the vanquished warrior over the balcony and rasped from behind his mouthpiece, "**Guests!**"

The justice fearfully readied his cruel blades and challenged the monster outright. From the floor, the Ziamon warriors armed with crossbows unleashed havoc upon Tenebrion, but the beast disappeared. The bolts lodged into, and some others through, the opposing wall. Then, suddenly, the demonic general reappeared in a burst of dark magic upon the elongated table and began his attack from the elevated position.

The hordes of warriors were on the constant defensive as Tenebrion mutilated some with the supernatural whip, immediately leading their armor to decay with each strike. In violent waves, the demon seized each soldier that dared to draw near to him. Swords and axes were bested with every next swirl and crack from the whip, resorting swords and axes to withering, crumbling fragments in their hands.

Tenebrion spun around to swat the weapon out from a stealthy attacker's sweaty hands, snatching him by the face and lifting him into the air. As the other warriors charged the demon to salvage their comrade, Esker watched the event unfold from the observatory's landing. He made sure to study

Tenebrion's fighting style. His whip degenerated inanimate objects, like weapons and armor, at will.

Tenebrion clouted six consecutive Ziamons and sent them hurling all about the hall. One soldier hit the stationary mirror so hard that he crashed through the glass without even nudging the loose frame. Most bolts piercing the demon's aged armor reached his tough hide but didn't stop his demoralizing assault. A crossbowman with exploding bolts fired for Tenebrion's unprotected skull, but, again, he vanished and reappeared someplace else like a sorcerer. The incendiary bolt blew open a crater into the opposing wall.

As Tenebrion had finished crushing a warrior's head into the floor, another met with him and, like a cutting scissor, swung his blades out to slice open the demon's exposed head. But, again, the general anticipated the assault in the nick of time and came around to snag his neck tightly. He was able to slice a portion of Tenebrion's bat-like ear off and his other blade deflected off the demon's dark armor.

The demon cried and flung him with ire. Fighting off the unrelenting Ziamons, Tenebrion observed his adversary soar high over the table, just missing the elaborate chandelier, and crash through the already devastated balcony's landing. Esker then, with his eyes locking on the chandelier, came up with a cliched, but effective plan.

Tenebrion did not wish to kill Esker yet. Instead, he wanted to finish mutilating his numerous opponents and leave their leader for last. Yet, for Esker, he was already working on a counter-offensive. He followed the taut wire that traveled from the chandelier and through the ceiling. He immediately found his demolition crossbowman and gave him a new target for which to aim.

Grappling his shoulder tightly, Esker said in one breath, "I will mislead the beast into the center of the table there.

Blow that chandelier from the ceiling when he's underneath. Not a moment too soon or too late! Hear it?"

"Yes, sir!" He nodded and positioned himself away from the fray and in perfect sight of the canopy and wire leads connected to the ceiling. Esker climbed onto the table and stationed himself directly under the chandelier above. In his open challenge to the demon, the justice pounded his blades together to get his attention. With a clear venue, the beast grabbed a wounded warrior and tossed him sliding along the table. The screaming soul glided along the surface and took the encased artifacts with him. Esker hopped over the oncoming warrior and allowed him to fall over the edge.

Tenebrion vanished and reappeared onto the table, weakening its stability. Esker and two other soldiers waited in the center. The demon struck from a distance, grappling a soldier's neck with Malevolence and yanked off his head. His corpse fell limp off the edge of the table, now sodden with blood. From Esker's left side, his comrade's blood had drenched his armor and face. He flinched and shakily cleaned his eyes of the splattered gore. Next, Tenebrion cracked his whip towards the soldier to the justice's right and placed a remarkable dent into his shield. He fell back onto the table, protecting his face, but the shield had already begun to waste away.

"Face me, you dick!" Esker shouted as he pounded his cruel together again. He didn't want to lose another man, for half of his team was already dead or mortally wounded. When his men became savvy to the scheme to crush Tenebrion under the chandelier, a horde of warriors hopped onto the table and rushed the demon from the other end. Stabbing him and shoving him backward with their shields, the Ziamons lured Tenebrion closer to the target. Nevertheless, the beast vanished and reappeared in the same spot on the table, blasting all of his oppressors onto the floor.

"Shield!" Esker plunged one of his blades into the wood and outstretched his arm to receive one. Holding the shield in one hand, he cast his blade forth and struck Tenebrion in his lower leg. The demon, with one ear and one more second worth of patience, spun around and yanked the blade out. Esker stood there staring him down with a sword and shield.

"So, you really want this? Okay!" Tenebrion cried out, enduring no more bolts from the crossbowmen.

Tenebrion stomped onto the table and shook it considerably. As Esker tried to keep his balance, the demonic general lashed out at him with his whip and slammed the tattered shield out from his hand. He fell onto his back and clenched his empty fist, desperately trying to overcome the physical pain from the impact of the strike. Now, nearly defenseless against the monster, Esker readied his single blade for close combat.

Enthralled, Tenebrion walked towards his rival, fighting off the horde of Ziamon warriors that tried to stop him along the way. As the demon neared closer, Esker crawled backward. He cleverly sized his monster up in the process. The danger was great as the demon sauntered closer. No matter what they did, they couldn't slow down the general any further.

With Tenebrion gaining on him, Esker looked towards the ceiling and cried frenziedly, "Shoot it loose—now!"

Tenebrion, sensing that something was wrong, stopped in his tracks. But it was too late for the creature, as the incendiary crossbowman fired the explosive bolt for the chandelier's canopy. It blew open easier than they expected. The tremendous piece came falling from the high ceiling straight for Tenebrion's skull.

Esker rolled off the table and took some chairs with him to the ground, hiding under them as he fell. By the time Tenebrion looked to the ceiling, the fantastic ornament smashed upon him with terrible power, devastating the table underneath. The sound and quake of the smash were empowering. Other Ziamons took cover from the shattering glass that seemed to engulf the hall.

Amidst the destroyed table, the heavy chandelier ensconced Tenebrion's body. The strike finished the demon's terrorizing reign on them. Esker looked over to one of his comrades and said to him, "Pick up my sword and saw off that disgusting head. I want a trophy for Ziamon."

The soldier retrieved one of Esker's cruel blades and readied the saw edge of the sword over Tenebrion's neck. Still alive and alert, the foul demon vanished for the last time. The chandelier crashed further to the ground and the warrior's first cut was nothing but shattered glass. Yet, the injured demon didn't return. He retreated in utter shame and agony. To where he escaped was impossible to know, but he learned not to take the Ziamons lightly again.

They were disgusted with Tenebrion's dishonor, but he was far from defeated. More important was their escape from the citadel. They could do no more in the observatory lab. After catching their breath and saluting each other, the team left.

After a thin line of ninja warriors, Predella escaped from the scrawny staircase and started to race for the exit up to the first level with Seth drooping tiredly in her arms. But the minute she departed from the thin stairway, an unexpected gate of old iron quickly fell and shut the exit off behind her. The loud slam of the metal-induced her to spin around to witness it for herself.

Holding Seth closely to her breast, Predella watched on as the ninjas behind the bars cried in apprehension. They were stalled inside the dark stairway with captors in desperate need of medical refuge. Ninjas before her had already dashed for the exit past the open vestibule. Sensing that the stalemate was no accident, Predella remained there, expecting something terrible to happen.

The cries inside the stairway persisted and it obligated Shioda to see the obstruction for himself. To his own dismay, there was no possible way for him to ascend the stairs now gorged with resistance. As his warriors feared the worst, Shioda sent his best to search for an alternate way out. It was not promising, but they had to try. With hope, there was someone on the other side who was searching for a lever or winch to lift the gate.

Predella couldn't understand how it dropped. Only after she ran out did the section close off. Panicking, she searched the wide vestibule for a trigger. Seth was too weak to tolerate her fast movements from corner to corner. He groaned pathetically. She stopped for a moment and appreciated that she could not help the others and save Michael's son at the same time. She had to make a choice.

She looked into Seth's fading eyes and knew that she had to save him fast. However, her dilemma had gone from worse to petrifying when she noticed movement from the thin alleyway to her left. Emerging from the shadows, Kaila promenaded her way into Predella's eyesight. The vampire was hardly clothed in a black leather lingerie outfit. Her thirsting eyes were locked on Predella with the most sinister of intentions.

Leaning onto one of her legs and holding her hip girlishly, the demonic general said, "**I thought I smelled a familiar snack. However did you creep your way into this place?**"

Predella held Seth tighter in her arms. She had battled Kaila once before, but could not overcome her power. This time, the demon was enriched by the paranormal energy of

Pommel. She would never permit Predella to escape with Michael Miuriell's son.

"**Going somewhere with my play toy? The Lord will not approve of that at all.**" Kaila moved in closer.

"Go to hell!" Predella scolded Kaila with nothing to show for her threat. She could not abandon the boy to load an arrow. By then it would be too late. Kaila moved in as she snickered.

"**But that's where you are, dear,**" Kaila mocked as she prepared for the pounce.

Suddenly, two smoke grenades detonated before the vampire, stunning her temporarily. Five swift ninjas rushed the demon from her right side and endeavored to slay her by way of their swords. Kaila was not impressed by the distraction but frustrated to the point of wreaking havoc. As Kaila fought off her fast assailants, Predella took her chance.

She set Seth behind her and unsheathed her bow. With careful precision, she loaded an arrow and cried out to those locked behind the gate, "Get back!"

When they did, she fired an ice arrow above the gate, freezing the wall and a portion of the gate to its core. When the ice expanded the inside of the mechanism, Predella fired another arrow of searing heat to thaw it out. In moments, the contraption began falling apart. She then picked the boy up again and darted for the tunnels that led to a higher level. She had to rescue Seth, leaving the ninjas inside to try and break the bars from the weakened gate to escape.

Predella valued the ninjas' sacrifice, deeming them heroes for taking on the vampire general. Many more lives hung in the balance. Thus, she refused to take the rescuers' timely offensive in vain. Predella ran out from the vestibule and held Seth close to her. She raced for the boy's safety and chance that she might return to save the others in time.

She left the sounds of warfare behind, fearing the worst for the warriors that were sure to fall prey to the demonic general. Predella ran down the wide tunnel until it led to the main voyeur, lying in ruins after Michael and Valkris had quarreled. A ninja had just escorted a feeble prisoner to safety up the steps in the distance. She would be there soon enough. Seth moaned from the uncomforting speedy escape.

But as she ran, a daunting feeling ran through her bones. The pattering of footprints was her first presumption. Almost instantaneously, Kaila, drenched in the blood of the slain, dropped from a loose grate in the ceiling and timed Predella effectively. The vampire held onto the grate's hinge bar and swung forward to kick the running huntress in her chest directly, launching her backward. Kaila let loose of the bar and used Predella's chest as leverage to flip backward and land onto her easy feet.

Predella could not hold on to the boy as she fell and slid on her back. The ground ravaged her smooth skin, but the unavoidable pain in her chest from the impact outmatched that. Seth collapsed, grunting as he landed. He was too weak to even attempt to run from the demonic general. He simply remained on his side in pain as she tried to catch her breath.

Seeing that Seth was not going anywhere, Kaila nonchalantly walked over him and headed straight for her rival. She wanted to torture her in front of the boy. Kaila wished for Seth to know that there were no heroes strong enough to rescue him. Predella saw the demon coming, so she rolled onto her side quickly to remove her bow and arrow. Turning back onto her spine, she swiftly loaded one and aimed for Kaila's head. When Kaila was but five feet away, Predella fired the shot. It jetted through the air like a bullet, but it only grazed through the wisps of Kaila's blonde hair.

She quickly went to try another arrow, but Kaila had already sprung into the air above her. She came down hard on Predella's firm stomach with her knee, constraining the huntress to soon expel blood from her mouth. She embraced her tight muscles for the blow, except Kaila's strike was too great. She coughed and whined as Kaila pressed deep into her body and snatched her neck by way of her vicious hands. Predella gagged and tried to break free from the demon's hold on her. She couldn't roll or flip Kaila off. It was a disgrace, for the stairway to the main level was only another twenty feet away at most.

"**Yes, cry,**" Kaila whispered into her ear as she started to lick her face. "**The boy will remember how you looked when you died without your precious dark skin, skinned alive. How traumatic.**"

Predella felt the vampire's sharp nails stab into the side of her throat. Kaila had her pinned well to the ground with hardly a way to gasp for air. She reached down to Predella's lower torso and inserted her claws just above her pelvis. The vile demon found her cries of pain to be erotic when she began to slowly tear four incisions up across her stomach towards her chest. Her blood crept out from the incisions as she squirmed, trying to free herself from the agony.

Seth could only sob as Kaila began killing his rescuer. Hearing Predella's heart-wrenching cries, Seth shouted for Kaila to stop. From his knees, Seth mustered up all of his strength and shouted. Kaila enjoyed his cries almost equally as much. Yet, Kaila's decision to torture her rival out in the open came to be a great mistake.

Predella's ice arrow did the trick moments earlier and droves of ninjas had come running through to escape. Even though she heard the warriors approaching, Kaila thought she would, at least, have time to gouge her beautiful green eyes out with her thumbs. She placed both of her hands on the sides of Predella's head, ready to slowly ease in her thumbnails for her eye sockets.

Instead, a flurry of arrows came whizzing through the tunnel and assailed the vampire. Struck by a half dozen in but a flash of an instant, she scurried off her prey and bounded back up the vent for whence she came, howling in anger. The ninjas shortly followed, guiding their allies who carried all the captives who were too ill and mangled to walk for themselves. One stopped and pulled Predella to the side so she wouldn't get trampled.

"The boy!" she barked with her back against the wall. "Go check on the boy!"

When the warrior finally went over to inspect Seth's condition, he saw that one of their arrows had pierced into his young chest. Barely alive, he opened his eyes and cried when the ninja pulled him closer. Shioda's division rushed on by, oblivious to the horrid scene. Predella caught of glimpse of him and was too stunned to say even a word. Wide-eyed, she fell onto her chest and crawled towards them, in shock.

"No. Oh, God, no!" she wailed, leaving blood in her wake as she crawled towards the boy, fading away from the fatal injury.

Michael easily heard the cries of Predella while he assisted the oncoming ninja team escape with prisoners. Worried that something happened, he slid into the wide tunnel of rushing escapees and saw his wounded son in the arms of a bloody ninja, removing his mask. The sight was terrorizing, feeling like he was living a nightmarish vision. Predella inspected the protruding arrow out from Seth's small frame, crying the whole while, was more than he could bear. Dropping his staff, Michael ran for them and cried for his son.

As Seth began slipping away, Michael slid over to them and found that it was his boy, after all. Seth was dazed. He could not appreciate the fact that his father had returned, for he appeared so different. It did not seem practical to him that he would actually be saved by his father. It did not seem possible that he would even see his father again. His vision was going black when Michael had come to look over him.

"Dad?" Seth uttered shakily. "You—came?"

Crying miserably, Michael held his son's head close to his breast and sobbed, "Yes, son. I'm here now. Everything is going to be alright, you hear me?"

"Thank, God," Seth mustered with a smile as his eyes began to close for the last time. "Mom is here, too."

His head went back and he was gone. Holding his son in his arms, Michael shook his head in disbelief. He had come so far, only to watch his boy close his eyes for the final time. No father would have been able to hold back. Michael kissed his son's forehead and held his body close, crying hysterically.

In the sordid moment, Predella, unable to hold her tears, put her hand upon Michael's shoulder, and said, "I am so sorry, Michael. Forgive me. I failed you."

Turning to her next, Michael saw the grief in her face. He saw the still line of ninjas rushing out to save the many victims of captivity and torture, passing by as he hoped they would so efficiently. Seeing the tormented sufferers in the backdrop, Michael looked back to his lifeless son and replied, "Predella, please bring my son out of this place. I came to get him out of Pommel and that's what we're going to do. Do this and you have not failed me."

Predella kissed him on the cheek and hugged him, full of guilt for not doing more to keep him safe. Michael hugged her tightly before handing Seth to her. When she received him, Michael continued, "When you leave with him, stay out there and get some medical attention. I need you to be strong for what's next."

Holding his boy in her arms, she followed the fleeing ninjas out to the ruined vestibule. Earlier, Michael had moved most of the wreckage to the side of the hall with Valkris buried inside somewhere. When Predella left with his son, Michael rose onto his feet, cleaned his eyes and went to help the rest of Shioda's team free every last survivor.

Shioda was about to investigate more of the torture chamber's suspicious perimeter until a ninja warrior reported, "We're nearly finished, sir. No more hostiles and Miuriell has returned to aid in our escape."

"Then get out of here and help the others. I'm just behind you," Shioda began, checking for any more survivors.

The ninjas ran off quickly while Shioda secretly prayed to himself. He was afraid for his team and the captors. While there was no need to search the gory torture chamber any longer, Shioda prevented himself from exiting just yet. He felt a cold shiver on his skin. A hissing sound began to strengthen and it was coming from inside the gruesome chamber. Shioda lingered his blue hand over his sheathed blade, sensing danger.

As the darkest fates would have it, Tenebrion had teleported in his torture chamber after his cowardly escape from the Ziamon sword. After a swift, but loud entrance, Tenebrion fully materialized from blackened smoke. Shioda would never believe what he had seen directly behind him but nine feet away. The demonic general needed to recover where he was most powerful.

Taking no chances, Shioda propelled himself from an operating table's edge and dashed straight for Tenebrion's hide. In midair, he promptly unsheathed his long slender blade and spun around to chop Tenebrion's head straight through the middle. The virtuous blow of the sword cut half of Tenebrion's ghastly head clean off. The demon did not know what did him in, for the master ninja had completed his move fundamentally well.

Tenebrion jerked before his corpse collapsed fiercely to the ground, emptying blood over the chamber floor. In the end, Shioda's steadfastness proved lifesaving against the first demon he had ever encountered. His human heart was beating faster than ever after such a strike. He looked over the carcass of the grotesque demonic general and recoiled. There was no room for triumphant boasts. The sight of the ghastly creature alarmed him.

A group of ninja warriors had scurried to uncover what the fast wrangle was about. They, too, found Tenebrion's corpse to be a disturbing mess. One of them exclaimed from the doorway, "Master Shioda! What happened?"

Before he could even begin to describe what had just unfolded, Tenebrion's corpse erupted into flames. The unfamiliar blaze carried a vengeful odor. His death had come with a lethal price. From the hot flames came a toxic gas that threatened to kill anyone who inhaled it. As Shioda rolled onto the ground and shut the chamber door with his foot from the outside, he warned all those near him, "We're all leaving right now!"

The final team of ninjas proceeded with their fast escape out of the dungeon level, carrying any stragglers as they went. From the Shadowland, the paladin lines covered their comrades' escape, though there was no need in firing any cannons. There was no real danger. Shioda's team escaped the sleeping horror of the Demon Plague's bastion in victory. He found it to be nothing more than a miracle.

While more ninjas escaped with feeble victims of the Demon Plague, a terrible feeling had rattled Michael's nerves. Amongst the cheers about the vestibule, a vision forced itself into Michael's psyche. The events slowed down unnaturally and it appeared that the ninjas were floating underwater rather than running on foot. Everything went silent. When his vision went black, Michael saw only the Demon Lord.

His helmet of blades and spikes glared Michael down with burning eyes of red, so hot that Michael could feel the heat on his face. The Demon Lord then spoke to him, "**So, you have come to betray the conquest *you* created?**"

"Whatever you are—wherever you are, I'm coming to crush you! One way or another, you're going to face me! So help me God, you'll answer for the lives you've taken! My wife—my child!" Michael cried back, then coming to realize that he was on his knees with his hands over his head. Shioda knelt by his side and tried to shake him from his spell.

"Michael, we have to go! Come on!" He helped him up.

Fearing that the Demon Lord was onto their invasion, Michael rose to his feet and said, recovering from his stupor, "Listen. I think the Demon Plague has awakened. You go. Get out now and run far away from the Shadowland! Go!"

Mystified by the news, Shioda answered, "Who has yet to escape?"

"I'll handle it, just go!" he screamed back, seeing to it that Shioda ran after his rescue unit. Paladins and Tinarians at the line ran into the Shadowland to help the warriors take the captives safely into the sun.

Michael shut his eyes and instantly sensed that Lai and Maxim's team were in danger. Esker and his team were on the run. Aramis was routed. Providing that the Ziamons could evade the demonic eyes that were going to open at any moment, it was Lai and Maxim that needed help. Putting aside the debilitating sorrow in his heart, Michael pushed on to meet the last rescue squad and save them.

Princess Shina remained unconscious under a protective blanket and Predella looked over Seth's body in another blanket. She took the boy's death hard. With teams in dire trouble and Michael racing in deeper to save them, she could not wait idly. She started to run off into the Shadowland to help the rest escape, despite her grave injuries. Saving her life before it was too late, Lana cried for her to stay with the boy. Stopping mid-stride, she broke down almost immediately and ambled back outside the demons' dominion.

When she returned, Lana noticed that her lesions were still bleeding down her stomach. She embraced her and said with compassion, "Michael wanted you to stay here with him. That's what you'll do. Besides, you desperately need stitches."

Lana called over a medic to look after Predella, sitting back between the possessed Tinarian princess and Michael's deceased son. She sat there, stunned and scarred from the disturbing ordeal. The arriving medic left a hectic scene just yards behind the defensive line. There was not enough staff to rightly treat the freed captives. Even Merrieu did not have the resources to help the wounded and so many others that suffered from malnutrition. The anxious line awaited three other parties still inside.

Meanwhile, Lai's team escaped from a chaotic creature beyond their comprehension. They all raced down a thin corridor lit by fragile windowpanes on each side six feet apart. Maxim ran directly behind, desperately trying to hold off Scythian, the reaper phantom. Its scythe had already turned six ninjas into sopping shreds. The girls had seen the demon before, so they were motivated to run for their lives.

Regardless of what he believed the demonic general to be, Lai tried to find the route they used to make their entrance into the bastion. Somehow, the manmade trail had faded. The mishap had made finding the exit route to the first level problematic, especially with an indestructible wraith hacking them down.

The ninjas without the burden of carrying females cast shuriken and throwing knives for the demon, all which soared straight through it. Maxim had tried to gain the monster's attention, rather than have Scythian focus solely on the escaping captors under its watch. With his Mad Phoenix ablaze, Maxim dodged the demon's blows and countered, though it did nothing. The phantom demon was unkillable.

However, the team was gaining ground with women yearning for freedom, thanks, in part, to Maxim's attention to the creature. There were some ninja warriors that simply could not keep the pace as they were forced to carry women as they ran. Some were cut down viciously as the females fell to the floor. Scythian's purpose was never to harm the sacrifices, only slay their captors.

Maxim saved a ninja's life when he deflected one of Scythian's devastating swipes of the scythe. Undoubtedly, the demonic general was losing patience with his human rival's skills. A sure number of ninjas without female captors assisted the Tinarian knight with the almost impossible task of stopping Scythian. The demon swung through the opposition, but the warriors didn't falter. Two were struck down. Their lifeless bodies tumbled while the swift battle persisted.

A familiar stairway leading to the lower levels was a welcoming sight. The team of ninjas dashed down steps with the weak females screaming. Already, Scythian had secluded a few women in the corridor, too afraid to run without a warrior escort. They knew they would probably be taken back to their tragic keep. There were six ninjas that stayed behind to challenge the phantom, their final mission to slow the demon down enough to help the rest of the team escape.

The ninja warriors fought the indestructible demon with honor. Dying one by one, the brave warriors infuriated

Scythian to no end. Maxim knew that he had to find a way to kill the phantom because it would never stop. There was no turning back. He vaulted bravely to slice off its hooded skull, but his fire-sword grazed through air and smoke instead.

As Lai's team took to the stairs for their hopeful freedom, Maxim and three remaining ninjas quarreled with Scythian. It roared chillingly and dropped its devastating scythe for Maxim's turned back. He just evaded the unnatural blade, rolling quickly to the right. Scythian pulled its weapon from the cracked floor and jostled a nearby assailant into the wall. The ninja lost grip of his blade and by the time the katana clashed before his feet, Scythian returned with a crippling blow into his abdomen. The scythe pierced viciously through his body and into the wall.

"Damn you!" Maxim steadied his fiery blade and racked his brain for any useful attack that could hurt it. The pair of doomed warriors blocked the way down the steps as Maxim dared to challenge the demon head on. It had to have a weakness somewhere.

The reaper demon glided forcefully for its intended target, roaring terrifyingly as it neared closer. Maxim charged his foe and evaded its primary swipe. He landed and swiftly spun around to watch Scythian's following moves closely. The demon swirled smoke about the air before challenging him again. This time, it connected with a strike and almost knocked the fire-sword from his grip. However, Maxim was a master of evasion. Scythian couldn't administer a crippling blow.

Maxim still tried to find a method of killing the creature. Because the scythe was tangible, it became the only thing he cared about. He briskly devised a ploy to steal the weapon and find out what made it special. After dodging a few more close calls from the scythe, Maxim put his back to the wall just inches from one of the corridor's windowpanes.

When Scythian swung its blade straight for his chest, he hurriedly rolled out of the way and permitted the scythe to crash into the stone, becoming lodged. Before Scythian could pull the scythe out, Maxim cried and dropped his blazing fire-sword down onto the weapon's shaft.

The flaming sword snapped the shaft in two and the blade remained stuck securely in the wall. As Scythian jerked backward, Maxim seized the opportunity and tried to pull the blade out. His efforts were not timely, for Scythian dropped its futile shaft and diminished the blade to smoke. As Maxim fell back from the loss of leverage, Scythian absorbed the mystical smog and formed a new scythe out of thin air.

"You crafty fuck," Maxim gasped, then turning to the others and told them to go while they still could.

As they refused to leave him there, Scythian came again to cut Maxim in two. On impulse, he clanged blades with the creature, forcing the scythe back to clang into its skull. The sound was like a blade hammering into stone. When he saw it, Maxim thought of, at least, one other method of stopping the demon.

In a last-ditch effort, he stood before the phantom with his arms stretched out to his sides, as if to surrender. On cue, the demon came with a vertical strike, as he hoped. When he dashed just inches to the side in order to evade the hack, Maxim chopped the scythe's shaft again. When the blade had fallen clanging to the floor, he scooped it up with one motion and threw it back at Scythian's unnerving skull.

The blade spun like a sickle all the way into Scythian's skull, lodging deep into the bone. His daring shot was perfect, apparently impairing the demon. Though he didn't know if he had a follow-up plan, black smoke that seeped out from Scythian's fissure let him know that the fight was over. The ninjas by the stairs didn't see it that way. They ran and told him to follow after them, as he just made the demon mad.

Watching the creature begin to implode, Maxim said to himself, "*He's mad because he fell for it. Not so many brain-cells in that cranium.*"

Scythian's skull then exploded, blasting Maxim back as he was off-guard. The detonation threw him across the corridor and into one of the window panes. He crashed through the colorful glass and was sent soaring into a larger room, falling down another story. As he screamed for his life, Maxim landed into an interior fountain pool. He splashed down unevenly, struggling to hold on to his sword all the while.

When he floated to the surface, Maxim swam to the edge and lifted his sizzling fire-sword onto the tile floor before his face. While gasping for air, he looked up at the shattered glass portal from where he was thrown. He rose to his knees only to find himself in an illustrious crypt. Coffins with names etched on each one made him take a second look. *Kirik Cainam* and *Vestilus Ny* were just two names that stuck out to him. He staggered through an old crypt designated for infamous sorcerers of years past.

Maxim retrieved his sizzling sword and tried to find a way out. He was forced to find a new route of escape, alone. Though a short upsurge of steps led to a transparent doorway, he was not certain as to where it would lead. Nonetheless, he needed to try the only path given to him or his hesitation could have cost him his life. He knew that the ceremony was probably ending soon.

Lai led his frazzled team through the ruined vestibule and ran into Michael who had just started to look for them. When the ninjas rushed past them with petrified women in their company, Michael asked, "Where is Maxim?"

Lai answered worryingly, "The angel of death cut us down and would be harassing us still if he—"

"Is he alive?" Michael asked in great trepidation.

Lowering his head, he replied mournfully, "Maxim distracted the demon so that we could escape. I don't know what became of him after."

Pounding his staff into the ground in anger, Michael caught his breath and said in a hurried whisper, "The Demon Lord knows we're here. He could unleash everything he has to snuff us out at any moment! Get out and tell the line to get as far back from the Shadowland as possible!"

"What about you?" Lai asked, following the remainder of his team out of the vestibule.

Michael ran deeper into the bastion and shouted, "I've got to find the others before it's too late!"

Lai couldn't fathom the bravery to venture into the demon-infested bastion alone when things were about to explode. Committed to his unit, Lai caught up to the last ninja warrior and supervised the escape. They unsuspectingly passed by the ruins of Valkris's downfall. The demonic general was buried under the smoking rubble, but the Seltek showed some signs of life. Its eyes opened and looked about, trying to locate its owner. In just moments, parts of debris started to move.

Running behind his team, Lai dashed over the rubble and bone of the Shadowland to catch up. His warriors raced to bring the females to safety when the paladins began setting up the cannons to cover them. The commotion compelled Lai to slow his escape and look behind him. To his dismay, the bastion's stable doors opened to reveal Kaila's full cavalry of vampires ready to run them down. On reanimated corpses of horses and rams, Kaila and her vampiric horde had come charging onto the main field.

Seeming like dozens, the multitude thundered across the Shadowland faster than the rescue team could make it out on foot. To help stave off the demonic cavalry, Lai and his warriors without captives formed a defensive circle. Without halberds or spears, they resorted to firing a volley of arrows. Before the cavalry could break through Lai's bold defensive, Thomas launched his full force of knights into the Shadowland. Tinarian and paladin soldiers rushed forth with Lana looking on in dismay.

"Shioda, stay back!" Lana cried. "They'll protect Lai! My brother will not die on that field, so help me God!"

"I can't take that chance!" Shioda shouted back, taking his ninja warriors back into the fray to support him.

When Shioda ran back into the darkened field, Lana screamed for him. She erupted in anger over his hypocrisy. The rescue team pushed the women to run for their lives, hoping to converge with the oncoming knights just a quarter mile away. While Kaila's cavalry was ready to slaughter Lai's squad, standing as one in the center of the Shadowland, Predella rose from her seat and felt a gust of opportunity.

In-between Seth and the unconscious princess, she equipped her elemental bow and loaded an arrow. Judging the wind and distance of half a mile, Predella fought through the stinging pain of her scalded palm and pulled back the bowstring at full draw. Eyeing Kaila's leading position high on her undead stallion, she released the arrow.

Kaila was too focused on the impending kill to see it, but Predella's arrow soared for her. It pierced her forehead, knocking her off the charging horse, and engulfed her into a blazing disaster. Like a detonation, Kaila's body exploded fire all about the field. Unsuspecting vampires in their general's scorching wake suffered the heat as they went. From over three thousand feet, Predella's single shot slew Kaila in her false moment of storming glory.

Dodging the vampire's unbridled horse, Lai endured the rushing force of her undead cavalry. When the stallions ultimately engaged his squad, they scattered. The ninjas cut and hacked at the charging horses as they ran and dove out of harm's way, but most were overrun. Their sacrifice bought the fleeing captives some time to scuttle into the care of Thomas's knights. Shioda and his volunteers ran up to break the demonic cavalry's second wave.

By the time the vampires started on Shioda's squad, it was too late. The knights safeguarded the females and made a stalwart barricade of armor and shield before them. As the cavalry rushed on, Lai and his scourged team fired a flurry of arrows from behind. The counterattack caught some of the demons in the back as Shioda's unit formed a defensive line. A thousand feet in waiting of the vampires, Shioda called out, "Grenades!"

His squad unclipped their grenades and then hurriedly pressed the pin loose, holding the explosives out to the sides. When the intimidating demons were nearly on them, Shioda cried out, "Launch now!"

When the explosive volley was finished, the vampires had lost half of their cavalry. Loud and overwhelming, their joint demolition strike blew gaping holes into the charge. Any of the undead that had fallen from their undead stallions were quick to take the fight on foot. As fast and fierce as they were, there was no hope for victory. Shioda's counterstrike proved to be an unexpected encumbrance.

When Thomas's knights rushed forward to crush the remaining force, the vampires withdrew from the field. They retreated back for the protection of the Pommelian stable in failure. Kaila was killed and the sacrifices had made it out of the Shadowland. The paladins abandoned their attack and followed the Tinarians back to the line, assisting the women and young girls in finding refuge. Withdrawing vampires had taken the charred remains of their general back with them.

While Shioda and Lai's squads converged in the hellish field, Predella sat back in her seat and rested her bow against the stretcher, as before. As she inspected her sore palm and the aggravated lesions on her torso, a small crowd started to form. None of them had ever seen such a miraculous shot in a time of urgency. Those who had once doubted her skills learned something. Lana nodded her head in gratitude. She returned the gesture from her seat.

However, Lana didn't realize her brother's dire injury. Rising to his knee in a painful groan, Lai opened his vest and found the origin of his bleeding from an open gash. One of his men put pressure on the wound when he grunted from behind his mask, "Go tend to the others. I'll manage."

Hearing his brother-in-law as he came nearer, Shioda removed his facemask and replied, "To hell with that. Your sister will kill me if I don't drag you back to that line."

"Good work back there." Lai coughed, feeling faint. "It was good of you to bring those."

"Always carry grenades, Lai. How many times have we been over this?" Shioda fought to help him up. "Now, let's go. Your heroics won't end here. You've got more insane things to prove, I'm sure."

"We lost men," Lai replied as his comrade helped him walk back towards the line, feeling to cry. "How many have you lost, Shioda?"

"Not now, man," he said, gesturing for his men to help support him as they went. "There's time for that. But we have to get out of this black cloud before they deploy a second wave."

As his team started to pass them, some carrying fallen comrades, Lai muttered, "Did you save Michael's son?"

With guilt weighing on his broken heart, Shioda pushed onwards and said nothing.

Eric dared not enter his sister's quarters, knowing too well that Shina was long gone. If Michael was strong enough to take her out of Pommel, then maybe the Demon Plague's talk of destiny and fate was all but nonsense. His own plans were shattered beyond repair as his soul was sold away. His primary motivations for joining the conquest had backfired, aiding in the corruption of his own sister. Eric, in shame, only peered into Shina's wrecked quarters without drive. He lingered there without conviction.

As his world finally imploded, he cringed to the sounds of the overbearing stampede advancing in his direction. Hundreds of shadow demons scurried passed him in an immense rush. Like a rapid river of hellish matter, the demonic stampede passed him by. Eric glared blankly at the wall as the demons rushed about him. At last, Sattka and the Demon Lord had awakened from their slumber. The bloody ceremony, buried in secrecy, was finally over.

As the demonic stampede stormed through the corridor in search for intruders, Eric considered his fate. He never imagined that Michael would lead such a daring raid on Pommel. Much of the Demon Plague had underestimated his army, taking them as nothing more than neophytes with false hope for survival. Yet, Tenebrion, Scythian and Kaila had already met their ends at the hands of his warriors. Eric, sulking in the midst of a river of demons, began to question his role in the epic war.

Loud booming shots echoed throughout the field as the party nearly made it out of the Shadowland. Bullets pounded the ground, some just by their footsteps. Paladin cannoneers spotted the sharpshooters firing from a parapet midway up the tower. Mad Legionnaires assailed Lai's unit from afar but were out of range. Thomas's cannoneers aimed to cover them with a barrage of artillery fire.

While the Mad Legionnaires fled from the salvo of steel hammering into Pommel's crenellations, Thomas shouted to his defensive line, "Get the captives and wounded far out and away from the Shadowland! We're wearing out our welcome, it appears!"

Just as Shioda fell into the line with Lai off his shoulder, he shouted out, "We need medics now!"

Lana came upon them with the Tinarian medics who put pressure on Lai's bleeding right away. The defensive line already started out as Thomas ordered when Lana grabbed Shioda by the face and said heatedly, "And now I'm telling *you* to stay back! Get it? Stay back and so help me God if you step into that black hell again!"

Finally, as the line withdrew from the border of the Shadowland, a thunderous clap took to the miasma above. A sudden storm, as evil as anything they had ever seen, brought their eyes up. Like a volcanic eruption, hundreds of flyer demons soared over the tower of Pommel. The daunting spectacle put a burning fear in all the hearts of those who saw it.

Thomas screamed, "God save us! Everyone get away! Take your lives and go—now!"

As soon as they emerged, the flyers had swooped down to the ruins of Pommel and picked up all kinds of rubble and debris. Before they realized what the demons were about to do, the flying horde launched a torrent of heavy debris for the defensive line. Out from the Shadowland, the debris came crashing into the outer field.

Fleeing from the bombardment, warriors closest to the Shadowland's edge came under heavy fire. Dozens were crushed by the assault. Tinarians carried the princess's body away from the barrage with Seth's covered corpse just behind them. Shioda, seeing a bulk of bricks headed straight for them, pushed Lana out of the way. She fell back as the rubble crashed. Paladins sheltered Lai from the carnage, enduring the bricks and rebar banging into their shields. But, when Lana picked up her head, she saw Shioda lying alone in the wreckage that nearly killed her.

"Shioda! No!" she cried running for him amid the falling rubble, tripping over the debris. Predella made it to him first and started dragging him away from the danger zone. In the pandemonium, people were running from the onslaught, not seeing that Shioda was hit. Cringing from the stinging pain of her fresh injuries, Predella fell to her knee and tried again.

Lana, dodging another missile of rubble, caught up to them and helped Predella heave Shioda out of harm's way. Pulling him thrashed, bloodied and broken, Lana started to cry over his body. They both lugged him, one arm each, away from it all until they couldn't pull him anymore. Coughing as they went, the smoke weakened them enough that they fell back. As far as they dragged him, it didn't seem far enough.

At last, teams of Shioda's division came to carry him the rest of the way. On her knees, sobbing amid the devastation, Lana cried out, "He's dead! Oh God, he's dead!"

Predella held her and said in her ear, "He's not dead. I felt his pulse. He's still alive."

Lana looked on as they carried Shioda's body out of the smoke and out of her sight. She squeezed Predella closer to her body in the greatest fear of her life. She clenched onto her with everything she had. The paladins that brought Lai out from the assault, shields up, ran past them. She then jolted up and raced after them, trying to find Shioda beyond the smoke. Predella, still on her knees in the debris, watched her until she vanished.

Among the knights that retreated, Thomas came upon her and yelled, "This isn't a place to get soft! Get moving!"

Shaking bits out of her hair, Predella stood up and cried back, "And what about Maxim and Michael and the others?"

"That's what *I'm* here for!" he replied. "Our forces are just redeploying further from the Shadowland! We'll cover them in their escape."

"And I'm a part of that 'we,' legate!" she said. "My bow is still somewhere buried in that line and I'm going to use it to put arrows of fire and ice in their chests!"

The last remaining team under Esker was dreadfully lost. Green beady eyes emerged from the corners and scrawny sharp claws rose from the floors and the walls. The shadow demons led them off course in their escape, running anywhere if only to save their lives. Terrorized beyond reason, the warriors swung their weapons in the hopes that their sporadic attacks would make contact. Attacking from every direction, the shadow demons wreaked havoc upon them.

The merciless slaughter drove them to madness. Esker pushed forth, thrashing mindlessly through any creatures that dared block his way. It was hard to see, for the demons had encompassed their escape. Their numbers were dwindling at a shocking rate as the hall became plastered with blood. Ziamons and demons slipped on the gore which they tread.

Finally, bright fiery lights illuminated through the hellish ambush. The creatures were slashing and clawing at them as they rushed through, but the Ziamons refused to surrender. Esker invigorated his team to rush forth with all of their combined might towards the shreds of light that teased them in the near distance.

Closer they came to the light, though their stamina diminished fast. Esker was cut and clawed. Other warriors fell from exhaustion but trampled over the bodies of their comrades. By the vigorous might and will of the Ziamons, they blasted through the weak fortification of a group of demons until they collapsed into a large circular room engulfed in flames. The plummeting debris of enflamed wood crashed down directly before the corridor's end, trapping the team inside the burning library. Archaic books, many of them collected from the old world, were kindling for the hungry flames. Smoke filled the archive, trapping a dozen soldiers that survived the demonic ambush.

Two heavy lead doors swung lazily from the other end of the library. Esker pointed for the exit and raced for it as their only way out. While they rushed forth, Maxim came into view, slicing another shadow demon in two with his blazing fire-sword. In-between the burning bookcases, he turned around with his Mad Phoenix raised high. Esker and his team stopped there, taken aback by seeing him.

"Cavallo!" Esker gasped. "What the hell are you doing in here?"

"Looking for a way out!" he screamed amongst the fire. "What the hell are *you* doing here?"

"Demons chased us in here!" he cried out, reeling from the intensity of the flames.

Maxim, cowering from the same fires, shouted back, "I got waylaid in here! The demons just came from everywhere! They don't like the fires, though! So, we're safe for now!"

"Safe? Are you fucking delusional?" Esker cried back. "And I gather you started this inferno?"

"I can't help it! It feeds off my anger!" he yelled over the roaring flames. "And you pissing me off isn't helping!"

"He really is a Red Menace," Esker told his men. "Get to those doors!"

As they ran past him, Maxim called out to his rival, "How do you think I got held up in here, you idiot? There's a pack of those things waiting for you through those doors if you're really interested! The fire kept them away!"

"Hold!" Esker shouted, inducing his men to stop, then coughed from inhaling the filling smoke. "Thanks to you, we are going to die in here anyway!"

"Me? Thanks to *me*?" Maxim countered. "There really is an asshole for every occasion!"

Suddenly, the center of the room began to quake. They moved away from the breaking floor as it ultimately caved in. From the gaping hole, Michael's Staff of Truth floated up into the library, gutted by the fire. In seconds, Maxim and Esker peered down the cavity to witness Michael staring back up. A sight for sore eyes, he opened his arms and said, "I see you've found the Library of Yesterworld. Jump down, if you please."

Maxim was the first to leap down, caught in Michael's telekinetic forces. Esker shouted for his men to do the same before the fires consumed them. One at a time, they jumped down. Esker being the last. Michael then reclaimed his staff and started out for the bastion's exit.

"Stay behind me and don't look back. As long as you're in my presence, the demons won't kill you. At least, I don't think they will!" Michael called to them as he ran, blasting holes into opposing walls as he went. Hordes of demons had swarmed all about the fortress, taking it over like the innards of an anthill. Closer to the side vestibule, Michael cried out again, "Stay with me!"

Calling upon the powers of his staff, he finally saw what became of the defensive line. Droves of flyer demons littered the Shadowland. He could possibly bring them through the field without the flyers picking them off. His newfound powers had him confident that he could control the demonic army. He felt them at his core. Like the Mad Legionnaires, he figured that they would have no choice but to listen to him as the 'father of the conquest.' It was just another leap of faith.

Yet, once he was about to turn the corner into the vestibule, he stopped short and put out his hand to hold off the others. He felt something wrong—an evil presence. The army held up with a hungry pack of shadow demons at their rear as Maxim uttered fretfully, "What is it? Michael, come on, we've got a horde of demons on our ass! We can't dally!"

"If you want to live a bit longer, you'll do exactly as I say," Michael answered.

Before they could process what he meant, Valkris declared from within the ruins of the vestibule, "**I know you are hiding over there, Miuriell—you and your monkeys.**"

Seeing the evident fear in Michael's eyes, Maxim asked, "Who is that? Michael?"

His vile skin torn and scraped from being buried alive, Valkris held his enfeebled Seltek to the side and continued, "**I know your false son is dead, all thanks to your allies' carelessness with their primitive bows and arrows. Your princess has turned completely to our side, leaving you as the only one out of place. Is this betrayal just to prolong the inevitable? I must say, your childish defiance has, at last, taken its toll on us.**"

Sensing the shadow demons advancing on their current position, Michael blocked off the corridor behind them with a telekinetic force field and replied, "I'll give you one last chance to make yourself scarce, or you'll stay dead this time."

Valkris laughed, then saying, "**As long as Seltek lives, so do I. You may have crippled it, but therein lies your real trouble, Miuriell. You can't seem to finish anything you start. Come on out and let's finish this.**"

His heart racing, Maxim asked, "Michael, what are we going to do? We're no match for that psychotic—"

"I am," Michael said anxiously. "I can fight him, but none of you will make it into the Shadowland without me."

"Just kill it. We'll be right behind you," Esker replied. "This battle would be a good death."

"**A good death. I admire that one's spirit. You've stalled long enough, Miuriell. I think I'll come to *you*,**" Valkris said, extending his Seltek out and charging a spell.

The ghastly rod began to glow and its erratic eyes had started melting. Each one bled out until the great lifeforce of the demonic instrument transferred into Valkris himself. The convergence doubled his power, making the Seltek nothing more than a hollow instrument. Its unnerving eyes began to emerge from all over his body. From his arms to his chest, restless eyes looked all about.

Throwing the empty rod to his side, the new Valkris breathed in deep and exhaled loudly. Even Michael could feel the change in him. The demonic general started for them and hissed, "**The lord has awakened. Now, instead of saving these helpless monkeys, you may want to consider how you will save yourself! Who will save you, the almighty Miuriell?**"

Out of nowhere, a bright bolt of energy shocked Valkris and heaved him to the side several feet. The blast rattled his bones, leaving him to shake off the spell using his own magic. Finding the source of the sorcery, Valkris raged, "**You fool!**"

Prince Eric, having teleported there just moments ago, charged his magic and proclaimed, "It's a dangerous flaw you have, not being able to tell the difference between a monkey and a human being. I'll make you understand."

Again, Eric discharged a powerful assault upon Valkris, who, in turn, deterred with sorcery of his own. Locked in a power struggle of dark magic, they illuminated the vestibule and sent deafening shocks throughout the bastion. Taking the only chance they had, Michael bashed in another way out and led his party deeper towards the tower's main atrium. As they ran, each warrior got their remarkable glimpse of the Tinarian sorcerer's epic battle.

Amongst the most formidable battle of magicians they had ever seen, the party dashed deeper into the bastion with the intent of running out the main doors. The intense power of the dueling sorcerers shook Pommel to its core, breaking walls and cracking floors as they ran. Though they couldn't know the victor of the bout, it hardly mattered when the main exit was just a chamber away.

There was no stopping Michael. He made his way in and then out of the large doors, uninterested in staying inside the bastion any longer than he needed. With his band of warriors closely in tow, Michael ran across the breadth of the Shadowland swarmed in flyer demons. They swooped down as a horde straight for them.

"Stay with me! Don't lag behind!" Michael hollered as they ran for their lives.

The ground hosted the grisly remains of Pommel's city. They ran over the rubble of the marketplace, the school, the church and everything that once served as a homeland for many of the people that were rescued moments earlier. A tricky landscape, the warriors had to watch their steps. One trip up and they were fodder. When the swarm of flyers came to pick them out of the fleeing party, Michael's force field repelled each one. The demons crashed into the invisible shield to hamper their escape, but Michael held strong.

One tripped over skeletal remains and fell, rolling into the ruins of the Shadowland. When another screamed to alert the others, Esker cried out, "Forget it! Save yourself!"

He proceeded to run with the rest of the party, hearing his comrade scream in terror as the flyer demons came down to rip him to shreds. Michael's protection could only hold so far for so long. They then ran past the corpses of vampires and ninja warriors, realizing that a deadly battle had ensued once already. They didn't plan on joining the dead.

The sounds of the sorcerers' battle reached the depth of the Shadowland. Eric countered a strike from above and jolted Valkris across the vestibule and through the wall. The impact wasn't enough to kill him, however, and Eric knew it all too well. He had to unleash a cataclysmic spell to bring the whole tower down. Nothing would survive. His eyes burned blue and a superior force emanated from his core. Valkris had to know what the sorcerer was planning to cast.

But as he charged his masterful spell, it had all drained away in an instant. He collapsed to the floor and groaned in pain. All his magic granted by the Demon Plague was gone. In a breach of loyalty, the dividends of his evil covenant had been stripped away. Finally, he had nothing left. His sister, his pride, his humanity and even his chance for redemption seemed like a distant dream. On his knees, Eric looked at his dirty hands and realized what had happened.

"**What the Lord gives, so can he rightly take away,**" Valkris snarled haughtily as he approached. "**How fitting an end for such a sniveling coward. How I longed for this day to see you diminished. I thought of a fitting way for you to die, you know. Like how you turned that old dupe into stone, I find it only fitting that it be the way you die as well. Don't you think? A stone monkey in the East and now a stone monkey in the West. How just.**"

With Eric staring up at his vile executioner, Valkris brought his cupped claw down to seize the prince's chin. With but a touch, his body would slowly turn to stone, like Drake back in Tinaria. When the claw just reached his face, Eric quickly grabbed the demon's wrist and held it in place.

Valkris gasped in dread as he couldn't break away from his clutches. Then, Eric lifted his right palm, charged with a havoc spell, and blasted the demonic general back twenty feet. Valkris roared in utter shock as Eric finished his crippling spell effectively.

Tired from the grueling bout with his adversary, Eric said boldly, "You still haven't learned."

It was true that the Demon Lord drained all of Eric's granted magic, but even he underestimated the exiled prince's lone mastered spell. Mimican Essent, the only incantation Eric ever learned to master himself, copied Valkris's entire arsenal. He copied what he could from the Demon Lord himself without being noticed. When his dark magic was taken away, Eric did not hesitate to replenish the combined powers of his enemies to enact a full vengeance.

Standing as the most supreme being in Pommel, Eric proceeded with his casting. Fearing the sorcerer's superior might, Valkris attempted to flee the duel by teleportation. Seeing his every intention, Eric was unimpressed. He only had to whisper a word and the demon was frozen in place. After failing to escape, Valkris desperately brought all of his magic into the fray. In a last-ditch effort to slay his adversary, the demon unleashed his greatest spell.

"**Burn in hell!**" Valkris cried, casting the Black Wraith Skull for him. Eric deflected the spell and fired it back at him, triggering a rolling explosion. The chambers ignited a black outburst of magic, destroying everything. The tower began to sway from the instability. Shockwaves from inside blasted gaping holes from every direction, nearly imploding the bastion from within.

The ground shook and the atmosphere of the Shadowland altered, sending flyer demons back. Michael was able to see the faint silhouettes of the defensive line far away as he endured the staggering repercussions of the sorcerers' battle. But the Demon Lord had seen enough. Flying high over the tower, he joined the legions of demons airborne and entered Michael's mind. Like a scourge, it rendered Michael helpless.

As close to the edge as they were, he held his head and screamed. His forcefield dissipated and the flyers quickly took advantage. They swooped down to annihilate the rest of the party. Falling to the ground in agony, Michael dropped his staff and writhed in pain. Visions of unparalleled horror stormed his consciousness. Everything he feared had come to fruition. His son's decaying corpse, half-buried. His friends all being disemboweled and torn apart. Shina foreseeing the mass murder of countless children, all hoarded into a giant mound of carcasses. It was torture, drowning out everything else.

Thomas's cannoneers unloaded everything to cover the escaping party only yards away from the Shadowland's edge. A valiant team of knights dashed in and raised their shields in an effort to shelter them from the air assault. Predella had fired arrows of fire and ice to keep the demons at bay. Along with the volleys of cannon fire, the flyers fell by the lots.

"Predella!" Maxim cried as he tried to hold Esker's arm over his shoulder as he ran. "You're hurt! You were out! You were safe! Why risk your life? Why?"

"Because I love you, you asshole!" she cried restlessly. "Help me with Michael!"

"They're breaking through!" Esker cried out, pushing away from Maxim's arm. "Get him fast!"

The cannon fire drenched his cries, but Esker stood fast and guarded the rest of his men. Demons came crashing down to bluster through to the edge of the Shadowland. A fierce clash of steel and claw ensued as Predella and Maxim grabbed Michael. Tinarian knights helped carry him out amid the violence. The paladins endured the crushing and scrabbling of the demonic army, backing up as a unit while the others brought Michael out.

Once the sun touched his face, the nightmarish visions finally stopped, leaving him unconscious. The Tinarians kept the pace to bring Michael as far from the Shadowland as they could when Maxim and Predella returned to the hostilities. Of the Ziamons that escaped, assisted by their Tinarian counterparts, Esker was not one of them. In the fray, Maxim spotted him and one other Ziamon soldier limping back. There was a hole in the paladin line, enabling a rush of flyers to break in.

Two paladins dragged Esker back, leaving the other Ziamon to fend for himself. Maxim and Predella fought through it, side-by-side, mounting blood of man and demon upon their sweating bodies. Maxim's fire-sword engulfed the ravenous creatures into flames. It spread like wildfire. In their attempt to save the lone Ziamon, they sustained angry gashes and lesions. Eventually, the paladin line turned and ran for the edge, pushing everyone back. When the army of blood-tainted steel made it out of the Shadowland, Maxim and Predella dragged out the remaining soldier and collapsed.

"Keep going! Run for your lives!" Thomas cried out, for he knew what the flyers were capable of doing with debris.

Out of breath and energy, the ravaged party trudged as far from the line and never looked back. Amongst the frenzy of flyer demons, Sattka ambled over to the Staff of Truth and picked it up. She peered out at the Angels of Resistance make their despairing retreat. In holding onto the mystical staff, the demonic general looked up at her father hovering above the tower of Pommel. Bemused by Michael's audacious act of defiance, the Demon Lord swore retribution. Both sides had borne a grave price, altering the course of war beyond any of their expectations.

PART II
CHAPTER XII
THE BELIEVERS

In the same murky woods, Opal gathered raspberries in a small basket. Michael walked cautiously as he tried not to disturb her. He didn't want to do anything to trigger his fantasy to end. Just watching how beautiful she was, Michael leaned against a tree and took in the moment. But then, from her side, Seth had come walking up to show his mother all of the blueberries he gathered. They smiled together, at peace.

Seeing his son for the first time in his dream reminded him of his fate. Michael covered his mouth and cried, trying not to make a sound to ruin it. It finally made all the sense to him. Like visiting heaven, he couldn't stay. Seth and Opal were, at last, united beyond time and space. Michael had no place with them in death. There was more he had to do first. Wiping away his tears, Michael laughed in gratitude for their tranquil reunion. He wished that he could have watched him grow into a man, but it was not to be. His spirit lied clear of the dreams Michael had in place for him.

When he opened his eyes, laying on a thin mattress, a paladin's voice emanated from the foot of his bed, "Master Miuriell, thank God you are awake! Are you alright?"

Feeling his body for wounds or scratches, Michael didn't know how to reply. Seeing him search himself frenetically, the same man spoke again, "Your body healed fast. By this morning, your injuries were gone, except for some stubborn bruises."

"This morning?" Michael gasped in bewilderment.

The knight said quietly, "You have slept for two days. We thought you were in a coma. The legate will be glad to hear of your recovery."

"Where am I, then? The Demon Plague follows me everywhere!" he said nervously from his mattress.

"Your friends took you away from Merrieu at sundown. The demons didn't harm them or us. Sir Maxim Cavallo and the huntress refused to leave your side," the knight replied.

After the knight started to run out of the car to alert the prince of his awakening, Michael briskly sat up on his bed and blurted, "Shina! Where is Princess Shina?"

The paladin let off the door and replied with his back to him, "She is imprisoned in a fortress due west. The princess almost burned to death in the sun. That was after she killed one of our brothers-in-arms. In trying to escape, she collapsed out in the field. Her skin—"

"That's enough, knight," Michael sat up on the edge of the bed, trying to get his bearings. "I'm very sorry to hear about your loss. I'm sorry that I wasn't there."

The broken knight cleared the lump in his throat and said carefully, "Your loss is far greater than any one of us. We pledged our lives to God. Your son didn't have such a choice. No father should ever have to bury a child."

Feeling like he was too bold in saying it, the knight had excused himself and said, "I'll let the legate know you're up."

As the paladin left his lodging, Michael massaged his neck and reached for his staff. He then realized that it was no longer in his possession, causing his heart to race. Tethered to it still, Michael felt the physical extension of himself deep within Pommel's bulwark. The Staff of Truth was not a part of him any longer. Like losing an old friend, Michael put his head in his hands and groaned in anguish. He had lost next to everything he ever held dear.

In hearing the muffled commotion beyond the door, he knew that many awaited his return. Much had happened since the mission and he needed to be a part of what came next. Exhaling deeply, Michael fixed himself and walked out into the barracks' antechamber. Standing around the lobby table, Maxim, Predella and a group of paladin knights lifted their heads. Because no one could find the words right away, the three heroes met in the middle and embraced.

By the time Thomas had made it into the antechamber, Michael and the others were exchanging comforting words. There was a great deal of guilt in Michael's heart for all that transpired days ago. But they would never let him sulk over their struggles, for he lost his only son. Upon seeing Thomas at the doorway, Michael asked solemnly, "Can I see him?"

Together, Thomas led him and the group down to the barrack's chapel where a slew of coffins waited in the foyer. Lit by torchlight, Michael came upon Seth's casket and rested his hand over his son's forehead, shrouded tightly with a white mantle. In taking time to pray and pay his respects to the only boy he ever had, Michael kissed his face and left his tears on the shroud.

"They called him my 'fake son.' They said he was never meant to be born," Michael said, broken-hearted. "But they could never have known what this boy was to us. He was our world. Seth was even stronger than I realized. He survived all that time, alone in hell, without his father, and without his mother. And yet, he knew I'd come for him. Imagine that kind of faith. Especially for one so young. At least I got to see him one last time. At least he saw me before—before he—"

Predella placed her hand on his shoulder from behind, giving him the strength to say, "He saw his mother at his end. In that dark place, he saw my wife. That proves heaven exists, doesn't it? Heaven can exist anywhere—even in hell."

"Amen," Thomas declared.

Michael then squeezed his wet eyes and said in sorrow, "I'm so sorry. You've endured more than I promised—more than all of you deserve. Forgive me."

Rebuking his guilt, the group rallied around him and made it clear that their choices in resisting the Demon Plague were their own. They all made sacrifices. When others prayed, they shed blood. Michael understood that. Catching a glimpse of the paladin that was there when he woke up from his long sleep, he composed himself and said to them, "I've missed a lot these past days, but I am here now."

Nodding humbly, Thomas followed, "We can catch up over breakfast. You need to eat."

In heading out for the mess hall, they passed a lone, unmasked ninja warrior waiting outside the chapel. He called for Michael's attention in the group, fidgeting with a black arrow in his hands. When he gestured for him to approach, the young man said to him, "Sir Miuriell, it was my arrow that killed your son. This is the one here in my hands. I have come to seek your forgiveness and your judgment upon me. It will be my honor to pay for your loss with my life."

The ninja knelt before him and raised the arrow above his head in shame. With the group watching, Michael took the arrow from his hands and considered it. Thomas then said in dismay, "This is not the time, nor the place for this, boy."

Michael knelt before the ninja and returned the arrow, eye-to-eye. He said to him, "I see no benefit in the death of another brave soul. Take this and let it remind you what we're all fighting for. I forgive you. Now, you need only to forgive yourself. We need you."

By the time Michael had risen, crowds started to form around them. They marveled at his emergence, knowing full well that his mission to save so many from the Demon Plague had come with a price. Some paid with their lives, making the ultimate sacrifice so that others could be free. In breaking through the multitude of onlookers, he heard some of them praise his name in gratitude, while a few others beseeched him to free them again.

Taken by their strange pleas, Michael asked the legate, "Why are some of these people asking me to set the captives free—again?"

Before Thomas could relay the disconcerting news, Maxim said over the growing masses around them, "The two darling sibling leaders deemed the captives cursed and threw them all in the dungeon."

Appalled, Michael gasped, "What is it with those kids and the dungeon? We make the sacrifice to save those people and they put them in cages *again*?"

"It has been frustrating, to say the least," Thomas said, finally ordering his paladins to push the populace out of the barracks.

"And where is Shina in all this?" Michael asked, fearing the worst.

Maxim answered, "We thought it best to keep her away from Merrieu. She's in a fort somewhere out east. It hasn't been pretty."

Thomas furthered Maxim's point, "We figured that the demons would follow her, even if she was unconscious, so we elected to keep her in Fort Andrews. For her safety and ours."

"One of your knights told me that she killed someone," Michael said, talking over the dispersing crowd.

"Indeed, she did. A good man," Thomas replied. "As my unit escorted her carriage out for the fort, she awakened. In her escape, she killed one of my best paladins and blew out of the carriage. Of course, it was during the day sometime, so she burned up pretty bad. I'll spare you the gruesome details, but she nearly died out in the field. They covered her up and gallantly delivered her body to the fortress where she, as you can expect, recovered. She is possessed by a strong demon."

Sighing from the news of the daunting challenges, he asked the party, "Is there anything else I should know before I ask the sovereigns for an audience?"

Predella then muttered into the air, "Should we tell him about the Mad Legion outside the walls, or let him figure it out himself?"

Thomas said, "And they're still outside, regardless of how many times we've cut them down. They apparently had attacked Merrieu when we were at Pommel. More of them arrive each day, just surrounding us."

"We had to fight them back each time we took you to and from Fort Andrews," Maxim added. "They could use one of your magical pep talks."

"My God." Michael went to use his staff to see the extent of the siege outside Merrieu's walls, forgetting it was gone. He then said somberly, "Perhaps you could schedule a meet with the siblings. I must speak with them before it's too late."

During breakfast, Thomas's paladins alerted him that the sibling sovereigns agreed to a meet, but only Michael and himself were welcome. Conceding to the stipulation, the two followed delegates up to the throne room's open veranda. The siblings sat side-by-side overlooking Merrieu's eastern field. As Thomas and Michael walked out to meet them, the scope of the Mad Legion's siege was in full view. Well over a hundred of them, afflicted men and women waited for some kind of order.

Catching him glaring over the sight, the prince regent greeted Michael from his seat, "So, you see our unwelcomed visitors? Just one of Merrieu's newest complications since you've all arrived."

Just into his twenties, Lucas Cachot, the prince regent, gestured for his guests to sit across from them. His sister, Luca, ruled jointly with him. They were identical twins with similar governing methods. In light of their families' blighted fate, it fell on them to uphold Merrieu by any means. Mentors guided their dual leadership with urgent advice to take no chances. The kingdom was seemingly just hanging on.

Accompanied by a line of armored guards, Prince Lucas began, "Legate Excallum here had informed us that you were awake and it was good to hear that. We were hoping that we could speak with you directly at some point. Because you had called the meet, I assume you want to know why all those people you saved a few days ago have come to stay in our dungeon?"

Michael answered, "I'm glad you brought that up first, Your Majesty. I thought it was clear that our mission was, in part, designed to rescue captives. Now, warriors from all over this world have come together, putting aside their differences, to invade Pommel. Some gave their lives so that those innocent prisoners could be free. Throwing them into another dungeon defeats that purpose. Those people need medical attention. They're malnourished—"

"Let me stop you there, Sir Miuriell," Prince Lucas cut in. "All valor aside, Pommel is cursed. Because you and your army infiltrated a cursed place, those poor souls you saved are no different than what they were as unwilling guests over there. They are unclean, like that legion of zombies outside our walls.

"The rations you brought from Falcus are just not enough. Advisors tell us that we may have enough for but two more days, at best. I'm sorry, Miuriell, but you and your 'Angels of Resistance' must think about returning to Falcus. Merrieu has suffered more than you can ever know."

"Let me stop *you* there, prince-regent," Michael replied. "There isn't a man, woman or child that I have met that is free of suffering. We've all suffered here. We've all lost a part of our lives in this war. Now that I am awake, by the grace of

God, I can go to work on the issues you just addressed. Like before, I can cure those people outside these walls. Tonight, maybe, I can even cure the Tinarian princess. I'll try anything in my power to take our lives back from the Demon Plague.

"Those prisoners in your dungeon are my people. They are your people. If we're going to win this war, we have to save each other. We need to protect each other. What we love matters more than ever before because it can all be snuffed out—like that. Pommel was my home and my entire family has been stolen from me. You've lost as much, but you still have Merrieu."

"And I intend to keep it," the prince retorted.

"And you will." Michael asserted. "I could not imagine the stress you must be under—the whole kingdom on your shoulders. Give me one day, at least, to prove that I am a man of my word."

Digesting what Michael had said, Prince Lucas yielded to his sister, asking her to weigh in on the matter. Looking at Michael intently, as if studying his face, Luca said, "Your eyes make a very different promise, Miuriell. This evil has changed even you. How can you expect us to believe that Merrieu will not?"

Thomas then lifted his hand to intercede, "I think I can answer this one for you, princess-regent. Michael has a very unique gift, one that saved our lives more than a dozen times. Our fateful mission rescued over a hundred captives from the grim lot of torture and ritualistic sacrifice. Three, maybe four of the Demon Plague's generals were assassinated in the raid. He may look cursed, but believe me, Michael is a blessing. Give him one chance. Then, we will return to the holy city."

The siblings looked at each other and came to a quick conclusion, just moments in their insightful eyes. Luca turned to them across the table and declared, "End the siege outside our walls and exorcize the demon in the foreign princess. Do those tasks and we will grant the release of the prisoners."

Lucas furthered, "There are conditions, of course. We can discuss them after you've accomplished your errands."

Though Thomas nodded in the appreciation of some progress, Michael said boldly, "I can agree on one condition. Medical staff examines and treats the captives today. If any die—"

"I can't concede to that condition of yours. We can't risk any epidemics," Lucas said, impudently.

Michael leaned in and countered, "Then I collapse that dungeon down to grimy sand and leave the Mad Legion out there for you and your sister to deal with. Understand that I am playing nice with you both in the hope that we can come to an agreement civilly. If we can't work together, then those demons in Pommel will take advantage of our disarray. That, I cannot allow."

His spine beginning to shiver, Lucas said, "So, we are a kingdom under occupation, after all?"

Michael then stood up and replied coldly, "That really depends on how you look at it, Your Majesty. You're both still young. You'll have the chance to make your own decisions that will affect the lives of millions after us grown-ups are finished ridding our world of a Demon Plague. We are *all* under occupation, regents. Please keep that in mind as I go and take care of the tasks you've assigned me."

Thomas bowed his head before asking to be excused from the table. Luca gestured for her guards to allow them to leave the veranda unhindered. As Michael and Thomas left, the sibling sovereigns looked upon each other again and then sighed, realizing that their authority was under attack. They grew up reading about and even meeting Michael at various events all over the realm. Their suspicion of him only grew.

Thomas, upon leaving the royal wing under heavy Merrier guard, uttered, "Well, that was some show back there."

Heading out of the castle, Michael asked Thomas if he received any word from Ellium over their participation in the war. Thomas said, "My scouts have yet to return from their journey, but I'd have to assume Ellium is ready for the assault."

"We can only pray that they are. Falcus can't do it all," Michael exhaled. "And what about Lana and the others? Are they alright?"

Upon descending the royal staircase, Thomas only said, "Best leave them to me, Michael. You have more than enough to worry about on your own."

In the medical wing of the barracks, Predella had come looking for Lana. The smell was foul as she turned the corner into the intensive care unit. In a large room guarded by three ninja warriors, Predella saw Lana sitting by her husband. As she came to the door, one of the guards asked if she was open to guests. Lana evidently agreed to see her.

When Predella humbly entered, she could sense that Lana had not left the medical wing since the first day. There was distress in the thick air and the closed curtains made the room seem bleak. Closer to the window, Shioda slept. He had bandages over his head and half of his face. Near the door, a nurse patted a moist rag over Lai's forehead. He, too, was in a deep sleep. Lana sat between their beds, hunched over her husband and facing the window.

When Predella neared closer to her, she turned around to greet her. She stood up and hugged Predella tightly as if recalling their last embrace on the edge of Pommel days ago. There was a fear about camp that Shioda had succumbed to his injuries, but he was still alive. Yet, there was no chance of him taking part in another battle in the near future.

"He was talking last night and he had his first meal this morning." Lana then started to sob in her shoulder. "But he doesn't remember me. He doesn't remember who *he* is."

Distraught to hear of his amnesia, Predella held her by the shoulders and looked into her tired eyes, streaming with tears, "Lana, I'm sure it's just temporary. He's just lucky to be alive after taking that hit."

"But when? When will he come back to me?" she cried. "You should have seen the way Shioda looked at me. It was like he never saw me in his life. He was scared. I told him what he did—how he pushed me out of the way to save me. He just looked right through me."

"Sit down, Lana. I'll draw the curtains just a bit, okay?" Predella said softly, guiding her to her chair. She then drew the curtains and let in some light, impulsively watching the Ziamons run laps around the barracks. She then took a closer look at Shioda laying still in his bed and said, "First, his body. Then, his memory. You'll see. After seeing your beautiful face enough—"

"I'm pregnant with his child," Lana uttered, holding her stomach instinctively.

"Oh, I see," Predella said, taken off guard by her reveal. She pulled up a seat across from her and smiled, "Then, he has a big reason to come back to you. Shioda will come back."

Wiping away her tears, still streaming, Lana turned to her brother and remembered what he said about the escape from Pommel. She said quietly, "Lai told me about how the Eastern heroes saved his squad from two different generals. He said Maxim offered his life so that they could escape with the women. Then, you came along and killed that vampire with one shot. I saw it myself from the line. What a sight. I've never seen a shot like that before."

Predella modestly replied, "How is he doing?"

Locking eyes with his nurse, Lana answered, "They say his wound is infected. He has a fever. The doctors are trying aggressively to treat him. As you would guess, they're going to have to sit out the rest of this war."

"Undoubtedly, I guess that means you too," she said.

Lana then stared at her brother's face, pale and damp, before saying unflinchingly, "No. There will be a Kai on the battlefield. I will don my armor and equip my halberd. On my father's honor, I will fight in my husband and brother's stead. And when this war has long ended, my children will know what their mother did to secure the world they love."

Finding the glimmer in her eyes, Predella then realized that her mind was made up. She said to her, "Wait, Lana, you can't be serious."

Lana brazenly answered, turning to look into her eyes, "I'm serious, Predella. One angry woman is worth five men in battle. That means they'll be ten men between you and me."

Still stunned by her mad resolve, Predella asked her, "I won't speak for them, but Shioda and Lai—"

"What if Maxim told you that you couldn't fight?" Lana broke in before Predella could get started. "What if he forbids you to take part?"

"Maxim? I don't—" she attempted to conceal her secret companionship.

"It isn't much of a mystery, Predella. You and Maxim," Lana said. "You're a perfect match—a perfect attraction. Can you imagine if you couldn't fight? Word has spread in Falcus about what you did for your people in Ziamon. You are a chain-breaker. You were destined to free those slaves. I can tell that you're someone who obeys the cries of the soul. You wouldn't stay your bow, no matter what Maxim said."

"Maxim is one thing, but you're pregnant. You just told me this," Predella replied with concern. "There is a time to fight and a time to preserve what you love. Let me fight for you, Lana. I don't have as much to lose. You have a family. I know what it's like to lose that. If I was pregnant with a child, Maxim wouldn't *have* to tell me. I'd stay with my baby, out of harm's way. That is how you secure the world they will love. They have to be there to see it with a mother to raise them."

"And what of the final battle? What of the battlefield?" Lana said quietly.

Predella looked at her intently and answered, "This *is* your battlefield."

Lana processed what Predella was saying when Shioda groaned just beside her. She rose from her seat to check on him, putting her face over his so that he could see she was there. He held her arm and looked up at her, trusting that she was who she promised. He peered into her eyes and studied her pretty face, trying to remember. With half of his face bandaged and his one eye still reddened from blood, it was even harder to make out Lana's features.

As Predella stood up to look on, crossing her arms in worry, a paladin knocked on the door from the outside. When she went over to him, the knight whispered, "I heard you might be here. Michael was asking for you. He is outside the main gate."

"What is he doing there?" she asked softly. "I thought he was meeting with the siblings?"

The paladin answered, "The meet is over. The siblings are collecting medics to send to the dungeons. Michael was able to arrange that, at least. But now he's trying to cure all the afflicted out there. There's got to be hundreds."

"I'm coming," Predella turned to let Lana know she was leaving, but, instead, left her alone. In heading out passed the paladin, she whispered in his ear, "I'll be back for her."

The knight nodded honorably. Predella then headed down the corridor, passing the other knights, to find Michael.

Just outside of Merrieu's gate, Michael stood with arms open. In droves, legionnaires came and knelt before him. He waited for the entire army to form in place, somehow willing them with only his mind. Men and women from every part of the realm knelt and waited in his watch. Some had joined in on the flash invasion of Merrieu days ago. Others just arrived but hours before. The madness brought them upon the Angels of Resistance's provisional base.

Thomas and Maxim, along with thongs of others behind the gate, watched cautiously as Michael seemed to meditate in the army's presence. They were at his beckoning call, even those from over a thousand feet back. He was able to feel the dark possession in their minds, driving them there. Finally, the sibling sovereigns had come to the veranda of the castle to watch the spectacle for themselves.

"We are ready for the attack, master," a self-appointed leader said from behind his Ellison mask. He had come from as far as Ellium to lead such a raid. The madness spread out even further than he realized.

Michael, in feeling connected to all of their minds, said calmly, almost in a whisper, "Go back to your homes and be free. Live honorable lives. Chase your dreams. But never heed this power ever again."

The masses from inside the kingdom's walls looked on in awe as, in scores, the legionnaires dispersed and headed into various directions. They left artillery and siege machines on the open field, some even dropping their own weapons as they went. The threat had ended in but minutes, leaving just Michael standing there by his lonesome. Yet, from amongst the crowds, a young girl remained while the others left. She seemed bewildered and anxious watching them all go. Either he missed her somehow, or she wasn't ever afflicted at all.

With hardly any legionnaires remaining, Michael went over to her, but she ran off. He lowered his head and sighed, for some succumbed to the madness and others just followed the herd, wanting to belong. For a young child to watch their family or friends go off with blind ambition, it seemed like the only thing to do was go along. Michael hoped that she ran in the direction of home.

When Michael turned back to reenter Merrieu's main gate, the waiting crowd amid the crenellations cheered and applauded his miraculous deed. Without another battle or even drawing a blade, the newest Mad Legion had simply broken away like an autumn leaf. His powers grew since his last curing of the madness days back. Upon reaching Thomas and Maxim in wait at the gate, Michael said, "One more task remaining."

"Michael, that was—astonishing!" Thomas gasped.

Amid the cheers, he proceeded to say, "Did you happen to bring your Paladin's Compendium along?"

"I don't go anywhere without it," the legate replied. "I must ask why."

"It has the rights of exorcism if I recall," Michael said. "Just in case. We have to get to her before dusk."

Maxim interceded at the gate, "If you're talking about the princess, I'm coming along."

"Of course, but we're going out blind. Without my staff, we'll have no insight. Antonis may have to join us as well." Michael headed into the plaza with Thomas and Maxim at his sides.

As the masses followed them in adulation, Maxim said in protest, "Under no circumstances can that witchdoctor get anywhere near Shina. He's been wanting to kill her since the Ghost Forest."

Michael smirked and replied, "Then I'll have to make a believer out of him."

"Shit," he grumbled, walking through the Merrier mob back to the barracks. "That means his babysitters are coming too. Look, I'm taking Predella as a buffer."

Thomas remarked with his head straight forward, "I bet you are."

"What the hell does *that* mean?" Maxim countered just as Predella was meeting them halfway.

"Thomas, we need only a small task force—just those I trust," Michael interceded. "You'll make the arrangements?"

"Consider it done," the legate said before going off with some of his knights. When seeing Predella walk towards the group, he then gibed, "Here she comes, Maxim. Don't be shy. Just be yourself."

"Ha. Ha," Maxim countered sardonically.

By noon, the task force set out for Fort Andrews by way of a carriage. A five-hour journey, all fourteen cramped inside. Michael sat at the head of the car with his back to the driver, while Maxim, Predella, Thomas and his three best knights sat to his right. To Michael's left, Antonis and his six Tofauti guards looked across the car at the opposite party. All the weapons and gear were strewn in the aisle with the exception of Maxim's fire-sword and Predella's elemental bow, for which they held vertically before them.

Pulled by a team of oxen, the carriage ride took them east along the road to Merchant's Pass. The view of Pommel's Shadowland made the Tofauti warriors lift the shudders and gawk at it. The sight was overwhelmingly sinister, regardless of how many times passersby had seen it. Antonis didn't need to look upon it for himself. He saw it in his visions. The sensation, alone, was enough to know its prominence.

For the others, looking on it gave them a great amount of grief. They knew that they would one day have to charge on that cursed land one final time. Michael kept his eyes shut while passing it, unwilling to look upon it from a distance. In seeing him avoid the Shadowland, Antonis cleared his throat and said, "I was very sick upon hearing of your son's death. If there is anything I can ever do for you, you need only ask."

"Thank you, Antonis," Michael replied. "Many made the ultimate sacrifice that day. That mission isn't over until those captives are freed from Merrieu's dungeon."

"Of course," he responded in accordance, then turning to Predella just across from him. "And you have surely made yourself the heroine in this war. A scarred palm, an injured torso—looks like the vampire got what was coming to her. How did you pull off that shot with a palm marked so deeply? I hear it was remarkable."

Her wounds still in sutures, Predella felt her sore palm, branded by the Mad Phoenix's handle. She replied humbly, "I find that any pain can be suppressed when one must save the lives of others. Maxim has saved mine more than once. And Michael—more than any of us can count."

"I know that well," he replied, then sighing, "and now we must save Princess Shina from herself. God be with us."

Just before Maxim could take him on, Michael declared, "Not herself, prophet. She didn't choose this curse—and I did not either. We were born into it. Yet, I believe, like the afflicted, I can very well cast out the demonic spirit from her body. My burden, this curse—I'll use it to bury the Demon Plague until not even a speck of their existence remains on this earth. But I need you all to help me. That's why each of you are in this carriage. You're my circle of trust.

"When I fell into oblivion at Pommel, the Demon Lord showed me things that would make any man's knees buckle. It lingers, still, in my mind whenever I close my eyes—all the torment, the suffering. But I also gained access to something they didn't think I'd see. There is something buried beneath Pommel, something from the old world. So old, in fact, that the founders of Pommel built the bastion over it, possibly to conceal it.

"There is an evil down there that is beyond anything I've ever felt before. It felt, strangely, like home. As baleful as it seemed, there was a part of me that believed I belonged there. It's hard to explain, but I think *that* is where the Demon Plague originated. That is how they surprised my people in the dead of night. They didn't invade. They lived underneath Pommel the whole time. I have to find out what's really down there.

"It begins with curing Princess Shina of her possession. What I've told you—what you see tonight, must not leave this circle of trust. Whatever happens inside that fort, you must never enter. Regardless of what you hear, you stay outside and remain there until Thomas or I summon you. For her and your safety, please promise me that. This is the endgame."

When Michael finished, the party agreed to remain at their posts at Fort Andrews. Maxim glared cautiously at the prophet all the while. Antonis only smiled back, then saying, "Your ally doesn't seem to trust that I will keep my end of the agreement."

Michael answered, "Luckily, Maxim's faith in me, offsets his distrust in you."

"Well," Antonis said, returning Maxim's stare, "isn't all that just swell?"

As dusk was approaching, the party's carriage made it partly up the rocky incline before the oxen gave out. Situating it just off the path with a paladin to watch after the driver, the group headed up to Fort Andrews on foot just a hundred feet up the way. Tall grass and shrubbery flanked the path as they went, seeing the fort just up ahead. Two paladin knights came to meet them at the stockade. Equipped with a vial of holy water and his compendium, Thomas met them first to learn about the situation inside.

The princess, possessed by demonic forces, was still fighting to break free from her bondage. Her chains were just at the breaking point and there wasn't much time left before she eventually busted out. Michael told the paladins to clear out the fort. They were more than happy to receive that order. All nine knights raced out, leaving Shina alone inside.

After discussing the plan with Thomas, Michael came down to address the rest of his party. He said to them from behind the stockades, "I place you here. Once we're inside the fort, there's no telling what she'll do to resist. Stay on your guards for whatever may come up that path. Antonis, you're my eyes and ears out here. Without my staff, you're all they have. Stay alert, all of you. And whatever you hear—"

"Don't go inside," Maxim declared. "We got it. Just find a way to save her."

Predella said earnestly, "Good luck."

"By God's grace," Thomas proclaimed, making the sign of the cross as he turned to Michael, "and that you know what it is you're doing."

Breathing in heavily before going in, Michael nodded and said, "Amen."

The two of them headed into the gloomy fort, leaving the rest of the party to guard the path. Just setting foot inside, they could already feel the concentrated evil swirling about. Like in a thick miasma, it was hard for them to breathe. There was no mystery as to where Shina was kept. Michael felt her in the dungeons.

On the way down the winding staircase, Thomas said, "In poor taste, but this was the only fitting place—"

"This is what dungeons are for," Michael replied.

When they neared closer to the bottom level, Shina sensed them and called out, "**More visitors? How nice.**"

Before they turned the corner into the open dungeon, Michael stopped him and said, "Whatever she says, don't take her on. Leave it all to me. Just stay back until I need you."

"Understood," Thomas said.

At last, they entered into the fray. Shina lay across the dungeon and against the cold brick wall, her wrists shackled. Wearing the same outfit for days, she looked like a prisoner. She cackled as they came forth amid the row of empty cells at their sides. Closer, Michael saw how the sunlight scourged her pale skin. Fractures ran along her entire body. Her eyes were still black, nearly hiding behind the strands of her red hair. Sitting on the chilly floor, she grinned at them.

"Shina, I've come to set you free," Michael said, leaving Thomas by a cell.

"You mean kill me, don't you?" Shina rasped. **"Well? Here I am—my love."**

"You're not my love," Michael retorted. "The girl that you are keeping hidden, trapped inside her own body—let her go. Now."

Shina then spat to her side and said furiously, **"You see, there's your problem, Miuriell. You just don't grasp that I *am* that girl. I could be a queen, but you'd rather I be this virgin twat. Look at yourself! Can't you feel it? Things are changing and you're changing with them! Grow a pair."**

"I'm sorry this happened, Shina," Michael said ruefully. "You didn't deserve this. But, I promise, when we're finished, you'll never have to fear the sun again. You will be Shina once again—once we leave this place."

"Because that sexless, pampered exorcist will *cure* me? Please, if you're going to try that, spare the theatrics and just kill me," Shina countered.

"Leave him out of this. It's just you and me," he said.

"Is it? So, you'll pee on me and tell me it's raining? What's happened to you? You're not a king—or a master.

You're a farce," Shina said irately. "**Whatever you're going to do, just get it over with. End this tragic tale.**"

Thomas looked on from his place, apprehensive of their ability to exercise her demon. Michael, however, raised his hand towards her and said, "This will be over soon. I swear."

Finally, he began reaching inside her soul for the dark segments the Demon Plague had awakened. She felt him as he rummaged for her, trying to segregate the bad Shina from the good. She fought back against his exercise, resisting every rush of force. The energy in the dungeon began to swell between them, compelling Thomas to brace against the cell bars. The rush of darkness was overwhelming, much like an unwanted rush of adrenaline.

Leaning forward, Shina growled through her teeth, "**I'm not one of your brainless disciples, Miuriell! You won't break me! You'll *join* me!**"

Outside, as the group waited for anything to happen, Antonis lifted his head and gasped, "It's begun. He's trying to rid her of her demonic spirit."

"As long as he doesn't rid her of her life," Maxim said.

The prophet then felt an evil dynamism growing from inside the fort, "But, something is wrong. Something is not what it seems."

One of the paladins muttered, "Now, there's a shocker."

The eleven fort knights assembled behind the party, their bodies facing the garrison, and waited. Not thinking anything of it, Predella neared the prophet and said, "Michael warned us against going in there. Everything is in his hands."

"For you, that may be comforting," Antonis replied. "I, on the other hand, don't think he knows what he's started."

Michael battled Shina for her very soul, feeling her fighting him with every breath. He pulled harder and reached deeper into her spirit. Like vines consuming a derelict house, Shina's dark entity would not let go without a desperate tug of war. The more he pressed, the more she pressed back. In challenging her demons, Michael shouted out with urgency, "Thomas! Pray! Read anything from your compendium! We have to diminish her—"

"**Pray for yourselves!**" Shina shrieked over him.

As Thomas somehow gathered his courage to read the right of exorcisms from the Paladin's Compendium, Antonis's warning came to fruition. All of a sudden, the eleven paladins charged with guarding the fort had ambushed them. Drawing their swords and maces with shields in their hands, the holy knights attacked without mercy. The assault took them off-guard, even the prophet himself.

Two afflicted knights charged the Tofauti warriors and were able to stab Antonis in the side of his neck. One of them pushed the knight back and pierced the maddened paladin through his face with an angry thrust of the spear. The fight was on, as Antonis's guards dragged him passed the stockade and out of danger. Another warrior hurriedly put pressure on his mortal wound. He laid on the ground in shock as the party fought the afflicted paladins back.

One of the defending knights cried out, "What's going on? Why do they attack?"

After firing another arrow turning an afflicted paladin into an ice statue, Predella looked to the fort and uttered, "It's the princess."

Thomas shouted the rites of exorcism with conviction, but Shina only became angrier. Her rage rivaled Michael's, still trying to free her from the evil. The dark power became too much for Thomas to bear, just making out his words and slumping over out of breath. Sensing that there was no way any holy passages from him were going to work, Michael had to resort to his second plan.

"**Shut up that true paladin wanna-be before I creep into his core and take his soul!**" she screeched.

Unable to pull out her demons, Michael recognized that Thomas was in grave danger. He desperately screamed back, "Thomas! You have to go!"

True paladins from centuries ago had the faculties to perform a proper exorcism, even as dire as the current one. But Thomas was far from one of those. A glorified cleric, the legate faithfully read from his compendium, despite his hurt. Dark energy emitting from the two powers were but instants away from consuming him entirely.

Finally, Michael screamed with all this might, "**Thomas, go! *Go!*"**

Taken aback by Michael's menacing powers breaking loose in the struggle, Thomas shut his compendium and then fled the dungeon. Leaving Michael to deal with Shina alone, he hobbled up the stairway and dashed for the main doors. He nudged into a toppled desk and fell, breaking his vile of holy water all about the floor. The disturbing sounds from below compelled him to make it out to the front in a hurry.

Breaking out through the main doors, Thomas beheld a horror he never could have expected. A despairing melee had poured out over the front lawn with his own knights being the maddened aggressors. He looked over the fight in horror. One of them, injured in battle, lobbed a live grenade into the throng of Tofauti guardians. A paladin shouted, "Grenade!"

Finding it in the air, Maxim swatted it up with his blade. It detonated twenty feet above them, its impact putting Maxim to the ground. Taking advantage of his vulnerability, a wounded knight came up behind Maxim to stab him in the back. Before he could surprise him from behind, a Tofauti spear skewered his throat just under the helmet, killing the assailant. Maxim jerked back to witness the warrior's quick actions in saving his life. He nodded in gratitude.

Antonis was fading fast, even with two of his protectors fighting to plug the gouge in his neck. Maxim stayed with the group to stave off any further attacks while Predella used her last three arrows to incapacitate the remaining afflicted. One final knight writhed on the ground, persevering with one of Predella's arrows in his thigh. To avert any more bloodshed, Thomas cried out for the violence to end. He came down to the stockades and knelt before the crawling paladin stricken with the madness. Holding him down, he said, "May God have mercy on you, lad."

Though wounded, the party prevailed against the mad paladins. Antonis, however, couldn't hold on anymore. When Maxim came to help, the prophet grasped him tightly by the arm and gargled his last words tailored for him alone. He said, "You must—die to—to win. Die, Maxim—to win—"

After revealing his last prophecy, Antonis finally died. In his death, the Tofauti guardians began to cry and shout. It was their doom. The Honor Quest was over and they, in the end, failed to keep the prophet alive. As criminals, it was no longer possible to return home to Tofauti as redeemed souls. They stood over Antonis's body, realizing that their hopes for salvation had died with him. Predella had joined the group, lowering her head to say regretfully, "I'm so sorry."

Not processing the prophet's last words, Maxim went over to Thomas and asked, "What's happening in there, legate? Shina controlled all these men, didn't she? She poisoned their minds—"

"She's too strong. God help us," Thomas sobbed from his knees.

Michael took on the princess's dark spirit for as long as he could without imploding the entire fort on them both. In a last-ditch attempt to cure her, Michael reached in and roared, **"Then you leave me no choice!"**

No longer trying to separate the demonic essence from her body, Michael sought to absorb it. Like a black hole, he extracted Shina's energy and drew it into his own. The power increased his strength beyond measure but swelled his body with a rush of evil. His skin, like hers, became pale. Black veins pulsated throughout his person and his eyes raged red. Shina could hardly breathe, sitting helplessly as if her all the air was sucked out from her lungs. Soon enough, her blackened eyes began to return to normal and her skin showed signs of some color. In mere seconds, her evil aura had been drained.

She slumped over in chains when Michael was finished. Collapsing to his knees, he held himself off the ground and fought the swirl of wickedness in his being. A bitter struggle of good and evil nearly tore him apart from the inside. While he wrestled with the surging power, Urik somehow entered his mind. A faint prompt of advice echoed, *"You are still the man you were. You will always be that man. No matter what, this unspeakable evil will never have the absolute power to make you something else."*

They could sense the tremendous energy bursting out from the fort, compelling everyone to back up. Maxim pulled Thomas away from one of his fallen comrades and retreated. Something sinister had awakened and none knew what it could have been. They only felt its effects. Flocks of birds had scattered from the region as they drew their weapons. It was but moments after that the doors blew off their hinges.

There, in the doorway, Michael ambled forth with the princess hanging from his outstretched arms. He carried her out from the fort and waited there for someone to come and relieve her from him. Maxim dashed over, sheathing his blade while Predella called for him to wait. When he ran up to him, Maxim looked upon Michael's dark countenance. It was evident how powerful he had become.

His reddened eyes glowing, Michael declared in a dark tone, parts human and demonic, "**Take her and leave. Make it as far as you can before nightfall.**"

Receiving the princess in his arms, Maxim uttered, "Is she? What did you—"

"She's alive and relieved from the evil that plagued her. Shina will recover. I must stay here—for some time," Michael said, exhausted and overcome with a vile lifeforce. **"Go on. God willing, we shall see each other again soon."**

With that, Maxim ran back to the group with Shina in his care and urged them to follow. Predella couldn't fathom what happened, but she broke away and led the others down the path. The Tofauti warriors all lifted the prophet's corpse and heaved him down. Thomas turned his head one last time before racing behind his paladin brothers, seeing Michael in the arch doorway watching them go. When they made it far enough down the slope, Michael withdrew inside the fort.

PART II
CHAPTER XIII
THE TIDES OF WAR

Sattka bore arms atop one of the high steeples of the citadel. Empowered by the dark miasma lingering over her, she peered out over the outer realm. With the dusk came a familiar figure walking alone down Merchant Pass. The scourged knight and appointed leader to the deteriorating Mad Legion, Garvin Kane, advanced. Intrigued by his return, Sattka glided down from the tower. Kane saw her as she landed up the way within the perimeter of the darkness.

Wielding a large broadsword he stole from a fallen soldier, Kaine's armor was burnt black and his left claw grew menacing. His eyes reflected Sattka's green hue as they finally converged under the miasma. They both stared at each other with very dissimilar judgments. Sattka said, "**I like the new you. Your wretched smell is gone.**"

Kane responded without the slightest showing of fear, "**Your stench is still there.**"

Laughing with disdain, Sattka contemptuously hissed, "**You missed all the shit.**"

"**What happened to this place?**" Kane barked when he acknowledged the destruction all around him.

"**Miuriell happened. Come follow me,**" Sattka uttered as she led him into Pommel's bastion.

She brought him through the sheer devastation of what once was the atrium. After Valkris and Eric's duel, the mere foundations to the citadel were weakened. Remnants of the Mad Legion slaved away at trying to clean the wreckage. She updated him on their losses, for they were staggering. Sattka was the lone survivor to the demonic generals. Kane couldn't believe the report.

When they finally entered the throne room, the Demon Lord said from his seat, "**It was only a matter of time for you. I knew you'd come back.**"

"**I came for vengeance,**" Kane replied, "**but it seems I missed my shot.**"

The Demon Lord removed himself from the throne and walked over to him, inducing Kane to step back. Towering over the slayer, the demon answered, "**Your magician counterpart betrayed the conquest and died, but not before taking Valkris with him. You failed at Falcus and you failed to return to your legion, now diminished. Why did you come back now, I wonder? To suffer justly at my hand perhaps?**"

Kane proceeded to step back as he fretfully responded, "**I came back with an ultimatum that might rejuvenate the conquest!**"

He watched Kane squirm away as he retorted, "**You have one last chance to impress me. Speak.**"

Kane wasted no time in arguing his case, "**My proposition stands this way. I want the swordsman with the fire-sword who killed me. But I also want the power to return to my human form again. I want to appear as I was before he torched me.**"

"**Abaddon's fire-sword,**" the Demon Lord responded. "**What do I get in exchange for reverting you back to your largely inadequate form?**"

"**You can then kill me or let me stay on the squad,**" Kane replied humbly. "**I only want my revenge.**"

"**That's the one who ended Scythian,**" Sattka added. "**I fought with him in Tinaria. He's a skilled opponent.**"

Thinking it over, the Demon Lord ultimately answered, "**I accept your proposal, Garvin Kane, but my mercy** comes with a price. Kill the swordsman and then you will return to your human form. If you return Abaddon's bow along with the fire-sword, then I will forgive your trespasses and let you live long after the conquest."

"A bow? Which bow do you want?" Kane asked.

Sattka answered in her father's stead, "**The bitch with a bow that shoots arrows of fire and ice. She killed Kaila with it.**"

Accepting their proposals, Kane held his demonic claw to his chest and said, "**I will return the weapons along with their heads.**"

Turning his back to him, the Demon Lord started back to his throne, saying, "**We'll see.**"

Looking to Sattka as if he dodged a bullet, Kane asked, "**What about the squealing red-haired girl? Do they still have her? You know how delicate she is in the daylight.**"

"**The girl is of no concern to—**" The Demon Lord had started to answer when a revelation came to him. Something happened. He could no longer feel her, let alone find her in the realm. Shina's dark spirit was absent from her body. In a crude twist of fate, he felt her power coursing in Michael. He clenched his claw and growled with searing anger, "**No. It can't be.**"

As night enveloped Fort Andrews, Michael sat upon the crenellations and viewed the dying sun to the west. Deep in his meditation, the war for his soul was never more serious. With the night came the immense power. His appearance had turned further to Abaddon's side, as even just letting go was dangerous enough to finish the cycle. He had to hold on lest he sway too far into the dark. Finding the little peace within himself was the only thing keeping him from succumbing.

Reminiscing his childhood, replaying his wedding and witnessing his son's birth reconnected him to his humanity.

Breathing rhythmically, Michael found that he had the ability to control the evil churning inside. Yet, in balancing the two forces, Michael sensed a greater evil joining him atop the fort. Not bothering to break his meditation entirely, he only said, "**It'll do no good pestering me. I have control over it.**"

"**Do you?**" In Seth's small frame, the Demon Lord stood behind him and declared chillingly through the boy's voice, "**I know that you're a geyser—a time bomb waiting to blow. It just takes a small push and you're there. That terrifies you, doesn't it?**"

"**You came to make sure, and you did,**" Michael said. "**Shina is free from your evil. She's far from your reach.**"

Looking out towards Merrieu, the Demon Lord lowered Seth's head and sighed, "**She was perfect. We selected that girl for you and you threw it away—your progeny. Now it all means nothing. You betrayed us for the last time.**"

Shaking his head, Michael retorted, "**And the cost was great. I lost my son, which you throw in my face. But even while you use his body as a puppet, he, too, is far from the likes of you. He sleeps in eternal peace.**"

"**I can't wait to see where this takes us. Either way, the conquest will be fulfilled. Prolonging it agitates me, but it'll all be worth it when you turn—and you *will* turn, Miuriell,**" The Demon Lord came closer and whispered into his ear with his son's voice, "**We can wait months, years if it takes that long. I can always build an army. How long can *you* last? Another night? Two nights? Soon, you'll be what your precious humans fear more than anything. You will betray them as you betrayed me.**"

Unable to take any more, Michael finally let out a loud, roaring cry and blasted everything away from him. Reverting the fort into projectiles of rubble and masonry, he obliterated the waterfront in seconds. Hovering high above the void of what once was the dungeon, Michael virtually envisioned himself as Abaddon. Yet, even after his profound exertion of might, Michael's rage had not transformed him into his ancient counterpart. There was still enough of him left inside. He lingered above the earth, fists loosening, as humanity's strongest weapon—one teetering on the border of supreme evil and noble discipline.

Deep into the still of the night, Merrieu's barracks were alive as ever. With the party's return hours ago, came droves of citizens who observed the Tinarian princess carried down to the safety of the clinic. They then watched the Tofauti take Antonis's covered body out from the carriage. The crowd had come to know the prophet as the mystic who predicted the Mad Legion's attack days before. After everyone had come down from the car, it became evident that Michael was not with them.

 Since then, the siblings kept their word and pledged the release of the captives in the morning hours. As Shina slept in the clinic, receiving urgent care from the barrack's dwindling medical staff, Thomas sat in a warm sofa chair facing the den's fireplace. Awaiting Maxim, for whom he summoned, the legate stared stoically into the crackling flames, mulling over the day's events and the new challenges that lied ahead.

 In time, a small team of paladins escorted Maxim in and left the two to themselves. He prudently walked over to the fire and sat in the sofa chair next to the legate's, exhaling all the trauma of the day. Nodding empathetically, Thomas said, "Some hectic day."

 The fire's crackling breaking the silence between them, Maxim replied jadedly, "You asked for me?"

 "I did," Thomas answered, just as tired. "How is Shina?"

 Taking time to reply, Maxim rubbed his eyes and said, "She's malnourished, and throwing up on top of it. But Shina is back to herself again. Michael likely saved the princess's life, or whatever he did. But I doubt that's why you called me here. What's going on?"

Taking a sip of rice wine from a small glass, Thomas passed a folded letter over to him to read. As Maxim unfolded it and started to read its contents by the flickering light of the fire, the legate said, "I received this message from one of my men upon our return."

Taken aback by its contents, Maxim gasped, "So, Ellium is ready to invade Pommel. They were watching us?"

"The emperor has the best technology at his disposal to observe us from a distance," Thomas replied. "They saw our escape from Pommel and were convinced that it was time to converge on the Demon Plague—jointly. Falcus and Ellium in one absolute battle to determine the fate of our world."

"But in three days' time?" Maxim rejoined. "It's just not possible. By the time we inform Falcus—"

"Even *if* Shadisha already knew, it would take two days to assemble the army and then three to march to Pommel," Thomas explained uneasily. "Ellium's army is massive and, to be sure, an advanced force to be reckoned with, but even they can't do it alone."

"You can take this up with Michael in the morning, if he returns to us," Maxim said, handing the note back to him. "If he is still the Michael we know."

"You saw him best, Maxim," Thomas replied. "What did you see?"

Recalling Michael's evil countenance when taking Shina off his hands, Maxim could still feel the overpowering force in his chest. Glaring into the dancing flames, he replied, "This dark force he's fighting—I don't know how long he can hold it inside. Ridding the princess of whatever possessed her may have tipped the scales in that battle."

"And, you fear, our last battle as well," Thomas said.

"We should all fear that battle if Michael loses himself," Maxim sighed. "Think I'll be praying on that from now on."

Thomas read between the lines on Maxim's spirituality and took another sip of his drink before asking, "So you *do* pray, after all. I thought I pegged you as a holy warrior."

Maxim uttered diffidently, "If you say so."

"I know so. Maxim, I've lost good men today and it just never gets easier. Having you as my paladin deputy may—" Thomas paused when he saw that Maxim wasn't showing any interest.

He retorted, "I mean no offense, legate, but you don't know me."

"On the contrary. I know you better than you think," he countered. "When the news came to Ellium that Malcusin had found a new disciple and he was able to wield the fire-sword, you can imagine the media storm. But for a young lad like me right out of school, it was more than intriguing. You were an orphan when Malcusin chose you but did he even know that you could wield the fire-sword? Did he know that you were a descendant of the Baelin paladin lineage?"

"The Baelin lineage went to shit after the Hessian Wars. Who knows who I am or where I'm from?" Maxim muttered.

Thomas, however, proceeded unhindered, "When the paladins were first assembled in Ellium, many possessed the ability to heal. Some could even resist magic. Those days are gone since the empire banned the order more than four hundred years ago. Now, we serve as humble soldiers of God—no healing powers, no glowing maces. I have brought the order back from dormancy to foster hope and salvation in a world stricken with darkness. The new paladin order needs a man with your gifts."

"You think I'm a Baelin, do you?" Maxim started as he ogled the fire. "I'm no holy man, legate. I'm a killer. And my heart lies in Tinaria."

Peering into Maxim's eyes, Thomas replied subtly, "I, too, am a killer. We're both killers, Maxim. Paladins don't take a business like that lightly. I have prayed on this for years. The reality is quite grim, I'm afraid. This new world we find ourselves in requires noble killers. This world doesn't need any more lambs. It needs lions. The Baelins understood that."

"Too bad Ellium didn't get that," Maxim scoffed. "What you need is a miracle, not a deputy."

Surrendering his glass of wine for Maxim to finish, he said, "We *are* the miracle. And Michael is our north star. Your princess is evidence of that."

Gulping it down, Maxim grunted before saying, "Well, I have been thinking about that. Michael could have killed her. He could have ended it in that way and Antonis would have been satisfied. But, he didn't. That seer wanted Shina dead if only to cut out a part of the Demon Plague. I get that. Instead, Shina controlled your paladins to kill us and he was the only casualty. It's a crude irony.

"Before those monsters are all just a bad memory, that north star could very well turn into our worst nightmare. He knows it just as much as we do. And yet, I still have to believe that he is going to lead us to victory. Somewhere, deep in my spirit, I believe we can win—despite the odds against us."

Thomas nodded with a crooked smile, "There's an old saying we paladins like to use when the journey gets dark. 'Trade fear for faith.' Another Baelin quote."

Handing the empty glass back to him, Maxim yawned, "Perhaps I'll meet them in the next life. We'll have a grand ol' family reunion. But, before then, I think I'll burn that demon nest of a bastion into smoldering heaps of bone and ember."

"Amen," Thomas replied, closing his eyes in feeling the warmth of the fireplace on his face. The two warriors simply sat there in silence, ruminating on the challenges to come in light of the mountains they already moved.

Having gathered in Antonis's quarters, the six Tofauti warriors reflected on their uncertain future in bitter silence. Three of them had fallen asleep while the others assembled in the study. Illuminated by lanterns, the small room served as a safe place to mull over the fateful day's happenings. The small group rummaged through the study, unwilling to sleep until they came to terms with what the morning would bring.

One of them, however, sat in the prophet's provisional desk and bravely spoke, "This is enough. I cannot go on with this any longer. I do not care if I break my vow of silence. Our Honor Quest is over."

Stunned by their confederate's admission and violation of the code, the two others turned to fire glares at him. There were no real repercussions, however, for their mission ended in raw failure when Antonis died in their care. Seeing that his confederates still refused to utter a word in protest, the same warrior went on, "I cannot return home. What was my home, or my place of birth, will no longer welcome me. So, instead, I shall migrate to Falcus and apply for naturalization."

At last, one of them neared closer to the desk and said in a whisper, "Shut your mouth. Tofauti will hunt you down without mercy if you do not return. We failed. We must then return in dishonor and face—"

"My name is Pingas and I will not return as the prisoner of my home." He rose from his seat to face his complainant. "I will gladly fight and die for my right to stay here in this land. They will not hunt what they believe to be dead."

"So, you will lie to save your hide while we become the prisoners again?" the other said, closing in on him. "Coward."

Pingas retorted heatedly, "Am I the coward for wanting to stay and fight the demons? Am I a traitor for making a new life for myself when the smoke clears? I have earned freedom just as much as the many warriors of this land. You do, too."

"And your family will suffer for your disloyalty! Is that what you call bravery?" he said, gnashing his teeth. "You had sworn an oath to the council—to Chief Madax himself!"

"Then I break the oath and make a new one." Pingas, in anger, pounded his fist onto the desk and said, "My family is long gone! I *have* no one to worry over! I am sorry if you cannot say the same, but my duty to Tofauti is over. I am free."

Finally, the other warrior clenched his fists and warned starkly, "Then, by the code, you know what we must do with you."

Pingas, guardedly, looked at the other confederate who bore the same threatening demeanor. Their dispositions had turned hostile, even in the stillness of the study. He eyed the lantern that hung by the doorway and then the other right by the corner of the desk. When they sensed he was skimming the small room in advance, the warriors pounced on him.

He seized a bare candlestick and swatted the lantern off the desk, snuffing it out. When the battle ensued, Pingas dashed to one edge of the desk and fought them amid the dimness of a single lamp. In the struggle, they rammed into the bookcase, toppling shelves of books and other items. One of them unsheathed a dagger from his boot and went to stab Pingas in the side. He was able to deflect the blow with the candlestick just enough to bear a small gash in his forearm. Letting out a grunt, he countered with a strike to the jaw and a hard kick to put him into the desk.

The desperate skirmish woke the three other warriors who made their way to the study with daggers drawn, still half-asleep. By the time they all came upon the bloody scene, Pingas finished crushing his former confederate's skull with a telling blow. When it was done, he retracted in pain from a broken finger and eye socket. Blood from the swollen eye had run down his face while he breathed laboriously, having survived his confederates' assault.

In dropping the blood-splattered candlestick at his feet, Pingas leaned on the battered desk and uttered, "I won't—go back—"

Staggered by the gruesome sight, one of the warriors gasped, "What have you done?"

"Survived," he replied, paining to speak. "No more. The quest—is over."

When one of them prepared to rush in and strike him down for his crimes, another held him back, sighing. Amid the tense standoff, the warrior declared, "Enough violence. We have to discuss this as a confederation."

"He killed them!" the other cried.

"I said we have to discuss what happens," the elder of the group proclaimed. "No one sleeps until we come to some agreement—as a unit."

Despite the uncertainty and surge of adrenaline about the men, they sheathed their weapons and agreed to proceed civilly. Having not spoken in weeks, they became something like impulsive soldiers, working on instinct and from a place of reaction. Deciding to finally use their voices to cooperate, harkening back to their free days in Tofauti, the four fighters lowered their guard.

One asked prudently, "So, what do we do now?"

The elder replied, "We return to our living quarters and start with our names and the crimes that made us prisoners in the first place. From there, we'll agree on a plan, opening with what to do with the bodies of these men. Can we settle on that for now?"

Gradually, the warriors nodded, including the injured Pingas in the study. They funneled into the place where most of them had slept with the intention of talking it out. There was much to discuss. Would they judge Pingas for his killing of their fellow confederates? Would they return to Tofauti in disgrace or stay in the West with the Angels of Resistance? If so, what then? Would they live in Falcus? Ellium? How far did their loyalty go? They hashed out their fate in the embers of catastrophe.

Morning in Merrieu, Thomas and the Merrier guard supervised the release of the captors from Pommel. Women and children among them, the freed people walked out of the dungeons and into the barracks where they filled the lasting garrisons. Filled to capacity, the barracks held warriors and civilians affected by the Demon Plague more intimately than others. Some were doctors, politicians, educators and, in many cases, widows.

Grateful that the sibling sovereigns kept their word, the legate greeted them in the plaza. Thomas, accompanied by a few trusted paladins, shook their hands and said, "Shina has been cured, the Mad Legion has scattered and, now, you have ensured that the many innocent Pommelians and Merrier that were saved from that evil bastion will remain safe."

Having shaken his hand last, Lucas said warily, "Well, it is a shame that Miuriell is not among you to see the fruits of his work."

Just then, a guard from the crenellations shouted out, "There! Miuriell has returned! He is approaching the gates!"

"Speak of the devil," Thomas uttered in amazement.

As he headed over to see for himself, Luca scoffed, "Or don't you mean 'demon?' Same thing, I guess."

Hearing her, he stopped in his tracks and turned about, affronted, "Watch your tongue, woman."

"Watch *yours*, ambassador," Lucas countered heatedly. "We heard about your old friend's transformation. Of course, you wouldn't know how we know, but that isn't the point. It is that Miuriell is no longer the—"

Before the sovereign could finish, Thomas had already turned to leave, uninterested in what the young rulers had to say next. The legate left them there as he headed for the gate. The guard came to stop him for his insolence when paladins stepped in. The tense impasse gathered a crowd, causing a stir among the populace. Even Thomas drew his blade, ready to resist arrest if need be. There was no telling what would happen if the siblings became reckless.

Crying out so that they could hear, Thomas hollered, "I thought we had a deal?"

With equal fervor, Lucas shouted back, "And what deal included allowing demons into our walls? Miuriell has become one of those things!"

Luca furthered with a bold roar, "And if he's coming to Merrieu, he's coming for blood."

Then, a loud commotion preceded one of the guards, "Incoming!"

As everyone looked to the skies for whatever had come upon them, Michael floated down like a superior being. His clothing tattered and ragged, electrical energy accompanied him during his descent. When he gently touched the ground, he said, "**I am no demon—and I am not coming for blood.**"

His voice was deeper and with an adjunct of something sinister behind it. Along with his glowing red eyes, Michael's skin had black veins crawling up his neck and arms as if scourged by dark vines. The masses that witnessed the scene gawked in awe, left petrified. Among the gasps from the mob, Michael proceeded, "**Your spy was right when he said that I have transformed. But, make no mistake, I am Michael Miuriell of true Pommel and the destroyer of the Demon Plague. To quench your fears, sovereigns, I have control of the dark power within me.**"

Immediately guarded by a small army of soldiers, Lucas muttered in a daze, "That doesn't exactly quench our fears."

"Spy?" Thomas said. "When was there a spy?"

"**The driver,**" Michael replied. "**And, Thomas, I am so sorry about your men.**"

Sheathing his blade, he said, "It's just good to have you back, Michael. There is news we need to discuss—if you feel up to it."

"That's it? News to discuss, as if everything is fine?" an advisor to the siblings struck out at them. "This man became a monster and you say 'it's good to have you back?'"

"**This monster is on your side.**" Michael retorted with no intentions of backing down or wasting any more time. "**I understand that you are scared. We're all scared, but our next hours together will determine the outcome of this world. You have kept your word and I have kept mine. If the tide of this war is going to turn, then we'll need to plan our next steps carefully. Any misgivings or cricks in our resolve may—**"

Lucas finally spoke out and cut him off, saying crossly, "Yes, yes, we must unite and this, that and the other. Clearly, you *are* the same Miuriell, as different as you may look. You drone on incessantly no matter what you sound like."

"And you can fly now," Luca inserted fretfully.

"**Evidently,**" he said.

The chattering of the awestruck crowd made the dead pause ever more awkward, like a stalled show. With no one knowing what to say next, Thomas stepped in and said, "I'm sure all of us can agree that a conference is in order? A meet to discuss—everything?"

Lucas looked to his sister before sighing, "After an early dinner in the palace. That is where we will discuss all these things."

Jumping off her brother, Luca said sternly, "But you'll have to stay in the barracks until then."

"**I understand,**" Michael replied.

"We have been more than accommodating," Lucas was sure to add.

"**No need to explain, sire. You've done everything I hoped,**" Michael nodded and forced a smile. "**Now, I can see my people—my friends again. Thank you.**"

He then started off for the barracks, knowing Thomas and his paladins would follow closely behind. There was just enough time to greet the many Pommelians that survived so long in the hellish bastion. His heart ached for them. Closer to the barracks, he saw the guards diverting the Merrier from the Pommelians as they left the dungeons. Pommelians had poured into the barracks and were greeted by the Tinarians.

As he approached the entrance, the freed Pommelians started cheering his name. His appearance did not frighten them. They all saw things worse than him. They experienced a terror for the likes that many would never understand. Even the young ones, still trembling and clutching their elders, felt a sudden hope in just seeing him. What better way to defeat a demonic army than to unleash the best one upon them? Their best was still strong enough to conquer his own evils with a heart of good.

Walking through the crowd of grateful Pommelians, he said to Thomas, "**I never thought I'd be reunited with any of them again. Perhaps they thought they'd never see the light of freedom again? Hope, alone, cannot be our only path to salvation. You have to walk through the dark and turn on the light yourself.**"

A Tinarian knight spat out the coffee from his mouth at the sight of him. While it was purely impulsive for some still to cower at his ever-changing countenance tipping evermore to the darkness, they trusted that Michael was still the man of promise. As the accursed leader to the Angels of Resistance, he revealed that his true strength lied in his ability to take what was meant for evil and use it for good.

"**Thomas, I fear that this meet will be our last. The siblings will not let our forces remain here for any longer than tomorrow,**" he said, making his way to the medical ward. "**I know it hasn't been easy for you, having to take over while I am gone. But you've done well.**"

Thomas stopped Michael before they came any closer to the hospital, saying quietly, "In confidence, there are some critical matters that you need to attend to before we focus on that meet. Yet, first, don't you think you should eat something before you walk into that hospital? You must be famished."

Seemingly disregarding his concerns, Michael asked in a serious tone, "**What of Antonis? Is he—**"

Groaning, the legate shook his head and responded, "He's dead. I haven't seen the Tofauti guards since. That could be a problem."

"**I feared that.**" Michael closed his eyes and bowed his head in grief, feeling some guilt for the prophet's death. Many people started to encircle them as they talked in front of the medical ward, trying to steal a better look at him. Wanting to check on Shina and his friends, Michael embraced Thomas by the shoulder and started for the hospital. More than food, he craved for the interaction. In battling for his very humanity in the solitude of the dark, he came to understand the reviving power of comradeship.

Shina woke up to a blurry group of people coming into view over her. Dreading their figures first, the princess came to remember that she was no longer a slave to the demons. It was strange. She felt the warmth of the sheets and the soft, gentle protection of her bed. Maxim came closer and held her hand as she adjusted to the light. The sun's rays illuminated her room and kissed her skin. She had almost forgotten the feeling of the daylight, having been scorched by it only days before. Maxim caressed her damp red hair.

After seeing him, she turned to her left side and found Michael in the doorway. There seemed to be an army outside in the corridor, but he came in and Predella shut the door behind him. Just the four of them in the hospital room, Shina started to cry. There was a time when she believed she was too far gone to be saved. Yet, she was herself again in the company of those she trusted most. It was overwhelming.

When Michael came to greet her, she looked over his new features and sobbed, "I'm sorry. Oh, God!"

Michael sat beside her and said softly so as not to alarm her with his voice, "**No, princess. There is nothing that you should be sorry for.** *I* **am sorry that you had to suffer the way you did. But you survived. The real you survived.**"

Looking into his red eyes, she controlled her weeping and asked seriously, beset with guilt, "How many did I—who did I—"

"**That wasn't you, princess,**" Michael whispered. "**You will have to remember that you weren't in control.**"

"But I *do* remember it," she said with shame, her voice cracking. "It was like I was peering through the looking glass of someone else's life like I was in a prison somehow. It was cold—so cold that I was shivering, but it burned, too. In that terrible place, I saw what I did, but can't remember if I did all of it or if some of it was just visions—nightmares. But then, I saw you. You're the last memory I had in that prison—that prison inside myself. And now look at what's happened to you."

"**That was my fate,**" Michael said, "**not yours. You are free from their grasp.**"

"But not from my sins," she closed her tired eyes, moist from escaping tears. "I'll never be free from that. The damage has been done."

Empathizing with her grief, he took a deep breath and replied, "**You can't blame yourself for not being strong enough to withstand what they did to you. You are just as much a victim as those you've harmed. The thing is that you can make a lasting difference now. You can find a way to make this world better. But, first, you must try to rest. Understand?**"

Shina wiped her eyes and whispered, "I'll try."

When the Demon Plague invaded Tinaria, her life had changed forever. They mercilessly hunted her since the first night and then inculcated the demonic spirit within once she was in their grasp. Taken far from her loved ones, Shina fell victim to their terrifying power, alone and in distress. There was no way for her to go back and reawaken the girl inside. She was gone. Having finally lost her brother to the Demon Plague, Shina needed to find a way to reinvent herself in her new world.

Maxim told her that she would have to try to keep food down for breakfast and she nodded. She had thrown up all of her meals the night before, suffering from nausea and fever. In kissing her forehead, Michael said softly to her, "**You'll be alright very soon, princess. I promise.**"

When he said it, Shina put her hand upon his face and looked intently into his eyes. Seeing through his malevolent countenance, she said passionately, "Thank you. Thank you for what you did to save me."

Clasping her hand on his face compassionately, Michael replied, "**Of course, Your Majesty. You're welcome.**"

When he gently pulled himself away, Michael voiced his plan to check in on Shioda and Lai. Shina told him to tend to them, having heard earlier of their conditions. As he took his leave, promising to return, Predella leaped up and told him, "I think I should come with you for that."

Looking to Maxim after she said it, Predella waited for confirmation that he would be alright with her on his own. He nodded and watched them both open the door to the loud corridor to leave. Once they were gone, Shina suddenly asked Maxim to come closer. Always faithful to his princess, Maxim leaned in. Unexpectedly, she met him halfway and began to kiss him on his mouth passionately. She put her arm around his neck to pull him in closer, feverishly kissing him harder. He broke away from her lips, leaving the princess to gasp like a fish out of water.

Shocked by her impulsive action, Maxim stammered, "Your Majesty, I—"

"Sorry. I couldn't help myself," Shina said, catching her breath. "I just always wanted to do that. Couldn't do it with Predella in the room. It's been burning up inside me."

Rubbing his neck nervously, he said, "Jesus, I can tell."

"I know that something's happening between you and Predella," she admitted with a sigh. "You can see it in the way she looks at you—and the way you look at her. Figured I had to take the chance on you before you're officially taken."

"Is it that obvious?" he replied, smiling coyly.

"I get it, though. You're both warriors. You're both hot," Shina pronounced with her eyes closed. "Do you love her?"

Not prepared for the conversation, Maxim uttered, "I'm not actually sure if we're that far yet. But, on the battlefield, I think she told me that she—well, it was a bad scrap and all of us were just trying to—"

"She said it?" Shina opened her eyes in shock, but then reared back her enthusiasm when she realized how far she reached into his personal life. She then put her hand over her face and laughed at herself, "Look at me behaving like some middle-aged gossip monger. Forgive me, Maxim."

"It's alright, princess," he said light-heartedly. "We all have been a bit on edge after the escape from Pommel. It's a miracle any of us got out of there alive."

After a brief pause, Shina remembered her ill-fated sibling. Knowing that she was opening herself up to sorrow, she solemnly asked, "Did you see my brother? Was he there when you escaped? Tell me the truth."

He knew he would have to deal with her brother's fate one way or another, facing the princess with the sordid news. Reminiscing the fateful episode, Maxim glared forward and replayed the scene out loud, "When Michael came back for us in that nightmare fortress, we got held up by a demon magus. Your brother stepped in and fought him off so we could run. In our escape, there was a massive explosion—"

"Did he die?" she asked fretfully, dreading the answer.

As gently as he could say it, Maxim replied with some hesitation, "I believe so. I'm sorry."

Shina then exhaled, partly relieved that his end was an atonement for his dark path, but also that he was gone. Eric was her older brother who loved her unconditionally, despite his torments of the soul. His love for her was such that he put her in the enemy's dungeon in the hopes of sparing her life. A lack of faith and reason opened his heart to evil as a way to heal his twisted mind.

Flashes from their youth, when times were simpler and innocent, pushed her to surrender to her emotions. She remembered him as that little boy, looking for his father's approval, but serving as a guiding light for a small princess. Fighting back more tears, Shina only moaned, "He saved his soul by sacrifice—I pray, oh God. Have mercy on him, Lord."

Sympathetic to her loss, Maxim stroked her hair again. Though driven to provide his princess with compassion in her most difficult time, Maxim couldn't help but think of the prophet's last words to him. Before Antonis died, he rasped one final prophecy. *You have to die to win.* His words brought him some worry. If he had to make the ultimate sacrifice in the battle to come, he would do it proudly. If that's what the prophet meant. Maxim couldn't make sense of it.

Feeling saddened, he held her hand for comfort.

Shioda slept through the morning, still patched up and with virtually no memory of who he was or what Lana meant to his life. She slept by him, her head resting on his chest. It did her well to pretend that he remembered her. The smell of the room became second nature—a natural scent for the new place she called home. Lai, however, sat upright and conversed with a medic. His wound, though yet infected, had shown some improvement. Upon seeing Michael at the doorway, he smiled.

Saying softly so as not to wake Lana, Lai said with glee, "Michael, thank God you're alright. I hadn't seen you since—"

With Lai unable to recount the horrors of the escape, Michael nodded with understanding, "**I know, old friend. Pardon what you see. My appearance—**"

"None of that matters, now. It's your heart we all count on, not your features—everchanging," Lai replied with a fast spike of pain coming from his bandaged side.

Michael then noticed his doctor. The medic had been looking at him intently since he came. At last, Michael knew who he was, recognizing his face. Had it been so long?

"**Doctor? Doctor Libe?**" he gasped. "**It's you, isn't it?**"

The old family physician met Michael in the doorway and embraced. Thomas and Predella watched as they both sobbed in each other's arms. Their regard for one another brought a flood of memories and deeds they never imagined would have returned in such a dire time. Lai understood that his new doctor was Pommelian, but never expected him to be so personally admired by Michael himself.

Taking a better look at him, Michael asked, wiping any remaining tears from his eyes, "**How did you get here?**"

"You saved us, boy. You saved *me* from that hell," the doctor said gratefully.

"**But here. How did you—**"

"The guards were looking for medics in the dungeons. I offered my services, so, yesterday, they released me and here I came," he said, glancing over at Lai in bed. "I've had the true pleasure of working with Master Kai and Shioda Shokan."

"Master Lai is my father. Call me, Lai," he pled.

Turning to Predella close by, Michael told her, "**Doctor Libe was our family doctor. He delivered Seth. We were very close.**"

Predella beamed with wonder, "You never told me any of that, doctor."

"And, for that, I trust you'll forgive me, dear," he said, then gazing back into Michael's sinister eyes. He saw deeper into the soul, passed the color and mysterious aura inside the iris. He grasped Michael's shoulder and declared faintly, "You are still in there, boy. Everything I saw in you then, I see even now—just brighter. Your spirit is so great. No matter the push from the dark side, the strength I see in your eyes will always be enough to push back."

Solemn, Michael didn't want to ask if he lost anyone. It would only have brought more pain. As the doctor examined him through his eyes, Michael saw the grief in his. Such hard talks were better suited in private. Instead, he asked, "**How are they doing, doctor? Predella tells me that Shioda has some amnesia, among other things.**"

Placing focus back on his renowned patients, Libe had escorted Michael into the room and whispered gently, "This man has a long road to recovery, but he will live. But, again, his fighting days are over. It's too early to tell how disabled he'll be, but Shioda will live to see the birth of his child."

"I'll see to that myself," Lai added from across the way. "My sister will not be alone in the challenges ahead."

"Lower your voice, you stubborn fool," Lana whispered from Shioda's chest. She was awake after hearing her brother insist on pleasantries with the doctor. Finally, she arose.

Michael came in to hug her and she obliged, unable to control her crying. She let out her grief and frustration in his chest, though as quiet as she could to avoid waking Shioda. He let her cry, squeezing her tight so she felt his embrace. In stroking her hair, soaked by her stress, he said to her, "**Lana, I am here for you. Whatever you need, you can count on me to get it for you. You may worry about him, but Shioda is going to remember. He'll remember again.**"

Lana said nothing in return. Yet, when he was about to separate from her, she whined, "I'm sorry for your son."

Looking down in her wetted eyes, "**Me too.**"

She looked to Predella and then to Michael again, "You know my request, right? You know that I will be on that field again if we fight once more."

Sighing, Michael replied, "**Yes, I know that's what you want.**"

Clenching onto his arms, she said fanatically, "And you will not try to stop me?"

"**Of course, I must try, Lana,**" Michael said. "**You want to avenge your husband and your brother and everyone else who gave their all on that unholy ground. If I wanted it, I could place you there. But you know I won't. For the sake of that unborn child, I won't do it.**"

Having feared that very response, she buried her head in his chest again, brokenhearted. Michael felt her pain when he continued, "**As a husband who has mourned his wife, as a father who now mourns his son, and as a man who has lost many periods of sleep over his people, I pray that you find it in your heart to forgive me. Because, if you** fought and died on that battleground, bearing child, how could I forgive myself?

"On the other hand, you deserve your vengeance, as we all do, I think. Later, this afternoon, there will be a conference. Every leader here in Merrieu will attend. I'd like you, Lana, to represent the Kai and the Shokan. Your voice is welcome. Together, we will discuss the designs that may bring the largest armed force down upon Pommel—ever. There are other ways to contribute to that end. Can we expect to see you there?"

The room fell silent waiting to hear Lana's response. In her angst, she slowly drifted over to her husband's bed. As if in a daze, she stood over him and held his still hand. Lai was first to say something, asking from his bed, "Girl, are you—"

"I'll be there," Lana proclaimed boldly. "And I *will* be at Shadowland's edge, like before. There will be a Kai witness of this final battle. If you won't give me at least that, then you'll need to put me in chains, so help me God."

"**Alright, Lana.**" Michael conceded, stretching out his hand to her. "**Let's go and get you cleaned up. Then, we'll have a bite to eat. Okay?**"

Lana then hunched over, feeling that some weight had been lifted, and kissed Shioda on the mouth. Vindicated, she walked back to Michael and took his hand offered. She put it to her face and whimpered, "I'm so tired, Michael, but I can't go to sleep. I'm always afraid to sleep."

Understanding her plight, he led her out of the room by the hand, "**Come with me.**"

Michael escorted Lana out into Thomas's care when Shioda started to moan. Predella looked on when Doctor Libe tended to him. She heard Shioda ask sluggishly, "That voice. Who was that?"

Libe slowly opened the curtains to allow some light to enter the room. Hearing Shioda utter something incoherent,

Libe said, "Don't fret, Master Shioda. Lana will return soon. I will have some breakfast sent for you if you like. Then, we'll take another look at how you're doing."

Shioda turned his head to see the blurry figure in the doorway. While it pained him to do so, he, with but one eye to work with, soaked in the mystical visitor. He wondered from where he had come. Was he another one of his 'friends,' as Lana had referred many times? Groaning, he tried to listen to him speak to the others inside the room, but his swirling headache and bandaged right ear just muffled the voices.

Returning his head to the center, staring at the ceiling, he closed his eyes and tried again. He fought to remember. A burst of memories flashing by, inconsistent and without any reason, besieged his mind. Still, some reoccurring moments played amid the gales, helping him to focus. He tried holding on to them, chasing the memories through the confusion. As a young woman, too fuzzy to recognize, tried pulling him out from a chilling melee, a voice called to him. *Now, let's go. Your heroics won't end here. You've got more insane things to prove, I'm sure.*

Shioda, after analyzing it deeply, realized that it was his voice. He couldn't tell if it was a memory or a dream, but his eyes welled up with tears. Quickly, he turned his head to see if the mysterious visitor was still there, but he was gone. In a way, he felt that the character awoke something deep inside. The man's unnatural voice, somehow, roused his own from the inner recesses of his cloudy mind. His soul cried out.

PART II
CHAPTER XIV
THE ATONEMENT

For the majority of the day, Merrieu and its guardians worked to organize a recovery plan for the freed captives. A great many of them were Pommelian, while Merriers made up the rest. Some families were reunited, though others were fractured by the news of lost or slain members. Resources were finite, as the sibling sovereigns had feared, and strict rules prevented medical staff from applying their potential on the patients that were deeply in need.

Aside from the big number of captives suffering from malnutrition, everyone appeared to have been in a state of shock. The horror that the people experienced would never leave them, like a parasite of the mind. They dreaded night, knowing full well that Merrieu was not far enough from the watch of Pommel. Yet, in truth, there would be no place of refuge far enough to break them from the trauma of what they experienced there.

After Shina told Maxim to go out and breathe some fresh air, he walked about the barracks to clear his head. A few minutes into it, he stumbled upon the Ziamon camp. Their morale appeared low, for the lot of the army was quiet. No songs or garish jokes, no war chants or drills. He had never seen them like that before, even in his past experiences fighting them. Maxim gathered a team of Tinarian knights and went to visit his fellow Eastern warriors, a move many of his men did not openly support.

He headed into the Ziamon sector of the encampment with the intentions of speaking with Esker, the acting colonel after Aramis was killed. The soldiers glared at them as they came through. Maxim led the unarmed knights through the scrutinizing horde until Esker came to meet them with some guards of his own. Unlike his Tinarian counterpart, he was fully armed.

Meeting him in the center of the camp, Esker shook his head and said lazily, "Well, this is a surprise. What the hell do you want, Red Menace?"

Permitting the slight, Maxim replied, "Look, I'll keep it brief. We're having a meet with the siblings about what our next steps are gonna be here and the final push on Pommel in a few hours. If nobody told you, I'm telling you. I'll expect to see you at the palace if that's what you want."

He had planned out what to say and how to say it when he was walking up to the camp, but Maxim couldn't recall any of it. After delivering the message a Merrier courier already gave an hour before, he started to leave. Before he could turn completely around, Esker called out to him, "Hey, I asked you a question."

Maxim stopped and looked back at him, his knights in a defensive stance with just daggers in their auxiliary sheaths. Esker came closer and asked more intently, "So, what the hell are *you* doing here?"

As the warriors of different sides watched each other vigilantly, Maxim answered back, "It's been a while since the escape from Pommel and, well, even with our differences, it's imperative that we stay in communication. We don't have to like each other, but we have to work as a unit. Now, I know a great deal about what happened to your divisions. Your units lost the most out of any other, so if you don't feel—"

"For shit's sake, stop talking," Esker hissed, walking up to Maxim's space. "I don't know if it's because your princess is back or you're smitten by that Waasi, but something kicked you real good in the balls to make you limp over here looking for a hug. You think because we fought side-by-side to get out of that shithole alive, it makes us friends? Get this right, Red Menace. We don't need your pity. For the time being, we just need your sword. And once that Demon Plague, or whatever you like to call it, is sent back to hell where it belongs, we'll have nothing to do with each other ever again. Hear me?"

Relieved that his rival opened it up, Maxim came even closer, saying unflinchingly, "Don't misunderstand me, desert dog. I don't give a damn about you or any of those fanatics behind you. I want to win this war and that means we have to work as a unit, whether we like it or not. If we lose this fight, it's all over and we can take our differences and bury them all in the bloody trenches along with our bodies. I just want to make sure your heads are still in the game."

"If you have to ask, then you don't really know a thing about us Ziamons. We're here until the end—until the very last man, if need be," Esker countered. "So, why don't you go and worry about yourself, or does the princess have to give permission for that?"

"Listen, Esker, you don't get what's going on here," he fired back heatedly. "Ellium wants us to be ready in just a few days for a one-shot chance at finishing off Pommel. That isn't going to work in our favor if it's just the forces we have now. Our meeting later could just end up being an advanced notice of eviction from Merrieu and then we're royally screwed anyhow."

Gnashing his teeth at the absurdity of Ellium's request, Esker finally lowered his guard, saying, "Those ignorant nobs think they're runnin' the show after everything we did? After all the blood we spilled and shed?"

"That's my point," Maxim said.

"Where did you get this information?" Esker asked with a sense of suspicion.

"Thomas Excallum is the ambassador to Ellium for the holy city," he replied. "That's why we're having this meet. We need to come up with a plan—together. If you're still willing to bring your men into the valley of death, I'd assume you—"

Esker started leaving the conversation before Maxim could finish, saying as he went, "I will attend the meet."

The Ziamons then followed after their colonel, ending the exchange there. Maxim turned and left, muttering to his fellow knights, "Yeah, you too, you Ziamon bastard."

They laughed, at least, to his jests of exasperation, but Maxim smirked at achieving his lesser goal. He felt that their despairing escape from Pommel's Shadowland revealed the prospect of a greater alliance. Despite Esker's hard demeanor face-to-face, Maxim found an opening to lobby for a mutual objective on the battlefield. If they were going to be victors against the Demon Plague, he knew that they would have to fight as one. As Michael urged a time ago, "A greater evil has come calling on us, so we need to wake up and join hands in resistance."

Maxim joined Michael and Predella in the courtyard for some lunch at the gathering tables. He updated them on what little progress he made with the Ziamons in the hope of unity on the battlefield. With the crowds of bystanders encircling them, Maxim was sure to keep his details discreet and brief. Serving as an open mess hall of sorts, the courtyard was free for all to eat a single serving. Rations were scarce, so tickets were distributed to each member of the army, including the newly freed Pommelians.

As they chatted before the big meet, Tinarians came up to the wooden tables with news that four Tofauti guardians had come for an audience with Michael. He looked over their armored shoulders to see the Eastern warriors waiting for his reply. Intrigued, Michael permitted them to come join his small party. The Tinarian guards waved them in.

All four of the Tofauti warriors came forth, unarmed. No one in the army had ever engaged with them since the prophet had breathed his last. Michael had borne a sense of guilt over Antonis's death, blaming himself for inviting him to Fort Andrews. He felt, at least, he could provide for the six Tofauti guardians who were cast into the wind thereafter.

When they came to the table, Michael greeted them and asked if they would like to sit. Graysonel, the elder and self-proclaimed leader of the group, stunned the small party by answering, "We'd rather stand if it's all the same to you."

Hearing his voice for the first time, Predella gasped, "So you can speak now, all of you?"

"Our mission is over with regretful results," Graysonel replied humbly.

Michael nodded with respect, "**Yes. I am very sorry.**"

"That is why we are here," he proceeded to speak for the group. "After discussing it, we have chosen to stay here and fight under you for the cause. Returning home would not bring us honor. It would mean a great deal if we could join your ranks for the remainder of this war."

"**The choice is yours,**" Michael quickly replied. "**You are all one of us if you choose to be. God knows we could use as many able-bodied warriors as we can muster.**"

Maxim then added, turning in his seat to face them, "I am assembling a combined force of Eastern warriors if you are interested. That includes Tinarians, Ziamons, a handful of Tofauti—and one Waasi. It's fitting that we battle as a unified force. It would be the first time that ever happened."

"And all of us would represent home," Predella said. "A united front."

Seeking the approval of his fellow warriors, Graysonel answered for them again, "We like that idea."

"**Then it's settled. That was easy,**" Michael beamed, feeling lighter than the Tofauti found purpose in his company.

With the warriors officially joining forces, Maxim went with a few soldiers who had already eaten to pick up some mess tickets so that the Tofauti could eat right away. Though Maxim had left, Predella remained and offered that they join her at the table. The four agreed to sit, grateful for the invite. Upon getting a closer look at Pingas, still wounded from the battle to the death the night before, Michael had to ask, "**We should assume that the rest of your brethren won't be joining us?**"

While Pingas refused to answer, Kulind, one of the four, replied in his stead, "They will not be joining us for the rest of the mission."

Understanding that hostilities must have ensued over the fate of the six, Michael held his tongue. It wasn't his place to challenge the tenets of their culture at such time. Predella, on the other hand, was familiar with Tofauti Honor Quests. She knew that the missing warriors were either dead or on the run. In an effort to change the subject, Graysonel looked to her and said, "It is said that you rescued many Waasi from their bondage of slavery in Ziamon. It is said that you did this while the demons attacked. Is such a thing possible?"

Thinking back on the horrors of their escape, Predella said, "Well, it was possible. It happened. At the time, none of us really thought about the odds—only survival. I suppose anything is possible once you have made up your mind about it."

Pingas, then, fought through his pain to ask her, "Then, I have to ask. Is it possible to defeat the demons?"

His concern was evident. He fought through the pains of his raw injuries to ask directly. Predella replied, "We already struck a major blow to the Demon Plague. As long as we have Michael, we can finish—"

The booming horns of the crenellations had suddenly sounded, putting their early discussion on hold. There was a problem at the gates. Again, Michael reached for a staff that wasn't there as a force of habit. He rose from the bench and began walking towards Merrieu's main gate, saying out into the air, "**Something's coming.**"

Predella joined him standing and asked nervously, "The Mad Legion again?"

"**I guess we'll see,**" he said, then taking flight. Predella had not seen his newfound power and he was not shy using it whenever necessary. The Tofauti followed her in gawking up at him as he soared effortlessly over the city. As citizens and soldiers alike stared, Michael hovered above the populace to observe the threat for himself. A massive caravan had come from the north with a long wagon train and flags of different townships. By the looks of it, there was no army, but a large band of peoples.

Michael settled on the ramparts, startling the soldiers there, and asked, "**I assume we're not expecting company today?**"

"No, sir!" one of them answered frantically.

"**Give word to the guard. I'm going to intercept the caravan before they get here. Better send some back-up, just in case,**" Michael said before drifting off again, leaving Merrieu behind. He glided down to meet the migrating party at its head. As he neared closer, landing gracefully like a god, the caravan halted its march. They all looked on him in awe of his power. Of all the stories they heard of Miuriell, none had ever included his ability to fly. To him, it seemed like a gift he had all his life. Nothing surprised him anymore. Even attaining a transcendent skill such as flight only reminded him of his ties to Abaddon. It felt habitual.

A few miles away from Merrieu's watch, Michael made his way on foot to the party's front line. As intimidating as he appeared, the assumed leader of the caravan did not show fear. He lifted his arm and stopped the march, hiding a smile behind his beard. When Michael approached him, realizing that there was no threat, a familiar feeling came over him. He had seen his face somewhere before.

Deciding that the caravan was consisting of vagabonds, Michael came closer to the leader and thought out loud, "**You are someone I've met once. But where?**"

With the multitudes of migrants looking on as if there was a celebrity in their midst, the bearded man removed his hood and replied, "Miuriell, you saved me back in Falcus. In saving me, you saved all of them, as well."

"**Falcus?**" Michael then started to remember. "**You are the man I cured of—**"

"The madness, yes!" he said with elation. "I was just a slave to the Mad Legion when you cured me. You told me to go and cure others like me—and I did. All this time, I've gone to towns and villages all over the realm and repeated those words you told me. Many of these people have you to thank for their freedom. So, we came here to pay our gratitude on our way to Ellium."

"**You came here for me? All of you?**" Michael said in shock as he looked over the masses. "**How did you know?**"

The caravan took a respite from the march when the man said, "'Michael Miuriell releases you from the binds of conquest. You are now free.' Those are the words that have set so many minds free. People said that your army traveled to Merrieu, which proved true, after all. We have wagons of donated food for your forces—plenty of rations that can help in some way, we hope."

"Rations of food? You all may have saved us more than you know," Michael said with appreciation, stunned by the caravan's generosity.

Another man added, "We just want to give back. You're all fighting the forces of darkness. We just wanted to help."

"And you did. We are in need of provisions," he said. **"If you give me some time, I might be able to negotiate asylum for a portion of travelers in your band."**

"No need for that, sir," the man answered promptly. "I am leading this caravan to Ellium in the hopes of a better life. Some of us have family there. It's a shot we have to take."

"Then, I suggest you keep as far west as you can. A major battle could break out in the next three days and your people could get caught in the crossfire. Ellium will be sending a substantial force," Michael warned.

"So, they may be reluctant to grant asylum," the man deduced aloud. "We thought of that."

Sounds of the Merrieu cavalry reached his ear when he took a longer glance at the caravan. There were families and lone refugees, veterans and merchants, farmers and smiths. There were flags from Shopville, Agora, Sadiq, and Inwood. A caravan of freedom seekers and freedom fighters. Directing his attention to the leader of the convoy, he asked of him in wonder, **"I never got your name."**

With the cavalry in sight, the man answered, "Frederick is my name, sir, and I am at your service."

Shaking his hand in gratitude, Michael replied, **"Your generosity as a group may tip the scales in our favor."**

By the time the cavalry caught up to him, Michael was already in the process of receiving donations of food. The soldiers couldn't comprehend such unconditional charity. It initially made them suspect some sort of poisoning plot, but the idea was deflated when Michael stepped in. He vowed to use the provisions for the Angels of Resistance and masses in the hospitals still recovering from their captivity in Pommel.

The caravan camped outside Merrieu's authority and worked together to make an organized pile of provisions for the soldiers to carry in later. Michael thanked each and every migrant that contributed to the cause as they came to offer something. Under the watchful eyes of the cavalry division, Frederick's band of free peoples gave their donations. The pile quickly evolved into a mound, convincing Michael that such a bounty of resources could have a positive influence on the meet. It was that more possible to extend their stay, only to ensure that the sick and wounded had time to heal.

Among the contributors, a hooded man came nearer to Michael and said to him, "Good afternoon, 'savior.' You look as terrifying as ever."

Not expecting the brash man to speak to him with such a familiar voice and out of the blue, Michael studied his face. When he lifted his head to look Michael in the eye, it became clear. The left side of his face was scourged a charcoal gray just barely concealed by wisps of his long white hair. Finally recognizing him, Michael gasped, "**Eric?**"

Offering a solemn smirk, the exiled prince replied, "It's obvious you're not hiding your malevolent gifts anymore. If anything, you've embraced them."

To avoid the leering eyes of the soldiers, Michael took the sorcerer by the arm and moved him away. He whispered to him when they were a fair distance from the cavalrymen, "**I thought you were dead.**"

"And now you know something the Demon Plague does not," Eric said slyly. "The bout with Valkris almost did me in, if that's what you're wondering."

"**If your intentions are to manipulate these people, then I—**" Michael spoke from his gut when Eric interceded.

"I'm here for no other reason but my sister," he said in desperation. "There was no turning back when I betrayed the Demon Plague. She is all I have left. I came simply to ask if my sister is alright—if she's safe."

"**No thanks to you,**" he griped. "**How many more people died due to your treachery? I lost my only son in that mission. I may lose even myself after tearing the evil spirit out from Shina's body.**"

"I came to my senses too late, I admit. There is still time for me to do some good—behind the scenes," Eric appealed.

Overwhelmed by his neglect to fathom the weight of his actions, Michael countered furiously, "**Have you that far separated yourself from reality? Do you really think you can just crawl back to us after all the harm you've done?**"

"I came for atonement," Eric declared anxiously. "For what it's worth, I've come to terms with my sins. As you must know, there is still a great deal of magic just burning inside of me, waiting to be used. For my penance, let me prove that I can help destroy them. After that, I'll surrender. I'll promise to turn myself into whoever. But, at least, give me a chance to be a human being before the end."

"**That may not be left to me anymore, Eric.**"

"You know that you and I alone can take down Pommel if we really wanted. Our powers combined—" Eric said in an attempt to convince Michael to go rogue along with him.

"**You know I won't,**" he countered. "**I'm on the verge of losing control if I'm not careful. The Demon Lord will try to coax me out. He wants me to return to Pommel. He can feel it just as much as I can. Abaddon is just beneath my skin.**"

"Oh yeah? Well, they're in my *head!*" he cried out. "I'm still having visions—nightmares at random! I'll do any damn thing to make it stop, even if I have to take them down on my own. I'll burn the whole thing down. You can accept your fate or become prey to it. You can't stop me from stopping them if you won't do it."

"**Don't be stupid. All of a sudden, you're fighting a holy war against them? This is *our* fight. You are just too late. Too many of us have died—and more will if we do not plan this final attack rightly,**" Michael thought out loud. "**Unless you can teleport our army in its entirety to Falcus and back to Pommel within one day, you really cannot be of any use to us. I'm sorry, Eric. But—**"

"I can do that," the sorcerer declared. "If I can teleport the Mad Legion into the Ghost Forest, I can do the same for the lot of you. You need only say the word."

After hearing it, a new enterprise swelled into his mind. Eric's sorcery could be a necessary evil to solving their issues with Ellium's war timetable. To gather with the Falcun army, then appearing at Pommel's gates moments later, ready for a final scrap, was the dream scenario. Michael was not willing to sacrifice that advantage.

Changing his mind, Michael said, "**No tricks. No more lies. If you can do this—**"

"I can do it," Eric answered with resolve. "I am, by far, the most powerful piece on the board. There isn't much I am not able to do—especially now."

Thinking it over, Michael stroked his bearded chin and said, "**Where will you be?**"

"There was some old castle by the creek up north. That's where I am right now, actually. If, of course, we have a pact, you can come by and see me," he answered, revealing that he was but a magical copy—a temporary clone.

"**If you mean what you say, then, perhaps. Meeting with you in the night is out of the question. They watch me very carefully in the dark. They'd see you,**" he replied. "**Although, I see you already take precautions.**"

"You don't think I'd actually travel with this rabble, do you?" Eric scoffed, then casting his gaze to the horizon where Maxim, Predella and the Tofauti traveled on horseback.

Two Merrier soldiers came up behind Michael to advise him that a small group of his allies approached. When he had turned to see them come, he found that Eric had vanished. It seemed that only he was capable of seeing him at all. The two soldiers didn't notice the exiled prince or anyone that was talking with Michael. He then returned to the caravan where he introduced his friends to Frederick and his convoy of free peoples. All the while, Michael kept his mystical exchange with Eric to himself.

In Pommel, when the demons were set to sleep, Kane followed the sounds of Sattka's groaning through the dark of the dungeons. He tracked her angry moans to the furnace room where he snuck up on her having sexual intercourse with a human. He watched as she rode him naked, grinding upon him with thirst and carnal rage. The man cried from the pain and terror of her vessel, as also her razor claws digging deep into his chest. Finally, at her climax, she snapped his neck and separated his head from the spine.

When she crawled off of her prey, she tossed him into the wild furnace where her other toys of men burned away. It was then that she noticed Kane peeping on her from the open doorway and turned to see him there. Totally nude in all her scales and feminine attributes, Sattka grinned and asked, "**Do you want a taste, or just want to watch?**"

On guard, he muttered, "**No thanks.**"

"**Just curious, then?**" Sattka said, nearing closer. "**Or are you bored?**"

"I thought you things were asleep during this time, or are *you* the one just bored?" Kane answered, trying to hide his angst with bravado.

Sattka looked over the three remaining prisoners left to endure her torture in chains and answered, "**Since Miuriell stole our sacrifices, there is a lack of fresh blood for us to bathe in. That is how we sleep. Yet, because his unique army of human scum killed most of our generals, we may ration that blood for when we really need it—like before they return to try and finish the job. Those pests.**"

"**Well, I hate to spoil your fun, but—**" Kane was about to relay his message when Sattka finished his words.

"**Father is looking for me,**" she said, expecting him to grant her with Valkris's authority now that there was a void. The males in bondage huddled in the corner of the room, had shuddered in fear with the hopes that she would leave them be. She leaned her back against the doorframe and stared at them in lust for more.

Sattka proceeded, "**Do you know how many times I could have killed Miuriell in his sleep—how many times I had the chance to gut him? I alone could have ended all this, countless times. But father—he'd never allow me to do it. His unwavering conviction in Abaddon's coming is still stronger than ever. His version of conquest is askew, to say the utter least. What do you say about this?**"

"**Nothing. I know my place,**" Kane countered, then in a wary tone, said, "**and I know when to keep my trap shut.**"

She then smirked and caressed the side of his face with her blood-sodden hand, "**What a devoted little thrall. Tell him I'll be up after I've had my last fix.**"

Sattka then went to seize another victim for her desires of the flesh. It served as a welcome replacement for her lack of sleep. Kane, repulsed by her unending hunger, called out as he started walking away, "**You can tell him yourself.**"

The appalling sounds of her raping another young man to death on a cold slab table resounded throughout the dank dungeon, barren of ill-fated prisoners. The madness attracted droves of hapless people from all over. Some became newly instated members of the legion of human combatants, but a slew of others were more suited for fodder.

The siblings permitted the trove of donations from the free people's caravan but requested that it be confined to the barracks. Merrieu would not share in the provisions in some fear that the bounty was poisoned or tainted. Such was the attitude of the sovereignty before the meet. The main leaders to the Angels of Resistance gathered in a conference chamber and took seats about the table decked with picking food.

Each of them nervously waited for the siblings to arrive so that the meet could begin. Two head chairs at one end of the rectangular table were prepared by their consultants as the group settled in. The other end was without seats, hinting that the sibling sovereigns were the only authority. Michael sat closest to the corner with Lana, Predella, and Maxim on the west side. Thomas sat across from Michael on the east side with Esker as his only company.

Merrier agents lined the walls and watched the group vigilantly. Esker returned each of their gazes with a stone-faced glare. Lana was no longer anxious, but indomitable as a force seeking retribution. It would take more than a generic psychological tactic to intimidate her. Thomas, on the other hand, felt that he had the burden of holding the spirit of the army together with this single meet. He, like the others, could not have known that Michael had a magical insurance plan in the event that the conference broke down.

Before the sibling sovereigns came in, Michael cut into the onerous silence, saying, "**No matter what happens, everything is going to be alright. If they suggest we leave this place, just follow my lead.**"

"Fair enough," Maxim answered. "But, to be square, I'd rather walk. These people have been pushing us closer to the exits since we came here."

Lana interposed at once, "But I'm not leaving without my husband or Lai and they aren't ready to be moved the way they are now. They'll have to get through me to do it."

"It won't get to that point," Predella assured her.

Yet, Thomas interposed regretfully, "But it may."

"What about all the rations those radicals brought? I mean, isn't that what they were bitching about in the first place—rations?" Esker rumbled, voicing his grievances more aggressively since Aramis had died.

Thomas humored him, saying, "Merrieu has endured a long bout of political corruption, spanning generations. So, in a way, these young rulers feel they have an obligation to cure the cancers deep within the fabric of the Merrier landscape. They're pushing hard against anything that may limit their ability to run the ship the way they deem appropriate. I guess in this case, we're the aggrieving factors."

Maxim countered irately, "When we came here, I can remember the sea of the afflicted—the Merrier stricken with the madness. If not for Michael curing them, those two kids would be swimming in aggrieving factors. So, I think we can agree that it's all a bunch of bullshit."

"**Let's keep in mind that we're not alone here. These agents are the eyes and ears of the sovereigns**," Michael interceded. "**We should be grateful they allowed us into their walls for all this time.**"

Shortly after Michael finished, elite guards entered the elaborate room by the double doors and permitted the chief advisor through. He came in to announce that the royals had arrived for their summit, inducing everyone to stand as they entered. Lucas and Luca marched through, followed by a unit of councilors for war, infrastructure, defense, agriculture, and others. In moments, the conference hall had seemed cramped by their guards and cabinet.

When the sibling sovereigns sat, they all sat. The meet had started with their attendance, though Luca thought to say, "Please, have some canape as we begin."

Esker already had been eating, long before the siblings came to join the table. Excusing it as naive barbarism from the Easterner, Lucas cleared his throat and started, "Thanks to all of you who have come to this meet. It is meant for us to talk about steps going forward. There are many facets to this, so I think I'll ask Legate Excallum here to get us started."

While the servants poured wine, Thomas obliged his request, saying, "Well, as you all may know, I received a letter from Ellium last night essentially informing me that, after our triumph at Pommel days ago, they have decided to go ahead with plans to launch a full-scale invasion of the bastion city. That invasion will take place, at their counsel, in three days, counting this one.

"Of course, gathering the main forces of the Falcun League would be impossible at this point. We're in too deep and they're out too far. By the time they've assembled their forces and trudged even as close to this valley, there'd be no time to organize and set out even basic tactics and strategy. So, we're at a sort of impasse."

"Not from where I see it, ambassador." Lucas cut in. "I find the Ellium Empire to be something of an intimidator. In nearly every matter, the emperor must call the shots. They do business with an utter selfish heart, selling trinkets and a series of resources only they have access to for high prices. Yet, they hold their technological advances of building and of war close to their chests. They've isolated themselves from the rest of us, even as Pommel and us Merrier are part of the principality. It is my suggestion that you just tell them that they need to wait until you are good and ready."

"I couldn't agree more, Your Highness," Michael said, "but that would mean we'd need to stay here longer, like, at least a week more. It was my belief that one of your aims for this summit was to expel our forces from Merrieu altogether. Unless I'm mistaken?"

Put into an uncomfortable position, manipulated by his own words, Lucas looked to his sister before retorting, "Yes, I realize the difficulty in hearing this, but after discussing the circumstances with your settlement here in Merrieu, we have come to a conclusion—"

"That you may have to confide in Ellium from now on," Luca cut in to finish his droning thought.

A great air had been sucked out of the room, bringing the conundrum into the forefront. Thomas wheezed, "So, you have gone right to it, then."

Lucas elaborated on his sisters' blunt words, seemingly nervous, "Well, you see, it just makes more sense to continue with all your invading business with them, only because you are dealing with their—"

Esker interrupted after gulping the last of his wine, "Is this the ramblings of a scared child?"

His crass outburst tore a deeper hole into the progress of the summit, making even Maxim sink into his chair. After hearing it, one of the siblings' advisors stepped forth with his hand over the hilt of his sword, "How dare you!"

"Well? Who is really in charge around here?" Esker had pushed further, unafraid. "You young sovereigns are clearly just marionettes—just puppets under these puppeteers. It is either you want us to defy Ellium or you want us to lie with them. It can't be both. Many have bled and fell into the ground to fight those demons that you have never seen with your own eyes! We've made the sacrifice while you sit about and complain. Why string us along? So, what is it you want from us?"

"What insolence!" the same official cried. "You would have the gall to—"

"We can speak for ourselves, Graign. That is what this eastern brute wants, after all," Lucas said crossly. "Speaking plainly, have you no decency?"

"Decency doesn't win wars," Esker countered.

"And war dogs untamed put their own squad at risk," Lucas replied angrily. "This mongrel needs a muzzle."

While Esker laughed, Michael came to defend him, "**He has lost many good soldiers, Your Grace. Forgive him.**"

"He doesn't need forgiveness. He needs manners," Luca spoke out from her seat, visibly shaken by his impudence.

"With all due respect, Your Highnesses," Maxim then interjected, "we're just tired and worn out from fighting this war for so long, only to be told that we aren't welcome here. We've caused no blight to your people. If anything, we've been a godsend. Your city was on the verge before we came and provided much-needed aid. We just ask that you hear us out."

"And so, we have, Tinarian. But now, our situation has changed," Lucas returned in defense. "Miuriell has changed. He now puts our people in danger, just by lingering about."

"Miuriell *has* changed, sir. He's gotten stronger," Maxim riposted.

Lucas answered, "Oh yes, he can fly now. Tomorrow he will unwittingly bring damnation upon us. You might find it advantageous, but the Merrier don't. We find it dangerous."

"**We may not have a long history, you and I, but I've been in the business of spreading lasting peace for you and every other citizen of this world. There hasn't been a war for decades, with the exception of this one. This army, I can tell you, is a melting pot of freedom fighters from all over. Rivals and friends from different worlds have come together to seek the greatest prize.**

"We are evidence that humanity can fight as one, despite our differences and creeds. The Angels of Resistance will need to prove that they aren't just an army of men and women. They'll have to prove that they were an army of *all* men and women," Michael proclaimed.

Digesting Michael's stirring words, Lucas sighed in his reply, "I do not doubt you are a great man. More importantly, Sir Miuriell, you are a good man. I'm not disputing that. What must be strewn out for all to understand is that you are now a demon-man. They're watching you. They're following you. How long before you finally give in and *become* one?"

"This is horseshit!" Maxim rose from his seat and cried, "We don't have time for this crap and all of you know it! If we aren't welcome here, then let's get the hell moving! Let's see how they do on their own again. Let's see how the madness creeps back into their minds and turns them into cattle! This whole thing is a bore and it isn't going to solve—"

"Stand down, soldier!" A Merrier officer shouted from behind the sovereigns, ready to use force if necessary.

Esker then warned casually from his seat, "If you're going to threaten him with your sword, you'd better be ready to use it. Trust me."

"Don't test me, you piece of—" the same officer finally unsheathed his sword, provoking most of the room to be on guard. A tense standoff then ensured, quickly putting most of them on edge. Michael and Thomas stared at each other in a despairing weariness from across the table.

Finally, when Lana had enough, she slammed the table with her fist and shouted, "That's enough! Enough!"

Her grief-stricken cry somehow wrangled the attention of the room, compelling them to quiet down somewhat. It was just enough for her to then bawl from her seat, "I can't—I won't listen to this! As I sit here, my husband lies in a bed with no memory of who I am or what he did on that field! He saved too many people to suffer like that, the way he is! Lai Kai, my brother, recovers from wounds inflicted by vampires on that same field as he, too, offered his life to save dozens of people! We can't leave! I'm not leaving with them like that! They deserve better!"

As the summit listened in to her angry pleas, Predella said coolly, "May I suggest we all cool down and try to find some common ground in all this?"

Amid grumblings from around the room, Thomas said with composure, "I think, if I may, we should consider that the free peoples' caravan earlier today donated plenty of food that can very well last the week. That was a miracle from God and a sign. Does that not influence the sovereignty in any capacity?"

"That was a wonder, ambassador, for sure," Lucas said. "That bounty can suffice for your party when you depart—"

Maxim scoffed, "You've gotta be kidding me."

Luca added in vindication of her brother, "Ellium has cast the die now. You must understand that it's—"

"No, it's just insane how adamant you both are in ridding yourselves of the one army that can actually do something to end the Demon Plague," Maxim said, still standing, hunched over the table. "I just can't understand it."

"It's a double-edged sword, Tinarian," Lucas replied. "I see your frustration and I raise you the welfare of hundreds of Merrier citizens that depend on our leadership during this difficult time. Put simply, it can't be Merrieu's responsibility to house this army of rag-tag fighters forever."

"But at least until the wounded can recover," Lana had appealed one last time. "I want vengeance, but leaving now will only put our wounded in danger."

"**What if *I* just leave and consult with my officers offsite? Would that be a sensible compromise?**" Michael suggested. "**After leaving at dusk, I won't ever return.**"

Before the siblings could ponder the proposal, Esker said bluntly, "If Miuriell goes, then Ziamon goes with him."

"That might sweeten the pot," Predella muttered.

Councilors discussed the proposition with the siblings, whispering feverishly as a pack. While they did, Thomas put up a resistance to his idea, whispering to him across the way, "What, in God's name, are you doing?"

"**Conceding**," he said. "**I have one more play if this doesn't pan out.**"

"We can't split up. Not now," Thomas rejoined.

Michael then smirked, "**If you don't like Plan B, then you're really going to hate Plan C.**"

Once the sovereigns had agreed on a stance, Lucas said, "I suppose that lies on the conditions of your dealings with Ellium. What will you do on that front?"

Michael averted the question to his second-in-charge, "**Thomas?**"

The legate adjusted his seat and revealed the plan they discussed earlier, "My scouts will ride south to the empire's checkpoint and deliver our message, which, in part, will ask for a postponement in the invasion. We were hoping that the Falcun League's main forces could march to us by then. From this valley, our powers would converge and advance towards the enemy stronghold."

"But that could take the week, maybe more," Esker had to interject. "I mean, from a military standpoint, the situation at Pommel could have changed by the time our forces came together."

Thomas responded, "Time is of the essence, I know, but what else can we do?"

"Let Ellium have at them on their own until your extra forces arrive," Esker said. "We did our part as those coddled baronets stood by and waited."

Predella subscribed to the idea, "He has a point. We all paid our dues on that battlefield—took some heavy losses. It should be fair for them to step up while we gather our—"

Thomas poured doubt on the plan, saying, "I could try, but we'd just waste time anyway waiting for their reply. And if they resist the plan, we could be left out in the water."

"You're the ambassador, aren't you?" Esker countered. "What the hell are you talking about with all this 'maybe' and 'let's hope so' crap? You represent them. Tell them what we need to win for fuck sake."

Luca then rebuked him, lashing out, "Watch yourself in my company, Easterner! I am a lady and won't stand for this gross disrespect! We were kind enough to let you settle an army such as yours in our barracks! Your men, running about the campus and lusting for our women, are crude enough! I can see why!"

"I honestly can't believe how much little experience I find just in this one room and there's a war secretary right behind you," Esker countered. "You're worrying about the wrong things, madam. If such language is too harsh for you, then perhaps you should close your ears."

The consul of war finally erupted after staying silent for long enough, "That is all I can take from this crossbred animal! No one has the right to speak to the sovereigns like so, especially our Lady!"

Esker retorted, "Again, there are plenty of resources here for all of the castle, including everyone in the barracks. There aren't any shortages. You're all just paranoid, probably because you've never had to rule during a crisis before. We'd be able to stay here for weeks on end and you'd still have a stable supply of resources. My men did the math—"

Lucas cut him off before he could say any more, putting up his hand, pronouncing, "I think it best if you leave. Now."

Maxim uttered amid the stark silence, "That's the most I've ever heard you speak at one time."

After looking to Michael for the sanction, Esker started up from his seat under guard and said, "And look where that got me."

When guard conducted Esker out of the room, Michael found the opportunity to end the meet before it became any hotter, declaring, "**I and the Angels of Resistance will leave by noon tomorrow. All I ask is that we be able to take the newly acquired provisions from the free peoples, and, of course, that you provide the necessary medical supplies and contingents for the sick and wounded in our party. That includes all the Pommelians in our care. If you can agree to those terms, we'd depart without complaint.**"

All heads turned to him in shock of his proposal. In an instant, he relinquished the fight, speaking for them out of the blue. Lana couldn't understand it, as she just stared at him in a state of dismay. Thomas, as well, glared on in a daze. The siblings didn't have to deliberate long in a settlement. For Maxim and Predella, keeping quiet and going along with him was never more testing. It felt like they were giving in.

When the summit steered for adjournment, Lucas had asked if they wanted to stay and eat. Michael, in declining, only asked if they could borrow the antechamber to discuss the next steps as a group. The monarchs agreed and shook hands with him, deeming it unnecessary to sign any official charters. They trusted Michael at his word.

Moments later, as the party filed into the anteroom, a guard shut the double doors and gave them their privacy for a time. Esker was there, waiting for them to return. He stood up to learn what transpired since his exit. Judging by their faces, it didn't look promising. Maxim, after he was sure they were alone, finally provoked Michael, asking, "So, what in the hell was that?"

"Seriously, Michael, you must have an explanation that makes a lick of sense for what I witnessed back in there," Thomas uttered, still taken aback.

Surrounded by his trusted cabal, Michael opened with, **"What if I told you we could make it to Falcus tomorrow and return to Pommel as a combined fighting force?"**

While they were cautiously intrigued, Lana spoke out, "I'd say you need to share a room in the medical ward."

"And how are we going to do that?" Maxim asked. "That must be some big magic carpet."

Predella sighed, "Really, Maxim?"

Michael breathed in deeply before saying, **"I'll ask you to have faith in me. Believe that I have a plan and that it's for the good of the cause and for all of us."**

"This is your Plan C, then?" Thomas uttered, detecting the uneasiness in the room.

"Afraid so," Michael said.

Lana asked, "But you can't tell us? There's quite a lot riding on this move, Michael. Shioda—Lai."

"If I revealed it, you wouldn't go for it," Michael said, **"but if I show you, I think you'll understand."**

Maxim sat on a wicker chair and groaned, "None of it matters now. We've already made a deal with the siblings."

"As I said, where Miuriell goes, *we* go," Esker spoke out. "Let's get outta this lost cause of a castle. I can just feel their weakness crawling up my boots."

Esker went for the doors, prompting Maxim to follow, saying, "I think that asshole is growing on me. Let's go, then."

"I'll prepare," Predella headed out.

When Thomas made his way out of the doors, Michael took Lana by the hand and said to her, **"I'll meet you in the medical ward. We'll make sure that everyone, including your brother and your husband, is ready. They will all be safe. I hope you can believe me."**

"I hope you know what you're doing, Michael," she said as she went after them, leaving Michael in the antechamber.

Before following them out, Michael voiced to himself, "**I can't be wrong. Eric, please, don't fail me.**"

PART II
CHAPTER XV
THE FAITHFUL

Sundown at Castle Greyhorn, Eric prepared a fire with a flare of his magic and cooked a plump rabbit on a skewer. On the veranda, he made use of a stone table and ate his meal. It was not ideal to have dinner inside, for he enjoyed watching the sunset away from the Shadowland. The cellar provided a bounty of wines from all over the realm, stolen from wineries and traveling merchants. Since he occupied an old derelict castle from a notorious team of bandits, Eric didn't have the burden of guilt.

Many people told stories of the stronghold's ruins. The prevailing theory was that it was haunted by the count that once resided there a century ago. Because of his cruelty, two witches visited his place and put a hex on it. Crops refused to grow and the cattle died. Even the creek's water tasted as if it was tainted, though other patrons fished and drank without concern. The only way to break the hex was for the count to take his own life before the witches upon their return.

But, a stroke of fear led the residents of Castle Greyhorn to rise up and kill the count themselves. Due to their unwise decision to murder him, the hex remained and the count was then doomed to inhabit his castle forever as a spirit. As some form of vengeance, Greyhorn haunted his subjects until they all left. The abandoned castle rotted from the inside, as there was no one who dared live behind its walls.

The tall tale was survived by the remnant gang members known as the Blackhearts, once a small army of bandits led by Kane, "The Slayer," himself. Since then, the ruthless band had dwindled to a gang of thirty-something men and women. A few of them kept watch of the castle ruins while the main force of the crew went out in search of prey. When Eric stumbled on the place, he made quick work of them and took the castle as his own until he had somewhere else to make his home.

In his solitude, as he was very much familiar, the exiled prince ate of his meat and vegetable sides, watching the sun fade beyond the mountains. He knew that Michael finally had something in common with himself, having to fly out to some distant place where his allies would not fall victim to raids from the Demon Plague. At least Michael had his reunions in the morning. Eric's morning was sure to be deservingly cold and empty, without the warmth of friendship or care.

Finally, however, he had some company. Though Eric expected his night visitors, he hoped to, at the very least, finish his red wine. Shouts and cries bellowed out from inside the castle, which then moved outside. Soon, he was surrounded by the Blackhearts, as he anticipated long before they returned. Cautiously, the bandits closed in on him from the veranda and others after climbing the ladders up the crenellations. They waited for their leader, Bone Keeper, to make first contact. It was a great offense to trespass Blackheart territory, especially Castle Greyhorn, their center of operations.

Eric continued to pick at his vegetables when he heard Bone Keeper come up from behind him, wielding a large battle hammer. His best fighters followed him onto the veranda from inside the atrium with weapons drawn. When he felt that the intruder was surrounded, just in case, Bone Keeper grumbled from behind his helmet of a hollowed-out goat skull, "Don't bother finishing that. We're gonna fry you in a vat of oil—one with a nice rolling boil."

While he stopped eating, Eric put up his head and gulped down the rest of his wine. He then exhaled to demonstrate his satisfaction with the brand and year. Enraged, one of the thugs shouted out, "Let's kill this bitch, Bone Keeper! Let *me* do it!"

As the gang cheered and cursed, Eric still said nothing. Bone Keeper then tapped the war hammer in his open palm and started his advance, "You're surrounded, maggot. We're gonna take our time droppin' you and your little white-haired pecker in that vat, too. You made such a big mistake comin' here, killin' my boys, eatin' our—"

"Bone Keeper?" Eric hissed, amused. "What sort of half-assed name is that?"

Seeing red after hearing the interloper's sudden insult, Bone Keeper dropped the head of his hammer into the floor and cried out, "You gurdy fucker! Stand up! Stand up or I'll put in your skull while you're sittin' on yer ass!"

Raising his hands up in surrender, Eric slowly rose from his seat and turned around to look upon the bandit leader. As he came about, Bone Keeper got a better look at his intruder. Eric's long, white hair parted down, concealing only part of the left side of his visage, burnt after the duel with Valkris. His tattered warlock's cloak of dark purple also endured the fight, blending the man he was with the man he chose to become.

Considering the leader's crude helmet and armor, Eric snickered to himself before saying, "You look just like him. Is your look an homage to that hulking buffoon, or do you really think you're the *new* 'Slayer?' One of him is quite enough, I'd say, but, I mean, it's uncanny."

Unwilling to hear him any further, Bone Keeper shook his head and grunted, "You know what, just kill this idiot. I'm already tired of hearin' his mouth."

Crossbows and smuggled Ellison firearms cocked and aimed right for him, Eric snapped his fingers in return, "Try your best, curs."

Upon firing, their weapons exploded like mines, blasting quaking holes in their lines. The shock of his shifty spell put the rest of the gang in a frenzy. Some cowered, while others rushed the sorcerer with blunt and bladed weapons raised. In their attack from all directions, the Blackhearts screamed and howled. Eric stood firm and took them on all at once.

"Blades, is it?" he conjured enchanted weapons to float and spin about him, making a tornado of edges. As the thugs charged him, he sprung his conjured blades for them, dozens at a time. They sliced, chopped and gored every assailant with but a flick of his wrist. Blood spattered from their bodies like gorged sponges belted with knives.

To make sure he killed all of the belligerents, Eric lashed the remaining ethereal blades everywhere. In the aftermath of his wrathful counter-attack, he fixed his ragged cloak and had gone off to look for any survivors. Bone Keeper fought to his feet, using the hammer as leverage, after taking a blade to the side. Eric kicked the blunt weapon away, inducing him to fall.

Finishing off the bandit leader, Eric summoned a molten fire from inside Bone Keeper's belly, snarling, "Eat this, you sorry-named scamp."

The brigand chief writhed and squealed on the ground as Eric went on his way, seeking out the remaining outlaws. When throngs witnessed their leader melt away from the inside out, they fled. None of them had ever encountered such dark magic. Braver bandits that remained to fight him found a greater rival than any of them could have imagined. Eric had endured surprise attacks and ambushes from various parts of the castle, freezing, scorching and pummeling them without mercy.

With his last incantation, Eric obliterated a fleeing goon, reducing her to dust, but also putting a cramp in his hand. Seemingly alone in the rotunda, he massaged his palm, "Hmm, perhaps I overdid it."

Brooding over the source of the spasm, he came to the realization of how quiet it became. Again, Eric was left alone. In a twisted respect, he enjoyed the company of his foes. To be around fellow humans in all their repulsive fibers of morality was a welcome feeling, compared to sulking in the company of demons. In the end, he'd rather be alone in a forsaken keep than in Pommel's hell on earth. With Castle Greyhorn cleaned of bandits for the moment, Eric hoped he could catch some rest. If Michael remained true to his word, there was a chance for redemption in the morning or the days to come.

In the dead of night, Michael broke free from his horrid nightmare, holding his pounding heart. He fought to catch his breath, high above the world in his solitude. Light rain fell on the crest of his modest tent, pitched hours earlier on the high foothills of Merrieu's westernmost county. His sleep, as usual, was disputed by a series of gruesome visions—flashes of the most grotesque hostilities. Recovering from the terror of his unholy dreams, Michael felt the presence of something evil.

Amid the soft tapping of the raindrops on his tent, he called out from his bedroll, "**So this is where you'll fight me now—my dreams?**"

The unsettling whispers from another one of the Demon Lord's puppets answered from just outside the tent's sheet, "**You ruined our sleep, so we shall ruin yours. It is**

fitting this way. Your lack of sleep will escalate the turning."

Still too tired to argue with the forces of darkness from inside a tent, Michael simply said, **"The more I endure these visions, the closer I come to learning your secrets. Keep feeding me, if you want, but I'm going to piece together the origins of your plague."**

"But that comes with a price, doesn't it?" the puppet whispered in return. **"The more you learn, the closer you will step into the truth of what you are. It benefits both of us—all, but your humans."**

Already frustrated with being awake, Michael uttered, **"Those humans kicked your ass some days ago. I would be very careful in underestimating them again."**

"Even now you speak of them as if you're not one of the herd," the Demon Lord parried. **"You know, Sattka was hoping to kill you in your sleep. I forbid it. You see, I still believe in the conquest. I'm the *only* one that believes in it. Must sound humorous to you, a demon longing."**

"Well, you gotta dream, right?" Michael replied. **"So, if there's nothing else, why not appease your daughter and let her come kill me? It'll be easier than having to invade that bastion again and kill the last of your vermin. Let's just get it over with."**

Unamused by his brazen dig, the demon whispered in reply, **"In due time, Miuriell. For now, sweet dreams."**

And just like that, the Demon Lord's puppet was gone. The taps of the raindrops hitting his tent was all that kept him company. Michael massaged his eyes and yawned, knowing that once he fell into a deep sleep again, his nightmares were sure to return. Every time it took over, Michael felt the urge to either vomit or embrace the carnage. Even in his sleep, there was a battle to fight. Though he would have tried harder to resist the horrible flashes of debauchery, Michael needed to pay closer attention. There were always clues to what waited for him in that ingress beyond the fireplace.

The morning brought a bounty of uncertainty for the waking Angels of Resistance, knowing that they had to leave Merrieu by noon. Michael had not yet returned when much of the army prepared for the journey back to Falcus. Still, none actually had any idea where they were going or why. Michael refused to reveal his plans to prevent the resistance likely to follow. While the army as a whole had every reason to hate the exiled prince, Maxim and Predella's motives were more than justifiable.

A large undertaking, Thomas, Lana, and Predella ran the medical transport operation just after breakfast. Dozens at a time, the wounded and sick were carried out on stretchers and moved into wagons and coaches. Medics followed patients in each transport stocked with the needed supplies and drugs. Those who were able, or had recovered from their prolonged captivity, walked. Others who were injured or malnourished took turns resting during the open march. Every fifth wagon in the train was gorged with rations and emergency supplies, including extra parts and clothing.

There was a daring degree of faith that went along with the army, particularly without Michael there to lead them. A disciplined horde of Ziamons marched on the right flank of the wagons as Maxim's Tinarians organized on the left. Merrier soldiers oversaw their company. Some citizens tried to come along, feeling it was better to follow the warriors than remain in the shadow of an unclear future. Thomas permitted only specialists to come along, but in secret, so as not to attract adverse attention from officers.

Thomas sent his last scouts south to deliver his reply in respect to the fateful date of their combined assault. Praying before letting them go, the legate dispatched his men and gave them orders to stay home after their mission was completed. Saving a few lives cleared his conscience before setting off north for whatever Michael had in mind. There was nothing he could offer as far as explanations to his lieutenants, for even he didn't know what came next. Departing Merrieu was all but a leap of faith. A rational mind could never conceive of such a plan to march north in advance of marching south on the enemy bastion in just two days.

Graysonel and his three confederates traveled amongst the Tinarians, fighting free and with purpose. They remained in Predella's company, as they shared Tofauti culture. It was small comfort. No one questioned the whereabouts of their missing confederates and they were never going to tell. Yet, if the Merrier wardens inspected the barracks dumping ground, they would find more than just refuse. There was a price to be paid for their defiance in staying west, but they would sacrifice anything to do just that. They joined the Angels of Resistance as sinners searching for salvation, ready to pay the ultimate price if need be. They reveled in the gravity of such a choice.

Under the supervision of the paladin legion, the party checked the wagons and coaches one final time before making the journey out of Merrieu. In a show of good will, the siblings donated fifty modes of transport for the trip to carry the wounded, the ill and the dead. The final carriages hosted the cleansed bodies of the fallen, including Antonis and Seth. It was the least they could provide since Michael and his forces ensured that their kingdom's chances for survival were better than weeks prior.

Lana was more hopeful than expected. Lai was up and walking, having shown signs of recovery. His infection seemed to have healed faster than anticipated. He took it as a good omen, concentrating on encouraging his sister. Shioda was in a critical, but stable condition in the third wagon of the train. Ninja warriors walked along the head cars, checking in on him and his sister. As a unit, the only piece missing was Michael himself. Noon was less than an hour away.

While some of the army was willing to set off, the greater part wanted to wait until the last minute in case Michael had arrived. Esker was adamant about holding on, as his mission was bent on following Michael's leadership and no one else. Before the debate reached the company in its entirety, some Merrier officers entered the barracks' main entrance with a bit of good news. Michael was in Merrieu.

Princess Shina, after hearing of his arrival, breathed a sigh of relief from inside her carriage. While she was urged to rest in one of the head cars, she preferred to show herself to her fellow Tinarians. The guilt of her evil deeds under the spell of the Demon Plague lingered over her like a black cloud. Against Maxim's wishes, Shina stepped out to mingle with her knights until the word was given that it was time to set off. Thomas led the train out of the barracks and through the Merrier square. Shina returned to her carriage for the moment, appeasing the soldiers' chivalric sentiments.

Taking the first steps into the main concourse and out of the barracks for good, the Angels of Resistance encountered the Merrier populace assembling along the sides of the path. Thomas expected there to be a crowd, but nothing like what waited for them on the flanks. Like walking the gauntlet, the army marched through the masses. Yet, as they went, sounds of applause began emerging from sporadic spots in the crowd. Progressively, the clapping increased and turned into some sort of collective ovation. It was a surprise wave of praise.

The Ziamons looked about the spectacle in shock. They were not used to such acclaim anywhere outside of their home state. Some of the citizens that came out to see the army even knelt before them, showing the greatest admiration. In light of such glorification, some Tinarians waved instinctively. When a small girl connected eyes with Pingas, still limping since his bloody bout with his Tofauti rivals, she broke away from her older sister to greet him in the procession.

By the time her sister reached out for her, the girl had already made it to the hardened warrior from the East. From a place of innocence, she smiled up at him and offered Pingas a small white flower. Her act was the last thing he would have expected during his march out of the city, but he received the offering. Such kindness was foreign to him in the West. While the Merrier guards pulled her away from the parade of warriors, she waved clumsily. Proceeding to walk on, Pingas considered the small flower and why the girl chose him from the rest.

All the while, the crowds clapped and cheered their valiant service, knowing the trials still ahead. In the distance, some of the army saw Michael floating a few feet above the square awaiting his allies. Surrounded by the cheering people encompassing the plaza, Thomas made his way to him first and said with a small grin, "Showoff."

Michael returned the smile as he looked over the state of his army from his floating high view. He then came back to the ground and addressed his trusted officers, saying, "**I made all the necessary arrangements with our contact. Just a short way north and we'll be in the clear.**"

"But you can't tell us who and where *can* you?" Maxim replied, helplessly tense.

"**Looks like you'll have to trust me once again,**" he answered.

"Always," Predella said.

Nodding in appreciation of the masses that came out to watch his army depart, Michael soaked it in and proclaimed, **"All these people cheer for us. They are grateful for what we've done and what we're going to do. You all deserve it."**

"Not what I expected, but I'll take it," Thomas replied.

Michael smiled again before ascending high enough for all of his company to see him, compelling the multitudes of the city to cheer and whistle. His own forces were in awe of his newfound powers. They believed that he was the best chance anyone had in crushing the Demon Plague once and for all. It was a boost in morale just seeing him float effortlessly above the earth, electric sparks, and flashes in his wake.

Just as he was about to lead them out, he had to ask, **"I should assume that you brought my—that you took care of my—"**

"Of course," Thomas said with compassion, finding it as hard as ever to see his friend suffer. Having lost a father, it was but a taste of how awful it must have been to lose a son. There was a warm, beating heart behind all the darkness of Michael's exterior and it bled for his only child. When hearing that his friends didn't forget to load his boy's casket, Michael exhaled loudly, as if fighting the urge to cry, and began moving out of Merrieu's square. In under twenty minutes, he and his army had left the kingdom behind.

The march north proved to be uneventful, stopping for lunch midway. With the exception of sporadic drifters heading south to Pommel, stricken with the madness, the army hadn't encountered anyone. Heading to Castle Greyhorn was often considered a death wish, as many outlaws took refuge there. It became one of the Falcun League's aims to deliver the final blow to the Blackhearts and any other bandit gangs hiding in that area. However, the region was deathly quiet.

Though the army was on alert, wary of Michael's choice to lead them northwest into the perilous territory, they saw the outline of Greyhorn on the horizon. It became clear that such a castle, shrouded in infamy, was their final destination for the day. Nearing closer to the place, Thomas finally spoke out, "I really hope this isn't our new stop, Michael. Ghosts aren't the only things that haunt that castle."

"**No, it isn't our stop,**" Michael said, bringing the party to a halt, "**but it *is* the catalyst to our final destination.**"

Maxim had just joined them at the front and overheard Michael's reply. He took in the surroundings and said, "This is some hideout for brigands, isn't it?"

"**Was it that obvious?**" Michael uttered.

"*It was, before I got here.*" Eric's voice emanated from nowhere and everywhere, suddenly filling the spaces between them. Even Shina heard it, prompting her to exit her carriage. In her spirit, she knew it was her brother. As confused as she was, seeing him was the telling proof. From the outer walls of the castle in ruins, Eric sauntered forth. Well over a thousand feet away, she saw him for herself. There was no mistaking it.

Covering her mouth in shock, overwhelmed by surges of relief and anger. Her eyes welling with tears, she gasped. Eric came with his arms open and his warlock cloak, fluttering in the faint gust of wind. His white hair, casting to one side and his face, scourged by dark magic, was all that Maxim needed. He knew it had to be him. Stunned, like the others, he said in a daze, "Michael—what have you done?"

"Is that? It can't be!" Predella came to see him clearer, passing Maxim at the shoulder. "He's alive. Michael, you knew he was alive—all this time?"

"No, since yesterday," he answered. "**Since he came to me, seeking redemption for his sins. He is the one who is going to deliver us to Falcus. Teleporting us will be his last act of free will. After that, he has agreed to surrender.**"

Maxim, shaken by the anger of feeling betrayed, said, "I see now why you wouldn't tell me. You pulled us here to work with this—this demon."

"**It isn't what you—**"

"I vowed to kill that man the next time I set eyes on him. And there he is," Maxim growled, making a fist that trembled at his side.

As Shina broke through the soldiers that tried to prevent her from leaving their protection, Predella shook her head and sighed regretfully, "After all he's done, you would trust him?"

"**He nearly died so that we could escape. Eric is not doing this for us. He's doing it to save his sister,**" Michael said. "**And so we can finish what we started. Bringing us to Falcus is just half of it. His last deed will be transporting our entire force right to Pommel's front door without any warning. They'll never see us coming.**"

Hearing Shina run up from behind, Thomas added, "So we'll make a deal with the devil to snuff hell from the earth?"

Shina finally scurried forth, obliging Maxim to restrain her. She didn't fight it. The princess was too broken to fight. When Eric saw her from the ruins of the castle's walls, he went to reach for her, as if she was just there at his feet. His emotion nearly brought him to his knees. Instead, he made a fist and let his tears flow down his face, much like his sister. She cried in Maxim's arms. He looked to Predella for what to do next. Like him, she was overcome.

Michael nodded his head, giving Eric the signal from afar to perform the casting. Eric almost didn't see it, wiping his wet eyes and focusing on his grieving young sister. But when he caught it, he turned around and began his spell. It was one of the most difficult incantations in his arsenal, but one he had performed before for the Mad Legion. Stretching his arms forward, and reciting the ancient words, a tremendous power burst from his core. The cape of his cloak rushed up. His hair blew back. A thunderous rumble brought the spell to the earthly realm.

With the army looking on, the spell of Cravat Foros had begun. A sudden crack, like the nucleus of a star break, formed from nothing before him. It grew larger, as if he fed the entity with just his words, forming into a circular lake of dark matter. Esker gawked at the unfathomable sight, muttering in terror, "Tinarians and their perverse capacities."

"**He understands that we can win,**" Michael declared, feeling the darkness of Eric's incantation stimulate his soul. "**There is no fate when there is faith. All these years, Eric tried to make his own fate,** *because* **he was faithless. Now, he'll use his powers for good.**"

"I truly hope you know what you're doing," Maxim said.

Thomas furthered his concern, "You do understand that we'll be bringing a very powerful traitor behind the holy city's walls? Unless you trust that man beyond a shade of a doubt, I think it's the riskiest thing we've ever done."

The portal was in its final stages of completion when he answered his allies' anxieties, "**Trust is one thing. Respect is a whole other thing. He knows that I can turn him inside out before he knew what happened. Eric will help us.**"

Another boom, reaching into everyone's chests, had signaled that the spell was finished. His large portal, a gaping hole in thin air, hosting a swirling emulsion of magic. There it waited for its brave travelers looking to voyage through time and space. Eric stepped away from his work, feeling drained. Such sorcery took lots of energy to sustain. He lingered by it until Michael decided the time was right.

"Just beyond that portal lies Falcus. Are we ready?" Michael asked with resolve.

"I don't know, Michael. *Are* we?" Maxim retorted.

Shina, after studying her brother's mannerisms, fought to compose herself. She said, "Eric won't hurt me. We'll make it through whatever that thing is. I know it."

While she was convincing, Predella glared at the exiled prince one more time before returning to her post, saying as she went, "We may make it to Falcus, but it's what happens once we get there that I'm wondering about."

"He'll be my responsibility," Michael assured her.

Predella didn't change her stride when saying, "There is no man I trust more."

"Really?" Maxim uttered.

"Make that two men," Predella called out, "but only one that I sort of love."

Thomas turned to Maxim with a thrilled expression and said, "The 'L' word!"

"The 'sort of L' word," Shina emphasized.

Maxim snapped, "Can we please focus? That thing won't stay open forever."

"That's true," Michael replied. **"You have followed me this far. Falcus is waiting."**

By the swirling portal, Eric threw his arms out at his sides, wondering about the delay. Despite the battalions' indecision, Michael encouraged them to follow his lead. He started up for the mystical gateway with his army closely behind. Maxim had urged Shina to return to her carriage, but she refused. She wanted to look her brother in the eyes to make sure he was a man seeking redemption and not the same one, plotting to deceive them. The nearer they came, the more distressed she felt. There was an uneasiness in their march as if they were cattle filing for the slaughter.

Yet, as they reached closer, the sorcerer fell on one knee and bowed his head in respect. Maxim, on the other hand, saw it as an eluding tactic to avoid the stares from the many he betrayed. There was a shame in the evil that he had done. As even when his sister approached, he cast his head downward. His cascading white hair concealed most of his face, especially the affected side.

When Michael reached the enchanted portal, he knelt before Eric and asked him, "**It's as you said, you will follow us after we've all made it through?**"

Eric lifted his head slightly, gazing upon Michael through the wisps of his hair, and said, "I will, as agreed."

Michael nodded, satisfied by his renewed allegiance, and continued for the portal. His army watched every moment that Michael walked towards the gateway. While there was a fair share of trepidation amongst the army, there was none more skeptical than Maxim. He was certain that he was on to Eric's sinister plan. Repulsed by it, he ran it through his head as the scene progressed.

It's a perfect plan. Michael will walk through the portal and vanish, leaving the rest of us vulnerable to that bastard's attacks. With his powers, we'd just be sitting ducks. He could wipe us all out, effectively eliminating the only real threat to the Demon Plague. That son-of-a-bitch will do the demons' work, as he plotted all along. How could Michael believe his shit? There, once he walks through that portal, it's on.

When Michael did walk through the fluid-like glass of Eric's gateway, Maxim looked to the kneeling sorcerer and put his hand over the Mad Phoenix's handle. He was ready to race over and cut down the traitorous warlock before he had any chance of initiating the attack on them. But, to his surprise, Eric remained there, waiting for Michael to return.

In seconds, he came back from the portal and waved the army in. It was a successful spell, delivering him all the way to Falcus in but one flash of a moment. Salvation was at hand.

The army followed Michael into the portal, then finding themselves at the giant walls to the holy city in the shade of a second. Everything was different on the other side—the wind, the sun, the texture of the sand under their feet. The wagons struggled after making the sudden transition. Abruptly, they came before the Falcuns, astonished by what they witnessed. Eric's spell had worked, funneling the Angels of Resistance into Falcun territory. Michael put the holy city at ease, then revealing Thomas Excallum and his paladins.

The Falcun League dispatched their warriors to meet the Angels of Resistance at their walls. It was a liberating sight to see. As Michael promised, they made it safely back to Falcus by the supreme power of a traitor's sorcery. The remainder of the army utilized the portal under thirty minutes, leaving only Eric as the last piece. Some didn't expect him to follow them all in, expecting the sorcerer to evade justice for his crimes. But, as the portal closed in on itself, Eric was there, standing in its stead.

Michael approached him just moments after with arms crossed, barely hovering over the sand, and said, "**The exiled prince kept his word, after all.**"

Looking past him, Eric considered the big reception from the Falcuns at the wall and replied, "Well, now we'll see if you do the same."

"**I have no choice. The very future of this world rests on our ability to work together,**" he said. "**I stand firm on my vow.**"

"Unless, of course, your friends beyond that wall cower in fear of your newborn powers and features and whatnot. You are a haunting thing now," Eric said.

"**Trust me, Eric. They will fear you over me any day. You've given them a reason to hate and fear you,**" Michael countered. "**That's why you'll need to behave and do all that they ask, even if that means a cell.**"

Putting up his hands, Eric replied, "I surrender."

Ill at ease by the sorcerer's sardonic tone, Michael came in closer and said sternly, "**Hear this. We've all made some grave sacrifices in this war. When we enter that city with the news of what's happened to us, they won't be tolerant of your—**"

"I get it," Eric answered. "So, why don't we just get this over with?"

"**Yes,**" Michael sighed, heading for the great wall of the holy city, still under repairs, "**why don't we?**"

Masses of Falcuns praised their swift homecoming with celebrations in the streets accompanied by loud victory bells and music. The Pommelians filed into the Tinarian embassy where they were segregated into different wings to continue their medical attention. Shioda was transported to the Holy Consul Hospital to further his treatment. Lai went along at his sister's request. She wanted the clinicians to check his wounds properly.

Eric, in chains merely for the Falcuns' peace of mind, followed Michael to his cell. Shadisha didn't feel safe with him outside of a cage. Paraded as a prisoner of war in the streets, he endured the swears, jeers, and projectiles from the public. He kept his chin up and looked straight on, unwilling to show any remorse to strangers. If he wanted, Eric could have tried to obliterate them with just a raise of the eyebrow.

Michael walked a few strides in front of him, though he, too, felt as if he walked the gauntlet. When the populace saw him close up, their expressions changed. It was not the face of the Michael they knew. Like Eric had warned, many of them saw only the darkness. His appearance was ominous after all. Unlike times before when he could charm them with just his words, even his voice had turned. It was always Michael's way to convince the world of his heart through action, nonetheless.

Ninja warriors of the Kai League followed Michael and Eric closely behind as Thomas and his paladins trailed in back. They all marched for the Principal Palace where Eric would settle in his new maximum-security dungeon dwelling and Michael would reunite with Shadisha and Urik at last. There was much to discuss with not a lot of time. Shadisha, as Falcus's master tactician, would need to work fast. Tomorrow was the last day.

Shadisha escorted Michael to the Excallum quarters to check on Urik's condition. Sadly, he had not improved much since they left for Merrieu over a week ago. He slept in his bed, gaining his rest. Several attendants monitored his condition, but she asked that they leave for just a few moments. They all obliged. When the last clinic closed the doors, Shadisha came in to hug Michael tightly. He reciprocated her embrace, letting out a sigh of relief. Feeling the warmth of her body and of her compassion helped him realize that he was still loved.

"I was so heartbroken when I heard," she whispered in his ear, tears falling onto his shoulder. "I'm so sorry."

Whispering back into her ear, Michael said, "**I know. He is at peace now—with his mother.**"

"Of course, he is," she pulled back and held his face with her soft hands. "They're in a realm where the beauty of love and peace we all seek radiates from their spirits. May we all find ourselves in such a place one day."

Smiling in gratitude, he uttered serenely, "**One day.**"

She then came to kiss him on the forehead and wiped her own tears away, leading him to Urik. At his bedside, he had left an old bible opened to a page in Revelations. Shadisha then sat him down and placed the book in his hands, saying gently, "Manna's personal bible handed down from the New Vatican centuries ago. Urik circled this passage for you to read. When he wakes up, you can ask him more about it, if you like."

Intrigued, Michael received the book and read the part his mentor highlighted. The verses were about the angels of Revelation that brought destruction upon the world. Urik had sent his attendants to research more about Michael's queries on Abaddon. It appeared that they found it in the Book of Revelation 9:1. Urik's intuitions had borne fruit yet again.

It read: "Then the fifth angel blew his trumpet, and I saw a star that had fallen to earth from the sky, and he was given the key to the shaft of the bottomless pit. When he opened it, smoke poured out from a huge furnace, and the sunlight and air turned dark from the smoke."

Michael couldn't help but think on the fireplace hidden beneath Pommel, hiding whatever secrets within. Still, he read on. Verses about locusts emerging from the darkness, stinging and torturing those who did not have the seal of God. Passages warned of ghastly creatures prepared for battle, some with the faces of humans, some with women's hair and teeth like lions. Others wore armor and bore wings. But the final verse brought the chill to his spine.

It read: "Their king is the angel from the bottomless pit; his name in Hebrew is Abaddon, and in Greek, Apollyon—the Destroyer."

Gaging from the look on Michael's face, Shadisha asked him, "What does it mean? Is it about the Demon Plague? See, it goes on to warn about an army and a plague around 9:16."

"**It's about me**," Michael gasped, closing the holy book in shock. "**It's about Abaddon—an angel of the Apocalypse. An angel of torment.**"

"You? I don't understand," Shadisha said. She couldn't understand it, for it was something only Urik and Michael had discussed before. If he was the re-embodiment of an angelic king of destruction, then his Demon Plague was his army of minions—twisted angels born to torment humanity. They did only what they were created to do, torture for Abaddon—for God's wrath. Yet, they were not sent by God. They were sent by a fallen angel of death.

"**I'm the reawakening, the second coming of a rogue angel of some kind. My minions are tormentors, but they aren't supposed to be killing anyone. They're meant only to torture. The destruction part is left to me. The Demon Plague is a corrupted, unbridled—unchecked—**" Michael saw the dread in Shadisha's face and stopped thinking aloud.

He held her hands and said, "**It's just a verse from the New Testament. He wanted it to give me some clues as to our enemy's secrets, that's all. I was internalizing it.**"

Still shaken by everything he said, Shadisha stammered, "So, you—what did you find out?"

Rubbing his short beard, Michael thought on it, making the connections as she listened in, "**There was a fireplace in Pommel's vestibule that was there for all my life and I never felt it had anything to hide. But, standing before it, there was something—hidden. Something dark. That fireplace is the furnace. The Shadowland is the smoke blocking out the sunlight. And the pit. The bottomless pit is where all the Demon Plague's secrets reside. That's where Abaddon dwells. So, that's where I must go. If that's where those demons were born, that's where they'll die.**"

"So, we need to get you to that pit. If you return there, they won't just welcome you with open arms, will they?" she said, already planning the attack in her head.

"**I don't know. Probably not,**" Michael replied. "**But if I make it there on my own, one thing's for sure. They'll do everything they can to turn me. Every demon—every last minion will be upon me then, pushing me to the limit.**"

"Then once we get you inside, we'll have to keep them distracted," Shadisha strategized. "It'll take thousands of our warriors to do that. *Can* they do that?"

"**They'll need to,**" Michael replied gravely. "**We have a sorcerer that can replace me on the outside.**"

She then stood up and groaned, pacing about the room, "I don't like this, Michael. That man is a demon, himself. What is to stop him from turning coats again during the battle?"

"**He won't do that,**" Michael said.

"He betrayed us once out of desperation. He'll do it again if he feels that the fight is lost," Shadisha rose her voice. "That man will bend for anything that scares him. And with his power, he scares *me*."

Hearing their commander from outside, two attendants opened the doors and crept in warily. One of them asked, "Is everything alright, Master Hasana?"

Shadisha exhaled and said, "All is well. You may return to your duties. Thank you."

As they entered the chamber again, Michael met her in the middle of the room and caressed her shoulders, saying, "**I know you're scared. So am I. But we must have faith. We will be victorious. We'll need to.**"

She muttered so that the attendants didn't hear, "I hope you're right."

"**Faith, Shadisha, not hope,**" he said.

After seeking the same faith in his eyes, Shadisha touched his hands and brought them down between them, "I will make the necessary preparations for tomorrow. All of us need to be there, including that magus, who I must trust only because I trust you."

He kissed his hands as she started to go, leaving him to spend some time with Urik. Among the attendants, Michael sat at his bedside again and perused the old bible for any further clues. But, as he did that, Michael felt drawn to other parts of the holy book. He turned to the Book of Psalms and began to read some scripture. If he was going to ask others to have faith in him, he would need to strengthen his own. Of his many tests in life, none had ever been harsher than recent days.

"**And you'd better be there, as well, old man,**" Michael said over Urik as he slept, then returning to the psalms, saying with emotion. "**For me.**"

At sundown, Predella looked out from the high balcony of the Tinarian embassy as Michael rode off. He didn't want to drift away and stir up anymore suspicion about his new powers. Predella, however, knew that a simple horse was nothing but a cover to hide his true gift. Out under the open night sky, she applied herbal medicine to her wounds. With Kaila's teeth and claw marks still taking its toll, she took up her elemental bow and pulled the string. She would need to be ready to fire every arrow at its mark. In a few days, the lives of many depended on it.

As she thought it all over, a voice emanated from behind, "So, you're watching the dark knight ride off into the void, as well?"

Turning around, Predella observed Eric come forth from the darkness of the lanai. Shocked to see him there, she said, "I doubt they trusted you enough to give you free roam about the city."

Stretching out his arms, he replied, "Of course not."

"Well, you'd be a bit more careful than you are now. Maxim is on his way up here to meet me and he's been talking about severing your head from your shoulders all day," she said coldly, leaning against the porch balcony with her bow in hand. "Then again, whatever your reason for coming here, you should know that catching me by surprise is a good way to get shot. What do you want?"

There was a loaded question. He had the opportunity to seek forgiveness from the woman he detested for so long. Seeing the light, even while it was dim, Eric had to take this difficult first step to salvation. Without it, he did not believe redemption was possible. His guilt could cloud his judgment during the final battle at Pommel and he couldn't be off.

When Predella tightened her grip on the bow, Eric folded his hands behind him and said carefully, "I have come to you with the hope of reconciliation."

Taken aback by the sorcerer's unexpected appeal, Predella could only muster, "What?"

Nearing inches closer before stapling himself in one spot, Eric began earnestly, "You spoke of the destruction of your people. I, along with so many others, would not believe your claim. Well, I believe you now. I believe you because it was my fault."

Predella leaned off the edge of the railing, gasping, "You had best choose your next words very carefully."

Taking a deep breath, he said, "In my exile, I thought it was only a hallucination or a dream, but it was real. My nightmares were real. The Demon Lord sought me out as I slept and agreed to a pact in a dream state. Fulfilling the covenant meant committing an appalling act. He gave me the choice of the target, much like a rite of passage."

"What appalling act?" Predella clenched her fists in ire, predicting what he was going to admit.

"It was I who destroyed your home," he started, welling up with tears of guilt. "It was the first time I ever used the sorcery that—"

"It was *you*?" Her body welled up in a surge of anger and sorrow. "Of course, it was you! You sick—"

Putting his eyes to the bow in her trembling hands, he said, "I came to clear the air in hopes of ridding the curse from me. You see, I've relived that day over and over sometimes every day—sometimes every night. Ever since I set foot in that wicked bastion—"

Incensed, she rushed forth and clouted him in the chin with a fierce fist. When he stumbled back from the blow, refusing to evade her attack, she tackled him to the ground. There, Predella straddled him and seized his white collar, raising her fist to finish what she started. She hit him again in the face and planned to beat him to a pulp for his evil crimes against her and her people. She felt that all the pain she endured would transfer from her fists into his flesh and bones.

Killing him meant that she had slain the one responsible for the murders of so many innocent people. Still, she remembered the reason Michael brought him to Falcus. It jolted her mind as if Michael himself caught her wrist in mid-punch. As her quaking fist lingered over his bludgeoned face, she realized that it was not him alone. He was weak and vulnerable to the Demon Plague's malevolent designs. Killing him would not end her suffering. It would turn her into what she was not. It would turn her into him.

Hence, she closed her eyes and exhaled, letting her tears rain on him rather than her fists. Predella grabbed him by the collar and cried out, roaring into the night sky. How she dreamt of how she would kill her people's destroyer. She had the warlock in her grasp and she couldn't do it. Ending him would end any chances of returning to Pommel in time to bring the war to an end—to finish the Demon Plague.

She sniffled and rose onto her feet, leaving him there on the ground where she put him. While the sorcerer looked up at her from his beaten position, Predella walked back to where she dropped her bow and retrieved it. Eric slowly returned to his feet, wobbly from the beating. In peering out into the dark distance as before, she wept, "Damn you, Eric. You killed my people. The survivors became slaves."

"For whom you freed from bondage," Eric said without even a hint of pain or swelling from his mouth.

She turned to see that his face had healed as if she never beat him in the first place. His face was clean, with the exception of the scarring since Pommel. Holding her head, feeling faint, Predella sighed, "I knew you'd never come face me in person."

"I made a vow to him that I wouldn't leave my cell," he said calmly. "Technically, I'm still there—and here."

Shaking her head, Predella loaded an arrow and aimed for his head, "Is that so?"

Eric found that her killing him was probably part of the healing process. It was better for her to kill the projection of him than the genuine article. Hence, he let go of his guard and said, "Shit, just do it, then."

She fired for his head, hitting the mark right between his eyes. The sorcerer fell like a corpse, the arrow jetting out from his bleeding forehead. Just the act of killing him worked like a stress reliever, feeling that she avenged the Waasi people in some way. As she came to salvage the arrow, Eric's clone had begun to disintegrate into ashy matter, dissolving to the magic from whence it came. Her arrow simply clanked to the floor.

There, in the background, Maxim had finally come to see the conclusion of the act that played out on the lanai. He saw how Predella was shaken from whatever transpired. Looking as if she was going to collapse, he ran and caught her in his embrace. She then grabbed onto him tightly and sobbed. He could only hold her for so long until she fell to her knees, too weak to stand. Maxim knelt with her and held her securely, baffled as to whatever happened before he arrived. But rather than ask anything, he just held her and pressed his face against hers. Beside them, lay the arrow that slew the enchanted copy of the sorcerer, seeking impossible redemption.

Shina, accompanied her Tinarian brothers and sisters, attended a prayer service ministered by Thomas Excallum himself at the Founder's Church. Hundreds gathered to pray at the mass, though more hoped to hear stories of the army's woes and triumphs from Pommel. Pommelians were there, of those who could make it. Falcuns joined in singing hymns as a choir of diverse voices echoed throughout the sanctuary.

Below the hall, the bodies of the fallen rested in coffins until they were sanctified for burial. They were all to be laid to rest in the Field of Honor, a cemetery dedicated to those who gave their lives in times of war or acts of great heroism. Yet, Michael swore that Seth be sanctified, but preserved for his burial in Pommel. Once cleansed of the Demon Plague, his son would sleep in the soil of his home.

Eric watched his sister from afar, hiding amongst the gallery high above the nave. She seemed at peace. Singing as a parishioner among the church community, the princess really prayed with all her heart. Royalty didn't matter. Shina was just one of them, beseeching the heavens for divine intervention. The most critical fight for the future of the world was at hand. Seeing her away from the demons' influences convinced him of his failure. He needed to obliterate the Demon Plague and play nice with the Angels of Resistance if he wanted to make the wrong things right. The chance for absolution had a very small window.

Lana, as promised, stayed with Shioda until he slept. It was her intention to meet Lai, released from the clinic, at the Founder's Church to pray. When he appeared to fall asleep, she kissed him on the mouth and prepared to leave. Yet, as she started out of the hospital room, Shioda whispered, "Are you leaving for good?"

Taken aback by his fearful plea, she sighed and dropped her things at the door. Lana returned to him and held his hand. Kissing it, she whispered back, "I'll never leave you. Don't you understand?"

Tolerating the agony to speak in his condition, Shioda said to her, "I don't know if my memory will ever return. And I can't promise that I'll ever be that man you married, but you make me want to try. You make me want to fight for it. Lana, you're an angel and I'll fight to come back to you if I can."

Crying again, she tried to conceal her tears in the dark of the room in saying, "Just try to get some sleep. Okay?"

She kissed his hand once more before leaving for the prayer service. But he held onto her hand tightly, preventing her from leaving just yet. When she came closer to assure him that she would return, Shioda spoke first, beseeching, "Don't go onto that battlefield."

Stunned by his request, she muttered back, "Wait, what did you—"

"I don't want to be alone," he said earnestly. "You're the only person that makes me feel like I'm not alone. If anything should happen to you on that battlefield, I'd be alone forever. There wouldn't be much reason for me to try anymore. I will do anything to keep you from going—I swear, I'll do anything you ask. Lana, please."

She saw in his eyes the desperation in his eyes, but also the sincerity in his trembling voice. While his memory had not yet healed, Shioda found true comfort in Lana's company. It was a genuine feeling of care. Despite his afflictions, Shioda was tethered to her with a love that transcended the mind. In feeling the warmth of his hand, Lana, at last, felt a fragment of her husband.

"Alright," she said, finally making her decision. "I won't go. I'll stay with you, okay? I won't go."

"Okay," Shioda said, relieved. "Thank God. Go on, then. Send your brother my warm regards."

Encouraged, Lana smiled and kissed him on the lips. It felt strange for him, but Shioda hoped it would jog his memory of their marriage. Regardless, he felt better knowing that he was able to spare her life and her baby's life by keeping her out of harm's way. Lai would have to approve. As she left him, Shioda uttered, "You'll say a prayer for me?"

Stopping at the doorway, she replied, "I'll say a prayer for us."

When she was finally gone, he considered the flickering light of the candles parallel to each other, breaking some light into the dark room. He found it ironical. The candlelight was much like his mind, fighting to illuminate the crevasses of all he once knew about his life. There were so many missing parts where the light could never reach. To remember anything, he would have to follow Lana's lead, trusting her unconditionally.

Even if he didn't remember her, Shioda would learn from her. He needed to keep Lana close as a beacon of light in the hopes that she would illuminate the parts he couldn't. Of all the love she hovered over him, Shioda so deeply wanted to return for her sake. Every kiss, every tear, every moment she shared with him had to lead somewhere.

. . .

As he slept amid the dark, early hours of the morning, Michael awoke to another brutal nightmare. The Demon Lord promised that the visions would not stop and he was right, but Michael counted on the dreams for any new clues to what had called to him from beyond the veil. Though feeling that sleep was a fleeting luxury as of late, he was able to catch something. Just before he woke up, Michael saw his Staff of Truth.

The legendary article called out to him amid the horror of his flashing visions. It was there somewhere beyond the furnace, waiting for him to return. Sitting up in his bedroll, he heard sounds from outside his tent. Still catching his breath, Michael carefully peeked outside. There, in his dismay, he saw his horse being eaten by an impious creature. It chewed up the animal's innards, having slaughtered beast earlier on its side. Upon seeing it, he blasted the repulsive scene away with his powers, leaving nothing in its wake. He cringed from what he experienced.

Like the morning before, he felt that he wasn't alone. A dark, cumbersome feeling encompassed his camp. Fed up with his stalkers, Michael crawled out from his tent and stood firm in the dead of night. His campfire had extinguished hours ago, leaving little light. He clenched his fists and shouted out, "**I'm not impressed!**"

In just moments, a myriad of green eyes materialized from every direction, closing in on his camp. An army of evil surrounded him, hissing and snarling in the darkness. There, where his horse was eaten alive, an angelic figure came forth, beaming with light. Surprised to see such a divine being out in the open, illuminating the dark, Michael covered his eyes, but then saw through the deception almost instantly.

The man's bright light was blinding, yet didn't drive the demons away. The radiance hurt his eyes, unlike that of holy light. When the light dispelled, showing a dying brilliance of what was a pair of wings, the handsome man spoke, "**Is this form more suitable for you? You *are* an angel, aren't you?**"

"**Don't patronize me,**" Michael countered angrily. "**It doesn't matter what skin you crawl into. You always stand out.**"

"**I beg to differ. Honestly, I find that I'm fitting in quite nicely,**" the Demon Lord replied. "**In fact, this skin, as you put it, is the perfect insult to mankind—a conjured lie that fosters false hopes in sinners—**"

"**Say what you've come to say and then leave me be.**" Michael cut him off, too tired to hear him any further.

With the demonic horde closing in, the Demon Lord, hiding behind a handsome face, ambled closer and said, "**We know you're coming back. When you do, come alone. Our forces have prepared a deathtrap for all your scum allies. Taking them along will only end in their suffering. And I believe we both know what they'll endure. You've seen it in your visions, night after night. Each one of them shall cry for death and they'll live on in torment, all because of you—*for* you. But you already know this, don't you?**"

Facing his nemesis with a stone scowl, Michael replied, "**Are you done?**"

The Demon Lord only smiled back after the snark reply, vanishing into light and leaving Michael alone with the horde of demons. His voice, however, lingered in the air, as if trailing off with the wind, "*I long to serve you, Lord Abaddon. May the sinful writhe in your righteous fire.*"

A parting shot to incite him, Michael cowered under the insinuation that his allies would suffer by his hand. Demons as his only company, far from Falcus's watch, he looked about his wicked cordon feverishly. Shadow and flyers alike skulked nearer, enclosing the circle with him as the nucleus.

It was as if they bowed to him, trying to convince Michael that they yet trusted him despite his confusion. He had his allies in the day and them in the night. The message was spitefully clear.

"**You think I accept you as my own? Is that what all this is? You'd better hear this—every vile, hideous one of you. I disown you! I hate you!**" Michael began screaming at the top of his lungs, enraged. "**Go back to your hole and wait for us there! We're going to kill every last one of you! Wait there for us! That'll be your grave!**"

Sattka listened to him scream on from deeper in the cover of darkness. She saw how there was no saving him. If her father thought otherwise, she would prove how he was wrong. Enhanced by Valkris's magic, coupled with her own powers, Sattka vowed to kill Michael the moment he set foot in Pommel—with or without the conquest's consent.

Before losing control, Michael stopped and realized that he was playing right into their hand. Discharging his powers could have tipped the scales to his inner malevolence, particularly in the hours of darkness. Breathing heavily, Michael caught his breath and snickered, "**Know what? Stay and keep me company if you like. I can't care. Can't blame any of you for doing what you can't help. We all have our demons. I suppose you're mine.**"

He then returned to his tent and left the horde outside. They closed in on his encampment, emitting baleful energy that would have overwhelmed anyone else in terror. Even the smell of the evil pack, the putrid odor of death, was enough to pester his sleep. But they would never harm him. Michael knew the code of the conquest.

Sattka, then, prepared to execute her mission objective. Though she wanted to kill him in his tent using her newfound powers, she resisted the urge and followed through. Clanging her swords together, Sattka swiped the blades and cast a fast-spreading wave of magic. The spell, like Valkris's Seltek, had transported the demon horde back to Pommel. Yet, the true nature of her task was to steal Michael along with them.

When the energy blast reached his tent, having already taken the demons away, Sattka knew that something wasn't right. She should have teleported back with him since they were not permitted to travel out without Michael's presence. Being that she was still there, Sattka realized her spell had no effect on him. With a fierce rush, Michael thrust the tent away in tattered pieces, exposing his crouching form on the ground-sheet. His red eyes smoldered intensely in the night.

Sattka suddenly enveloped in fear of his ability to resist the spell, gasped. Michael rose to his feet and growled through his teeth, "**I've teleported once already. I refuse to go along with you, the new Valkris, I see?**"

Before giving him a chance to crush her into nothing, Sattka swiped her blades again and hastily teleported home. A last spark of magic dropped to the ground after the demonic general vanished. Michael was alone in the dead of night, as he was every night, but without a tent. Transported back to his home would have led to ruin—for Michael and the world. It wasn't clear if they knew Eric lived or that he switched sides. What was clear, clearer than ever before was the desperation.

PART II
LAST CHAPTER
THE FINAL CRUSADE

Morning light awakened warriors to a final day before the fateful invasion of Pommel. There was enough time in the day to plan and brood over it all. Even hardened soldiers had found it difficult to draw the line between dread and honor. Such an attack was unheard of in the chronicles of any war before it. Officers ordered their troops to report for duty with the promises of spending the night with family and friends. An operation like the one to come was the kind that made widows and fatherless children.

Everything had to be right before the sunset. Humanity depended on their victory over the demonic army and the warriors depended on their leaders to strategize the perfect attack. Before the mobilization of the vast Falcun army could get underway, the greatest minds and warriors of the new world had to meet one last time. There could be no mistakes. The very fate of the world hung on the outcome of one battle. Even if the demons subsisted for the day, there would be no second. Not winning the first battle, meant losing the war.

In the Tactician's Prudence, an enclosed courtyard in the center of the Principal's Palace, they gathered. Michael and his most trusted company, Maxim, Predella, and Esker among them, made their way into the courtyard. Thomas and his two paladin sergeants were already at the large stone table, along with Shadisha and her strategist scribes across from them. Her scribes were tasked with copying everything she asked of them during the meet, solidifying the true scope of the attack.

There, in the midst of Michael's procession, Eric walked through, unshackled. The idea of pretending that he couldn't perform his sorcery in chains was readily dismissed at day's first light. The impending mission required a lofty degree of trust. Looking upon the traitor stirred up different emotions for her, but Shadisha trusted in Michael. She had no choice. For Predella and Maxim, on the other hand, such trust was tested beyond all merits. She never told Michael about Eric's visit or his admission to her last night. They both kept it to themselves for the good of the mission. Predella felt sick.

Lai and his captains stood up out of their seats to greet Michael as he came. In spite of his injuries, Lai insisted on his role in the incursion. He knew his ninjas as he knew himself. It was his duty to be there, regardless of the risk. Representing his sister and brother-in-law on the battlefield, no wound or smarting pain could stop him. His obligation was first to his people, then to his petty ailments.

Over three hundred Falcun soldiers guarded the yard, though not to protect the party from the sorcerer—but the other way around. When Michael reached the large table, he asked Shadisha with concern, "**Urik, is he—**"

"I urged him to sleep in. There's nothing I can't tell or show him after we're done here," Shadisha replied.

"**Very well,**" Michael said, sitting at the head of the table. "**I suppose we should start. I'll begin if we're all ready.**"

Everyone seemed to watch Eric cautiously as he leaned against a column, refusing to sit with the rest of them. It was for the best that he kept his distance anyway. Believing that everyone was prepared to flesh out the master plan for the momentous battle to come, Michael started speaking from the heart. He said, "**Before we do this, I have to tell you what an honor it has been to fight alongside you—all of you. I'd be proud to storm the gates of hell with the likes** of you. You are brave, selfless people. You've overcome differences, made peace with your enemies. No matter what takes place under that dark cloud, you're all heroes to me."

His words touched them, bolstering their purpose in the entire war. Each of them had made sacrifices. Each had risked their lives to bring the fight to this point and they were going to do it one more time. Thomas, finding it impossible not to say something, replied, "I think I speak for the rest of us here that we would follow you into those gates because we trust you. You've led us through the fire and, by God's grace, you'll lead us into victory tomorrow."

The prominent members of the party nodded and felt it was a fitting tribute to Michael, the man who battled his own demons while uniting so many against the Demon Plague. It would have been easier for the demonic forces if the kingdoms of the world remained divided. Eric couldn't believe just how genuine their faces were around the table. In being away for that long, he missed all the adversities Michael pulled them through. The admiration for him was unquestionable.

Planning out what he was going to say and how he was going to say it in his head first, Michael looked about the table and said, "**For this battle, it would be better if I wasn't there at all. To tell you truly, they are expecting me. They want me to come alone, but I couldn't do that. *If I do that, they will swarm me until I—*"**

"Turn," Maxim interceded, compelling Michael to nod with regret.

Esker then added, "And then we're all fucked."

"Essentially," Thomas uttered in agreement.

"**Which is where the Angels of Resistance comes in,**" Michael began. "**Once I infiltrate Pommel's bastion, you'll need to commence your attack. The Demon Lord will be** preoccupied with me, which will keep him off the battlefield. That's one good thing. The bad news is that Sattka, his daughter of sorts, will likely be leading the horde."

"Daughter?" Shadisha gasped. "They have daughters?"

"**Call her what you want, she's our greatest threat—more than ever before. This is where Eric comes in,**" he turned to him, compelling everyone to direct their attention to the infamous sorcerer. At last, they would learn his role in the decisive assault. Hearing it with an open mind, they allowed Michael to proceed. He said, "**The Demon Lord has granted Sattka with Valkris's powers. This complicates things for us. Eric can't cause havoc with an opposing sorcerer on the field.**"

"I can if I kill her first," Eric replied from the column. "I'll take her by surprise. She doesn't know I'm still alive."

"**We don't know what she knows. One thing *we* know for sure is that you'll be no good to the army that way. Is there any spell in your arsenal that can make her inept?**" he contemplated aloud, hoping Eric had something devious up his sleeve.

"You mean drain her magic," the sorcerer muttered. "It could be possible, but it's risky."

Maxim said, "This whole thing is risky. Can you *do* it is the question?"

"In theory," Eric explained. "I copy magic, not steal it. If I were to drain her powers away, I'd have to retain it in my core. That spell isn't meant to drain that much sorcery at once. It could kill me."

Esker rejoined, "But you *can* do it?"

Slighted, Eric snapped back, "And I can drain the blood of men, too. I can demonstrate if you—"

"That won't be necessary," Lai said, sensing the meeting was about to veer off course.

Eric then shouted, "You really don't want me to be dying prematurely! Keeping myself alive means keeping the rest of you alive! I'm the only shot you have out there when it gets bad! So, pardon me if I don't feel like committing suicide!"

To quell the rising tensions, Predella interjected, asking Eric directly, "Can you drain just enough of her powers until you feel you need to stop? It would, at least, be a shock to her system."

For Predella to suggest such a compromise took both Maxim and Eric by surprise. With all she discovered about the destruction of her people by Eric's hand, she had every right to scorn him. It revealed her willingness to cooperate with her enemies if only to help the army fight as one.

Eric considered her simple proposal and conceded, "I do believe that could work. I'd need to get in close, but it could be enough to work."

As the friction eased, Michael said, "**Then that will be your first priority—neutralize Sattka.**"

"Or just revert her back to her typical awfulness," Maxim added. "Trust me. She's a one-demon army."

Eric remained on task, "And what's my second priority? Kill everything while defending all of you, I presume?"

"That would sound about right," Shadisha replied utilizing the battle map on the table. "As Michael is inside, doing whatever he must do, Eric will fill the void outside. We'll need to keep away from the Shadowland's edge, as Thomas detailed what happened last time. Keeping our distance from the Shadowland will prevent the flyers from flinging debris into our lines, but it will also have us at a rather significant disadvantage."

"How so?" A ninja captain asked.

Leaning over the battle map, she revealed her plan for the attack, "For those that are going to invade the bastion, it will be harder to provide artillery support that'll cover them."

"Cover them?" Esker uttered in dismay. "You mean we are going into that hellhole again?"

"The battle needs two fronts—inside the bastion and the teams to cover them from the outside," Shadisha explained.

"Why go inside the bastion at all? Isn't that what Michael is for?" Esker contested with concern.

"**There is a finite amount of demons. Taking the fight to the bastion's interior will force them to split up their forces. With Ellium's assault from the south, Sattka would need to place forces outside to defend the bastion and inside to protect the citadel**," Michael illustrated on the map. "**Sattka is the main target. She's tired—sleep deprived. If you can kill her, then the demons will be without a general. With any hope, I'll have dealt with the Demon Lord by then.**"

"But you don't know what's down there," Maxim said. "For all we know, the Demon Lord will be lying in wait for the battalions invading the citadel. He could replace Sattka on the field once she's gone like Eric is doing for you."

"**I'll lure him in. He's expecting me**," Michael justified his designs. "**Where I am, the Demon Lord will surely be.**"

Exhaling apprehension into his clasped hands, Maxim sighed, "I hope to God you're right."

After the party reflected on the weight of the oncoming battle, Thomas spoke, "If this is a battle of annihilation, there will need to be distraction, encirclement, a decapitation force and, of course, a constant barrage of artillery in support. There will have to be a cavalry brigade that flanks the demonic horde and keeps them at a distance while—"

"We'll have all that, Thomas," Shadisha interjected. "It must be carefully planned, one step at a time. That's why we're all here. The perfect victory, one division, one brigade, one battalion at a time."

Anxious over the scope of the one-time battle, Thomas said, "I understand. It's just—if we lose this fight, if we don't defeat them before the sun goes down—"

"We're doomed," Lai blurted out. "Dead in the dark. The stakes were never as high."

"**Which is why we'll win,**" Michael iterated. "**We must.**"

Smothering the rising anxiety of the meet, Esker stood up and leaned over the battle map, saying, "So, what's it gonna be? Where do we all fit in?"

As the Falcun League's tactician, Shadisha obliged and compelled the others to gather around the battle map as well. When she saw they were all there, the plan unfolded before their eyes. Thomas and his Paladin Legion would need to converge with the Ellison army, serving as the communicator to both forces during the battle. His Holy Emblem Riders had the task of traversing the outskirts of the battlefield to deliver messages both north and south. Notwithstanding Thomas's initial objection to his role, he agreed to do his part.

After the theatre of battle was assessed, the push for the incursion of Pommel could begin. Michael needed to breach the bastion before the invasion started. Once inside, the Falcun League would deploy the East Rangers, warriors from the East led by Maxim and Esker. The company's charge was to storm the gates of Pommel, destroying anything that wasn't human. Kai League cavalry would push any resistance out of the path of the rangers' advance. Ninja warriors would follow in support, flanked by gunners on each side.

Suppressing fire from artillery outside of the Shadowland would have to be relentless, long after the East Rangers penetrated the bastion. From that point, interminable waves of divisions would rush the battlefield like breakers on the beach, attacking the Demon Plague's ground forces. Archers would prevent demon hordes from flanking the warriors or surrounding them. Coupled with the Ellison assault from the southern front, the battle would be a perpetual attack unlike the world had ever seen before.

As Eric neutralized Sattka and obliterated any airborne threats, Predella would provide him with cover fire as needed from the defensive line. Such a strategy, centered around the current battle arena of Pommel, would continue until Michael had destroyed the heart of the Demon Plague from within. It was a fundamental, but tentative plan. Shadisha left space for countermeasures, certain that the demons were preparing the Shadowland for a massive encounter. Anything was possible and the Angels of Resistance had to be ready for it.

Painstakingly, each of them added a different scenario to the battle, forcing Shadisha to come up with resolutions. A team of scribes wrote and drew feverishly as they deliberated. Hours passed, they broke for lunch and then went over the plans again. Their dialogues, soon enough, were more therapy than plotting. Talking about the fight ahead brought them closer together while reminding them at every turn of the warrior's prospect: Not everyone at the table was going to make it back alive.

The prospect of living for one more night before fighting the biggest battle of their lives had its effects. Some spent the rest of the night with family—others with their lovers. In the Tinarian sector, Maxim and Predella spent another night with each other. Lying under the sheets, the two bare lovers embraced as if it was their last chance. Sweating from their previous lovemaking, they looked up at the timber ceiling, thinking of tomorrow.

When neither of them spoke, Predella broke the weary silence, "I should be there with you in the thick of it."

"No, it makes sense," Maxim said, catching his breath. "I think this tactician knows what she's doing."

Sighing in disappointment, she uttered, "You *would* say that. Your conscience will be clean. But for me, I'll have to wait to see if you live through it—like Lana and Shioda."

"Don't say that," Maxim snapped. "You don't get it. It's not going to be like that."

"Oh no? You'll just rush into hell and I get to watch from the outer—" She stopped before starting to cry.

"Listen, Predella, you said—when you dragged me out of the Shadowland last time, you said you loved me. Then, just yesterday, you said it again." Maxim turned to her and stroked her hair. "I know you have feelings for me, but—maybe you shouldn't."

Predella only looked at him, taken aback by his hurtful admission. As she tried to find the reason behind it in his eyes, Maxim went on earnestly, "When we saved Shina from Fort Andrews and Antonis was killed, his last words, I think, were directed to me. He said that I would have to die to win. For all this time, I didn't understand what he meant, until now. I am going to die tomorrow and there isn't anything we can do to change that. I died once, so it's not that scary. This time, I will give my life for a purpose—"

"That's bullshit," Predella spouted, refusing to allow him to continue. She said, "Forever, you said you didn't trust anything he said. Then, suddenly, his dying words are your destiny—your fate? Tell me something, Maxim. Are you haunted by a dead man?"

"What?" Maxim gasped.

"It's not hard. You either believe that prophet's dying words or you believe what I'm telling you. I fell in love with a man who carved his own fate, sometimes with a sword and other times with his bare hands. Yes, I fear for your life out in the midst of the Shadowland, but that's *my* burden. I must be afraid for you because I've fallen for you. You don't have to admit that you love me back," Predella pulled his head closer, "but don't you dare tell me that I can't love you. I will worry about you and that's my right. I get to panic."

Hearing her lay it all out reminded him why he fell for her in the first place. She was able to see through him. And in seeing the dark parts, she cast no judgment. They found the lost pieces of themselves in each other. Maxim kissed her on the lips and said, "I love you, too."

Predella muttered, "Don't just say it because I—"

"No, I want to say it. It feels good to say it without fear or regret," Maxim replied with a new sense of conviction. "I never said those words to any woman in my life. In some ways, I never really knew what love was supposed to feel like. I didn't know how it would happen or what to do if I found it. It was just easier to go it alone and avoid hurting you. So, if I did die, I wouldn't have to worry about you crying for me. But I see how that was selfish. I *do* love you, Predella. You showed me that."

They converged in each other's arms and kissed again, leaving whatever words that could be spoken further on love and hate for the day after Pommel. Even if Maxim's confession was coerced at the moment, Predella was content with living the charade. Stradling him as he clenched her by the waist, they made passionate love. The shadow of Eric's fate was left to linger in their hearts, somewhere deep where love couldn't see it. It would pour out altogether—the love, the anger—after the defeat of the Demon Plague. All they had to do was survive until then.

Lai walked in on Lana and Shioda cuddled asleep in his bed. They held onto each other as if there was a chance they'd be forced apart. Though his eyesight was never good, he could see their future together. He went over to them and pulled the sheets up to their shoulders. Once kissing Lana on the side of the face and rubbing Shioda's back, Lai walked out and shut the door behind him, his spirit alive.

The Tofauti rested their weapons and found peace as a unit of brothers, drifting off in what could be their last night in a foreign distant land. Freedom was theirs, in triumph or in death. The sins of their past were but flickering fires, longing to be snuffed out than burn low forever. They would make a fateful charge with their new brothers in the East Rangers. In the morning, they could be baptized in battle. A new life was just beyond the dark horizon.

One would think she was going to battle in the morning the way she could not sleep, but Shina understood the cost of victory and defeat better than anyone. With her father gone and her brother having betrayed Tinaria as a sorcerer for the Demon Plague, victory meant that an Ellison uncle would vie for the throne. The life as she knew it was long gone. Even she was no longer the girl she left behind in the East. Yet, defeat at Pommel arguably denoted the end of the human race. Most of the world's greatest champions would fight for their right to exist. All Shina could do was pray.

As she looked out over the dark abyss of the western realm from the embassy balcony, Michael found rest. Anguish led him to think of any way of avoiding another visit from the Demon Plague and get a good night sleep. His desperation put him into the Great Pacifica, resting comfortably on a lone boat where the demons could not reach. Coming full circle, he laid on his back with his armed crossed under his head and slept. The serenity of the open water and the universe above were his comforts. But instead of wandering without direction or of a clue as to how he came to be there, Michael slept in the steadfast belief that his destiny waited at first light.

Lord Bravus, Lieutenant General of the Munitions Corps, led his Ellison army through Hessian Falls, a rocky outlet to Pommel's southern expanse. A force of shock and awe, the munitions divisions brought Ellium's glimmering soldiers of armaments and gunner specialists north. Armed with automatic shotguns, grenades, and pistols, each soldier was a one-man army when compared to the outer world's forces.

Massive rolling tanks were equipped with the finest cannons and rocket launchers capable of blasting gaping holes into stone. Other drivable machines hosted mortars and ballistae. Altogether, the army of thirty thousand bore down on the infamous Shadowland of Pommel, bewildered by its profound evil. Just staring upon the fixed miasma swirling high above the tower put them all in a state of dread.

Lying in wait within the rocky pass, Bravus expected his scouts to return with news of the Falcun army. Instead, sounds of galloping horses delivered Thomas Excallum and his Holy Emblem Riders to Hessian Falls. Over seventy paladins rode into the Ellison camp, bearing news of the Falcun forces and their convergence just north of Pommel. When Bravus's spies challenged him, having not seen the Falcuns for miles, the paladin assured them. The attack was imminent. The time had come. Thomas hastily explained the plan.

At Pommel's north battlements, vampiric lookouts bore witness to a mystifying spectacle. One after the other, gigantic whirling portals emerged about the perimeter of the Shadow-land. Strategically placed, the magical gates reeled, seven of them. Before the vampiric guards dashed off to alert the Demon Lord, an eighth portal opened. It was smaller than the others, barely recognizable from the bastion. From it came a thunderous missile, screaming across the Shadowland.

Michael soared towards them, shouting as he came, and pounded through the walls. Amid the great explosion, there he stood. His tattered cape waving behind him, Michael's eyes glowed red. What vampires that survived the blast had all but vaporized with just a flick of his wrist. They turned to ash in his wake. He then dashed through the corridors of his home to find the cryptic gate that led to where he could not see—the door beyond the fireplace.

When the crash of Michael's dramatic entrance echoed throughout the land, Thomas knew that it was time. Warning Bravus, he yelled, "That was it! That's the signal!"

Watching the undead murder of crows squawk and fly away amid the explosion's aftermath, Bravus flicked away his cigarette and said, "You better be right about this."

"Shell away," Thomas declared confidently.

Once the Ellison shelling of Pommel began, the Demon Lord teleported Sattka and Kane to a southern lookout. From there, they watched as the massive army fired their artillery. Explosive shells shook the bastion and made the tower sway. Sattka gawked at the thousands in the distance and said, "**It's beautiful. Look at all of them—like a delivery service.**"

"**That's the Ellison Munitions Corps,**" Kane said from behind his dark skull helmet. "**They have enough firepower to level this whole place.**"

"**Except, they won't do that—not with Miuriell here,**" the Demon Lord said exuberantly. "**He *is* here, sooner than expected. Our time has come. I am not to be disturbed.**"

Amongst the bombardment, the Demon Lord vanished, leaving Sattka and Kane to hold off the impending attack. But, for Sattka, it was a bittersweet objective. Her father, obsessed with Miuriell's destiny to reunite with Abaddon, offered too much mercy. If it was her choice, she would have already had him strung up and bled out. It vexed her that Miuriell had such a hold on her father. At the very least, she could revel in the slaughter of mankind. Perhaps, her father would be right.

"Today marks the end of the human race," she said in a staid tone. **"This show of force is a distraction. There will be more to come—the best ones. When they do, their sad resistance will be over. Get the army together. It's feeding time."**

She then leaped off the lookout and flew away, mingling with the crows amid the Ellison barrage. Kane wasted no time in following her commands. He withdrew into the tower and went to organize his forces. Unlike the Demon Lord or Sattka, he couldn't teleport or fly to his battle station. So, he jumped. He finally slammed into the parapet walk seven stories down, crushing some part of his armor. While it should have killed him, Kane's inhuman regeneration healed his critical injuries. In but moments, he recovered and went off to make his final arrangements. There was little time, for he knew that the main invasion was looming.

The Angels of Resistance, however, had already come. From the many portals about the Shadowland, humanity's last hope rushed forth. The soldiers and ninjas converged into the northern front with haste, racing through the mystical doors to come face-to-face with Pommel's hell on earth. Taking their positions one thousand feet from the demons' turf put the true nature of the mission into perspective. To defeat evil, they'd have to charge into it.

Pommel's northern and eastern towns were nothing but baron fields of rotting corpses and devastation. Much of it had been compressed, where some other parts rose like landfills and dipped like pits. The topography of the battlefield was a haphazard theatre, save the northern sector. It was the route of their escape days ago and would serve as the route of their main offensive. Sattka perched atop the tower in wait.

Upon shrieking, thousands of flyer demons soared out of the many openings of the citadel. Like killer bees about the hive, they circulated the fortress and emitted a collective hiss. The thousands of warriors that never saw such a sight almost didn't believe their eyes. The scene was overwhelming. Bravus, taken aback by the shocking spectacle, ordered his mortar and rocket tanks aim for the swarm of demons in the air. Soon, Sattka and her minions glided about the sky to evade the explosives.

"It's certainly worse seeing it in person than dreaming it up," Shadisha gasped from her chariot in the back of the line. "Get the sorcerer up here now."

Floating by her side with his arms crossed, he replied, "Already here. Shall we get this underway? Every minute passed is a minute closer to sundown."

"Sattka is circling the tower," Predella said from Shadisha's left side. "Can you get close to her?"

"Of course," Eric said, looking up at the booming war in the sky, "but I'd much rather she come to me."

Shadisha then shouted amongst the exploding shells in the distance, "Just go right now. Ellium can't keep up their firing forever."

"Oh, surely, master tactician," Eric retorted as he started for the Shadowland's treacherous atmosphere, "I wouldn't want them to waste any more shells than they have to."

Enchanted wings jutted from his back as he darted into the fray, cutting through flyer demons and avoiding explosive shells. When he saw that Sattka was onto him, he shouted, "I'm back! Tell me, sprite, did you miss me?"

"Traitorous filth!" Sattka swiped her blades together to project a magical cross capable of cutting him into fours. Eric withstood the blow with his own incantation, setting off a big wave of power that blasted flyers away. Both armies of north and south watched as the battle of sorcerers took place in the hellish firmament of demon and fire. Bravus commanded that the artillery cut down to half of its salvo power to conserve for later strikes and so there was a less likely chance of killing the sorcerer collaterally.

As the supernatural duel continued, Lai spotted a huge threat springing up from the Shadowland. Hordes of flyers had started pulling up a giant metal beam from the ground once utilized for skyscrapers and bridges before the apocalypse. Having dug it up days ago for such a purpose, the demons carried it through the air and lifted it higher as they came. Dreading the incoming attack by a projectile, Lai shouted in a dazed stupor, "There is nothing worse than when demons work together! Everyone, fall back!"

"My God, that'll do the trick," Shadisha muttered in the fear of what was about to ensue.

Stunned by the demons' maneuver, she could only look on as they dropped the nine-hundred-pound beam into the sun. The giant beam came pounding onto the ground, sending plumes of dirt and rust into the air. Just as the girder rolled and bounced for the front line, Eric materialized out of nowhere and cast a powerful spell for it. His sorcery clashed with the colossal beam but sent it soaring back into the Shadowland. Bemused onlookers nearly fell on their backs when Eric said, "Think I'll take this off your hands."

And just like that, he was gone, teleporting back whence he came, fighting the she-demon above Pommel. The girder hurled through flyer demons that tried to avoid it when it had finally reached him. Eric only touched the old beam with his open hand to take full control of it, regardless of its weight. In targeting Sattka, he sneered, "Surprise, bitch!"

Eric swung the beam for her, swatting flyers along the way, and ultimately striking the demonic general in the side. Sattka careened down for the citadel and crashed through to the eighth level, screeching all the way. Eric let the beam drop into the Shadowland as he pursued her below. He flew down to where she fell and entered the gaping hole, still coughing up smoke. Once the beam settled into the battlefield and the loud clanging was finished, the mystified army erupted into cheers. The infamous sorcerer saved their lives and offered a telling blow to the she-demon in the process.

Their cheering couldn't be heard from inside the tower, or from the pounding of the Ellison assault, but Eric knew his triumph was at hand. Sattka fought to break out from under the rubble, her eyes raging a fiery green. Eric closed in on her and proclaimed, "It's not all your fault. You were granted this power only a while ago."

Then, as he leaned over her maimed form, regenerating more every second, Eric said, "It isn't for everyone."

He quickly grabbed her by the throat and began draining her magic, absorbing its powerful contents into his core. The casting paralyzed her, permitting Sattka only to squeal. As she lay helpless in his attack, Eric started to feel his core overload. As he agreed, he bled more than half of her powers before aborting the rest. Taking enough to weaken her, he stumbled back and fell onto his knee, reeling from the unstable volume of magic inside. Eric teleported back to Shadisha's side, where he groaned from the strain of holding it all in.

Fearful bystanders retreated from his spot as volatile energy leaked out in perilous flashes and fluxes. His eyes had become bright flames of power and veins jetting out from his chest started creeping up his neck. In a deified voice, Eric cried out, *"Hurry and send them in! I have to get rid of this magic!"*

Shadisha shouted without wasting any time, "That's it! Send in the rangers! Let's go!"

Two demolitions specialists fired colorful mortars into the center portal, which soared over the East Rangers' heads from the other side. The signal received, Maxim unsheathed his Mad Phoenix and hollered, "Here we go! Prepare for the charge!"

Kai cavalrymen placed their horses at each side of the battalion before the East Rangers charged off into the portal. When the army was in formation and ready to make the most pivotal invasion of their lives, Esker looked to his Tinarian ally and then shouted madly, "Bring the pain!"

The Tofauti warriors cried out amid their Tinarian and Ziamon brothers, ready to make history or become it. They all rushed into the portal, transporting into the hell of war. The change in conditions came as a shock to each of them. Demons inherited the sky as earth-shaking bombs detonated all over the Shadowland. Parts of Pommel's tower and bastion fell off and slammed into the ground after taking enough hits from the Ellison munitions corps. Eric hovered above them with a god-like disposition and discharged crushing currents of lightning into the army of flyers. The scene was wildly overpowering.

Esker loved the idea of it, charging into Armageddon. He hosted a wide smile on his face as they neared closer to the Shadowland. With Maxim's enflamed fire-sword raised high in the air, the Eastern Rangers entered the cursed battlefield. A dark, overbearing sensation took them all by surprise. While the last of the rangers had come through, the Kai cavalry had finally started to meet them at the center. They ran for their lives towards Pommel's bastion with flyer demons falling all around them and bombs pulsating the atmosphere.

Eric ultimately closed six of the seven portals, leaving only the one behind them for emergencies. In their rush, some fallen demons hadn't died from the impact, leaving them free to lash out at the rangers. The warriors hacked and barraged them as they went, trying to keep the monsters away. Flanking cavalrymen safeguarded the battalion as much as they could.

Seeing that the dropping flyer demons posed a problem from them, Eric conjured a wind tunnel just above their heads by a few meters. The forceful gusts pushed the falling demons to the far sides, clearing the way for the warriors to make it to the bastion. But, Sattka, maddened by the loss of her sorcery, called her minions back. She had a plan in place in case of something as such happened.

As the flyer demons returned to their dens in the high levels of the citadel, Sattka summoned the shadow demons to rise from the darkness and snuff out the incursion. Kane, from his lookout, commanded the vampire general, "**What are you waiting for? Kaila? She's dead! Get your horsemen on those assholes, straightaway!**"

"**They are in route, even as you bark at me,**" the tall, slender vampire riposted. "**They don't need you to tell them that. You're not truly one of us.**"

"**You can bitch about that all you want later! Just do your job!**" Kane screamed. "**You remind me of that dick of a sorcerer—that traitor cunt!**"

"**Is he a dick or a cunt? He can't very well be both.**" He cast his red eyes downward at the cavalry of undead horse and ram, his black ponytail falling to one side.

While the two generals bickered over the employment of troops on the ground, the vampiric cavalry charged for the advancing rangers. From every direction, hordes of shadow demons surrounded them. The Kai cavalry stallions became spooked by the sudden ambush of creatures and many started to run wild. In moments, the cavalry became virtually futile, which left the rangers out in the middle of the Shadowland to fend for themselves.

As the vampiric cavalry sprinted closer to their stranded position, Maxim called for everyone to form in the center. The Tofauti knelt with their spears up so as to repel the charging horses and rams. The Tinarians lifted their shields while the Ziamons prepared for a bloody scrap. Predella saw the grave situation from her chariot and beckoned Eric to come back down to meet her. When he returned to ground level, Predella fretfully asked him, "What are you waiting for? They're about to get overrun!"

"Can't risk using any magic on them from here," Eric had tried catching his breath after slaying so many flyer demons.

"Then get in there!" she cried back. "They're all going to die out there!"

Eric countered, "And risk getting picked off by their sharpshooters? No, I don't think so. Besides, Sattka is up in that tower waiting for me to make that same mistake you're trying to—"

"Screw you, then. I'm going!" Predella was about to alert her charioteer that they were going to roll out when a horn sounded off to her side.

Shadisha held her by the arm and cried, "Predella, you aren't going anywhere! I need you here to guard the lines! The first wave is going in now to support the rangers!"

Eric smiled at her scornfully and said, "See? There's a plan for everything."

She answered only with a scowl, as the first wave of the army rushed into the Shadowland to stave off the demons. Maxim held his blazing sword out in anticipation of the attack from all sides, ready to kill anything that came close. When the cavalries collided, a one-sided battle ensued. The vampires blasted through the Kai cavalry and galloped for the rangers' formation. Shadow demons harassed them from everywhere.

Embracing for a brutal fight, the Tinarians raised their shields and readied their blades. Maxim, however, found an opportunity. He screamed for the nearest knight to hold their shield steady and jumped from it. As the knight pushed him off, Maxim sailed directly into the vampiric cavalry and hacked through them with his flaming sword. He was lost in the fire after the attack, but his countermeasure steered some horses away from his allies.

The bulk of the vampiric charge devastated the rangers in the first wave, knocking most of the warriors to the ground. Pingas was able to stab a rushing skeletal horse in the neck, forcing it to fall over and throw the undead soldier to the ground. Esker sliced one of the vampire's arms off as she came, though it didn't stop her from leaping into the group of rangers and attacking. With the constant assault from shadow demons, the attack seemed to last forever. Over a dozen soldiers were dead when the vampiric cavalry turned back to charge again.

The first Falcun division met heavy resistance on their push to support the rangers. Shadow demons materialized from every dark crevasse. By the time the undead cavalry had come rushing for a second attack, the ground was saturated with blood. Horses kicked it up and soldiers became stuck in it like red mud. Corpses of all kinds piled up around the perimeter of their anti-cavalry formation. The demons were relentless, like ants swarming its prey.

Maxim fought his way to the north so that he could face the undead cavalry a second time, his face already splattered with blood. But, before the second wave could hit, a violent flash of lightning struck the space between them, revealing Eric in his full power. A wave of his arms emanated a dense current of energy that scorched the advancing vampires, practically annihilating each one. The undead cavalry turned to smoldering ashes.

"That woman of yours can be persistent to the point of annoyance, can't she?" Eric said.

With the Falcuns' first division in sight, Maxim slashed open a demon's hide before panting, "Cover us! We've gotta get into that bastion!"

When Maxim raced back to his rangers, Eric muttered, "You're welcome."

Inside the citadel, Michael floated before the infamous fireplace that held the secrets of the Demon Plague. Walking closer to it, he felt its radiating power. The bastion sustained heavy attacks and he knew that there wasn't time to waste. Many risked their lives so that he could uncover the demons' weaknesses and crush them from the inside. Feeling around the extravagant fireplace, he looked for anything that could resemble a lever or button. There was nothing.

Then, as he thought on how he would break through, a soft whisper came from the furnace and gently blew by his ear, "*A star has fallen and he was given a key to the shaft of the bottomless pit.*"

It was then that Michael felt his Staff of Truth near, somewhere beyond the fireplace. Thinking about the cryptic whisper and what it meant, he knelt before the hearth and saw only stacks of wood. Yet, as he pondered its austerity, he felt drops of his blood fall from his nose. It had been so long since he bled, but, at last, there seemed to be a greater purpose than simply warning of evil to come. The drops of blood that fell to the floor seemed to run towards the hearth as if some force pulled it. Even on his fingers where he wiped some of it from his nose, the blood moved in the fireplace's direction.

While he could have tried to obliterate the entire room just to unearth the entrance, Michael inserted his hand with what little blood remained. Stronger, like a magnet, the pull of the hearth lured drops of his blood off his index finger and into the offering grate. A rumbling from underneath his feet and the fireplace transformed into a mechanical opening for some hidden stairway below. All it wanted was a drop of his blood and Michael was granted entry. From there, a mysterious, but evil power, beckoned him to enter.

As he ventured into the dark unknown, the motorized gateway closed him inside. A strong light awakened in the far reaches of the descending staircase, which sparked a virtual chain of lighting to guide his way down. Michael cautiously braved the stairs until he made it to the bottom, where there appeared to be a large chamber door with a bright screen just above it. Somehow, as he simply stood there, the digital panel scanned his entire body—his eyes, facial features, heart rate and even temperature. In moments, the steel door slid open.

A bloody, horrific mess awaited him in the vestibule. It was as if a thousand people were slaughtered inside over time. The rank smell of death and tinny blood inundated his senses, inducing him to gag. While the chamber was large, hosting a slew of passages and doors in a hexagonal pattern, it all began to close in on him. The sheer evil of the vestibule, coupled with the stench of the dead, nearly brought him to his knees.

As he tried to understand what happened there, Michael found his staff. The artifact floated in the center of the gory hexagon, bewitched by some supernatural power. Amid the gruesome display, he didn't recognize it there. He knew, in the scheme of things, that the Staff of Truth was put there by design. The Demon Lord wanted him to have it back, but for a deeper purpose. He hovered inches over the floor, stained with dried blood, and pulled the staff over to him as he came. Once reunited with the illustrative extension of himself, what he expected came to pass. A rush of understanding overcame him, flashing the past, present, and future into his mind all at once. In an instant, he was connected to everything.

The dried blood all over the vestibule was nothing more than a crude style of wallpaper, making the setting for rituals homelier. The floor under him was a filtration device for fresh offerings of innocent blood, drained from young women and then dispersed in the complex vessels and conduits deeper in the perverse facility. Further down, a massive lab collected the blood and stored it in individual tubes fit for bodies. Despite its immorality, the technology was superiorly advanced.

How old was this facility? Based on its machinery, it must have been built during the Primeval Tragedy—maybe even earlier than that. This place could be over a thousand years old. But why? For what reason would anyone create such a depraved lab? What was the Demon Plague doing with it? Michael fought for all the answers to his questions right there where so many sacrifices were offered to the bizarre machine.

But as he ventured through time and space to uncover everything he could about the facility and its creators, a ghost of his former self had come walking by him with staff in hand. Somewhere in the past, Michael wandered into the chamber and entered the door directly ahead. He seemed to be under some spell, blindly following an urge to be there.

Seeing himself wander the cryptic facility cracked his version of reality. The hard truth broke his heart. It was him. It was all because of him.

Michael watched himself amble through the compound as if it was his home—as if he had been there before. There was no greater pain than knowing Lord Drake Vitan was right all along. Michael followed himself deeper into the facility and traveled down a large working elevator to a lower level. It was his first conscious experience in such a transport machine, but he had clearly ridden in it before. Numbers and terms from the old world alerted him that he had arrived at the main level of the test center. Again, he followed his past self into the wing.

The door slid open fully and welcomed him into a diffusely lit lobby with old and broken furniture littered about the tile floor. The smell was rancid, giving off the scent of old death and mildew. Once he walked out from the elevator, Michael felt closer to the nefarious secrets hiding somewhere within. The walls were white at one time, but decay had consumed them. Some areas were splattered with blood, ancient blood. The one to the left had a picture of steps with odd writing under it. The door to his right was unmarked, but his past-self used the one directly ahead.

Bullet marks riddled the entryway. Upon pressing the red button, the door slid to the side and revealed a large spacious observation room with a wide glass window. Lights from the ceiling were dead or blinking, testifying to the battle that must have taken place. To his astonishment, he watched himself amble over to a control center and press buttons. Michael followed him to see what he had done.

The place was practically destroyed and many people had undoubtedly met their end some time ago. Pieces of the walls were destroyed, some with gaping holes. Thousands of bullet holes riddled the room. The only things missing were the bodies and whatever weapons they used. But when he saw himself press the red button on the command console, his old vision had vanished. It was then that he noticed what was on the other side of the great observatory window.

A sizable machine, similar in shape to Eric's magic doors, called to him from the other side. The sounds of cries and screams echoed through his head. Explosions and gunfire had resounded from all over. Abaddon terrorized the lab during the Primeval Age. It was where the Demon Plague was created. It was where Abaddon was born to the world. It was where he came to reopen the portal, permitting darkness to enter his home.

Somehow, the underground lair was built for Pommel. There was another room beyond the portal. Michael barely saw it through the darkness and floating flakes of debris. The button had been pressed at least one time every day since he started up the portal, allowing for all of it to happen. Using his staff to see, Michael found Sattka as the one operating the old apparatus. The gate formed, like magic, from just the touch of that button—its programming saved for a thousand years.

Utilizing his staff again, Michael observed what lied beyond the gate. Many stations, all of them destroyed, were situated around the large portal. Age-old blood was everywhere, but fresh blood-soaked in a small tank inside the vast chamber. In order to trigger the portal again, it required the fresh untainted blood of human sacrifices. Somehow demons materialized from the gate, but something had to happen from inside those chambers first for it to work.

Yet, as he peered beyond the gate, a wicked sensation ran up his spine. When Michael turned around, fearing that he was not alone, he realized that his intuition was rarely wrong. From the shadows of the control room, the Demon

Lord came into view and said, "**Impressive, I know, but it's much more profound in person.**"

He propelled Michael with a great force, smashing him through the observation glass and down into the dim lab itself. Barely surrounding himself with his telekinetic field, Michael fell sliding onto the floor below, but twenty feet from the old portal machine. The sinister magic that shocked his body put his nervous system in overload. He used his staff as leverage to rise, at least, to his knee.

"**Welcome home, Miuriell.**" The Demon Lord's voice came from everywhere and nowhere. "**Welcome to where it all began—where *we* began, thanks to you.**"

"**That wasn't me!**" Michael shouted from his knee, still rattled from learning about his role in the demons' awakening. "**Something possessed me to start this disgusting—**"

"**Abaddon,**" the demon replied. "**He was reborn in you as we awaited your second coming. We waited so long for you to finish what you started. When you restarted your project down here, I thought you had returned to us. But you could imagine our confusion when you repelled our arrival.**"

Michael used his staff to revisit that fateful night when he awakened the Demon Plague. He was possessed by a dark force, but only until something broke him free. When Opal was slain before him, her heart torn right from her chest, it severed Abaddon's hold on his consciousness. His overwhelming sadness and fury over her murder snapped him back into himself, burying Abaddon so deep that only the demons were able to sense it afterward.

"**My wife.**" Michael seethed from the ground. "**That was all I remember. When your monsters killed my wife. You made a mistake—underestimating me. You undervalued my grief. And my love for her—for my son!**"

"**Yes, perhaps you're right.**" The Demon Lord's voice had softened. "**We didn't anticipate your sentiment.**"

"**My sentiment?**" Michael growled as the floor started to crack from his anger. "**Let me show you what sentiment can do for us humans.**"

He shouted and detained the portal device in a fury. In seconds, he crushed it to the ground, laying its smoking, sparking heap onto a conveyor belt that ran through it. Michael tore the concoction from the floor and threw it into the broken glass of the observation window. The machine was smashed and rendered inoperable forever. Nothing would come through it ever again. The demons remaining on the field were the last of the Demon Plague. Though the triumphant destruction of the satanic machine was fulfilling, Michael had to wonder why the Demon Lord failed to stop him in the act.

As he breathed heavily after killing the gate to evil, the Demon Lord said from somewhere, "**You think destroying your greatest achievement will kill the conquest that you, yourself, put in motion? It's irreversible. Look under your feet. That is where you were born. You can create a gate far better than that now. Abaddon never finished what he sought out to do.**"

Michael looked down at the dried puddle of blood and tightened the grip on his Staff of Truth, "**And why not? Didn't you ever think on that? He never finished it, because he never wanted a conquest! If he wanted you, he would have returned to this evil place and unleashed you then! What was he waiting for?**"

Trying to pinpoint the Demon Lord's location proved to be fruitless, as he answered ubiquitously, "**To test the world. He wanted to see if it was as vile as he presumed. And, as you well know, it was. Your world ended.**"

"**But not before his campaign,**" Michael retorted. "**He stopped—abandoned you here.**"

"**Your humanity has made you weak and so stupid,**" the Demon Lord declared. "**His time is now. Don't you see it yet? Humanity, in all their vile wickedness, has fallen. Their rule over this planet is dead. Now, it is Abaddon's time to torment the unmarked. It's all your God's will.**"

"**No. If it's Abaddon's time, then it's *my* will!**" Michael cried out wildly. "**And I just want to kill you!**"

"**Then prove it, Miuriell!**" the Demon Lord cried from the other side of the lab, through the remnants of the portal machine, with his red eyes blaring in the darkness.

In what seemed like a flash of light, Michael soared into the mysterious laboratory and smashed through his nemesis. On impact, the Demon Lord broke into hundreds of glass shards that transformed into black moths and beetles that flew and scurried away. Michael slid into the vast chamber as he realized he played into his enemy's hand. The ploy to lure him into the extended laboratory succeeded. Searching for the Demon Lord somewhere inside, Michael utilized his staff and frantically searched the breadth of the entire facility.

While he couldn't locate the grand demon, Michael came to understand where he found himself. Thousands of dimly illuminated body-sized tubes hosted preserved avatars of shadow and flyer demons. A strange green solution conserved the creatures for hundreds of years by some means. Many of the glass containers were already empty, some still wet with claw prints tracking on the floor. Michael searched more of the enormous facility, finding the larger tubes from where the demonic generals had awakened.

As he examined the evil laboratory further by way of his staff, the Demon Lord's voice resounded, "**Welcome to our birthplace. Your greatest achievement was always us—an army for the ages. These husks hold our spirits** and we sustain them like engines to a machine. You gave us life."

"**I didn't do this. I don't understand—**" Michael could hardly comprehend his role in all of it.

"**Your fiendish avatars proved to be the most perfect paradox. Divine souls of vengeance armored with the evil casting of humanity's wickedness projected back upon them,**" he finally revealed himself in his daunting form, his giant wings spread out like a dragon's, blocking the only way out. "**It's time to choose, Miuriell. Finish the conquest you started centuries ago, or die with the human race that has debased this world. I warn you, this is your last chance.**"

Still overcome by the perplexity of the Demon Plague's origin, Michael wrathfully answered, "**I must avenge those who died during this madness. I caused this hell to be unleashed. I brought this calamity upon us. So, it's up to me to make it right. I can't explain how all this could have possibly existed under our noses for so long. What I know for certain is that none of you belong here.**

"**You think you're angels fighting some holy war against us? What kind of heaven would send monsters like you? No, you don't belong here. I'm sorry you waited this long for bad news, but this 'conquest,' or whatever the hell you want to call it, ends right here—right now. And may God forgive me.**"

When Michael concentrated his powers for his chance to kill the Demon Lord as fast as possible if only for the sake of his friends, the grand demon channeled his own awful power and said, "**Then you've elected to die. Challenging me in this place is a useless endeavor. You'll lose yourself and Abaddon will finally be unleashed.**"

"**We'll see,**" he replied, holding his staff out before him.

The Demon Lord wasted no time in dashing for him in the hopes of disposing of Michael quickly. Their collision inside the murky lab blasted nearby consoles and tubes into shards of debris. Alarms sounded after pressurized tanks erupted. In their duel, waves of their malevolent power pulsated about the incubated demon avatars, filling them with life.

Two divisions of Ellison tanks invaded the Shadowland, breaking through barriers and fences built with human bones. Shadow demons swarmed the vehicles to slow them down for flyers to swoop in for the attack. Remnants of the Mad Legion fired rockets and cannons from the bastion's southern line. The egregious exchange of artillery from both sides generated a massive smog of sulfur. Chaos inherited the field.

From the north side, Maxim and the East Rangers were able to make it to the main gate, leaving demons and vampires in their bloody wake. Eric had produced a forcefield that kept them safe from flanking shadow demons. Legionnaire sharp-shooters picked off rangers who struggled to make it into the door. Shadisha, noticing the perils of their desperate attempt to breach the fortress, commanded that cannons obliterate the snipers' perch.

Anticipating the incoming barrage from artillery, Kane and Lucero, the vampiric general, took evasive action. While Kane fled deeper into the bastion, Lucero jumped down into the brawl of the battlefield. He landed on his feet, splashing bloodied mud, and unsheathed his jagged sword. When the cannons began their bombardment, Lucero began his attack. Pingas saw the vampire's swift assault upon his fellow rangers and intervened. He charged the undead assailant and thrust his spear for his back.

However, Lucero effortlessly evaded the strike, rolling to the side, and accepted the Tofauti's challenge. Seeing his confederate take on the vampire singlehanded, Kulind tore away from the front line to help. Amid the frantic fighting in Eric's forcefield, the rangers killed their last demon and started pushing through the barricade leading into Pommel's main atrium. Rubble rained down on them as they fought a horde of demons into the bastion.

"This is a goddamn mess," Eric muttered, holding back droves of demons from overrunning the East Rangers. Flyers returned to the skies amongst the cannons' salvos, pouring fragments of debris over him. Losing his patience over the infuriating stalemate, he shouted, "Fools, back away from the barrier! I'll do it myself!"

Tinarians pulled Maxim away from the barricade before Eric discharged his spell. Rising into the air, he stretched out his arms and emitted a whirling inferno that thrashed the barricade of metal, wood, and creature. Charred shadow demons scurried away from the blast site as Maxim led the charge inside, bringing his own source of flames along the way. Esker raised his bloody blades and shouted for any lingering troops to follow him inside.

Eric then turned his attention to the hordes of demons eager to rush in and decimate them. Considering the resurgence of the flyers above, he decided that he had enough. Manipulating his own forcefield, Eric propelled his magic wall outwards into a devastating pulverizer that eradicated hundreds of shadow demons at a time. The first wave of the army slowed their advance to avoid getting vaporized. There was still a myriad of demons crawling about the Shadowland, keen on massacring their human intruders. The army had taken advantage of ground and rushed deeper into the field with their shields out front.

Hearing of the East Rangers' successful incursion of the bastion and her first division gaining ground, she launched her second division of six thousand troops to supplement the first. When the warriors charged the battlefield, roaring to bolster their courage, Eric took notice and returned to the sky to kill the resurging flyers. Burning through the opposition, he focused all his power and opened up a superior dome of magic energy, electrifying the flocks of demons in his vicinity.

While the East Rangers had almost entirely invaded the bastion, Esker waited for the Tofauti that challenged Lucero in the field. Masses of shadow demons were converging on them. The brothers-in-arms fought as one to slay the vampire, but couldn't overcome him. When the last of his Ziamons entered Pommel, Esker finally shouted for them to abandon the fight and join them in the safety of the bastion's atrium. They were too engaged in combat to hear him.

Graysonel landed a successful strike into Lucero's thigh, but it barely slowed down the undead general. In but seconds, the new wave of shadow demons would be upon them. Pingas knew it and decided to take it on himself to keep the vampire at bay so his confederates could escape. Calculating the best opening for his attack, Pingas reared his spear back and took in the fight from paces away. When Lucero kicked Kulind out of the melee, Pingas threw his spear. The strike pierced Lucero in the back, tearing through his tattered cape. After throwing it, he rushed the vampire, trying to reach him before he knew what was coming.

Once the vampire pulled the spear out from his lower back, he sensed Pingas's advance and anticipated the assault. Lucero spun about and smacked him to the side, putting him into the bloody ground. By that time, it was impossible to stay on the field, for the shadow demons scampered in. Esker slid into the scene and pulled Graysonel back, risking his life to rescue the war-bent Tofauti. Ziamons and Tinarians alike came to help drag Graysonel through the reddened mud and out of the fight. Kulind ran along with them, leaving Pingas and Boma there to face the horror. There was no saving them.

Graysonel and Kulind's last sight of their brothers-in-arms was of the demons consuming them as Lucero snapped Pingas's spear in half. The Ziamon crossbowmen then stood over the Tinarians' crouched shields and fired bolts to keep the wild demons back. As the Ziamons reloaded, the Tinarian knights lashed out at the creatures until the crossbows were ready for another salvo. But there were too many of them and they started crawling over the soldiers to scurry inside. Maxim and the others desperately sought to kill any that breached.

"Why? You should have left us out there!" Graysonel shouted at Esker over the mayhem of the atrium's conflict, "They were torn to shreds out there!"

"And you would have joined them!" Esker shouted back. "What were you thinking challenging that guy? You could have gotten us all killed!"

"Pingas was the first! He was the first of us to choose to remain—" Kulind started mourning the loss of his friends while panicking over the seeming hopelessness of present circumstances.

Esker cut him off amid the hostilities, hollering, "Then you fight on in his memory! You carry on for them! But, don't you dare pull that shit again, or I'll leave you there to get minced by those things! You get *one*."

Spotting the vampire general through the violent fight at the main doorway, Graysonel vowed boldly, "I will kill that bastard!"

Esker replied before joining the others in pushing back the demons, "You'll get your chance again! Believe me!"

When it seemed that the demonic horde would finally push through, for sheer numbers alone, the creatures began to turn their attention to the field. Shadisha's opening division of ninja warriors reached the bastion, bringing their bloody rage with them. They clashed with Lucero and the demonic army of shadows, alleviating the East Rangers' brutal battle inside the bastion. Esker ordered that the human barricade remain at the door to deter any further attacks and then hunched over to catch his breath.

"You alright?" Maxim asked, recovering from the serious bout just moments ago.

Esker cleaned the blood off his blades as he returned, "I think we bit off more than we can chew. You should watch the Tofauti. They're the only ones left and they're sour about it."

"Dammit," Maxim sighed. "We've lost many a good man so far. Gotta hope the worst is over."

"Nothin' is over until we clean out that nest upstairs," he said. "If we can station some arrows up there—"

"Good call. I'd like some of the first division to come and join us in here before we spread out deeper into the bastion," Maxim said. "Let's just hope they can hold them for now."

After discussing tactics with Esker, Maxim commanded a task force to neutralize the verandas and crenellations to obtain the high ground and eliminate the enemy forces there. The Shadowland had become a nasty arena for fraught battles of demon and man. The first and second divisions of the army brought the ferocity that they promised, skirmishing with the shadows, flyers, and vampires in open combat. Much of it had already changed them forever, ingraining nightmarish visions in their memory that would haunt them for years to come.

Eric practically chased the flyer demons away a second time, slaying over a hundred more than before. Yet, from the large hole of the fortress came a hastening flash of green, rocketing upwards for her target. In sensing something after him, Eric turned towards Pommel, but not in time to stop the demonic general from stabbing both her blades into his chest. Sattka, having recuperated from his draining attack, skewered the sorcerer and plummeted down with him, screaming as she descended. Vengeance was hers.

Though Eric tried to fight her back, there was nothing he could do with her blades piercing straight through. Finally, like a meteorite, Sattka and Eric slammed into the harried battle-field, creating a great boom and a wide crater. After the smoke and debris had cleared away, the she-demon flew off and reclaimed the skies. Even the Ellisons felt that something was wrong. The dynamic of the field had changed, tipping in the Demon Plague's favor.

Having lost their greatest asset in the battle, a collective gasp rung out across the battlefield. In such a sudden turn of events, the warriors in the Shadowland became hazardously vulnerable. The East Rangers in the bastion were stranded. An entirely different strategy was needed and fast. In response to the heart-wrenching loss of their sorcerer, Shadisha ordered that her third division enter the field prematurely in the hopes of engulfing the demonic army with their combined strength.

Lai sent out his reduced cavalry to retrieve the sorcerer before the demons had at his body. While he was once a traitor to the cause, Eric fell as an angel of the resistance. Thirteen of them galloped out amongst the carnage of war to find where Eric had been routed. Heavy infantrymen pushed for a clear pathway for the horsemen. Predella had already picked off a dozen flyers that came too close to the line when she noticed that the demons in the air had radically decreased in number. Eric's efforts made a difference. Over a thousand demons had met their end by his hands alone.

But moments later, scouts from his Holy Emblem Riders reported to Thomas that Eric was defeated. The need for spectacular aggression was in order. Lord Bravus approved a special black operations force to invade the bastion and meet up with the East Rangers to take over Pommel's citadel in case the first division couldn't risk leaving the field. It was a gamble, but Thomas was able to convince his Ellison allies that such a tactic was necessary for the stability of the joint attack of both forces.

Their agreement came as Lai's cavalrymen returned in full form with Eric's body, bloodied and beaten. Predella ran over to see him for herself. Seeing him spread out on a sheet in the back of the line came with mixed feelings. He was her people's destroyer, but also a reformed freedom fighter for the resistance. Eric saved thousands of lives during the battle up to that point. It seemed surreal watching the exiled prince lay motionless without uttering a quip or a snark. The portal that delivered the East Rangers had closed as a result of his defeat, making it clear that any chances of an emergency withdrawal were out of reach.

However, while inspecting his critical wounds, Predella felt for a pulse and found it in his neck. She then felt a faint one in his wrist. She impulsively shouted, "He's alive!"

The chief combat medic interceded, "That's impossible. Look at his wounds, girl. You saw that spectacle earlier. This man is long gone."

"Or you can just feel for his pulse like I just did," Predella retorted from her knee. "He's not gone yet."

"He was dead just moments ago! He had no sign of life!" the same medic replied in shock after examining him a second time. "She's right. Somehow, he's breathing!"

Predella, amid the stir around Eric's body, thought out loud, "Sattka has the ability to regenerate. I saw it for myself in Tinaria. When Eric drained her magic, he probably absorbed some of her regenerative properties as well."

Lai uttered from his horse, "Clever son-of-a-bitch. That means he could recover from this. That's what you're saying."

"That's what I'm saying," Predella declared.

Shadisha then commanded the party, "Get him into a medical tent and watch him carefully! We still have one hell of a war to win here!"

Soldiers carried Eric away with a throng of medics at the ready when Predella counted six arrows left in her quiver. The Shadowland was a loud, horrendous theater of war and it was only going to get worse with Eric on the sidelines. She ran over to her fletcher and asked for an abundance of arrows, as many as he could find or make. More demons were going to test the line and she would need to be ready. Predella was prepared to answer the call, one scorching arrow at a time.

The Demon Lord and his newborn minions propelled Michael through another wall, setting him into a different lab sector. Bleeding and exhausted, he steadied himself and put out his staff before him. Red blinking lights and a blaring alarm warned the inhabitants of the underground facility that its stability was at risk. Yet, Michael stayed firm in his stance. An army of newly awakened demons followed him into the new lab, but not as disciples—as hunters.

When a multitude pounced for him, he let loose his staff and let it twirl about the room, cutting the monsters in halves. When over thirteen had been sliced apart, Michael beckoned the Staff of Truth back into his hands and waited for another wave. Hundreds had burst from their long sleep, hungry for blood. Michael tried to control them, but it was no use. There was something different about the new creatures.

The Demon Lord materialized from the far corner of the large laboratory, unphased by Michael's best tricks in combat. He advanced towards him and said with his wings stretched out, "**These children will not obey you, Miuriell. With our dark auras expelling all about this place, they awoke under my control. Since you've chosen death over your true destiny, they smell only weakness and fear.**"

"**I have no time for this,**" Michael countered jadedly. "**I will kill all of them if need be, including you!**"

"**Look around you. This facility was created to make husks for an earth-ending army. You'll never destroy all of them and walk away with your life,**" the Demon Lord proclaimed as he advanced for him. "**This room is where we store the offerings of blood. Those two cisterns alone have served as our sleeping pods, rejuvenating our avatars. An army such as this must feed to attain the same benefit. It was you who brought us here, Miuriell. Now, we shall be the ones to end your life.**"

Foreseeing the grand demon's crippling attack, Michael counted on his staff to show him something he was missing—anything that could turn the tables. His omnipresent sight scoured the entire facility for a weakness. In just seconds, he located, at least, one last ditch possibility—a final recourse. It prompted him to find the same hopeful device in the current lab. All he needed was a fire.

"**You're right. I made this place, or some form of myself did, a long time ago. And if I made it right, I would have included a basic failsafe for that time period,**" he said with his eyes on the power unit in the wall. In a sudden pull, Michael yanked the electrical wires from their foundations and combusted a tank of compressed gas from several feet away. The small spark ignited a flame, setting off the anti-fire sprinkler system inside the lab. Though the archaic system was slow to start, there was enough water in the reservoir to shower the room.

Throngs of shadow and flyer demons fled the sector, fearing the degenerative properties of the water. Even the Demon Lord winced from the water's burning effects. Putting out his palm to catch the droplets, Michael stood amongst the shower and said, "**This little project wasn't finished yet. I know that, because the creators installed a genetic defect in your avatars that made it susceptible to water, just in-case the specimens went rogue. And, to prevent them all from fleeing the underground lab, they made your husks vulnerable to direct sunlight. So, you see, demon? You're just an incomplete experiment—the whole lot of you.**"

The sounds of screeching demons rung out from around the facility as the Demon Lord slowly learned to withstand the cold downpour, vanishing from the room. Michael only had to find him under the falling rain of the laboratory to finish it. As weak as he was, however, the grand demon transcended the basic laws of its husk. Slaying him would be no easy task, but, for once, it was possible.

Maxim's task force, dispatched to eliminate the enemy's perch atop the bastion's crenellations, claimed victorious. A well-timed, expertly driven ambush overwhelmed the Mad Legionnaires and few vampires that commanded them. After staging the daring act, the squad set up a nest for two Tinarian gunners and a bowman. The insanity of the ongoing battle below proved to be disturbing. Smells, coupled with the sounds and sights of the violence, induced the squad to cover their noses and mouths.

However, from their advantage of height, they noticed a peculiar formation of soldiers assembling yards behind the line. When the squad leader donned his binoculars, he saw what appeared to be the remainder of the Mad Legion flanking the Angels of Resistance's forces. The surprise maneuver put the army in a bind, trapping them between the Shadowland and the legion. Over thirty cannons lined the front, ready to open a deadly volley. It was too late to warn their allies of the impending attack.

Just when some of Lai's cavalrymen noticed the enemy formation behind their lines, the artillery began firing. Taken by surprise, the army took emergency defensive measures not taken into consideration beforehand. The legion had ample time to aim their cannons accordingly, so they hit most of their marks. Like sitting ducks, Shadisha's remaining two divisions endured the brunt of the attack. In droves, warriors met their end before ever seeing battle.

In a panic, Shadisha instantly employed the fifth division with annihilating the Mad Legion before they caused damage that could not be remedied. Lai sent out the rest of his cavalry ahead of the fifth division in the hopes of preventing another round from legionnaire cannons. After the fifth division set out to take on the remnants of the Mad Legion. Predella came over to Shadisha's side and protested, "I should go with them!"

"Predella, I've already told you that I need you here! At any time, those things can—" Before Shadisha could finish her reprimand, Predella saw Sattka soaring for them and aimed an arrow for her. The front line watched the demonic general swoop down with great speed, charging a magical aura about her. Like a comet, Sattka planned to plummet into their very position. While Predella fired an accurate shot for her, the she-demon burned right through it and fell upon them.

"Watch it!" an officer cried while they all dispersed from the incoming collision. As the demon screamed with might, Shadisha watched in a daze, bewildered at Sattka's risky attack out from the protection of the Shadowland. She slammed into the front line like a meteor, causing a loud and devastating detonation.

From the destruction, Sattka urgently crawled towards the shelter of the Shadowland before taking to the air again, regenerating her razed skin. The sun ate into her scaly flesh, but the comfort of the miasma rejuvenated her in seconds. When the pain subsided, she cackled in the war-torn sky, pleased with the demoralizing counteroffensive outside the battlefield.

Predella, although rattled and shaken, crawled on all fours, alive. The dust lingering in the air and the ringing in her ears altered her interpretation of what really occurred. All that she was able to make out through the remains of the front line was a winded officer desperately working to revive Shadisha. Ultimately, the army's efforts were in vain. Their master tactician was dead.

Hearing about the sudden attacks upon the line, Maxim ran up to the third level balcony to see the chaos for himself. Smoke concealed the devastation from afar, leaving only the sounds of desperate battle and artillery fire. He tracked Sattka as she soared amongst the flyers, knowing that she had dealt at least two death-dealing blows to the resistance already. It was clear that something had to be done about her.

Warriors from the first division began entering the main atrium occupied by the East Rangers, finding fleeting salvation and a place to rest. The rangers opened the way for them as they sporadically came, battle-weary and shaken. But, as they expected, the respite was short-lived. Lucero and his flock of vampires and shadow demons also returned, seeking another chance to reclaim the bastion's main atrium. Soldiers of the first division took up arms again, unwilling to allow the evil forces any hope of breaching their asylum. Esker took charge.

"There are plenty of giant holes in this bastion for those things to sneak in from! We're not going to stop that vampire asshole!" he shouted so that the multitude of soldiers could hear him. "The only way to stand a chance is to let them in! We create a death trap in here, enclosing them from all three sides at once! Understood?"

Just as the wave of evil started to rush forth, the party assumed defensive formation, as Esker outlined. Then, like a hurricane's tidal surge, the beasts entered. Half a dozen at a time, the demons scurried in, thirsty for more blood. Ziamons, Tinarians and Falcuns alike held their positions and locked in the creatures for as long as they could, keeping them trapped at the atrium. The fighting was intimate and fierce, pitting human and demon against each other in close quarters.

Lucero entered almost casually with his jagged sword dripping blood from the blade as if it was leaking. He killed over thirty brave men on his own and looked to extend his tall tally inside. Graysonel waited for him to come. He grabbed his ally by the arm and pointed him out. Pingas and Boma had to be avenged and they had to be the ones to do it. Holding their spears tightly, so as not to miss even an inch of the target, the Tofauti brothers stabbed and pierced their way to the vampire general.

Maxim heard the ruckus from where he was and knew that the atrium was breached. Peering down on the battlefield showed the influx of demons, hordes of them. He ordered that the squad fire everything they had down upon the monsters in the hopes of slowing them. The flyers were getting closer to their position, so they also had to be cautious. Two Tinarians threw percussion grenades down into the unholy cluster. The bombs' detonations shook even the bastion's crenellations.

As Maxim left them there to help his allies in the atrium, the four knights that guarded the entranceway to the veranda were left in the corridor, butchered. He stopped there and un-sheathed his fire-sword, making it blaze violently. Then, from the darkness of the passage, a familiar voice came, "**Tinarian scum, we have unfinished business.**"

Maxim realized that the murdering traitor he thought he killed had come back as a stronger foe. The broadsword in the monster's other hand suggested that he was no longer human. Incensed by the killer's new ghastly form as he stepped into the light, Maxim shouted, "I see you finally turned into what you are on the inside—a deformed monster!"

"**I wanted you all to myself this time. No distractions. No conditions,**" Kane growled haughtily. "**Just you, me and that sword.**"

"You'll come to regret that!" Maxim dashed for him and offered up a flurry of scorching blows.

Kane, bearing the weight of his heavy armor and sword, withstood Maxim's attacks. They clanged blades and parried critical strikes, but with Kane always giving ground. Finally, Maxim leaped and kicked his foe through an old wooden door, sending the Slayer into another room somewhere. He jumped into the broken doorway and pursued Kane further, lighting up the dark hall as he went.

A critical battle emerged at the bastion's main entrance, making for a tight mass of blood-spattered fighting. The survivors of the first division that didn't make it inside

Pommel's citadel withdrew and merged with the second division locked in battle within the middle of the battlefield. As the third pushed inwards to relieve the first and the second, the East Rangers fought to hold their positions inside the atrium. Systems of communication broke down after Shadisha was killed, leaving the warriors in the bastion to fight until the very end.

Finally reaching Lucero amid the carnage, the Tofauti took their chance. Spears were not ideal in such close combat, but Graysonel fought through ally and enemy to fight the dark general head on. Lucero smiled pertly and accepted the new challenge, certain that he had the advantage in every aspect. Graysonel jabbed at him, but couldn't land a single thrust. The vampire deflected close calls with his jagged blade in the game of perfect precision. Graysonel needed just one good fake and jab to slacken his adversary.

Then, Lucero caught one of his last thrusts of the spear by the shaft and yanked it, pulling him in closer. Abandoning his primary weapon, Graysonel spun into the vampire's space and drew his dagger. When Lucero went to drive the warrior through with his blade, Graysonel rolled to the side and gave one desperate thrust of his knife. The vampire kicked it out of his grasp and pummeled him with the butt of his own spear. Lucero cast it for him as he fell back, keen on piercing the man with his own weapon. Esker, however, repelled the spear upward just in time.

While the Ziamon saved his life, Graysonel gave his all to keep Lucero's attention on himself for his confederate to get into position. Amid the bedlam of the battle, Lucero didn't sense Kulind sneak up on him from behind. Fearing that the vampire would detect the stroke of his spear just as it came for the back of his skull, Kulind aimed for his leg. The strike was on target, perforating the back of his thigh. On impulse,

Lucero cried out and swiped his bloody blade to hack his attacker in two, but Kulind just barely deflected the strike.

Esker put one of his blades in Graysonel's hands before pushing him towards the vampire general. Dashing forth with momentum, he stabbed Lucero in the side of the throat. The serrated blade pierced all the way through, stunning Lucero right where he stood. Kulind followed up with a direct thrust into the vampire's mouth, breaking clean through the back of his skull. They both pulled out their weapons at the same time and let the demon fall on his knees, dying.

"For Pingas," Graysonel said.

"For Boma," Kulind provided the telling blow, stabbing Lucero through the heart and ending the fight.

Graysonel then lobbed Esker his serrated blade as the Ziamon lobbed his spear. They both retrieved their weapons and nodded in gratitude during the heat of conflict. With their confederates avenged, the Tofauti resumed battle with fellow rangers-in-arms. As fulfilling as it was to slay the vampire, it only gave way to scores of shadow demons that rushed to take his place. The steady stream of lethal creatures never seemed to subside, hinting that the last valiant acts of the East Rangers and first division were fighting off the Demon Plague until the last man.

But from the interior balcony of the atrium came rapid fire and percussion shots. Ellison commandos appeared by the dozens in black armor and enclosed helmets. Their converging fire upon the entranceway overpowered the demons, cutting them down. Soon, the Ellisons provided enough firepower to push out the remaining demons back onto the field, essentially saving the rangers below.

The captain spoke from behind his helmet, resting the smoking machine gun on his shoulder, "Figured you boys were fighting the good fight down here. Looks like we made it just in time."

"This is where the party is," another Ellison added from the opposing side of the atrium.

From the interior balcony, the full scope of the intense battle's aftermath was in clear view. Fatigued warriors tried to recover from the burden of prolonged combat amid a room gorged with the corpses of demons and soldiers. A thin layer of blood lined the atrium from corner to corner. The wounded moaned and howled. In seeing it in all, the Ellison captain had his medics go down and inspect the injured. His tone changed. Ultimately, the entire squad was rendered speechless, aghast by the horrific scene.

"Establish a perimeter. Place a half-dozen machineguns at the entrance point. Don't let those things enter here again—only fellow humans," the captain said intently.

The commandos had only seen a fraction of what Falcun forces endured thus far. Upon witnessing the hell of war out in the field, their legs began to shake. Once the captain saw it for himself, he pulled in five men and told them in private, "I don't think Lord Bravus really knows what's going on in this end. We need reinforcements, a load of them. Deliver that message now—and be careful."

Esker took care to check the status of his fellow Ziamons when one of his best came back with word that Maxim was nowhere to be found. Instead of doubting him, Esker spit out blood from his mouth and said, "Wherever Maxim is, he's got a reason to be there. Our orders are to hold this position, so sit tight and stay alert. We're in the safest place to be right now. Go figure."

The fifth division, not yet learning of Shadisha's death, raided the Mad Legion's artillery unit, practically butchering them in minutes. The cannons quieted during the strike, but it wasn't the victory the Falcuns readily expected. Sloping down the hill, not far behind the cannons, lied the true nature of the legionnaires' flanking maneuver. Over a thousand of the mad soldiers, lying in wait, received the signal to launch the full-scale attack. The shocking discovery came too late, as the rest of the legion executed their counter-offensive.

"Heads up!" a ninja warrior shouted from his horse. "It was a ploy! Prepare for battle!"

For weeks on end, the Demon Plague assembled its possessed minions for the daylight army, rationing their best for drastic measures. Programmed to carry out the biddings of the conquest without fear or choice, the Mad Legionnaires rushed up the hill as mindless beasts. As they stampeded into view, the fifth division withdrew from their position to form a new line several yards back. Their duty was clear. Under no condition could they withdraw from the field. Failure to hold the ground meant leaving the fourth division exposed.

Echoes of war came calling on the last line in reserve. A cavalryman rode over to warn Lai of the ambush, compelling him to send the last paladins of the Holy Emblem Riders out to petition Thomas for help. They rode off with a firm ferocity. All the while, Predella fought within herself. Shadisha's last order was for her to remain on the line. Yet, thousands gave their lives in the Shadowland and hundreds more did the same against the full force of the Mad Legion behind them. Having had enough, she abandoned her post and jumped onto an open chariot with but six arrows in her quiver.

Though the charioteer chided her for leaping into the car, Predella loaded an arrow and aimed for his head, saying crossly, "I don't give a damn what you have to say, you're just going to ride north or I'll find someone with bigger and better balls than you to do it for me!"

"Crazy! I have orders to remain here! You'll shoot me?" the man gasped, threatening to draw his sword.

Glaring back at him, she said, "Enough have died, but I'll lose one more to save hundreds! Don't test me!"

Taking Predella at her word, the anxious charioteer took to the north where the fifth division met the Mad Legion in dire combat. The other charioteers called for him to stop, but they didn't have Predella in their car. She was not going to stand by on the defensive line any longer. Her strategy made tactical sense, even if the charioteer couldn't see it. There was no gain in riding head-on into the fray. Predella told him to ride off northwest and then circle back around to flank the enemy. He was not going to argue.

Observing the legionnaires' charge from a distance put their attack into perspective. Opponents were going to leak through the fifth division one way or another. Predella was set on breaking the legion's resolve before they could gain ground on the defensive line. When the charioteer turned around, he followed her directives and closed in on the charging legion on a forty-five-degree angle. When she felt they were in range, she let loose her first arrow.

Soaring into the brigade, her arrow sunk into a soldier's side and exploded on impact. His enflamed corpse propelled into the charging line of his fellow legionnaires, spreading the flames across the way. As the chariot neared closer, she fired her second arrow—another explosive shot that sent enemies flying into each other. Again and again, Predella let loose her fury on the army, blasting scorching holes in their lines. When she felt her car was close enough to the action, she told her driver to slow down so she could jump off.

Two arrows remaining, Predella bounded from the car, rolled onto the grass, and fired another accurate shot directly into a charging legionnaire's breastplate. Hurled backward as a conduit for expanding ice shards, the slain soldier fell into the company of his fellow men. Fast-spreading spikes of solid ice impaled nearby soldiers and blocked the way for any other charging foes. Her last arrow, as she took care to aim it, met another enemy directly in the forehead, spreading several feet of perilous ice shards into the army.

Out of arrows, she finally joined the Falcuns in battle and brought forth a wrath none had ever seen from her before. In sliding to pick up a fallen soldier's short sword, Predella came in like a demon. Screaming and squealing, she cut down all her adversaries with unforgiving cruelty. A one-woman army, no soldier dared to face her alone. Instead, she killed legionnaires in droves, spilling their intestines and hacking limbs—slitting throats and gouging out their eyes with cold, blood-sodden steal. Before risking losing the blade due to the freshly shed blood dripping down into her palm, she threw it into the belly of another unlucky recipient.

With her elemental bow as her only weapon, she stood before the fifth division and cried out so every member of the Mad Legion could hear her, "Is that all? Is that everything you can do? You're lambs! All lambs for the slaughter!"

Even some Falcuns thought it best to keep their distance from her. Advancing legionnaires, though they hardly knew fear as mindless pawns, began to learn the hard lessons of the battlefield. Swathed in the blood of her enemies, Predella let loose her wildness like an unleashed tiger. When the Falcuns were close enough to see the panic in the legionnaires' eyes, the conditions of the battle changed.

In the atrium, Ellison commandos felt the floor shake, as if there were detonations below their feet. Other troops felt it as well but assumed it was due to the Ellison Munitions Corps and their battery of the south tower. But the Ellisons knew the corps suspended their barrage a time ago. The trembling was coming from somewhere inside the citadel—a place below.

Deep within Project Gambit's underground lab, Michael obliterated everything left standing. Under the falling water of the ceiling sprinklers, he finished off demons too feeble to run away. The progeny of the Demon Plague was nearly finished. But, as he destroyed everything he came across with just the flick of his wrist, Michael frantically shouted, "**Come out and face me! You are a coward, demon! Many of the humans you despise are sacrificing their lives as you hide away—stalling me! They'll be nothing left of this experiment by the time I'm done! It'll all be just a bad dream in years to come!**"

The Demon Lord, however, materialized behind him as the rain fell. He raised his sinister claw and executed the most devastating spell, driving Michael into a wall of equipment, triggering new explosions and scattered fires. The staff knocked out from his grip, Michael fought to stand amid the devastation. He groaned from the pain taking over his body with water and fire besieging him as he rose to his knee. The grand demon's spell provoked the evil within him, forcing it out from deep inside. Michael tried to suppress it, but it was overpowering.

Ambling forth, the Demon Lord tolerated the stinging water drops in saying, "**And here we are again, like the first time we met. I saw Abaddon in you then. Now, I see only some wretch who squandered his calling—all for sinners. That, alone, is the greatest sin.**"

"Do me a favor and shut up for a minute," he groaned from his knee, struggling with the darkness inside raring to emerge. "**All you do is talk.**"

"**Then, let us end this meaningless exchange.**" He expanded his vast wingspan and charged a devastating spell, one that would cook Michael from within. **"Let this place be your grave!"**

But Michael had sensed his staff somewhere nearby and beckoned that it return to him. He directed the artifact to come by way of a detour, straight through the grand demon's torso. Like a missile, his Staff of Truth tore out from his adversary's chest and landed firmly in his expecting hand. Staggered by the surprise attack, the Demon Lord grunted from the burning pain. The shock of it brought him to lower his helmet and sigh.

"This is pointless, isn't it?" he said, inspecting his open wound. Coming to terms with Michael's stubborn resolve, the grand demon continued, **"There is no reason for me to fight you any further. I know what you need."**

After receiving his staff, Michael fought the visions of the past surging irrepressibly into his mind. He heard the Demon Lord proclaim something, but couldn't hear it due to the swell of baleful memories. There was so much that the debased lab wanted to show him. It became burdensome.

While the demons kept their distance, tormented by the sprinklers, Michael felt his blood begin to boil. Breaking free from the staff's outpouring of omniscience, he opened his eyes to witness the Demon Lord's undesirable gift. He declared, **"I'll help you."**

A surge of power came from the grand demon like a hot gust of malevolent energy, rushing over Michael. Like he did with Shina, absorbing her evil spirit, his lifeforce soaked up the Demon Lord's request. There was no escaping it. Michael tried to resist, but his darkness drank it in. Already on the precipice, he felt himself fall away. His worst nightmare crept deeper into his being, taking hold of who and what he ever was in life. In moments, Michael couldn't take anymore and cried out, expelling a vast amount of wickedness.

The outburst destroyed everything in his vicinity. From top to bottom, the lab's ceiling had caved in along with the floor. Nothing in his immediate area survived. But, when some of the smoke had cleared, the Demon Lord returned to the physical plane and beheld the fruit of his sacrifice. There, floating in the midst of his devastation, Michael awoke to the body, heart, and soul of a new creature. He opened his eyes, a deep crimson red with black pupils, and exhaled slowly. From his mouth came a pall of heated vapor.

Throngs of demons that survived his slaughter moments ago had scurried over to bow. The Demon Lord, himself, had fallen to one knee in prostration and bowed his head. At last, it seemed that Abaddon had come after all.

Maxim opened the doors to what appeared to be an old, but enormous auditorium of some kind. Much of it made of wood, the two-story theatre was chocked full of seats facing the large stage in front. In the center of the place, an aisle of bare wood floor cut through to the theatre's platform complete with curtains and lights that hadn't worked for centuries. Holding the thirsty fire-sword in his right hand, Maxim searched the place for his adversary.

Suddenly, Kane dropped from the balcony to cut Maxim in two with his broadsword. Maxim rolled out of the way and just evaded the plummeting warrior, letting him smash the floorboards. Wooden fragments danced all about, as Maxim rose onto his feet, raising his sword up to his waist.

Kane followed suit, covered mostly in armor, and faced his enemy. There, they studied each other, trying to find any weakness for the duel that was to come. Breaking the silence, Maxim angrily uttered, "You were dead. So, are you undead?"

"**More like born again, I'd say,**" Kane replied as he steadied his heavy blade before him. "**The Demon Plague is** generous to those who swear their allegiance to their conquest. That is how I received my special gift."

"How sweet. Does your special gift include running away from a fight to hide away somewhere?" Maxim barked from his guarded spot.

Kane snickered, "**I wanted you all to myself. You're the challenge. You're my ticket back to humanity. Then, that black whore.**"

Igniting the fire-sword with his hate, Maxim said, "In some way, I almost pity you. You're nothing more than a pet to them, a plaything. They have no use for a thug like you—neither do I."

Not caring to converse any further, Kane cried and lunged for the knight. Maxim repelled the attack and evaded his next swipes with ease. He blocked the final strike with his sword and then counterattacked with blinding speed. His blade cut Kane's throat clean, spouting blood like a fountain. Gurgling to his knees, he removed his helmet to breathe. Shaking his head, Maxim peered down on him and said, "With all your new 'gifts,' you're still a loser."

Kane's body fell thumping to the floor. Blood poured out from his vessels and painted the ground, almost following Maxim out towards the exit. However, when Maxim thought that he defeated his enemy a second and last time, something didn't sound right. He stopped and turned around to see, Kane straighten his head, which had been severed almost clean off. His eyes glowed purple and his skin turned to a darker red. His teeth were sharper in some places like fangs.

Kane began laughing in his dark, demonic tone and signaled for Maxim to return to the fight. Maxim, stupefied, saw how his foe had changed since regenerating. He walked towards his nemesis a second time, looking to chop him up enough times to prevent any more rebirths. Kane readied his blade and anticipated Maxim's next strike.

Kane chuckled, "**You see, Tinarian! I can't be stopped! Throw over the sword and I'll end you quickly.**"

Enraged by confusion, Maxim engulfed his sword and had at Kane again. This time, the battle seemed nearly equal. They clashed blades and clanged each other's attacks assiduously, compelling steam to rise from each strike. The two warriors battled fiercely for a long two minutes until Maxim parried a futile attack and came around to slice through Kane's thigh.

The cry was not enough satisfaction. Maxim immediately concluded his assault with a rising hack to his inner knee. When Kane fell to his back, Maxim raised his inflamed sword, shouting loudly, and plunged his flaming sword into Kane's chest. Backing away from the torrential flames of ferocity, Maxim overlooked his work with falling beads of sweat threatening his eyes.

By the time he wiped the beads away from his brow, Kane rose to his knees and then to his feet again. Repairing in front of him, Kane screamed in a demonic tone and went on the offensive. Maxim blocked and parried what he could from his charging enemy. The clash was matched with both combatants overtaking the other at any opening. The fight gradually made its way to the stage ahead. Just evading Kane's demoralizing strikes, Maxim withdrew to the rows of seats nearby. He ran on top of each one, staying above ground without trouble. His balance was faultless.

But Kane wasn't amused. He raced up the center aisle and tracked Maxim's movements atop the chairs. Finally, he bounded into the air at least ten feet and came down upon Maxim with crushing force. Maxim had just leaped out of the way, missing the explosion of smashed chairs. The loud crashing of the wood and ancient metal sounded in the background as he recovered from his diving evasion and slid out of danger. Kane bashed his way out of the rubble and into the side aisle, beginning his walk towards him.

Maxim advanced into the aisle and clashed swords with him again. This scuffle lasted no longer than ten seconds, for he evaded a vertical swipe of the broadsword and returned with a rear stabbing thrust, cleverly hidden from Kane's sight. Maxim twisted and pulled the blade from the armor, ensuring that Kane would feel the pain and bleed out. Blood erupted from his stomach, following some entrails.

Crying out, Maxim dashed away from the fallen warrior and ran onto the stage, planning out his next plan of attack. Kane cried from the agony on the ground. He fretfully tore off his armor and witnessed his vicious wound heal right before his eyes. He threw the heavy mail into the seats behind him and ran in Maxim's direction, bare-breasted. He bounded into the air and came down onto the stage, cracking the wood planks, to continue the swordfight. Kane was growing stronger and faster with every mortal blow. His demonic form gradually consumed him.

Maxim received two strong blows to his face from Kane's defensive elbow before kicking the demonic warrior in the shin to slow him down. Kane winced slightly, which was enough for Maxim to unleash hell. He lopped off his armed wrist and then spun around to kick him in the torso, sending him soaring off the stage. Kicking the armed hand behind him with a strict watch on his foe, Maxim then knelt over the fallen broadsword and rushed his fire blade down upon it. The sword failed to break. It only scarred black.

Suddenly, from behind him, Kane dashed for him. In a sudden flash of attack, he rammed Maxim into the short stairway offstage. He quickly recovered to see Kane reattach his hand. To give himself time to think about how to proceed, he broke through a door nearby and followed the steps up to the second level. Kane, though, was directly behind him and made chase all the way up.

When Maxim reached the balcony's entrance, he dove out and immediately defended one of Kane's prompt attacks. The Tinarian was jostled, but he regained his balance and punched his enemy in the jaw with his armed fist. Kane withdrew and recuperated before continuing the assault. Maxim raced up to the center balcony where the seats were positioned in a gradient slant. Again, Kane vaulted to kill Maxim quickly.

He evaded the attack and countered with a deep slash across Kane's back and a perfect thrust through his kidney and out from his lower belly. Kane growled from the agony as Maxim pushed Kane's helpless body up the steps, igniting his blade along the way. Finally, Maxim shouted angrily and tore the blade from his lower torso, engulfing Kane in flames and jetting him up the steps.

The searing traitor cried powerlessly and slammed into the back wall, breaking a segment from the brick. Kane was overcome by fire, though not for long. His hardened skin scorched for a while but ultimately quenched the flames. In the end, his demonic skin smelled rank, like dead flesh. Kane, growling like a bear, became infuriated by Maxim's amazing skill. This time, it was he who backed away. He backtracked up the aisle to a stained-glass window, still aching from the crippling blow.

Maxim gradually followed him up the steps, taking extreme precaution. His grizzly exit wound was healing fast and his skin had fully recovered by the time Maxim raced up the stairs. Meeting blades again, they engaged in desperate combat. Kane deflected his fire-sword to the right and then answered with a defining slash to Maxim's side. His armor split open, revealing Maxim's bleeding cut. Kane then grabbed him by the throat and lifted him off his feet, strangling him one-handed. Kane's demonic claw around Maxim's throat was like nothing he had ever experienced before. His eyes were swelling and he couldn't inhale.

In the gist of his blurred vision, Maxim realized that his enemy was going to impale him like a snared pig. Before Kane could impale him, Maxim ignited his fire-sword with all of the might he had left and blasted his sight. Blinded by the intense heat of the sweltering flames, Kane threw Maxim through the oval window, blasting the glass into dispersed shards.

Maxim fell into an empty storehouse for the theatre entirely made of wood. Strong posts supported the weight of the ceiling and floors above. Maxim scurried away from the rose window and crawled on the glass to achieve safe distance from the enemy. When Kane presented himself before the obliterated window, Maxim hurriedly removed his slender armor and threw it for him. Kane effortlessly knocked it to the side and sprung through into the second story storehouse. Maxim charged his sword with flames and dashingly charged his enemy, weakened from battle. Kane obliged and met him halfway.

They fought fiercely for the upper hand, blocking and parrying at all costs. The contest spanned all about the room, bashing planks into pieces and slashing boxes into shavings. With great fury, Maxim unleashed a terrifying inferno with a swipe of his sword. Kane evaded as much as he could, but the aged wood attracted the flames in seconds, spreading fire all about the room. In the attack's aftermath, Kane had vanished.

Maxim held his fire-sword close to his body, expecting anything. He tried to hear or even feel the movements of his enemy. Yet, his nemesis was faster, stronger and quieter after each death. Kane snuck up behind him and punched Maxim in the lower back, then slashing the fire-sword out from his grip. The blade whizzed across the depot and landed near the gaping window leading back into the balcony.

Following his wrathful offensive, Kane thrust his sword for Maxim's spine, hoping to kill him promptly. Instead, Maxim evaded the sword, which smashed through a sturdy post of wood and locked his arms around Kane's outstretched elbow. Hastily, he broke the arm with one ruinous move. Dropping his blade, Kane screamed and tried to pull away. Maxim let go and clouted his adversary square in the face. Kane was heaved back, holding his broken arm. Maxim would have proceeded with his attack, but the filling smoke from the surrounding fires reached his lungs. He covered his mouth and dashed to a safer spot, coughing up smoke.

Amongst the fires crackling about him, Kane replaced his arm with a snap and shouted furiously, "**Why do you continue to fight? You can't kill an immortal!**"

"I fight to the end, regardless of your gifts! I've got more pain to give until then!" Maxim charged him with a vehemence of punches and kicks. Kane blocked the first few strikes, but Maxim connected with two blows to the stomach. More demon than man, Kane returned a blow with his enclosed claw, striking Maxim in the head. He fell back but rolled onto his feet.

Kane chased him and proceeded with a punch in the chest and an uppercut to his jaw. Maxim groaned agonizingly and fell onto his back a second time, visibly hurt. Kane jumped into the air to drop down onto Maxim's shaken body. His knee crashed down, but met only with the floorboards, like all the other times. Maxim rolled over and regained his footing, willing to fight on.

When Kane coughed from the filling smoke, Maxim ran and jump-kicked his opponent in the face. Kane covered his broken fangs while Maxim propelled off a burning post and walloped him in the side of the face with a dropping punch. The half-demon spit blood from his mouth and then dispensed a responding fist to Maxim's gut. The punch was brutal, bringing him to his knees. Kane then kneed him in the jowl, putting Maxim on his back yet again.

The fires were eating the storeroom to nothing and, in turn, pieces of the ceiling began falling down, breaking the floor below. The battle site deteriorated along with them. The loud breaks of the detached floorboards reminded them that their foot placement was never more critical. Maxim swept Kane's legs out from under him, sending the brute crashing to the floor. Maxim rolled away to distance himself.

The fires were enclosing in on him and the gaping stained-glass window was his only escape. Maxim first needed to reclaim his sword from the burning ground, if he could find it. Kane spotted his blade, but it was on the edge of a burning hole in the floorboards. Balancing the fate of his weapon, Kane dove to save it, but it fell off the edge of the scorching hole and clanged to the bottom of the theatre.

Maxim luckily spotted his blade. It hid under a shattered piece of lumber. Running to reclaim his weapon, Maxim slid over to the piling wood and freed the sword. Taking it by hand, he spun around to cut Kane down without further delay. Regrettably, the fires weakened his senses and Kane was right there to weaken him further.

Wielding a blazing plank, Kane smashed Maxim on the side of his bare body and compelled him to dive to the ground. His skin was blackened and blistered by the flaming strike. Feeble, he dropped his sword, permitting Kane to claim it for himself. It sizzled in his demonic claw, but Kane's tolerance withstood the unbearable burning. Maxim watched him endure the searing pain of the fire-sword's handle in horror.

However, smoke began to rise from under their feet. It was not long after that the wooden floorboards began to buckle and give way. They both fell a full story with blazing wood clusters in their midst. Crashing to the ground, both combatants lost consciousness among the seating below, stricken with flaming lumber from above. In seconds passing, the sounds resonated with the destructive crackling of the flames above and below. For once, the fighting in the antique theatre had finally stopped. From the ruins, only one man rose from the debris.

Kane shoved the extinguished pile of lumber off his body—his human body. All of his demonic attributes had begun fading away. His purple eyes returned to blue and his fangs to teeth. The claw was gone as a new human hand replaced it. Standing about the wreckage of the auditorium, Kane raised his arms and laughed gratefully. The obvious cause for his revived humanity was Maxim's death.

He remained half-covered under a pile of scorched wood between broken seats. Seeing his fire-sword near his own feet, the gleeful Kane retrieved the legendary sword by the blade, still hot. He began walking out of the theatre, dazed from the great battle, but pleased with the result. A fiery explosion from above let loose another pile of enflamed planks of wood that fell upon Maxim's chest. Kane left his defeated enemy there to bury in the ashes of a theatre hundreds of years old.

But the impact of the fallen debris had a unique effect on Maxim's condition. The blow to his chest restarted his heart. In moments, he awakened and gasped for air. Blood sprayed from his mouth and he lived again. He shoved the heavy wood to his side and snuck out from the oppressive splintering heap, shaken by the ordeal. Falling to his knees, he held his aching chest, but then looked on to watch Kane amble off with his Mad Phoenix.

Kane thought he heard his enemy, but shrugged it off. It was his last mistake. Maxim dashed up behind him, seized his armed wrist and snapped it with little exertion. The crack of his bones, coupled with his squeal, was music to Maxim's ears. The fire-sword slipped from his hand and dropped into the waiting grip of its rightful owner.

Flowing with his attack, Maxim spun to cut through Kane's side and then again to make another slice just two inches above the previous. Kane gurgled and collapsed to the ground, holding his oozing entrails. Spitting up blood, the Slayer looked up at his reborn killer with astonished eyes and moaned from the shock of losing everything so fast.

Maxim stood over him with his bloody sword and said jadedly, "I guess we both have something in common. We've both risen from the dead more than once. What's different is that you're dead and I'm not."

With one exact swipe, Maxim lopped off Kane's head, finishing him. The corpse fell over and ended an unforgiving era of evil and betrayal, a testament to the Demon Plague's duality in covenants. Maxim then limped away, understanding the meaning behind Antonis's prophetic advice at last.

The Ellison Munitions Corps advanced further into the Shadowland under burdensome demonic resistance in the hope of breaching the bastion's dense walls. The battlefield was bloodied, but soldiers were gradually pushing the demons back. The diving flyers swooped in and threatened their advance for every step. Cover fire provided by the war machines kept most of the creatures at bay. The fight was hostile, taking several reloads of their guns to take meters of the field.

In the northern realm, the battle had become fiercer than ever before. Mourning Shadisha's death, Thomas finally arrived and took over her divisions. In discussing the battle ahead, Lai suggested that the divisions of the second and third had been fighting for too long. The gallant fighters refused to surrender any ground to their demonic adversaries, working in unison to survive. Flyer demons savagely swooped in and harassed them from above, leaving holes in the lines.

But then, from a medical tent, Eric came staggering. The army applauded his return, though he looked half dead. From the line, greeted by Thomas and Lai, Eric saw the silhouette of his nemesis flying amongst her kin. Looking past his allies, he rose his arm and conjured an isolated storm amid the miasma of the Shadowland. When he had her sized up, Eric let forth a single, but loud clap of lightning. The bolt struck Sattka by surprise, cooking her as she glided midair. She descended from the powerful strike and slammed helplessly into the battlefield not far from the bastion's main doors.

"That'll ground you, crone," Eric muttered. "Let that be a lesson to never underestimate Eric Orgento."

The army hailed the sorcerer's thunderous return. Their morale boosted almost instantly just knowing he was back. It was far too soon for him to engage in battle, but the flyers had scattered after learning of his presence. Soldiers of the fourth division helped him stand, for he was yet weak from Sattka's earlier attack that near killed him.

Esker watched the daring display of warriorship from inside the atrium when Sattka fell to earth. Though he assumed the second and third divisions would be able to finish her off, it appeared the demonic general was not ready to claim defeat. Scorched and maimed, she recovered to some degree and planned on fighting her way out of the field. Flyer demons guarded her against the warriors who tried to deliver the final blow. In but moments, she joined the defensive and hacked down any challenging warriors herself.

Unable to lay low in the comfort of the bastion any further, Esker had to answer the call of the soldier crying out from inside. Thus, he dismissed himself from the East Rangers and rejoined the intense fight outside, commanding his Ziamon brethren to hold their positions. Armed with his two serrated blades, already stained with blood of the demonic, Esker joined the dense bulk and partook in their demanding task of slaying the she-demon.

The Ziamon warrior passed by brutal warfare. Two shadow demons tried him, but he was able to hide amongst the heavy fighting and ward them off, only wounding them. He had no time to kill his enemies, for it was Sattka that he wanted. War drums pounded loudly in his spirit, virtually beckoning him to give in to his primal instincts. Sattka killed her last challenger and watched the bold Ziamon come for her head on. She studied him carefully and licked her lips, knowing that he was a worthy kill. Sattka twirled her dual blades and waited for him to reach her, signaling all of her minions to leave him for herself.

He jumped over a dying shadow demon, compliments from a Kai marksman, and entered her combat zone. They met blades inside the cordon, matching each other's swords strike for parry. For the first bout, Esker fought off her attacks with a frenzy only a Ziamon could provide. Her demonic presence instilled fear in his heart, but it only fueled his performance. Sattka wanted to finish him off quickly, but his fighting skill forced her to be more cautious. A duel of will and tactics, each pined for any opening to make their first attack. While her strength exceeded his own, Esker managed to strike first with a sawing swipe to her right arm. Sattka winced for a moment.

She answered with a rising kick to his waist, taking him to the ground. He rolled over and speedily bounced back to his feet, just in time to parry her next attacks. One of her blades barely grazed his face. He returned with a cunning stab from behind. Sattka evaded the sneaky strike and clobbered him on the back of his head with her pommel. Esker reeled away from the battle to gather himself after his head started to bleed. She would not provide him respite.

Sattka ran him down and unleashed all of her wrath upon him. Her golden blades became too fast for him, ultimately trouncing his chances. She viciously pierced one of her swords into his stomach and compelled him to collapse onto his knees. Esker, run through, raised his blade to return the favor, but she swiftly hacked off his right hand by the wrist. His armed hand dropped to his side and he cried from the pain as well as the creeping defeat.

Still, he was too stubborn to admit to his failure. She crossed her swords across his throat and said with a sickly smile, "**Now be a good human and die for me.**"

Just before she could slice off his head, Esker secured his left blade tightly in his grip and peered exhaustingly at her scaly, flat stomach. With his last chance of defiance, Esker lunged his cruel sword up between her legs, sawing into her evil vessel. Her arrogance was bled. She immediately abandoned her finishing blow and cried out from the most horrific agony she had ever experienced.

She pulled away and staggered about the ground until she ultimately collapsed to her side, crying further from the anguish of her vessel's mutilation. Esker held the newly bloodied blade in his hand still and took lasting pleasures in watching her squirm. Leaning upon his plummeted blade, he felt himself fade away. His vision blurred and his mouth became dry even when filled with blood.

In the end, he slid down the hilt of the blade and fell to his side, overseeing the war in his sights. Amid her squirming, Ellison tanks began bombarding the demonic defensive from both sides of the bastion. Sattka, along with her minions, became easy targets for the timely Ellison reinforcements. In the mayhem, the she-demon was overrun by raving warriors that passed the smoking necropolis and invaded the main entrance, shouting valiantly. Esker slowly lost consciousness with a sneer, dying a warrior's death.

The Angels of Resistance had begun to achieve the upper hand. Forces besieged the bastion and stormed through its many corridors and levels, defeating the undead as they charged. The fighting was manic inside Pommel, but it was a fight that the armies were raring to win together. Predella, though injured considerably, joined the invading warriors in the hopes that she would find Maxim among them. Her nasty work of the Mad Legion helped the fifth division take them out under fifteen minutes. Without Shadisha to stop her, Predella rushed forth into the Shadowland and thought only of Maxim.

"This could be it!" Thomas cried from the line. "God be with us!"

Under great duress, Ellison soldiers risked their lives to plant explosives along the northern wall. Shaking the battlefield, the massive eruption shaped an enormous cavity. Amidst the dead, surviving soldiers knew their brazen duty. Upon the desperate calls from their superiors, the brave men dashed into the gorging smoke, armed with rifles. The resistance inside the castle was savage, but never enough to stave off their courageous mission.

Bearing the colors of Ellium, flag bearers raced forth, admittedly in fear. Shouting for victory, the heroes of their time invaded the evil fortress and offered their valor for the fate of the world. The citadel had been breached from both fronts. Triumph, in the end, seemed possible.

"Where is Michael after all of this? Have you seen him?" Thomas asked from his horse, concerned.

"Better we don't see him," Lai answered. "As long as we don't see the Demon Lord out here, we know Michael is doing whatever he has to do in there!"

Abaddon finally touched ground and basked in the new world he helped to create over a thousand years ago. Walking on towards the Demon Lord, his dark hair seemed to flow on after him as if gravity didn't apply. Parts of his armor and cloak were torn to shreds in his transformation, allowing parts of his lean, muscular physique to show through.

Sensing the Staff of Truth somewhere, he outstretched his arm and claimed it. The article he created to focus his powers in the earthly realm had rushed into his hand. When it settled into his grip, archaic symbols along the shaft glowed a bright white. Demons followed him as he walked onward, beaming with incredible power.

As the grand demon awed at the return of his supreme leader, Abaddon said chillingly, "**Peer into my soul, my child. Tell me what you see.**"

Doing as his father asked, the Demon Lord gazed into his core. Thereafter, he trembled in trepidation, overcome by what he saw. Within the greatest demon lied Miuriell's noble soul, for his spirit defied even the fallen angel in the flesh.

"**Impossible!**" the Demon Lord gasped, unable to fathom it. "**Miuriell? How?**"

Michael answered from Abaddon's lips, "**Will you deny the human spirit now? You were right about one thing only. I am not one of you. I am greater.**"

Without raising a finger, Michael tore the Demon Lord's black heart from his elusive armor, letting it float in the air between them. As the Demon Lord collapsed to his knees, Michael effortlessly turned him into ash. He fell apart into a collective heap of dust.

On impulse, the staff finally upheld its famed reputation. Michael, in a flash, learned all of Abaddon's secrets. How he became the father of the Demon Plague. How he created each demonic minion in perfect detail within Pommel's labyrinth. How he sacrificed himself then to recreate himself today for the conquest. How sorcery spawned from his creation. It all became clear to him.

And with all of this knowledge, Michael felt no more fear. He looked down upon his bested enemy and tapped the suspended heart aside with his staff. It drifted off lazily. Most of the creatures about him continued to bow, yet knowing that their creator could easily dispatch them with a single thought. With Abaddon's vast power, Michael turned them all into piles of ash, then blasting their disintegrated forms away with a forceful pulse.

While the fighting raged on outside, a great series of detonations emanated from the tower, scaling upwards. Upon gazing at the sky, both human and demon alike witnessed the profound emergence of Abaddon hovering above the earth. Roaring from exploiting all of his incredible power, Michael determined to wipe the Shadowland clean of all evil. Rescuing every warrior from the burden of battle, he diminished every last wicked creature to dirt and ash. Blades cut through nothing but dust as the hellish army rose high into the miasma, ultimately swirling into oblivion.

While some claimed victory, many others feared that the sovereign creature above would turn on them next. The army from the depths of hell had vanished in seconds, stunning all who remained on the field. The bodies of thousands fallen were scattered about the barren land, signifying the real sacrifice of the quest.

The Angels of Resistance were silently astounded, observing the supreme being erase all that was left of the Demon Plague. When it was over and only the casualties of the crusade remained, Michael dropped from the sky, shaking the ground like a quake. None were stupid enough to confront the demon, for they could only surrender their weapons and pray that he came in peace.

For certain, Michael was the greatest peacemaker. When rising onto his feet, he outstretched his arm and caught the Staff of Truth, triggering the inscriptions to glow as before. Amongst the speechless masses, Michael raised his staff in triumph. What followed was the adulation of the being that saved them. It became clear that it was Michael Miuriell, the true savior of the quest.

The thousands of exhausted warriors that fought without rest or provisions had realized what transpired. With no demons to fear or fight, the united human army raised their weapons and cried out in the elation of their magnificent victory over the Demon Plague. Pommel, once a refuge for the evilest beings that ever inhabited the planet, had become holy ground.

The idea seemed impossible that the Demon Plague could be defeated, but their faith proved that all things were achievable. Taken by his incredible new appearance, warriors of all races joined in meeting him. They jumped and cheered, reveling in the miraculous ending to the awful war.

"Michael? Is it you?" Predella gasped, covered in blood.

"*It's me*," Michael replied in a weighty tone.

She shook her head and cried, overwhelmed by all that had happened up to this fateful moment. Predella said to him in tears, "Is it over, Michael? Is it finally done?"

Caressing her face, he said, "**The war is over, yes, but there is still one demon left.**"

Along with others who understood what he meant, she pleaded with him, sobbing, "You? No, Michael! I know you don't mean you! You won't do this!"

"**We have won this together as a united force—as humanity's resistance. It's time for me to finish it on my terms. This is the way I want it—the way it has to be,**" Michael said.

She countered frantically, "There must be another way! Can't you just—"

Moved by her compassion, "**This is the way, my friends. You all must vow to me this victory will not be in vain. Heal this world with your compassion. Spread the word to the farthest lands. Please, remember this for the sake of what we have accomplished here. We sacrificed too much only to revert back to the sins of our past. On this hallowed ground, make a new covenant. Let love lead the way.**"

After those about him showed him gratefulness and praise, Michael offered Predella his staff and said with an endearing smile, "**To remember me by.**"

Predella received it in honor. In order to save the world, he needed to perform this one final deed. The throngs of warriors realized what was to happen. They all hushed and conformed around their savior and friend one last time.

Amid the tears of sadness and joy, Michael Miuriell soared high above them all for the dark miasma. In that uncanny climb, Maxim looked on from an opening in the fortress. He watched his greatest ally close the book on the Demon Plague forever and bowed his head. Eric, as he looked on at the monumental event transpire, couldn't believe the man's character. He realized that Michael was unlike any other man he had ever known. A leader by example—one who defeated his demons.

Michael soared further into the miasma and broke through the dark overshadowing clouds. But in his ascent, he saw the lights of the two most precious people in his life. The figures of his wife and son beckoned him, making him feel the beauty of sacrifice. Finally, he was able to see them again—to hold them again. Forever.

Closing his eyes and finding the one image he wanted to hold onto before leaving the world he knew so well, Michael used his power to finish it. He blasted himself away along with the wicked miasma. They saw the overwhelming spectacle as a culmination of everything he believed. The dark cloud faded off into nothingness, proving that the hell had been washed away once and for all. The ash of Michael's body gently fell over the silent battlefield. Thomas bowed at the sight. Then, others bowed. Hundreds more fell on their knees to honor the man who united the world against evil and saw it through to the end, selflessly.

When the sun broke through, kingdoms buried hatchets and embraced each other, knowing that they were brothers and sisters on the same side. Like Michael had hoped, the hardened soldiers embraced each other and reveled in their joint triumph over a common evil. At the end of the day, when the night had come, it came without fear. The hellish conquest that was one thousand years in the making had been defeated within months. There was a faith revived in the new world.

PART II
Epilogue
Veneration Day

A year had passed since that extraordinary day. The city of New Pommel was bursting with thousands of patriots who gathered in the streets to celebrate the first anniversary of the world's liberation. The day was warm, though the start of autumn was not far away. The refurbished kingdom had been decorated weeks before for the great holiday. There were still years of work to be done, but the bastion had been turned into a temple—a place of reflection. That was the first step in the restoration process.

Many different heroes returned to New Pommel to celebrate Veneration Day. The honoring of the bravest of warriors was the true purpose to the recognized holiday. The unification of the world on that day had sparked a worldwide movement towards the pursuit of peace. It served as a day of reflection and unity, remembering The Resistance Period.

Everyone remembers where they were when they heard that Michael Miuriell saved humanity, overcoming the evil that consumed him. His valiance and light of heart challenged mankind to face their fears and faults. Urik, having recovered from his dire illness, attended the ceremony. Under his charge, Lai had become the honorable Ninja Commander. Shioda followed in the temple with his wife, Lana, at his side. While needing a cane to walk, he recovered from most of his egregious injuries. Though he never regained his memory, he fell in love with her all over again. For him, it was the first time, but Lana found a new kind of love for his husband. She became Urik's new hand. Together, they raised a healthy infant daughter, Sayuri.

Legate Thomas Excallum maintained his admirable title of Commander of the Holy Emblem, having been awarded the Medal of the Empire for his steadfast duty and bravery during the Resistance Period. Maxim Cavallo, returned to Pommel as a father-to-be with his love, Predella, carrying their child. She was glowing in a bright Tinarian gown, revealing a small protruding bump. Her royal gown didn't only conceal her pregnancy. Scars from the many battles against the Demon Plague riddled her body, telling stories of her sacrifices and bravery. As for Maxim, he could not hide his scars. He wore a patch over his left eye to mask his broken eye socket. His combat days were long gone since the Battle of Pommel. Surviving the duel with the Slayer left his ribcage permanently damaged. Yet, as a war hero, he had more to live for off the battlefield with Predella as his wife and a child on the way.

The Orgentos retained control of Tinaria as the queen refused to abdicate the throne. Princess Shina, having survived her possession a year ago, had become a new commanding voice for peace between the East and West. Ellium did not challenge their right to rule Tinaria as long as Shina agreed to marry an Ellison noble of her choice. Shina was in the process of thinking about it, potentially for a long time.

Prince Eric was never seen again after that fateful day in Pommel one year ago. Some say he made one last appearance in Tinaria before disappearing from the public forever, disgraced. Others say he assumed a new identity and traveled the world as a vagabond. What became certain was that his magic slowly began to disappear after the Demon Plague was wiped clean from the earth. Queen Orgento, as well, felt her powers waning ever since.

Predella determined that hunting for Eric's ghost was a fool's task. She tried to move on as a bridge between Tofauti and the Waasi tribes. Though she could never forget what he did to her people, Predella had used her time to honor Michael's last wish and make peace with enemies. Since coupling with Maxim, she saw the world in a new light. For the sake of her child, planned for delivery in six months' time, she hung up her elemental bow for a time when it was required of her again.

The Ziamon soldiers that fought the Demon Plague had become honored figures in their society. Their attendance at New Pommel's commemoration was in an effort to represent Colonel Aramis and Justice Esker, as their sacrifices became an inspiration to all of Ziamon. But, secondly, as their tribute to Michael and his last wish for peace, came to announce the abolishment of slavery in Ziamon. Predella and the Tofauti delegates longed to hear them issue such a decree. The only thing that would have made it better was if Master Ayden had come to make the humiliating announcement for himself.

Chief Madax of Tofauti, the reigning empire in the East, made a rare voyage to the West in order to help dedicate the new temple. Representing his people, he brought pardons for the six Tofauti warriors that guarded Antonis for their Honor Quest. In accordance with his new decree, Graysonel and his confederates were honored for their brave stand against the Demon Plague and forgave their defiance. Posthumously, their allies and their families were exonerated as well. Madax was in the West for a few weeks after the ceremony, scheduling summits with leaders in an effort to join the global theatre.

Beautifully lifelike stone monuments were placed all around the temple, idolizing the heroic sacrifices of the Angels of Resistance. Emulating Pommel's original intention of showcasing the old world, New Pommel was dedicated to honoring the late world, as well as the one to come. It was a museum of artifacts and revered articles that played a part in defeating the Demon Plague. The three legendary weapons belonging to Predella, Maxim, and Michael were kept there on display. Since the end of the incident, they were virtually average weapons.

Walking through the center of the vast place, memorial statues of stone lined the walls. Each statue was created in the likeness of major fallen heroes during the quest. Names of the fallen, hundreds of them, were etched in the walls themselves. The temple, in essence, was a living memorial of those who made the ultimate sacrifice.

But twenty feet up, Shadisha, the appraised tactician of Falcus, raised high above many. In full armor and wielding her saber, she mounted a raring horse in the heat of battle. It was her final service to the country she loved that much. Up further was Justice Esker and Colonel Aramis, sharing a statue for their dramatic valor. There were simply dozens of other warriors and key players that were praised with memorials down the path, including Antonis the Prophet. But the largest of them all stood out in the back.

In the center of the path against the back wall of the edifice stood the venerated sage apprentice, father, hero, and founder of the quest, Michael Miuriell of Pommel. Shina walked up to his raised statue and touched his feet, remembering all that he had done to save her life. There was no greater hero. She cried for him, shedding her dear tears, and embraced his feet lovingly. Buried beneath his statue, his son, Seth, rested in eternal sleep.

Etched in the stone base of his remarkable memorial read the phrase, "Savior of our time, unifier of our children."

Veneration Day was celebrated in New Pommel every year since, attracting more visitors than Pommel ever had in its height. It was only fitting that they display the figures of humanity, flawed and complex, to show that everyone was capable of humbling themselves to find common ground in the common good. They, as a reunited force, obliged Michael's last request and vowed to ensure that the world never fall to war again. In that act of discipline, they respectfully remembered the Angels of Resistance in times of trouble.

When the days were done and the temple had closed, a servile custodian swept the floors clean, content with a job so close to the embodiments of human greatness. Every time he swept before Michael's statue, he would remove his hood and bow his head in reverence. There was much he had to do to fully atone for the sins of his past. Believing his close call at the Shadowland was a second chance at life, he swore a new oath. His days of sorcery behind him, he found new power in the still presence of fallen comrades. The beauty of gratitude.

About The Author

Born and raised on Long Island, **David V. Mammina** grew up in North Lindenhurst as a young boy having written various free writes inspired by his exposure to comics, video games, and good books. Currently, he teaches history to young students with disabilities—and many gifts. He was awarded the Presidential Call to Service Award.

OTHER BOOKS BY DAVID V. MAMMINA IN PRINT

The Angels of Resistance
Parts I & II
(Earlier editions: 2005, 2007, 2009, 2012)

Protector of Children:
Assassin's Dreams
(2008*)

Paltronis
(2010)

Redeem the Knight
(2011)

Redeem the Knight: Blood Ties
(2013)

Redeem the Knight: Parts I & II
(2014)

Redeem the Knight: Eden
(2014)

Protector of Children
(2015)

Redeem the Knight Trilogy
(2017**)

*2008 is original version of Protector of Children
**2017 is the combined trilogy of the books listed.